THOSE WYRD

— AN HONEST THREATS SAGA —

AND WONDERFUL

Trent Lindsey

ISBN 979-8-9882096-0-7 Paperback
979-8-9882096-1-4 Ebook

Printed in the United States of America. First Edition: May 2023.

Type sets used: Cover, Charles Swarel Regular, Iowan Old Style, Hunter River; Titles and headers, EB Garamond, Iowan Old Style; Body text, Minion Pro. Book design by Trent Lindsey.

For more information and to contact the author, please visit honestthreats.com

Dedicated to all those wyrd and wonderful.
Those folk with their head in the clouds.

It is those same quirks which define us.

HERE THERE BE MONSTERS

— ACT ONE —
Mad River Junction

. . .

— ACT TWO —

Warrens of the Mortuary Cult

. . .

– ACT ONE –

MAD RIVER
JUNCTION

I

DAY LATE, DOLLAR SHORT

Far off in the distance, a bison's bellow grips the air, and within seconds, the ruckus is drowned out by an overzealous tolling.

Clang-clang, clang-clang, clang-clang

William's whole body shudders upon hearing the hand bell, and his eyes open with a keen sense of urgency. That's not the day-break alarm, it's role-call, and he is already hurtling out of the cot. Several other bodies around the chambers remain groggy, stocked to their beds, frankly flipping and shunning the early ringing cry. He sweats as incessant voices clamor down the hallway, a few other early-risers, clearly in a rush.

The roiling rackets of dawn dredge all manner of fond memories. His chap-pop would often rile the boy Jones so that they may take full advantage of otherwise scarce daylight. While it's easy to lament the daily grind, he has now grown accustomed to it.

His parents took all the necessary cautions, molding him into an earnest lad that craves for their own responsibilities, ready to take on the world. William often reminisces of his early teenage years and sensations of travel, for they were the endearing type, and sponsored an assortment of coming-of-age ventures. Boarding caravans and convoys alike, he voyaged like true vagabond ilk: sightseeing quintessential landmarks around the frontier, such as the renowned Tom Fry Eddy, mountains of yore, and posh orchards of white-capped pines called the Anderean Ozarks, only to mosey quietly into the next town over yonder. They endorsed his journeys on a subtle promise, a pledge to thwart boredom and delay his imminent adult responsibilities.

Through childhood tales of grims and gremlins, they ignited his passion for exploration. A fervor towards broadening his horizons, and experiencing everything that the world can possible offer. Emery and Concorde Walder loved their son beyond a reasonable doubt, and were overcome with emotion when he fantasized about saying farewell. Rather than condone leaving the nest, they embraced this flight of fancy, dreaming of their little guttersnipe's stories and fables after a grand gambit around the territory.

William has always been one with his head in the clouds, a dreamer with such an incredibly ripe and vivid imagination, that it tastes impossibly tart to everyone else. He devised battle plans on even the most moot notions, becoming a scissorsmith of regal intentions that will never come to fruition. This is why his family trusted him so generously: he's an overthinker, envisioning every scenario down to the slightest ills, there's was never a warrant of suspicion against him- *betting men beware.*

With the waning of the bloom and waxing of the barrow, the northern settlements seasonally seize with an abrupt cold. The air feels brackish and dense, like inhaling raw needles, a vile bitterness that would strangle a babe in its crib. William has sealed himself inside several jackets during the night, acting akin to a suit of armor. These weighted blankets and formidable sheets of bison pelts do little to halt the constant, creeping chill. One may only whimper while the fleeting feeling of heat is so painlessly sapped from the body as an all-consuming draft. Scribes detail impending weathers in their logs, preaching that the circumstances grow more dire each year. Bodies uncontrollably shrivel in the ensuing cold, contorting like mannequins- puppets controlled by malevolent forces and calamitous circumstances, buried within a casket laden of leather and fur.

The lad instinctively pats himself down, stowing hands until he clasps a wrinkled slip of parchment stashed carefully in his ensemble. It's a coveted travel ticket, permission to board the caravan's final outing. There will be heavily limited seats, and as the Bannermane mercantiles are never associated with charity, they will be eager to transport as many commodities as possible.

As an ever-talented individual, he had appropriated his precious voucher nearly a fortnight ago. William only recently joined the Crooked Men's outfit, a notorious band of highwaymen across two territories.

Desperate to procure permits, he is not proud of what he has done, the extreme lows that he's resorted to: setting about burglarizing homes for their charcoal, an elusive and scarce source of fuel; most residences lie in utter abandon while their former families flee from the oncoming storms. Should anything had gone wrong with the local constable, the gang deemed him an ideal patsy. Awarded by Crooked Eli the Stockpile himself, this delicate paper is inscribed for Bonaventure, the underground home station and residing seat-of-power for all Bannermane.

While the local residents are renowned for their uncanny ability to hunker down against any inclement weather, the constant all-season onslaught has dried up fleets of trading convoys throughout the territories. As they cower behind twenty-foot bulwarks, caravans sink among disaster, their precious payloads are swallowed into an endless seas of white. Clan Bannermane price gouges their prized painkillers to a nigh endless stream of frostbitten victims, and continue to operate the exclusive line left in town, presumed to be the final sled-wagon for a dozen months. They'll have to endure until the opening of sutler's paradise, when the snowdrifts finally retreat, revealing the weather's ill-gotten gains.

William clutches a pewter locket threaded around his neck, only before booting a yellowing portmanteau lying at the foot of the cot. The hotrocks inside briefly careen into one another, producing a staggered, stumbling sound and ensuring that his haul is still safely stowed away. After grinning and bearing eighteen years of frontier grit, then four of vagrancy, practically living door-to-door as he toured the settlements, no one is as eager to leave Mad River Junction as he.

William recites, "'Agen tis time tah return tuh roost," while clutching his amulet and chain. Several links have been previously sheared-off, now artfully rigged with carabiners of various shapes and sizes. A borderspiel insignia is meticulously etched onto its cover: the iconic hunting horn, sigil of Boar's Band- one can't help but wonder who carved it. The locket itself is a simple, down-to-earth contraption, unceremoniously prying open to reveal portraits of his beloved parents. They smile at each other from across the clasp, their faces animate, gesturing in a series of nods before meeting William with a welcoming gaze.

Some bannerfolk, an enlightened-few, behave like true kin; they thrust unwavering faith in those that stand among them, united against all odds, yet he's selfishly abandoned them, choosing to instead wander the vast frontier for spoils. Ides of night often bring perilous thoughts, his mind wanders, mulling over why he would ever leave them and their cherishing sanctuary. It's a rather festering disposition- self-destructive even, but he's always felt at home in the white wastes, even if it acts as nothing more than a purgatory between paradises.

The Bannermane people retain a penchant for exploration and staking their claim, not maintenance, as that know-how is reserved for stewards, leading them to strive for the bare minimum before treading onto the next subject. They often reject trivial matters, those necessary upkeeps that ensure frontier dwellings are habitable and safe. Pioneers are sufficient with letting properties gradually decay, trying to peddle prospects prior. Business magnates shed no tears for welfare, as their train of thought typically pertains to: if it's not demonstrating their wealth or worth of the family business by attracting moneylenders, why should lift an ounce of effort?

There's a nook in the corner of the bunkhouse suite, furnished with a teensy cabinet stand and mirror disturbingly crusted and cracked with age. A wrought iron candelabra, flanked by a dozen tiny braziers, dimly light those impending years of neglect. Mirrors are a bane, luxury items in residence of the rich, as no ordinary person desires to glimpse their wretched destitution.

William's reflection is naught a pale imitation of the original curio before it. The likeness creates a ghastly presence, as his visage is hideously warped through the array of fractures splintering the glass's surface. The frozen hinterland of Mad River has certainly taken its toll, the boy Jones skin is a sickly, discolored matte; arid, and crumbling into thousands of tarnished scales.

He inches closer to his reflection, parting wiry hairs and chapped lips to reveal a staggering arsenal of yellowed, raw, and worn-down ivorywork. They were armaments in another age, now nothing more than whistling toys. Yet his eyes sparkle at this distance, some brilliant gleaming amber composition with flecks of gilded gold, like a ferryman's bribe for safe passage. The right eye is a puzzling conundrum of wounded burgundy, as several blood vessels have popped, permanently staining its white emptiness. However, there's more to these pleasure-seekers, they're moving pictures able to share the genuine sincerity of one's character, acting as gateways teeming with life and imagination.

Burly whiskers tickle the underside of his nose, curling outward and dancing across his face. His facial hair culminates into an unkempt, scraggly, t-shaped beard and sideburns. The language of men is spoken through their iconic bristles, this makes him a bonafide vagabond.

Unveiling a rotund roll of fleece, William proceeds to decorate his figure in a series of spectral-white wrappings. Careful to avoid any commotion, he unfurls the roll, cupping the wooly strip within his dominant left hand, clasping it firmly against the ear, and drawing it against the circumference of his head. Covered skin is a comfort for any outdoor venture, this is a regular morning routine and today is no different.

He winces when every now and then, a natural flex that only spurs further jolts of pain as fingers accidentally press into patches of dry skin. Broad crevasses permeate downwards, revealing rich veins of bruised ichor, a dermal blight that tightens further and further each day like the trappings of a noose.

Now bound tighter than a wrapped cadaver, nimble fingers frill at the bandages inhibiting his vision, creating lengthy slits just wide enough for his eyes. The occasional strand of beady auburn hair meddle their way outwards, burdensomely poking through otherwise considerable lashings. They are nippily packed away, and the fabric trimmings are rearranged in tight succession.

That greasy hair of his coronates into an iconic cowlick, a mop so matted with knots and tangles, it ought to be a helmet. Proper headgear is essential after all, vagabonds must wear coverings for those vulnerable areas like the ears and neck. William hoists the padded coif latched around his collarbone, tying it tautly within the bow of chin, and encasing his entire head and neck in rigid, well-defined bullhide, resistant to all manner of spoiling weather. An embellishing tier of feather-shaped buttons adorn his collar, golden jangles that accentuate an otherwise ordinary padding of fleece.

He keeps his personal stamp straddled firmly around the wrist, wrapping thread around thrice, the last thing anyone would want to do is misplace these trinkets among packsnow. It's a trivial detail at first glance, as Bannermane seals are quite the oddity, easily to misplace and just as easy to covet, unique to every person. They're used to identify frontier rank and status: gold for those elite regiments of renown, namesakes in every scholarly textbook, while silver addresses business magnates, and bronze is the material typical between pioneers, scissorsmiths or anyone good with their hands. In William's case, copper denotes vagrancy, urchins and those who make regular use of charity. Once given a lick of ink, they're used to certify transactions, refraining from certain borderland taboos, such as removing a glove in the cold to bestow some janky, hand-scrawled signature, as a majority of vagabonds can't write.

There's an additional fabric guard woven over his left shoulder, protecting a large portion of collarbone. In hindsight, there was one wound it could never shield William from: an intricate birthmark, a red blemish awfully similar to the symbol of ruination, the dreaded Mark of Dayne. Braced by the rumors of his eldritch upbringing, fellow urchins believed that he was tainted, and their parents felt convinced that he was deviant spawn of fell. Bannerfolk have the tendency to shun the viscerally queer, from the crook of one's eye or the gait of their walk. Caught in the crushing vice of normalcy, William grew up in the adversity of his peers- a communal animosity of sorts, there was no compromise between others of age. In time, he embraced and revered it.

The boy Jones was raised among the frontier settlement of Lucy's Isle, some routine destination for Impair Ultra, a traveling troop of miscreants who scour the wasteland for oddities, items of interest to fuel their makeshift carnival. They fared north during the bloomtide seasons, excavating snowbanks around the Kiss for frigid treasure. On occasion, their roving band would break stock above a long-forgotten crypt. He flocked to their theater upon their return, a novelty tent fixated onto a sled, familiarizing himself with never-ending curiosities. William began idolizing stories of fantastical creatures, heeding tales from beasts that go bump in the night; ne'er-do-wells that father once faced- a welcomed break from reality.

A short-lineage of Walders staked a claim in an otherwise unremarkable settlement, just another dot on a boundless map; lying on the precipice of danger, yet a stone's throw from the safety. Lucy's Isle is an island redoubt, completely encircled by thick glacial ice, the frozen remains of Mad River and its endless tributaries. There are numerous settlements across the territory, yet each homestead is decisively anchored to the frozen freshwater shores. While creek trout attract fishermen in droves, the frozen streambed is used as a highway. Sled caravans are able to traverse this icy terrain, a lifeline stretching between the hamlets, including those towns of Mad River Junction, Endmost Kiss, Ozark, Whitehorse Crossing, Malham Tarn, and farthest hitchpost, Wayland. Convoys of Mandonmen and Mastersons, routinely two burdens wide, made stay in this frontier settlement, as kin of the company often partake in carnal delights.

Every season, frontiersmen flock to its soapland. These folk, numb with the vicious whippings of the wilderness, eagerly welcome the scalding, yet tender sensations of the bathhouses. The constant feasting of flesh by primal beasts drove even the most dastardly zoo of horrors mad. William was coming of age, guiding his own flames and raw vigor, yet stayed away from the rage; the wise were eager to escape the raving whims of lesser men, as creative minds tend to flourish in adverse circumstances.

So as the year's inevitable bloom bled to barrow, William found himself in similar straits, only substituting for a change of scenery every now and then. Whether bound at the frontier settlements of Tom Fry's Eddy or Wayland at the river's end, the north is a truly unkempt land, ravished by the winters and wild fell. This realm of opportunity can only be tamed by the Bannermane, a ferocious folk whose hearts and whims wail like possessed beasts. Their kin harbor sensational willpower, an abhorrent eagerness that strokes every fiber of earthly being. Not even a raging inferno, consuming the utmost verdant of libraries, could dare to compete. This uncanny influence stretches to common rabble, unlanded vagrants, and those without hearth nor home; all stave the thickest ice in order to be the rawest truths of themselves, asking who they really are at their core. But the realm of feral gods is just as ruthless, testing mortal coils, and too many break under the strain.

· · ·

Gorgeous golden rays of morning daylight begin bleeding from cracks in the timber roofing, giving William's dreary lodging an otherwise mild hint of life. Specs of dust slowly filter between them, casting gentle shadows across nearly a dozen cots, mostly still filled and slightly stirring. One of William's bunkmates, Mandel Haggerton, shuffles in his cot, using a pillow to prevent the sun from glaring across his face. He can tell one among them is already stirred to action, proclaiming, "Shut the door on yer way out, 'Liam. Some o' us are tryin' to blink an eye 'ere."

The young boy chortles, and strides towards the nearest exit.

"See ye nevah, 'ag-man!"

He's ecstatic, finally escaping such an unpleasantly foul-smelling prison cell. The stench of soiled grime will forever stain his clothes, and not even the hardiest launderer would dare take the challenge.

William briskly rushes past the bulkhead leaning ajar and bolts towards the stairwell, briskly trawling his luggage across the floor behind him, attempting to surpass the men heard earlier. As if on call, every doorway swings outward, and with brief glances, he can spot scores of other folk.

People stream single-file from rather untidy lodgings, unifying in due course like a ruling tide. William is swept up in the moment, but takes casual glances towards their sorry state of affairs. Between awkwardly flung, arm toting carry-ons, he can peek within nearby quarters. Each suite is filled to the brim with able-bodies, packed snugly within niches of their neighbors' packstuffs, stocked like an artist's pencase. A painful number of excursionists drowsily lounge about, others eccentrically glide towards the first-floor stairway.

Those following are crass with retched stenches, bearing spew and urine, suitably tracked into the halls by numerous parading feet. This justifiable rank spares none, gouging all eyewells alike, and compelling those unseasoned few into indecent, blubbering fools. Rancid smells degrade the guests of any sensibility, they rashly coat themselves in patchwork outfits and pieced together articles of clothing.

There are plentiful supplies of jackets that are inherited from recently expired loved ones, or gloves bartered in exchange for hours of quaint toiling. While the destitute can only manage so much regarding their questionable choices of attire, William cannot make out a single hat among the flock. Of course, there are hoods, coifs, and furs, however he spies no headpieces. Notable townsfolk procure pompous wide-brimmed hats, they become relative status symbols, and are adorned with luxurious plumes of fowl origins as a showcase to their class and worth.

Outfits of atrocious taste tend to divulge more modest natures, vagrancy is despised by most influential Bannermanes, especially by the Mandonmen, who considered sootwrasse lamer than a two-point buck. Every settlement is deemed property between one of three mercantiles. Mad River Junction is under the steady guise of Charlie Mandon, a ruthless financial maven, and convoymaster of the western reaches. She is instrumental to the Bannermane cause, and minted her trading empire merely by tickling two coins between her fingers.

Charlie is a fearmonger at heart, and no matter leaden legs or frostbite wrung hands, her squall-dogs would howl, "If ye can't pick up an axe, yer not worth ah notch in the ledgah."

Preaching adversity and 'fair-shares,' her creed is succinct in abandoning those infirm, considering them quirks and troubles. It's not pride they pour into their labors, but selfishness, an inherent need to lavish in privilege.

There's a limit to their patronage, a precise number before they sever stakes and split. In Bannermane society, those are nickel, fingernail-sized pieces called trademarks; ten can be yielded for a brass tenmark; one-hundred and one-thousand ceded for silver billmarks.

William has negotiated a hefty premium his departure, the contents of coal appreciating upwards in the ten-thousands of marks, even prior to an esteemed assayer's evaluation. He's overwhelmingly optimistic, confident enough that there will be a bill of sale, officially stamped with the seals of House Sauder and the reigning seat of Bonaventure station. A boy Jones is always disgusted with the notions of looting, although 'appropriating' may be a term more befitting of his style. The stairwell takes offense as an oversized suitcase slams atop each creaky step with blundering *thumps* and *wallops*.

Reaching the bottom of the flight, William briefly stumbles with his luggage, as the bosun's trunk is rather unwieldy, completely worn down on its corners over the years. He was very fortunate to acquire it, even after the ferryman's awkward incident.

Several heads perk towards the blundering noise inside his hardcase, a notoriously clumsy scraping. Only he immediately dismisses them, his sole goal is to be out the foyer in a matter of minutes. Dozens of feet stomp across the upstairs hallway, with many others rising to action in their wake.

He descends into a dismal scene of poverty, men and women are strewn about the floor like verminfolk. They sprawl about on patchy blankets, while others idly wrap themselves underneath layers of clothing, throws, and pelts.

Bittersweet noises of bard-like luxury distract and soothe the ears of its residents, these are the charitable fancies of some tavern howler. Subject to incessant noises at the bunkhouse for these last few weeks, William knows the ire of this trouble-maker. Hearing the finale culminate into a rousing chant, Cillian finishes with a riff on his hurdy-gurdy, an otherwise rabid machine of crankshaft, keys and string.

That shrill, off-pitch voice churns out, "Break out the growlers, talk for hours! Lilly-liver chuckpeas make an excellent stew!"

Upon sewing the last note, he immediately cradles the instrument into his shoulder, anticipating a righteous applause. A few awkward seconds later, Cillian is reminded he's entertaining the wretched people of the Junction.

With the spirit of contention, he spouts, "Well, if that's 'ow it's gonna be, maybe next time I should play ah sad song for all ye sad people o'ver there."

Cillian strides for the door posthaste, clambering with the handle, and blurting out, "Too late now, I've got places tah be. I 'ear the patrons rilin' 'ready!" Before promptly shutting it behind him.

The dining hall itself is an incredibly lofty room, staves of timber are embellished with pig-iron chandeliers, shadowing several towers of luggage and travel gear in a rather bleak scene. The desolate bar is naturally devoid of spirits, and instead features dozens of empty platters under torchlight whilst vegetable compost is scattered all about the floorboards. There's a sizable, cauldron bare of any broth hoisted over the bunkhouse pit. Many huddle here, dedicated themselves to the warmth of the dwindling flame. Dark forms silhouette around the perimeter, carefully avoiding the windows even if they were sealed with fabrics long ago. There is no staff to be found, the innkeeper herself must be preoccupied somewhere else.

Destitution and poverty runs rampant as people attempt to escape the unrelenting storms. However, there's no short amount of politeness, the ambience fills with "'Ow-do-you-dos" and "Good-tidings." Passing shabby assortments of kin and acquaintances alike, William sidesteps around, acknowledging those with an impulsive, "to you as well" before hastening towards the front door. He emerges to a recently shoveled deck lacking numerous sets of bootprints. Shivering with delight and glee, he must be one of the first few outside, it only betters his chances on making the wagon train.

There's a flyer nailed onto the entrance's trim that flaunts the caravan schedule, a note which has become otherwise unreliable, some sporadic arrangement over the past two weeks. Four large lines of prose taunt him- missed opportunities, he had only just attained the voucher from Eli the Stockpile. The notice itself is crafted in weighty woodblock text, of which the numbing cold has already dilapidated. Rich black ink has begun to fade, giving it a distinct matted appearance and texture. In whole, another lackluster stain on a lightly yellowed sheet paper.

Today's departure is the last prospect to leave, there are no other options. This hitchpost has been a blunt, but otherwise necessary end to his recent promising venture, he plans to return to Lucy's Isle and conclude his tour. William knows when it's time to call it quits, soon Mad River Junction will be engulfed in the brackish swells of barrowtide.

Sheltered by the wooden bastion and unassailable mounds of snow, the Junction's boardwalk is a slender avenue, strictly housing a few prestigious estates, the square, and magistrate's station. Scores of buildings stem from here, gradually ebbing away from the extreme weather. The wooden porch of the inn is set just alongside the main promenade, offering a glance of the morning trek to come. The trading depot is slightly less than a twentieth-league distance- a winding path through the burgeoning settlement, yet William can't help but feel appalled and intimidated. This is no simple trek, every step outside encourages the reality of the situation, the road is paved with fine layers of pale earth. Nearly every walk of life is combed over in lofty sleet, it would take hours of excavation to uncover. Numerous homes have been lost, as the weight of the snow easily crushes households into frozen crypts, displacing and forcing families to live out the sorrowful weeks in the bunkhouse.

A particularly brawny fellow is driving a wedge-shaped plow, clearing the tidings from nearby walkways. An abundance of snow rests at his forefront, making his efforts remarkably slow and steady. His figure appears fairly abominable, clad in numerous layers of thick furs and wool. Upon noticing his presence, this man pauses from his strenuous work with a gentle wave, pulling down his fabric mask, and revealing piercing amber eyes.

"Mornin', 'Liam. Fancy ah kiss? Been dustin' dis burg since first light."

"'Ere, Bywata! I can't catch-up, see ye in the next coon's age. I mustn't miss muh train!"

"-can't blame ya. Git luck on ye advent-ah, ahvent-ah, anuver gud venture, suh!"

William often ponders that he doesn't belong among such delightful people like Bywater.

After these prompt goodbyes, the quirky vagabond resumes his mundane task, propelling himself forward with the aid of his own two feet. They are overly exposed, with each of his seven toes leaving their unique imprint in freshly fallen snow. Unlike the common man, Bywater is a true miscreant and oddity. Denizens of the frontier can be victims of peculiar affairs, influenced by corrupting magiks which alter the ichor of mind, body, and spirit alike. Some possess uncanny abilities, like an acute sense of smell, others will flawlessly strive due north; Bywater is immune to the taxing chill, much to the demise of ordinary folk. His existence threatens the Bannermane way of living, he is different, awkward, yet better than the average man in every way.

The surrounding promenade has been stripped of its identity, lying empty, and near abandoned. Folk would once flock to its stores, the Hinds Woolier Shoppe, aromatic bathhouse, gamekeeper's office, confectionary; even the taps of the local soda jerk and birch beer merchant, Bourbon, had her warehouse pilfered. Crime is becoming rampant, and thankfully, hasn't escalated past petty theft. There's no town guard to keep the peace anymore, most have ducked away, turning into pathetic villains themselves. During the occasional, erratic visit, mercantile agents are responsible for keeping the fragile balance between order and chaos. They're undeniably efficient, and merciless- the settlement reverts to its swindling episodes. The amenities of society are souring by the day, frequently snowfall reminds the bannerfolk that they reside in shambling dread.

Redoubling his efforts, William shortly finds himself traversing a trench, there's a narrow but brief opening amid the top. With the consistent blizzards, no one, not even Bywater can keep up with maintaining the roads. Day laborers do well to focus strictly on the essentials, that means street paths are only cleared a couple shoulders wide. This trench he trudges through is fortified by snowbanks twice his height, and looks as if it could tumble at any moment. William's thoughts are jarringly interrupted by someone hollering further down the passage, could this be a member of Bywater's company?

A quick-whipping shout careens down the trench, "Clear!"

Some perverse moment of silence follows, coercing an earnest lad into believing they imagined a voice on the wind, until, "Clear! Clear now, bison on the path!"

The voice echos harshly from the drift, it could be coming from either direction, the constant curves in the path only give him twenty feet of direct sight. William panics, intensely debating what he should do. He's heard the stories and can't risk running into such a gnarly beast head-on. A thick white cloud pummels into his face, as the mounds of snow start to tremble, snapping him into action. Aggressively digging into the snow bank, William carves out a shallow niche to scurry in. The little suite completed in record time, he now sits on a throne of long-preserved, flattened grass and permafrost. William tries to reheat his delicate hands inside one of his inner jackets, while using his legs to pull in the luggage box.

The trembling intensifies, more or less refilling his temporary hideaway with loose pack snow. An immense steely hoof drops down, nearly the size of a human head, keeping pace by another, and another and another, sinking deep within the solid ground; these steps continue to trample further down the path. After casually sticking out for a glimpse, William returns to the fray. This wooly terror is now coasting a corner, its hulking berth reaching the height of the snowy sidewalls, dense overgrown fur eloping in tow. Its head turns backwards over its shoulder hump, letting out a booming guttural bellow.

All accounts show that bison have only been domesticated within the past few decades. They should be treated as reckless, endangering wild creatures, but this regard doesn't stop common folk from rearing them for their precious meats and furs. Even the Bannermane elite attempt to domesticate bison early on, imprinting young calfs known as red dogs. These laborious beasts-of-burden are raised into lives of heavy servitude, trained to be ridden as armored calvary or pull lengthy caravan sleds when they come of size. Bison can withstand brutal temperatures, conditions that scold the wickedest mongrels, tame. Among the grandest creatures these badlands have to offer, they are absolutely extraordinary, and are the only beasts able to surmount the nigh-impassable, northern mountain ranges. Bison are dire breeds without a doubt, beasts that never concede and would sooner march unto oblivion.

Caught in its awe, William admires such a magnificent creature- but suddenly, a crowd envelops him, all hounding the giant beast's lead. It's too dense to see where they're going, but one could only assume. A few overly-packed individuals tumble with their belongings, accidentally stepping into the bison's oversized footprints. Securely straddling both hands around his carry-on, scores of stranger folks and neighbors are pushed aside as William eagerly surges forward. Having been caught in Mad River Junction for a stint of time, there are familiar faces among this crowd.

There's the furrier, Marlene Hinds and her butcher-hashing husband, Kirk; a tailor going by the name of Ayers Beechworth, then Galvin, Mandt, Sassafras Pache, Rabley, a few debtors and laymen further dress this awkward cast. Each one anxiously exchanges their qualms with William before mustering into pace. Mandt hastily strides alongside William, bickering like birds of a feather, and hurtles a friendly punch into his shoulder. She's a familiar stray, habitually haunting the boulevard borough for prospects like a pesky crow. This alley-cat favors herself as a curator of admirable ancillaries, an exaggerated item broker, and is a frequent patron of William's fetch-quests.

Mandt has a penchant for mischief, particularly around gremlins and their meddlesome tempers, having them scrounge for fiddle on a jumble of zany stints. There's a refractory flanking the Junction's broadway, a spacious, walk-in kiln used as safe harbor for Mandt and her stock cronies. She's always lurking around the oven, it acts as a vault for all her procured wares: baubles, jewelry, and trinkets able to be sealed away on a whim. This gives her, and the higher-end items, the placating aromas of copper and evergreen oils. Clients ante when their affairs are dabbled with more successful scents, it makes them appear faintly exotic. William can tell she's spent the early morning tucking goods away, she possesses a distinct, earthy aura, with a soothing hint of dried wicker.

Two bronze chains are strung around Mandt's neck, while an owl's head pendant gently sways to and fro. The horned one clutches a glass vial between its beak, corked on one end, allowing the solution to ferment. The viscous, lilac-tinted liquid fosters a single lavender wand and several dancing elderberry beads. Through a trick of the light or reflections from the snowfall, the elixir appears to be glowing with misty cerulean haze. Occasionally, nearby clerks can be overheard speaking borderspiel, a rough dialect of common tongue.

It sounds like nonsense, like chucking a perfectly, well-versed conversation through a gin gang. Caravanhands splinter their words out of necessity, as out across the flatlands, while the wind tickles at their throats, convoymen tend to speak as little as possible. Instead these bannerfolk focus on practical hand signals, body language, and flags.

Quite a number of vagabonds loiter around the statue of Charlie Mandon, their unbridled champion, a true vanguard of the plains. As a woman of unwavering might, her likeness is cast entirely from bronze. Dubbed, the Maven of Lucre Dawn, she poses alongside treasures with a billhook thrust upright into the air. While her feet melt into an ivory brick plinth, they shine brilliantly with gleaming golden patina. The convoy's merchantmen rub the caps of her boots for good luck, some even close their eyes in brief prayer, begging for fortunate tidings. William and his entourage criss-cross around decorative hedgerows, their once vibrant green colors are hardly decipherable, permanently encased within ice. The courtyard is littered with wooden crates and lockboxes, the bulk of which are being packed onto sleds, heaps of provisions to be towed by their beasts.

Not nearly five minutes down the promenade, visitors begin to arrive at the town's most prominent landmark, Mad River's local caravan post. It's a monumental sight, highlighted by a colossal double-door, able to withstand even a bison's gait. A wrought iron gate is stretched across the span of these planks, coiling and sprawling like tress, giving it an artistic, yet mangled appearance. The walls of the Junction's station are supported with raw timber, pillars of scaly pine that seep fresh syrupy amber sap. It drains from the hampered tree in clumps, catching the sunlight as if they were excreting precious gemstones. Bannermane building practices are new, crude, and precarious, with architects operating strictly on a 'as-needed' basis.

The outermost surfaces of dwellings are protected by thin, metal sheets, some buckle off walls in entire patches. The cold consistently strains lumber, goading each nail until they eventually ease themselves out, and every panel along with it. Burnished copper is practically universal, and flattened into a foil for construction. They retain the sun's heat, and prevent build-ups from pack snow, which collapse roofs with sheer weight. The roof has another exclusive resident, a limbic flue, which helps cycle heated air throughout an entire building. Recognizable from their iconic horsehead beam, they regularly bobble up and down, spewing a furnace's waste and roiling fumes into the sky. Clans of the territory revere machinery, commemorating the ingenious industry of the brighter minds that have come before. William's parents were fascinated with history, these inventions remind him of the steel horn stories that would draw black bile from the earth, draining it of toxins.

As the morning crowds draw near, the handbell once again proceeds to furiously shout.

Clang-clang, clang-clang

Distracting them towards crew-controlled queues.

The complex is compartmentalized between three sections: a boarding shelter, reception, and storage. Two clerks are nonchalantly calling out for tickets, affirming that they be out and ready. Once waved through to boarding, every traveler is greeted to the inspiring sight of three towering bison at the end of the hall. The withers of each beast reaching high into the rafters so that they must duck upon exit, and their horns regularly scrape at the sheet tin roofing. Many clerks seem to nip at their heels, snaking swiftly underneath as they port nearby cargo.

There is nothing more grisly or intimidating than a Judah Steer, the largest is decorated in a vicious assortment of deep scars, its horns adorned by permanent red staining. Travelers from far and wide flock among them in macabre adoration, a few young children brave and dare one another to touch their hairy hides. An unexpected and harsh snort is enough to drive them away, fleeing back to their families. The beasts periodically stomp their hooves, testing the firmness of their cleats by scraping them harshly against permafrost. These spikes provide additional friction on the ice and help guide their strides. They continue to shake while their lead is hitched, yesterday's snowfall still clutches to its mangy beard like a mongrel to meat.

The bison herd is nestled securely in dozens of straps, hitched to the helm of three, blatantly over-packed carriage cars. Their reins recede into the gaping mouth of a winch, this distinctly-carved figurehead is a totem in the silhouette of a screaming wolf. A metal buggy intended for the rider is placed at the forward, the ferryman's booth is a mastercraft of status, dashed with a variety of strongboxes and assorted containers. The covered passenger coach follows next, much longer and complete with two lengthy rows for seating; passengers are already boarding, some even overflowing onto the slick roof. No convoy expedition is complete without a caboose, the third car, lashed as a low-bound sled, it holds another collection of storage boxes and also a few luckily seated patrons. Any cargo deemed valuable- abet too large, is securely fastened in rope, and attached to drag behind.

A few caravanhands can be clearly seen struggling upon a chain of knots. They intensely focus on their handiwork, one is of measly stock, too anxious and repeatedly misthreads his rope. The clerks are under the scrutiny of an enforcer: a strong and silent bosun with terrifying presence to match. While a pair of orange-tinted goggles may mask his eyes, they can't avoid his dreadful gaze. He is burdened with traditional padded armor, twenty pounds of gear that grant a weighty and impressive stature. The lower half of his face is skewed behind an oversized neck-guard, while thin, curated strands of mustache hair barely weave their way around.

Unlike the Underdark factions, Bannermane cannot brawl in plate armor, the cold renders metal brittle and liable to snap. It is second nature to sheathe weapons and stow equipment when not in use, instead to be saved for when the moment's right. An ornamental broadsword remains stashed onto the guard's back, carefully shrouded inside a vibrant and luxurious fox skin. Bannermane troopers are often awarded animals pelts to signify rank, this man-at-arms identifies as a captain. Their pommel has been replaced with a carabiner, keeping many stray keys, and a personal seal used for stamping official letters, close at hand.

The trooper routinely cocks his head from side-to-side, maintaining a full field-of-view over the boarding area, and religiously monitoring every departure line. His mere presence vexes any would-be, tin-pot soldier, those that would test his mettle, attempting to lay their hands on the convoy's meager supplies. There are no exceptions to his intuition, even the crew are suspect.

William has a keen eye for the caravans too, watching for passengers every duskday, only to discover their emptied houses the following dawn. The wealthy bided their time long ago, retreating to their bountiful seasonal hearths in the Underdark. He recognizes most aboard the convoy as honest folk alongside their kin, venturing to escape just as he. In typical frontier fashion, the women dress in pelted cloaks crowned with oversized headpieces and unfurling plumes, every man wears tightly stitched leather-pieces, with rolling bundles of cloth adorning their upper arms.

Ah, he'll miss the Barrows dearly, especially Herald. He was very grateful for their company as not many families would willing take-in some reckless stray. Mad River may have been a tad tumultuous, but it was a charitable lifestyle for a decent knave like he.

Boarding at the caravan post is an extremely delicate operation, and those waiting are firmly instructed to form lines as a belligerent Mandonman howls on.

"Ticket, ticket, ticket would ya! Quit yer lollygagin', 'ready. Stow all dem shouts n' bellyaches. Some o' us got places tah be, dontcha know?"

William is drawn into a group of anxious villagers while a clerk reviews their corresponding papers, afterwards delegating them towards the passenger car. There's plenty of lounging downtime, folk are sparing morsels of food among their family members, humming hearty tunes or reciting poetry, rustling intensely through travel bags, then stamping papers atop their forearm with a personal seal or the like.

Their line is paltry, continuing forward at a snail's pace until William reaches that cusp. This is his moment, respite within reach.

Over this slow admission, the crowd has swelled into nearly a hundred folk. Their fluttering commotion briskly reverts into a crescendo of caterwauling, each person attempting to speak louder than others nearby. The distant sun proves an adequate distraction for William. He embraces this rare comfort, bathing in its warm rays, stretching his arms taut and arching his head back. It's the scarce calm before the storm.

The solispyre is indubitably revered by all Bannermane, their gleaming beacon over an otherwise desolate wasteland. A prosperous omen, children born under its grace are rumored to be gallant and pure of heart. It appears erratically, almost prophetically in nature, on select few occasions to scatter wicked blizzards and gales. Undiluted sunlight sears everything it touches, an inherent danger behind favorable weather. Not only does it completely eviscerate human skin, but reflects off the ample snow causing blindness. This fleeting sickness is avoided by wearing goggles and routinely resting the eyes.

William habitually pulls at his face wrappings, attempting to give his sight much needed relief during the wait, however it grows dimmer by the day. The waning solispyre dictates an end to the dry and prosperous, aptly-named bloomtide season, as sunlight will eventually ebb into darkness, bearing way for wanton weather, cold spells, and brackish tides that leave soaking wet barrows. Mystics treat the winter season as a great cleansing, a linger frost that dulls the senses, drawing kin closer to the safety of the hearth. Scholar's recognize this critical juncture, and anticipate the longest season on record. Everyone appears eager to wait out the coming storms at Bonaventure, in the relative safety of the Underdark's vast network of passageways.

During such incredible busyness, an official finds himself strolling the grounds with urgency. Checking that clipboard manifest, he records the number of passengers and makes consistent calls to fellow clerks. He's dressed in traditional Bannermane garb: a tightly-bound maroon bandana slipped around the right forearm, a hefty matte snap-buckle strapped around the torso, and a crest stitched into the largest lapel; a knapsack drapes around his shoulder. Recognized throughout the northern expanse, an elderflower blossom, decorated within twisting lines of buds, is the iconic sigil behind Mandon's mercantile.

What sets him apart from the other clerks is a very distinguishable pauldron, draping down of his left shoulder into a leather guard sewn with royal red threads. This distinct armor doubles as a sheathe, holding a short billhook, the perfect weapon for hacking at ice or wood. Outfitted for battle, these additions make him very intimidating and menacing.

The Mandonmen themselves have always occupied a very commanding nature, an aura of self-arrogance emanating with every step. Unlike the Masterson and Sauder guilds, the Mandon mercantile habitually contends within the farthest reaches of the north. They uphold much harsher lifestyles wherein the strong rule, firmly believing they hold humanity's destiny in their hands. Their company operates on whims, appropriating whatever property they wish as compensation for their efforts, often overstepping their jurisdiction against frontier settlements, in acts even deemed sedition against Bannermane authority. On those fringe settlements like Mad River Junction, they are considered by magistrates and magnates to be a necessary evil, the Bannermane avoid usurping them for fear of the backlash that would follow. Often Mandonmen are responsible for granting them such a prestigious position in the first place.

Clearly distraught, the official calls over his caravan team and the two additional clerks that are overseeing the crowd, and ten men huddle around in frank, subtle discussion. William can only decipher bits of their conversation while they continue gripe and insult one another, speaking haphazardly.

"Oi, ye fancy git playin' tin-pot!"

While the caravanhands are distracted, there is no sneaking about or mob mentality. No one is daring enough to bite the hand that feeds them, any altercation would jeopardize their ever-valuable seat. As the situation grows ominous, everyone simply remains quiet.

The huddle breaks at once with a few men dispersing, returning to that nearest coach while a handful of others succeed with their ferryman. This extraordinary gentleman approaches the crowd, slouching his shoulder to remove a slingbag. Fondling around for just a brief moment, he pulls out a metal hailhorn no larger than his forearm. Halting himself thirty feet from everyone, the clerks position themselves in preparation for the announcement as another drops a two-tier stool onto the ground. Gently clambering on the platform, the conductor adequately judges that he's ready to speak. Mere seconds later, his once mellow voice booms through the device, resonating over the entire audience.

"Greetin' common rabble and 'bonds, mah name is Morgan Pikewise, ferryman o' this 'ere outfit. From da bottom of muh heart, I bear da most unfortunate tidins. We will nah longa 'onor any furtha tickets."

The mass of passengers, including William, begin to groan and clamor.

"Settle down, 'ush-up ya barnacles. Der 'ave been ah numba o' counterfeits discovered and 'agen we don't 'ave 'nough of dem seats."

A wave of panic ignites the crowd, some desperate and dedicated individuals heave forward against the clerks. Frustrated shouts linger into the air, "Ye 'aven't checked mah ticket!"

"Mine either, tis stamped- official!"

"-there ain't enough bloody room," the conductor responds with dreary vindication. Perhaps he even shed a tear in the moment, as Mandonmen are ruthless actors.

Another figure among the crowd pipes up, "Check the tickets that 'ave 'ready rung! All the fakes 'ave gone first. Kick 'em from the wagons!"

Williams spins around to a light tapping on his shoulder.

"Let me bark at ya. Those fakes 'ave ah lick o' red 'round the top cornah. See, see the black etchin'?" Marlene exclaims, showcasing her voucher under all the commotion.

"Big 'oss, we got families o'er 'ere!"

"Tink o' da children!"

It is at that moment the conductor bends over to whisper in the ears of three clerks, he has spotted something elusive, and points towards the center of the crowd. They've had this kind of talk before, a bridge crossed one too many times.

These men forcibly surge forward, avoiding pairs of clingy and grasping hands- ducking and weaving until they locate a young girl, no more than five years old, kneeling on the ground at the feet of her parents. As throngs of people continue to merge closer, it's exceedingly difficult to make out exactly what is happening, some are aggressively pleading with the convoymen, and situation quickly turns into a huddling mess. Arms outstretching towards the center like a maddening prayer, everyone is reaching towards the men to separate them and the child.

The ferryman's voice continues to eerily linger on, "We understand dat does stayin' will face 'ardship… der-for we 'ave decided tah take da young'uns."

Deep amid the group, the clerk unsheathes a polished theater knife, some thin, six-inch blade, threatening those around him as he frantically attempts to draw some breathing room. This empty space reveals the two other caravanhands, one nursing a fresh head wound, and a tiny river of crimson seeps into the snow.

The infuriated spectators, realizing they can't directly confront the official, instead grasp at the child's coat, attempting to pull her back into their swell. The girl is certainly engulfed by the crowd, partaking in a primitive game of tug-and-war just prior to the clerk's landing. There's a groan of desperation, and suddenly the gleaming shine of silver disappears.

"Back devils!"

A woman's ice-shattering shriek pierces the air, some shrill more intense than any broken steam pipe.

Ah-gah

"Nah… oh no-"

Suddenly the air is rife with some sickly gasp and grotesque sputtering. A man is frantically grasping at the dagger forcibly set in their throat, blood oozing rapidly around the gash until he begins frothing from his mouth.

Using this alteration as a distraction, the officials rapidly collect the remaining children and usher them towards the convoy. The young girl involved is sobbing uncontrollably, unfortunately old enough to understand what has occurred, especially as the victim's other hand still remains latched around the frills of her coat.

This man tumbles forward into several inches of snow, collapsing to his knees while the clerk works frantically to undo his grasp.

The caravan's enforcer has keenly finessed his way into the ensuing conflict, and hurtles a kick towards the victim shoulder, sending him careening into the permafrost. With a vicarious *scoff,* "Filthy bleeda," he nabs the clerk and daughter, escorting them from the fray. They swiftly retreat with the child, consolidating with other convoymen and their prizes, whom are all ushered towards the passenger carriage.

Reaching at his leather guard, the ferryman unclasps and draws his billhook. It's an exotic looking weapon, fashioned with a gnarly blade that tips forward from the handle. The hilt is embellished amidst fitted gold studs, imbued with a faint ashy-blue glow presumingly enchanted by an artificer.

His shielded left-arm braces toward the crowd in one flowing movement, his feet part to shoulder's length, and both hands tightly seize the billhook's handle, rearing the weapon defensively- a posture reserved by foremost accomplished veterans.

Even with such a dreadful action, no one retaliates against the clerks. Blood has been shed, a treaty broken. It is only with such a cunning act of remorse that they're reminded about the fragility of life.

The mother is profoundly dumbstruck, a real Calamity Jane, and is seen weeping onto another's shoulder as her daughter is escorted away onto the caravan coaches. The sole comfort she may muster are simple gestures, a goodbye wave choked with grief.

In all, they make room for eight remaining children, most are caught-up in the abrupt sense of urgency: a sudden direction that has distracted them just long enough to avoid confiding with their families. Some relatives have to be restrained by townsfolk.

Dark murmurs openly fluster about, they are left with one unfortunate consensus: there's no point in attacking the last lifeboat, it's inhumane either way. A shrouded figure grumbles a series of unrecognizable, borderspiel mutterings. There are certain standards to be met on the frontier, including common law against murder. This clerk will meet his fate, but at the timely action of his own people. In some corrupt sense of frontier purpose, the people are unwillingly grateful, as the whole town will be buried within a fortnight. No one pulls any punches, there's no hint of struggle, the world remains still and watches as bystanders to a perpetually harsh reality.

The perverse awkwardness is only broken by those bisons brays while they nip at their harnesses. The conductor pulls at his cloak and strides past in an intensely powerful movement, heftily climbing to take his place atop the lead car, then wrapping those monster reins tightly around his wrists.

Since there's no additional room for boarding, his crew struggles to notch themselves around the sides of the passenger coach. One particular Mandonmen hitches themself into the loose cargo dragging behind the caboose, lashing hefty amounts of rope around his waist. There's an overwhelming sense of desperation. Cascading from the glacial face like a towering waterfall of clouds, an oncoming storm can be seen past the lake in the north.

"Pay 'eed tah mah words, as I don't be pridin' muhself ah villain, nor fancy murdah. We all worship da frontier's divine law, dat does endure persist, and does dat fall short perish. This may be yer end, but take comfort dat yer names will live 'notha day. Now ye fools, stop fluffin' 'bout 'ready. Thin does crowds and tend swift visit 'ome!"

Hailhorn in hand, a seated ferryman turns to address his company.

"Flanks secure. Gales at da rear. Liftin' for the 'venture by mornin'."

A clerk responds atop the rear sled by waving a yellow flag.

"Garrison nigh-no time tuh waste, all 'board and 'eady!"

With his bosun's approval, that ferryman finally casts aside the metal instrument, and with beaming pride, reveals a sharp bullwhip stowed beneath the seat. In one malicious movement, the cord cackles and weaves, *ca-rack, ca-rack,* snapping at the leading bison, the cracker nearly searing the Judah Steer's hind.

What starts as a mere tug is driven by pure instinct now, the beasts of burden heave and surge forward. Each hoof sinks through three feet of snow, the frigid earth trembles after every tremendous step. The cables that bind the cars together strain under the pressure, brittle metal groans audibly in response.

The convoy inches forward at first, a snail's pace for those clerks still feverishly attempting to lash themselves aboard. They trudge alongside frivolously, a moment of opportunity soon turns to peril when the convoy rapidly outpaces them. Two men are left in visible anguish, they ache and *groan* while the sled hastily distances itself.

The couple lunge in one final discouraging throe, grasping for any loose ropes dragging upon the loose white glaze. Even if they had the momentum, there was only another hundred feet of opportunity before the terrain shifted to unassailable ice. The tributary's frozen rivers are unforgiving, and bison caravans erect a certainly abrupt, jagged surface in the wake of their travels, a steeplechase of sorts. Untimely pits easily catch feet and sprain legs, leaving travelers completely stranded from the shores.

At last, the three-coach convoy's immediate departure leaves many rattled, but none so much more so than the stranded crew. Aghast and thrown asunder, they lie among the snow in a state of complete defeat.

Minutes bleed to hours, the caravan line becomes another ominous silhouette on the horizon. Now no larger than a speck of dust in someone's eye, if one were to blink or lose their concentration for a split-second, they'd miss it.

The withdrawing convoy miraculously bleeds into the air, folding over itself and becoming formless. Blending into the sky's vast ocean, beast, buggy, coach, and caboose alike vanish without a trace. The crowd bears witness to the cold's most recent, dazzling phenomena, a fleeting mirage reflecting off the river, a true Fata Morgana. No one dare breaks their stare, it's not so much the disbelief as it is penance- dreaded realization: the culmination of their entire lives is now rendered void. There will be no further aid, no help is coming, all hope has evaporated, such are the ills of frontier living.

Life is undoubtedly bleak, and this particular series of events is built with unfortunate happenstance. Severe seasonal storms frequently batter the flatlands, incapacitating and unjustly starving many local towns. Countless migrating vagabonds, those desperate to make a living, find riches rediscovering what was once swept away by the wilds. Rambunctious folk known as trailblazers cling to the notions of limitless freedom, then are swift to be reminded: that on the bleeding edge of society, there is a broad line separating the have and the have nots.

A sparse, considerate few stock themselves around the newly-nominated widow, comforting her through this irredeemable act of tragedy. She cannot swallow the frog in her throat, once howling in rage, her fresh cries are nothing more than sputtering whimpers wrung from a wet rag.

Snow can be perverse comfort; the pain helps people forget: numbing the body by portion and parcel, depriving those senses until there's a complete absence of emotion- no feeling, rumbling in the gut, neither dreams nor mulling thoughts, just an empty void, a husk of who the person that once was.

This widow lies sprawled on her back, wallowing on the ground, and staring absentmindedly at the vast sky. Her eyes are completely bloodshot, nearly rendering the poor woman blind with a combination of poisonous guilt and grief. Her complexion has been scarred and hideously warped from the ongoing trauma. The mother treated her little half-pint as royalty, a precious mink among the marshes, presence to treasure. Now she had lost her true Charm and joy in this world, still somber, but however grateful that the innocent lass got out.

They been watching this sorrowful stent for hours, and their remorse is broken by someone's feverish attempt to address the crowd. The figure's routine outdoor outfit is comprised between cloth fabrics and furs, cradled by some thick leather apron wrapping around the speaker's neck with spare twine, while their skirt lounges entirely below his thighs. This smock lining has an over-abundance of pockets, granting the blacksmith the decorated appearance of padded bulwark. An additional bandolier straps against his waist, draping a dazzling array of wrought tools, specifically suspending a one-handed hammer, which is soundly clasped on his right-side.

The man is a genuine artisan, even crafting his own rigidly-set, smithing mask, his upper half of face is draped underneath an overbearing leather cowl, allowing for his facial hair and chin to flaunt openly. If it wasn't for classic, jet-black tint of the goggles, any objects in his spotlight would be prospected by a pair of stark, evergreen eyes. The smith's burly, mahogany-shaded, squirrel of a mustache is truly iconic, commandeering an explosive five o'clock shadow following the curvature of his decisive brass jaw. In some gutsy act of self-ordained dentistry, a curated selection of copper canines seat themselves alongside an arsenal of creamy-yellowed teeth.

Between hide and hair, the empty space on his face is rocked by wrinkles. Smiths often have worn complexions, and this burly character is no different. This trait is especially prominent on his cheeks, where patches of exposed skin are dominantly dry and flaky. Easily distracted by the Fata Morgana, William had missed the beginning of this smith's rousing speech.

"Beans," the boy Jones mutters under his breath, now intently listening while the wright jabbers away, "-we are bound togetha by some common creed: just fightin' 'gainst impossible odds, through thick n' thin- even gotten our rears 'anded to ourselves one certain way or 'notha, but we always bounce back, we always endure. 'Agen tis day shall be no different, nor tomorrow or the next. Oi, this ain't no wienie roast. We're wrought of stern stuff. As long as those continue tah act n' cooperate, our dawn will always rise the comin' morn."

Attempting to lighten the mood, his tone becomes very inquisitive.

"Where is that greasy magistrate o' ours, eh? Prolly took our coin n' fled off tuh Hearthland so, blather-on 'bout legerdemain."

There are numerous- understandably, foul expressions about, along with a few innocent mutterings, confiding that this was indeed the case. Losing children and being left for dead tends to be a traumatizing misadventure. Regardless, the smith affirms their struggles and gives his people a temporary sense of direction.

"All lookin' ah bit dreary. Perhaps it'll be best tah spoil spell under ah touch o' rest. 'Ush-up for now, 'cause tomorrow we'll 'ave ah bit more sense. Letta gatha in ah place somewhere like the square- or nah, the inn 'stead. Might get chilli after tis eve. In the meantime, letta have the eldahs return tah their carehouse, everyone else make for those bunks o'ver yonder."

Vernon turns his attention to the abandoned mother, "Ma'am, that nearly-tolerable brute, Jerome, has offahed ah stroll and stay 'round 'is 'earth. Someone tah give 'onest company, watch over ye, and ah goon who crisps decent pork rind."

Strangely enough, these words are comforting to the widow, as those that experience loss too often become lost themselves.

His address is met with a thunderous applause of moans, but no one actually detests the smith's thoughts. Not only is this man's voice reassuring, but his face beams with a sense of prestige. After all, he's a familiar face around town, crafting all this hamlet's wrought iron fittings, hinges, and nails. Wrights train under Ignis Lampblack's hierarchy of metals, demonstrating their fondness of copper, bronze, brass, iron and steel. Young tikes always linger around Vernon Waulbellow's forge with delight, dancing among its intense heat and sparks. If it weren't for his charity, Mad River Junction wouldn't be more than a stain on a map. Vernon had nothing but ill-repute for those Mandonmen, as they too often sold him materials at exorbitant prices, then treat his craftsmanship as cheap goods.

"Ain't all but swindlers n' thieves," he'd often declare while drunk as hurley to common patrons at the bunkhouse bar.

He isn't quite wrong, nor is he quite right. To the avail of countless trailblazers, Charlie Mandon is a regular fortune finder, not an idol any decent folk should be looking up to. She is a true bonanza king of the north, conniving and ruthless. By making a hobby of crowds, and becoming bully-rooks with betting men, Charlie acquired her illustrious land, mines, and some rather explosive tendencies. One quarry in particular produces reddish-blue gemstones, and when they are duly-blessed by mystics, these rocks can produce disastrous results. She exploited this weapon like a bag of cheap tricks, sowing wrath upon her self-labelled enemies, until she seized an entire swath of territory without consequence.

It's a diabolically shrewd business strategy, as since bannerfolk strive for their independence, no one dared unite against her. In Charlie's hands, the Junction is just another exploitable asset. However, with Alexander Bannermane's rise to power, a new dawn approaches: maybe there's an opportunity for change, and those honest threats will finally be dealt some worthwhile frontier justice.

When the sun descends westerly and the air subtlety bleeds into throes of twilight, a destitute horde begins slogging their way back through the caravan station. There's a dear old mum singing hymns among the alleyway, cordially enchanting innocent passerby with her odes of better times.

Others scoff at tract so frost-perous, and untame.
Rile and bum to the caravan trail's dull flame.
Cross the wold wake, in the gait of glaciers great,
A Warwick family stakes their claim.

But alas, such cold drudgery,
Swindle friend, foe and dear company.
To the brink and led astray, still the Warwicks stride way,
To fill their hearts with gold, lavish luxury.

With their heads hanging low, leaden with sorrow, the ground becomes painstakingly noticeable. Those wooden floorboards that decorate the trading post have splinters that dance jarringly upwards, along with an occasional hole, to which these features catch the loose snow tracked-in by dozens of stumbling feet. The townspeople have no remorse, confessing, "So be it," should Charlie Mandon's place of office become mangled. A pity of sorts, the Bannermane flag drapes over the exitway, it would make a wonderful buff.

Hoisting the hefty trunk towards his side, an incredible cloud of frustration greatly looms over William's head. This evening he'd be halfway towards Bonaventure with forty pounds of luggage strapped safely beneath his feet, he had never conceived a notion otherwise. Instead, the stars now align for a fabled return at the bunkhouse. Another stay, coddled in some dank, dingy room with wild men, spirits tilted to their mouths and laid low, drinking in praise for the end. He could make proper certain, half of those drunkards never escaped their beds. To be fair, stormtide season bears forth over eighteen hours of blanketing darkness, regardless of alcohol abuse, schedules tend to get rough.

Large portions of the streets are engulfed with a lingering nighttime gloom, with those scattered lampposts providing a meager amount of illumination, barely surpassing the steely-blue glow of the waning moon. This cairnmire dangles heavily, clipping mountain-peaks in the far east as a totem of phenomenal sensation, flooding the wilderness with radiance and shadows distant stars. The shamans chronicle the moon as both a vast ocean, and an unfrozen oasis in the sky. It stirs illusions of splendor while beasts lurk amid the midnight gleam and spirits flourish. Under its gaze, droves of people quickly spill onto the promenade, leisurely trailing in the stead of those before them.

Very few travel homeward, instead notching themselves firmly into nearby snowbanks in destitution, without a respite or proper place to rest. The town is decaying, there are plenty fearful to return home. Dwellings on the fringes of the Junction have been already gutted, looted and ransacked. There's nothing for them, not even kindlestuffs for a fire. It's safer to flock, and take their chances in crowds.

Several people are edging away from their audience, mingling instead towards an isolated bluff; after waiting all day, this has been the only opportunity to use the privy.

From the corner of his eye, he catches wind of a certain, lone hearthbound smith. After showcasing his wisdom and astounding confidence, it's a wonder why the wright is not among dear friends or an entire entourage. William attempts to mingle closer, shadowing merely steps behind, thinking that this well-connected stranger could be his ticket out of here. However, the jostling of the boy's hardcase is enough to warrant attention, and the ironwright procures a fleeting glance over their shoulder.

Continuing at pace, the smith makes a glaring observation, "Oi, this roost 'tween me ears may be addled n' ould, but I be 'errin' ya, lad. Bark-up, were ye needin' somethin'?"

William finds himself stumbling over his remark, not necessarily expecting such a retort. He decides to present a petty question, some query with an obvious answer.

"Yes-'um, yeah. I was wonderin' if ye knew when the next train will be arrivin'?"

In response, the smith closes his eyes, and taps thrice between his eyebrows with his left hand.

"O' gosh, apologies there. I think everythin's finally catchin' up tah mah, didn't intend tuh come-off so blunt."

To appear amicable, nonchalant and fairly human, William pulls down his wrappings while he speaks.

"No worries, mate. All us 'bonds 'ave been rattled good. Say-nay to those bogarts, act as if it didn't 'appen."

"Ah-ah," the smith momentarily stutters, treading carefully upon which details to disclose.

"Ah-actually there won't be some'notha caravan for ah coon's age. Us hoosiers are on our own from 'ere on out. With 'ow those Mandonmen cut thread and ran, I expect this tah be our worst season yet."

Not apt with casual conversation, he swiftly turns and continues on his way.

"'Erring that ah storm's been brewin' all week, and it's gonna 'it big tonight. Get all quiet and spent, 'ead on 'ome!"

William keeps pondering to himself, an inquisitive feeling that 'perhaps he knows something else,' and the earnest lad continues to pry somewhere between interrogation and politeness.

"Wait, please wait!"

Scurrying to catch-up, and promptly halting once they are shoulder to shoulder, William openly flusters on.

"There's no way they'd skew us like that, leave 'em bleedin' all season. The Bannermane gotta send someone fit. Last year we spent two weeks at most-"

"-that was with stocks 'pon stocks o' medications and rations, now we got nothin'. Those thieves stripped the Junction, liftin' supplies from the storehouses right under our noses. Noticed muhself after some chaps misplaced- or so they say, some charcoal o' mine. So I says, oi, and took it tah the big loaf, Morgan 'ikewise 'emself- wouldn't even let me intah the caravan post. 'Ad to be why that hoosier packed up and left too- Hoosierfeld Char, our magistrate, I mean."

Perplexed by this information, and feeling quite ignorant, an awkward silence fills the air. He had no idea how bad their situation actually was. The bunkhouse must be a festering pit by this time, folks gnawing away at one another for scraps. In times of frequent hardship, William himself can go lengths without nourishment, yet he's famished. It has been almost a full day without a morsel, and nary is he besieged by thoughts of hunger. Fending starvation is about keeping the mind occupied for a bit, finding a prevalent obligation to focus on: constantly worrying about the convoy and its traumatizing series of events were sufficient enough, until now.

"I can't 'elp but notice yer 'andbag there, were ye pilferin' for ah place tah roost and steed the night? Can offah-up some floorboards o' mine. Can't imagine it's too safe sleepin' at the bunkahouse."

Deep in thought, William shakes his head upon finding himself staring at the ground.

"Uh, actually I'll take ye up on that. Such ah prospect sounds delightful."

Then, remembering his manners, the lad enunciates his appreciation, "Thanks. What do ye need as tenda?"

"Oh, nothin' yet. Don't mean there's ah lack of 'ard work, we'll find a use for ye yet."

From what the wright had just divulged, William is extremely grateful of the opportunity, the Junction will rapidly descend into fanaticism and chaos. Common law or not, people are bound to get hurt. Besides, it's no burden to Vernon. The wiseacre seeks apt fellowship, lest he be some lonely, greying man drowning sorrows at the end of the world. And you never know, being band with such a sincere soul may part William a bit wiser.

An ominous, encroaching stormfront hastily coerces the sun into an early grave. This prompt descent bathes the promenade in immediate dusk. Twilight beckons forth copious amounts of intense, murky gloom, a clout that yanks at every ankle, nook, and cranny, hauling headway until it swallows entire figures, and douses residents with darkness. There are those forced to navigate around once familiar objects, cluttered barrels and crates aside the walk which are now, simply confusing shapes. This botched assortment litters the area with inky shadows, obscure illusions that loom just out of focus.

Not one body reaches for the streetlamps which draw oil, but supplies have ran dry ever since the drovers pushed their cattle to pastures southwardly. The bunkhouse has an overside brazier fueled by pitch, however that sludge burns with foul git, it makes all kin within sniffing distance ill.

There are few folk lucky enough to lodge at home, specifically with enough hotrocks to tender flame. Because of the occasional crackling blaze, a windowpane or two shimmers with scarce radiance, just enough to line ruinous faces with envy. This subtle glow gives them the appearance of draugr, withering and mindless beings, pale impressions of their former souls.

Much like the aching permafrost, there are those who rightfully fear an eternal night: the soothing solispyre- the life-bringer, shadowed by eons of raging storms. Even the pastel luminance of auroras appear to retreat during the barrowtide. Instead of sprawling across the vast night sky, their godly craftsmanship and breathtaking, glittering and glistening performance is ceaselessly bound to the ground. Perhaps it's to mock those who carefully steer their travels, fleecing their journeys home into something dimly foolish. From here on out, the tundra will flow with rivers of emerald and teal.

After a few minutes of pacing together, they finally part from the frigid main avenue, cutting ties with any nearby audience. William is anxious and clever, sizing-up the smith's character through their straightforward small-talk, providing prose to avoid any suspicions, and lying when his conversation gets too personal. Old men are happy to divulge the finer details while those young'uns are weary of it.

The boy Jones would much rather focus on the obstacles at hand. These sidewinding streets are encased in torrents of waist-high snow, transforming an otherwise casual hike into a strenuous slog. Heaving forward, their harsh breaths frequently sow their conversation, and the wrought drops a subtle reminder that this is a common commute, everyday at dawn and dusk. Decrepit rows of abandoned timber townhouses surround them, and on occasion, their second floors have imploded under the ample weight of snow. Even though the world is decaying around them, with ample debris strewn about, the smith continues to lead William confidently to the farthest reach.

There's an obscure stairwell descending onto a patio below. Several inaccessible doorframes line the permitter, blocked by an endless cascade of pack snow. This area is coated in an obscene amount, acting no more useful than an inescapable pit. The duo immediately plummet, snow seething into his outfit, finding its way into every opening originally thought inexistent. Expelling a muted *shriek,* William finds the frigid cold overwhelming. Snow only exacerbates the intense cold, an invisible, unnerving toxin that seeps from fingertips to toenails. Their heads barely break the surface, and the earnest lad actually clings to his hardcase like a liferaft.

The mounds of snow are remotely traversable by attempting to tread, fluttering arms and kicking. He discovers this by frantically trashing, careening his available arm wildly around. While the boy Jones recovers, the iron-wright has already made his way about, opening an available door ajar and coaxing him inside. Being submerged in precipitation is the strangest feeling, William has never had an intention to swim, but roughly imagines this must be similar.

Through an awkward combination of hopping and squirming, he catches a second wind and reaches the entrance. Surging forward, his heavy footsteps collide loudly onto the wooden floorboards. With the extreme change of pace, William grows a little disconcerted, and tumbles onto his knees. Layer upon layer of fleece garments cushion this abrupt fall.

The door is forcibly shut behind him with a struggle. Those battered wood planks *creak* and *moan*, trembling very loosely on their hinges. A distinctly broad strip of lumber squarely leans off to the side of the nearest windowsill. The smith takes this particular timber stave, sliding it within two precisely installed brackets, bracing the entrance firmly shut. William stumbles to his feet, conquering the three inches of slick that has flooded into the studio.

Unfortunately, there is no pleasant furnace to greet them or warm their spirits, instead the room is tainted by severe cold. A couple oil lanterns are encouraged to illuminate while his eyes pry at shattered windows, where sleet leaks in through the gaps like soot.

William tears apart his facial wrappings, every binding densely soaked in an unfavorable mixture of saliva and sweat. His dry, wilted nose is assaulted by the age-old smells of cinders, meat, mold, and rot. This shelter is worse for wear and under constant siege.

There's nothing around but bare furniture- no chairs, or sheets; just an individual cot lined with furs, a basic stove with its exhaust piping out a nearby breach, a cupboard with empty provisions, then lastly a single workbench surrounded by piles of lumber peelings and two bottles of varnish. With the appearance of a dingy closet, this hole-in-the-wall is a stay nowhere notable: the ceilings droop, making everything feel more akin to a cellar or crawlspace. He might pummel his forehead into some rough-cut timber rafters, and come off this affair rubbing his noggin, a tad bit worse for wear. However, even with his cantankerous attitude, William's appreciative to be finally protected from the wind.

The smith is by no means naive, and notices William's curious, instigating eye.

"Know it ain't much o' an ensemble. That table o'ver yonda is where I whittle. Busy carvin' 'andles, tikes enjoy special tokens 'ere and there. Ain't 'bout the marks. Anyways, welcome tah mah rough and 'umble 'earth. Put yer trunk down- well, anywhere really. I'll see if I can scrounge up lil' somethin.'"

With a calming nod, the smith forgets the foyer and heads directly to that awry cabinet. For roughly a minute, the greybeard finds himself scarcely rummaging between scores of empty cans, just to reveal two dusty pieces of jerky. They've been cached on the second shelf for at least a year, if that's to be believed. Contemplating to himself, 'as ma said, beggars can't be choosers,' this preserved meat should be roughly safe to eat, maybe even with a subtle hint of flavor.

He swings back to address his company, "If ye don't 'ave anythin' packed, ye can 'ave these. The grime builds characta, ya see? Adds tah the flavor."

"No, no, seriously I couldn't- shouldn't. Please no. What will ye 'ave?"

"Oh, nothin' tah fret over. I'm not one tuh worry, usually somethin' comes 'bout soona or later. Just gotta be patient."

Despite the hospitality, William successfully coerces him into taking a portion. The two men idly relax their backs on the wall, and stretch their legs out on the floorboards. With a sensible chuckle, the smith stares at the piece of jerky before taking a bite, "Congratulations on survivin' yet-'notha day on the frontier, 'ere's yer 'ard-earned reward. Cheers!"

They raise their pitiful meal as if knocking glasses, both breaking out in a fit of laughter while scoffing it down.

The boy Jones leisurely confesses, "I nevah did catch yer name, wright."

"Tis Vernon, Vernon Waulbellows. Now, I've seen yer ilk 'round 'fore, but can't match name tah face nor face tuh mileage. Ye are-"

"Ah, beg pardon, yes 'deed. I'm William, 'Liam Waldah-Fields, nary ah score."

A fleeting grimace crosses his face, "Fields, 'uh? 'Aven't came 'cross one out 'ere, why aren't ye swole in Bonaventure with the rest o' them orphans and urchins?"

William constructs another fib- 'no,' he tells himself to ease the guilt, 'more like an exaggeration.'

The boy Jones exaggerates to the greybeard that had never known his true parents, instead he grew up in a chapter carehouse, was adopted by a paramount looking to swell his company. And how, like the usual fry, he avoided school like a plague, and once becoming a decent age, embarked from convoy to convoy, passing through almost all the Bannermane settlements. Wasn't long until the Crooked Men took a liking to him, and eager for coin, worked a few odds and ends before finding himself in Bonaventure on their tickets. This immediate compulsiveness and swiftness to lie frankly surprises William.

"Actually, my fatha was ah Fields, took me all 'cross the nine winds.

Course, only adopted me for the labor. Though, gotta say, 'e was ah mighty fine caravaneer. Good with 'is 'ands, lots of jobs 'ere and there for some layman."

"Awfully strange that 'e would 'ave 'is kin take ah bastard's name. Sure that always got ye ah lot of glances 'round town."

Vernon clutches a dwindling flashrod, indistinguishable from his very sooty fingertips, just enough kindling to light a single wick upon the brazier between them. It sparks as a numb, sandy orange, until seconds later, steadily blazing with hues of ruddy rose. Vernon continues to query, "What 'appened tah them, why are ye 'ere famished and 'lone, young'un?"

William relinquishes a hint of truth, "Man, just wanted tah stave out on mah own for once. Ould'em I'd meet 'em this Moorseason, at the Giles Carnival in the 'venture. Where is yer family, wiseacre? Ye don't seem like ya enjoy bein' 'lone yerself- too young," he jokes, chuckling.

"Tis a spiteful tale, lad. Mah maiden grew red with the rot. We dredged out o' Urbana, 'owever sickness is ab fret ye can never seem to escape, n' tis easy tah get caught by the Underdark's guise of safety. Aye, no 'aven there, just plenty o' painful memories. The clans ate away at muh family 'til notha was left: gaffer starved durin' the great debate, meema married-off for packstuffs, bruvver conscripted, guttersnipes lost and nevah found 'agen- stolen by those pigs of war. All I'm left with is their names: Wells-Doubleday, Lyn, Victor, Clyde, Clifford, Camille, Marilyn, until it's just me n' muh shame. Lived in the Junction twelve years now just tah leave that place 'hind. Thought I could leave it all, everywhere I go, death follows, like it's inescapable. All I want is ah life of peace, somethin' to build 'gain-create, and maybe I can outlive ah life of loss."

William's stunned, solemn silence consoles the trauma, because sometimes that's all that's needed: an ear to the wind, someone to talk to. Vernon never expected a real response. There's nothing compared to familial love, it's true compassion, greater than any victory, a warmer feeling than the morning sun or kindling fire.

He knocks the back of his head on the wall, staring straight into the ceiling rafters, eyes gently glazing over in thought.

"They buried 'em already, ya know? That man skewered by way o' dagga drew the throat. Nothin' tah bark 'bout, decent eitha, 'is corpse is restin' 'neath three feet o' snow. They 'ushed it up, marked it with ah flag not steps from where 'e was slain. What ah nasty turn of events."

"Tis the way of things, it could always be worse."

Vernon mulls over in thought, "Yeah, but it ain't 'ave tah be, things could be betta too."

This evening's weather sets-in harshly above the junction, granting gale-force winds a fierce howl, shifting between the shuttered buildings. This massive, regurgitating stormfront drapes the entire town with an onslaught of snow, immediately extinguishing any ambient light and plunging the settlement into murky blackness. This sudden torrent of flurries prevents anyone from making trivial ventures, barricading every doorstep in copious heaps. An unhealthy chill stalks these pioneers, unlike any cold they've encountered before. It snakes around for vulnerable prey, seeping through the tiniest nooks and crannies, paralyzing victims in lull of the hearth.

Given the gravity of the situation, these two sit in good company. A duo of able-bodies, one with the necessary experience to steel any situation. Their basement dwelling trembles against the skewing winds. Ample grime pours from rifts in the floor above, coating the cot's furs in a fine layer of lampblack filth. Vernon stirs into action, directing his protege towards the lumber pile of scrap near the stove.

"We'll fangle these rods 'round openins we find for insulation, force 'em in as tight as possible- ya 'ear? Especially 'round the door. I'll prop ah few pieces of timba to 'elp brace it."

William rolls his eyes with visible frustration, without a hammer, he'll need to rail the dowels painfully with his palms.

Vernon reacts in adamant surprise, "What? Those Mandons stolen all muh nails, and not the ones on mah fingers! If we don't cramp these planks intah these gaps, it'll get tah be ah pretty uncomfortable night."

Most of this woodstock is bark and trimmings, perfect kindling, and adequate size to wedge in every split. Between smidgens of brother-like banter and bonding, these two bully-rooks finish their crude handiwork in record time, though nothing a true carpenter could ever be proud of. Three sturdy staves now reinforce the door, while behind it, the snow's steep height on the plaza grows ominously immense.

Continuing their conversation about the territory's distinct settlements, Vernon simmers on, "Ye evea been tah the Isle?"

To which William nods.

"Must've been a sorry sight, lad."

"Oi," the boy Jones affirms, "Poor taste- bettah scenery."

That old greybeard sputters into laughter, "O, right ya are!"

While they may have prevented the unbearable, immediate cold, there's still a lingering chill. Only a fire could offer respite, the stove is unquestionably alluring. It's a chance to cleanse the soul, an opportunity to dry otherwise drenched boots and gear. Vernon has been having difficultly setting anything alight. He'll approach the furnace periodically, attempting to flare a certain spark from his meager supply of flashrod, but is unfortunately unable to tender any real flame.

While the wright made his latest bid, retreating henceforth to warm his mittens, William struggles around in his luggage. Storing his portmanteau on the other side of the studio, he flips the forty-pound hardcase to reveal a slew of essentials items. His clothes are bundled tightly in a transparent tarp, confined inside a great heap of charcoal. There are quite a few sizable chunks, some pieces that have jostled enough, fragmenting into smaller lumps. Grabbing a handful of this debris, William makes an effort to light the stove himself. He kneels into the cast-iron kiln, ensuring that the charcoal is cradled by loose bits of moss and trim debris. With a swift strike of the flashrod match, the bedding ignites into a suitable flame, and he shuts the grid-iron grate proudly.

This culmination is enough to warrant Vernon's direct attention, who appears more frustrated than delighted. He spies inside the carry-on, which fills him with visible disgust and sours his expression into a nasty scowl. He grabs the boy Jones by the fringes of his coat and exclaims, "What injustice is this? N' don't go lyin' tah me boy!"

Caught by such surprising aggressiveness, there's weariness in William's response.

"Ah- ah, I stripped them from the Wellesley Quarter. Those meisters won't be missin' it!"

"This right here! See this?" The smith clutches a fistful of charcoal, caking his hand in soot which slips through his fingers. "You're no betta than those Mandonmen, lootin' hotrocks from every storeroom. This is an obscene 'mount, and yer 'oarding it from othas who needs it!"

"I 'ad tah, Mr. Goodsir! Tis the only way tuh get ah ticket n' job for the Crooked Men!"

"Even worse, William! Those hoosiers are ah gang of 'ighwaymen, the robba barons o' Mad River. What made ye think that they could be trusted? Where's yer 'ead? Betta be gettin' rid of 'em."

It's an honest question, they're felonious fiends, a frontier cabal of knaves and dastardly thieves. The common rabble of these flatlands crave order, sowing law from the wilderness. It's easy to find a place in society, acting as a simple cog and working one's way to complete the daily dredge, but to William, that's nothing more than a slow death. The Crooked Men is just another clique, a method to earn his passage and travel the vast expanses of the world. Perhaps, Vernon is justified to debate the ways and means, even if no fortunate soul is harmed along the way? Is it not the obligation of young men to push boundaries, and wiser men push back?

"No, Vernon, don't spew this venom n' nonsense! We need these 'otrocks tah trade. Tissa flatiron and neitha o' us are prepared. We're famished, runnin' on empty, and there's barely two slivers o' exhausted jerky 'tween us. Then we 'ave tuh worry 'bout canteens, bedrolls, lantern-"

The studio reverberates with a series of interrupting, abrupt curses.

"-Consarnit, wretchman! Ye-yes yer correct, but that doesn't make it nearly right. Keep these spoils to yerself, I'll figure it out in the morn.'"

He's very rattled, covering his eyes with the palm of his hands in visible frustration. Vernon aggressively strides towards his fragile cot, blowing out one of the lanterns hanging along the way. Now, dressed in a draping darkness, the smith kicks his feet up, and the whole bed slinks another six inches lower, shrouding himself in skinned fox and hare pelts with a *hmmph.*

William exhales a long-awaited sigh of relief. Graced with an evening's shelter, he didn't expect his generosity to be so callously tossed aside. The dingy floorboards are dilapidated and splintered, nary a comfortable rest but a respite nonetheless. Adorned in vast fleece laters, William sprawls on his stomach, resting his forearms awkwardly underneath the chin, uncomfortably stirring every few minutes or so, burrowing his vulnerable face into an elbow or staring aimlessly into an ominous corner. The soft, lounging berth of the fire hardly hinders the intense, amassing chills that skulk soundlessly above the ground. The raging light is already dying, yet they need support of the hearth, and William rekindles the flames' coal much to Vernon's anguish.

"Oh bother," the wright cries, half-asleep from across the room.

II

RECIPE FOR DISASTER

William awakes to nasty shivers, immediately keeling his knees upwards into his abdomen as frightened, shuttering whispers escape on his breath. The quivering frenzy begins inside the chest, where muscles tense and tighten, rattling every tendon from fingers to toes. Midst the night, a thoughtless, traumatizing bitter lie with him.

Both nearby lanterns have faded to fumes, dwindling down their rationed oil fuels. With no one to tend its flame, the stove has gone out too. There's no way to tell how much time has passed, every window is a portrait of white paint framed with ice. Fierce gusts rage against the building, which quivers, crying those desperate groans. Calamity can be heard outside, as timbers fracture and snap when footfalls of snow leaden their roofs. In this waking moment, he peers towards Vernon resting in a cradle, blissfully unaware of the ever-present, invisible, bone-chilling geist.

Attending accruing shock, William emits a paltry string of pained whimpers. He feverishly jerks his arms from within their sleeves, caressing his chest with numb limbs. A dulling fog overcomes him, a grinding delirium that saps the restlessness from his body, and bleeds his thoughts nearly unconscious. At the moment, the heavens and earth themselves collide. An intense, soft light floods the room, it seeps through every gap: windows from across the room, ventilation around the ceiling, and every opening from the floor above. This sudden illumination blinds his eyes shut, leaving every other sense open for intrusion. The rank whiff of death, decaying rancid meat, overwhelms both nostrils. His eardrums are struck by the discordant scream of a woman, a mundane life or death trill, yet far worse, easily eclipsing the events at the Junction's trading post. With a crashing thud, his brain rages and swells with pressure, as if some brute bludgeoned him over the head, and William finally falls into a restless slumber.

He unexpectedly finds himself in a foreign, yet familiar tract, muddling in a quarry of stone. The yawning crater is shallow, surrounded by an endless acre of ominous, obtuse woodlands. William is unable to find his bearings as these copses tower above him, clipping at an aurora above, which is a compelling verdant green. Their vast thickets are dense, each branch forking into a mindless, innumerable array of timber tongues, threatening to swallow him up. The rind of every nearby tree is scarred in a glaring parade of lacerations, remnants of foul git. There's an assortment of loose cobble that lies at his feet, and a miniature monolith in wake, an assembled pyramid of craggy rock.

This rekindles faint memories of the outlying cairns from his childhood, and as William attempts to gather the stone around him, he distressingly finds that every fingertip has been worn down to their nubs. The profound lack of linen around his limbs, gut, and feelers is just as frightening. Wearing next to nothing, he instinctively starts to jitter and twitch. William has no memory of this journey, nor his intentions, only that he must escape, and flees in the opposite direction towards a twisting crevasse.

Appalling clouds haphazardly brew together as noxious cold grey. A fierce gale immediately sets in, howling all manner of cursed and foul language. It calls forth the most tempestuous fury of primal hate, an elemental rage orchestrated for only death itself. Those that hear its heinous call are met with despicable eldritch horror, a voice that engulfs victims like a tide to ocean. His ears are overwhelmed with their piercing screams, an unearthly manner of anguish and grief. This call seeps deep within the skin, turning flesh frigid and weary, the blood pulpous, and bones bleaker. It's an intense and formidable warning, a siren's scolding shriek; for something lurks amiss, hidden by nature's wrath.

William's eyelids completely glaze over, encasing themselves within a grizzly coating of frost. Icicles creep upon his face, congealing ample streams of mucous, and searing otherwise fragile, dry skin. The constant onslaught of squall and sleet allows strictly for an inches' pace every few minutes. He gradually grovels ahead, patiently biding for the next opening. William battles the ceaseless fray, enduring the absolute worst the world has to offer. Battered and bruised beyond heart's content, he continually drudges on, legs shuffling forward, one after another. A formidable amount of flurry grapples towards his waist, a sheer snowfall that leadens his feet in place, and fully halting his advance. The ever-cursing winds shriek, attempting to bury him within a pale, white grave.

There are fleeting moments, fervent desires of escape, but the body acts as a puppet with every string cut. It's as if thousands of blighted hands tug sharply at his heels, attempting to drown him into the earth, another victim filling a silent tomb reserved for the dead. Like the echoing laughter of arena spectators, the winds continue to holler their profane encouragement. The gods gawk and jest, yearning for this destitute mortal to succumb underneath several layers of fresh, pureblood snow. So many before him have fallen, trampled by such bleak reality. He screams a subtle cry, a perverted gasp that falls just out of earshot of every listener. Year after year followed by day after day, survival is a daily pursuit- it's all trivial, a human being can only bear so much.

As swiftly as the proverbial priest counts their blessings, these foul gusts shift and welcome timid weather- however so brief. Could it be a roguish, unscrupulous taunt? The flurry openly flusters yonder, hastily lashing itself to the boundaries of forest, and forming a momentary eye of the storm. The bitterness of the temperature goes lax, steering away and receding just like the winds. The gales have manifested into a physical barrier, preventing escape.

Occasionally a billow bursts into this serenity, becoming nothing more than an opaque mist that fades just above the tundra floor. It's as if nature itself grows arduous of the encounter that approaches, and has firmly decided to retreat. An awkward amount of time passes, anticipation that begins to churn far sour. The seizing terror of an unexpected guest leaves a persistent shiver, an anxiousness that rattles every bone, a nausea irking its way into his very core; crowning within his mind as a discord of maddening voices.

Amid the edging brush, a brawny, hairless head breaches forth. It is both breathtaking, and dumbfounding. There it lies, a behemoth of disgust, uncharacteristically attached to a slender neck which frivolously snakes and surveys the frozen permafrost. This ghastly array begins to gasp, then abruptly snaps upwards, uttering a guttural clicking cacophony fathomlessly within its maw. Other than the rows of jagged icicles that fill a gaping jawline, the bodiless beast portrays a truly frightening human-esque visage. The eyes, an unholy culmination of golden citrine shimmering ill-omened gemstones peer energetically across the steppe, analyzing every nook and crevice. Consuming rich scents, the nostrils flare with every croaking breath, needlessly expelling pine odor and clouds of warm mist.

Even from this distance, the putrid stench of rotten flesh coddles its gums, while the skin is rife with musk mellowing in brine. The creature reeks of fell, an unholy matrimony, a binding of men and pure chaos. Now the beast curiously gazes towards him, appearing absolutely riveted. The skin antagonizingly crinkles around like a mask with each curl of the lip, an occasional tooth perforating an unholy smirk. This burnt umber expression tightens further as it openly stares, eyes untimely blinking out of unison, indistinguishable from a broken record.

Oh woe, what an ailing fate, just encountering this fiendish creature is punishment enough. The hideous tendril-like neck, which pulses with every largo swallow, cranes to blot out the hazy sun. Its insurmountable necking easily exceeds the height of three men. This avidly appalling devil sneers, locking its gaze with Williams. He is a tortured soul, entrapped by an endless watcher. Even worse, it bellows a gravelly cackle to rile the scene.

Such situation grows incessantly dire, the noise it emits sounds vaguely human, like a man trapped inside a circus costume for twenty years, even while it perpetually crumbles away. In a declaration of malice, the beast speaks from the perspective of an unfathomable nightmare, lips curling unnaturally to simper upon the far reaches of its cheekbones.

"Amid great emptiness, what do you fear more? Do you dread the loneliness, or the answer?"

There's a vile, gripping silence without the nipping wind to interrupt. A tell-tale heart dares not to reply, any response may be too provocative. It readily grunts in utter anticipation, continuing to prod while smiling to unnerving ends. Depravedly, the situation dwells on for minutes unto the hour; even if there was a chance for escape he cannot summon the audacity to try. Under its ever-watchful gaze, each breath and upheaval of his chest brings a fresh glaze over its eyes, as if this wicked fell recognizes the tenderly value of what lies beneath, bone, flesh and sinew.

Sinisterly, the beast conjures another trick, almost repeating itself.

"Is it the furnace that drives the heart of the desire to do more?"

There's a subtle promise for an exquisite adventure into the great beyond. As a true patron of lost causes, he emits an untimely and distinct *groan*. Not simply in fear of his tragic life, but the discomfort of holding such position for the better part of daybreak, the hours are glancing by. The creature's presence vies a mortal coil, every fleeting moment is a reminder:

this is a monstrous beast, charading as the form of man.

With no answer to its query, a wicked smile now contorts into a grimace, toying has led to frustration. It strides forward, emerging into the clearing at full breadth. All fears have been confirmed.

There, in his gaze lies some supernatural bastard, a true fell beast and prophesied spawn of ruination. Instead of relaxing abroad on the shoulders, the snaking, behemoth-sized neck is instead a tongue, and stretches into a gaping maw. Spewing rows of serrated teeth, this unholy gullet stretches underneath the collarbone, wedging far inside the abdomen as if split with a godly axe. There are numerous, human arms dangling around, vile appendages that quiver in anticipation, waiting to toss carcasses down the all-consuming throat. With barely two identifiable torsos, flesh is fiercely twisted upon one another, bones skewed where they shouldn't. Pieces of gristle openly gawk through the skin, which is wound ever-tightly across the stomach, particularly inching as barbs along the spine. Like some unnatural knapsack, the beast's back bulks into a considerable hunch, adding to an already formidable visage. It clambers ahead on two brawny, bear-like limbs that are dusted in pale fur. The hindlegs are just as malign, peculiarly arched to pounce on lonesome, ensnared prey. Whenever it lumbers forth, these feet linger on the ground- a maddening movement, consummated with a sharp *pop* as the tendons stretch. Perhaps it's some form of perverted showboating?

It beckons a heinous call, there's a sort of ominous guttural chanting emitting from the mass of fleshy teeth, even as the head openly dangles above. Striding closer to the entrapped man, this unnerving melody rapidly swells into a chaotic chorus with every step. His audible whimpers are barely interrupting the auditory plight, he can hardly begin to withhold such dread. Facing a terror five times his size, screams of desperation only catch in his throat.

"What do ye want? Stay away! I'll hurt ya!"

It's a trifle of a threat, but pure anguish is a gratifying curiosity to fell; so it abides, abruptly halting in place with scarcely an effort. It's difficult to believe this seething abomination is capable of eloquence, yet, it decides to speak once more- gravelly and hoarse, just like every other ordinary man with an unusual face.

"*Hmm.* There is something awfully awry, you seem almost too familiar."

Even at an impeccable distance its mammoth-trunked neck swiftly swivels downwards. Positioning itself just within just a few paces where the nearby air immediately reeks with the rancid odors of detritus, salty sweat coats its skin and congregates among patches of hair. At nary a glance, putrid wells regarded as eyes brutally attempt to determine his identity, piercing right through what remained of his steadfastness. William braces, but can't help to remain powerless, utterly devoid of hope.

"Yes, yes! You are the alderson boy, the one forgotten among the vaults who strayed from his flock. You have scoured the farthest reaches to my domain. My-my, what has become of you? Speak child, and receive my blessings, my mark."

Conquering the distance in a moment's notice, the twitching, bloated corpse manifests itself straight before him. The acidic breath of its maw singes his clothes, melting any ice around his goggles' frame. A single claw draws near, whose talon easily exceeds the length of any saber. It rests itself upon his coat where it promptly skewers through, bestowing a corrupt sigil on his chest. This causes him to writhe with pain, violently churning in place. His blood seethes from the wound like a grotesque beacon. Capitalizing on the moment, the fell beast howls with pompous excitement. Its heinous call rattles the old world. The sun starts to fade and everything appears to grow grim and quake as life itself quivers. The world is only as dark as imagination, and lulls for a deep sleep.

This isn't William's first vision, and sometimes, it feels more akin to a memory. Hours later, his eyes flutter to the sight of chalking white footprints, and a pair of salted boots by the door. A charming orange brilliance radiates around the room, the feeling of balmy hearth, with an inviting mellow aroma fade the traumatizing nightmare. It soothes his senses and relaxes an otherwise stiff body, consummated with an extraordinary yawn.

Sunlight, a sporadic amenity amid the basement dwelling, gingerly wafts through recently shoveled windowsills. A deliciously smelling marinade tickles his nose, emanating from a plate of salted meat and vegetables lying atop his luggage.

"I know it ain't mine tah spend, but betta be grateful now, these meals gotta be few and far between. The sprouts may act ah bit tenda, but they're scarce. It was ah reasonable trade after all, got 'em from that squirrelly neighbor o' mine next door. I still expect ye tah get rid o' the rest."

Forgetting his arms are snared within his jacket, William rises only to promptly hurtle over. As his face presses into the wood, he crawls within reach of his hardcase, setting the tempting grub beside him, and unfastening the trunk to divulge its contents. He had acquired nearly forty pounds of charcoal, or hotrocks as Vernon insists on calling them. There appears to be a decent bulk missing, approximately a quarter had already been used as fuel or traded for breakfast.

The boy Jones is indeed grateful, scoffing greedily at his portion while his hands unfurl rifle through his coat, but that doesn't end the disdain. This bountiful meal drives an unexpected bargain, overcoming William with a slothful penchant. He flusters about on his back, idly relaxing and resting his eyes once more under the subtle, waning presence of candlelight.

An abrupt, well-placed kick promptly wretches him out of this lingering stupor. These are unprecedented times, there are places to be, and he had been taking too long to wake! Vernon prods at his sluggishness, flustering William in a rash outburst of scolds.

"Up, up 'ready ya goon! Gatha yer woolies, scoundrel! Some red dog ye are, 'bout as useful as ah bison's rear-end!"

Upset by these blithe attacks, he shoves the iron-wright towards the entrance, "I'm on mah way, get goin' ya lug!"

Yanking at a pouch pocket on his chest, William retrieves a quaint, red leather-bound journal. It's coated with a thick film of black dust that keeps the distinct residue of several fingerprints. This pocket-sized notebook isn't just a grocery list, but catalogues entire swathes of indulgences, all the comforts that he had intended to spend with newfound riches. William blames the Mandonmen for his current predicament. Now sure that it's on-person, he once more, hastily stows it away. And with that notion, the boy gives timely chase, coddling his suitcase under his arm without delay. The clashing duo are out the door within a jiff, taking substantial advantage of the break between squalls, even as dense clouds heave and shift overhead.

William emerges to a harrowing landscape, and is dreadfully reminded about the ides of winter. There is a trifle of light, as the glacier overshadows the entire territory, perverting the morning with a riling cold. A definite sign of the changing season, a massive avalanche of snow, perhaps two feet or more, drown and lay siege to the Junction.

Even if granted safe passage, these circumstances still wouldn't be enough to rile folk into leaving, as if they have a deathwish: adamant and hell-bent on their own self-destruction. This is the true way of the north, become trail-blazers, magnates, or die trying in an endless cycle of creation and destruction. Humans are bound to be savagery, goaded by those seven drivers, elder gods that predate all of history on this earth. They are fell patrons that prey on human emotions, reaping the souls of the weak-willed to fuel their innate, incomprehensible desires: envy to incite them, lust to enthrall them, greed to drive them, pride to praise them, wrath to break them, gluttony to feed upon them, and where sloth only sleeps upon their bones.

Alderman archaeologists and Saltseer scribes describe scriptures once thought forgotten by time. Few can decipher the secrets of written language, and even slighter can translate helvetica, the original tongue of the old world. These learned men vividly detail beast-bringers of yester-yore as evil incarnate, and the root of worldly woes. Their presence beckons unnatural snow, and those around them are corrupted as vessels.

Of course, this could all be nonsensical hearsay, fables preached to children as cautionary tales. Orphans and urchins often weave fantastic gossip, bragging about colorful critters spotted amidst the corner of their eye. Alongside rumors of grand monsters, kindred spirits account for the whereabouts of grims, the menagerie of monsters; trollfolk that burrow underneath the glaciers and rooted groves of alder carrs; gremlins, thieving junk-hoarders of the Underdark and hinterlands; ghuls, terrible cannibals trapped in the endless slew of passages; and the stillmen of old-city, those encased in ice since the first major freeze.

The constantly-shifting weather breathes life into the frontier's frigid hellscape, terraforming the terrain, for better or worse, with every waking breath. Blizzards surge forth at whim with winds that completely sear flesh from bone. These events have little regard as natural phenomenon, they migrate, and seemingly disguise areas of interest: abandoned structures of antiquity, trenches of unfathomable depths, writhing tar pits that contain the detritus of cryptic creatures, and gaping maws garnished with scattered stalagmite-esque teeth. In contrary to the mesmerizing, gilded auroras, the unrivaled enigma of the north would be the heinous, crimson cloud, an impermeable, mystifying aura that corrodes the lungs of its victims, leaving them disoriented and nauseated. All those caught within its cruel haze are incapsulated by the intoxicating aroma of copper and sulfur.

The north can be surmised as a cruel and vindictive realm, evidence of which is strewn across the Junction as pure, fresh snowfall. It settles in mounds, bit by bit and inch by inch, like the ante of an all-stakes poker game, until an otherwise inconspicuous strip mall is nothing but a snowbank. The adjoining alley lanes and streets aren't simply dusted, but lathered in a generous coatings of ivory deluge. Thick, rolling dunes span from spout to gable, makeshift ramps that slope upwards towards second floor risings. It is as if the silken fibers of spider webs are aggressively intruding on ever aspect of ordinary life. This brackish tide swallows entire turf, burying anything along the permafrost for years to come.

When navigating polished tracts, it's far safer to tunnel through pack snow, where the flaking flurry compacts under its own weight. People of the Underdark are brash, and consider it rude not to trust the finer things of life, however, Bannerfolk are seasoned with grit, and simply scoff at such audacity. They unquestionably understand that this sort of vain demeanor is liable to get you killed. Countless folk ramble the white wastes, making one simple but ultimately costly mistake, and thus never return home. Treading on fresh snow is like hobbling on loose sheets, travelers are liable to fall completely through and get caught underneath. Most victims asphyxiate and drown in this dreaded onslaught. If one is forced to traverse the surface, snowshoes help distribute a wearer's weight without abruptly collapsing the tide.

Vernon had labored the waiting hours of daybreak by clearing a thin trench through the plaza, their newly ongoing hike instead becomes a brisk, winding stroll. Bundles of snow shore up like walls around them, easily surpassing the height of their heads.

Vernon shouts towards a nearby apartment, "A stout farewell, Jerome. Thanks for the breker, and say goodbye tah the missus for me!"

They receive a muffled, but very angst holler originating behind some window on the upper levels, *thump* and a glass pane is thrust upwards in response.

"There's always ah catch tah yer well-wishin', I don't trust it. There shall be no more gifts or gratuity from muh. Now off with ye, Vern. Yer not gettin' anythin' else!"

The blacksmith glances at William during this response with perplexity, and simply shrugs, "Whelp, mayhaps we 'aven't parted on those best ah terms. I volunteered Jerome to house that widow, and that wiseacre will prolly send 'er tah the bunkhouse in our steed."

The pair continues their journey by ascending that same set of stairs from earlier, only discovering that their returning route is near impassable. A formidably frosty enemy confront them, surpassing the heads of men, and reaching aimlessly at the powdery-blue sky.

Taking immediate action, Vernon nabs a metal shovel resting at the bottom of the flight, with the tip of its spade firmly encrusted with white, and begins excavating a tunnel and exercising plenty of colorful language. His practiced hands make the whole endeavor appear effortless, yet his age shows, a dip around the shoulders that bears worse with each heaving throw. Vernon cleaves into the nearest mound, assaulting snow clearer than the whites of their eyes. He gradually advances, fashioning a consistent shallow egress, just enough where it's necessary to bow their heads.

They're surmounting an endless barricade, like an avalanche from the cliffs of Doyle Rock had stricken the junction overnight. Snowbanks deposit a sheer endless amount of white wealth. Entire houses are buried, with their contents preserved like treasured troves. In rare instances, rooms can become capsules preserved in time, making them the target of scrupulous few, and archeologists alike. No matter the morality or self-righteousness, alderman nor harlot, everyone is casualty to that unforgiving Nana Nature. She wishes harm, intending to maim and fester wounds on those who rage against her malign games. Yanking the taut strings between friends and foes, the untamable wilds manipulate those who memorize its board by always playing with a few extra pieces. There's little regard for those that inhabit mortal coils.

Peering just over the summits, a few townhouses appear to have weathered the night- an incredible feat, as adjacent buildings have suffered far-more disastrous consequences. On numerous lots, nothing more than the occasional wood beam remains above the surface. The aftermath of this storm is the toothpick that broke the boar's back, signaling the coming of days, the settlement's end-times and encroaching doom. It's painfully obvious, the evidence surrounds them. The glacier appears menacingly above the carnage, shrouding the far horizon as another flurry of storms approaches the brink. The townsfolk will divide against one another in envy, goaded by their instinctual survival; they'll falter to lesser natures, driven by desperation. These people refuse to leave out of stubborn pride. It is their own hubris, even the worst of nature's wrath fails to convince them otherwise. In some perverted primordial law or twist of fate, humans are strangely enthralled by death, savagely bound to an endless cycle of creation and destruction. In the end, this selfish, gluttonous nature will be their ultimate demise.

Vernon's livid panting hastily quells these dark thoughts, his efforts are utterly vain. Their expedition is undeniably clumsy and slow, with frequent slogging pauses, just before stomping down snow or hurling it towards the side. Several awkward flings find their way near William's face, prompting him to use his hardcase as a shield.

He proposes taking Vernon's place with vigor, but is rejected with adamance. The duo's procession eventually uncovers a minor clearing, populated with the footprints of recent passerby. It's a lucky break during the voyage, and Vernon promptly collapses to the ground with the opportunity.

Teased with this brief rest, he immediately rethinks his prior decision, promptly handing over his shovel to his youthful acquaintance. Between his stressful gasps and heaving, mucus expels with every breath, grossly freezing portions of his facial hair.

"Up friend, give me yer 'and."

With a timely yank and pat on the back, his traveling companion is propped firmly back on his feet.

"I'm not feelin' too spry. Percilees, o' per-sah-lees, that whatever word. Mah whiskers turn greyer by the day."

Under new leadership, the remaining journey is relatively easy-going. William occasionally widens the one-person trail, collecting a spadeful, and lobbing snow beyond his right shoulder for appearances. The previous visitors have already excavated a remarkable path, an intense chore for any amount of people, a blessing to William that he'll take credit for.

According to last night's voyage, this trek should take no longer than twenty minutes. They emerge from a horde of precipitation, two hours after the dawn's daybreak. The trench pathway leads directly onto the main road, which is an ailing sight to stumble upon, Mad River Junction appears to be sinking: brittle lampposts gauge the snow's true extent, which loftily caresses heights around their vacant oil lanterns; front porches and storefronts lie immersed in utter abandon, as nature erases the defiling human presence. Strangers rally behind common camaraderie, armed with picks and spades, crumbling fort bastions made of fine sleet. They have erected another tunnel, adequately-sized for human quarry, as with the Mandonmen's disappearance, bison won't be of concern anymore. Townsfolk hustle upon this causeway, heeding directions from those scissorsmith laborers toiling nearby.

"Lay tah the bunkhouse, all-lay tuh the bunkhouse."

"Funny, peeks at that. They took yer speech yester-evening tah their dear 'earts. C'mon Vernon, we're 'eading tuh the inn too."

With shovel and suitcase hand in hand, William leads their meager company through the promenade. Nowadays, this boardwalk is an empty shell. Prior to the offseason, this strip was a bustling hotspot for mercantile and trade, vendors peddling wares of numerous local goods like handmade, mastercraft sleds from local wainwrights, along with delicious exotic meats, distilled oils and pelts.

A hooded entourage of mystics bind the Junction's latest casualties in indigo-stained wrappings, and are quietly left to their own devices.

"Ah-see-o, ah-sigh-o."

There's at least a dozen corpses strewn about a cart, patiently awaiting their turn. Once bound, the remains are gently lowered into a shallow rectangular pit, one parallel to another. Afterwards, they whisper a quiet blessing, entrusting trademark coins upon the sockets of each eye, a stiff fee for passage into the next world. Every carcass is thoroughly frozen, and immune to timely rot.

If- or when, the Mandonmen return, it is Bannermane tradition to exhume the dead and lay them to rest in sanctuary outside of town. Dying by the frost is the purest demise, the cold is illy comforting: a salty bath that dampens every sense of self, leaving fond memories that taste so terribly sweet. The wisest among revel and reminisce in these prior deeds, cradled like babes. Even life's greatest enigmas seem to melt away, the relationships wrought and those individual puzzle pieces of personality.

The approach to the bunkhouse is nothing like William remembers of his departure. The facade has rapidly deteriorated since, sleeves of bark have been entirely stripped from their timbers, and numerous windows now compose shattered panes. There's a thunderous commotion somewhere on the second floor, a rowdy riot complete with fits of rage and incomprehensible bawling. A stool hurdles out the window, landing between the duo's boots with a dulled *thud*. Loud screeches emit from the opening, and with what sounds like a dresser, a sliver of furniture can be seen firmly positioned to close the gap so that the cold won't seep inside. Appearing as a subtle invitation, the front entrance is actually propped ajar out of necessity. Various soupy odors of sickness seep outside, permitted by an unremarkable vermillion brick. These rancid fumes reek of acrid smoke, body odor, and sodden clothes with a subtle hint of feces, unfortunately nothing out of the ordinary.

Approaching this obscene entrance, a woman anxiously barges forth. She grips several produce bags, leafy greens spilling over the brim, and barrels from the building to the fresh, airy street outside with a nearby vagrant chasing after her. William braces his shoulder against the closing door for Vernon to enter, and they are greeted to a dire spectacle. The first floor has been converted to a market of sorts overnight. Makeshift, waist-high stalls balance on plentiful piles of abandoned luggage, displaying a gross amount of trade goods. There are some who lounge around on flattened tarps, swindling the last traces of forgotten booze, lazily hollering and perpetuating business in a semi-lucid state. All official clerks and vendors have long since departed, replaced by scores of costermongers that hawk d-grade cuts of meat and produce stock, camping supplies, oils, pelts, and small arms like daggers and hunting knives.

A particular knave is advocating their fine pewter canteens, "Don't trust 'em filthy mittens, stay safe drinkin' straight from ah flask!"

Across the room, the bar has since been dismantled into a stand-up stage where an alluring skald recites her verses of enthusiastic, optimistic poetry. This lector's voice is tinged with heavy accents of borderspiel, an uncommon frontier tongue spoken by caravanmen. This causes her to momentarily pause, carefully pursing the accentuation and pronunciation of upcoming lines between her lips before voicing aloud. A busker strings along, strumming melodic tunes on the skald's careful cues. It's the howler from earlier, that sour Cillian Lore, who now paces around with a merry gait and wide grin, absolutely enthralled by the skald weaving numerous far-fetched tales, leading with childish excerpts like *The Fisherman's Fox* into *Gossamere*, where a debtor discovers a long-lost treasure hoard. However neither of these stories could compare to the quintessential fable, *Magellan the Tower*, spoken true by all Bannermane pioneers and amusingly recited in rhymes. The metallic snapping of Cillian's supportive hurdy-gurdy's magpie chords and keys makes the entire experience reveling and wholesome.

It begins with an arrogant warrior, a quartermain of profound dispute and phenomenal mettle. He brandished an enchanted axe, wieldable only because of his herculean strength, an armament that is said to cleave winter itself away. This towering figure boasted about his battles against legendary frontier beasts: the Carrstein Bear, Manspite the Pale Terror, and his clashes with all manner of serpents up and down the glacial-wrecked coast. The Bannermane people plead for his services, describing a massive abomination that torment their skies and dominating the land, bawling forth as a tempest scourge. Only by venturing deep within her territory, a desolate cliff-side land of permafrost and rime, did the warrior stir Regina of the Whipporwills. The herald had finally met his match, bearing witness to a hulking bird of prey and gripped tightly in her claws. She stole the quartermain away to her roost, which rested beyond the farthest summits atop tears of clouds. This is where she introduced her fell brood, a clutch of three unhatched eggs, adorned with ancillaries and trophies from her prior guests. Regina festered and fled above the mountainside, anticipating the man's demise. However, her timely return was instead met with dismay, her three shrieking chicks starving without any bones to comfort them. The quartermain had discovered a gaberdine cloak among the remains, allowing him to glide upon a recent storm to safety. She shrieked to the heavens in anguish and cursed the warrior, vexed by the loss of her children's alluring spoil. They say her offspring seek vengeance, tracking him to this very day. That their beaks pierce thunder, claws roil mountains, their wings beseech whirlwinds; yet the man has defeated and thwarted them at every opportunity, coveted away by his magikal ward, a vermillion mantle, the same color as the birds' eyes.

There's a modest face among those gathered here, that of Mandel Haggerton, a charming acquaintance and Mad River Junction's finest cordwainer. Relinquishing the hardcase at his feet, William provides a gentle tap on his shoulder, to which Mandel acknowledges his presence with a stark hail.

"'Ere ya is, ye dandy rogue. Thought ye staved-off for good, stiflin' in one o' those awful coaches to 'venture or whatnot."

This earns him a sarcastic retort, "'Ey now, ye true rascal in return, I wasn't gonna stay willingly. Tis ah true displeasure tah see ya 'gain."

They brace arms in a familiar greeting, firmly locking their right hand around the other's forearm, and the left on their elbow. His friend bides a question with a shallow whisper, "Ye got anymore o' that charcoal still? I may be dull, but I ain't dumb. We should trade some with that costa o'ver there. Sure am getting 'ungry."

"Yeah, mate. Right 'ere," William then uses his foot to give the trunk a slight tap. With a swift glance around the room, he notices the distinct lack of Mandel's typical accomplices. "Where is Sir Bywater, or Eli the Stockpile?"

A sorrowful scowl blankets his face, "Ould Eli is just being petty, run-in' somewhere, off with his squall-dogs. Bywater 'imself is gone too, at least I haven't seen him this morn'. Plenty o' poor saps flounda'd in their sleep. Mayhaps two dozen or so expired late yester-evening, some throats were slit, bleedin' bodies were all dragged outside. Twas ah rugged mess, but 'water is a hoosier 'imself, wouldn't get caught gud by someone else. Nah, 'agen that 'is regular work on our powder mill will do 'im in sometime soon. Nay-say track-talk 'bout immunity."

William spends the latter part of an hour casually bantering with Mandel, perusing stall upon stall of the bunkhouse emporium. He bargains away all his remaining charcoal under such a delightful ambiance, trading that stiff, charcoal-grime encrusted hardcase for essential tools, a hardy pack of supplies and satchel of rations. He auctions his red, leather-bound journal with glee, shaking free of his earlier indulgences. Not only is this knapsack filled to the brim with breads and salted meats, but he has managed to procure a quarter-pint bottle of frontier rye too. An elixir that Mandel eagerly helps himself too. William's tanned belt now bows wearily with gear, but instead of the typical hunting knife or theater dagger looming at his side, William opted for something a bit more extravagant.

After belaying Kester, the arming costermonger, and that rogue ordnance dashed upon a sled, he acquired an antique pikehead from some desperate couple- at least that's what they called it. It's the ideal size and weight to wield with one hand, like an axe of sorts with a troublesome nib at the end, a better choice for chipping away at any unruly ice.

"'Ere Hagger, 'err me out. I'd like tah introduce 'notha kindred soul. 'E's our ironwright, and I believe that 'e'll get our company in short order. This fellow would be-"

William turns to no avail, wrongfully assuming Vernon would stick by his side. Instead, this 'stalwart' companion of his is thoughtfully conversing with the skald, preparing a speech.

"-I mean, that gent o'ver yonda."

Vernon surmounts the stage, standing a full head above everyone else in the parlor. His morning audience encompasses a slew of motley personalities, each adorned with dreary dispositions. Faced with similar-reaping circumstances, every one of these able-bodies are outfitted in sagging, sopping wet clothes and garments. Casting anguished expressions between one another, their faces are incredibly worn, skin damp, tattered and peeling, some afflicted by the early stages of red rot. With neither hope nor vigor, they aimlessly wander around from booth to booth, their glances firmly cast along the ground. A once proud people lie in full-view, presently broken, battered, begrudgingly accepting their slow, all-consuming demise. Now, more than ever, the bannerfolk of Mad River must unite.

"'Ey folks. May I 'ave yer attention 'ere?"

With this sudden disturbance, a few heads perk upwards with consideration and calculating scrutiny. It's almost like a steam pipe had burst, and the onlookers are contemplating whether it's significant enough to fix or not.

"Listen, and 'arken me townspeople. We're now marchin' through uncharted territory, dire straits- so iz call it, that will only be gettin' worse by the moment. I assure ye, unlike those recent years, we cannot weatha this storm. Yesterevening was simply ah taste, ah mere glimpse tah come. While I have faced my fair share of mileage, and peered perilous odds, this is the squall that will break us. Even if we were gonna cowah, and by some profound miracle- survive, things wouldn't be swole. There's no proof that those storms on our 'orizon wouldn't be even worse. We must gather togetha, and bark. We cannot live on permafrost and spite alone. These grim times often dictate our decisions for us, and this is our definin' point: do we accept the terms chosen for us or rave against the close of day, fleeing forth unto anotha tomorrow? I mustn't speak for ye, but I for one do not intend to be buried in my house, sealed-up like a tomb. Instead, I vouch we journey south, retire tis junction and seek Bonaventure's Underdark for refuge."

Now the once bleak halls of the inn are challenged with more remarkably upbeat sentiment. Residents, neighbors and laymen alike find themselves agreeing and resonating with Vernon's choice words. Families whisper among brood and knaves murmur to their constitutes.

"The winds 'owl and I angah- I rage, cause my bones ache and I am grey. I am fortunate to have greeted so many years, n' even while most were lonely and depressing', I found life beautiful and fulfillin' nonetheless. 'Err me, I am ready tah die, but I do not tender an early resignation, and shall leave no call unanswered. I will rest in due time, but ain't 'fore my kins' safety, this is why I must tread on. I loathe perishin' forthfold, and fear wadin' among the dead, therefore I volunteer myself tah be yer beacon of light. I shall see this trek through, destiny proud."

An elusive woman, skulking in the corner shadows, decides to speak up. Her impressively imposing figure burdens draping robes of silvery-pewter, the collar is decorated with a patchwork sash of golden accents. Her devotion to otherworldly spirits is accented by her totem, a magnificent helm and furred mantle, contributing to their towering frame which gently rattles the rafters. William is not familiar with her ilk, but mystics are indeed superstitious, consulting with geists on matters regarding the mortal realm.

She appears like an ordinary woman, just egregiously tall. Her sizable figure stands a full, four heads taller than anyone onstage. This proper is different than the priest lectors outside, and not just by garb. Her blood is imbued with magiks, a giant's boon, making her susceptible to taint. Fell influence tends to tweak those around it, causing men to do wild things, such as becoming feral and more distasteful towards other people. William's heard stories of folk taking with animals, distinguished by their livid, yellowed eyes. They really shouldn't be doing that, the normal amount of conversations alongside droves of critters should be zero.

"Orderlies do well tah remember their places. No one dares speak for Austerlaund but 'erself. The scrys 'ave nevah shorted mah, who are ye to judge otherwise?"

"I'm Vernon Waulbellows, the iron-wright."

"- a blacksmith, of course. And I am ordained, why would someone like myself bow tuh the whims o' common folk, some hoosier? My wards do not foretell o' any catastrophe: the solispyre will rise tomorrow morn, as it always has. Those forefathers o' yers settled this Junction, and just like them, we shall endure. I am but a vessel, an agent of ordah tah avert the sway of chaos, and I say that the spirits bless our stay. Only by the sight of prophets, like muhself, may we eva reach salvation."

"Prophets be damned, this is serious. We 'ave very lil' fire, food and medicine. The dead lie in droves 'bove n' below, either litterin' bunks or lyin' limp the street. Dusk and dawn may follow the sun, but who's to say that we'll be there tah see it?"

The crowd seemingly vies between these two leaders, do they usurp the recent traditions, or flee for safer sanctuaries? Emigration is a core tenet of Bannermane culture, settlers fled in mass exodus, departing the Underdark nearly two decades ago. Bonaventure station itself was originally founded as penal colony, imprisoning an entire host of political dissidents, those unfortunate souls from Hearthland who accidentally stepped on too many toes. Now, the emerging barrowtide season is coercing them to return, twenty years of grandstanding for naught. Will they face persecution, would they be responsible for crimes of generation's past?

The territory's first settlers trekked towards the farthest reaches of this expanse, they defied nature itself, risking their lives and more to found the towns in the very epitome of freedom. Among the wilderness, anyone can be anything, no one is bound by a family name or duty to society; every individual is the weaver of their own fate. The entire livelihood of bannerfolk revolve around the unforgiving hinterlands, adapting to its harsh behaviors, and conquering the wild unknown. Every aspect of frontier life is worn as a badge of honor, even the most trivial of pursuits, like shoveling snow or baking bread garner the respect of others; these little accomplishments stand as a testament of their triumphs, as against all odds, they persevered. Residents of the Underdark would never understand the struggles of the surface world. The townspeople would rather perish as free kin than return to the oppressive world below.

Bannermane don't believe in any other way, and surrendering open skies to dwell beneath ground would certainly feel like incarceration again.

They stubbornly mark this day, ranking their grudges, debating the difficult decision, is life more valuable than their morals? Countless have perished in the pursuit of happiness, and their names only exist while the settlement continues to succeed. Will their extraordinary trailblazing be forgotten? Was it all moot?

"We must tenda this decision togetha, and rally in the comin' days; lest townspeople divide into packs, and compete like wild animals. This isn't the first time, we've been down this path 'ready. 'Eed my words, cause I've seen it 'fore. Eventually those few pace out of line, step-by-gradual-step, until brothers-in-arms thirst at each otha's throats. If the Junction sevahs, then- I say, we're as good as dead, but togetha we glean chance, and may yet persevere. The indecisiveness ends tonight, I pledge tah unite us. If the world refuses to change, and storms swell with fury, then I shall move the earth."

William had just met the man, and he already wants to tackle the bison by the horns. He carefully ponders to himself, 'If not 'im, who?' And, 'If not 'im, who betta?'

"Our society dwells 'pon stretches o' wasteland, everyday we face uncertainty, and everyday counter impossible choices. As a man of resolve, let me carry this immense burden. I will lash-out 'gainst any wrath that dare strike our journey, y'all focus on survivin'. I can do betta, we can do betta," states Vernon, "Now who's wit me?"

The blacksmith has proven persuasive as the inn hollers in consensus, a thunderous applause that shadows his own booming voice. Very few hesitate on this dramatic course of action, and Vernon is swathed in a sense of new-found enlightenment. The townsfolk have made their decision: they will abandon their pride. Various members approach the stage, including the distressed widower from yesterday's caravan swipe, greeting the speaker with their uplifted spirits.

Only a handful of sour individuals depart the inn, carrying shallow baskets of goods to fortify their abodes in the hope for a closer blackberry winter. Strangely enough, the mystic chooses to remain, intrigued by Waulbellow's fine patter of encouragement. With an untold number of strangers surrounding them, he kneels down to elaborate further on his plans. Their fellowship is a rather odd assortment of characters, there's Galvin Broad, the haberdasher; Cliff Fetherhaugh, a high-stakes gambler, who regularly wages by and large property and livestock; Rabley, a fence; then the widow, Lena Tillstead; and lastly, Austerlaund, the giant, spiritual shaman of Mad River Junction.

"I'll start by addressin' the obvious. Frankly, everyone 'ad their chance tah opt-out, so I'm delighted to have you all 'ere. The more, the merri-yah us hoosiers seem tuh gawk. 'Right, 'right, I'll get on tah this 'ere point. Just like those vile Mandonmen, we ought to high-tail it straight outta 'ere, grab whatever we can port and flee the Junction altogetha. Now, in ordah tah do that, best course o' action is tuh split up intah teams. Bless those strangers up 'fore the crack of dawn, ye lot saved us allota precious time by clearin' capstone. Our priority needs to strappin' togetha sleds. Once we 'ave the means, we can begin evacuatin'. Saw a couple wainwrights 'round 'ere earlia, plenty o' laymen too. I need all 'ands buildin' and renovatin' scrap at the tradin' post. There might be a carriage tucked away- best method tah move the most people. Every able body should be scroungin' for pig iron and hotrocks, check every 'bandoned 'earth n' lazy mercantile. Once I get the materials, I'll craft some wrought- some way or otha tah reinforce the runners. River-travel is tricky, rough timba won't last an hour on its own."

Vernon takes a moment, and like he's talking to an invisible personality, mutters under his breath to determine if there's anything he had missed. A signature smirk crosses his face, before making an additional announcement, "Questions, any ideas for mah tah blatha-on? If there's anythin' betta, 'olla by all means. We're fightin' on the same front 'ere."

Mad River has been on-edge since the final caravan's excursion, for most of the common rabble stand at the brink of oblivion, and unfortunate extinction. There's literally nothing for them here, as their value of supplies grow ever-scarce, stretching the rabble to their breaking point. These remaining residents are angered, frustrated, and frightfully concerned as one question mulls over everyone's minds. A woman straying at the audience's fringes casts a scornful glare, piquing Vernon's interest. He stands at attention like an unparalleled therapist, "What's on your mind, lass?"

"'Ow many o' us are bein' left behind?"

With an almost possessing stare, he gazes square at her eyes, conveying the upmost certainty and confidence, declaring, "Once I can 'elp it, not ah single soul. Those friendly tah the Junction and infirm shall be protected. If ah single life is not meant to be worth livin', what was the point of starting at all?"

A man breaks out in clamor, "That's wut we 'ike tuh 'ear! C'mon folks, show yer praise!"

The room suddenly erupts in a second rave of fervent cheers and clapping. Vernon nods and smiles in appraisal, parting his hands in an attempt to settle these rousing patrons. He speaks again, and this time, scrupulously paraphrasing from his notebook full of sketchy, scrawled notes.

"Now I've got them roguish plans, an ire tah fight, and the drive tuh live on. 'Eed this call tah action, we must rally and divvy tasks. From this moment forward, every single hoosier 'ere is our vanguard! Tis finally time tah pull ourselves from the brink! There is plenty of work ahead n' we must stride at careful pace."

The ironwright directs his attention to an odd, forgotten individual of the crowd. Upon Vernon's direction, waves of men part, revealing a stoic renegade. His figure is shadowed within a weighty pelt, disguising his arms and torso, lunging downwards towards skirts of boot. The lavish remains of a lynx is cast around his neck, the pelt clad amongst smoky grey clouds in company of brilliantly charred speckling. Its head remains prime, propped on the victor's right shoulder, while the ends of each ear stand at abrupt attention. Two, potently crimson orbs have replaced its beastly eyes, which became casualties of an honest scrapping. The draping limbs of this lynx are harnessed with ropes, sinews that display the trophies of previous hunts, dangling talons, teeth, claws, and feathers of all sizes. One these knick-knacks is a curved horn clamped with a bronze seal, the medal and mark of all wickerwalkers, awarded by Alexander himself in recognition for battling foul, grudgebringers across the wastes.

Wickerwalkers are foremost hunters of the frontier, seekers that pursue prey to the farthest reaches of white earth. Those commissioned by the mercantiles are at the steed of Creedance Fairplay, gamekeeper of the north, who maps the the territory's abundant migrations and predators. While wickerwalkers battle beasts that go bump in the night, those true nightmares are left to the employ of quartermaines, ruthless trackers who never flee in lieu of death, tackling elusive great game like bears, boar hordes, and whipporwill raptors. These prized hunts command the attention of lesser men, and the boots of those merely wishing to share the room.

As the hunter's piercing gaze finally meets Vernon's, he possesses a quiet demeanor, and meticulously scrutinizes the events of the speech, as it's the wicker's responsibility to shield the sons and daughters of Oestergaard.

"Ye sir- yes, the wise bumpity codger! I call 'pon the aid of ah wickerwalka, a man who treads 'tween the realms o' beast and betta men. Take stock o' current affairs, feed our starving populace, and smite the wild stray."

The burly brute is a being of few words, "ight then," and responds with a singular nod. Since this hunter has been thrust in the same boat, he might as well do the deeds asked of him. As the wickerwalker departs, the slew of his personal ornaments softly cackle with each step, boney claws rap against one another. Vernon is resoundingly pleased by this farewell, and soldiers onto his next topic.

"Back tah the docket: visiting the aviary. We must immediately 'lert the magistrate of Bonaventure 'bout our endeavors, dispatchin' ah courier might beseech their charity- needless to say, prompt some propa evacuation. Rabley, fancy flight, don't ye? See to it then!"

Fowl are the most forthright, and reliable means of communication between stations. There are two breeds used as messenger birds, the fuss and feathers kite, and those marsh ospreys. The kite is an amber-eyed, cotton-colored avian; males, indicated by their darker, marbled plumage, frequently bicker between themselves. They have become truly domesticated, completely dependent on human interaction, feeding off table scraps and roosting in the rafters of homes. Some owners treat them as devoted pets, gently holding them within the palms of their hands, fitting the fowl with custom leather headpieces, ornate feathery tufts and manes decorated with buttons or beads. Kites trained as messenger birds are distinguished by their sleek goggles, lenses that can be dimmed with the flick of a switch, to instinctively calm the bird. They often have harnesses strapped to their fragile frame, the perfect size pouch for transporting a letter or odd scroll.

Marsh ospreys are too stubborn to be keep as dutiful companions, and are wilder in nature than kites. Native residents of Mad River, the Slaughterbound Fens and glacial mires of the unkempt north, these raptors are meandering opportunists. While their diet consists primarily on pygmy rodents, they patient observe the whereabouts of beavers, minks and otters. These particular critters stake holes in the ice, where ospreys will use this opening to nab trout fry just underneath the surface, pilfering prey from the mouths of other hunters.

Since settlements regularly fall to malign forces, numerous, intuitive contingencies by the Bannermane already exist. One such prospect is to fashion a guide beacon, an emergency balloon of sorts that floats high above the town. These signals are sewn with bright materials, indicating danger in the area, and spottable over vast distances. Caravanhands and convoymen often implement miniature versions tethered to their lead cars.

"Where's that dasha, Galvin? Yea, yea! We need ye to deploy the emergency beacon. Should be somewhere in the trading post- maybe ah closet somewhere, yellow-crate lined with reflective tape. Emergency provisions, lotsa wire n' ah slippery canister o' 'elium… ah-ah, heel, heel- heel, helium will be inside. 'Itch it to the anvil around my smithy- the perfect mooring, ah simple anchor bend knot 'round the cleat will do justice. Be sure tah patch any o' does 'oles!"

"If push comes tah shove, and nah 'elp is coming, we go out on our own terms. I will lead our remainin' craftsmen and wainwrights intah framin' the sleds. Now, jump tuh it! While we don't 'ave any bison or hounds, we have sheer grit. These coaches will 'old all-em basic supplies and foodstuffs, n' be boarded strictly by the infirm, all those unable tah pull their weight. Any othas, we're relyin' on yer broad shoulders, yankin' the chains, closin' the distance 'tween the Junction n' Venture Depot."

He beckons towards the woman at his shoulder, "Lena, could ye gather company n' run door tah door? Scavenge what ye can, then direct anyone 'ere tuh regroup. I'm lookin' for dem dry provisions, tinda, sleeves. I'll strip timber n' nails from these very dwellings Most have already been 'bandoned. Go, see to it n' go now."

"Absolutely," answers Calamity Jane, commandeering the situation by piping shouts for volunteers, "Alright, need some folks to answer the draft," and her call-to-action is met with a resounding amount of hands.

While their outfit swells in numbers, all motioning towards the entrance, Vernon paces to the far end of the stage, conversing with his traveling companion, William and Mandel Haggerton.

"'Liam, o'ver 'ere, 'Liam. I need someone I can trust for ah job. We need a small team to dispose of those bodies upstairs. Drag 'em ontah the arcade n' bury 'em out tah sea lest they rot- just warm 'nough tuh go makin' us all sick."

William feels slightly bitter at this command, and contends the fact that his caliber of qualities are being ignored. While he's a breed of young stock, his extraordinary salvaging skills are absolutely unmatched. The boy Jones would be much better suited helping Lena and the others scavenge for supplies, and is about to debate this fact with the ironwright before he notices someone anxiously treading through this mass, wading in the opposite direction of those departing, emerging closer to the platform.

The newcomer urgently shouts, "'Err mah Mr. Goodsir, someone must reach the local chapter. If we're are tah leave, we must recover those records housed at the magistrate's office. The three charcoal tomes."

As remnants of the crowd descend outside, they leave the skald standing among the wainwrights left in the parlor. She announces, "My name tis Arabella Gaberdine, and the language of Mad River is my upmost responsibility."

This poet does not pander for approval, simply providing discretion, and heads hastily towards the outdoor opening. Sensing a fortunate opportunity to escape his dreary work work with the dead, William prods the smith.

"Um, Vern? Mandel says 'e can 'andle those sleepas all by 'is lonesome," to which Hagman gives a firm, taunting wallop into William's shoulder.

"Youch! Bella o'ver yonda will need 'elp burglin' the clerics, and ye know 'ow I am. I should go with!"

Vernon lets out an exceptional, unraveling *sigh* at his protege.

"Fine, 'right fine. My team will be workin' the post plaza. Stave-off 'ready, fool."

Under the wiseacre's prying eyes, the hotrocks thief gleefully bounds around the stage, catching-up to the skald with exuberance before a timely exit onto the nearby street. Truthfully, he dons a greedy, ulterior motive. Breaking into the administrative station would also give him access to the Junction's vault, a room keep under lock and key that protects those long-desired treasures of- who exactly knows, perhaps the room is full of fine furs, silvers and sacks of precious gems? One could imagine that this vault has already been looted, but William likes to believe that he has the upper-hand, and those Crooked Men couldn't dare compete. Even a mere pocket of riches would be enough to book a room at Bonaventure, some decent stay in the Underdark.

As they depart the bunkhouse, the wispy frigid air does little more than goad these illicit efforts, and the two march with an abrupt gait. Arabella, dressed similarly to all dignified Bannermane lector, is a defining symbol of posh glamor; elegant, refined, dangerous. Her flowing locks of auburn hair are pierced atop by a lengthy, elaborate, needle-like pin. She is tightly bound in numerous layers of sleek fleece, toned with ashes and pitch. A mantle of creamy-beige stoat fur lines her shoulders, bundled in tufts, engulfing her neck as a sleeve and accentuating against otherwise murky satin attire. Three novels of spruce-blue bindings are steadily buckled across her chest like a corset, a sheathed theater knife is strapped alongside the right ankle. The skirt of her clothing is a dazzling array of fine tools, an assorted roll of paintbrushes and fountain pens, plus a chest containing ink wells and loose blotting paper. William is easily distracted by the fierce mid-morning sky, a masterpiece which enthusiastically competes for his attention. There has been a noticeable shift in the light, and those characteristic rays of rosy red and muted lavender now dance just beyond the jagged peaks of faraway mountain ranges.

As that distant yonder leisurely fills with brimstone, an uneasy tension riles the air. These vivid colors churn together like fingers seeping into gloves, their intense sheering beams pierce through broad daylight. The limelight of the sun is dramatically outshined by this luminous, vibrant brilliance, gradually bathing an otherwise golden glow into an ominous crimson sheen by the stroke of the dusk. Books of antiquity, clad in a writ called helvetica, an otherwise ancient tongue distinguished by Hearthland's forbearers, prophesizes the red sun. Their scrolls illustrate the end times, entries which describe incredible turmoil upon anything the bleeding solispyre touches.

William can only recall one strict line, 'Then the skies blaze with anger, raining tears of hate and poison.' Although menacing, children pay heed towards a variety of nursery rhymes; those petty, patron parents often weave tall tales. As the weather churns for worse, it reveals foul imagery strewn about as clouds, shapes of agonizing things and twisting trees.

One peculiarly lively wisp dances around its neighbors, busking on the ocean sky. It depicts the sorrowful portrait of a grim, or puffy-faced trollfolk, temporarily immersing the streets with shadow before gingerly dissipating against the sunlight. This momentarily gloom manifests over the worst ruins that the Junction has to offer, various storefronts have imploded, just like the townhouses prior. Their wooden timbers dilapidate and collapse in such manner, acting as an abrupt, untimely casket for those occupants.

A distinct handful of buildings still stand unabated, having withstood a slew of vicious storming gales, but unfortunately not the plentiful robber barons. Barricades of planks and wrought have been torn asunder, littering the ground with debris before vagrants smash the front windows, helping themselves to the property's priceless contents. After all, if a proprietor took the time to board-up their business, it must be harboring something special. These scroungers had ample opportunity for their misdeeds, precisely striking during the inn's gathering, which emptied the streets of witnesses and occupied scores of townspeople for hours. Lying agape, splintered, and decorated in a visage of detrimental graffiti, these empty emporiums echo their grief, a ruthless reminder of the chaos at bay. The people are inches away from absolute turmoil, only their morality glues them together, so what will take to finally push them over the line? What tragedy is left to endure that won't result in that finally shove? At such extremes, life on the bleeding edge is just another tipping point above the abyss.

William's boot catches an odd panel in the scruff which reads, 'Millwright Pioneering Co. EST'D Mad River, authentically handcrafted cooper and carpentry.' He scans the destructive wake, peering ahead through a nearby alcove. It takes a moment for his eyes to adjust for the darkness, subtly giving the illusion of a silent, respectful pause. The abandoned premises is populates sole by lines of deserted shelves and scattered sculptures that were too hefty to carry. Someone has defamed an elaborate caribou bust with maroon paints, wasting more than just a beautiful beast, but that of the taxidermist's livelihood. Several supporting staves obscure his view, they've each been whittled into animalistic figures, but with the distinct lack of limelight, these once glorious totems are foreboding figures amidst the gloom. There is an undoubtedly barren presence, nary a rogue hammer or wrench.

William spots a body in the farthest recess, stripped of their furs and garments, slumped sprawling alongside the wall. What was once a thriving family business, the Bannermane ideal, is now a decrepit wreck. Poor Wedge Royal, he was once a kindred spirit and frequent patron of the Junction's delicatessen, an establishment which has also been devastated during this recent unrest. William had only attended once or twice, tempted by the everlasting aroma of sugary sweets. Anise's Bakery had been a bustling hotspot, inviting clamors of townspeople every morning with delectable muffin morsels and comfy, homespun scarves.

The pastry chef there, Mabel, avidly leads a double-life as a seamstress, having been taught by her aunt, Lucille Pearl, a greyhair from Tom Fry Eddy. That ole wiseacre would often goad her niece with thoughts of marriage. Saying that, "Tis the role o' ah woman tah take the helm. Expand yer horizons, keep the men at 'ome."

Harassing William whenever he ventured too close, telling him to "Get ah real job."

In Bannermane society, men typically operate the homefront, while women have a more quintessential role, expanding business prospects from settlement to settlement. This is usually accomplished by marriage, where a wife will find some lucky bachelor in a new town, incorporating their assets into her portfolio, across any number of husbands. The end goal of of a mercantile is to be diverse and prosperous.

Mad River Junction is connected in an endless slew of businesses, products and services that traverse the territory. It is known as a trade town, where raw resources are refined, as how animal carcasses are stripped-down to their pelts, and shipped back for upper-society. Mercantiles focus entirely on profits, not people. No amount of lives or back-breaking work are of concern if it implores upon extravagant whims and lavish luxuries.

The pair navigate through the desolation, arriving at the magistrate's station in swift manner. Unlike other buildings of the Junction, the municipality's refined timber frame is thoroughly fashioned with gridiron and sheet metal. Ample spans of thin wrought iron bridge the gaps between windows, paralleling the direction of innumerable wooden boards. The iconic, I-shaped building is outlandishly top-heavy, an upside-down cake looming upwards eighty-feet. Its sleek copper roofing steadily reflects brilliant orange-fire, accentuated by a dazzling array of steam pipes and valves that burrow into the complex. A bulk of the tubing hurtles into a massive exhaust tower, a chimney of sorts, that sports little to no fumes. This building sits at the foot of the Junction's metal bulwark, a barricade that persists and protects the settlement's financial district from any blizzards that cross the flatlands. Despite being an engineering masterpiece, the local chapter couldn't withstand the elements without this additional fortification. The reinforced entryway of the magistrate's building houses a formidable set of double doors, crowned by a weathered relief of a bison's head ascending into a lofty, multi-story window. Peering past the first floor, three more levels can be spotted inside.

The skald swiftly directs herself upon the ingress, gripping an enormous handle cast in imitation of a horn, and the door shutters in place with each tug, with bitter frost latching this portal tightly in place. Only with their conjoined efforts, do Arabella and William finally fling the wooden shutter wide open. To their surprise, the immediate vicinity is lit by scones of raging torchlight. The antechamber before them is immersed in the soft shimmering, revealing two limestone statues of men dressed in quartermain garbs. These extraordinary hunters remain nameless, as there are no visible inscriptions. This reception comes as a bit of shock, they had expected every office to be relinquished in response to the magistrate's predictable disappearance.

As they carefully stride forward, the air inside is filled with the stench of bureaucracy, freshly pressed papers and inks. The oncoming ringed gallery is reserved for several clerks and the registrar, workers who compete with the daily grind, recording the comings and goings of the entire settlement. The floor is a dense packing of fine, polished board and oddly clean. Each desk is immaculately tidy, every sheet of paperwork is organized in neat piles rather than being peppered around the ground. This main hall is a breathtakingly vast, tiered chamber, each level with a protruding balcony, complete with an elaborate chandelier dangling far above their heads. The fixture is merited with dense, prolonged strands of wax, demonstrating its chivalrous dedication to the craft over these decades. Three dovetail-shaped standards auspiciously droop from its rigid arms, each depicting the sovereign factions: Avery Sauder's piercing arrow, seemingly springing from its beige canvas; the elderflower, sewn with bold reds, sigil of Charlie Mandon; and lastly some golden star lying on an endless sea of turquoise, symbol of the Masterson house.

While these three merchantiles all stand united as Bannermane, it's not always a flawless coalition. They occasionally skirmish, vying over herds and scarce resources. These banners wave and flutter to one another despite the absence of wind. Their hems drape and sway just above the floorboards, keeping the area immaculate, and free of dust. A private niche lingers between the colorful drapery, a sanctified refuge of sorts housing a single, brazen orb about the size of a typewriter. The surface of this crystal ball is pristine, skewing the contents with a ghastly, glazing haze. There's a precious elixir held captive, a peculiar syrup brimming with life. It's constantly ebbs and flows, a fickle fluid of midnight blue. Bits and boggles of ivory glitter periodically bind together, forming flashes of visions to those who are arcane adept, however it's nothing but static to the boy Jones, the same never-ending image on repeat. A twisting pillar of ice guides the ancillary to waist height, then five finger-sized icicles graze across the glass, forming the ache of some frosty palm. In this mellow, heated auditorium, the hardened ice is most unnatural: there are no shallow puddles of water lapsing among the floor. The entire shrine reeks of magik, part in fact to its volatile aura, a shroud of mist that dissipates a few feet from the artifact.

On account of the visitors' curiosity, they discover a weathered man lounging upon the outskirts of the room. He is settled among a lowly scribe's desk, elbows pressed with scrolls at hand, basking alongside a lulling candlelight. A lively glow bathes his clerical pursuits in ample droves of ginger. The author's body remains remarkably placid, yet his feathered pen amusingly dances across each spread of paper. This solo artist is startled by their footsteps, and cocks his ear towards their approach.

"Mah, mah, mah watta pleasure- I didn't see ye der, gave me ah bit o' fright."

As a man of written word, he possesses no earthly endowments but a journal, and appears incredibly feeble. When pressed against the hefty pine frame of the chair, this author seemingly sinks further into its limber leather cushions. Every bodily fiber croaks and strains, his skin is so taut, it's like dressing a skeleton. Some humble garb, a certain generational cloak comprised of sewn patchwork penmanship engulfs his fragile figure. Aside from wits end, the dainty skullcap gently caresses a whipped-topping of hair, however does little to hide a hastily receding hairline. Groomed, crow-greased facial hair, with tinges of steel wool, loom considerably off the base of his chin, culminating in two wiry wisps that part in different directions like a bowtie.

While the visual drudgeries leave senile men worse for wear, it is a gift to reminisce in the distinct, fragrant aromas of ash, parchment, and ink. Guided by a petty lash straight-through his brow, the left side of the author's face is marked by a fading sore, it's an expressionless, visual burden to be blind in one eye, and the orb is permanently coated in wax. There are countless dusky freckles across his face, like someone had graffitied trivial minutiae by throwing clouds of somber soot. Abundant amounts of nosy wrinkles string themselves like wire, impersonating the handiwork of tanning leather, tracing a rather permanent, studious perplexion.

The old man introduces himself as Jeremiah, curator of knowledge, and speaks like a pompous reverend.

"I am an all-fatha o' fate, grand eldah o' dis Junction. Jeremiah da prophet o' truth. Well- got tah be 'onest, tis all dreary, n' gets ah bit blurred with age. That tends tah happen wit anyone o' muh mileage! Children, 'ave ye come tah ponda da orb, summonin' secrets like countless othas 'fore ya? Dis device is blessin' from da gods, able tah scry beyond comin' times. Few can herr whispers, and even fewer behold tah fantasies within. Yet, only I can interpret tis wisdoms, weatha, and myriad threats. Tell me, does it also call tah ya, invite ya, tempt ya? Can you 'eed tis words? What do ya see?"

Jeremiah is a knave at heart, possessing a penchant for promising mountains, but delivering molehills. The man regularly guises under ordained illusions, but scores of townspeople recognize his habits, coining him as just another a sleazy con-man. He is potentially the eldest ilk around, this being the sole reason residents deal with his abrupt, cautionary antics. Vagabonds believe there is always a shred of truth behind the myth, and revere the elderly. The orb is one vessel for his insane trepidations, and preaches obscure visions. It's renowned for being able to predict the weather, a sight not just limited to Jeremiah. Austerlaund has recorded mystifying images for twelve weeks straight, and the crystal has only shown one thing: snow, a constant slew of storms. At one point, the magistrate himself felt insulted, lifted the entire globe and shook it, leading certain magi to believe that it's simply broken. Even from across the court, William senses the midnight oil's agony, almost as if it writhes in pain.

"Oi, ye wretched scoundrel! We're ain't 'ere for any crystals so don't go hasslin' us. 'Eed way! We're nosin' for brass chairs, left ah bit o' our 'andiwork in 'is office."

"Char, dat magistrate? Coo-coo, 'right, I step 'side. Try not tah make constable's quarry. Simply up dees stairs, two flights on yah left."

The author raises his arm, awkwardly coronating the direction of the central staircase with a deposing grimace.

This flight is beautifully decorated in peak Bannermane grandeur, a pair of brass, avian wings adorn each turnout post. This counter-clockwise, ascending staircase lines the permitter of the chambers, conveniently displaying a nearby, handprinted sign that Arabella has no need for. 'Official Business Only," it declares.

William takes a brief gander at the directions, if they continued straight ahead, they would reach those forgotten quarters of watchmen in no time, maybe discover where the constable is. They're in dire need of someone to keep the peace, and as a man of character, William doubts that he fled like the mayor. Arabella divulges that the magistrate's station is located on the uppermost level, overlooking the adjacent properties of Mad River.

The staircase is heavily worn, as an innumerable amount of feet tread these very steps on a daily basis- well, not anymore. Without the busy-bodies, the consistent warmth feels misguiding, uncanny. They've been without a proper hearth for ages, it feels almost troublesome to trust it, as regular townspeople are strictly accustomed to unforgivingly cold, raspy air. The bitter and frigid temperatures have hardened their lungs, prompting the rising climb as nothing more than a pretentious inconvenience. Their trek guides them passed several landings, each serving various sectors, industries, and inner-workings of the settlement unbeknownst to common folk. The Bannermane are industrious and mercantile kin, two floors receive undivided attention towards the settlement's fiduciary interests, including trade caravans, and the like. Outposts are careful in regards to taxation, attempting to stay competitive against similar towns by encouraging low-rates with higher yields.

As Ayers Beechworth once iterated, "We needin' more guds flowin' through our hands than othas."

Apparently, the same thought applies to furniture too. The traveling duo reach the top flight, only to be barred by desks and bureaus in a sort of scandalous feat. With no other alternative, they must awkwardly clamber over the makeshift hurdles, to which William sarcastically prods, "Say, 'ow very considerate o' them!"

"This is no small-time undertakin', imagine what they're stowin' away up there."

"Oh, I absolutely couldn't. What if they 'ready emptied the vaults n' we're trekking all this way for nothin'?"

As his tongue utters the final word, William quickly covers his mouth and winces. Not only was this rampant thought selfishly embarrassing, but expresses his true scheme. Before Arabella can even begin reprimanding him, an invisible, timid voice lashes out from the platform above.

"Stay back foul git. Fiends! There is nothin' for ya 'ere!"

This demand startles them, however it's an underwhelming trifle, and the sheer lack of grit to accompany the insult does little to waver their advances. Thwarting the crude barricade only takes a momentary lunge forward, or a curt shimmy to and fro. They overcome every obstacle within minutes, however in stead of Arabella's advance, William could swear the skald went out of her way to hinder him, that an additional chair leg or two struck clumsily at his shoulder. The duo scales the final few steps, immediately peering for the origin of the jarring remark. As an adjacent door cautiously creaks closed, William impulsively rushes headfirst towards it. His left shoulder sharply collides with a dense *thud* that reverberates around the chamber, followed by a hoarse cacophony of clattering bolts and latches.

"'Ey, 'ey there," he chides, peering through the keyhole. "I'm just lookin' tah chat."

"Good grief, yer as dense as stone. Nah different than those poor sods earlia comin' after muh meister's treasure. Get out of 'ere. I ain't 'ad nothin' for them, and I 'ave naught for ye."

The skald pulls at William's unblemished shoulder and shakes her head in dismay.

"No need for a darin' plan or 'oneyed words, I'll handle this," she insists.

Arabella directs her attention solely towards the woman locked in the magistrate's office, sealed behind three inches of solid wood. This recess on the top level is nothing more than a waiting room, a glorified lobby; the overabundance of dust reveals several chairs, and an antique printing press. It's a machine of creative ingenuity, worn in all the right places. Fabricated from metal plates and alder wood, however the press is too hefty to be handled by anything less than a half-dozen chivalrous men.

"'Ere, Rylie. Please way the door. Itsa that sister hoosier 'erself, Arabella."

"'Ush-up! Bella, no shame? Is that really ya? Oh my gosh, thank the 'eavens. Ah, I am so sorry! 'Ere, give me but ah moment, I'll get that door."

There's a profound groaning from the clashing pig iron and her very own exertion, with the whole lot choking upon an adamant cacophony of grinding metal. She emits a disingenuous chuckle, "*Umm*, it's now gotten stuck- ah bit loose, but still stuck. Might be able tah 'ave that shifty, 'eavy-'anded wastrel kick it in."

William rolls his eyes in vehement disapproval.

"Fine, fine, though if she gonna call me wasted 'gain, I'll do some me some good and lock the rest of ye unruly lot outside."

Rylie must've heard his comment, because a bubbly chortle can be heard once more. He reluctantly directs his attention to the gummed-up door, knocking twice forthwith.

"'Right, back off there, lass."

Precisely pacing three steps back, William suddenly springs forward and rears his gait. This decisive lunge drives his heel home, landing reliably beside the doorknob's bracket. The door immediately severs, creating a loose gap with a *thump*, enough of an effort to pry the entranceway fully ajar. It had to be the weight of his clothing, pounds upon pounds of layered fleece and fur adds up, and William doesn't possess such burly strength on his own.

Once they emerge into the highly-anticipated room, Rylie joyously exclaims, "Thank ye, muh savior," before promptly gliding forward, wrapping William in a tight embrace, and condescendingly planting a kiss on his cheek amongst joking limerence.

He's a little jarred at the notion, but pleased to finally match a face to such a soothing voice. She is relatively middle-aged, and of average stature, amicably nestling her head against the base of his neck in a mocking jest. Rylie is an inviting figure, graceful yet feeble. Her skin demonstrates hefty milage, an exceptionally weathered combination of tested mettle, overly dried skin and wrinkles that accentuate the contours of her face. Even amid the chaos, she possesses a delightful demeanor, wholesomely welcoming her guests to this temporary living arrangement, and beckons them towards a lively hearth that flanks the door. Sweeping strands of hair are keenly knotted into taut braids, they spread downwards in an orderly manner, bunching at the ends of her shoulder blades. These locks are carried inside a transparent veil, eluding, but showcasing threads of gorgeous copper. A circlet, adorned with a blemished ruby-green tourmaline, weighs this insulating hood, preventing it from being blown away outdoors.

Like all clerical habits, her clothing is rather reserved. She exhibits a plain dressy tunic that flares towards her thighs, bundled further by a collared jacket of fine pewter. This entourage of attire can only be seen through the thin sliver of her cloak, an overwhelming drape, glazed in a pale cerulean that is clumsily stained with oily washes. It's clasped by a silvery chain, while a trophy hare's pelt- a righteous prize, lies unfurled on the left shoulder. She has gathered the ends like a shawl, fastening it into a brilliantly stout bow around her stomach. Her raiments do little to distract these new visitors from a pungent, lingering taint. The bitter musk can be detected an elk's length away, a rather unfortunate trait that she has become accustomed to, regularly bathing in the salty brine of her own sweat. Becoming the princess of her own tower has only distracted her from previous duties.

Until two days ago, she kept busy handpressing those authority-approved flyers around town, broadcasting directories in popular parlors like the bunkhouse, caravan post, soot depository, and plenty of whereabouts between. While most townsfolk cannot read, and media print is typically considered minutiae, her words continue to cast iron. She is immaculately idolized among town-criers, gathering a fine menagerie from their hearkening patrons, cajoled by the profound sense of hospitality that emanates from her keen assortment of words. The skald, Arabella Gaberdine, is a burgeoning maven of prose, and has been guided as her apt apprentice for years.

Originating beneath the corridors of Monument Plaza, Rylie conveys illustrative thronepatter, an appreciation of finer culture and sophistication above ordinary kin of the Junction; an especially rare treat among borderspiel-speaking residents, whose language utters the most unintelligible gibberish. Her notices have grown dire in recent weeks, acting akin to warnings. These general posts regard the eveningtide curfew, points of contact during an emergency, directions to the nearest soup kitchen, and petitions for heating the debtors' prison while before being swept away in the recent storm.

However her most important task was appointed by the magistrate, Hoosierfeld Char himself. She details a daily log of noteworthy events and happenings, a draft or personal diary of sorts summarized in coveted novels. Mad River's very own tome catalogues nearly a decade's worth of discourse, every entry reviewed and endorsed by the magistrate's personal seal, a stamp of acknowledgment that has been mysteriously absent for the prior eight entries. Frontier settlements find themselves in flatiron quite often, those hard-pressed circumstances with no good choices. Rambunctious trailblazers get caught in the glory of it all, disregarding the risks, and leading their towns to noiseless ruin. Entire homesteads have been devoured by ceaseless chill, the ground quakes, swallowing every instance of man and replacing it with fathomless snow. A charcoal tome is reserved for periods of great upheaval, some quiet, last-ditch resort to chronicle the history of the settlement, lest all the hardships have been for nothing. These manuscripts are rumored to be lodestones for misfortune, acting as a grimoire of calamity, frankly from the ill will they entitle. Lingering geists, spawned of raving wilderness, are left with only hope, a hope that their archives and personal odes may be recovered before all evidence of their past life perishes.

In her self-prescribed duty of historical preservation, she rallies against Junction's watch. Once their constable went astray on Ander's Route, there was no weight barring them steady. It's a menacing stretch of badlands, ceremoniously named in lieu of its discoverer, a raving man who now loiters around the local chapter. The path itself remains elusive, residing within the wake of advancing glacier, firmly rooted against endless amounts twisting crevices and tunnels. Formidable beasts roost in these halls, and with each hapless sightseer, hallow the ground in which they tread.

"N' 'fore ye pipe-up 'bout it, yes-yes the magistrate's gone. Up and fled upon the nicest wagon Rochesta eva crafted- that's 'omestead money ain't it? I've been sitting idly on mah toes since then. We actually 'ave this place to ourselves. I believe that constable got lost too, 'broad the craglands, far westmyr, outta past Andah's Route."

"Andah's Route? Ye main Ander's Route? Why would be trekkin' out there for? Nothin' but permafrost and grisly rime."

"'Ey, can't really tell you. I just 'andle the papers. Course, these ordas must've been paramount, 'cause the envelopes were sealed with Tryas, direct from the Bonaventure's magistrate. Last time I saw crimson ink was some banta 'bout a consolidation prize, only after an unlucky sap turned up deada than birch on bark. Found 'is body iced, over a league from 'is dwellin'. Don't think they 'ad any suspects though, a straightforward case of slippery sickness and alls that, man just went delirious."

Rylie appears to become further distracted by every sentence. "Percilees, it's splendid to finally talk. Thought I'd break, go crazy from loneliness soon 'nough. Simply chatin' with othas is one of those few things folk don't miss 'til it's gone. Mayhaps wool socks too- I'm grateful to 'ave only 'ad frostbite once, near lost my ear, but losin' yer toes too, I shudda just thinkin' 'bout it."

"'Ey, 'ey!" In a bid to warrant her attention, Arabella abrasively grips at her left wrist. She then sharply snaps her fingers thrice in brisk succession, evoking a *snap-snap-snap* until the printmaker turns to face her. The two face another in front of the unlit fireplace, messily surrounded by heaps of books, ledgers, and manuscripts that easily exceed waist height.

"Rylie, we're retrievin' those tomes. I will be leavin' with company towards Bonaventure. There, I can turn them o'ver tah the authorities. All these stamped pages are the proof we'll need to request relief supplies."

Whilst convincing her, the skald accentuates each phrase, continuing to calmly caress her hand and forearm.

"Please look at me, togetha we can save lives- ye may 'elp save the souls of Mad River's bannerfolk, but only if ye decide to 'elp us, or betta yet, come with."

"Bella, we've known each other for years, but I ain't sure, tis unprecedented." When Rylie was first bestowed her title as keeper of the sacred texts almost a decade ago, she had been specifically instructed to never allow them to leave the premises, let alone the Junction!

"People are dyin', they've been at it for weeks, even if some settlas refuse tah open their eyes and admit it. The 'venture needs their offerin'- they need the tomes. This is serious, we need 'elp, so are we gonna let ah few dingy rules get in the way o' savin' lives?"

Rylie paces along the grounds of the office, deep in thought. The room's soot-toned paneling bleeds dreariness, doing very little to aid her comfort. Almost every wall lies frivolously empty and barren, stripped of their worth by the previous occupant, bearing numerous similarities to that of a cell. One single piece breaks the mundane atmosphere, an oil portrait of the first magistrate, Hoosierfeld Char, which had been bolted to the wall, unable to be removed through conventional means. An oil painting sporting their likeness is adorned inside an aureately bejeweled frame, an opulent ancillary where guests can revel in heirloom heritage. His accomplishments are rendered in the company of an ambiguous crowd, where he is clad in feathery affairs, leaning against that same winged, staircase figurehead from the lobby, with tome in tow. That manuscript appears as an unyielding thing, the same size of a loon, the generally slumped shape and weight tween a sack of potatoes, only Hoosierfeld can bare its burden.

The plots of the nearby partition are a bleak, foreboding reminder, the color of cinders and sterile, leaving ample space for his future successors, moreover those that will bear blessing. His lone pair of eyes are ghastly, appearing to stare down its visitors and force their gawk. As if the legacy screams at the top of silent lungs, witness me. Having been stranded for days, no wonder Riley has found wits-end. Frightened, cold and alone, this portrait definitely does not help.

She hadn't expected it, but the responsibilities of the absent magistrate's office have finally passed down to her. Laced with this unintentional burden, her body quivers with anxiety. As Rylie swerves around the entire room, her steps quicken, each more feverish than the last. Shortly thereafter, an otherwise brisk, comforting ramble rashly tallies into laps, doing little to aid any concentration. Under the gentle light of hanging lanterns, she veers around the room, brushing beyond sparse end tables, only to collide into her lounge-sofa sleeping-quarters and nearly tumble beside the lulling fireplace. She heavily *sighs*, recognizing this uncanny stress and decides to take a seat with her palms against her eyes. Rylie upholds her prestigious title with sanctity, however she cannot allow any innocents to be taken at the sole expense of her stubbornness. It's a difficult, in-the-moment determination, but she remains resolute, and stands to address her company by pitching the duo her newfound intentions.

"I shall allow ye to take the books, seal and all, but I must come with the two of ya. I've sworn to protect their contents, tis muh duty."

Arabella joyously resounds with, "Only if I'm by yer side."

The trio acknowledge their freshly-minted pact with nods and slightly bobbing curtsies.

"In that case, I oh-ficially authorize ye both as 'andlers. As impromptu Mandon office-suhs, yer entitled tah benefits includin' mealstamps for mornin' rations, discount caravan ticketin', and o' course, yer very own seals. Now, there must be some 'round 'ere somewhere... oh, forget all that jargon. Thank ye, thank ye, thank ye, I'm grateful for the company!"

William interjects with blatant commentary, "'Ad tah be lonely, campin' up 'ere and whatnot?"

"O' course my dear boy, I ain't an 'ag yet! It was necessary to block that stairwell too- buy me some time if brigands came near, thankful there was only you two. I was going to ould this room even if it took all barrowtide. Truth is, I debated leavin' muhself, back when Hoosier was first mentioned something 'bout mandatory evacuations. Tis all outlined in our manuscripts. Should've all gotten-up and left together, gatherin' folk of the town 'long the way. Trouble was, 'e freaked with word of those remainin' convoys, left us 'hind with 'most everythin' lashed to 'is sled. Pretty soon, the only person left in this station was little ole me- which I'll remind ye, is ah recipe for disaster. Now come, there's still work tah be done. Follow now!"

The visitors accompany Rylie to the utmost end of the room, gathering just past a bureau crafted from exquisite cedar planks. The desk is positioned firmly before a circular, ornamental windowpane, glazed with the Mandon flair, namesake and colors, flanked by several ornate wall sconces. They're crafted from stalwart slabs of peppery pewter, sporting several paunchy hoods to hold a lingering flame.

The scribe yanks at an unlit lamp, a disguised secret switch, until it drops with a fitting *clang*. An obscure niche of the room responds with a resounding *tick*, as if a latch had just released. Hoosierfeld's portrait above the fireplace's hearth is now subtly jutting out, only noticeable from the magistrate's point-of-view.

Rylie strides to its location, swivels the painting on hinge and reveals the front of a steely safe, an impressive slew of armor and dials. All Bannermane recognize the engineering of Clan Penn, their labors are utterly unrivaled and second to none. This vintage, vault of ironsides leaves a distinctly enduring impression, completely impregnable. While it's rather dull and drab: a military-like, olive green, as it was never intended to be a center of conversation. Originally curtailed by an illustrious yellow signature, the maker's markings and embellishments have since faded orange.

"Avert yer eyes, ye bully-rooks and muppets. No distractions. This'll test my memory, lest my 'andiwork too."

Rylie stands upon the tips of her toes, and setting attention towards a row of defining brass knobs, each engrained with a hundred or so subsequent digits. These six separate discs must be meticulously dialed to their correct keys, so she rotates each one with utmost ease, yet maintains a creeping pace, methodically biding her time, assessing each of their unique tunes and quarreling pips. Upon every successful digit, a choir of steel clamors from inside the mechanism until the final combination culminates into an unlocking panel, manifesting a lackluster keyhole.

The scribe is giddy, she loves this part and reveals an overly crowded keyring stashed within a tunic pocket. Rylie then casually, but persistently, begins scouring through dozens of metal slivers; an overbearing amount- large and small keys all-around, made of brass, copper, then those bits and bobs in-between; some are ornate, others simple- it would easily drive a layman mad. As the most trusted lackey, she has special access to the mercantile's operation- every portion, including the private affairs of their local- now remotely-employed, magistrate.

As the questing duo patiently tend to cooler heels, William glances outside and begins to brood. He's greeted by a despairing scene overlooking the Junction's square- a landscape of dreary white and greys, tinted ever-so slightly by some rosy hued glasspane. An earnest lad can spy upon all the hardships and indecencies from this perch. There are numerous isolated incidents such as street-corner bonfires, herds of bootleg mobs, and vandalized dwellings, overall a rather gristly sight.

Past those frigid avenues and alleyways is a vast domain of barely palatable nothingness are stretches of wilderness rarely seen, as cloudless days are few and far between. These breathtaking, salted plains which rile Bannermane to action have always harbored less than tolerable weather. The ferocious tenacity of these blizzards craft a spectacular series of rolling dunes spanning the entire length of flatlands. This yawning expanse is dotted with the occasional rocky outcrop, hardscape diminishing among the constantly swelling white tide.

Aptly known as Mad River Junction, the town's border is nestled between the shores of a resting lake, and those silent, and motionless frozen waterways. The river's icy tributaries provide an excellent highway route towards each of the eastern settlements, as sled convoys avoid treading the thick snowbanks of unsheltered, dry plains.

Leagues unto the west are true craglands, a stretch of inhospitable territory littered in tar pits and mires. These lands split apart like shaggy fur, withholding trenches that thrust far within the bowels of the earth, where an odd, misplaced step is met with an eternal plummet into abyss. This corroded landscape of agony lies at the foot of a glacier, a monument to all sins that grows greater by each passing day. Those walls are insurmountable, rising thousands upon thousands of feet and scraping at the heavens themselves, brewing storms in a manner most foul. Winding gales cascade from the ice, propelled with spite so that they may bleed onto the plains with ardent savagery. Unable to cross the terrain of craglands, blizzards trespass across the lake and then take to the south, giving pioneers a shallow opportunity to brace against them.

With an abrupt, 'A-ha!' Rylie produces the key, rubbing the promised piece succinctly between her fingers. She thrusts it squarely within the vault, twisting it three-quarters clock-wise before the mechanism finally yields.

They are humored by an unexpected hoard of rations, leaving William to burst into a slight chuckle. There are salivating forever cakes, extra-canned kidney beans, bits and gobs of Blue Tang fizzy sticks and sweetened cola caramels, then several bottles of Medallion Red, a decanter of herbal gin, and even candied doses of the narcotic hush-hush. In haste, Rylie digs through this absurd collection and pockets the remaining packstuffs, dressing every available pocket, and padding the lining of her two coats. This is her stash in a way, and William grows rife with envy.

Behind this nourishing facade of provisions is the town's true treasure, three black books bound in cherry twine. As ordinary townspeople cannot read, those of the common rabble would reckon these records as fuel for the hearth. Nonetheless, for those shrewd and cunning enough, these charcoal tomes detail an exact manifest for lost cargo and buried treasures just waiting to be excavated.

Coveted by merchantmen, liegelords and taskmasters, manuscripts such as these contain unfound wealth. Despite famed fortunes, the poetic skald is humble, striving to preserve the Junction's commentary, safeguarding Bannermane culture and history, however brief it may be. There are other precious artifacts tucked away in the vault, lavish luxuries that would fetch good bids at auction. Modest vagabonds like the scribe call these objects of power quite ruinous, foul trinkets that drive the wedge between kin, and blur the lines between that of friend and foe. Spotting the glint in William's eyes, an ambitious desire, Rylie firmly flings shut the safe's door, mitigating any feverish attempts at loot.

The unearthed compositions are quite hefty, and Rylie's forearms tremble at the mercy of their weight. Each cover is visually roiling, bound with a carmine, lacy twine that stitches together medleys of patchy skin. The awry nature of sewn patchwork is eclipsed by audaciously studded engraved emblems and text, artistically branded as, *Juries of the Junction, Volume 1 of 3*, and so forth. These novels have miscellaneous minces of jutting metal to protect their hardcovered corners from any potential misuse, yet dozens of interior pages protrude out, the result of countless oversized additions and folds. It is the scribe's ordained duty to log these albums, at the magistrate's timely discretion of course. These pages are filled to the brim with Rylie's scrawls: mercantile tallies, clerical habits, weather reports, residents titles and occupations, records of every vagabond and passerby. It was truly impeccable work, jotting the every passing thoughts of Hoosierfeld, those memoirs that constantly required her to revise, and make additions to prior counts, resulting in myriad scraps of glued parchment. One such sleeve details Mad River's ancestry, a family tree that could easily be pulled into a six-foot scroll, seamlessly bound within its great book. There is fifteen years of history between their binding, content that may have been registered by Rylie, but withholds the wealth of knowledge derived from the skald's orations, enchanting poetry and ceaseless storytelling.

Not eager to leave these prospects nor weigh down arms, the trio take turns lashing tomes upon their backs, towing the tomes between spare reels of cord. Arabella tugs at the line binding print to William's ensemble, culminating with a mighty heave while the strapping constricts around his chest until he's nearly short of breath. Once properly situated, and before anyone could question their position, the skald addresses her underlings.

"Tissa pity tah take this chore 'pon us. These are not delightful endeavors, but toxic. As instruments o' their divine might, only the gods may judge us. We must return these tuh the caravanhouse, whetha by boon friends, or that o' the family, our faith shall always be rewarded. On now, lest you be."

William pardons one last glance out the window, and scowls. Boggling fumes of inky smoke contend with bushels of milky clouds upon the sky. It's remarkable that these burgeoning criminal enterprises have beguiled such copious amounts of kindling. He's not one to contend with unnecessary dangers, yet he finds himself treading into the beast's lair with beef pinned on his chest, and jerky lining his pockets. This is not what he had intended, a real pilfers-player would be pleased on skulking about the back lot.

As they slowly approach a descent into madness, all the boy Jones manages to ponder is how his original thieving opportunity has become a proper stint of penance. In fact, having this much history strapped to a person often remind folk of their very own. Those pioneers and young tykes were always so keen at mentioning malpractice, regurgitating his eldritch upbringing, notoriously ruing the day of their meeting and further cementing life as a loner. While William has always savored those moments alongside his foster father, Emery, paramount of the Walder family, Bannermane abide by the rules of finders-keepers, the blame can be sifted entirely on him.

When they proceed through the lame office door and onto the auditorium's upper concourse, an intense rustling can be head downstairs, the distinct rummaging one often finds when a rat buries itself through trash, coupled with daft tidings from the author. Peering over the balcony railing reveals an ant of a man slugging a ladder five-times his size across the auditorium.

"What on earth? Wordsmithy, are ye seein' this? What is that brute afta?"

"There's only one thing 'e would pitch for, must be plannin' ah caper, pilferin' our bloody bannas!"

The crew's rambling return down the staircase is familiar act of incoordination, as they clamber a mess of furnishings and tidings of equipment. Their knees quiver atop the balancing acts, often accidentally sliding a foot or two between cabinetwork, and stumbling. Arabella mutters with frustration at her dear friend, Rylie regrets her efficiency.

The whole scenario takes around ten minutes, entirely warding the thrill of their chase. At the endmost stretch, William takes a dreadful tumble. He completely somersaults once before landing on his rear, gliding down the remaining staircase by the sheer bulk of pages on his back. As he haphazardly slides past the bottommost flight of gaudy newel posts, William's heels strike solid mortar, hurling him headfirst towards the center of the chamber with boundless energy and reckless abandon. The polished floor tile does little to stop his advance, and instead causes him to reach terminal velocity, before ultimately colliding into a spewed span of ladder. Up until this point, the wickerwalker intentions were candid, and was plainly minding his own business.

As a learned vagabond, this stranger on stilts brought a plentiful variety of pliers and shears, gear to that may easily remove these flags from their chandelier. His knees suddenly buckle from the blunt force of William's impact, and the equipment is launched into the air without a moment's notice. He instinctively hunkers down, gripping at that top step, desperately attempting to steady himself in fear of taking an untimely plunge. Upon realizing his tragic mistake, William feverishly cradles the foot of the ladder, clutching a leg in the feeble attempt to keep it stable.

The two crescendo into a bizarre, impulsive, spurring scream, only ending when their voices finally strain, and the fear dwindles down. William releases his arms, and collapses to the ground in an exasperated *sigh* of relief. Now that the threat of collapse has subsided, this outlander clambers down, scrutinizing every rung for safety. He huddles over himself, placing his hands on his knees, and queries the earnest lad.

"Could-could ye not, n' I mean nevah, do that 'gain?"

With a lamenting sneer, William casually chimes, "I make 'solutely nah promises."

The clear impression of footsteps command the chamber, and while still lying on his back, the boy Jones peers in the stampede's general direction. He sights Arabella and Rylie lacklusterly striding towards them, before addressing the artistic troop.

"Oi, awfully right o' ye two laggin' 'hind? I was waitin' for someone tah catch mah on those steps, wrappin' muh up like ah mere babe."

"Stow it, ye halfwit dunce."

"Zippin' it up now, skaldie."

Always crafting conversation inside her head, Arabella is a woman of prose, never struggling for that perfect word. Examining this fresh face, she bluntly probes for his purpose.

"Fancy a bit o' thievin', don't ya? Waited 'til the guard ranks 'ave been thinned n' while ould Jeremiah is distracted, eh? Where's that madman author?"

"There's nah trace, nary ah sign o' 'im now."

"Oi, yea. I be doing ah bit o' thievin', but nah. No, no you've got it all wrong. I may be ah filthy wicka, but I'm a filthy wicka with purpose, ya know?"

The huntsman gestures towards the chandelier.

"I wanted tah have Galvin string these up on the balloon 'fore I 'ead out on me expeditions. Merchant cloth makes our endeavors somewhat granda in respects- official, in ah sense o' the word."

Concerns of finer things are customary, dredges leftover by rubbing shoulders with clan partisans. Wickerwalkers are creatures of renown and people of heroic repute. As a frequent of bad country, these breakneck-connoiseurs convey a certain 'je ne sais quoi'. His garb is an ensemble of trophies, gifts of sensational prestige, and pay homage to excessive patronage. They are extremely influential members of frontier society, and the Bannermane mercantile will often sponsor their diligence. The broad brands use them as walking adverts, self-started celebrities, promoting their exploits as knights loyal to the common cause, and the realities of their lord.

The huntsman draws at his copiously groomed mustache, a certain no-nonsense, bristly frill, shaped into the curated character of a handlebar, much to the ails of some six-inch, scraggly beard that meanders down his jowls. A slick, greasy mullet seeds the hinds of his head, dressily dancing downwards until it reaches his lobes, then it sprawls into an awry thicket. This dandy styling is polished by a wide-brim cap, a horseshoe-shaped mushroom, black as the color stout. Three threads of feathery white plumage pierce the hat's brow, aghast with the vibrant display of a cockeyed peacock. Like an acosta of irons, his impressive and burly ancillaries swindle an otherwise thin, gauntly host.

As a true champion of Oestergaard, the wickerwalker is victim of circumstance. His ensemble is a ragtag assortment, pilfered over a variety of campaigns; ancillaries awarded in due diligence under the guise of Charlie Mandon. From the most basic bracers, to the hardiest helms, his mere presence gives ordinary pieces exceptional luster. A fox pelt swathes his throat, giving the appearance of a red mane, its fiery furs dangling atop his leather chest plate. This cuirass is handpainted, in hues of soft blues and rosy reds, depicting the figures of twin salmon: the uppermost fish shifts abruptly backwards, as if just breaking the surface, while its partner dips underneath, each revealing their vicious maw of teeth. Certain portions of the wickerwalker's chestpiece are decorated with wax, stamped in various official-looking seals, tokens of favor from the folk he has saved. Immense billowing sleeves droop around his biceps, uncharacteristically stuffing themselves inside elbowpads, giving way to hulking bearskin gauntlets. His denim pantlegs are just as flattering, patterned in dozens of pasty vertical streaks. They cascade into a pair of knee-high leather boots, their cuffs are ludicrously swollen with wool. There's a bizarre blade straddled to his waist, a weapon guaranteed to make Kester wash with envy. It's a wicked cross between some gaudy meat cleaver and machete. An additional grip has been tempered at the end, allowing it to be easily carried within two hands.

"Say, I recognize that fur, yer that odd fella, Redmyne, right?"

Despite her use of honeyed words, Arabella is aiming for a scrap, as a man wouldn't be clad inside hide and steel without foul intentions.

The stranger retorts with some silvery plea, "Aye lass, that'll be me. Edmund Redmyne at yer service. Red-men, not red-mane or reed-mine. It's Redmyne, quite simple actually. I thought 'bout comin' 'ere searchin' for packstuffs in the chapta cellars. Got ah little shortsighted when I passed by the auditorium. Couldn't pass-up an opportunity tah dash these flags, these overgrown carpets are awfully expensive tuh weave. Love me ah bit of that Mandon red muhself, eh?"

"'Ey, 'aven't ye sworn yerself to the ruby woman, Charlie Mandon, who scourges 'pon all our 'omes?"

"Yea, tis true," the wickerwalker woefully admits, but not before nonchalantly changing his tune, "but I ain't chippa 'bout it, though. In nah manner do I prize payin' tithe to villains. She's ah connivin' devil in disguise, for sure I tell ya. 'Ave ye met the witch, even seen 'er 'fore? 'Er eyes are sinista and wild: one is the color of cherry wine, the other a mute ginga- marks of ah 'untress!

"We 'aven't had the pleasure of 'er acquaintance yet. I don't believe she'd ever range all this way, vacationin' at our lil' 'ackwater Junction," Arabella insists.

"Consider it ah blessin', sista! Now, will ya three keep fussin', or y'all turn tail and let me nab some nifty keepsakes?"

"We'll take our scripts and depart. Don'tcha 'ave better things to do than toil in these chambers? 'Aven't ye found much grub yet?

Edmund heralds his findings, "'Fraid not, not anymore at least," waltzing around them, conceding, "An 'onor 'as been fated to me. Now, I only 'ave the entire Junction to worry about. So thanks for that. As those bountiful caribou 'erds have returned Westergaard, I must direct attention elsewhere. I fear fishin' for scales off our rivershores and paltry poultry. It's all unreliable, like castin' doubt intah the unknown."

As they make way to the exit alcove, otherwise whence they came, William bids adieu and a fond farewell. "So long, rationtenda," he says, then begins to ponder, "by the way, why do they call that Charlie the ruby woman?"

The wickerwalker warns the young man, "She's ah purveyor o' lavish treats, especially precious gemstones. 'Er dresses are lined with red rubies. Avoid the blue bittersweet ones, they're curious jewels, 'avin' the tendency tah blow people up."

William is viscerally disturbed by that comment, and can't help but cringe. It's a faintly unimaginable exploit, although, perhaps he intended to mention something else? Could he mean other stones? Surely he can't mean real people, that wouldn't be true. Still, a trial by fire is the deadly culmination of expression and temperance. To be in the presence of something alive and breathing sounds oddly enlightening. The warmth imbues those around it, invigorating anyone brave enough to brace its companionship, while the cold belittles and erases them, destroying their little dignity.

Now that Edmund is left promptly left behind, the team duly surrenders themselves to the elements. The wind howls, accentuating around every alley and corner until it's a cacophony of rage. Even the broad double doors ache and struggle to close behind them. With nary two steps outside, the air immediately retaliates against them, harshly lashing at their faces, stifling every orifice. Arabella and Rylie briefly cry with anguish. The boy Jones is grateful for the facial wraps binding him from crown to collar, even if they gift a somewhat suspicious persona, they alleviate the cold's severe nipping sensations.

Thunk. He can feel the butt of a club wallop into his back, causing him to wince in grotesque pain, his kidneys have been suddenly speared in an accurate duking fit. This opponent catches him off-guard, twisting his right arm behind and grappling tightly as another adversary lands a firm impact cleanly against William's midriff, barely missing the binding and protection of the thick book.

The frontier territory is ripe for plunder, therefore Bannerfolk must be undeniably eager to safeguard their prospects. Veteran troopers are kept on retainer, including those iconic dragoons, enlisted, able-bodies that never concede, and more importantly, never surrender. William has seen his fair share of martial arts, but never consider himself a fighter.

Those who possess remarkably ill-mannered, aggressive natures may be taught combat from an early age, specifically lockja, the grappling sport. Competitors attempt to stun their opponent through a sequence of chokes or locking limbs, inspired by breaking steer and wild game. Tourneys are huge ordeals, as local chapters tend to harbor fighters, sending them to brawl with rivals abroad.

The pair of brigands deliver another merciless body blow, riveting William's viscera, riveting every innard until those hordes of butterflies in his stomach are sedated. Emotions run rampant, and he can't muster the energy to kick into a frenzy, hardly letting out some frightened whimper while his vision wanes into a dull trance. Even in this lucid state, William comprehends trivial insults between them.

"Da audacity of dees thieves, burglin' da burgh 'fore us. Sock 'em 'gen, cleat!"

His assault is rendered by the Brothers Jack, the siblings Brace and Boot Billhook, those two notorious Mandonmen left behind from the ferry. The boy Jones can scarcely stand, instead collapsing promptly in a heap, causing Arabella and Rylie to wince with attrition at the hounds.

"Filthy lil' insects, do-ya tink buggas steal from us? Ya lot wouldn't 'ave any-tink if it weren't for us n' Charlie. Othawise yule build 'ovels tah die-in next summa, 'onestly sah borin'. Outta all those tinks left, sum numbskulls still draggin' 'round useless wads o' wipa papa," lectures the boisterous Brace prior to bursting into a hilarious fit, some prompt laughing spree.

These two highwaymen bicker and quarrel constantly, lapsing into their usual bullying, shoving the two women firmly into a nearby snowbank. Boot smacks at his sibling's shoulderblade, egging his attention and points, a familiar necklace of an owl and flask which clatters around their neck.

"Quittit! Dat brat's one o' Eli's goons. Ya outta reckon der collar, has dat buff on da back like da rest of dem Crooked Men!"

Realizing they shouldn't continue to torture the trio, those Brothers Jack sling a few crude insults as their closing remarks, and depart in a rush as swiftly as they appeared.

"What is dat 'oisted 'round 'is belt? Is dat supposed-ah be ah blade?"

"Oi, dat's a shitty knife."

The earnest lad's head is still ringing from this brutal confrontation, and the skald eyes caution when William finally returns to his feet. His usual bundle of clothes now carries profuse strings of snot, sweat and still. This encounter has sewn distrust between them, poor William has has been dishonest with his current company, ensuring that the boy Jones isn't in someone's best interest to keep close. He appears further and further unhinged, cementing himself as a stone-cold opportunist, not a savior, nor a helper. Yet, the fact remains that the Brothers Jack left them alone. Shouldn't that event be worthy of compliment?

The skald gives-into her humanitarian, and more forgiving inclinations, calling upon Rylie's assistance in an attempt to wrest William from his stupefaction. She procures a bottle of bitters from her handbag, that safety clasped, plaid satchel, just for toting the essentials. She strenuously wrestles with a green glass bottle, attempting to loosen its screw-on cap. Once finally freed, a foam violently erupts, immediately seeping down the whole neck of the bottle. This elixir has begun to visibly bubble, producing a transparent, sandy-brown, miasmic mist with a staggering, noxious odor. In one steady move, Arabella cups the vial's rim with her handkerchief, swilling it around twice and further aggregating the frothy ingredients inside. She flings the glass upside-down, emptying the contents into this makeshift sleeve, and exposing a citrusy-yellow bit on the fabric.

Gingersnaps are toted as quintessential Bannermane cure-alls, an iconic, home-brewed concoction and remedy well-known for its pungent properties. Stowing the bottle, the skald hovers this fermented fruit beneath William's nose, halving the peel and splitting citrus rind with her fingers. The wafting, questionable odor instantly revives William from his semi-conscious state. His eyes suddenly open in excitement, and then lets out a grotesque groan of pain. *Ugh*, he moans, demonstrating those lamenting woes and the pain raging amongst his abdomen.

"We'll get ye properly cleaned-up. Next time, think twice 'fore takin' on those brutes."

Rylie shambles over to their newest casualty, suffering the after-effects of frontier swill. The two of them hoist that boy Jones by his armpits, propping the lad upwards in short order. As William weathers his feet once more, their group is struck by another brisk squall, removed from the sanctuary of the local chapter.

The wind is abusive, tugging at their hats and hoods in the attempt to weasel below, demonstrating pressures akin to grappling invisible geists. Contending with the elements is a wholly impossible feat, and those that challenge its reign are liable to become the latest victims, survivors wretched and riddled with frostbite, often forfeiting extremities like fingers, toes, ears, and in the worst cases, entire chunks of their facial features, commonly their nose.

Relinquishing a limb isn't the end of the world, just a temporary inconvenience to those bold enough; because they regularly send their men into the white wastelands, the mercantiles have fabricated prodigious medleys of prosthetics: iron jaws, veneers, faceplates, hooks, harpoons, hammers, claw-foots, and pegs. The Underdark weave tales of Magnolia Men, those chaps who are fonder of these modern mechanizations, exchanging their personal parts for dare-say upgrades. For men and women of the Oestergaard who particularly wish to avoid sacrificing life and limb, these malicious- yet, breathtaking gales are quite threatening.

As the trio depart the local chapter, the Junction's townspeople are busy making themselves scarce. An unfortunate vagabond is plighted to the ground, smashed by an intangible bull, propelled haplessly about the thoroughfare. Gusts shear emporiums of their siding as easily as shepherds tend to their flocks, all while those neighboring residences are expertly stripped of their shingles. Barrels, crates, sleds, and other abandoned property that have been littering the fairway are now thrust into the air with utter abandon. Fragments of debris are driven home, hurtling through awnings and windows, launching slews of infinitesimal crystal shards into its fray. These extreme hurricane-style winds are vastly convincing of retreat, confining three intrepid navigators to traverse the Mad River Junction's numerous back alleys.

As they clamor into the nearest passage, and collectively breathe a sigh of relief, William discovers with angst that several chunks of glass have lodged themselves into his outermost jacket. While straying from their original route, Rylie is steadfast, mentioning, "This corrida couples tah the promenade."

"Tis the usual, easy-goin' racket. Take that side gullet," she spouts, steering them towards the nearest track. However this passage feels discretely forgotten, conveniently tucked away from the life-line landmarks of the town. The wind whistles overhead, trapping swathes of shadows onto the walls and permafrost before them. This gloom undiscerningly ebbs away at every detail, as there are no doorframes, wrought ladders and stairs, signs, those distinct stacks of lumber, pallets, garbage or refuse here- not even any characteristic color, just looming darkness. William presses his hand against the adjacent brick bulwark, allowing the delicate building contours to guide the trio in the direction they need to go, only occasionally causing them to stumble over pieces of undefined rubbish.

Arabella procures the helm, taking lead and stating, "'Though I can't gawk, I feel an assortment o' footprints under my boots. Call me 'Bella Bloodhound," the skald demands, jokingly calling herself the Junction's foremost tracker.

It's an extremely comforting feeling to crush the icy hallmark of those who have journeyed before; as if, traveling in the safety of an invisible flock. Even as their soles lapse in these sinking depressions, plunging a well half-inch, they continue to keep an unwavering pace. Treading in the imprints of another is a simple practice, superficial to the touch, up until Arabella slogs into an odd texture. Instead of the characteristically weaning *crunch* of thin ice, their ears are instead greeted to a bizarre *squelch*. If it weren't for the murky blindness of the alley, the trio would be staring at one another, wide-eyed and in disbelief. What could this mysterious substance be? Maybe loose lantern oil, booze or nectar?

Turning the corridor's corner gives them an abrupt answer. As sunlights bleeds through the passage's spillway to the main promenade, it also carelessly dawdles across the ground, manifesting over an ill-fated afternoon. A certain thickening stream of gore that has begun to still like a glacier, trails of blood ink their way towards a cluster of carrion: five fresh casualties feed into this frozen river, the deceased are lined with inescapable, fatal wounds, leaking heinous amounts of ichor from their brawn. As clouds of steam roil off their flesh, the heat dissipates under a pale gaze.

Three victims have been slashed across the throat, another completely run-in with a blade through their chest. One final figure, presumingly the assailant, dons leather fixings; yet, this makeshift armor has done little to yield the troll's toll, as the brigand's skull has been remarkably caved-in. William focuses on the assailant- no one he knew, nor could tell, as the front of this shrew's mug is hideously warped, with two now-absent eyes commemorating hysterically bloody pulps.

The outright onslaught of this confrontation has unsettled masses of packsnow, almost like battling inside a cratering caldera, the raging fulmination of fur and gristle. This catastrophe has been recorded on the walls, as copious flings of blood now garnish both cinderblock and stone. Those corpses have been stripped of every valuable garment and possession, and where one would expect a warm wool of fleece, a gallery of onlookers are instead greeted by patches of exposed skin, toned-blue under frigid breaths of the wind. Their deaths feel cold, even with prompt disregard to the weather. In the end, the lack of their belongings instills emptiness, and these townspeople could have perished for next to nothing. The ice only prolongs the crime scene, it engulfs the encounter with whitening glaze, everything remains oddly preserved and sterile.

When pioneers are pitted in the face of an antagonizing unknown, there is nothing worse than violence met against their fellow man. The unsurmountable danger comes not from the barrage of storms, nefarious creatures, or the torments of slippery sickness, but from what you hold dearest. Betrayal strikes at the heart, just as much as the soul. The loss of one's humanity is an unjustifiable demise, the beginning of greater evils. Is this despicable nature the work of the Brothers Jack? Could those villains have goaded those untimely fates?

Rylie whispers a few near-silent prayers, a collection of borderspiel mutterings preached by wards in residence. Although there's truly nothing that can be done: the ice has set, immortalizing their conflict in those days of yester-yore. Together the trio strives past these five hushed omens, narrowly slinking around the bitter confines of alley, towards the ominous exit to the promenade. The wailing gales continue to compose their baffling tunes, causing everything within earshot to tremble.

III
—
PATRON SAINT OF LOST CAUSES

At this point, no resident would be caught dead braving these elements; all risk, zero reward. However, much to their disbelief, their eyes glimpse upon a lone figure belligerently brawling the breeze. This can't be no Bannermane native, as the outlandish figure flaunts midway on the concourse, actively taking the brunt of wind.

They are adorned in reddish linen, similar, yet vastly different to the traditional Mandonmen hue. Felt threads furls through every opening of personal bulwark, distinctively ruffling around their neck and elbows. The identify of this stranger is clad in a bull's head, not that of a bison steer, but a forgotten beast of old. The helmet is an exceedingly ornate masterpiece, even the craftsmanship of Vernon's wise-old maester couldn't dare compare. Every feature upon this scarguard is exquisite, yet frightening: a pair of mighty ten-inch horns curve from their position on the brow, the ears stretch outwardly, endowing a modest steely crown while a brass nose ring quivers and chimes with every aching step. The northernmost pole of its head exhibits a decorative crest, whose plume gently sways, brushing against each separate shoulderblade, sweeping from pauldron to pauldron.

Those vambraces double as bucklers, tightly-wrapped in crimson leather strips. A ceremonial belt and sash pulls the armored herald's midriff taut, causing a metallic skirt of chainmail to billow. The lounging remnants of robe needlessly tickles their knees, polishing an otherwise disadvantageous, hefty couple of greaves. Their brigandine is shimmering, those thousands of grating, ornery scales competing alongside one another, their metal sheens which reflect the solispyre's throes of dying light.

A walking suit of armor wouldn't be caught without their signature armament: a greatsword of unwieldy size, almost the entire length of a man, stowed safely among a backpack scabbard. This sheathed double-sided blade is a Clan Claremont original, complimented by an iconic, crescent-shaped guard above its hilt. The knight marches akin to a monster, stamping fiercely into the snow, consummating all their strength strictly to move one pace more.

The paladin's gait reminds William of those ancient divers and their metal carapaces, as father always delighted the young boy with riveting tales of adventure and treasure. This ensemble is utterly unsuitable for frontier roaming, and alas, and the latest step in a series of trembles sinks firmly below the snowbound surface. Their weighty, plated boot drops several inches, then an additional foot until the traveller is forcibly rooted in place. They appear to be in agonizing pain, thrusting their arms wildly into the air, and cursing.

The tempest storm heeds their insults and responds posthaste, quite unforgiving in their plight. That profuse volume of debris brewing in the clouds finally makes landfall, clashing into the Junction's promenade, delivering loose lurching furniture, sizable fragments of wood and splintering clouds. This rackety mob careens into the paladin, bursting into thousands of smithereens against their fully-armored casing. What was once a wooden cask becomes nothing more than a fine powder, but not without cost. The occasional cauldron or metal casting bowl punches through, punishing the knight with ample bludgeoning. After enduring twenty-minutes of trauma, the flurries finally wither, dissipating from a haze of visual static to a crystal clear picture, like nothing ever happened in the first place- yet, there's still some strange visitor sprawled across the clearing.

Onlookers are delivered a clear episode of torment, for the agent had been struck in the head by a typewriter, delivering him straight unto the ground, and sending the calamitous character into a state of full-blown panic. They crawled to the nearest residence, hand in hand, legs in tow; sheltering underneath an unremarkable deck in a desperate bid to escape the pandemonium. Nonetheless, their body has failed them, and the paladin struggles to maintain control. Flipping onto his back, this newcomer begins writhing in pain, barely able to summon words and incoherent screams. His own hands spasm uncontrollably, violently assailing his face and chest in a bout with their worst imaginary foe.

As soon as the storm's subsides, Rylie launches herself into the quell, racing towards the knight-errant's direction, to which, Arabella and William promptly pursue. From this distance they may only gasp and gawk at the trauma, for these injuries would silence an audience of even the most accomplished of the Riviera's doctors and sawbones surgeons.

The herald's once radiant raiments are tarnished under the spell of a thousand campaigns, snuffing the earnest spirit of his ancillaries. This fester white-rot of decay gouges every inch, splitting the tinniest hairs of chainmail, to pruning pauldrons alike. Their helmet's bull-like brow and visor has been caked with icy rime, and the metal brittles, fractures, and achingly crumbles apart with nary a glance. Each horn severs like icicles snapped from their hitching post, and the steer's muzzle immediately implodes. As his helm ebbs away, the paladin's visage bears passing resemblance to that of a man. Whilst Bannermane are as enduring as pine, for others, the cold is utterly demanding, and the prosecution refuses to rest. Without a mask to keep the frigid frost at bay, it ruthlessly commandeers his face, freezing all evidence of moisture, and a copious amount of tears.

The hapless man's eyelids innately throb in place, wincing with despair. His skin is painstakingly etched in bands of blackened brawn, flayed by thousands of wraithlike whips. These somber slivers proceed to waver from his face, stretching like rags, and leeching from their features until his appearance resides in a discord of tatters. These gnawed remains are covered in juicy, overgrown boils, and any ward sporting a lance would expose oozing purple slimes, as viscous as when magnate strikes oil. This secretion dribbles down onto his once prominent threads, every article of clothing has been sheared from his body. As they mend approach, the trio swiftly spot the source of his fatal woe: a hulking beam that protrudes through his chestplate, embedding itself within his flesh with the spite of a giant harpoon.

"Poor sap's been gutted like ah fish. William, yer shoulders should warrant the weight. 'Elp us get 'im tah the trading post!"

Despite his incessant clamors, the two maidens tug at the knight's arms, bolstering the frail host until he burdens William. Having practiced lifting a stunned vagabond moments earlier, the pair strain almost effortlessly, and without prompting any additional strife upon the victim. Once leaning against the boy, in spite of the horrendous commotion of agony he spews, the boy Jones is distracted by the man's lanky height.

Admitting to himself that "Thankfully- sure as ah stoat, 'e mustn't be much more than five 'ares 'eavy." Most of the knight's heftiness was tucked inside his armor carapace, which has since fallen apart.

A plethora of shallow wails flee from the ever-ripening corpse, whispering dark tidings in William's ear. The herald's half-conscious, delirious and senseless condition coaxes forth a few final mannerings.

"Osbourne… quest to… Till-the Warden… must find," before petering out.

Each existential muttering tears at the very fragments of his soul. Arabella attempts to console with warm words, swiftly producing another gingersnap, juice and all, to keep him lucid. They stride for the caravan station in one conglomerate mass, frantically lagging alongside the causeway, huddling for heat.

The paladin's greatsword, strikes at the nearest posts with a deafening *thump, thump, thump*. A few inches of the blade peek from the scabbard, captivating William's eye for detail. It is an arrogant thing, harnessing some four-inch wide, double-edged flat of burnished steel. The blade is worthy of smiting monsters- that is, if anyone else is capable of lifting it. This oversized, cantankerous stalk is more cumbersome than a fit man, nearly the wingspan of an osprey. When wielded with ferocity, those tempered edges can cleanly cleave opponents in two. It truly is a stunning ancillary, some certainly distinguished reward for services rendered in the name of their liege lord.

Knight-errants pledge their life to their clan, devoting themselves in decades of decorated military service, although one nary has the tendency to dawdle that long. Armored heralds and knights are vindicators of the Underdark, bound to a ceaseless struggle as warrior throngs battle in destitute masses of tunnels and passageways. Why would he venture out this way? This is no inexperienced volunteer, but a well-accomplished retainer. Could he be in search of a quest, looking for something of renown?

As their ragtag entourage approaches the trading post, four men with makeshift weapons stop them. These are peasant volunteers, conscripted under Vernon's whims, who halt their passage by way of kitchen cutlery taped flimsily onto the ends of shovels. The elder among them mistakes them for common knaves, and chirps.

"Oi, ya lot! What's yer fancy for all dem dressy scripts?"

Before noticing the maimed figure dragged between them.

"Utta damnation, 'ell and eight balls, git this man tah the sawbones!"

In that moment, two hands press into their backs. A familiar voice ushering them forward.

"Quickly now, with 'aste! There mustn't be much time, Austerlaund is just inside. Take 'em to where those magik-buggit folk can see."

William peers over his shoulder while those other forces surge forward, and the wickerwalker approaches from behind, carrying various totes and bundles of tarp, waving them through the watch and escorting their wildly assortment towards the caravan post's entrance. These rolled sheets are those banners form the local chapter, no-doubt, and will be a fitting addition to the emergency beacons. He promptly hands-off these materials to vagabonds, those more needly-inclined who wander too close, before trailing the others inside.

Now that the entire Junction's adheres to a few measly buildings, neighbors rekindle their relationships, and people mingle with strangers they've never met. The station is abuzz with menial labor: kin take stock of current supplies and rations, ex-innkeepers sling hash in the makeshift mess hall, former arkwrights assist the maester wain with sleds of timber ply. It's all hands on deck, everyone is contributing to these chores, between drover, knave and distraught vagrants, there's always some part to play. A grocer clerk has taken to marking ink on the walls, illustrating an emergency calendar, and biding the days. Mystic wards adulate and bask in the main corridor, paying homage to obscure gods in its corridor. Their esteemed leader, Austerlaund, towers over her congregation, that by-product of occult constitution and giant's blood.

This arch lector immediately sights the cadaverous calamity, casting her entourage aside and propelling ahead to seize that poor paladin without a moment's hesitation. She works quickly, plucking that metal shaft straight from his chest until awry with pulpous bile. This beam collapses onto the ground, not reverberating with a *clank* or *clang* of some hollowed, lightweight scrap piece. It constitutes an agonizingly dull *thud*. The man regurgitates rancor, fetching a nerve-wracking scream as the crowd watches in horror and disbelief. This warping shriek sharply drains his energy, and the paladin goes limp under such impromptu medical procedure.

Residents of Mad River Junction always have had animosity towards that which they cannot comprehend, frequently antagonizing Austerlaund and her supernatural practices. She is routinely visited by comments like, "You bastard, ye've killed him!" And "Why would she do that?" Nonetheless, the diviner's deductions will forever be shrouded in mystery.

Disregarding the audience's ailing remarks, She remains silent to this commentary, and actually signals for her accomplices to escort the ragdoll to their improvised medical wing. Those loyal wards lift the knight-errant onto a stretcher, then jolt down the hall with urgency, surging toward the trading post's stables come hell or high water.

As they enter the caravan barns, treading upon the same route used during the boarding process to which William spied the Judah Steer, those closest available beds are nothing special, albeit routine, cushioned by a bundle of four-month hay, formerly the bedding of a bison stall. The patient is blatantly laid loosed on a thin layer of blanketing linens, narrowly separating them from that stained hogwash and grime. Austerlaund's assistants surround them, scouring those few metallic pieces still strapped to the knight's body.

Together they flaunt hammers and chisels, intending to splinter open these coverings, and expose those fresh wounds beneath. It's a tedious process, and especially considering their nonexistent experience with plate armor, there's no guarantee that any of these strikes hit home. Many mallets miss, instead walloping and tenderizing half-frozen flesh. The whole process is excruciating, even while operating on a desensitized, almost brain-dead client. A priest proceeds to whisk broth in a cramped, earthen vessel, spilling hundreds of beads until it congeals in an obscure, slop-like substance. This cryptic solution is separated into four shallow dishes, with the knight's hands and feet submerged into these salt baths.

Once free of the steel chitin, every wind lash needs cleaned in a medley of homemade salves. Austerlaund herself takes a formidable, four-inch painter's brush and garnishes the herald's body with oil from head to toe. She kneels right above the paladin's fairly indistinguishable head, claps her hands thrice, spreading them across like wings. Chanting a few fruitful phrases, the arch lector initiates a summoner's ritual. William has never seen such discourse, but recognizes the foul magik.

Austerlaund draws upon guttural words, awful verbose that leaches from the throat, almost loathing off the tongue and lulling into the wind. Inky tendrils manifest in her tear ducts while a black venom dribbles out her left nostril. Glacial-blue eyes darken, invaded by an otherworldly presence. She grabs at the paladin's temples in a swift, explosive movement. The sheer size of these hands overwhelm her patient's face, covering his smitten ears, brow and hungover eyes. Though, that is the least of his worries.

Calling upon the eldritch powers that be, Austerlaund invokes an azure gleam. Her hands emit a flowing magik, much like the ebbing course of a stream, that seeps from the sides of his head into every available pore, liberally overrunning into his nose and mouth with the work of attercops. The room is taken in a whirlwind of spiritual energy, a nonexistent draught that extinguishes braziers and chandeliers until the priests are operating in almost complete darkness. A chilling aura sweeps over the spectators as forces of the World Pillar wax and wane.

William strains against its pressure: the clashing of life and death as Austerlaund bids to upset that titular balance. Being in the presence of such potent arcane energies is enthralling, exhilarating, almost electric. He can feel these ethereal sensations soaring, frisking between threads and skin, rousing every hair on end. While her illusions are captivating, this is no mere theatre show; the hulking mystic isn't a charlatan, she doesn't dabble in folksy shenanigans or tricks. Although this raw sway may charm, conjure, or hex at whim, sorcery is both a blessing and a curse, as it attracts greater evils.

Magik remains the art of ruinous powers, as behind its glamorous, mesmerizing masquerade, beings of twilight prowl behind the curtains. Diviners must pay heed, remaining cautious, and incredibly vigilant not to abuse their eldritch gifts. Every supernatural spell, no matter how large or small, makes them susceptible to foul influences. The looming barrowtide, and absence of life, only riles corruption. Fools caught within the aura of occult phenomenon sporadically stem otherworldly experiences. William can already hear their heinous calls: it starts with whispers, fragments of phrases that allure towards his dreams and desires.

"Alderson-"

"Mark of Dayne- his pride"

There are multiple voices hidden in this speech: one ravenous, another who's speech is strained through a blender, then a third that is blatantly aggressive, triggered and arguing to him that something "-has locked away your past," instigating with the others until they stir screams inside his head.

"Only fear will find the key!" And with it, these clamors fill the boy with anxiety and intense paranoia.

At this stage of the seance, a member of her fellowship notices William's plight, and accosts the gathering onlookers, abruptly shutting the stall door as another ward hectically attempts to shoo them away. While the crowd disperses among the main alley, William strides into a nearby showroom, just as his breathing reels into an uncontrollable stupor. This whole event has humbled him, and the boy finds himself absolutely dumbfounded, gripped with horror upon how easy it was for darkness to invade and overwhelm his mind. A stray hand clasps itself against William's shoulder, suddenly startling, and causing him to choke and gasp.

"Relax, 'Liam. We were all there, but tis o'ver now, tis all o'ver now."

Rylie hypes up a narrative of what the voices personally told her. "Somethin'-somethin' 'bout lionhearts they told mah. Though, one got loud. Like, really loud. I didna mind that brute much."

"Stow it 'ready, ye addled 'ag! 'Liam isn't quite feelin' up tah 'imself. In fact, think ye gone and made things worse. Say, why don't we go 'head and nab that book, take a stroll, and leave ye alone with yer thoughts? Wouldn't that be swell?"

William stares blankly into Arabella's eyes, and simply nods several times before pointing to the manuscript anchored to his chest. The skald understands, instructing the boy to take a seat, and hustles some certain pocketknife across the twines transfixed around the tome.

She takes this blade against fibrous grains, gnashing them thoroughly through until Rylie proceeds to wiggle their particular manuscript free. The whole hardback slips into the scribe's illustrious hands, allowing those sundry-sized sinews to gingerly drop from William's chest. After all, Rylie outright adores her work. Adorned in a sense of gleaming pride, she handles the book gently, dusting those covers free from a slim lining of snow moments before passing it to the skald.

"-can't begin tah describe 'ow grateful we are, ye gone 'bove and 'yond! Our trek went sideways at times, and those things could 'ave gone much, much worse. Ya might've even saved that tin-pot sold-ya's life. That 'unta is all bulls and bravado. I'm sure 'e'll thank ye, as I thank ye."

When the two literary critics ultimately depart, Rylie gives William quick embrace, patting him thrice on his backside.

"Thanks babe!"

The boy Jones does little to respond, his grimy mug is still stunned and expressionless, yet the scribe retreats, beaming with a fiery smirk even as the wooden entry closes behind her. Coarse gears manifest in William's head, they constantly rewind over and over, cruelly replaying the reels of his memory, and repeating the same old gist about a marking. The scar on William's chest becomes increasingly tender during this revelation. Distracted and lost in thought, he idles for the better part of an hour. A lively warm glow has shined upon him, now it ebbs through an array of pristine glass windows. Light, once more, bears way for darkness.

The illumination grows distant, ceremoniously dawdling away into noticeable throes of crimson. Superstitious folk pay heed to the red sun, its sky blazes like a raging inferno, tearing apart and bleeding into the dreams of others. William's field of vision is fashioned with contrast, dominated strictly by two hues: a chronic red, as if life itself had been dipped in broad strokes of blood-soaked scarlet, accentuating his loneliness by making him tone-deaf to the natural beauty of the world; and there's black, a sort of all-inclusive, inky stain that outlines familiar, ordinary objects with a profound nothingness: the complete lack and absence of everything worthwhile.

Lengthening shadows tend to wander over yonder, sprawling across various spans of neglected, worn decking. This congealing mass rapidly begins to swell, aching over every fissure in the floorboards, and each widening crevice, unmistakably spreading towards the nearest sustenance to sate its needs. The shade pursues in his direction, gliding across the real estate until a pair of phantom hands clamber close to the boy's ankles. William finds himself completely vacant of resolve, his body has no initiative, and floats amid the murky emptiness. He can scantily produce a whimper, nor withdraw his legs as they are swallowed by the taunting gloom.

An intense *thwack* ripples though lounge and leeway, causing the unsightly geist to recoil. With a swift kick in the rear, the adjoining door spontaneously swings ajar, flooding the suite in the rogue glimmering of candles. William can spy the illusion for what it really is, his own subconscious anxiously eating away at him, a visceral betrayal- to what end?

This showroom, in all its glory, is a well-conditioned masterpiece, once shrouded by William's depressive shadows. The Bannermane mercantiles pay thoroughfares to the lavender glow of love, with still blooming chrysanthemums dotting the expanse. A myriad of sled models are on display like a museum walk. Numerous caravan cars that are charmingly-constructed, polished works of art, others are instead delicate prototypes, promising mountains but delivering molehills. One of the more decent convoys is ornamented with the timber figurehead of a bear, a dominating paw thrusts outward, able to hold reins just past the driver's arrangement atop the car, funneling those thread to whatever beasts tow their car. There are three, remarkably empty slots of grime, these must have been the models dragged off for the wainwrights, and those are diligently working on their opportunity at escape. At the far end of the demesne, alongside the lofty windows, is a crafty booze bar where they serve howlers to seasonal patrons. Its countertops are propped in a menagerie of distillery casks and gilded bird cages. Certain armaments are on display above the watering hole, oversized forks known as boarding pikes for keeping wildlife at bay. Around the bend of the bar is a particular dining table for entertaining guests, some seating for a rousing soirée are plumb and barren. The typical arrangements appear to be missing, no silverware or dishes to be found, nor anything that could be considered remotely valuable.

A mobile workbench has been set-up in middle of the chamber, carefully distilling a wealth of information over several, carefully curated charts in attendance. There's a meticulously detailed, hand-drawn to scale, map among them, a clever introduction to the four territories. Each settlement is marked with tiny miniatures, with intelligence straight from Mandon command, these baubles distinguish the current position of Bannermane troops on retainer, while colored ink-lines illustrate prior destinations and voyages. These numbers forecast the incredible distance that the Junction party intends to travel, and just how hidden the subterranean stretches of the Underdark really are. This guide flaunts the honest truth: that the northern frontier is a vast expanse of desert, and filled to the brim with follies, born of grit, snow and stone. It's all a tremendous odyssey, as one could trek a fortnight in any direction and still wouldn't escape its clutches, especially while traveling on foot.

Trailing the Mad River is definitely their safest option to Bonaventure. It would be a night's-ride with a bison lead, although pulling sleds by hand- a trifle of a pace, it must be at least a three-days' journey. To be perfectly clear and fair, Vernon jiggled the doorknob to a certain extent before dubiously deciding to sledge the door clear. William barely shirks in response, and instead, Vernon is aptly bewildered by a figure festering alone in the dark.

"Ga-ah, ya brazen buzzard! Dead on leadin' me ah fright there. Almost thought my coffin-dodgin' days were 'hind mah," he declares with gusto.

Incandescence from the candle-laden hall filters over their excursion, tenderly lapsing over the boy and revealing his face. The smith's eyes widen with excitement, bountifully applauding at this happenstance before bursting into an innocent tirade.

"'Liam, ye rightful lad, goin'-off and missin' all our fun! Yer in luck, there are still so many more errands on our rostah. Come, come, we 'ave ales tah down and venom tuh purge. These days are rife with drudgery!"

Vernon surpasses William in leaps and bounds, distancing himself towards a collection of odd containers molded alongside the nearby wall. Gripping the handle and pulling taut on the showroom's freezers reveals a basket of the sorts, cordoned off by a perilously radiating mist. The technology of these devices is nothing but frank, coolers chill their contents by exposing them to outside air; a simple pipe cracked open, funneled through the wall. No insulation, electricity, steam, weekly chores, or that of a layman's manual labor are necessary to maintain the necessary preserving temperature. There he procures two, maybe three burlap sacks from the freezer, each coated in a thin veil of ice, hare carcasses to be defrosted for tonight's dinner shindig.

William attempts to take a stand, fairly eager to join his company, only to break into an abrupt stumble. His limbs fail, a foreboding pin in his heel causes his ankle gives way, still groggily lazily and asleep, causing the boy to collapse in a decisive heap.

"Oh nah- youch!" He exclaims, attracting Vernon's fatherly gaze.

"Now what are ye doin'? Tis nah time tah take a nap, we gots a feast to prepare! Nah seasonings nor scallions… 'mm. I guess it'll be mainly ah broth then."

The wrought-iron blacksmith has a petty disposition for admiring the obvious.

"Say," he inquires, "What's with all the 'ope? That sure is a fine bunch of thread."

William is quite disgruntled by his demeanor, shedding the twine that bound the charcoal tome and spurns, "Ah, ye know 'ow it is, just fancyin' ah bit o' spring-cleanin.'"

"Eh boy, ganda at what we got o'ver 'ere," riles Vernon, identifying the coops on the counter.

"That wickerfella must be some real big-shot 'right. Fed our party live lemmins too. Shored-up the plankin' 'neath our feet and there they were, burrowin' unda the floor! Now 'e's talkin' of an expedition. Let 'em goes I say. He knew where that Mandon aviary was, 'ready dispatched several birds. Course, 'ad 'em stagga the dispatch. Wouldn't want the whole flock tah be caught in the same windstorm, 'uh? Increases their chances o' somethin' makin' it out. There was an eagle though- young 'un, but ah huge trucker. Some kites too, maybe four or five birds total."

The greybeard loafs on, an expressive gent who's never lost for words.

"Always kinda fancied raisin' kestrel meself. A lil' shoulda-bud, somethin' that I could feed tiny lickins o' protein bars or shrew, certainly annoyin' pigeons not afraid tah speak their minds. Those sorts are prolly troublemakas, but it'd be my troublemaka- ya know? My very own accomplice, complicit in my crimes 'gainst 'umanity. No doubt bugga-off at the first sign of trouble, like so many otha charactas 'round 'ere. Well, everyone's talkin' 'bout gettin' one of them new fangled pups. Dogs seem tah be gettin' smalla and smalla every year. People are breedin' whiskery tykes called poochies, 'ear they're all the rage in tunnels. Those ruffians are kept as status symbols, 'nothea 'and-'eld trophy for them to parade 'round. Whole lot of them must be real dolts. 'Eard an 'andful of unsettlin' rumors- troublin' really, tad o' them can run 'round on two legs. Smart enough to buzzard at 'ints of food, then clamba intah the walls. Sounds spiteful tah me, can't be more than ah fantasy though, myth of sorts tuh tell the babes: the gremlins will find their way-in at night, and teeth on yer knickas. Nonetheless, these wenches would nevah survive up 'ere, gotta be a 'eal vicious mongrel, somethin' like ah- uh, like ah wolf."

"'Eard a tale one or two times back of a greenie actually feedin' wild stray. Course the luckye swinda brought its pack tah play and slaughtered that whole caravan troop. Now, that's what wild animas do up 'ere, yer eitha predator, or a lollygaggin', bound-tah-be-eaten sooner-or-later walkin' sack of chow. Besides, Junction folk'll start snatchin' up anythin' they can reach: hogmeat, hare, and all. We're just as bad as those monsters."

Vernon can sense William's silent ire, "What, was it somethin' I said? The whole thing's true, I ain't nah liar like that Glennson ilk of yers."

"Anywhoose, the company's been kinda diligent. Time's ah wastin', high-tide we joined them," Vernon warrants, querying an earnest lad with his open-ended hand, "What do ye say?"

At this point, William has always intended to follow along, like some adept pupil or a reliable bosun to ferrymen.

"Aye, I might do that," he remarks, catching Vernon's mitten and casually shaking. This brings out the boy's typical banter, and William mirthfully quips at the smith, "Don't mean to worry ye. Been spurnin' fears on tinge tah rats and butchas."

It's all a welcome distraction, stemming William to return into his usual, buoyant- but never-too-sunny, self. After their grand ole adventures apart, the reunited pair easily recognize the traces from those three absent sled cars. Each model left a distinct impression in the hardwood floor, extensively gouging the planking, especially by being towed away. With Vernon's ample experience alongside the joys of a hand-sander, he asserts that these blemishes are "Nevah gonna buff out. Wouldn't want tah be in charge of refurnishin' this post. Too much work, I gotta say."

The boy Jones then strikes-up a proposal, "Follow 'em, mate. Tag those trails tah the main-stay, find-out where all those people 'ave been campin'. It must've took plenty more than six 'ands to tow these monstrosities from 'ere."

Vernon mockingly congratulations his young student, "Aye, William, that's what we'll be doin'," before wheezing into a sparing chuckle.

"You ould man, 'avin' the cruelest sense of 'umor. Next thing that'll make you laugh are ladybugs dancin' on the ceilin'. Why are these carriages missin' anyhows? What makes 'em so special o'ver the othas?"

"Honestly, I dunno. Couldn't tell ya if I wanted! These were the displays Rochester was especially interested in, so talk to 'em later. That fool, kept braggin' 'bout weight, sleeknee, slicknee, and the rest."

Undeterred by the mocking flattery, the duo sharply return their attention towards the showroom door, and proceed through. The timber frame itself is nothing spectacular, however it must have been just barely wide-enough for the sleds to inch through. A crude proportion of this trim has been splintered apart, no wonder Vernon had such troubling booting the door down. Incidentally, this proves that the fuller, finished models would've needed to be meticulously dismantled with a majority of their special odds and ends cast aside. It's truly a shame, these carriages in the showroom are outfitted in luxury.

A bulk of the models sport a closed-bay for six passengers, each seat cushioned in copious leather and lit through an ornate array of horned lantern scones; the prone driver's box juts out of the chassis with ample spacing for footwork and taxing gear; rooftop railings can clasp secure any overburdening luggage, engrained with lavish woodworking, further coated in a commandeering, stylish red-and-gold color scheme; and no doubt, heavy! Despite their case, William daydreams over these indulgences, fantasizing about a relaxing tow out of town, and now, knowing what he had to go through, that the ticket wasn't worth all this trouble.

IV

—

REVELRIES AT
THE TIN HOUSE

Vernon breaks into an immaculate gaunt, weaving around every corner, and careening down the hallways like a possessed madman. In briefly the span of a blink, the smith stumbles upon a rabble gathered in the corridor. Fueled by his ordinary and aching, self-righteous fury, the smith is unable to stop himself, and nearly launches himself straight into Austerlaund's hip. Vernon barely avoids her thigh, swaying to the side at the last second, and tempering himself against the closest wall. He collides with such sheer force, that if the lemmings were listening, they would have heard the partition fracture above them. Accompanied by her regal posse of mystics, the half-giant's looming presence dominates the concourse. The priestess greets this circumstance with jovial laughter.

"Silly bristlehair, ya gone and almost lost yer 'ead."

Her eyes are propped like immense torchlights, lucent gemstones that pierce every fiber of being, peering through their whims as if they were utterly transparent. She surveys Vernon specifically, and almost mockingly, inches her gaze down, sizing him up head-to-toe with hardly an effort. There's a prominent bundle of blankets in her arms, a prestigious bulk that shifts with such grace and ease into the eve of Austerlaund's arm. To their spectators' surprise, what was once thought to be a simple tote of laundry is actually her newest patient, the knight she intends to port to the commissary. He slumbers in these linens, fast-asleep under an arcane spell, quietly hushing all sorts of gibberish. The priest condescendingly leans over and pats Vernon's head with her freed hand.

"Yer ah tiny fool."

Vernon is completely flabbergasted, an embarrassing expression of shock clads his face. When the realization of her insult finally rings true, he spitefully raises his fist in outrage.

"Why I oughta-" he exclaims, gruffly muttering a handful of curses under his breath.

"-ya 'ear me, lecta!"

However, their exchange is eclipsed by bouts of shouting, as down the hall, their pretentious argument is not the sole argument to lapse from the far double-door. They distance themselves from the caravan post's gangway, heading in the opposite direction of the bison stables and towards this newfangled commotion. Vernon and young William heed the way with Austerlaund and her mystics following in their stead, carrying the unconscious warrior prince.

The chambers strewn before their outfit emanate a steady mellow heat. As Vernon and the others barge inside, there's a slew of townspeople already basking in its blaring warmth. The commissary is secluded deep within the trading post, an essential respite keeping wayfarers properly cozy and fed, enthralled under the furnace's grand eminence.

"Wuh, what the-?"

William is momentarily distracted as his shoulder graces an icicle completely crafted from wax, causing it to snap and collapse promptly to the floor. Above the entryway is a gleaming shrine, a magnificent altarpiece is incorporated into the doorframe. It is the life-sized bust of a rather imposing snowy owl, and the bird's crooked maw gnashes at a stocky scroll, while the fowl's wingspan stretches to an awe-encompassing twenty-feet wide. As an ornate coat-of-arms cast in mottled grey-gold, this sweeping mass of gilded game is pronounced with the finest details. That marble plumage is without compare, every individual feather is distinct, straying just out of line or popping slightly from frame. Oil-like glaze dribbles beneath these downy tuft, lengthening the likes of each feather until they seep into ever-hardening puddles of wax residue amongst the floor.

There are several candles mounted at its helm: one carefully perched at the top of the airy raptor's head, and another six hitched to its wingspan, acting in unison as a beautiful candelabra. It's a weekly clock of the sorts; as each candle burns, the wicks deliberately denote the day, and even the hour. When maintained by the local bellringer, this device is precise enough to measure the passage of time down to the nearest minute! Every candle is unique, representing a specific occasion, and nestled into placement on the roost. They are color-coded in peach, coral, tangerine, ginger, burgundy, a pastel pink, and lavender hues, burning in bone idle glare with incense, a sensational cranberry aroma.

The Bannermane mercantiles operate on this one-of-a-kind calendar, and start their business week by chasing Dawnsday. Next, costermongers and clerks take their goods to market, staking claim that so-called Moorsday. The third day, Hailsday, is typically reserved for events, and is known as Framersday or Fyresday by their Underdark brethren. Midday indicates the distinct middle of the week, only to be chased by Pactday, a span for when business arrangements are commonly closed. Fifthday itself is remarkably unnotable, a time for family convening tailed only by Dusksday, the relative end of the week. Just as the caravanhands of the Gaards that have walked these very halls, Vernon and company have a bit of business to attend to themselves.

A half-flight of stairs plunge directly ahead of them, descending into a tiered, rectangular basin. This recess is subject to an immense fire-pit, its roaring lavender blaze is fueled by refuse: the hindmost handful of logs, scrap that acts as kindling, and combustable garments; a combination of which concocts a lucid rank. A cauldron roosts right out of reach of these leaping flames, and a roasting spit just above that. The succulent, sweltering meat has been smoking for the better part of a day, indicated by tinges of caramel glaze, probably before residents began throwing rubbish onto the fire. Rich dabbles of sweat and fluid seep underneath its belly, adding an intricacy of flavors to the boiling soup below, hopefully with the tinges of garbage. Though William is accustomed to moderate fasts, his hunger has yet been humbled, a feast such as this attracts the services of the Junction's lamest men.

The room's farthest reaches are inscribed with a series of wiry, second-floor scaffolding withdrawing to tunnels towards private lodgings. Spectators gawk from these perches, twisted in the pipe railings, and dangling their legs in the air. The occasional onlooker is missing a shoe, as their footwear lies abandoned on the ground beneath them. All the furniture in this demesne has been repurposed, the slew of seating and dining tables that once adorned the commissary have been assorted onto the outskirts of the basin or burned entirely. The vast majority has already been broken down for kindling or to be refurnished into their jury-rigged caravan.

The ample array of chairs are now dissembled into piles of loose lumber, along with lots of skewed straps and ropes. Rochester has ensured that the three carriages benefit from the arrangement, yet his whole creative process is rather obtuse. He has committed to the necessary modifications: there are upgrades like reinforced windowpanes for the winding gales, plows in front of each ski for maneuverability, and furnace stahls to keep the booths heated; nevertheless, the wainwright fitted certain amusing thrills, painting bold pinstripes so each carriage goes faster, and lumbering bells to intimidate any potential predators.

Rochester enabled a host of laymen and vagabonds in his pursuits, constructing additional flat-bed sleds for cargo in the process. One such platform is for the fellowship's massive cauldron pot, and a makeshift stage of sorts, another pulpit for Cillian's performing antics. Without bison to yank at the helm, in the wake of carriages, dozens of earnest hands stitch together towing harnesses, sizing their own chests.

The room is a vast, moshing pit of materials. Cartons of supplies tower upon on the lattermost wall, shipping container crates, degrees of plywood, and pallets all spray-painted with a variety of symbols, designated as fragile delicates, flammable fabrics, heavy loads, or temperature-controlled packstuffs. Certain boxes double as cages, drilled with crude holes, restraining droves of hares for the journey ahead. There are several dedicated muster stations, or distinct areas where they can stow gear: a tarp full of makeshift weapons, heaps of furs and blankets, and vessels containing their remaining lamp oil. Collectively, these rations sustain the livelihood of several dozen, remaining Mad River Junction residents. The smith intends to goad them into an impromptu meeting, taking stock of their collaborative efforts, yet finds himself acting as a marshal between two rash combatants.

A couple of men break into a harsh brawl, recklessly shoving one another back and forth. One person is fiercely propelled towards the hearth, and lands in its conflagrating mess. His leather treads are consumed by the fanning flames, gifting them a distinct char on their soles. While he flails about, the embers dance with him, coruscating every step. His elbow thunders against the stewpot's rim, almost capitulating its generous bounty, goading everyone to *gasp*, caught between shock and awe. Cinders openly writhe about, showering the paved stone in spells of firebrand while the scoundrel heeds his escape.

With a brief hop and a skip, these scorching furnace begrudgingly allow recess. As the patsy recovers from this surprise simmer, their antagonist continues to banter, pacing around like a brigand and sharply hurling insults. The enchanting glamour of the commissary is now outright absent. William recognizes that the common decency and camaraderie between fellow folk has been undisputedly expelled from the room. Their situation is extremely tense, strung like the tautest tightrope, and could be cut with the dullest blade.

These two men vie for each others' throats. One is a massive brute, two crowns grander than his competition, broader than the average man. His opponent is something worthwhile too, though a figure befit for a stage. The lesser of the two sports a slicked-back, arctic-white mohawk, it drains facetiously from the upmost portion of his headpiece. Fringes of hair flounder into a padded, fur-lined jacket which is several sizes too large. These frontier threads are known as rustlewear, perfect articles of clothing for surface treks. A broadly braided, corded belt firmly straddles together the ensemble, latching his commandeering overcoat to a tightly-woven, insulated wool suit. The portrait of this character is adorned in an overweight mask, a girthy patched capsule that is impervious to any harm, consigning to guard its handler for numerous years to come. He addresses his assailant by spreading his arms wide, proclaiming with an adamant gusto that grapples the heavens.

"Yer profound act o' 'ate spews venom in every direction, tarnishin' the reputation o' our dear fellas. Seek spite and ye shall be rewarded in righteous fury. Witness me, ah testament against yer stride! 'Arken and 'eed warnin' gent, as I greatly admonish debates 'tween fists."

The instigator is enraged, and demonstrates his intent to rattle sabers by pummeling at his own barrel-sized chest. He reeks of peat, and various earthy stenches. This brawny, beast of burden possesses leather pauldrons that only accentuate his gargantuan gorilla shoulders. As his torso heaves, scraps of olive green drab lurch in rebuke, and a flowing linen cape billows at his rear. The cloak outlines his backbone, pinned underneath a weighty, double-bladed axe, a contending labrys.

A man of true grit, he dawns an iron hood. There's an obvious dent in its cap, some bygone battlewound that's sure to cut off circulation to his brain. This helmet merely shields the upper portion of the face, plunging over the very bridge of his nose in an eccentric ridged guard, while wings dawdle and spread wide protecting his cheekbones. The remainder of staunch skin is coated in burly, razorback bristle, an exalting burnt umber. Blood-red beads stare through the ellipse slits of his helmet, possessive eyes that glare fixatingly at its next, imminent mark. A pair of pronghorns consummate an otherwise quintessential Boar's Band outfit, they hastily pierce from the temples and furrow his brow.

Above this squabble, bystanders persistently howl and whoop, describing him as an, "Obscene jackanape!"

Edmund Redmyne can't help but egg them on, the wickerwalker could be described as a betting man.

Ra-aagh! The insolent fiend readies a wargarbl, uttering a wailing war cry that sounds like buggit nonsense, prior to casting his swole fist. This warrior is a professional at enthusiastically handing out naps. However, as a fellow of petite frame, the featherweight anticipates this throw, and whimsically weaves.

The blow attains headway, although not where originally intended, in lieu of the target's dodgy disposition the rushing surge instead lands against a nearby sled. It careens with such force that the carriage door immediately buckles, imploding the adjacent glass, and sending the whole device a handicapped furlong away. The totem at its helm quivers upon impact.

Seeing that his adversary means business, it's the contender's opportunity to demonstrate his innate battle prowess. In one swift move, he accelerates towards the rowdy bruiser, dodging a glancing hook, wrapping his own forearms around the throat and applying pressure. This maneuver catches the vandal by surprise, and he instinctively surges forward as the oxygen lapses in his throat. As the smaller patron continually wrings his neck, driving him unconscious, the brute collides directly into the wall. His face smashes the brick with substantial force, causing the scaffolding to tremble and the crowd to stumble and waver.

The horned helmet loosens its grip, revealing the stunned aggressor as Korralack the Kable, a roving highwayman who has coined the phrase, 'More heart than technique.' The other character must be none other than Morbin Evershade, an urchin turned probational nuisance, William's personal rival in these recent days.

Spewing from beggarly roots at the East End, Morbin became a rather shady trafficker of mischief. He's always had sticky-fingers, it was just a matter of blossoming into them. They say that even as a babe in the shelter's crib, he pilfered his caretaker's badge and seal. Naturally, the swindler condoned his grift, frolicking to the niche field of archeology. As the Underdark is buried deep beneath the old city, hallowed inside bulwarks of asphalt and concrete, this labyrinth withholds immeasurable treasures. Ancient ruins reach towards the sky, skewering the heavens in tracts of rebar. Hearthland's boroughs have stood for thousands of millennia, and will withstand thousands more, even while slew of storms batter these estates, but never seem to sheer its impenetrable hull. Nana Nature grows ever-vengeful, burying the irons in copious snowfall, preserving the depths of old city for countless years to come.

Those caravans and freshly-founded settlements who trek on the surface are victims of brackish weather, caught in crossfires of frost and sleet. Originating from the earliest days of some great cataclysm, eldritch snowstorms incessantly plague the hinterlands and northern territories. Travelers caught in their midst will be suddenly frozen on the spot, as lonesome navigators are given trivial warnings. If water vapor suddenly singes the air, and the temperature steeps churning breath into thick, roiling clouds of mists, those vagabonds do well to immediately panic.

The chillrend doesn't discriminate between innocent nor guilty, ice is eternal, and there shall always be rime. Those entangled within its ire become nothing more than taut mannequins, frozen in place for all eternity. Mutilated corpses are cocooned in a casket of ice, still clasping at their collars, and hinting at their bygone lives. Known as stillmen, puppets are permanent residents of the old city, populating the fringes of Urbana. Common sights include residents in their ordinary rituals: waiting in lines, at a desk or once commuting, waltzing down the avenue or snared inside a steel tube.

Scholars speculate with wonder about these quarries; that those struck while asleep, clinging to their beds, actually dream. Statues can be rather harmless, nothing to fret over, it's the infermieri that navigators must fret about. The faceless dead are indiscernible geists, an obscure blur out of the corner of someone's vision. Witnesses beware, apparitions present real danger. They are ghouls that nip at roving ears, the weight on burdened shoulders, those that tug on laymen, the hands that grab at poor souls and yank them underneath snow. With the ample peril, archeology remains a lucrative industry, perhaps one of the few remaining professions in which practitioners volunteer, repeatedly throwing themselves into jeopardy.

Morbin devised his racket in which salvagers survey surface terrain, excavating beneath the ice and pack snow to uncover any valuable artifacts. The barrowtide beckons forth brackish malcontent, shimming its foot in the door whenever pioneers reach the safety of hearths, showcasing a relentless and lengthy season of strife. Only during the reminiscent sutler's paradise, can those august opportunists dredge the white wastes in search of fortune.

The merchantiles typically employ finer folk as sutlers to recover their goods, amateurs whom swindle their company, and plunder ill gains. This burgeoning thief always brags about his findings at ill moments, constantly celebrating those dishonest splendors, and William grows exhausted of these tall tales.

Interestingly enough, Evershade boasts about looting a crypt further down the Oestergaard. Mentioning how it's a despicable ruin, following an ambiguous, decrepit ladder through trodden sewers, to a particular depository deemed as "Retcon" by the fabled Atticus Dour. Morbin himself was never able to pierce the vault, but maybe that's a good thing. Whenever the quartermain describes this ancient room to scribes, "I stumbled 'pon company of the ould world, many mutants that slumba and ache. Few 'woke, forced me intah untimely retreat."

Evershade is some certainly couth, yet devoted kleptomaniac, bringing a welcomed, dandy flair to the profession. Townspeople rely on Morbin for such illicit character, hiring the adamant to assert their family heirlooms from moneymongers and pawnbrokers. Both William and his association eventually found themselves at the rapport of the Crooked Men.

Morbin the moonlight procurer possesses a lucky knack for grand larceny that should never be described as anything but expertise, while the boy Jones is a charity case, goaded into petty theft moreso from his desperation. That amateur archaeologist is several degrees slicker than William, always attempting to one-up him in some sort of fashion. They aren't enemies per say, yet the boy finds himself religiously annoyed by his presence, their rivalries prompting those routine *sighs*.

Under Eli the Stockpile's order, one of William's earliest heists involved pilfering a handful of iron fittings. Morbin, always up to his classic hijinks, pilfered all of the blacksmith's pins- his entire stockpile, not five minutes later. With all this foolhawking, the boy Jones couldn't believe that he didn't recognize Evershade's grinning mug sooner.

Now that the fleeting, but enticing conflict with the brute has entered a fitting resolution, Vernon attempts to sway the gallery of gathered onlookers flaunting above the nearly knocked-out Korralack. These patrons have their qualms and due diligence composed against one another.

"People, people," the iron-wright preaches, "Pay regard! Calm down with all this ruckus. Periclees, for pity's sake, yer kin 'fore all! Turnin' on each otha like babblin' spawn. Dontcha go slayin' giants where they don't exist."

Vernon takes heed of Austerlaund scowling nearby, "Present company excluded, o' course."

His audience continues to banter and chant, riled by the ensuing fight and frustrated by their current climate. However, his convictions do very little to quell the venomous congregation this time around, they are barely capable of comprehending Vernon's presence. This entirely provokes the blacksmith, a barb that pierces his chest and lets loose an onslaught of rage. He releases his pent-up frustration by screaming at the top of his lungs.

"By the divinas, we're not animas!"

The Junction's untitled lockja champion, Morbin Evershade, is lulling in his victory. He cruises underneath the scaffolding and scrutinizing gaze of Edmund Redmyne, springing to station among a throne of strongboxes, his personal coffers brimming with capital coin and paper trademarks. These are Morbin's self-described winnings, not just trophies of his sparring bouts, but his vanity too. These funds are barely worth more than the paper they're signed on, they would make better kindling.

The thief exhibits a sarcastic rib, "Ah, we're just playin'. Don't be so drab, chief. I assure ye that we've finished all that work 'ready."

"Yer such a scoundrel, there nevah seems to be anythin' right with ya. There are more pressin' concerns than that degenerate sense o' superiority," Vernon declares, gesturing towards the fraudster's state of affairs.

"I'll have none of this paradin' 'round, we aren't gonna be worshippin' ya anytime soon."

Morbin Evershade condescendingly bows his head to bid adieu.

"Farewell, yer eminence. Best o' luck."

When Vernon departs, he can't help but notice that convenient heap of cushion and chainmail, the defeated Korralack. The wrought takes an arrow to his knee, a respectfully slight bend of attention, taking note of the blockhead who brandishes another disorienting dent along the curvature of his helmet.

"And ya? 'Arken brute. Does the light still creep intah yer eyelids? Can ye see me?"

Korralack slouches beside a nook in the wall, where his legs are contorted to odd angles. The jarring rubberiness of his body shares the same binding numbness as his mind. Blank, expressionless eyes heed Vernon's advance, however focusing in entirely the wrong direction, even as the blacksmith bows within spitting distance.

Korralack's mouth can barely muster the nonsense, "Ye sound awfully famili-yah. Oi 'aven't talked tah mah dear ole mum in quite sum time."

Even after receiving a stretch of mental trauma, the plighted pugilist,

Kable, bars no ill will towards Morbin. These affairs bar ordinary causeway, as bullyrooks rather enjoy brawling, bickering like siblings is an amusing thrill, and builds a sense of camaraderie. This joust had been a true testament of strength, a clear and clever victor has been crowned, and youth has triumphed over strength. Yet Vernon returns to his agenda, where a certain degree of age and expertise is required.

"Roosta- err, Rochesta! Where are ye?"

Fellows of the flock gander amongst themselves, shuffling their feet awkwardly, and dancing between shoulders of one another. These excitable creatures finally complete the puzzle, separating enough to reveal the timid jack, a man who's distinctly allergic to crowds. He resides elusively underneath a set of scaffolding stairs, chewing anxiously on a stick of rubber-like, birch sap. The constant gnawing, a mastication of gum and teeth, produce an eerie moil.

The racket surmises as a definitive series of *sloshing, schlorps,* and *schloops,* as if someone stepped in a substance most detestable. Vernon addresses Rochester, the grey-haired wainwright, commanding him to attention.

"Whatdoyamean, me? Really, ye need poor lil' me? Are ya sure?"

"Yes, o' course. Don't ye remember, when we were jabberin' earl-yah? That stress must be gobblin' at yer brain!"

He motions with a wave of his arm, "C'mon, closa Rochester. Let us gossip."

That aforenamed Rochester may be the vagabond's real title, but Rooster is a bit more fitting. The wainwright has always been wary of sticking his neck out too far, possessing a complete amity towards craftsmanship and profound respect of the trade, these fears are completely trivial, people adore his work. These sessions with the blacksmith have been a rather enlightening, an endearing gift itself. With what spectators could strictly describe as boundless drivel, bantering alongside a master with his hands, Vernon comprehends his incredible vernacular. After all, stray dogs find their stride together.

He normally exclaims at the opportunity, "'Ot-'eeled slubberdegullions! Finally some madcap who fathoms talent! To tink, I almost got an offah tah bunka barrow o'ver at Whitehorse."

Rochester is a man of scarce prospects, the Mandonmen routinely kept him busy managing their fleet of caravans, where he hid from more commonplace residents, never mingling or engaging with. The sole ingredient of his stew left him more troubled than certifiable. Scarcely venting the floodwaters of his knowledge, the wright is a quay that can handle an endless deluge of scrupulous factoids about dredges and shanties.

They casually parley regarding the state of their projects. Vernon has acquired some specialty parts left among his smithing shop, enabling the wainwright's provocative innovations. To William, it all sounds like gibberish- strictly sparse borderspiel, just intricate language that's difficult to discover.

"The sleds are done," he'd seem to say, "'Ere are the changes we made."

Rochester's handiwork has been assisted by several dubious laymen, though he could barely muster the courage to command them. These are valuable scissorsmiths, a type of vagabond familiar to the blueprinting field, Swiss-army-knife humans who can craft all sorts of goods. Hoosierfeld Char kept them at employ, committing their labors all across the promenade and Mad River Junction. Together they've installed all sorts of ad hoc, jury-rigged industrial roofing, laying a variety of snow guards to safeguard the uttermost essential properties. That wasn't their only lucrative, dynasty project, they're also responsible for the steam piping linking the suites of the trading post to the basement boiler of the local chapter.

The trio must've apprenticed with the fire-breathing wrightlords of Clan Penn, no ordinary layman should command such knowledge. As ice relentlessly batters the heating ducts, this system will soon shut down, it immediately frees the superheated vapor, fracturing the valuable lines of copper. They might have gotten away with patches during the bloomtide, but the entombing packs now will ensure that they're not a viable solution anymore.

Clerks, from auctioneers to hucksters, beseech scissorsmiths to compose typewriter their keys. If it wasn't for due diligence of laymen would the brethren of Charlie Mandon be able to dots their i's or span any t's. These censors draft ledgers of goods for distinguished records and bills of sale. To them, printing is an iconic agent of professionalism, a symbol of yester-yore, and therefore a medium to strive for.

Their final affair of renown embraces rugged novelties, pioneering frontier innovation and just like real Bannermane grit, a technology that fails within the first few years. The telegraph system had been introduced in the Underdark within the prior decade, ironing a name for itself as an expansive, yet expensive communication concoction corresponding point A to point B. They work by tapping a transmitter in such a distinct way, that it can be heard and interpreted by operators on the receiving end. Lines of cable traversing from settlement to settlement have severed and long since frozen over, but for the brief period of time that it worked, instant messaging was an ingenious invention.

As Rochester, Vernon and company are distracted in throes of blue-collar discourse, a disgruntled rabble steadily streams into the room. This gang of guests eventually trickle netherward into the basin, and crowd the fireplace's tender hearth. These wayfarers are dingy in appearance, but no strangers, tiding to the generous first impressions of the furnace's tepid warmth.

"Oi! Oh my, what a smell," townspeople seem to say, either spurred by the garbage or insatiate odors of broiling venison. Their vestments are coated in snow, frolics of fabric strewn over rosy pink skin, a common symptom of worsening weather.

A range of folk retain prosthetic fingers, casualties of the cold, nonetheless certain burglars meet the same fate. Everyday, to wits end and no avail, residents of the northern territories are thrust into the frigid temperatures. Unlike their wild, hairy counterparts, human bodies are susceptible to intense traumas. The frontier is all encompassing, people track its residue into their dwellings as easily as snow. Their skin deteriorates into sour spreads of reddened skin, a destitute prognosis known as frostnip, which in its tardy form, will result in blistering skin, swelling and shakes. The ivory coast thrashes with a worsening degree, permeating the skin and leaving an aching echo of dead flesh, before advancing to its ultimate form, the black death. This is the point of no return, as once this disease reaches its conclusion, the tissue can no longer be revived.

Sawbone surgeons specialize in taking tokens of hypothermia, trimming meat and gristle to save the overall life, not necessarily guaranteeing the limb. However they're no psychologists, and attest that prolonged exposure deteriorates the mental condition of its victims. There are two phenomena that conspire under the guise of frostbite, both pace along the self-destructive agenda. Inspiring dementia, mania and psychosis, "madness that melts the brain," becomes apparent when those affected peel off their attire, and run bare-naked through the sleet.

Bywater had such an event, a sudden reflex propagating imminent death, and fled into the woods for days before discovering his fortunate immunity. The other is the complete opposite, designated by reigning authorities as hide-and-die syndrome. Afflicted individuals will abysmally burrow into snow or enclosed spaces seeking comfort, only to be greeted by death, and gently expire afterwards.

The beacon of light in the center of the room summons an exquisite diet of people, an unanimous symposium of individuals thrust into dire circumstances. William recognizes many as familiar faces around town, even habits from the day before. The bard, Cillian Lore presents himself, attempting to soothe the parade, but in spite of everything he exemplifies, only infuriates the surrounding persons. Perhaps it's his abrasive personality, that listeners cannot comprehend the decisive dedications in his work. Each lyric, every stroke of oral eloquence is a sheer masterpiece in his very ears. Somehow, those in the audience seem to suffer from pesky lobewyrms. Acting like an authentic town crier, he harshly hollers, before inciting an exhaustive rake at his instrument.

"Hear ye, hear ye. I welcome y'all to 'notha moor-is-day. A buoyant occasion o' business and barbaric reckonin'. Ya know, almost reminds me of when-"

"Enough of yer fetid showmanship," Vernon suddenly interjects. "Place a pause on this fanfare. We got plenty o' otha propositions tah address. Tissa traditional audience any'ow, fava them shamisen o'ver yer metallic cacophony. So we'll call on ye when the need arises."

Using his harness, Cillian swings his hurdy-gurdy directly onto his back, immediately seating himself in the vicinity of nearby loons and proceeds to pout.

"I surmise our affairs, and glance at these proceedins. Rochesta, we 'ad a good chat, so keep up the good work is all I gots to say! Fellas and femmes, 'ere it is as I see it. We've made significant progress on our caravan, it'll be finished for ah trip in the comin' morn'. I'll be requestin' scouts, and other dependable lads commandin' our packstuffs. There are those I trust, but also those who treasure more traditional values. I implore all whom share mah regard for merit o'ver opportunity. There are still a few maneuvers tuh review, these must be ready 'fore departure. I'm personally preppin' the carriages for any infirm, and strappin' towlines tah these craft for the intended evacuation. Our travels will be 'ard and dauntin', this route eastmyr- er, easterly, for all ye thronepatter folk, is treacherous without bison steed. Sabercats chase flocks of sheep down the mountain channels, danger findin' themselves closa to our settlements, nestled in these craglands 'long Ander's. As we desert the Junction, tundra terrors will stalk our every move. O' course, that's assumin' we're not surrounded by rovin' bands of man-eatin' boar and wolves first. Mayhaps, we'd be 'apless if ah bear strayed our way. Their pasty-white coats mask 'em, makin' each n' every meat merchant o' the campaign nigh-invisible 'til they're right on top of ya. Alabears are frightful in nature, much worse than sallow southern cousins. I 'ear they actually forage on diets of berries."

"While we're on the topic of 'onest threats, some of ye may recognize otha ergonauts 'round town. Ye know them as dreary folk, vagrants- those unwillin' tah change or cope with our current predicaments. Such fools are belligerent, and almost always come up with ah reason not tah do somethin'. They may have once been acquaintances, friends, even family, but now- avoid them like the plague, consida em 'ostile. Mad River has balkanized 'tween these factions, includin' a Mandonmen cabal led by them Brothers Jack. Crazy tah think there are folks crooked enough tuh join them. These brigands wouldn't botha sedatin' you, soona cross yer gullet for the lint in yer pockets."

Vernon asserts his sentiment towards the hunter, lashing out in a series of berating barbs. "Eh, wickahman, ye must be nothin' special if ye'd soona allow varmints tah rummage through yer garden. What kind o' wiseacre would permit vermin tah festa?"

As a bonafide breakneck-connoisseur, Edmund Redmyne sternly stares on, rolling his eyes at the blacksmith petty abuse. He's gotten this far by choosing his own battles, and knows when to hold his tongue. The sharp, trilling voice of Rylie Hess echos from the loftiest leanings of scaffolding.

"Vernon, yer not 'elpin'! 'Ush 'ready!"

An awful, trickling sneer creeps through his stretch of face. The wright raises his arms in resignation.

"'Right, 'right. Oi, pipe-down inklin'! On a lighta note, tissa time tah celebrate best we can. We've made progress by leaps n' bounds. By bandin' togetha we 'ave given our struggle meanin'. A few of our folk, that duad Hinds, gatha supplies as ah soup kitchen. Think we're all deservin' of ah meal with all the real fixins. Marlene 'as stood vigil ova the fire's tenda flame, she'll see that everyone gets some propa meal. Go, go-on now!"

An altruistic figure wielding a manageable array of kitchen utensils makes herself known. If it wasn't for the delicate aromas of garlic, the traditional vices of gluttony, the sous-chef swinging a ladle around certainly captures their attention. Marlene Hinds is quite the character, an ingrained, eccentric type. The variety of grey woman who quickly befriends those around her, giving baba quite the reputation as a lesser-known league of celebrity. Though her ranking is sure to improve with this earnest charitability. It isn't long before she finds herself wedged between shape and arms, a hammer of anvil, eagerly forming a tidal wave against her, causing the elder to shout with exasperation.

"One at ah time, one at ah time, ya fiends!"

This ensuing crowd produce dishes from nowhere, momentary, makeshift bowls and reconditioned mugs once used for liquor or nog- quite forward-thinking, these crocks don't even need bother with spoons, and it's all less likely to spill.

Bannerfolk nourishment is quite speculative, it's easier not question the source. A typical broth features notions of a prior hunt, then the mixture goes on to include gross cuts of meat- more undesirable parts of a bison such as its flank; high-fat trimmings known as laudermilk; and a bare minimum of over-ripening, bland fruits and vegetables imported from Underdark hothouses. It doesn't matter in the end, as all of these juices simmer and mingle in a perpetual, concocting stew. A true maven of the flame can keep their dish acquainted for weeks, adding in dashes of spice and fresh protein when the opportunity allows. Frequent patrons say that the flavors blend together, one would hardly notice a rotting fare.

This is Marlene's folksy bone-whiskers broth, bits and bobbles of hare dance on the steaming surface. Even when pestered, the crone carelessly continues to curry favor upon her cauldron, refusing to cite her source of protein, but William is relatively sure those rodents were once a drove, a bunch of lovable pets. Alas, Sassafras Pache must've broken down with tears at the donation of her beloved companions, raising her little companions since they were mere, suckling kits. She was an enthusiast really, and once described her elaborate set-up, the colony nested in a special multi-level cage inside her dwelling, and were fed the freshest herbs and greens that Sassafras could muster in her makeshift, indoor garden.

Each time the ladle is thrust into the stewpot, the swill looses a barrage of droplets. These burst and sizzle onto the flame, peppering everyone's nostrils with the fumigating, yet tantalizing odor of singed Fuebian Reserve cheese. The smells congeal in a physical cloud, immersing the nearby tracts in a dense atmosphere of miasma. Marlene's husband, Kirk is stocked behind a generous bounty of caribou, a frolicker's rump that has been roasting on a spit, ceremoniously donning an apron around his paunchy gut.

The surface of sweaty, succulent flesh is punctured by a two-pronged carving fork, then by a probing blade, which see-saws its silvery edge to and fro against the clear grain of meat. It takes an antagonizing amount of time to prime the round. Kirk engraves the hindquarters, rendering trimmings of rear shank, steak, tips, sirloins, and exquisite tenderloins. Each perforation releases streams of tallow, consummating the deer-roast in its own juicy innards. As patrons eagerly approach the scalding pit, the tailor finally separates flesh from bone, often needing a hardy grunt or two to sever the last few, remaining tendons.

As the meat greets their plate, diners can't help but pause and take in a whiff of fireweed and pine. This is no ordinary grub or dull, packstuff provisions, this is fine dining. Most don't bother with dishes, however as a gentleman of culture, William impetuously searches for a plate, finding an odd assortment of saucers underneath an empty chair. It takes him nearly the better part of an hour to assert his prize, as people savor their moments.

When William advances to the cauldron's wake, he permissively scrutinizes Kirk, who discovers the distracting gleam in the boy's eye. The Junction's impromptu butcher responds with a nod and pointing of a finger, reassuring William with a tender rump of roast.

"Welcome, dis bludga of ah deer and I 'ad sum sort o' scuffle," he tends to stiff, delicious rump of meat.

"I wun by da way."

Carefully casting aside his knife and fork by nonchalantly impaling them into the roast, he is left with a hot meal. One he would ever-so graciously extend to William, if only he may pay the slopshop's toll. Kirk's free palm extends egregiously, shifting his fingertips in a motion that says, 'Gimme!'

"That'll be fifteen trademarks," he casually chides.

"Fifteen?" William remarks to himself, is he serious?

"Fifteen, are ye sure? That's an awful lot o' money."

Even if the boy had anything to hedge, he's been led to believe that Vernon assembled people of character, vagabonds who wouldn't dare to extort chumps like him.

"What do ya mean? This ain't nah soup kitchen," Kirk condescendingly sneers.

"But Vernon said-"

"Ye don't got any money? We're Bannermane for pity's sake. Hagglin's our blood! Heavens tah betsy, so don't go tellin' me dat yer askin' for a 'andout."

"Umm," William gripes, "Well, yes-yes sir. Guess I am."

In that moment, Kirk's complexion is cast in a litany of agonizing grimaces. He looks away, thrusting his gaze into the rafters and cries out.

"Oh! Oh, woe. Marlene, come quickly! Dis da sort o' folk we've been warned 'bout. Shiver muh timbas, dis lad is ringin' our charity bell."

"A handout?"

"Oi, now dat's what I said, lass!"

"No! Oh mah. Oh mah, 'deed. *tsk-tsk-tsk* That just won't do. And tah tink, ye were totin' 'round that ticket earlier as if ya just won the lottery."

The pair of cooks are livid, and somewhat disgusted by this childish jest. Marlene stares at William fastidiously, peering from the greasy range of unkempt hair to the leather clasps of his boots. She notices a peculiar, silvery glint straddling the boy's abdomen. She pipes up with the confidence of a choir.

"What be that fancy piece of metal? Buttons, belt buckle? Are you stowin' coins from us?"

He shakes his head from side-to-side in response.

"Not at all mah fair lady. Tissa brigand's blade, meant tah drive off the worst 'ighwaymen on this side o' the Oestergaard!"

William's face is stoked in glee. Finally, an opportunity to show off his trophy. He grips steadily at the halberd, and propels the armament from its sheath far into the air. It catches the ambience, reflecting the limelight for all to see. The weapon is not to be expected, and isn't an ancillary worthy to boast about: there are countless smudges crossing the oversized bayonet, its point has been whittled down to nub, and the shaft, in which it had been shattered from, is prominent as ever. His zealous attitude is swiftly shot down while the greybeard vigorously critiques.

"Broken, wut sense wuld bear barta for dat useless token? Ye gotta nose for reek, ain't no business 'ense at all. Tell ya what, do us a fava and empty yer pockets, we'll go from there."

He emits a *sigh* of defeat, "Really? Okay, sure-sure, sir."

William profusely detests this request, yet abides by Kirk's command, showcasing the insides of his coats, and overturning every pocket until copious amounts of herbs fumble out. A particularly shunted, tanned, peachy branch plops out onto the rugged stone floor.

"Ginga root and rosemary? What useless banta! Dontcha got anythin' o' value, even loose change? Anythin' but lint!

"Oh darlin', this tragedy got mah temples throbbin'. Quite painful to watch."

The two, salted and peppercorn seniors craft several taunts William's way, hassling him for his transgression, ridiculing the boy's request.

"Yer really testin' us. Wut are day teachin' kids nowadays? Tis like der tutorin' dem tah become simple-minded folk, knaves sold by the bunch. Day should pack ye right-up, tight as sardines, n' ship da lot off tah does amber pits. Does mines temper yer mettle, awfully arr-arr-arduous. Give ye ah fleetin' feelin' for sum decent, 'ardwork. And who knows, might actually earn somethin' for yer squalor."

A normal teenager would find this belittlement discouraging, a tear may graze their cheek as the other townspeople around the commissary chuckle and sneer. Although, the insult was superficial, and nothing more than skin-deep, the whole situation doesn't quite click-right in his head. It's like processing static: he's there, but rather absent-minded, neither frustrated nor egging conflict, instead blighted by an unemotional stent.

The greybeard finally hands his fellow sailor some supper.

"Take dis n' enjoy! Don't come back."

Kirk's annunciation is rife with sarcasm, and this offering profoundly irks William- not for the awkward circumstances surrounding the meal, but at the loss of his independence, forgetfulness, the lack of decency, and taking another's toils for granted. He ponders, why does he feel like the antagonist of this and not the victim? The boy Jones takes this plate and retreats towards the soothing edges of the hearth. He was once so keen to abandon them: Marlene, Kirk, and everyone else in the Junction, even with all their trouble, he now shirks at the thought. Perhaps it's a disposition formed of dependency, a constantly changing decree of survival. Occasionally settlers find safety among a flock, unified through their common troubles, then their survival triumphs against the aspirations of all.

There's a suspicious lack of furniture in the commissary's basin, most of the typical fixtures has been hoarded for the carriage caches, and the prevailing form of seating arrangements turn to barrels and crates. As bannerfolk depart from the hearth, scores of people idly mingle and chat. Some dine alone, instead finding a nice quiet niche in a corner of room. Humans are naturally social creatures, burdensome events pressure those to become hostile or vulnerable. Chaos is the driving force of nature, crafting roots that wind and weave, often constricting the meager lives of all those that toil within the Underdark- violence under the guise of a merciful god. However, strife can breed correlation. Conflict may draw people together, and just as easily rends them apart. In circumstances of turmoil, families are separated, children cast asunder, yet humans always find a way to see the light. The red sun is a seldom-seen sigil, pressuring strangers to find their stride with one another, but those that do form a bond tighter than twine. They become outlanders with similar bearings, and common causeway.

Residents and deserted drifters alike shout and mock, caterwauling, "Cliff, ye salty dog. I 'aven't seen ya in ages! Still up tah those shenanigans 'round the felt?"

There's a friendly face among the crowds, that of the cordwainer, Mandel Haggerton, who salutes with a wave, competing for William's attention. He natures a small gathering around the muck and refuse of a bin. Most have their backs turned to the boy, but he recognizes them as familiars few: Sassafras Pache, Rabley, Lena Tillstead, and her patron acquaintance, Jerome. Arabella Gaberdine also strays close-by, though William feels more comfortable sticking to the shadows, as he has routinely humiliated himself with selfish sentiment.

Mandel prods and complains, "Come n' join us for the feast, 'Liam, lest the 'unga gnaw at yer bones. 'Member, when the stomach jitters, that only means one thing, opportunity- something will soon be there tah fill it!"

The boy unenthusiastically gives-in to his peer pressure, but more importantly, perceives this as an uncertain chance to reunite with remaining band of so-called, fellow confidantes. A majority of those are seated on top of comforting, bundled tarps.

William approaches a cask of Brauhaus Bluddraught, some specialty fermenting mash of blood and rye. He spryly lurches his left leg over the keg, resting a free-hand on his belly, a lively maneuver of sorts. The others acknowledge his presence with nods and pithy whistling. Jerome condescendingly smirks and snorts before bringing a bowl to his lips, the soup must be tastefully sublime, because this regularly belligerent cohort mumbles to himself.

"Oh, that's delightful."

The dish binds his lips for an unprecedented time, finally departing and leaving a clingy wrap that decorates his whiskers. Lena is utterly famished, and chirps ahead of her plate in response, scoffing and greedily consuming the spread in a rite of desperate hunger.

This fellowship is famished, no one resting in the fire's bearing has eaten for the better part of the day- say, for Marlene Hinds participating in an occasional taste test, and the scraps Vernon parted with for breakfast. William gingerly abides to this company, raising a thoroughly-charred tip of venison between his fingers, and biting into its aromatically-seasoned flesh. His teeth are graced with pulpous rind, and his tongue is greeted by sweetened nectar remains of slow-roast tallow. A hidden clove of garlic saps the flavor of steak with an overwhelming taste of tangy suave. Sapid delectables such as this are an utmost rarity, and the boy revels in its bouquet of zesty seasoning.

William's appetite is so rudely interrupted by a tapping upon his backside. He whirls around to witness a mysterious chameleon behind him, this woman is adorned with daunt ancillaries of feather and fleece, hauling a weighty tote with various appendages sticking out. This magpie drops her luggage and swiftly unclasps it, revealing an aberrant stash of horns. It's an avid collection accumulated over the years, tusks and antlers of beastly bison, boar, caribou, elk, fang apes, gamut, and formidable terrors. The hex-charmer has a particular trophy in mind, one most peculiar in nature.

She reaches far into the depths of this carryall, uncannily rummaging around for what appears to be minutes. The horn that the magpie distinguishes would easily render Mandt purple and bitter. It's an awfully prized possession, only suitable for exhibition by prominent Bannermane magistrates. She bestows it to William with awe, then bows and quietly mouths words of encouragement while he graciously accepts the gift. When her scrutiny turns to the remainder of the gathering, she considers them with lesser intent. She blindly grazes through her bag before disturbing remnants of the wild hunt to others in their party.

William takes a gander at the blackened bison horn he received. This piece is about forearm's length, while the tip has been sanded down to a blunt nib. Thick, horizontal bands race around its fringes, with intricate meshes of lace web amidst them. These abstract shapes bizarrely debut forms like the constellations. Two bolts pin a strip broadly to the tusk, this fragment of leather is obliged to cup the knuckles, and bare fare for a better grip. The inside has been almost completely hollowed, it features a deep, winding crevasse spanning its length and narrowing towards the tip.

An audacious, almighty, wooden rumble overtakes the commissary, this rousing cacophony of sloshing booze, timber and metal frame thunders unconditionally against their ears. Kirk and Marlene must have left sometime after their showing, because they have just returned towing an over-encumbered cart. This rig is absolutely laden with barrels, simply hauling it around without at least two chaperons is an absolutely stunning feat.

They ferry three large, hogshead drums which rest on their caps, each distended to the extent of a household, coal-fire stove. Countless, showroom scores of growler-sized kegs are stacked among them, a wealth that strains the cart's feeble frame. Numerous drums fall off the wagon, landing with an abrupt *thunk* and rolling into the waiting arms of an opportunist.

The married pair deliver true mastercrafts, a crowning magnum opus for any and all arkwrights. Their handiwork is rigorously immaculate, bent timber underneath burnt iron, wrought rings, the distressed, tarnished, amber-brown tone of the wood flaunts its contents.

A burly man approaches this inebriating distillery display, and sets to work with a ball valve and hammer, tapping each and every kegs. William's sightseeing is curtailed by a masked man, a fabled party-goer motions at the boy to shoo. It's Morbin of course, thirsting after the very drum of draught he presides on.

William retorts with a trifling *snort*, and obliges.

Two men appear forthwith, gripping the keg by its cast rim, angling the piece ever-so slightly to wiggle their feelers underneath and nab the bottom, just to suddenly haul it away as quickly as fluttermice in the limelight.

It's finally coming together, these prizes are drinking horns. William scolds himself, the handle should've made things quite obvious.

With one stern swing of his mallet, the gin-milling host sends the taphouse sprawling. These tiny kegs, nicknamed growlers, pertain an intoxicating nog that dirties the humors. This is the last of Mad River Junction's precious alcohol supplies, soon their wells shall run dry.

A lowly brass spigot pierces one of the remaining, tinier barrels, unearthing a lucrative, foamy-white spray which disperses in a moment's notice. This mist clashes against his overcoat until the valve takes hold. To satisfy the culmination of his efforts, the keep places a horn underneath the spigot, braces for impact, and simply turns the knob. A steady stream of nog cascades from the nozzle, filling his vessel with divine ambrosia.

The ale is something else entirely, unlike grog, which myriad townspeople consider to be pale, watered-down slurry. It retains a ginger orange cause, so brilliantly rich, almost as if it was dyed. The flickering glare of light causes the surface to gleam with a slight golden tinge. This deep-amber draft has such a pronounced aroma that William can notice its stimulating vitality from a distance: the crowning crescendo of hothouse grains with hints of caramel. It's an invigorating elixir, a mild sweetness that possesses its drinker, blessing them with bouts of ethereal intervention.

Alcohol is seductive, not just due to its intoxicating properties, but the brimming life that bears with it. It is the essence of fate, drawing eyes from across the furtherest territories towards the energetic tonic trapped inside the glass. Portly drinkers don't seem to notice the trifle, the exploding agony, the soft illustrious noise when thousands of bubbles waste away, rather commenting on its iconic 'pep.' Hardier juicers tend to stiffer liquors, tonics and harsh spirits, bluddraught among them. In truth, it's a distasteful brew and few find the stomach for it. This vivid red concoction parts profusely sweet sorrow, a stain on every lip that bears it, the kiss of death.

After what feels like a fortnight, when those final, remaining wrung open and pleading palms receive their drink, a booming voice pierces usual hub-bub and rambunctious humbingings, competing for consideration. Korralack the Kable firmly evicts himself from their seat, thrusting a mug into the air and spilling his ripe nog in a rowdy, Bennet wave. His usual, intimidating profile, from jackboot to endmost prongs of horn, vents quite passively in the soft, supple underglow of the nearby bed of charcoal. Korralack's pitch clamors, flaunting aside labors of stone and timber.

"I prose' a toast," he declares, with his drinking horn quaking at every syllable.

"This noxious brine is fashioned from da sweat o' our brows. There's ah taste gingered with da blood n' tears o' fella patriots. Bannermane brews fermented by does impish-impeachable convictions, living proof dat inna-insuh-insurmountable odds can't be distilled without 'einously forthright sacrifice. May dis drink bestow greatness- ah boon, blessins o' health for da men 'side me. Ooh-gah!"

Vernon raises a glass in standard honors while Edmund joins their salute.

"Aye," comforts the impeccable leader, "I could drink tah that. I offa petitions to our chief, 'ail the gods of 'earth and 'ome. May they bless fortunate tidings on our families, those lost on travels prior, those 'ere with us today, n' those that may get lost tomorrow."

The trio of accomplices immediately shout in unison.

"Ooh-gah! To dah brink!"

Before chugging their brews.

The crowd raise their glasses on this ultimate note, bashing their own mugs together. It's a friendly wager, a slight diversion as neighbors begin jousting in competition. Aspiring contenders seek to keep their drinking horns high and dry, while adversaries challenge the strength of their grip and fortitude. Slim slivers of bone suddenly collide, twisting and intertwining, racing against one other until an odd notch of elk antler catches, and their opponent's horn abruptly plunges upside-down, wetting every inch of ground cobble with precious nog. To the victors belong the spoils, so is the guise of Bannermane society. These prizewinners gulp their ale with ferocity, a desert seasoned with caramelly-infused bitters that rejuvenates their parched throats.

William can't comprehend the nonsense of this tradition. His mind contests, in a time when they're urged to bear brother-arms, folks can't help but sport. So many growlers have gone to waste, what was the point of drinking horns while nog soaks the ground? At this rate, it would've been easier to suckle straight from the spigots. Still, after everything, the commissary is stricken in throes of jovial attitude. Some victors are regretfully benevolent, and share sips of their drinks to those who have lost. Brethren bully-rooks are packed shoulder-to-shoulder, as tight as sardines in a tin, laughing alongside tiers of play. Prominent residents of the Junction take stock alongside their peers, flicking at each others' ears, track-talk rife with belittling banter and taunts. Townspeople rally as William takes stock of this scenario, it's all vain venom. These companions are crammed in a drab, make-shift workshop, all within a stone's throw of each other. They each partake in jubilant festivities, though in their own extraordinary tack.

Vernon draws an immense crowd towards his table, the ironwright is overseeing an intense arm-wrestling match between Edmund Redmyne and Korralack the Kable. These two drifters are among the leading brutes of the north, it's truly an event of the ages. Wickerwalkers are preeminent huntsmen, brushing across the fray and all sorts of wild foe, while Boar's Band are crusaders of opportunity, constantly campaigning for freedom yet bickering amongst themselves for pillagers' prizes. Each competitor has their earnest thoroughfares and titles, experience in the highest regard. Korralack is drawn to contest, and absolutely loves to brawl, it was inevitable that he'd find rightful dealings, sooner-or-later, in the Junction's defense against wild beasts. This area of gloomy pit is bathed in the stenches of dither and grease, indistinguishable from a priest's corpse cart.

The two clash over a cinderblock wrapped in a wooly jacket, even the concrete stressed under this demanding strain. With their right hands firmly clasped against the other, the elbows of these overbearing competitors burrow erratically into the bundle of fleece. Muscles ache and quake, their forearms hastily quiver as sweat beads on furrowed foreheads, culminating in their facial hair and jowls. Their audience screeches with excitement, driving their fists into the air and fostering words of encouragement. They culminate into fathomable roars, up until Edmund buckles under the pressure, and collapses his face into the table with despair.

"Winnah!" Vernon declares.

An assembly of arms furl in frustration, with too many onlookers stating, "Ay! Redmyne had that in da bag, someone musta been ticklin' his wrist!"

The wickerwalker held bay for as long as his body could muster, barely lifting his head sideways to glance around, his face strained and rigged with a wretched disposition of their losing battle.

At another hustling diet, Mug Maxwell, the classic swindler, is demonstrating his astute legerdemain in a roiling game of cards with fellows, Cliff Fetherhaugh, Ayers Beechworth, Rabley and several others. A player recoils during his turn, taking a hot second to peer at the two cards in his hand. With a devious smile, he mistakenly opts to call Mug's bluff. They've been wagering candles and matches, and there are piles of incendiary combustibles- rather obscene amounts, all things considered. Cliff's decision simmers the ante in the round's final moments, distributing a handful of dice with five-sides up into the center of their table.

"Ah, bunch o' ladies' luck right 'ere," he chides, reveling his pair of queens by flipping them forward.

Coupled with a pair of kings, a jack and cards of other nonsense already strewn across the bench, this is a formidable hand. A silent spell descends upon their tourney, only to be broken by a profound muttering, eventually contorting into broken chuckling. The hustler, Mug Maxwell can hardly contain himself. His laughter is distraught, abhorrent, almost as if he'd be stabbed with a red hot poker. He's not the ideal patsy, this game has shown familiar insight as a cardsharp and paper driver.

Maxwell has competed in tourneys throughout the territories, to the heart of Hearthland and the furtherest fringes of Underdark. His bouts are driven by money, and worst so, the sheer will to live. He wanted a taste of the good life, and swiftly found that anything business involving Bannermane trademarks is well-worth the risks. With a swift kick to the balls, highwaymen will find that he weeps gold. However, tonight is no standard. There's certainty in this gambit, this draw showcases a king and jack of his, granting a total roster of three kings and two jacks, the winning hand. Cliff nods his head as palms furl shut, dancing a complimentary jig.

"Tis all fish and flounda, boys. Ye had absolutely no chance!"

His lively cheers are drowned out by bewildered gasps, a, crowd gathering behind the table, paying no heed to their gambling.

"Ye didn't, there's no way!"

"Oh, oh, but I definitely did," Morbin Evershade excruciatingly teases while lounging on his throne, "See, tis all 'bout confidence. City watches are nothin' but volunteers wantin' to return 'ome to their babes. If you wanna get through, all ye gotta do is grease ah few lobes."

The thief is detailing his various escapades of adventure, hearsay of antiquity, and certain reflections which sound similar to heroic tales around figures like the skald, Arabella Gaberdine, and Rylie Hess, the magistrate's scribe. These astounding artisans wonder at such chronicles, reveling over stories that they would, in-turn, incorporate into their own compositions.

"All of ah sudden those lil' gremlins popped straight outta the wall. Maybe ah well, or an 'ole in the ground I couldn't spy at least- can't 'member," Morbin dramatically spouts, "and Gaiden's skewered leg with 'ung tooth and nail. Nasty devils they are. Very kickable runts too."

Jeremiah Anders, the eccentric author from the local chapter, eagerly eavesdrops in the background. Armed with quill and parchment, he records even the most trivial minutiae for his nefarious schemes, intending to capitalize on whatever extraordinary fiction he tends to overhear.

"Oh, now dat's ah gud one," Jeremiah whispers quaintly to himself, underlining the striking phrase, "'Ung 'ead or 'igh-water," believing that's a particularly attractive, snake-oily verbose.

A pair of consoling cohorts have their backs turned to these transpirations. Mandel Haggerton and Sassafras Pache find themselves in good company, birds of a feather fluttering about, a budding romance in a world where it would be denied so.

The modestly distressed shoehorn finds pure bliss in her presence, sheer childish joy. If he was regular with his Haggerton brood, Lady Callie would be utterly furious with this development. They reminiscence over their usual, daily drudges, boring chores and labors. The bunkhouse by no means caters towards the palatable type, instead it is a place of poverty, dressed like a burrow and brimming with vermin. Though as a cordwainer, Mandel's has never been short of side-gigs. Sharing a room with various vagabonds has its perks, nevertheless a certain smell. He has spent a majority of his time mending felt for fleece, and valuing leather on behalf of brokers. Woodsmen are his typical patrons, as lumberjack calk boots are always in need of repair. These veteran foresters scale lush conifers, hacking at timber and trunk as sharp, evergreen needles pierce their soles. As an anxious man, Mandel's awfully afraid to stride out on his own. He blames copious amounts of stress, a series of ongoing Peaterbrick lawsuits, as his bedside regularly receives couriered notes in their name.

In contrary, Sassafras is a courageously bold breed of woman, never apprehensive to tread new ground. She's a standard sight at the institution, Mad River's fairly-independent mercantile. Clerks of all categories cater to the fancies of merchants, striking deals of desire at the whims of those greedier, whether that be acquisitions, commodities, debts, logistics, wages or upkeep.

As a premier moneylending clerk, maven of tender and crucial to commerce, Sassafras Pache is the leading accessory among them. Staged behind a desk the size of a wolverine, she daringly hedges alongside parts and parcels of trademark coin. Moneylenders weave destinies, forging new paths and dooming entire enterprises when they choose not to invest, yet her apt business acumen is begrudgingly pinned underneath Charlie Mandon's thumb. There were those who doubted their resolve, briefly glancing at a green curator with little regard to her determinations. Yet, Sassafras managed to up the stakes, securing prize-eyes, besting the odds of Bannermane scrutiny through audacious entrepreneuring, profiting over last season's proper bloomtide through leaps and bounds.

Mandel often spied her exploits through a stately stretch of windowpane, undauntingly commanding a babble of bookkeepers to audit with the authority of registrars. Whenever they racked together investments, this drove would intimidatingly rouse with cheers. Their gazes have never intertwined before due to one simple fact, Mandel has always been too nervous.

He confesses, "To nah 'asty march, I would nevah believe ah gal of yer stature tah take me seriously."

They reconcile over spotty grub, each jesting about their meal, and which ingredients could make it genuinely better. There truly couldn't be a more-perfect couple, the cordwain and principal negotiator act like twins in tandem, completing each others sentences, hooting at the other's embarrassing moments, and giggling as sprouts. They act upon their reveries, discussing what things could be, what hearts yearn for, and most importantly, what the pair aspire to become.

As Sassafras takes a quick peck at Mandel's cheek, a befitting reward for young philanthropy, William notices a lingering gathering around the cast cauldron. Drizzling bone marrow in the last residue of broth, Kirk and Marlene Hinds finish serving their last guest. Their devotion is legendary, some mileage thirty-years strong, an incomprehensible mark to strive for. The empathetic duo hand a spoonful of drizzled meat-chunks to Austerlaund, who is flanked by three of her mystics picking over scraps of boney sinew. She takes this morsel in good conscious, clarity not for her own person, but the infirm and semi-conscious knight-errant.

"This is Osbourne Bullheaded," she graciously elaborates to the 'volunteer' cooks, "an injured Claremont agent of the Underdark. They found 'em meanderin' the village roads, caught in the rippin' tempest of a storm. 'E'll be in mah company for a few days, at least, 'fore I can submit him to the real practitioners at Bonaventure. Ye know, that palliative pharmaceutical forum? These injuries are testin' the limits of muh flair."

Her hype does little to shave the mirror's edge, the paladin's mental state has rapidly deteriorated, becoming a shadow of his former self. The herald is completely vulnerable in this state, unarmored and exposed from his steel carapace. His eyes are sullen and spoiled, souring in complexions of frogtongue nausea. Each lid flutters uncontrollably, offering a gut-jerking glimpse while they seize, lapse inside the bowls of brain, and roll upwards. These sores are surrounded by stippled rings, portraying a familiar revenant over this empty vessel. The priest whispers an incanting chant to her patient, whom rests in the nook of her giant arm. If it wasn't for the generosity of gallivanters, he'd be another neglected corpse. Austerlaund elegantly parts his lips with her index finger, before gently pouring the burgundy medley between his chapped lips, and into an arid maw. However, in this situation, even a meager supply is absurdly generous. A bounty for remedy, and soothing ointment for the soul.

The mystical physician determines that Osbourne needs put to rest, finding him refuge in a nearby carriage car. After laying the ailing wreck in the cabin, and wrapping a throw around him. She closes the bulkhead door with a *clunk*, causing the whole contraption to shake. A stuffed otter plush dangles above, strung to the velvety ceiling. The ornament sends it careening into a sway, cuddling a treasure chest between its paws, with a huge grin stretching from cheek to cheek.

There are two patrons perched in the driver's booth, a party of an untimely trepidation. Behind the protective helm of a caravan lead, a stunning conglomeration of frontier innovation and design, is Lena Tillstead, and the Junction's most stubborn mule. As a mother painstakingly plagued by sorrow, it's reassuring to find a trustworthy mentor to confide-in, and in Jerome's case, this unlikely scenario has granted him a hint of humility. As grey and white whiskers grace his face, this resident has become bitter, a regular antagonist after the passing of his own daughter, Allace.

"'Agen, can't thank ye enough," the woman shares in confidence.

"Tis nah harm, lass. I'm just grateful- 'umbled even, tah be reminded wut I've been missin' all dees years."

With their ample time together, the two crafted an ancillary in memorium of Calamity Jane's daughter. There's a beautiful premise to it, that even while she's gone, her mother would always have a relishing thought to cherish. These waning hours have brought together a subtle concentration of hope, a guiding light that offers therapeutic radiance. This trinket may not appear special, it is an abruptly ordinary accessory after all, a seemingly unpretentious hair comb. Fashioned from wicker, thin strands of sinewy wooden fibers bundled into a neck of wiry coil. Its handle is entirely ornamental, the shape of a flower, featuring a folkish petals as its tip.

As an aging peregrine, Jerome has never been a craftsman per-say, nary a gent with talented hands, but he is an incredible tutor, an unorthodox librarian of comprehensive ramifications. Lana did all the work after all, the Junction burgher has a remarkably slothful manner, a history of peanuts and tendency to trifle. He observes the habits of those around him, particularly scrutinizing the journeymen, scrupulously adding their movements to his repertoire. It's a completely inquisitive parlor trick, able to perceive the slightest step, specific and detail, reproducing their knowledge to his benefit. Fortunately, there was a prolific bosun with a penchant for homespun things, and by proxy, taught Lena how to whittle scrap into a work of art.

This wiseacre would critique her every stroke, the ones that were too broad, as well as the motions that were too strict, when the blade of her theater dagger became dull, and when the edge entered harshly against the grain. An outsider would consider his remarks paltry, as journeymen know better than to bend their ears for knaves. Abet few opportunities, sometimes Jerome's observations are oddly satisfying.

"Lena," he'd begin to say, "dees strokes remind mah of muh dear ole maw. She was ah haberdasha, ah marvelous connoisseur of da art, and boy, 'ow I 'ated 'er."

William's favorite line always surfaced when others seem to be having a bad day.

"Well, ye still got two legs, dontcha?"

This commentary is lustrous, and forces onlookers to chuckle with signature grimace. These are eccentrics, Jerome has his moments, and can be quite passionate.

"I 'ad ah daughter muhself once, she was bright n' full of life, so much so dat da firmament followed 'er footsteps. Whatever fancies she set 'er mind tah were accomplished within da blink o' an eye. My kin musta been sent tuh conquer da 'eavens demselves, much tah da jealousy o' lessa men. Da fell filled 'er body with useless prattle. Pretty soon, der was nothin' o' 'er left. Allace's mind 'ummed, as if she was burstin' with ideas but unable tuh speak. Da tenda warmth of 'er skin since faded- felt foreign. The world is ah strange place. Life is miserably intoxicatin', n' wut remains o' it is fleetin'. We are defined by our most brazen moments, nah matta 'ow delightin', frightenin' or terrible. I've always 'eld tah 'eart dat even in our darkest moments, does uttermost convictions shall be rewarded. If yer Charm possesses dat very same desire, da world will bow tah 'er whims. Maybe our children will find each otha someday, as visitors in the ceaseless 'arbor, in their journey 'yond our wildest imaginations towards da Gilded Gates o' Guldourame."

A certain peregrine finds their conversation rather daunting, all this talk of religious eminence does little to quell common fears. For the time being, Rochester is leisurely lying underneath the carriage, a bolstering arrangement of cast metal and timber, comforted by its iron curtains. He has never paid heed to dusty soot and grime, instead he lounges in the squalor without a hint of trouble, warmly nibbling on a piece of deer backbone.

On the surface, it's a dull and typical overlooked portion, however the creamy tension of bone marrow makes it an all-worthwhile treat. His bliss is rudely discarded by parading boots, with a high-strung *twang* produced at every pace. Rochester is scorned by this annoying, auditory blight, scampering further underneath the hideaway for solitude. Cillian Lore pompously marches around, weaving between rows of furniture, and blatantly ducking into conversations as a tavern howler. Modesty is poetry's greatest failure, these serenades can only be described as bombastic.

His presence hinders against their placid pretense of gossip and riposte. In these circumstances, the posh vocal memoirs sound adverse. It does indeed pique their curiosity, but not in the way he had intended. Listeners venture a guess towards wounding plots and schemes. Nearby folks spit at his feet, ruining the sheen of his ferries. Cillian is completely livid, dropping his instrument until the straps sways stiffly against his shoulders, and twiddles his thumbs in a bout of frustration. He curses at these fellowships, rambling at his latest personal sufferance.

"May yer ale be warm, and champagne flat," describing the time he spends in Mad River Junction as an unparalleled stent of torture. Every lyric he bestows is a true work of apocrypha, "Y'all respect mah when I'm dead, ye really don't know what yer missing."

With his departure off the scene, Arabella casually decides to fill the void, and unlike a bastard who competes for coin, recounts a vivid cantos of bitter rangers. It is such a tragic telling, rather boisterous. Amid amity of duty, danger, and devotion, William praises her rathe composition.

"What ah divine album. Ye 'ave ah lovely voice and wit to match."

To his unanticipated posturing, the skald declines these compliments. Arabella responds wishing that people don't read too deeply into things, "Just live and enjoy the moment."

Maybe she's right, William has become his own worst enemy, always scrutinizing, over-analyzing, searching for faults on every little dilemma, and defrauding himself over the quandaries that present themselves. Here he is, at the end of the world, surrounded by jovial festivities- might as well consider humoring a brief act of depravity. With a drinking horn full of nog in tow, William is in a recreational bind.

He has never been on equal footing, nor tolerant of illicit waters before. Staring absently at his drink, its surface ripples with the slightest quiver of his hand. He spots his own reflection peering across its subtle waves, a blurry, depressed veil that lapses over the trivial details. This precious elixir absorbs all immediate incandescence, his vision is interrupted with tinges of umber, overwhelmed with gold, as this visage gleams.

William takes an insignificant sip at first until wet sustenance parts his lips and drowns tongue from bow to stern. His mouth is assaulted by a savory caramel tonic that tinges its tip, and one satisfied by its behavior, is compelled to continue with another taste, then another, and once more. Soon thereafter, with his mug despairingly aching upside-down, the last remaining drops of alcohol leach from the basin and onto the cinder floor. This tastefully distilled brew offered a sense of sanctuary for a trivial amount of time, an escape from the common slugs of reality.

In a sudden onslaught, and unfortunate act of vice, this scorching wash reaves his gullet. Much to William's inkling, this is the encroaching symptom of brown bottle flu. Medication is a flight of fancy, careful blends of raw vigor to use sparingly. Fortifications alleviate concerns of illness, infirmity, wounds or scarring, the dispositions in one's head, and when imbued with arcane properties, even forfeit concerns over death, managing frontier remedies is all the worthwhile. In the conflict of constitution, it remains absolutely necessary to moderate, as scarcity lies betrothed as an antidote to punishment. Binging solutions only dilute their effectiveness, and as unfortunate as it is, William has abused too much. While others may judge, the gods tend not to harbor favorites.

The denizen of hearth and home does not to bestow mercy, even during a first treading. In the gaze of those greater, those that indulge must be punished. Both eyes of the afflicted redden, cordoned-off by vast labyrinths of crimson webs. Only a mirror would reveal the extent of his damage. The two wells across his face begin to shore up, encasing each eye underneath a glossy varnish. Identical strokes of salted tears descend helter-skelter below his cheeks, flooding the assortment of wrung bandages tugging at his neck. William's pupils dilate with tremendous uncertainty, producing a foggy field-of-view, and presenting the nearby demesne in intense juxtaposition. Colors bleed, mix and blend into one another, profiles bend and shatter as perspectives collide; indistinct objects such as a bench flatten, becoming absurd visual wrecks.

It is a ridiculous circumstance, unparalleled to anything William has encountered in his ventures thus far, as if the jester began imitating, mimicking the same ordinary belongings over themselves, dozens of times apiece. The left side of his gut stirs, flooding with an uneasy apprehension. It pulses concerningly, throbbing to an irregular rhythm, oddly reminiscent of today's earlier brawl and drudging all sorts of equally unfond memories. This radiating discomfort ripples energy throughout his body, every muscle aches, the awkward series of events is overwhelming.

William collapses backwards onto a barrel of pig iron, reclining further and further into his seat with every passing moment. His headache is preposterous, even though it may be nothing more than a tingling sensation. There's a nagging feeling in the front of his mind, like he's able to remember something important, a fleeting conversation of the sorts, but is guilty of barely touching the thought. William can't remember things here and now, the exact date or quite where he is. The characters in front of him are merely strangers, nothing more than silhouettes.

If there's one word to surmise these events, it would be 'disappointed.' It's upon his failure to recognize opulence, or anticipate the effects is up for debate. He questions the entire experience and sheer strength of the aftershocks, the failure of these notions is paramount. The effects of the nog suddenly capstone, William's vision goes intensely dark, and he passes out for an undefined amount of time.

At one point during the evening, he finds himself gently shaken awake, stirred from an abrupt slumber. He can't recognize how much time has passed nor spent, and finds himself asking whether or not it has been several minutes or hours. William's positive that he's drawn a crowd, but rather unsure of its size and sincerity. An unknown voice drawls on, straining his ears by claiming that William appears as if he's already one foot in the grave. Considering his current state, thrown over a rim of cask there, and limbs strewn about here, he really can't argue against such sentiment. It's an awkward position, and going to lead into a very sore draw the following morning.

As a welcomed distraction, even through groggy lens, William attempts to focus on other pressuring matters. With the simple act of opening his eyes, William dreams of an entrancing treat, reviving into a burgeoning realm of warm paradise, complete with live greenery, trees, soil underneath his toes, and the whole nine yards. Instead, he wakes into a hardly palatable scene and is reminded that life on the frontier is confronting.

The fire still blazes, the air is filled with droning fritters of conversation. Maybe this could all be a hallucination, as it muddles all clarity, blending together what is real and which features an illusion. These concepts are inspiring, rather than guilt, William feels foreboding elements, as if chronicle have yet to pass. The thought is rather stirring, granting a moment of rousing tenacity. Is it a masochist train of thought to be so utterly fascinated? This incident is extraordinary, an enlivening query that while the world begins crumbling, the human mind wanders free.

A pressure builds behind William's eyes, enough of a disturbance that he rubs his brow with tenacity. There's a cast of character before him, fashioned from a multitude of ominous shapes and forms, and adorned in milky flames that spread apart like feathery wings. This fire is lucid, more of an ancillary or decoration, then hurdle. Their faces are intricately grand, emanating with intense beams of light. The only notable feature they reveal is a slew of vibrant white speckling. These pips flash spontaneously, giving the presentation of thousands of dreadful, expressionless eyes. William mistakenly recognizes the dignitaries advancing out of line, his brain believes the most prominent to be Vernon. In a state of drunken stupor, the boy Jones salutes this geist, signing-off with a signature.

"Ready tah disembark, capt'n," before striding off again.

His mind wanders, once more unto the breach, and a final narrative tickles his thoughts.

"Ye ain't needing muh permission," the apparition murmurs.

As he rests his gaze for the final time that night, the stiffness of the air is pronounced by a frightening forecast. This darkening gloam conceals another onslaught of inclement weather. Snowfall carried forth by a persuasive wind, the tempest gales howl with atrocious, nipping shrills- a vicious cycle. Ignorance is a gracious boon, those residing in the commissary are stocked with bliss.

A misty cloud of remorseless cold manifests, roaming the frigid avenues as a foil, an invisible predator that invites ruin. This threat is impossible, a constant enemy that probes for any weakness, no matter how puny or frail. It seeps through every fracture of the caravan post's timber, pooling in auras across the floor. These haunts are known as the blight, and are deadly in every sense of the word. In their worst aspect, these phenomenon migrate in search of hapless victims, permeating boots of leather and fleece, sapping venerable feet with frost, and subjecting flesh to the horrors of frostbite.

Thankfully the basin's balmy braziers keep the blight at bay, immediately releasing the chaffing gaff into clouds of vapor. The ceiling collects loose ice crystals that float into its rafters, reflecting ambience in a hazily abundant, dazzling array. In this sanctuary, it's awfully easy to forget the fatal nature of these exploits. The Junction hasn't come all this way to perish in a slurry of bitterness and ice, it's gotten this far thanks to the due diligence of journeymen and scissorsmiths.

In a quite blissful chant, the regular townspeople remain benign to the truths of the frontier. Even the most insignificant residents have done their part, there's always a part to play, idle hands to tug at the line. Some particular folk have welcomed their tutelage, eager to participate as patrons grasp at their wealth of knowledge. William is finally starting to come around to the impression of trouncing about with a group.

V

TRIALS INSIDE THE MATCHBOX

As another twilight slowly wanes away, the murky stains of night bleed to the complexion of a blushing sun, the faint glowing, pastel carnations of the coming duskday promptly emerge. The period of conclusion, and end of the week. However, unlike the preceding fortnights, the curtains fail to completely part for the morning's opening act. In this novel circumstance, the solispyre cannot shine through a never-ending slurry of storms.

A familiar pain returns to his chest, a longing sensation which recalls yesterday's exhibition. It ebbs within the placemark on his shoulder, the scarring blemish from his childhood, deep amid tissue and viscera. Could this be a consequence of the celebrations? This malady feels almost phantasmic, a quite unreal feat. He cannot name its origin, nor its precise affliction. All William can briefly hope to accomplish is to summarize that it wears down on him, braving the weight of a freight train and its wrathful cargo- others could not possibly bear his pain.

Mad River's trade outfit is in paramount danger. The posturing recession flaunts new torments each and every day. Snow sows itself like the once-fabled salty seas, a tearing torrent of cream that buries the town in excess. The Junction's wooden bastion is no match for this pasty deluge, easily overtaken by the barrowtide's white earth.

Its demise was preface, and simply the maiden offerings of brackish, northern squalls. First-floor windows, once offering an electrifyingly lively scene of the bustling hamlet are rendered moot, now better described as submersed, granting an unparalleled view of the ganky, unknown depths. Some people peering upon the abyss describe darkness, others fear to stare, as they heed the approach of unfathomable horrors that lie underneath.

The town loses more and more in a ceaseless struggle against the wraths of Nana Nature. It isn't the animals, nor sickness or brethren betrayal that residents fear most, but that of hypothermia. Exposure is the most common death on the frontier, as it ransacks the body, sending tragic martyrs into bed-ridden squalor. As bodies are torn apart by the diseased three: black, white, and red, people become desperate.

The cold enemy is relentless, one cannot save their own soul by bartering with death itself. In their last throes of life, dumbstruck fools contort into agonizing shapes. The blood vessels conducting bountiful elixir shrink and shatter, each and every muscle seethes as stiff as a board. This once fragile, human life induces brawn as tough as boulders, a distressing constitution, but the luxurious favor is for naught. At this stage, the victim's nerves had been frayed, and with it, their elusive, lingering feelings. Perhaps, the final, ravishing thought is iced over in callous, translucent tinges. The last fragments of personality vaporize into hazes of irredeemable memories. Strangely enough, those plagued by grief describe the cradling sensations of frigus-finem, that there is no suffering in the cold end.

> *Harken dear company, these eyes lie still,*
> *A victim of happenstance, the changer of ways.*
> *I fear the wilds, an endless chill,*
> *A placid harbor to waste the days.*
> *Alas, our voyage has ended,*
> *Leaving another lonely sailor at bay.*
> *You and I shall meet again,*
> *Sometime, somewhere, on a mid-summers' day.*

The august farewell commemorates those lost to the chill, it's a venerated poem that often decorates memorials, and uttered in passing to those who perish as the Butchers' List is bound to grow- a promise during these tumultuous times, even while the eldest townsfolk are prepared with well-prepped and organized winter contingencies. The fiercest turmoils set-in with malice, drowning the town in snow, collapsing remaining refuges like matchsticks as properties eventually sink beneath the waves. While they seek to avoid being buried alive, the residents are hidden underneath indiscernible hillsides, corralled about piles of clothes and luggage. They wail and lament, hung-over in debt to the auspicious struggles of their drinking games. Meager peasants loll on the cobblestone, huddling together in alms, conspiring, whispering, gossiping to one another. These rumors flourish in the crowded commissary, overtaking vagabonds whom dangle upon the scaffolding, conversing with their peers below.

William overhears a spiteful truth, that the onslaught of snow has collapsed the bunkhouse, coercing more people into propped-up factions around town. An overwhelming majority of these refugees have immigrated to the commissary, easily doubling the basin's population, a swell of a couple dozen to more than four. It is awfully crowded, the boy can barely stretch his legs before prodding a host of impoverished rabble, people packed as tightly as sardines.

They've coined this tract as the sanctuary district, lining the permitter of the room furthest from the fire with rows of shabby tarp tents. While it is a much larger, more accommodating space, no one is seeking refuge at the local chapter, merely because of logistics: its sheer distance from the post- too much effort, a massive waste of time to frolic and dredge through the snow. However, in their indulgence, the fickle flames of the furnace recede.

Now that the community is dwindling to the last remnants of their supplies, there is next to nothing fueling the fire. Wood from nearby buildings, businesses and residences is being buried faster than they can recover it. Armed with primitive shovels and pickaxes, excavation is a fruitless endeavor, lest archaeologists make themselves susceptible to exposure, in addition to their mires refilling in a matter of minutes.

Edmund best describes this route as a flatiron, a situation with no good choices. Maybe he, sporting a bit of generosity and his infinite wisdom of the badlands, can guide them to safety?

Optimism isn't a bountiful crop around Mad River, yet Marlene Hinds flouts a venture for greener pastures. Trying to ease the tension, she produces a lulling hum, something soothing and tranquil to remedy their waters. The lullaby is serenading, nothing more than a calming melody sung to children, but even the slightest impressions are monumental. After all, a single snowflake beckons the fury of an avalanche.

Others are keen to observe, taking note of a rhythm that swells their hearts and soothes souls. Mandel, keeping the beat of the bounding ballad by stamping his heels, points at the man dozing beside him, stoking at Galvin Broad's ego with a broad inkling of expression. This chant flickers ears, piquing the interest of interlopers, meddlers, and busy nobodies alike. Several kin are eager to clap their hands at pace, widening their graces until they drift into a certain jubilant jig. There are those among the crowd who begin to perk up, much to the demise of those drinking yester-evening, who stand to match bouts and competitive fervor.

"Oh, 'ey!" They cry with resounding cheers, crafting a wonderfully exuberant chorus of glee. The intensity is so severe, that one would believe that they were being strangled inside a chanting hall. For those more musically inclined, and apt towards tunes, strive towards a flaring concert.

Buskers are lively folk, possessing wild imaginations, these captivatingly clever and resourceful. Several sport clanking bobbles, knocking silverware together, hilariously striking at casks and luggage as fellows entranced by the rousing beat. Peregrines of the plains are rather audacious, even the background-droving of the lot, are producing instruments of renown seemingly out of nowhere. Marlene's melody added some delightful ambience, now it has been dutifully appropriated by self-appointed band barons and their booming voices.

The demesne riffs with gruff and gritty borderspiel accents, voices more attuned to the open frontier than luxury stages, mangling the otherwise simple phrase, Clan Marius, into "Bang Ah-roose!"

"Those crag-bearers naught bow to any flatfoots," they often say. Their callous is well-earned, etched by bards, chaperons and theater troops, tales ripe with pride and righteous honor, demonstrated over their intense love affair with musikcraft.

Travelers tell that mountain ranges of the northwest territory are inevitably burdened with commotion: the whistling tune of whipping winds, gangs of bellowing gamut clambering across the rockfaces, sending tons of tumbling scree down their slopes, hoards of voracious boar that hollow the earth; yet, all are shadowed by some calamitous roar.

The ceaseless ridges rise and trenches echo with booming voices. Spectators scout stalwarts perched among the campaign trail, the austere cliffs of Alta-vista, poaching on its perilous slopes with tusks winding from their distanced silhouettes. The rime of their ears melts with every melodious note, a song so beautiful, as it can be deadly. Members of the Junction partake in unveiling a generous bounty of manglehorns and bagpipes, instruments so ingrained in musikcraft, that their mere presence is awe-inspiring. Blaring bugles drive the camaraderie of company, egging ranks of duct and file into the fray with the sharp symphonies of thrilling victory.

Men of the mountains wield ungodly-sized trumpets, carriers of the mountain gales. This instrument features a slender, snaking eight-foot spanning tube, and inspired by stag tusks, curves at the far end into an iconic hook. The yawning bell takes the form of an animal, or in this case, a ram figurehead.

A performer tilts the instrument vertically so that the mouthpiece is positioned at the bottom, and thrusts it straight into the air. All of the weight is centered near the top, inside the totem's helm; it's an awkward affair to hoist the colors, as the leading lady dances to and fro, balancing an obnoxiously large trophy far above their head. She stops just past her ribs, resting the manglehorn's receiving end on the chest as she gathers steam. As the sweat wretches her brow and neck, this trooper cranes the leaden manglehorn distantly into the air. With one final heave, using every remaining ounce of strength, it towers above the clamoring crowd throughout the basin, and goat horns tickle the rafters releasing waves of attic residue.

Pressing her lips strenuously against the trumpet's token, she strains the entirety of her lungs into the tube, making the head yelp loud enough to shake the Junction's very foundations with shrill wargarbls. Piping a loud *vahroom*. The horn's craftsman found the time to add in quaint additions like a tongue, which flusters whenever the ram bellows.

Vahroo-roo-rum. The performer pours all ichor into the act, as this cacophony pummels through the loft, waves of damp dust descend upon the audience, lining shoulders with heaps of soot.

William finds this outing vastly vainglory. All these frostbitten characters seem quite cavalier about their circumstance, sacrificing the last of their physical ability for some bright tune. However, it's a true blessing to behold when vagabonds still retain their pivotal sense of humor.

One gregarious handmaiden tugs at their hardcase to no avail. Desperately wanting to join the venture, she comically hurls her baggage at a nearby stretch of uninterrupted cobble. The pressure snaps the distressed lock, allowing her to plunder her own packstuffs, looting a hurdy-gurdy from the trunk. Much to the demise of Cillian Lore, it wouldn't be a true Bannermane score without railing a wound harpsichord and twanging its strings!

There are plenty of people dancing around, skewed amok tiers of loose drabble, having themselves a grand ole time. They take to the forums, rigging a so-called stage, and cavorting in the limelight. William spots the adversaries of this congregation, a ragtag band of misfits who confidently stray from its gaze. These knaves stick out like a sore thumb, only every once in awhile perking their heads up and poking around, with all the festivities, they're the only ones who are suitably distracted by something else. Instead of flamboyant ranges, their instruments cackle and chink from the inside of a flagon, competing against the restless moot of music.

The loafing gamblers are mainly those of young ilk, distracted in their exploits, and participating a lowly contest of pilfers. These matches operate under the guise of luck, the otherwise casual love affairs of dice. The talent is trivial, as in reality, challenges are a consummating parley of luck and coercion, only ending when the victor has accumulated all gamepieces from their rivals.

When broken down, it's a rather straightforward game, writhing from roots in back alleys gambits, caravan cabins, the floorboards of dwellings, and even the grand gaming tables in Bonaventure. Each player begins with five several-sided dice and an opaque jar, they may hide however many dice they choose under said jar, and tumble it. Others field and survey their surroundings, probing the competition, and take turns wagering how many dice an opponent has under their jar, often using persuasion or trickery. If they guess correctly, they steal their dice; however, for those not appropriately qualified at bluffing, if they successfully guess the exact dice faces, they win their foe's entire amount and knock them out of the game. In the event that they unsuccessfully made such guess, that player would lose a die in consequence, or all their wager- depending on the game.

This contest is built entirely around grandstanding, savoring the moment, and dealing animosity between opponents. Pilfers has an almost cult-like following, featuring some pretty prominent players whom travel across frontier settlements, each with their own playstyle, pastime and eccentric nature.

Against better interests, William decides to pitch purpose and test his hand, asking to join with bravo, to which they unequivocally respond, "O'course!"

He takes a seat alongside a paltry lot, the fella to his right embodies a gauntly expression, jerking tracts of skin and facial hair scurry across an array of angular, skeletal features.

"Welcome. I'm that gamekeeper Mug, Mug Maxwell."

His style is sickening, an image that jerks at the pit of the boy's stomach, because William's own frame isn't an audaciously-thin, faulted mess. Maxwell's figure uncontrollably trembles in place, as if the tinges of every hair has been frosted, and he's shivering from the cold. A pair of fumbling hands nab at his stash of earthly possessions, towards a billfold, reaching into the depths of tailcoat pockets. Falsely believing himself to occupy the spryness of a swindler, this player deposits three ivories into their cup, and immediately pitches the glassware upside-down onto the floorboards. On the contrary approach, the woman to William's left hedges several strips of jerky, payment from a former fair, a proper penance thrown at the cobble. He had truly misheard the introduction, and acknowledges Mug by the wrong name.

"'Ello Mags," the boy Jones declares, "glad tah play," then he slyly remarks and mutters under his breath that it's "Surely, a pleasure tah meet the rest too."

They squabble amid themselves, and determine whether an earnest lad may participate, that without anything to gamble, if he were to win on his turn, he'd instead forfeits all bets.

Their confrontations are legendary, advancing patterns of play for the next twenty minutes, although it feels like hours!

"Bonanza!"

They caterwaul with reams of glee. There have been plenty of dashing opportunities and fleeting attempts at victory. William has been routinely beaten for the most part, making his boasts unexpectedly coarse. Slews of dice have ferried about, exchanging hands, each one unique in their shape and weight. Some are no larger than a marble, hand-whittled out several scrap scourings of pine. These trinkets bring an extra challenge to the game, as each bobble hits different. The sounds inside the flagons are never quite the same, making it tougher to guess the contents each turn. Starting with an original five dice, at one point William was able to accumulate eight total from his neighbors, but now is down to a dangerous amount of three.

The betting pool is unusually enticing, a proper frontier fortune. There are the common items like trademarks, candles and matchsticks, but then pygmy journals have thrown sunder into the ring, fishing hooks, a compass, some rather strange voucher for a two-day stay at the Arbor Island Resort. 'Paradise,' it announces in a fashion which sounds almost fake; then there are hand-scribbled coupons regarding future favors.

Most Bannermane can't read nor write, favoring pictograms instead, depicting stick figures performing various chores such a shuffling snow. 'Will steward for an afternoon,' or 'tend hearth.' Many lines have been crossed out or scrawled over, changing over the course of the game as the tides rise and fall, erratically based around opinions of their opponents.

The rivalry is captivating, and as unlikely as it may seem, William finds himself eager to ante without any shirts to lose. The competitiveness corrupts him, allowing him to devise less than honest methods. While the other members of the troop are distracted in a casual bout of quarreling, his hand coincidentally discovers itself aground. In one swift motion, he scoops a trifle of debris and distributes the contents into his jar. As Maxwell motions that its finally William's turn to parley, his mischievous grin proceeds to stretch, smiling coyly from ear to ear. All drums are fixed, anticipating the clattering and painstakingly awaiting fate.

Nonchalantly swaying his hand to and fro, numerous curiosities chink against the jar. *Clack, clack, clack.* A newcomer would assume that he's wagering high, and wouldn't dare bet against these odds, rather forfeiting their gamble. However, these are seasoned bookies, scoundrels drifting all over the northern territory.

"Der's nah way dat's possible," they accuse and hound him of cheating.

The gamekeeper is absolutely disgusted, deception is fraud, a lie by omission and a fate far worse than losing. William doesn't take this brazen pin lightly, and accosts them in return, placing the blame all around.

"Ey, what are ye doin'? I'm not the only guilty one, take ah ganda! Can't believe y'all ain't sharin' the tab," viciously pointing at the fellow across the party, "There are gremlins in yer pockets, and ye… won't even settle usin' six-sided dice! Y'all know this- been sharin' the same throws."

"Way tah go, fool. Yer the first person that can't handle the pressure. What ah blunda. Go on and git! Take yer filthy tricks with ye and leave!"

With a lamenting *sigh* William shoves those bits and pieces away, stands to attention, and strides off. He rues in this disdain, a victim of his own undoings, and has only ever felt this alone thrice before. At the height of having fun, when there's zero risk, bias or skin in the game, the boy Jones makes a habit of self-destructive tendencies. The sparring masses consider him an expert at sowing backlash, casting doubt, and squandering opportunities. In times of ecstasy, his mind wanders, overthinking and scrutinizing, he has the tendency to trip over trivial details.

The absolute gall, he asks himself, 'Why would he dare pull such a stunt?' It certainly wasn't for the publicity, there were real prospects. William was a hair's breadth away from reeling in palatable companions, maybe even foes to call- in the best and extreme cases, acquaintances. Could he just be at that age, the critical juncture when fellows exhilarate in the throes of life? Guttersnipes have the tendency to scorched the entire earth for the briefest bit of experience. Years among the rabble has demonstrated how to sift through all the unpleasantness, squeezing every ounce of racket from it. They bathe in glory, no matter the awkward or taut situations. Urchins are taught at an early age that Bannermane are not immune to rakish qualities, these brazen entrants only drive their stride, and temper egos.

"Damn the consequences," they exclaim! Despite the wavering opposition, for an intents and purposes, trekking through the white wastes is preferable to this personal thrashing. The gamemaster known as Mug Maxwell has precise prejudice, this episode was definitely a blunder. This company treats cheating scoundrels as slag, something to be wiped off and tossed aside, threatening to send him to the brig, or at the very least, its equivalent, an accompanied stay in Jerome's hovel.

It's a rather traditional offer, like all Bannermane brood, he has the decency to offer amenities, yet it's barely hospitable. Everyone hates these lodgings, leaving them to wonder, what sort of deranged mind can cope. In time, all fortunes part ways, agony can be considered an appropriate penance.

With barely a glance behind his shoulder, the ostracized adversary returns to the fold. In a stent of solemn, southbound expression, William vainly glues his gaze towards furrowed calks, the leathery dressings bound about his feet which are also caked with debris. Although, his eyes can't help but wander, occasionally peeking at the ensuing antics, he passes gaggle upon gaggle of waltzing denizens whom still dance to the buoyant tunes. His recess is spent dodging rogue elbows and stamping boots unscathed, a gratuity granted by the good graces of the herd.

The jarring stench of defeat is ridiculing, crafting a harrowing illusion, that the people around seem to stare while he's not paying attention. William can feel their scrutinizing glares burrow through sturdy patches of skull, and into the back of his head. The gambling aficionados were conversing, quite broadly, that the first loser had so-called, 'membership-dues,' and would be responsible for aiding the mystic, as her warding chore. With nothing better to do than seek her study, the boy begrudgingly teases the thought: that he may as well accept his prize, before deploying forthwith.

Pinpointing the whereabouts of a fabled half-giants is a task much easier said than done, the commissary is burdened in tiers of bodies, litter, and wreckage. Propped by a sturdy pair of boots, he stands a full few inches above the ire of everyone else, and in this common struggle, still is unable to sight walking monument among the carriage coaches and hoards of luggage.

An occasional rumbling can be heard, enough of a rousing clamor that it collapses the tallest mountains and flogs of leather to shower forth. Hardcases and loose packages pelt passerby like hail. The pacing reverberates through the halls, escaping the claws of the sprawling owl monolith, beckoning William to locate its source of profound power. He grows impatient with zeal, and adamantly pursues in ardor; proceeding so fast, passerby could claim that he is almost skipping upon the mist.

The abundance of debris forces him into scramble, scampering over an erratically-landed portmanteau. These hurdles are overbearing, causing him to lose sight of the oncoming gate, and notice a stray hand across his starboard side. It sways feverishly, wishing William well, and waving him on until he flusters through the navel, passing through in a fury.

Only after the fact does the boy stand at attention, and recognizes the mirage as Kester, muster station in tow, brandishing his cart of silvery armaments. How rude of William, while the keelhauler may not be the most upbeat of folk, they are certainly a vigilant individual. He is peeved, and silently mutters to himself, promising not to ignore the likes of which again.

The return venture to the medical ward is untaxing, and itself, mainly uneventful. That particular boy Jones retraces his steps, passing the site of Vernon's impact, rounds a corner or two, and this time, strides past the showroom floor until his grit is greeted by the bison alley dwellings. Austerlaund's impromptu hospice is a rather morbid sight to behold. There are four stalls lining each side of the walk, which themselves are stocked with a roster of infirm and elderly affiliation. They jerk and tremble with pain, more patients to count than teeth on a trout.

The ceiling is an absolute mesterpiece, riddled with holes in its awning where surges of air and moisture billow through. An attendant clears the build-up of powdery snow, almost brushing away foam, encouraging Austerlaund to address their concerns.

"Won'tcha do somethin' 'bout dis deluge? Can't sweep sleet foreva. Gonna bury mah at dis rate."

After lodging her complaint with the service department, the arch lector focuses her endeavors into patching those pitfalls, brandishing a hammer in one hand, boardwalk planks under the elbow, and six-inch jam nails clenched between her teeth. It's a fugitive fix, a temporary alleviation of the root cause, because the weight of precipitation mounting on the roof will eventually loosen the barricades, and yield another onslaught of elements.

The head priestess persistently peddles arcane treatments, touting that her potions mitigate the cold, at least for those recovering few. Elixirs can't sustain their generosity forever, each subsequent dose diminishes the potency, and tax the conductor whom enchants them. Thankfully, the half-giant's strength and connection to immortals, both the tempest and the tame alike, refuses to ebb in the slightest.

It's a surreal circumstance, mayhaps an illusion. She appears to grow stronger in the wake of those incredibly weak, as if Austerlaund relishes in the animosity of others- a cruel jest to the denizens of heaven and earth.

Vernon's notion of fleeing with these bedridden souls, withdrawing from town and saving those ill, bolsters a ripe bookmark in William's thoughts. Only owing to the wisdom of a competent healer can these impressions begin folding into fruition. The wards around the boy Jones twitter their tongues, conversing in hushed voices. Refusing to alert the acting physician to his presence, William casually mingles among this entourage instead.

If it weren't for the staunch snowbanks straddling the trading post, they'd be able to yank their jury-rigged caravan straight from the commissary, and out onto the river with haste. Alas, they'll eventually need characters bold enough to fleece windows from frost, some jinxed soul to play dress-up and brave the elements, spending the later part of the day heaving chuck. If they're particularly savvy, familiar with the temperament of weather, they should have a route for the coaches excavated and cleared well before nightfall. Those recent rumors spread among the wards mention that the convoy will make headway at first light.

Braithwaite, a fledging nurse as she so casually presents herself, is weaving wicker around the frame of a stretcher. This ward explains how to thread the strands among one another, creating a mesh of woven-fibers that may bear weight like a basket. She prides herself on the project, having hardly slept a wink, working almost nonstop under dainty candlelight to ensure they'd be finished before departure.

Her works are notably waterproof, allowing the blood of an unfortunate patient to pool instead of seeping away, as they might need to inject the vital fluids back in. The stress congeals underneath her eyes, creasing them with fissures.

Williams sizes-up her recent triumph, which is perhaps two steps from finish. Braithwaite introduces the practice to William, hand-in-hand, and an earnest lad proves as apt, proceeding through the motions among the remainder of their group.

Someone snickers on several occasions, cackling in a hysterical fit that could compete alongside a jester's repute, their vocal cords occasionally miss their mark, blaring a jarring, high-pitched squeal.

This stretcher in particular has been reserved for the knight, and assembled with droves of sympathy. Braithwaite is a chivalrous soul, and chaperons those who can't be treated as equals. In her regard, this pity is not just a gift, but a personal extension of self and love of kindred spirits. By treating it as a cast, she composes a medium in which to pour her heart into, writing messages of encouragement and symbols that are spaced far apart on the mesh.

Staves of protection are constructed from complicated shapes, but the ward can't seem to get the lines rights, surmising the lack of early-morning energy, as these scrawls appear like nothing more than nonsense. Her penmanship is rather erratic, as if someone has been tugging at her fingers, causing lines to curl when they should have been straight. All is well, it's charity after all, there's a certain credit given simply for trying.

Some townspeople believe treading on the finer side of life is futile, arguing that these sentiments are a waste of time. They cite language that flies truer than arrows, inappropriate claims about the horrors of frontier life, that the most carefree residents repent their grievances at the slightest case of terror. This commentary has a certain degree of truth to it, there are those who regret their selfish actions in the end, but just like every grand aspect of life, there is much reason to doubt it.

Death is often a culmination of experiences, a winding collection of coincidences that lead to an untimely demise. It isn't as trivial as making one dire mistake. One does not die by the bite of a rot fly, rather by the pestilence that follows. Warriors dare not perish from a mortal blow, unless they've ceded every opportunity to avoid it. The bane of human existence can be surmised by happenstance.

The wilds are truly unforgiving, and while injury isn't a surefire ride unto the end, it often grants the swiftest accommodations. Even if the trauma subsides, or a sawbones reprimands the immediate mutilation, rehabilitation is routinely threatened by disease.

Slippery sickness is an infection which spurs riling sweats, coercing vagabonds to simmer in their own juices and join the freshly departed. The salt-sages of the south, including the fabled Adelaide the Meddlesome, and those dead-lectors of Cinder Keep- honorable mentions all, and to each their own. These maesters and mavens are better healers than Austerlaund, nevertheless her guidance is reserved as a last resort, and the residents of the Junction will take what they can get.

Mystics have the tendency to favor a variety of soothing tonics, potions that help regulate body temperature. Ayers Beechworth is a recent addition to the cast of field hospital patients, and admitted himself during the waning twilight hours. Blanketed in bulks of linens with a pair of empty, crackling jackboots at his side, he grips at a flask of orange swill with swollen, liquified fingers. The hired-hand leans forward, pouring the salve upon his lower extremities which are rife with condensation. This apricot-colored concoction was brewed with the intent of keeping his toes balmy, yet persistence isn't rewarded, and continues to shiver with no avail.

Ayers is a man who beams with intense pride, a being driven by envy, who finds this current climate completely disconcerting. Unfortunately, as Mad River Junction has been plundered of prescriptions and remaining medical supplies, Austerlaund must be crafty, the townspeople wholeheartedly rely on these mystic concoctions. The whole practice is questionable; addicted might be a more accurate word to describe the Bannermane condition, as they've learned not to query the source.

Those dour glacial mires of the Westergaard have the tendency to hitch all manner of beasts in inky pitch. Lazy scavengers trust in the tar pits to snare potential victims. Though, they're a shallow class of wickerfolk, farming the creatures that wander way into sticky situations, manipulating short work-orders and leisurely fruitful exhibitions. Pack rats harvest these ingredients to be used in crafts and ceremonial rites, features like powdered boar's tusk, foxhorn teeth, brittle beak, rot root, muskrat fat, iron flecks, carpet moss, bitters, grimace and oils, before bison tongue, cheek, and tendons.

Alchemy is a favorite past-time for learned men, used to distill philters best described as brine, as there is always minor flotsam around, a bit like thawed sea water. Saltseers may dredge these ingredients together, grinding them up in order to generate a plethora of tonics and bitters.

Tonics are restorative brews favored by underground kin, their potency exhilarates the body into healing old wounds. Bitters are derived for their tartness, some sharp, tongue-in-cheek aftertaste similar to alcoholic beverages that those frontiersmen regularly indulge on. Although, they'd still much prefer a mug of nog, even if liquor wouldn't exactly be an inappropriate choice.

Bitters may tend paranormal properties when mixed with certain ingredients, especially those alder carr herbs farmed by the hags in Nettletown. Fennel fronds are harvested as magikal charms, fond for fortifying against spells and warding spirits. Caraway is a very similar-appearing sliver of greenery that offers tremendous boons when its fruits or seeds are pressed into oil, as consuming this bliss bestows clarity, comprehensive memory and visions. Pungent cloves of garlic lavish the gift of sight, or darksight specifically, illuminating otherwise obscure elements of the night. Lambs' ear is a delight when steeped in tea, and their velvety leaves of fleece, which are a shade between muted mint and lavender, incite pleasant, citrus aromas.

The violet purse, described as lavender by laymen, is considered a potential cure-all, sporting medicinal properties when applied as a soothing balm towards abrasions, burns and inflammation. That herbal smell is comforting, then generally ground and bottled as a cordial to be barter as an essential housewarming gift. Certain strains accentuate the lavender's essence, producing a certain dangerous, pacifying narcotic coined as tweedledee, psychedelics rumored to ambush users inside an overwhelming, dream-like stupor.

Hexes such as these can only be undone through illicit means, another boot-legged concoction or magik incantation, therefore strands of rosemary are preferable as remedy. Originally thought to be meddlesome weeds, flourishing amid the Underdark's furnace climate, sprouting in narrow crevices and spreading from a single fiber in one day, to encompassing an entire shrub the next. Whenever these brambles emerge, pesky hoards of gremlins flock, engorging themselves among the leaves in a banquet.

The territory between Bannermane mercantiles is vast, a unforgiving expanse of flatlands that stretch to the furthest domains of glacial mire and craglands unto the west, to the avenues of long-abandoned Urbana towards the south, finally landing at the feet of terrible mountain peaks north and eastmyr of the river tributary. Nothing more than a procession of yawning teeth which gnaw at the spewing sky, the land beyond is completely uncharted. Few have ventured passed the distressing domain, unwillingly to sacrifice live or limb in senseless stride. Above the trodden trails of the Ice Champion's Folly resides the stronghold of Cinder Keep, perched precariously above a canyon, fortifying the sole passage unto those out-of-reach realms and all miscreants which dwell there.

Cinder Keep is a full league past the pioneer settlement of Manspite, nestled among frost-ridden peaks in a voyage that grows more perilous by the step. This muster station is not some luxury retreat, Clan Marius estate or villa, there are no perks or amenities catering to travelers. It was constructed for one singular purpose: enlightenment, the cultivation of wisdom through unadulterated research. When one treks further then the horizon, magik becomes volatile and unstable, fringes of the World Pillar whose ley lines intersect and joust, flooding the ethos with uncertain energies. Cinder Keep has been outfitted for research into the arcane, erecting ritualistic chambers ethereal in every regard.

This was a site renowned for experimenting with the wyrd, where mystics study and hone eldritch knowledge, far from the bounds and confines of the material realm. Here, weathering spells, transmutation, enthralling auras, enchantments, wards and unnatural medicine are taught without restraint. They test the limits and consequences of the human element through methods ordinary Bannermane considered taboo. The people of the Oestergaard are typically preoccupied, concerned with trivial matters, luxuries or precious gems. Perhaps, these affairs are blessings in disguise. Cinder Keep is the last bastion of mortal folly, not just a refuge of study, but the pupils stationed here were presiding guardians of the realm.

Those that campaign and escape the ramparts' gaze are beseeched by monsters, true unparalleled horrors. Those distant hinterlands that comprise the Motley Mountains, Rimeweather Range, Slubberdegullion, and Balding Meisters of Moorland are guardians to all of humankind, keeping not just the rabble, but all fiends at bay.

Grims are an exhibition, bringers of death, and bearers of catastrophe. These beasts dwell in ruination, foreign lands that are stripped, barren, and would only be considered holy by those rendered insane. In the ceaseless battle between the tempest and the tame, those desolate wastelands are treated as their own personal workshops. Immortals experiment with chaos, becoming familiar with the poisons that taint bodies and minds alike.

Those slaughterbound warp with terror as their very own gristle and sinews tear. Bones are nothing more than afterthoughts, considered to be byproducts in a visceral stew. Shredded to pieces and cast aside, portions and parts are traded, displaced, and transfixed to become new fledging horrors. This sinful trade harbors sport, an otherworldly artistry that combines the most vicious elements of creatures, procuring an ensemble of perfect predators. It's as if a hooligan took a hammer and chisel to the zookeeper's marble, defiling the laws of nature, and appropriating grim, grotesque guises of their own design.

These miscreants are akin to shambling jetties amid a sea of pandemonium. The musings of fell gods are vile, yet impressively pertinent in design. Immortals possess an outrage for coloring inside the lines. This carefree experimentation renders no compassion, nor tender grace, simply exasperation, as their creation claws its way to life.

As the drones and playthings of higher powers, they are driven by the most basic instincts. This corruptive influence has nurtured them in the ways of wrath since composition, fueling their quest for domination. Every expression these cretins convey is a spiteful one, a bottomless fathom capped by anger and frustration.

The beasts aren't bothered by banal, mundane concerns, they rarely pay pardon to vermin that tread at their stead. Instead, they are attracted to affluence, artifacts of power, vessels containing ichor of the gods themselves. The influence they emit is profound. It calls towards grims, beckoning foes from the furthest ranges. This is the order of things.

Not even the greatest defenses can withstand the sudden stampede of a bewilderbeast in rancor. During one blackberry winter not more than a generation ago, their studious assembly awoke to such a clamor. Concerts crescendoed attention, heeding all the right warnings, but all was for naught. The hills were alive with calamitous bellowing, a rousing whirlwind that causes orchards to shudder at the thought. The wards seized at the profound, unmistakable cacophony, all the while an engine of war burst through their barricades. Fissures split across the mortar, a series of webbing not once larger than a hair's breadth, emerged into a gaping wound. The cliffsides tumbled, the mountains heaved, releasing a spew encore of rocks and scree. Within moments, a legendary bastion of earth and stone became a locus of torment.

A bear, unlike those the world had ever spied before, loomed forth. It was the ultimate manifestation of pure, unabated evil, eagerly answering the summons of bastard fell. This roving ursid laid waste to a kingdom of plenty, the epitome of mankind's probes upon the workings of the universe. One single predator, this pale horse, lashed the souls of two-hundred in the swiftest siege known to modern man.

As a meat-eating extortionist, grims are susceptible to otherwise gluttonous tendencies. Embedded in gore, engorging itself on a diet of scholars. The notably white pelt, pure as glacial powder, reddened in a sour worse than wine. With each hapless victim, it gained their strengths, and none of their weakness. Historians would be so bold as to proclaim the foe's intent, however, their crude minds simply cannot conceive the desires they lust after.

Monsters and grims act upon the slightest notions, rampaging after the faintest inclinations to bestow the favor of nefarious immortals. In all this sorrowing upheaval, the bear indulged on unnaturally latent properties, receiving blessings by the tempest in exchange of its unjust actions; an ample rally of rewards that continue haunting to this day.

Members of the ink-frame army frivolously depict this mesterpiece's endowments, poetically emphasizing unholy creations with piercing blue eyes, an exposed spine, and toothy tusks protruding from its maw, guiding flesh into an inescapable, bone-mashing gullet. In an exercise of divine intervention, denizens of the sky acted as the enemies of men, pouring all their venom and malice to mold true terror. This is the design of something sinister, the flagship of all things fell, and champion of death. It sows fear among the campaign, dredging spite in the hearts of all bannermen, causing them to curse and rue the frontier.

The retreating sons and daughters of the Oestergaard are fools to pity, they've spent the last league mortified by one somber fact, that the fall of Cinder Keep was not the first instance of incursion, nor the last. There were no witnesses, leaving fools to ponder where the beast really ran aground after the slaughter. Perhaps the menageries immediately began lumbering towards its next meal, or discreetly returned to the wastes whence it came.

The Raging Icon of Manspite, an alabear of renown, has been immortalized in a series of writings called *Tales Requiring a Great Leap*. It's Rylie's favorite anthology, a play on words that really stretch the horror. These depictions further embellish an occasional, sanguine painting or hand-sewn quilt to be passed between forefathers. The rime of a wayward bosun, spinning nightmares on misbehaving children.

The territory in which vagabonds tread is a gruesome one, full of frightful horrors, beings they dare not rally against. Each of the three mercantiles has their own unique struggles, unable to carry a good conscious: Avery Sauder cowers in an Underdark hold, distracting herself by playing with toy trains; Guster Masterson has been scarred by his exploits, and shores defenses; Charlie Mandon prods at the dreams of common kin, striving to strengthen character, fearing they cannot weather the oncoming storms. These thoughts are not a simple regard to ponder. The looming darkness that descends upon the hinterlands sends the Bannermanes quaking in their boots, threatening them with a prompt return to Bonaventure, and sanctuary of the Underdark. It is quite easy to revel in dark feats, because people tend not to notice good times.

These beasts are in contempt against the very laws of nature, yet are not the only corruptible creatures in existence. Humans, in particular, grow weary, sensitive to a siren's call. The denizens of heaven and earth consider kin as blank canvases, chess pawns, a lucrative resource to be molded in an endless amount of ways. They draw upon swarms of followers like moths to flame, appealing to an individual's greed, their envious tendencies and craving cries for power.

There is nothing more convincing than a demonstration, an alluring feat to ease temptations. Those onlookers who become utterly devoted to the cause are gifted special trinkets. These ancillaries showcase their faith, curry favor, and prove utmost fealty. They endow generous bounties of jewelry, all qualities of circlets, pendants, bracelets, and rings. Misarcana could be instilled in the lucrative gemstones themselves, even cast metals and fabrics.

Their greatest champions are granted weapons, helms, pairs of gauntlets, and various assortments of armors. The grand deceivers are utterly relentless, attempting to collude with them, goad them into committing indecent, immoral acts. Marks will begin to hear the dark whispers of the night become spoken aloud. As immortals compete, each defiled soul is another medal to hang on their wall, a figure to boast about. These people become mindless insects, worshippers of the false idols, instrument and tools that cater towards their master's every whim.

Rank in this line of work are accompanied to ridicule, leading live strings of bad luck as constant trials and tribulations. The candle burns at both ends, they witness both its splendor and inexplicable deeds, often prodding at one another, asking themselves, "With all this danger, why do humans continue to practice magik?"

Saltseers, or those scholars of the salt coasts and western forests, routinely dispense infinite wisdom. Their elders can't help but vex the white crows, remarking necessary risks, colluding that the ends eventually justify the means. They express that one soul may suffer the sins, so that all ships weather the storm.

Morality is core tenet of human nature, so much so, that the gleam of a stranger's gaze may determine their intent. Mystics that dwell among the forests, straying far from their mountain kin, remark that one step forward should only be considered when it's done together, a method supposedly better than one champion striding ten steps alone.

It's easy for romancers with a roof over their heads to debate philosophical thought. They have never experienced the pressure to perform, or anything truly riveting to believe different. They comfortably define material greed over refreshments at a lavish canteen, and how some certain, unsavory prospects choose to beget opportunity before all else. Although, this notion fails to conceive the Bannermane perspective: that they openly flaunt the dangers of the frontier, not to simply line their own coinpurses, but rage against the burdens others place on their shoulders.

The borderlands are yet another political platform, a stage offering an endless array possibilities. Players tour this territory to reinvent themselves, uncover the depths of their personality, and escape trauma, even at the risk of possibly inviting more- a gamble where, win or lose, the mysteries of life begin to unravel. Yes, the folk that roost here are selfish, they are ravenously opportunistic, rising to become bonanza kings. However the currency they tender is not all nickel and trademarks, but promises and heart. Vagabonds believe in utilizing everything at their disposal to further their position and extend their freedoms, sacrificing everything in the pursuit of happiness. While those may fear the powers of gods, the fear of doing nothing is something darker still.

As the followers of despots vet one another over their illicit, secret wars, they are oblivious to a front far more obvious. The luminance makes its presence known to those who possess vivid imaginations, and are the demented kind, persistently determined enough to find it. This glory appears as a tumultuous force, the auroras, a vivid phenomena flowing from the snowy seas of white unto the stalwart blue-grey skies. Lofty swathes of blue, green, purple and red culminate in a glorious epicenter, a manifestation of the fight between immortals, the spilling of godly blood. Ears withstand furious carronades, while lightning bursts forth from the heavens with every slash of their holy swords. This racket is not simply another clash between creeds, and instead hasten the end times. The embodiment of rage thrusts itself towards the bowels of the earth. This ordeal rattles the Oestergaard, sending the ice sheet that harbors the north into a frivolous sway; as when awkward lads are asked to dance during the theater reception, and will barely part their knees.

The unending chill cannot be responsible for terror alone, it is the great schism of the land that sends folk reeling. Chunks of ice the size of entire stations tumble off the glacial faces, delivering catastrophe, and opening webs of crevasses through the permafrost. The lands of beast and men tremble, the province parts, and the mountains anchored on the horizon quiver to their core. Those that bear witness are bestowed hideous trauma, and advised to seek counsel. Only dapper, pompous knaves would grace an audience, dissuaded by acts of mortal peril, consumed with morbid satisfaction. They pay no heed when crossing the Rubicon, declaring their foolish intents from the start.

Kindred souls do well to distance themselves. Instead, these people are thoughtful- cautious, staring at such anguish, and fearing that their lives in jeopardy. Disheartened countrymen dare ask, "Why would the gods have us bear these burdens?" Yet, time and time again, their query fails to stir answers or regards.

A local chapter may set alight in freak happenstance, or an estranged sinkhole swallowing-up the nearest orphanage, sending the homestead reeling. They collapse onto their knees in prayer, pleading to the heavens.

"'Elp us o' blessed storytella, for we are yer most devoted n' 'umble servants!"

The innate truth of the matter is that the divines aren't here to quell fear. Rather, immortals drive it. As the tempest and the tame wield powers beyond mankind's comprehension, bending all states of being, apathetically willing life into existence, and commanding the elements themselves. Despite the odds, they are not immune to petty squabbles, opting to build bridges, then quite as easily torch them to cinders.

Companionship among the firmament fares skin-deep: pactsworn in favorable moments, garnering alliances whenever their fates may align, just to henceforth squander opportunity. The Trickster god is particularly familiar around daggers, inching a blade between another's ribs for their own fond amusement. Their whims are fickle, conditions convulse swifter then a ferryman lashes at his steer, faster than the raptor in its element, and a haste demise. To cosmic icons, these fleeting fancies are law; everything else is in the way, much to the demise of those lesser.

These antics stretch to the farthest reaches of the world, sowing utter calamity. Whenever tragedies become personal, and those plain, ignorant folk finally hear the music, they tend to discover the simple truth of the matter: that it's outright every man for themselves. It is only when a victim suffers constant degradation, haplessly watching as their dearest tip the drink, or lose family to the blight, do they finally shake the stick at god. When they proclaim such outrage, that the menace they've endured isn't worth the wrath, learned-men realize that gods do not pay heed towards the trivial agendas of ants. These endeavors tip the scales, building and building a coming rage, as men can only take so much.

Some consider the raging winds of the north medicine, as they sear the flesh, hallow the body and numb pain. Masters of the hearth and home tend reasonable tempers, devising that forces of nature can't be inherently bad. However, the sovereigns of kingdom come cannot be inherently good either, when they continually fail to act, swatting at the nobody gnats they never considered from the start.

There are plenty of beautiful, defining moments to rescue vagrants, uplifting those poor, weary souls from poverty and prejudice, yet they do nothing. Criminals are guilty of the lie because they omit certain facts, or refrain from sharing the truth of matters. While immortals are superior to humanity, they share often fatal flaws, too busy battling one another to notice.

Wherever veterans may cast anchor, and fools haunt, does trouble toil. These types of people are not bound to the same ink, the subtle promises of simpler men, featherweights have no need of divine punishment nor reward to justify their character. They can conceive the notion that power is wrought. It can be harnessed through the insurrection, treason, and a declaration of war against beings far greater.

There are the weaves, the lifeblood of all magik, persisting through every element of the natural world, both perished and living alike. Auroras are the embodiment of the World Pillar, a web of raw energy and vigor that probes the confines of scientific posturing. This is the medium of the immortals, the material fruition of all magik: a convenient term whenever unexplained abilities present themselves. The firmament is subject to manipulation, while a special breed of bloodlines may draw upon it, others are cursed for just plainly existing. It is inherently unpredictable, and magik is the most basic act of turning erraticism into fortune and good tidings.

Opportunity presents itself through a procession of headaches and nosebleeds, wards may begin realizing their potential when crude-red ichor leeches into their ordinarily drab routines. Weavers with hemophilia often don't last long, as the rosy winters cause kin to wipe at their nose, dabbing taint that escapes nostrils, tickling the fringes of whiskers; or rather, these adepts discover a peculiar arcane prowess during an all-encompassing moment of anger. It's a suffocating process, as blood beckons, gushing forth like a broken spigot and drenching their figure, turning burdens of clothes into a flushed, vermillion ensemble.

They shout in retaliation, speaking in riddles of wind, nothing short of the roiling crack of thunder. Their voice careens through the piping halls and passageways, booming off its own intense echos, hawking such despair that the fleeting snowfall changes direction, avoiding such a fury, even just for a split-second. Demonstrating fiery, supernatural talents only ushers new adversities.

The subject is no longer an ordinary mortal, bound to the very confines of coil. They have become preeminence, beings susceptible to the higher plane, and are taxed with limitless potential; it takes gall to believe otherwise. Reality bends to their fingertips, akin to the conductor and the livid symphonies of an orchestra. If the world is an oyster, wards are the pearls.

Only the most gifted, yet deranged minds submit themselves to the company of spectral magiks known as the dire. These weavers regularly consort with phenomena reminiscent of conjuration, summoning long-forgotten geists to attention; divination, scrying over the hardly palatable visions of things yet to come; illusions that manipulate shadows or blur faces into intangible expressions, hiding figures that should be painfully obvious, right in plain sight; and necromancy, resurrecting fallen allies as they march across limbo, attempting to reach those sacred, Gilded Gates of Guldourame on their quest to the underworld.

The illicit arts are preached by the Alderman, denizens of the deep warrens at Westingate Proper whom delve into the desires of common rabble, and perform eldritch desires in their favor. While these privileges may appear alluring, they cannot possibly compete with the potential of fell fortifications. Mystics have only just begun to scratch the surface, and barely comprehend the true extent of these misdeeds. Spiritually-attuned scholars experiment with abjuration, wards and unnatural healing before ascending into blessings and hexes; enchanting arms, armor, enthralling auras and shrines alike; evoking weathering spells, dictating the chillrend; and transmutation, granting warriors traits suitable to creatures of fantasy.

What begins as a desire to protect kin, hearth and haven is cruelly manipulated by ruinous powers. Each magik charm they cast or utter connects them to the heavens, like strings on a puppet that cannot be severed. Immortals use this rigging to drip venom, corrupting dreams into nightmares. Through this method they craft another mindless thrall to do their bidding.

Their egos truly are a poison on the world, a toxin that animates malign tumors opposed to gaping wounds, preferring a slow, choking death. In spite of the adversity, these perversions can be treated. The first step is isolation, establishing a protective presence, a barrier of sorts that ousts villainous influences. These beings offer salvation to those in paltry states, eminence may gift gab, irresistible charisma, urges of impulse, the epitome of vigor, clairvoyance, the chiseled figure of a freight train, the strength of boar, bulls and bravado to the homely, or make their ward a fortune finder of brilliant and lavish luxuries; even if they persuade for promises of a better life, these desires are unattainable. A promise to move mountains yields valleys of unintended scree.

There is a definitive method to thwart threats, arcane staves draw upon the World Pillar, granting guidance, physical protection against malign forces and respite for the weary. Voyagers depict a variety of sigils scrawled into stone or timber, claiming that they emit a fine cloud of mist whenever a figure approaches. Coats of runic symbols impart wisdom, intended to warn of impending dangers or inclement weather. It takes a trifle of dedication to read them, and a distinguished stonesipher ages to learn, especially as the growing library of whipporwick exceeds thousands.

Vagabonds may navigate the frontier, discovering an awkward, stray crescent bend dotting the occasional evergreen. This shape is waxing miremoon, attempting to swallow the solispyre, similar in method to how wolves surround their prey. Another figure to come across is a triangle, some peculiar wedge with a line slashed through it represents Doyle Rock, the broken mountain with a magma core, denoting danger in every sense of the word.

The existence of staves and whipporwick is common knowledge, townspeople regularly identify them. When exploring town, an expedition should take the time to iterate symbols etched near the doorframe. These shapes help wrangle costermongers, whether they are true to compassionate folk or less than agreeable to deal with. Shopkeepers typically adorn their mark with pride, a bare of honor and their authenticity, very few attempt to shave it away.

Residents are familiar with the Mark of Dayne, the borderseal trademark for empty, decorating the bulkheads of nearby neighborhoods and residencies. These hollows are barren, picked-over wasted space, worth little to a sutler. In spite of panic among paradise, this impression is an ancient scrawl. It has been well-documented among the academy, hardcover journals, scrolls and scripts alike, and through muddles inked by hand, notes worshiped by men of science. Enlightenment is drawn in helvetica, language of the ancestors, actually predating the stillmen and great catastrophe. Although the sigil may grace prestigious studies, it has always possessed a negative connotation. Laymen rumor that it sports bad luck, regularly entertaining a disposition for disaster. Certain others are weary to look upon it, rather averting their gaze, and reluctant to merely mention the detail. The occasional artificer is commissioned to bestow the mark, furnishing entire medleys of arms and armor, however a worthy wright would never think twice about it.

Whenever a weaver delves into enchanting, the repercussions are severe and carnival. A wielder who parts with their gifts may complain of a depression to their person or parish, almost as if a cloud hangs heavy from ear to ear, blotting out the sunshine and draining the happiness of life; or in the worst circumstances, an aura of mischief that hexes nearby audience, wishing harm upon others.

There is a nigh-limitless assortment of staves harnessed through phantasmagoria, an acoustic entourage of proceedings, relying on a certain, magik-infused participant who can string a perfect tune. By vocalizing spiritual incantations, a manner of raspy warbles and wails, runes can be composed onto compliments. Modest belongings may instead become extraordinary objects of power, powerful ancillaries that can both aspire and sow spite.

Criers twist tales that romance all the Junction's weak-willed, envious townspeople, emphasizing equipment that barrio boys and beauty queens would do absolutely anything to attain. Bannerfolk lash their meager assets together, conspiring that their entire enterprise, perhaps decades of effort, was intended to fuel this transaction. They barter trademarks, assets, stocks, properties, even going as far to promise faithful personnel on retainer. The grifts of business can only go so far, eventually magnates yield any and all of their possessions: remaining provisions, supplies, riches, heirlooms that have been in the family for generations- everything must go. Desperation for the cause gradually crowns into a jarring, brother-betray-brother breach of faith. Whole companies riot to no avail, campaigns and paltry wars are fought over them. Whereas all this strife isn't pointless; the sad part is, it's usually worth it.

In a short stent of time, they become creatures of caliber, emissaries in the presence of eminence, wielding godly abilities, hurling bolts, and throwing caution to the wind. A good number of these items relay potent, protective temperaments, offering respite in some obvious, or occasionally obscure method, shape or form. While objects of power are revered by the Alderman, their countless conscripts and demesne does not extend onto the frontier. Bonanza kings contend over puzzling anomalies, artifacts such as an enchanted pelt.

Upon first glance, it appears like an ordinary trophy, a shaving from the withers, hemming tufts of fur that curl in dusky, bronzed mats. With this coat, Magellan the Tower is impervious to physical prejudice, reflecting deadly blows and parrying the impossible. He has no need of sustenance, wrestling vines of the Briarheart or contending with the elements; by all regards, this champion has become death-defying. He slew the fabled bison because in all its glory, bovines are still vulnerable at the belly. Retreating down a corridor of crag, crowded by confines of ice, the brute was cornered in the Antlers of the Earth. At least, that's what Magellan preached among an exhilarating conference at Mad River's bunkhouse, before he was never heard from again.

There is no reason to doubt his intentions, the exuberant commodore probably got lost on the way home. Retracing one's steps is for naught, the cackling glacier ensures that a journey home instead lapses its quarry further into the labyrinth. William is quite familiar with this tale, he had arrived at the Junction last bloomtide, merely a day late to witness Magellan's departure.

A wild flurry of enchantments weave their way through the mortal realm, offering all sorts of boons if the trooper can weather the begrudging envy. They most commonly fortify, increasing the damage threshold against perils, especially when traversing tunnels that normally make venturers sick, queasy in the caverns of their stomach and intestines, vomiting meager contents of bile a few hours later. Artifacts confer incredulous emotion, almost as if they have feelings of their own.

They overwhelm liege lords with despair, humiliating jealously and insecurity, cold-blooded emotional numbness, or a constant, riling frustration into anger. There are certain chronicles that sound oddly artificial, those circumstances that propose without consequence: shallow betterments such as becoming wiser over the years, or favoring animal companions in the steed of their human counterparts, stealing casual conversation with the nearest fox, lemming and otter.

Bannermane babes are taught stories when they are young, tales that iron their grit and shape wit, because in the white wastes, there is no room for error. They are warned of divines and the charity they play. William has always been keen to tragedy, catching wind of these particular second-hand treatments from some spiteful caravanhands. "Lost in the wildaness," they'd begin ominously, "and sent awry, dat remainin' party keeps tah dwindlin' fire."

An individual among them possesses a personal effigy, a certain pendant from her late wife, enchanted to ward that same rampart and unchecked frost that stole their love away. The gods relent, forging new manners in which to corrupt the citizenry. Weeks from the nearest outpost, this company is subject to borderspiel mutterings, every glance becomes privy to the remaining folks, any expression sacred, the placement of their hands and gear they stow. As the dusk toils unto dawn, midnight brings somber thoughts. They plea, desperately imploring to escape the chill, suggesting to sacrifice meager tributes, but it's not enough to quell divine comedy. The mental state of that navigator stowing the pendant deteriorates, becoming unbearably selfish, despite the cries and immediate concerns of her fellow companymen.

Compassion is of no consequence, she isn't eager to let present company borrow her token, or part with this precious pendant. A certain scandalous buzz tickles their lobes, fetching whispers that capture attention, alerting the swain to the powers that be. These pressures are egregiously persuasive, convincing their victim that the others nearby are not just accosting eyes, but deceitfully filled with envy; that they seek to murder her, and steal the heirloom for themselves. Hopeful listeners to this frontier tale believe that she hesitated, that her mind mulled over such intrusive thoughts, however others would affirm that she embraced her initial impulses, that the gods goaded her into the notion of striking first, swiftly, aiming to end the competition before they have a chance prospects.

One of the layman in their caravan complains that their tea tastes remarkably bitter, approaches their campfire, and nabs the kettle, ready for another cup. As the pitcher lifts from the rack, it emits a timely *croak*. A frozen frog had thawed in the boiling water, leeching wicked toxins into the blend. Members of the wagon train gurgle and scratch at their raspy throats, they had fallen for a plain ploy, a poisoning.

Those that survived the outburst, neglecting the community pot, frantically searched for the woman to no avail. Fully under fell influences of the tempest, she had escaped into the night. A fortunate few squall-dogs scrapped together their meager morsels, packstuffs from the very mouths of their dead, and managed to navigate between good graces of gale. Most expeditions that endure such plight never greet the following day.

Bannermane law is rigid, a decisive contrast amid the wild and untamed hinterlands. Any vagabonds that wish to voyage the Oestergaard must must declare any artifacts upon their person. These ancillaries are duly noted on the caravan's cargo manifest, and promptly locked away, tucked beneath the ferryman's key. The sort of people who wield enchanted items are often delirious, tainted of the mind, body or spirit. After all, it is only human to make mistakes, however, it is awfully inhuman to err upon others.

Objects of power tend to grant unintended side-effects, consequences that compound as time carries on, so artificers favor briny brews as an alternative medium. These concoctions are relatively safe, controlled through a series of repetitious, by-the-book experiments in a laboratory. At least, those that are exported from the Underdark and Saltseer alchemists. Here, among the contraptions and grimoires, they enchant potions across similar mystical verbose.

Philters are curios themselves, essences distilled in oil, with each ingredient given the breath of arcane to achieve restorative means. Mixtures are more medicinal in nature, able to negate the effects of alcohol, heal wounds, or offer major resistance to the crackling, bone-chilling cold. Even while these brews should be consumed in moderation, the lion's share of clients swig the swill whole, not bothering to read the how-to instructions and recommendations stuck to the surface of the bottle.

Flasks feature a removable crown, a trailing wick attached to the underside of the lid. This thread soaks in the conception, and when held above the tongue, relief is only a few drops away. These potions offer a glimpse of paradise, liquid excellence that tastes like ashes, burning the length of throat, until it stokes the belly as if it were a furnace- a reward alone. All problems suddenly make themselves scarce, the ethereal feeling is addictive and fleeting.

William and the wards are spent, having exercised the better part of this morning as a rush of drama and stage theater: diagnosing affliction after malady, finessing clean bandages, counseling kin through their withdrawals, and coaxing seniors through the unabated pain of hypothermia which accompanies the lack of sufficient medications. They can't help but remind themselves of their severely vapid patient. Even though she possesses a penchant for mending mind and body, the spirit is something else entirely.

Austerlaund wouldn't dare consider herself an accomplished physician, she'd much rather concentrate on enterprising like true Bannermane. The mystic once operated a fledging venture, dispelling roguish weather for teams of excavators and journeymen among the territory, stalling sermons stirred by the lord of earth and stone with the ever-valuable, antagonizing art of thwarting, nulling any arcane trepidations.

While townspeople may honor the Junction's reigning, resident sawbone, maidens of the Oestergaard's Riviera are usually pompous, public icons, not an erudite to be secluded in some stronghold for study. This arch lector is nothing of the usual sort, resenting her trade when taught among wardrooms. She favors working with her hands, not her head. There's a distinct lapse between medical knowledge and application, and if graded on the latter, she'd certainly outpace any maester. The mystic has been busy producing a number of salves, enchanted healing oils that she pours onto the knight-errant, and massages gently into his perforations, with the paladin's skin now appearing as a homage to outwear everywhere, a gnarled, gritty leather-like coat in lieu of real skin.

Being raised in a stationary band of giantkin, Austerlaund was raised to be weary of the outside world. These roving bands of titans are famed for their tusks, bits of bone broadening curious clefts of lip like boar, comparing them to the latter of beasts. Yet, the arch lector has always been spurred by spectacles, eager to spot monuments of the land and rather enthused by travel. Often stowing away to escape the shelters at Malham Tarn, she retains a certain affinity for sightseeing. As tempered metal bends in the heat of adversity or severs under frigid fright, hardship breeds burdens, and times are tougher than ever.

These untrodden lands of opportunity beckon ilk to transpire as trailblazers, pioneers whom selfishly revel in their own deeds. These vagrants often become nothing more than beggars who bicker for packstuffs, provisions and prospects. Hand-in-hand with the staunch aspirations of greed, the common Bannermane riffraff cannot atone the past, nor comprehend sights outside their binoculars. The true greatness of the frontier lies embedded between men of character, those that stride in the face of danger, and despite the odds, these champions sacrifice for the greater good. As martyrs, they are defined by their prestigious moral code, graded by the bounties and colors of all men. The channelling rages of the frontier quickly separate fat from the wick.

Braithwaite has been watching how the man-at-arms draws William's gaze. Of course, a figure of renown would draw an urchin's ire. The medical ward sassily remarks, mentioning, "Osbourne, that's Osbourne Bullheaded. Didntcha catch sight o' 'is helmet?"

The agents of Clan Claremont have bolstered ranks of pride and privilege, not tempted to flee during bouts of inclement weather. While the knight-errant's state has vastly improved, he has not yet reached any clear meadows.

A burgundy tarp engulfs his figure, a clever disguise for absorbing ambient blood and rancor. It envelops the edge of distressed jawline, parading down until the peaks of toes emerge, which are a contorted mauve mess, congealing in pools of its own blood. Osbourne Bullheaded's eyes are abruptly sullen, sunken beyond the depths of nasal cavity. They produce a jarring sanguine tinge, a pale turbulent redness that swallows otherwise normally burgundy-rose pupils, similar to a cranberry spritzer, dowsing inner-complexities of the paladin's very soul. A thick, greasy slime has begun to develop, and not just from the soothing balms, this tallow douses the fleece blanket like oil to cloth. His body dredges-up a ludicrous amount of toxins, covering his visage in a fierce sweat.

This slippery sickness, a term floating among caravanhands, is when the victim cannot retain any fluids, as these perspirations soak layers of garments and equipment alike, another medium for deep freeze, ensuring that any venture into the cold would be futile. Lacerations have collapsed portions between his facial features, wounds already imbued in scar tissue. The ill ravages of tissue is compliment of these peculiar ointments, giving the vast majority of skin a callous nature. Purple bruises embellish the remnants of old felt, centering across his forehead and temples. These sores barely clot the gore, or what riles beneath the surface. The gristle of veins and arteries frantically desire to depart this feeble frame, the confines of carcass, and limits of human ingenuity.

The farthest reaches of Osbourne's nose are grafted in a silken web, the dreaded ivory coast, the emerging conditions of frostbite and often irreparable injury. His jowls have receded towards both cheekbones, dredging the possibility of any wrinkles, drawing the hide taut because there's less to use. The knight's contours are nothing more than a funeral procession, jagged, restless bounds ebbing towards the upper-limits of his face. Each ear is wrapped in patchy gauze, a husk that emanates with serious, mangy ooze. Imagine the tirade of severed flesh as it begins to scream, and oceans of ichor that escape from its maw. William shudders at such a perverse notion.

Ooh, aah. Osbourne groans, inciting the ward to take several steps back. Braithwaite is appalled, frankly frightened that this patient- so worse for wear, is still conscious. He continues to mutter about, mulling more minutiae, almost appearing to quarrel with himself. There's a distinct lack of emotion trimming his face; not that it's possible to flex any muscles or tendons, nary a show of teeth. With a deep breath, the knight-errant's stare seeps into the ceiling rafters, eyes closed, damning his darkening sight and these ramparts.

He speaks alongside raspy, strained vocal cords, and the air brims with breathy, monotonous melodies combined with such quivering tongue. Those nearby fall victim to its prose, captivated by such distress, a voice that hardly carries the sanctities of life. Too often does his stuttering banter break into a coughing fit, droplets spawn as if they were venom, spewing forth from droves of teeth. Despite all evidence to the contrary, the paladin feels vaguely exhilarated.

"I hear the *hrrking* bells, t-they toll for me, not just for denizens of the d-deep warrens and seers of the coves, but all champions, com-em-manders, vanguards and visionaries alike. There is a voice in my head telling me that I'm destined to do great tha-things, rambling about prophecy and try-try-tribulations. *Aagh!* I hear their mockery, yet can't quite make it out. I am a clan-clad man, so few aspire, hoisting their banner to be-become heralds just like me. It is a welcome honor to be recognized in such a manner. This trumpet seem to lapse over, even condone my shattered, crumbling estate. I can hardly move, yet could take on the world-de."

Osbourne nests his head to shoulder, hawking phlegm in the gut of his throat. *Egat* and *sploot*, as if a levee had finally burst, a stifling amount of greening mucus suddenly erupts from his faucet. After a momentary lapse, he regurgitates his resounded degrade.

"T-they ask if I would leave my taxing luggage behind, shed these restraints on the platform, and it shall lift this cur-er-rse. Then, and only then, will I be released, no-no longer bound to the albatross that peers have wrung around my neck. I am not a victim of honeyed words, nor prone to nuisance- an agent of caliber agen moved by tru-truth."

Austerlaund warns that the spirits may have induced hallucinations, delusion and paranoia, yet another unintended side-effect.

"Rest now, renounce yer claim tah those brethren o' the Gaard, 'eirs tuh all that is permafrost n' rime."

Plagues frequent the frontier, as sovereigns of kingdom come often spit in each other's general direction, unfortunately drowning mortals or those caught in the middle, with their heinous blight. While a single bout of pestilence may quickly swell to hundreds of cases, sickness can be confined from town to town, kept in check by throes of menial logistics. Those feeling unwell are likely to perish en route, sparing any number of souls from dreaded anguish simply because of this distance between settlements. However fancy the hassle, the same can't be said for creatures of the wilds, who dispatch their own illicit dread.

Sickness is not just limited by whom wear boots, but spreads through megafauna like mortar's wildfire or the spark of flashrod, as livestock may easily submit to beastly afflictions. The rat flu is an all-consuming disease, carried by all manner of vermin such as lemmings, rabbits and foul rats. It's not the pests themselves which are the problem, plague doctors recognize the insects they tote around as the actual harbingers of disease. As the mercantiles dispatch gurus to investigate, these medical expeditions often arrive too late to be of any assistance, rather discovering residents keeled over on the ground, and the towns populated by critters that scurry on all fours. Those afflicted by the virus are certified by a vicious, dry cough and severe, reddening discolorations: the pooling of blood as their organs hemorrhage. There is no finer torture than watching your loved ones fade away, as when the life dulls from their eyes, and the furnace driving them dims- a sudden waste.

Diseases can also be contracted from consuming afflicted meat, ignoring the purplish blot on a skirt of bison may be a heinous mistake. Swine is especially perilous, as boar are truly filthy creatures. Once the poison has been ingested, they'll become lethargic in nature, slowly sapped over the following weeks of their strength and muscle; these are the agonizing affairs of tinder rot. If the butcher is lucky enough to be spared the indecency of soured protein, the next concern involves mischievous and microscopic tapeworms, beginning their life cycle as eggs which are invisible to the naked eye. These parasites demand tribute, pilfering organs of their essential nutrients.

These pests appear intimidating, but corruption is no match to flame: tempering the worst scourges in existence, even as Bannermane sack the beauty of the land for their own financial gain, they have reason to fear the safety of the hearth. Vagabonds are bloodsucking parasites themselves, leeches to Nana Nature. The gods have bewitched these pioneers with pestilence, spreading banes from person to person as easily as trademarks, a fitting punishment for fervent greed.

Inherited from father to son, mother to daughter, and countless kin in-between, hemophilia is among the worst crutches mankind has to offer. It grades the root worth of familial love, what kind of monster would let their children bear their weakness? Hemophilia is known as the bloodletting disease which prevents wounds from clotting, ordinary injuries instead become life-threatening, and even a bruise is a cause for concern. Those afflicted dare not traverse on the surface, as any laceration would leave a visible trace of crimson laced among the snow, trackable by any predators in the area. Those same scapegoats testify that the warmth of their bodies feels as if it's quietly draining away, coining this process as the feeling of charcuterie.

A victim may notice a trifle, some nick on their elbow that emanates a steady stream, this is the snakebit beginning, as the dribbling leak on a faucet eventually bursts into a gushing deluge, physicians watch helplessly, the best they can offer is a tourniquet around the bicep or thigh, then otherwise plentiful amounts of gauze. It is a very visceral occupation, chopping through gristle and severing tendons, any patients they come into contact risks contracting the calamity. Hemophilia is not just a blood disease, but blood-borne. Using a sullied handkerchief puts those in harm's way, increasing odds of infection.

There are burdens of the body, as well as afflictions of the mind. Insomnia is known by commoners as a kingly curse, which sports the saying, 'the lines are fraught with jagged edges.' This illness dulls the mind's edge, whittling their personality away with sleepless nights, croning at the fringes and sheets of bed. The total affairs of their kingdom wane into the least of their concerns, waves of insomnia swell into sensory deprivation, the lack of common sense and chronic assault of irritability, twisting unemotional stents into instant ire. Burning the candle at both ends, fraying the wick and losing wit after wit.

Occasionally, word travels the parkways, garnering crowds in anticipation as knaves know how to work a crowd, peddling their confidence to fleece gullible sheep. However, these bothersome pests often run afoul, guilty of conning the wrong mark, and find themselves victim of a cruel hex. Without hesitation, their once sane mind utters gibberish, suffering an emerging ailment, the acclaimed twisted tongue. These vagrants undergo a torrent of muscle spasms until the meat weaves into knots and they eventually lose the ability to speak. Regalia of the robe are confounded by this disability, as the disorder renders a nauseating bug, a feeling in the back of the throat, like the root of the mouth has gone rotten.

Poverty begets sickness, pandemics flourish amid reek and repulsive gutters. The Underdark sports its fair share of dehabilitating diseases, and dabs of medical monotony, almost as if kin were brushed with slick, putrid malaise. The black spot ranks among the worst offenders, fungi that thrives on damp surfaces, including the skin of those unfortunate enough to live in constant wet squalor. What starts as a rapidly-darkening rash easily spreads around the body, necrotizing any flesh it comes in contact with.

Those flush with funds siphon freshwater straight from the berg, while the desperate wretches must find loathsome, unfiltered swill sufficient.

Standing water is a gross omen, a breeding ground ripe with bacteria. It's not just an old wives' tale, any who partake in this illustrious drink are blighted with fetid blossoms, poisoned by toxinlurgy in a bout of frogtongue.

The disease is a very real, amusing contraction, making it almost impossible to speak- a valuable tool in a prankster's arsenal, spiking the drink of their forlorn target. Draining from their sinuses, mucus pools in the bay of the mouth, swelling the cheeks and giving the illusion of a disproportionate fattened, fleshy frond. Plague is eternal, residents must be quick to combat the grotesque with a purge-or-be-purged mentality.

Consumption ravages lands of gut and paunch, a battlefield dictated by vague, imperceivable commodores, where all affairs are kept tongue-in-cheek. Infection is guaranteed, at least in one form or another, and rages until those smitten welcome night with open arms. Those underground tunnels are brimming with life, microscopic organisms that settle on surfaces, seeping into the stone, water and eventually lifting into the air as an invisible veil of death itself.

This cloud permeates the densest fortifications, all a pilgrim can dare do is brace for impact. Pestilent vapors infiltrate the maws of ordinary men, forcing their way down their esophagus like feeding tubes, and lay waste to burning lungs. Diagnosed by a routine, asthmatic cough, tissues wither and rot into liquid goop, churning fluid until patsies drown on a chemical cocktail of their own broth. A prominent symptom of inferior air quality, the creeping cough is commonly caught by children, this mild sickness drys out esophageal lining. Magistrates would rather funnel smog towards station poorhouses than finance the necessary drilling rights and piping pollution above the surface. Meisters and mavens of science have yet to understand the long-term effects of living in rot.

This problem is unique to Underdark urchins and whelps of the warrens, as frontier babes are usually stricken by common colds, accompanied by sinus infections, sneezing, watery eyes and disorientation. Those infected are left sensory-impaired, making them susceptible to the elements without the safety of lulling flames. Those that march to the rhythm of feuding feet must ensure their gear is properly treated and stowed. Damp ensembles congeal bodily juices of sweat and buboes, trapping puss-leaden rime underneath layers of clothing. It creates an overly-humid environment, the perfect medium for gestating the red rot.

This strain of bacteria thrives on moisture, absorbing any sources of water to fuel its deviant germination. The skin cackles into the consistency of leather, wearing down into deserts of abrasion. Rot manifests from prolonged exposure to damp, unsanitary, and cold conditions, especially if one's Peaterbricks are improperly conditioned and dried, garnering its notorious reputation as trenchfoot. There is no real cure, physicians tamper with proper medicines, hoping that drugs will take, and the body overcomes any degenerative disease; patients of the plains are easily remanded into hospice carehouses.

Veterans praise mending salves, homeopathic remedies for fixing them up, right as rain: a slap on their back and they'll be as good as new. The lasting effects of physical trauma are convalescent, to a lesser extent, scar tissue may tell their story. Most alternative therapy and procedures are cosmetic, although a sawbone may lop off afflicted stretches of skin, and favor complimenting prosthetic replacement. There are some who do not wished to be corrected, claiming that these wounds define them, and make them stronger for it.

Those rogues in the alleyway can't help but pity the knight, even though getting hurt was consequence of his own volition. He's not just another patient to them, this is a man of the establishment, patron commander of Clan Claremont and worthy of high regards. These onlookers are alarmed by the foul scenario impending his skin, they believe it to be torture, involving whatever armor casting that couldn't be removed by the nursing team. This guard is now generating an environment rife for infection.

While the riddled, decaying flesh exposes itself as a blight to the errant-knight, crafting an ecosystem of revolting matter, blessing and safe harbor for those morsels that delight in lapsing tongues, the generous bounties of bacteria-rich saliva, any oozing pores, and maladies that consider noxious rashes delightful perfumes. As rot gives way to rebirth, these wounds are holy grounds, sacred to the waxing and waning of all life-forces except that of the hapless host. The very wards that administer treatment to the patient must minimize their window of infection. As contagious, stomach-churning spores take flight, medical practitioners are forced to wear their facemasks, bandannas and buffs indoors.

Nevertheless, wind seeps through every opening of planks midst the wall, the frigid wisps cajoling their noses to run ripe with goo, flushing the color of faces until they take the appearance of the walking dead.

There's a crypt running alongside the Junction's stray superstrata, but those caught paying fares towards the ferryman rarely wish to bunk there. Coffins and tight-knit spaces are bad omens among open plains, confinement is an awfully foreign concept. Trailblazers would rather lay anchor among the stars, content with oblivion as they suffer with melancholy, up until their ears are buried by volleys of snow, where they await cremation the following season.

This bunker is one of the oldest sites around, a certain field-day for archaeologists, remnants from before the settlement even existed. It is composed entirely of mythos: the halls are drab grey, floors marbled in concrete, there are recesses in the ceiling that sport pairs of translucent, cylindrical tubes- or so they say, William has never investigated before.

Regardless, this crypt houses a dilapidated arrangement of hallways and dead-end doors, organized in such an insatiable manner, that it feels like a dreadnaught has sunken beneath the waves. These warrens coax claustrophobia, as if the tunnels could be cordoned off at any time, and this vault suddenly becomes a mausoleum for the living. Most of the aisles end in a suddenly-steep stairway with a railing to accompany them. Another downwards descent to a deeper level, only occasionally starboarded by an odd door or two. These rooms are dark, dingy showrooms that present the occasional, odd rug, although they are usually emptied of anything that isn't flooring. There are no lights or sources of running water, the labyrinth offer no safe refuge other than the fact that the doors close.

Prospectors camp here in a futile quest to explore the grounds, but fall victim to their own nightmares; the fools fear that some stalker lurks midst these halls: this dreaded caretaker of sorts that prowls these halls could also pay them a visit, checking-in on its weary visitors, then they become kinsmen never heard from again, and there shall be no revelries in which to share in their stories. Traversing this maze and its crypts preserved in time, are on par to an immaculate museum exhibit, nary a spec of litter, lootstuffs or refuse. The bunker is residence of the mortuary cult, Bannermane scholars can only speculate how deep these vagabonds embark, or where the cult is located for that matter, as no one has actually laid eyes on them.

Mortuaries are responsible for embalming animal trophies, those prestigious showcases for the wickerwalkers. There are those who live on the fringes of wilderness, particular clientele whose drove herds of jackrabbits only to be harassed by a fox; these homesteaders are their most frequent customers. They catch the varmint through a variety of traps, crushing their frail game and making their entrails become out-trails. Taxidermists prize pristine pelts, flawless trimmings, remains of skin free from the slightest harm. It's not just an important feature, but absolutely essential, or else the entire process is a bust, even for expert.

Mortuaries treat the skin impeccably, brushing it- or rather dousing from bow to stern with a viscous draught. Some tailor-tenders believe that too much evergreen oil will frack the surface, and in spite of this narrative, it is best to be thorough. Tannins draw-out the hide's moisture until a pelt renders drier than a hull, forming an impenetrable casing. Only when their pet project reaches this manner, will they finally inject a series of chemicals, fluids that immediately eat everything underneath the brimming leather and strands of fur.

This embalming process is brief, and doesn't take long to digest its quarry. These vagabonds peddle a hilarious arrangement, emptying the contents of a hunt, stuffing the hollow form full of wool-filler packing, as firm as a mannequin. Taxidermy is a fitting end for such pests, now the critter doesn't have to hide, adopted as a foreboding scarecrow sticking among the very crowd it once stalked.

The source of Mad River's mortuary cult is not a concern to the common man. In lieu of traversing the tunnels, they venture a furlong easterly, approaching some skeleton frame of scaffolding and exposed gridiron rebar. This venue features a lift, a platform of lumber twined together.

Wickerwalkers arrive to bestow carcasses and a meager offering. There are no trademarks to exchange, just a sampling of frontier cuisine, supplies, and whatever wares that can be spared. As if inspired by magik, the mechanism jolts, beginning its plunge, swallowed by the murky blackness within moments.

The art of the Mortuary Cult takes days to perfect, and eventually a model will emerge, striking some original pose. William has bore witness to an assortment of genius: an exalted tundra terror, with their forepaws burrowing firmly into the frost, and yawning towards the iridescent sky; mammoth-sized caribou, true guardians of the steppe; though his favorite had to be Eile the bison. It was among the rarest variety, the highly-sought albino steer. The mercantile had to be sponsor, as a trio of armed guards arrived to receive it.

Mortuaries do not spare their efforts, townspeople commission them to save their beloved pets, such as a leashed goat they kept admitted a post. At the absence of a proper butcher or abattoir, certain bands of huntsmen may request to split their winnings. In due time, the lift emerges with hunks of meat shrouded in parchment, their pelts comfortably folded, and any extra ingredients are preserved. Eyeballs have been replaced by black, sew-on buttons, and certain distended fuss now floats comfortably in jars of fluid.

The stalls of the trading post are reek and rife, ripened by rot, that foul stench of death. A pestilent green giest waltzes across the alley, wafting underneath William's nose and causing the viscera of his sinuses to burn. It portrays the presence of a jester, jeering with mortal folly, summoned to claim souls for the dark lord. He hears a voice calling nearby, as the spirit struggles to emulate.

"Jones, dear Jones."

William nabs hold of a brass handle, sliding a portal of iron and fittings to the side. This bulkhead is a magnificent-sized contraption, intended to hold the mightiest of bison at bay. When an earnest lad sweeps the door wide, he inadvertently reveals a patient lying flat, prescribed to an odd angle on the floor with some strictly thin sheet of fabric between them and stained concrete.

Their face has been abruptly contorted towards the stall entrance, and visage meant for presiding over gravestones is now leering directly at him. This tensely wrought complexion feels lost out of time, as every vein strained into a vexed position. They talk with pained gusto, yet their jaw doesn't move the slightest.

"Ah-hah, dot I 'eard sum man wash wit da wards. Reminds mah o' ah much more sunny-ah time. By muh board at da Arbor Island Resort. Give mah dem feasts n' luxury steam baths. *Ooh!*"

He winces, his jovial demeanor struck by pangs of pain and stinging sensations.

"*Sis-ahh.* Say-'ey, please Jones. Mah-muh chest really 'urts. Will ya take ah looksy?"

The bed-ridden doormat winces again, now asking the poor boy to lift their blanket, and give a prognosis.

"Take dis sheet off already! Sorry, sorry, sorry. Can tell-ah bad news. Dat dis ain't gud, nah sir."

He does so with remorse, apologizing with guilt beforehand, as he is not one to zealously accept responsibility. The trauma is sickening, just as expected, but also a degree worse. This resident's abdomen is adorned with a gaping mouth, stretching from nipple to navel, an open would that could swallow William whole. Instead of plentiful amounts of healing puss, it is coated thick with slick black char, pulpous bubbles and leaky innards that ooze antifreeze. Royally purple strings leach under his dermis, secreting ichor into the hole, yet to no avail.

"Yer expression says it all, must be ah lost cause. Dat good ole doc 'as 'ready made 'er rounds, they-ey-ey musta be confident o' mah dispatch tah da morgue. Lookie at me, bound tuh trodden-off like sum lucky bloke at da lottery. Pity dat oi can't stay, then-then 'gain, fortunately I won't be der to greet da cleaners of dis stall. Bloody mess outright."

He dozes off for a few seconds, distracted by his gruesome pain.

"Mah whelps o' ah son, ye 'aven't seen 'em, 'ave ya? Can't tell from down 'ere, but prolly 'bout yer 'eight. Dem green eyes, frazzled 'air, bit slim 'round da waist. Nah? Dat's unfortunate. 'E was pulling mah tah safety 'fore I 'ad lost 'em in da fray. Like everyone else, dot best dat we tried our luck n' marched outta town. Even drew straws tuh determine the line, and which figure wuld play victim at da front and back of our expedition. Wasn't long 'fore we were set 'pon by devilish beasties. Nevah forget, daring da open expanse is ah fool's errand. All started with sum shriek, 'nough o' ah blast dat we cowered tah our knees n' covered ears. Then, as if sum-one wound mah stoppawatch, the sun became ah blot 'til we entered throes o' midnight. My cousin n' their spousa were yanked offader feet, nevah tuh return. Sum otha vagrant dot dat dey fled from battle, not knowin' da couple 'ad been dashed intah da sky."

"Please stay, laddie. I'm sorry tah ramble. Letta talk ah bit with wut lil' time is left. Der's nah one tah rememba mah story, nary ah book in muh name. I delight tuh 'come memory, neitha ah burden- dat's all I ask. Da name's Glennitch, or Glenn of da Grotto, as I've always have fancied fishin' out der. *Ooh*, twas born tah arborists durin' ah heatswell. If I wus cherry-pickin' 'rough an artist's arsenal, muh favorite color wuld 'ave tah be violet. Listen, *umm*, ye prolly don't wanna be bored with dem trivial details, but I knows dat I won't be makin' it much longa. Da sun 'as already begun tah settle 'mong da loneliest shore, n' I'm wrestlin' towards da way-after. Course that sheerwind 'ad tah knick me. Der's no recoverin' from ah filet 'cross da belly, gutted like sum dull harbor trout."

"Da graces o' ah slow death allow tuh part wisdom on mah own terms, inform-information dat isn't normally muh gift tah bestow. I can grant ya riches, all da valuables dat kin 'ave amassed 'cause death doesn't ferry fortunes. Tis ah lousy time for an ethical debate. Der is treasure buried 'mid does tunnels o' da mortuary cult. Take da gate, not da lift, knockin' thrice upon the door 'til it opens. Don't forget tah greet the caretaker n' petition 'em for safe passage, otha-wise ye'll nevah make it out; does walls will twist n' thwart any chance at escape, confinin' ye tah quarta for da duration o' days. Take da first left after da entrance, four-score steps towards da end of dat hall, den two flights down, n' da first bulkhead will cough-up a prize."

Glennitch the no-longer able grabs at William's hand, guiding it into his palm. The whole disgusting appendage is riddled with flotsam, almost as if prodding a wet sponge.

"Do me a favor, lad. Free yerself from dees affairs, n' nevah settle for anythin' less den absolute freedom. Life ain't fickle, nobody's savin' sum ticket-to-ride or askin' permission tah die. We exist in spite o' da odds, as minuscule specks o' atoms 'cross da grand designs of a universe, n' 'ave tah do everythin' in our powas tuh persevere. Bannermane rally 'gainst adversity, dis our way."

The frail, humbled man spies the coming of his days, lapses his head to the side and recites a poem, original writ from the clan's roving days.

Thou hast rung without luggage,
Naked, afraid and ugly.
"Witty as oatmeal porridge,"
Do folk rumor rather bluntly.

Once-long company had run afoul
Fendin' menace from these ages.
Faced with utter ruination,
They reckoned to retrace their paces.

This beast aims to devour.
Fierce breath do blaze.
Departin' even men-of-the-hour,
With their villainous gaze.

Our quiver holds no arrows!
And all I hurl are darts.
It's a hasty demise to swallow,
Nary chance to start.

Once a weakling at the seams:
Bowed, bent and broken.
Finds that when pushed to such extremes,
Their spirit has awoken.

In life or death battles
Nary be 'fraid to bite.

Scant rhyme nor reason,
Better men dare fight.

Damn the ramparts!
Fear the fell and cry.
What gall? Defying destiny,
Rackin' gleam twixt one's eye.

I fight the few that weave my fate
For I fear the long farewell.
Treading ground tween malice and hate,
My courage dast swell.

Cast forth into the furnace,
Is the cure for nature's malpractice.
A quest for vengeance doused with oil
Quenched 'neath roarin' flames.

Tis true, heroes harbor great feats,
Catchin' lightning in their bottles.
They climb mountains, mocking bitter retreat,
Even meteors dare not dawdle.

These deeds compete for eminence.
Soothing rewards for the soul.
What these scars can't destroy,
They shall define, and brand forever bold

Vagabonds make face with stiff upper lips.
They do not slump nor pray,
Rather choosing to quip,
And rue at the seeping of this day

Facing these straits with bitter determination,
They dare not yield, nor tender their resignation-
Trapped in a vicious cycle, the wheel does turn,
This lantern may dim but forever still burns.

"Jah-Jones, when I finally succumb tah dees wounds, dontcha let 'em eyes close. I want mah final glimpse tuh be dat o' light, not darkness."

"Aye, Mista Goodsir, I'll see it done."

"Dontacha worry 'bout this auld soul. Wheneva I'm finally laid tah rest, dis funeral procession shall be bare."

Glennitch peacefully closes his eyes, lifting his guard now that he's in the presence of a thoughtful companion. However, it is in that moment, something goes wrong, when the arrangement becomes plight, and situation dire. William's surroundings buckle within a split-second's notice and bat of the eye, his perception hazes away while everything around- anything that fills space, seems to slow down.

The air is swallowed by rhythmic whirring, an audio tinnitus that aches the eardrums, causing him to reel his hands away, crashing onto his knees and covering ears. There's a bucket of standing water just beside them, the ladle inside spins back and forth violently, the surface oscillates as if a bison is rampaging nearby. Nearby timbers of the stall warp, he can focus on each splinter as they weave and snap through one another. Nails sheer from the walls, bolts burst out of their sockets. The metal links of leashes, chains and reins shake feverishly, however the percussion's raging racket is the least of their concerns. A flash of lightning careens by, webbing past fixtures and debris dangling from the rafters. This is no ordinary, it is flame from the miasmic pyre burning into the very fabric of reality.

The release of energy pivots into the sharpest turn, exploding in a beaming burst of light into the farthest stall, Osbourne's stall. A sudden *gasp* can be heard, reseting the illusion. There is no trace of the light, its magik has been wiped from existence, no cargo has been pushed out of order, or belongings in the slightest.

William is of young stock, the freshest generation of brood- rather spry, and ingrained with adventurous mettle. His mind yearns for excitement; being trapped in a bleeding settlement like Mad River Junction has left his bodily humors a bit worse for wear. This is a barely palatable detour on his chronic, coming-of-age odyssey. If the world is a game, it is most gruesome- no, this world is a machine, relentlessly turning urchins into able-bodied men. While his skin grows callous and ripe with rind, William's blood still boils with a sense of exhilarating ardor, all tendons, gristle and sinews jolting with the everlasting electricity of life.

He reacts swiftly, abandoning Glenn with haste, dashing down the passage to retrieve help. The boy Jones then knocks into some sturdy door with his shoulder, completely slamming the gate open wide to find the paladin writhing, entering his final throes of pain.

"'Ey, 'ey, will somebody get the ward? Lector! I saw somethin' strange. Need ah lector o'ver 'ere!"

The entire wing quivers in response, jolting in place with each heave of Austerlaund's massive footsteps. She accompanies William with scarce consideration, shoving him to the side while he bombards her attendance with questions.

"Can't ye do somethin' to save him? Somethin', anythin'? 'Urry!"

The priestess places her thumb atop her patient's carotid artery, and this single digit presses against a whole scarred stretch of neckline. The elixirs have done their work, yet taken a toll, Osbourne's pulse is steadily weakening.

An audience has formed in the wake of the giant's march, and they can hear the pressure echo throughout the room. There's a faint monotonous beat, *dum-dum, dum-dum, dum-dum,* followed by one-second pause, *dum-dum,* two-second pause *dum-dum,* three-pause, *dum-dum-* before nothing, at one point the knight-errant's heart entirely stops.

It is during this stressful situation which William's lobes find themselves lulled by a baffling melody. He looks around and scans the stall, no one else reacts to this tune, they are transfixed by the medical entourage. It is unlike anything he has ever heard, in fact, it is the only sound that he can currently transcribe. While a ward rails away at the agent's chest, desperately shoving the palms of their hands deeper into his diaphragm. William grows entranced by this soothing speech, it's like a quiet, bewildering whisper, the subtle screech of a lemming, but bold, emanating from deep within the gullet of some monstrous hind. An awful impression staggers into his head: a lullaby, it's a lullaby… but why?

> *I see through your eyes, the gateway to the soul,*
> *I possess no moral quandary, this body is mine to mold.*
> *Stoke the furnace, oh herald to the flame,*
> *Chimera of my creation, pawn in our great game.*
> *Your nails shall become talons, your bones steel,*
> *Enough power writhe through to make all enemies reel.*
> *Rest now vessel of wrath, and weep!*

No longer lulled by false pretenses, William weighs-in on a seemingly-conscientious dialogue between the wards. The bulk of these practitioners and medical entourage aren't much wiser than teenagers, yet the weariness of the job has already impounded their complexions. Wards are adorned with frowning scowls, hilariously pitted bags under the eyes with each of their foreheads notched with wrinkles, and creases strike into several distinct ridges upon their nose. They argue and rattle, debating one another, announcing crude remarks for all to see.

"'E's unravellin', we're losin' 'im!"

"It's nevah so simple… 'is injuries were just too severe."

"'E 'ad nah business waltzin' intah town. Sure sign o' delirium, wearin' dem colorguards n' metal 'round 'ere. Was 'most beggin' for anguish if ye ask mah."

"Nah, nah one's petitionin' for yer 'pinion, dolt."

"Der wasn't ah snowball's chance in 'ell dat 'e'd make it through," gesturing vaguely to all of him, "Well, dat. Dat sorta trauma."

An abrupt demise can only be undone through abrupt means. When a rodent finds itself stuck in a glue trap, every instinct urges it to scream. Life finds ways to relent, raging against a quiet night, just as the winds will always continue to howl. In a streak of realization, William pips up, crescendoing at the top of his lungs.

"Magik! Can't ye can save 'em with magik? Can't ye do some magik or somethin'?"

The arch lector hands remain transfixed upon Osbourne's head, and Austerlaund's solemn expression turns rightfully flummoxed.

"Yer right, I know o' ah spell or two which may 'elp," she iterates, but not before her optimism quickly sours once more. "'Though they're plenty dangerous, foolhardy incantations, somethin' old, unwise n' untested. A wanderin' mage shared their experiments with mah as ah word of warnin', not a form of treatment. Ye don't make magik from nothin'. If ye allow creation, there must be room for destruction."

She dwells against the nearby crowd, prodding them for affirmation. There's the subtle nod or shake of fist akin to haggling during an auction, enough of a draw that Austerlaund feels confident enough to proceed.

The proper once again dredges ancient, ancestral spirits in an fascinating display. In a demeanor of lesser dismay, wrought with junction of confidence and curiosity, some presence looms strongly still, and a shadow extends into the far boundaries of ceiling rafters.

"I 'ereby plea with those o' restless feet, I beckon all bygone wonders," the head priestess clamors as the room swells alight with fluid, tainting all space in-between with a viscous blue dye. Although, something is different this time around, a charitable course of action is swapped by mechanisms of malevolence. In an instant, arcane trepidations turn the body into a subject of study. They drill deep into the pit of stomach, coaxing beads of sweat to surface across his hide. The arch lector converses with the firmament that strings the sky.

"Strange, I don't recognize the forces at work. They feel… fiendish tah degree, but that can't be. What darkness would ever choose to bear life?"

Under a guttural chant, these droplets turn from a shimmering transparent sheen to shades of black, soon covering Osbourne in inky oils. They seem toxic, causing the flesh to steam and char. These foul liquids abruptly burrow back inside their host, leaving gaping valleys in their wake. The majority of what used to be skin is better described as hardened leather, decorated in thousands upon thousands of depressive, pin-sized lesions. The paladin's eyelids flutter aggressively during this stupor, yet his head itself is incredibly still, held in position by lengthy, prune fingers. His body begins to contort violently, almost as if a mad man of science yanked a lever, suddenly delivering the everlasting electricity of life through its body; arms flail and legs kick, fighting against an invisible enemy, or worse off, fleeing from one. The man finally opens his eyes, reviving with an immediate gasp of relief.

Ga-ah! His wheezing is fairly harsh, as when a tunnel-borer breathes sulphuric fumes, suckling on their few vestigial figments of oxygen. The audience remains silent, scared of what has transpired, is this a moment of tragedy or triumph?

Braithwaite breaks the silence, congratulating the mystic by patting her back, "Alas, the dreary fool 'as returned!"

Austerlaund completely hunches over, barreling atop her own thighs, exhausted, her bedside manner drained.

"-there, warded off any spirits that came tah claim 'is soul. This wasn't dire magik or necromancy… 'ad nah idea it would work. Nearly knocked mah unconscious, let muh catch ah moment, or 'ave- 'ave ah moment. Gosh I'm so tired."

The boy Jones is overwhelmed with awe, "That was incredible! I've nevah seen anyone returned from the gates. Let alone, 'eard o' such phenomenon."

He finds himself consumed with a sensational attitude, filled with boisterous vapors and vigor, perhaps a little of that lightning struck him too! For the first time in his life, William's eyes are finally open, keenly observing the hidden wonders of the world.

There are those few occasionally humbled out of concern for others, that is why makes us human, our urge to explore: trekking into the furthest expanses of wilderness, furthering technological advances, cultivating a community, and the relationships people delve with one another.

"When yer feelin' up tah it, would ye consider curing all the otha afflictions? I should go check on Glenn, that dashin' rogue."

Overall, it's a rather short trip. William weaves way through group of spectators, begging pardon, passing the wards who don't have enough grit for the real, hands-on experience. Strolling through the alley actually fills him with remorse, as every stall is filled with one or more infirm patients. These Bannermane vagabonds are in desperate need of aid. It's awfully quieter than before, perhaps suspect to distress.

A sense of dread invades him, anxiety that crawls around his brain, granting an awful headache reaching from the roof of his mouth, to the very top of skull. This brisk walk ends in more of a sprint, where William finds Glennitch sprawled as before, yet weakly and further rotten. He had passed during the struggle, a victim of eldritch power and hapless condition. Austerlaund warned them, that is the price of magik. Existence is painfully futile, life ebbs and flows, and just like the innocence, can be stolen away.

William is victim to old haunts, a figure looms over him, sabotaging every chance encounter for the worse.

"Woe to the Storytella, the being that safeguards the souls of men!"

He claws frantically at his comrade's wrist, desperate to find some sort of pulse, no matter how weak. That ward and practicing lector, Braithwaite skulks nearby, stumbles upon them, and yanks at William's shoulder, affirming the situation.

"Stop-stop! 'Is 'ands lie still, 'e's 'ready dead n' gone."

The boy Jones petitions and pleas with Braithwaite for assistance.

"No, nah it can't be! We were just talkin', tellin' stories o' 'is family."

He cultivates the profound question that also lingers on the medic's mind, "Can Glenn be brought back? Could Austerlaund save him too? She can, can't she?"

"I don't think it works that way, 'Liam. The knight's soul has passed away n' was caught 'fore it reached the Underworld. With Glennitch 'ere, there's anotha story: 'is life was pilfered, n' cannot be returned."

Jones imagines shelves stocked with miracle cures, bottles of green draught just sitting there, completely useless. When magik is involved, all conventional means are thrown out the window, not even the greatest conviction can preserve the realm.

As a man of exploration, William is built of sterner stuff, and often refuses having a heated resolve. He doesn't get angry often, and is rarely a victim to pent-up rage, but this posturing right here makes his blood boil. Tossing gear around in a sore deal of spite, he blames himself for proposing that the arch lector defy the laws of human nature. Osbourne must have the graces of beings far greater, a pawn caught between the grand scheme of gods and an instrument to broker.

These affairs don't burden everyone, nor should it, and that is why Glennich had to flee, he didn't curry enough favor. For a candle to burn again, it must be struck with a match. A match, who's destiny is to serve others, then promptly perish.

Before the boy can succumb to his despair, the priest pulls him back into reality.

"Come brother, let us return. Dwellin' 'pon misdeeds is tah ask for maul, praise the bloody, fools cry havoc and let loose the rats of wrath- no sense dawdlin' o'ver the dreary."

A shirtless Osbourne rises from stead in the main stall, contorting both hand and hide upwards. His feeble frame shambles forth, twisting each ankle with every aching step, and reels himself firmly on a sack of root vegetables, lounging on a makeshift couch. He doesn't rave, nor repent while contending with the facts over of what has happened. Speakers unfold their versions of events through a self-conceited act of charity, faithless observations that they believe would be therapeutic, but in reality, are only sound to themselves.

The knight-errant feels very little clarity, he is a withered husk, a tortured soul whom is remarkably unemotional for being returned to the vigor of life. It takes awhile for him to muster the effort, as his lips part sweet sorrow, the composition of stress and strain grinding the voice. Those spectators that crowd the room are taken back by such brute speech, it shakes them to their core with terror, almost causing them all to rout, the prose cuts from his tongue like knives thrown in the air.

"It boarded the coaches, joining somber crew for ferry to the world over. They made headining to gates, yet took detour across the plains. A stretch where the people danced, yet those could hear no musik. This one was carried to the pit of trials, beneath a totem of ice and bone. The winds lashed-up and brought storms with it. Although, there was an excuse to worry, as I has stared up at god, and god blinked."

The fools whom remain within earshot shed their grimace, while they weren't expecting anything jovial- this, overly distraught tragedy is bleak and confrontational, the epitome of awkwardness. The wards choose to resign themselves from the fray, and stave-off their audience, now focusing on attending the priestess' ill omens, and preserving the newly-minted corpses.

"Oi, that hoosier is right, we should all leave when we can. The whole ordeal was getting grim anyways."

"Dat paladin is stranga 'nough, 'e culd use sum rest- speakin' bits o' nonsense now."

"'Ey, did ye catch a glimpse at that guy's chest?"

There's a brief moment of silence before the elderly, Marlene Hinds speaks up.

"Now I 'adn't expected that. Such commentary isn't really an appropriate thing to ask."

"No, nah good ma'am. There's some peaky-natured scar 'tween his pecs. Looked as if the trooper was run through with a harpoon, 'aven't seen a ploy like that since my days 'mong the wickerwalkers."

The boy Jones take one final look behind him, spying on Osbourne from the intimate space between planks on the alley. He recognizes a symbol straying before the paladin's abdomen, this isn't an amorphous blob retaining some hint of artistry like the vague, bear-shaped birthmark that strikes William's person, it is a twisted and warped mark of ruination in the relative figure of a trident. The taut poker pierces their flesh, leaving a firm bruise where their heart is. However, these aren't the most alarming changes in Osbourne Bullheaded's arsenal, his complexion has grifted, each eye turning from its original wine-red tone, to become fierce amber orbs. Perhaps his mind is playing tricks on him and he's seeing things, this wouldn't be the first time.

Suspiciously, there's a Bannermane tale to fit every quandary. If there isn't, they'll modestly scribble a footnote or something in the Book of Sages, advertising it as advice for nex'ter year. The mercantiles use these stories to influence those inside their kingdoms, to dissuade independent trailblazers and the divide of territory.

"We should all abide by these rules," leaders preach, "lest the wilderness divide and conquer us. Unlike the moles that cower 'neath the earth, we are rooted of one blood, men cut from the same cloth."

They float precepts as sacred knowledge, keeping denizens under their umbrella, safe but dumb. Bannermane shall not fall to the forces of evil, whatever madness lies beyond the realm's borders, outside the mountains and gait of glaciers. Yet the unknown will always find ways to supersede them, thus becoming far more devious over the decades. Experiments from the academy have revealed dire warnings once before, meisters of the white robe researched and documented their studies, recording what influences the iris into changing colors. It is not only a philosophical conversation, this occurrence is an existential debate.

Jeremiah Anders' retains the mentality of a jack-in-the-box, even when prescribed medication and the best of sleep. He is a comedic wiseacre entertained by all and respected by few, someone who may ease their tension, just as easily as he may yet mend it. As the self-governed, de facto diviner of Mad River Junction, he records the wayward whispers that petition travelers. He is more than eager to share such track-talk.

There is an ancient legend which begins like too many before it: a myth about a boogyman who roams the frontier, threatening to snatch those who have lost their way. The Bàs Athair Kardu as it has come to be known, Balacaud or Father Death in common tongue, is no tall tale. Laughing matters do not portray monsters with eight limbs, wielding axes, flayer, great weapons and mutated appendages among them.

He was once an ordinary man, vile and cruel as all things come, unparalleled by any mortal in being. This challenger marched towards the dead north, not to simply find their path, but blaze glory. He constructed a monument in honor, a place of worship, but to what he did not know. This act was enough to earn ire from the tame gods.

Those burnt patches of pineneedles would race into the wind, granting debris the resemblance of razorblades. Pools of sap inked its way from through permafrost, turning the fool's sweat and blood into the sweetest nectar. This syrup attracted rodents and critters from afar, while birds pecked out his eyes, eager to sample the succulent honey.

These herds of game summoned wandering hunters and wickerwalkers to his far-fetched domain. Slews of men contended his hill, yet all in turn were defeated, beaten into submission through heinous, brute strength; the throne growing taller with every skull- all tame were frightened by this sight, but alas, tempest gods were drawn to it. They did not prescribe such carnage, so that's how they knew it was sincere.

What started as an honest debate, wounded disposition into open competition, hurtling blow after blow across the midnight sky. These immortals were eager to come to blows, battling with unmatched ferocity. They aren't vying over another simple-minded, follower of chaos, this a willing host: a body that they can finally inhibit, able to bend the entirety of the mortal plane to their liking.

One geist stood out among all the others, the essence of wrath, rousing its champion in human form. Fell magik manipulates the traditional features of form, severing each arm and leg into two, the back spine into bonemold, forehead horns graze horizontally past the brow, a maw that stretches past the jawline and length of neck, yellowing both eyes into something sickly, blight incarnate. This experiment withdrew his few remaining sanctities of sanity, and welcomed a maddening mind. The procedure drove the warrior into a primal, force of nature known as Balacaud. It haunts the hallowed expanses of wilderness, picking up any stray navigators amiss its fray. They are bestowed visions, hallucinations that depicted the eight-limbed harbinger of Black Death.

A story in this regards doesn't often stir inconsistencies, certainly not as the original intention. Mandel Haggerton finds himself in attendance, perpetrating a curious prose to fend-off belligerence.

"*Umm*, well that don't make ah lick of sense. If nah one survived the encounta, then 'ow do we know what it looks like?"

Humankind has the tendency to deny its own imagination. Once dreams and nightmares become real, it becomes routine to deny the reality of what fates befall others. When living on the frontier, it is best to keep an open mind.

The wickerwalker is a man of character, not of virtue, living proof that it's necessary for outdoorsmen to keep their morality in check. Acts of kindness, no matter how big, may seem noble at first. Every optimist wants to become a paragon of goodness, chivalrous exemplars that are protectors of the weak, yet not even superheroes can save them all. It's best to make decisions based around strategic sense, while the needs of the many outweigh those of the few, so do their expense, and when the situation reaches that pivotal point, folk are quick to turn on one another.

Every Bannermane must learn about each other's purpose, it may just save a life later on. A vagabond that makes regular use of the carehouse may hold a background in jury-rigging, or residents of the bone orchard may have something to skirt misfortune. So stop and listen every once in awhile, young brass and petticoats never quite know when certain counsel may come in handy. That arrogant priest preaching on the village corner may appear crazy at first, but maybe once patrons delve past her messages of worship and doom, they find a silver lining. There are those who could gain a piece of wisdom around the topic of whipporwick. Not always though, sometimes they are just poor and rattled vagrants that have conceded under the stress- but now they know, that's something they weren't quite sure of before!

There are those rugged folk who regularly throw themselves in harm's way, wayfaring travelers who navigate the fiercest of what the old world has to offer, yet always seem to come out on top. Travelers must heed their instruction first, likely that these lessons might be especially worthwhile.

Edmund Redmyne tugs at the fringes of William's sleeve, pulling him aside for a strict, one-sided conversation. The hunter has taken notice of Glennitch's untimely passing, and the boy's gloomy reaction.

"Let this be ah lesson to ye," the huntsman proclaims, "the dead straddle their latest keepsakes. That man has committed to ah series o' bad decisions. That is why 'e lies 'ere, and not ye. I can tell that ye 'ave been crafted with sterner stuff. 'Eed these words, just as I did alongside my father, all those years ago. Even when faced with the worst circumstances, dontcha take for granted that one, mocking fact: that yer still alive- breathin' at that. Ye must move forward no matta the cost. One day ye'll feel the faint in your legs, they'll take to the consistency of jelly, and there shall be nah reprieve. Every fiber shall turn tah rubber, overwhelmed with tantalizin' static. It'll be like lugging cinderblocks, only yer feet leaden as if doused with glue, totin' litter and everythin' else that's been left behind. In that moment, ye'll feel as if ya made some mistake. Could it be vigor, or the ichor that flows through yer furnace? Nah I say. Now, if yer gonna go dancin' with the devils and dwell on the past, embrace those certain experiences- it's crucial. When ye trip, take a tumble; wheneva ye fault, live ah lil'. Dwell on these moments, because when all seems lost, they'll remind you of the gratuities in this world. It's when we forget these lessons, that these chronicles tend to lose themselves; 'cause when you stop, you die."

"'Liam my boy charity-case, or whateva I should call fellas who are this sloppy, n' require ah stiff kick in the rear-end. This is yer wake-up call! Ye need tah start gettin' serious, 'specially if ye'd wish tuh remain 'mong those who survive. So hoard, conserve yer resources, neitha fret nor strain tah unnecessary exertions- refuse the rogue ferryman's call tuh board."

"I do not possess any desire tah die, oh 'onored 'ost. I am not o' the mad sort, yet I will not stand idly by while those 'round mah perish," William pronounces apologetically. "If these folk desire warmth, then I will be the one tuh light the kindlin' n' fan the flames; when those are in need of nourishment, I shall strike at beasts readily. Asylum? Then these arms are obliged tuh shake the stick at god!"

"Hmm, 'ow very noble of ya. Some worthy sacrifice may earn ye ah footnote 'fore ye know it." The breakneck-connoiseur flaunts his assembly of scars, "Those mercantile dossiers make legends known, 'specially for feats, whomeva may lift ah mountain or force that Mad Rivah tah flow once more. Tell me, 'ave ye split records lately? 'Ave ye committed any acts worthy of 'igh regards?"

"To be 'ad, I ain't doin' this for the recognition. I'm just ah ratha regular guy, or as the people of antiquity used to say, an average Joe. Nothin' special 'bout 'em, the goldbands shouldn't- or wouldn't, invest in mah triumphs, and whom the beauty queens won't grant a second glance. Edmund-Mundie may I call ye, whom is by nah means an earnest lad, we're all in the same boat, treadin' the same waters that are these white wastes. While I may roll with the punches, I dare-say don't get discouraged by 'em, they shall not ruin mah, and as muh fatha would say, 'da sword dat breaks in da forge is worth more as two daggas.'"

"May I part with ah bit o' advice?" The Bannermane leans-in, patting young William on his back, "Ye are o' rare stock, best not bleed yerself dry. Remember tah treat yerself first, then your leftovas will be determined as generosity by othas. Watch closely as I prepare for the 'unt. This is my worthy cause!"

He's been polishing his trophy ancillary, an artisanal weapon assembled with wood and twine, some furious carronade that flings barbs, not buckshot.

"This is my 'arpoon launcha- er, I believe Penn engin-ahs describe it as pneumatic," Edmund attempts to brag while tapping the ballast tank tightly-strapped underneath.

It's a grand design, carved to briefly resemble a howling wolf; a butcher that strikes quick, that kills clean. The gun's extraordinary length well-exceeds his own height. It takes one hand at the base to let its volley loose, and the other grips around a leather-bound handle, giving a rough opportunity at aiming the contraption. Armed with three, two-flue harpoon shafts, timber staves topped with cold-rolled steel, these oversized-arrows will still make the bee-line, and pierce bison hide even during the most inclement weather.

He finds that metal projectiles snap at greater distances, it's like hurling some greatsword towards an enemy foes. As javelins with unmatched velocity, these missiles easily tear through the air, warping time and space just before they sink themselves into gamey flesh. The end of the first harpoon is fastened with rope, hundred-feet in fact, granting him the ability to retrieve that very same blade. As the barb finds itself trapped in lucrative prey, a sturdy, brass crankshaft allows him to return his ammo, hauling his immobilized quarry along for the ride.

"Oh my, what ah wicked machine. May I venture with? I must, absolutely must see this launcha in action!"

The wickerwalker explodes into condescending, smug laughter, "Boy-oh, yer not one to lash ah sled, even pitch tents or stitch waterskin! 'Ave ye eva tracked game larga than ah lemmin'? 'Ave ye tanned ah wata moccasin 'fore? Their bite may be deadly, but their 'ide is prized. If ye 'aven't sought for any o' these feats- then no, I wouldn't 'edge any bets. An untrained porta makes for liability on any party."

There are two fellow trappers, who in this moment, make themselves known. Suddenly, these huntsmen clank much more loudly, retrieving gear for an evening expedition. They are leaner, much more gaunt, and unlike their brawny leader, wield recurve bows for the hunt.

Each man is stocking their quiver with screaming arrows, twenty apiece should do. These are projectiles with an ear-shrieking whistle tied to the shaft, that way if they find their mark, they can track prizes through a raging storm. Other than their ranged weaponry, the pair sheathe theater daggers, the Bannermane do-it-all tool that can sever, stab, gut, disembowel, and skin in one go. If there's one thing this town isn't short of, there seems to be a surplus of armaments.

It is safest to travel in trios, that way if a comrade is maimed during an expedition, one person is assigned to carry their brethren, while the other may scout any treacherous terrain ahead.

They travel light, but are well-equipped for the hunt for any beasts grazing across the open expanse. Tracking megafauna, especially caribou is relatively easy, wickerwalkers just follow the mile-wide trail of footprints. However, it's an awfully exhausting chase, the herd doesn't appease predators nipping at their heels. It'll take days to catch-up with stragglers, the bulk of which are elderly, their muscles chew stiff; afflicted with disease, making them extremely weak and likely to cause taint; or unfortunate young, which are too inexperienced, they lose the scent of their mother and make all the wrong turns.

William is taken back by his brunt honesty, and can't help but comment on the wickerwalker's new, shifty-looking acquaintances.

"I wouldn't trust 'em. 'Eh got ah nasty look, prolly pilfer my coinpurse given the chance."

However, this slur does little to dissuade them.

"Oh for sure, these scoundrels will rob ya blind," Edmund discerns.

The trio heads to leave, inciting approach towards the trading post's main entrance.

"Doesn't matta what ye think, though. These men are fluent muskinvarnin, they could catch ah steer's musk n' tan hide by the followin' morn.'"

It takes bravado- truly, they are out the door with nary a glance behind the shoulder. Maybe the wickerwalker gestured a fleeting, goodbye wave, even out of spite, yet it was too swift to truly notice.

The team departs to trail southbound, avoiding the dangerous tracts of lands such as the craglands and glacial mire, instead opting for open expanse. This isn't the usual humbingings, ever since Charlie Mandon cut her losses, they've been unable to tend information from the gamekeeper.

There are three roustabouts spread throughout the Oestergaard, one for each mercantile, and they're all highly politicized. Those of the demesne speaking ill of their superiors may find certain licenses revoked. All hunts and the trophies produced shall be rendered forfeit. The Bannermane lose their way of life, no longer able to sustain themselves, like the rug has been pulled out from underneath them.

They'll either peddle a job underneath someone else, slinging as a cobbler, mending boots and shoes, or suffer real jail-time, kept under lock and key in a barracks barge. This isn't an ordinary debtor's prison, vagrants find themselves chained to the oars, underfed and overworked, rowing until they're nothing but wasted skin and bones. Dreadnaughts are the mercantiles iron-clad, sailing yachts, propelling through the snow by way of wind and fin to hunt great beasts of burden. When facing such punishment at the end of the line, one finds the tunes of a companyman quite hollow. How ironic, the Bannermane preach all about freedom, then are willing subject their underlings to bureaucracy.

There are magnates so exalted that they perch upon gilded thrones. Men who with a wave of their hand, purchase domains that rival empires. They monopolize the very essence of greed, that whenever they wish, goad laymen to pounce on opportunities that themselves so graciously provide. These endeavors frequently bankrupt coffers and entire family fortunes. Possessions amassed over generations often vanish without a trace, sons and daughters pry wallets which only spews cobwebs. Their opinions are thrust as absolute, unerring fact, as a majority of Bannermane have been sucked into their whirlpool of propaganda. Those who cabal in rank and file revel in the freedoms of the few, utterly convinced by crone messages: that their prosperities are also the fellowship's success, and good tidings will trickle down, as they share their wealth with those less fortunate.

They heed the words of those flush in riches, yet poor in character, and urge everyone else to fall in line. Worshipers of divine treasuries believe themselves to be drovers among a flock of sheep, while in reality, they are all lemmings to be snacked upon. In the Oestergaard, defeat is routine, starvation reigns supreme, and those that blame have become mainstream. Given a length of time over the decades, it's a wonder how nothing has improved. Despite ample evidence of the contrary, decent folk venerate magnates in the hope that they too could attain such legendary status.

However this appointment is akin to winning a lottery, and conquering those million-to-one odds through sheer luck of the draw. This begs the question, why worship what they will never become? This isn't a metamorphosis where liberty is guaranteed, and residents hedge much closer to the poverty line than that of a trademark.

Value is subjective, it is banter trawled by icons and stiffs alike, but worth, that's relative to the working man. Vagabonds labor, they are those who put in the hours, struggling to put food on the table, keeping their families safe from impending danger, and most importantly, warm. Maybe they are hexed, unaware of a magik spell cast over them. That's the only explanation as to why men would reward such moot notions.

The gamekeeper's purpose to wickerwalkers may appear rudimentary, they have a unique responsibility: maintaining a map of sorts, a ledger that records game and migrations around the territory. Willing hunters ferry notice to them by way of messenger bird, questing for an expedition, inquiring, registering, and declaring trophies. A gamekeeper distributes the wickerwalker entente, ensuring that livestock are not hunted into oblivion. They occasionally tread in the sense of duty, employing quartermains to deter a bear or wolf pack that threatens their realm, foes that regular hunters wouldn't dare attempt to sway.

Muskinvarnin is a borderspiel lingo coined by caravanhands, the 'language of smells' some folks call it, but the 'art of pungent, lingering odors' would be more truthful. Veblen merchants find it useful to distill aromatic fragrances and perfumes for the Underdark's high society, while exterminators in the trenches below track shadow the stench of gremlins and rats, quelling plague before they have garner prospects, though muskinvarnin has always retained a higher precedent among the frontier.

Miscreants hunt across the pale league, their company guided by maladies that manifest from oily hides to straddle sinuses. The chase is easiest during the bloomtide, when aggressive animals keenly mark their territories.

Those adept to muskinvarnin may sense the whiff of pheromones in the air, it's normally nauseating, although in a perverse way, enticing to them. The reeks produced vary from situation, maybe maturing into auras that are bitter or fetid, these scents enlighten wickerwalkers to what their prey is doing.

The rawest, most recognizable stench is wrought by pure instinct, the mere act of survival causes prized quarry to take flight. Their heart drums, pace quickens, attempting to put distance between them and their naysayer. The snow refuses to cede nor reward efforts, instead leadening their coat, stalling prey in earth's greatest tragedy: an inevitable demise. There's the occasional quarrel as dubious teeth lash towards their hindquarters. Saliva coats their own muzzle, and the victim enters desperate throes. The ground is granted fresh detritus, the creature releases its last supplies of urine and shits themselves. It's all fair game, the difference is that a normal human can smell it within thirty-feet, a muskinvarnin mutant, within thirty-thousand.

"Mayhaps, they'll find flock o' nice, juicy timberfowl? I would settle for some grouse giblets, ah dash o' spice, soaked in creamy brine," William candidly contemplates.

That caribou cut was his first morsel of real food in weeks, as can't live off dried, salted, whatever-mystery-meat-this-is, forever. Small birds are kind enough to keep to themselves, not exactly wanting to be turned into poultry. Spruce grouse nestle in pine groves, far from the havens of the ancient alder carrs and old city. Frequents of the carnival, particularly urchins, love the way sap tends to stick to their feathers, dousing the meat in a treasure trove of earthly delights. Evergreen oils imbue the skin and give it a soft, amber sheen. When pampered over an open flame, the skin seemingly melts away, presenting pieces of poultry that *pops, sizzles* and glistens with charm.

One can't help but wonder, when people delight in their food, what do predators imagine when munching. They pick their teeth with our bones whenever tendons and sinew wrap their ivories. Do they savor their meals? Do they salivate with a mere thought, licking their lips in anticipation as jaws clench around meaty limbs, and the juice that frees itself as they clamp down? Is it more than just plain nourishment? Can they feel flesh pass through their gullet, plunging into the stomach, dissolving in a pit of corrosive acid as brawny meat and tissue is meticulously torn asunder? These thoughts are dangerous affairs, there are plenty of opportunists on the trail who would love to pounce, partaking in human delicacy.

The southern trails are safer than the north grasps, but not safe enough.

Cautious kin have erected waystones to guide their paths, minor retreats, constructed with odd curios and whatever nature has to offer. Each stele is struck in a congregation of staves, boons that bestow blessings and luck. The stone of strength is a lovely oil masterpiece, it depicts a blind tundra terror casually investigating a man's arm. It does not seek vengeance, but that of sustenance, and fastens itself on the closest arm within reach. The sullied canines seek deep, routing arteries and striking marrow. A master of courage, the man isn't worried, and confidently raises their free hand high, ready to strike.

When departing from Bonaventure, coaches may request an excursion at the bluffs. The shrine of judgement lies a few steps above an abandoned inn. Visitors to this open reliquary seek truth, and address their guilt. The booth itself withholds scarce effects, particularly a handwritten, bound manuscript. Its spine is worn, scrawled with the title, 'Yellow Pages.' It's only companion cannot read, a lonely cranium of consequence. The skulls sits atop the book, and features a peculiar eye carved into the center of its brow.

Bannermane are footloose, taking pilgrimage to sites all across the northeast. The Lover's Altar is a prominent landmark, an essential destination for any vagabond ilk. People often leave behind personal belongings, trinkets that are a burden, and bind them to trauma. Thousands of feet trample in joy, ensuring snow is unable to garner stock this holy ground. Numerous pledges of honor and marriage are officiated here, relationships forged at major crossroads. Polyamorous mergers of bonds, family and company take their vows in front of a frame of painted glass. This intricate artwork portrays two chairs, a person lounges in one while sipping from a chalice, as their partner's remains empty.

Campaigns as these influence young'uns for years to come. These ventures are awe-inspiring, a privilege to embark-on, and it's quite reassuring that on the relentless frontier, there are still safe havens, even so few. If scribbles imbue such confidence, one can imagine what words do to the human condition. In traditional borderspiel greeting, siblings palm gently at the other's temple, close their eyes, and bow in adoration until two foreheads touch. They meld cordially, "'ere and now, now until nevah." While two Smithers of kindling find they burn brighter together, the darkness strives for balance, and contorts into something dreadful.

On the fringes of frigid flatlands, Gaard and beyond, a red dog dragoon tours narrowly ahead a burgeoning cloud of flurries. Warded astray with little but bison as company, her stomach heaves in anxiety. "Fasta," she exclaims into the beast's ear, barely eluding the blizzard at bay, "Must go fasta!" The ice gives way, collapsing under the extreme weight of hind hoof. No one is accused of fault when the severing of tendons eclipses the cacophony of crackling rime. This unlucky duo is pressed into a tumble until beauty and brute collapse into a heap. The dragoon screams at the heavens in angst, cursing this fatal misstep. Immortals mock her vain shouts, wiping their hand through the sky to advance the storm, they sure love to watch mortals squirm.

The situation at Mad River Junction is ever-dire, and the residents dream-up various escapades and treks of note, all dumber and further deranged than all those that have been thought-up before. Visionaries bring the wickerwalker's posse to light, in a mere half-hour, the outfit has surpassed every hurdle laid before them. The outskirts of the Junction are jumbled with wrecks, the first thousand-feet are perilous, liable to grant injury, and boots may be impaled by pinkie-sized splinters. As structures succumb to the sheer weight of snow, their lumber and scarce contents continue to shape the landscape into something befitting of a battlefield, an appalling no-man's land. Myriads of men have perished beneath the waves, their only remainder is a memorial constructed of hazards: leather caps, feathery hats, or fingers frantically grasping towards the sky, grisly hands undoubtedly tied to a corpse just beneath. The march of the graveseeking trappers encourages others to try once more, because in spite of what has proceed, they were able to depart with immediate danger ease. After all, it should be a cakewalk, the trail is nearly a straight line out of town, so why is this journey fraught with struggle?

There have been several foolhardy struggles since the Mandonmen fled the coop. The first band of residents strapped on their snowshoes, and made considerable distance before a foul mist descended upon them. Swirling, smoky-grey vapors plagued their campaign for minutes, then dissipated into dawn's early light. Five far-flung silhouettes now dot the distant horizon, figures that haven't moved for days. A second grievous attempt followed not long thereafter, Rochester the wainwright's fledglings plundered his unfinished, personal garage project. Overlooking the necessary rigmarole, they charter a coach leaden with cargo and passengers. Not long into their journey, the wood beams splintered, and scattered the troop. Most of the remains were pulverized, then set upon by packsnow, and swiftly sunk under white tides. As the bulk of the sled fled into the ground, those unfortunate tugging at the reins were lashed by their own ropes, and doomed along with it.

The final group to brave the trek was Glennitch's brood, brought low by a vicious and unseen sky-bound predator. Mad River Junction is situated in the middle of large, extraordinarily flat expanse, therefore the remaining residents profusely watch those who leave. There have been other departures in-between, but these were mostly lone navigators. There are probably around twenty or so- still living of course, that have surpassed no-man's land, crossing the all-encompassing steppe of ice and snow. Frontiersmen leave for worthwhile opportunities, waning smaller and smaller until they are simply amorphous blobs vanishing towards serene vistas.

Jeremiah approaches to seek patronage, and settles down next to William, awkwardly bumbling into his sore shoulder. Their gazes contemplate upon Edmund's journey, that hunter venturing closer towards a copse of timberland, like ants delving into an avenue of lushly evergreen bundles of paintbrushes. The author, Anders can't refrain from commentary, his passion for drama stemming from the stages at CAPAh Express, and peddles his usual bumbling nonsense.

"Corporal Bannin' n' da Road tah Redemption, our 'ero is thrust in-tah ah world of 'onest threats, as 'e contends with da monsters dat threaten da rivah gates. This theata production 'eadlines Ballard Sterlin' as Corporal Bannin', also featurin' otha intrepid exploras, like Farrell da Bard n' Quill Davenport as supportin' cast… it takes ah village? *Hmm*- nah, perhaps, just muh-be. Ar' Bard n' Quill even da right actors tah cast? Wut do ye tink, culd it work? I shuld sell da rights tah dis story, gots tuh be worth at least three marks oar two."

The boy Jones never considered himself to be indulgent of culture, and could care less about any performance writing. He responds with a cautious, "'Eh," knowing that it wouldn't affront the man's desire.

"Wut makes dis ah so-so remarkable- such ah phenomenal exploit is da stretch. Gotta be nearly two leagues from 'ere," knocking William on the chest and then his own, pointing to the two of them, "to der. It's an incredible distance on foot, even giants wuld 'ave trouble, one specific 'alf-breed in particular."

The author must've been a performer in another life, an affinity for the stage would lead Jeremiah to the Giles Carnival in good ole Bonaventure.

"Oh!" William cries, how his mind has been wandering, now realizing that this scryer is signaling about their wickerwalker, Edmund Redmyne's expedition as he continues to prattle on.

"Dey culdn't 'ave gone north, der's nothin' on da lake save a couple o' abandoned shanties. If dey travelled towards da Westergaard, der'd be plenty o' trenches tah vault, tarpits tuh mire 'round- seems like stressful work. Nah one wuld root to Bonaventure, hikin' the trail east on foot- sah-suh-successfully I mean. Da ancient river is allurin', yet no shelta for the weary. Does otters der are ruthless, 'ave ye ever been mugged by an otta? Right, dat's wut I thought too, sounds like nonsense 'til it happens to ya. Yes, ya-huh indeed, roamin' southwardly was da smart decision, ah wise route tuh take."

"No guarantee, sir. That party's out searchin' for fare, they'll be back soon, lest we 'unga."

"Oh, boy-yo, dat's where ye prolly wrong. If I was any younga, these legs wuld take me der, but nevah back 'gain. Smarta choice wuld be tah run."

They idle for an unprecedented amount of time, and the day's waning light ebbs to that of a flush magenta glow. The already meager beams of sunshine that pierce the intimidatingly thick, roiling cloud coverage patrol sporadically. Dusk approaches like some stark afterthought, a period of solemn reflection, the polar opposite to yesterevening's boisterous festivities. This morning's activity kept the trading post quite lively, heaping jaunts with the townspeople, and while it hasn't been a splendid skipping tune, this momentum is overly-satisfying.

William's company has seen reams of familiar faces take their chances and flee, streaming from the exchange over the course of the day, retreating onto the plains. These residents flee from bad omens, considering that, once a glimmering beacon of hope, the medical ward is now a sanctioned morgue. Vernon Waulbellows and his temporarily hopeful leadership have made that difficult designation, ordering kin to leave the expired, determining it's not worth the difficult manner transporting them to the resident mortuary cult. Those townspeople that remain commune for a wake, taking careful note of those not in attendance, whether that be for hell or high waters.

Without the essential supplies for a candlelight vigil, they burn their thoughts, prayers and memories, reliving personal encounters with those deceased: all those heartfelt moments that they laugh, dreamt together, and cried together. Austerlaund cranes along an edge of partition, using brute strength to knock aside timber she had once fastened shut. They'll need to barricade the adjoining hall following the reception, but these openings in the wall will flood the room in a frigid freeze, preventing the corpses' eventual decay. Her imposing frame dominates the scene, splintering planks of wood as if they were thin dowel rods. Now that William has seen the worst of her incredibly eldritch power, he imagines the arch lector exhibiting her portfolio.

"Look 'pon my work n' shudda. Be 'fraid, be very 'fraid," the thudding of boots to hardwood floor jolts him back to reality, and the boy finds himself frantic just being in the practitioner's vicinity.

These deaths have been entirely avoidable, humbling experience with only one conceivable bright side, that William won't need to compete for a place to sleep. In desire of solace, away from the usual anxieties that encumber crowds, he best believes to lie his head alone tonight, and retreats to the showroom for rest. He is distracted during the commute, plagued by a sort of dastardly brain fog.

The days' stressful incidents have been taking their toll, tugging at his conscious, and the very morals of his soul. He waltzes along without much care, passing each of the sore spots, whose cobwebs used to feature an entire transportation enthusiast's museum paradise. Rochester and his volunteers will finish their work on the sled, they have to, it's only a matter of time and a question of resources.

At the farthest end of the room's demesne, there bides a condensed, single-person carriage, a certain, long-forgotten display that was shuttered and cordoned-off with little respect. Instead of a traditional greeting, when William tugs at the cab's door handle, and shortly after, the entire piece tears free.

He drops the bar and explains to himself, "Tis just ah model after all," in some vain effort to relax his frustration. Following careful consideration, the only other route inside is through, and vandalism will become a necessity.

The boy Jones positions his elbow, takes aim, readies in anticipation for the sure and sudden jolt of pain. With an exerting grunt, he strikes at the coach's sheet of glass. William was expecting a flurry of shards, not for the window to lift from its frame as one solid piece. A transparent, rectangular pane now flies fast at the carriage floor, and upon impact, let's out a jarring, cartoonish *twang-twang-twang* as the whole sheet undulates uncontrollably.

"Plastic, o' course. Who would've thunk it?"

He emits an exhaustive sigh, now realizing that he'll have to reach in, pry for an inside latch and yank the door with his body weight. It's not even a rewarding enterprise, the seat is an obviously uncomfortable faux leather, crude, poor-grade hide stitched together, filled with copious, bouquet grass stuffing. William yearns for a decent night's sleep, lying flat on his stomach at first, cradling face into the pit of his elbow. Unfortunately for the boy, his guilt has begun to catch-up with him, and he rests with one eye open, weary that the crinkling of leather and the creaking ribs are the ghost of Glennitch paying visit. Shadows animate around the room, mocking him over his droll inability to protect others.

Strangely enough, William still ventures into a stupor. This slog of events have been demanding, arduous tasks, drawing him further and further into the bog. Today's recent events have twisted his heart from vibrant sanguine to a lifelessly dull grey. A normal mindset of optimism and enthusiasm has fouled, the factoids of his daily life are recited with emotionless exclamations.

The torrents of snowdrift that pelt against William's evening do little to quell feelings of impending doom. He harkens the melody, an intense, fervent tune that generates the thunder of drumbeats. These aren't the usual droves, this is the big un' as they say, which fall in clumps as large as bison hooves.

An all-consuming downpour reigns upon the trading post's dilapidated rooftop, which demonstrates signs of stress, the sheet metal buckles and the rafters sag a head or two. Each snowflake meticulously settles and composes, biding its time, waiting for some fault, the copper frail breaking point. William confides in thought, that if the roof were to yield under the engulfing precipitation, the carriage may yet provide comfort as a provisional coffin.

Nevertheless, it's safer inside, because in the definite throes of midnight, the distant shapes of frozen, contorted human bodies that lie on the outskirts of town begin to fall through the ice. However, that is impossible, and frankly it's too far to be sure.

The temperatures have always been furious, a coercive, oppressive tendency that builds rime on the skin, but ignores the vulnerability of liquid fuel such as alcohol and kerosene. No matter how much kin may praise the sun, not even the warmest bloomtide summers will dent it. There must be something out there, a warrant more nefarious than Nana Nature. If these disappearances were to be witnessed, citizens would clang the bells in terror. Something must have took them, enough of a nightmare that quartermaines would be scared straight, and freeze with fright. What manner of beast would feast on permafrost? Inches of hoar straddles those corpses, these beasts feature fangs that pierce beneath, dining on the ice-cold ichor beneath.

VI

RUBBING SALT IN THE WOUND

The boy Jones awakens during the early morning in a serious disposition, a combination of stupor and stupid state of being before the crack of dawn: profusely tired, frazzled and much more worse for wear, almost as if he has been lumbering through limbo, treading nothingness. Still as of late, these temporary sleeping arrangements haven't been help, the crick in his back is all too extensive, and each shoulder blade snaps into place. His eyelids crack open, just barely, to a certain methodical quivering of his own two boots, startling him enormously. William had been hidden away for the length of night, and good ole Mandel Haggerton found cause to go exploring, and root him out. The cordwainer was especially concerned for his friend, watching as William chokes himself and stops breathing during his nap, so an earnest lad wakes him with upmost urgency.

"Oi boy, ye worry me greatly. 'Aven't been 'ere 'fore. Why'd ye 'ave tah go off and 'ide in ah place like this? That wallpaper is disastrous."

William contrives a smile and attempts to speak, however only emits an unruly cough. There's a distinct lack of saliva in his mouth and throat, as he tossed and turned, drooling all throughout the night, its usual contents have instead been smeared around the cab.

The Haggertons were once an industrious ilk, operating a burgeoning mercantile amid scores of Bonaventure warehouses. Father and son produced footwear for all shapes and sizes, taming iron machines to mold and press their work. Replacing laces in favor of clasps, each boot was so finely threaded that they became waterproof. Together they coined the term, Peaterbricks, as pioneers pioneers always enjoy a good bit of trademarked style, especially those Veblen goods, and calling them Haggertons doesn't seem to roll of the tongue. These shoes became synonymous with reliability, better than the standard clogs, and essential gear of day laborers. Knowledge of the brand quickly outpaced their abilities, and attracted the guise of far greater proprietors. Lady Callie was one such figure, surpassing her interests as a magnate capitalizing on a fur-skinning monopoly.

She merged into the family through name alone, inheriting their business as matriarch, and adopting the Hagger ilk. To her, their two-generation success story was simply another enterprise for her umbrella, another seal on a rich racket. Callie was no stranger to backwater dealings, but her frequent ballroom brawls attracted lesser men. These riveting affairs drew flies, there were those attempting to settle old debts as others siphoned off the situation; regardless of their reasons, a terrible company descended upon the Peaterbrick depot. The irritating crowd stirred like vicious bloodhounds, frenzied at the scent of money, the type of people who lost a hedging bet, but decided to take an arm and leg on their way out in a petty act of impromptu revenge. The father had a callous personality, and sacrificed his namesake in defense of Lady Callie. Taking stock of their foolhardy decisions left their boy Jones cursed and thrown out of the family. Once heir to father's pride, Mandel was one of many coerced upon new lands, consequentially stumbling through the Riviera and into Mad River Junction. He's not an ordinary character, there's certainly more than meets the eye.

"What? Got that mind for design. I'm ah craftsman not ah magician, I 'ave that basic sense of schemin' n' grasp on composition- those colors clash! Ginger on sage- egads! Why would I expect anythin' else?"

This ruse brings the boy into a comical uproar. It takes a half-dozen hawking quips before William's language becomes somewhat decipherable.

"I am gettin' quite sick of yer banta, 'ag-man!"

"Ye have no room to complain, I go blind everytime mah poor eyes glance 'pon yer face. 'Ave ye looked in ah mirror lately?"

Mandel offers his hand, a friendly gesture to tow William out of the coach. The two of them start prancing along the floorboards within a moment's notice, dancing a merry jig to shake off the widespread drowsiness. They are quick to denote farewells towards daily chores, and stride for the door, marching with fancy at the chance to eat. Amidst an adventure out past the showroom's hallway, Mandel whispers into the boy's ear. William's expression immediately sours, their once cheery tenors are contorted with irritating thorns.

"Let mah tickle yer lobes for ah sec'. Call muh crazy, but I thought I 'eard a voice in the night. Brushed it off as the brewin' storms, wind whistlin' through a fissure in the window n' like. Wasn't 'fore long that I 'eard it elsewhere too. Lil' tiny scrapes 'cross the deckin', almost as if I caught a lemmin' burrowin' inside. This voice 'neath the floorboards called mah name. Thought I was hallucinatin'- o' course, wouldn't be the first time. If it ye didn't help earlier, I'd still be stuck frequentin' herbal remedies. Whetha or not it was actually real, still clear 'nough that I gripped the edge of muh blanket and stared at the same spot o' room for minutes. Then I heard it mutta 'Mandel' 'gain, 'Mandel' n' that's when I knew somethin' was wrong, that this wasn't natural. 'Gain and 'gain, it'd call tah me, until these spouts filled breadth o' room. It told muh malevolent things, that I wished ill and harm on othas-"

"That can't be true, Haggerton, ye must be in err. I'd brush it off as sickness and stress, we're all 'avin' ah difficult time copin'. This could even be withdrawal symptoms, mayhaps. Come now, let us join company once more. Bannermane find their stride togetha!"

William never once thought of himself in this precarious position, offering counsel for a dear friend. He finds the circumstance enlightening, yet troubling: he is not a wise man, and often prone to mistakes.

"Yes- yes, I do believe yer right."

Yesterevening's feign weather has deemed further excavations impossible, nearly everyone is bunkering indoors. The passageways ahead are full of commotion, that whenever they can spare, promptly jury-rigging materials that they have scavenged.

Kin of the Junction are an ingenious lot, they lapse on the ground, assembling various contraptions to aid their quest. One strings together spans of timber scraps, crafting a ten-foot pole they'll thrust into the packsnow, gauging its depth in the likely event they fall through. Another empties a slender tube for scrolls, carefully rolling a collection of local charts from around the river's edge. Nobody would give these maps up in a pinch, other than the carriages, these simple scraps of paper are the most valuable items in the entire Junction- paper trademarks be damned, not even a written check for ten-million could sway a vagabond. The dead have forfeited remainders of loot, including savory linens they were once bundled-up in. Marlene Hinds works frantically, interweaving these threads, stitching bedrolls and fleeces into makeshift rope in a pinch. It seems that only folks residing at the caravan post are those working on the sled or their own equipment, and those exhausted, nearing the brink of death.

"'Ere mate, take these 'andouts."

It has been a while since they've last eaten, and Mandel offers his cohort a generous bounty of preserved birch sap embellished with jacket lint. Other residents around the Junction have kept busy hoarding drugs and paraphernalia to make the coming days a slight degree more tolerable. They'll snack on dried healing herbs, enthralling alcoholic tonics, and whatever mind-numbing agents have been spreading around.

The two finally catch-up to the main body of activity, sighting the journeymen masterpieces, madly masticating their chewing gum all the way. Several thick, hawser-sized, leather-bound moorings extend from the front of each coach, intending to bind beasts of burden to tow their vessel, instead are pulled by half-a-dozen people, apiece. These vagabonds flaunt their soles in the banded boards below, damaging lacquer that once brightly for scores of visiting caravan traders.

"One, two- 'eave, 'o," they call out. "'Gain, one more time!"

They yank in unison, lugging the three carriages completely through the front doors with not much resistance until the wooden siding clings to the vestibule as if they don't want to go out into the cold, scraping the finished veneers of each coach. Rochester's red racing stripes have been cruelly whisked away. Oh, if sir Bywater were here, that stoic laborer would've made this project a simple chore, toting the entire haulageway in less than a jiff.

The three premier carriages halt in front of Charlie Mandon's glorified statue. The iron-wright, Vernon Waulbellows rapidly approaches, heaving a quarter cask above his head. He sets it to rest, say tenpace from the lead vessel, motioning for residents to come and take a gander.

"Friends, allies n' comrades, once we were strangas, only now we move mountains. Aye, 'ere's cheers to small comforts, n' yer kin!"

Upon these momentous words, Vernon snatches the rim of a growler-sized barrel, and flings the whole container, timber, fittings and all to ruin against the coach's clubbed figurehead. It splinters, although not by much, to where the butt of the keg is now a gaping rupture. Of course, it's purely a symbolic gesture, they ran the cask dry during the course of revelry. The smith had to indulge in christening the vessel, otherwise he wound the pride of all like-minded greybeards.

The remainder of Bannermane kin refuse to match Vernon's enthusiasm, and there are several in the crowd who find his optimism misplaced. To these townspeople, this isn't freedom, and a free voucher to safety, this episode signals the otherworldly trek they will need to take, and without bison steer, it will be a journey directed with scraps and strife, causing untold many of companions to not grace the following day. However, they should seek accomplishment from this ordeal. Certain scholars will record this sacrifice, and recognize that not all is for naught.

If the three Bannermane lords of the mercantiles saw this dedication, they would be overwhelmed, ripe with envy. This is the northern expanse's first independent caravan in decades, vagabonds that may roam wherever they wish, and to any untold respites that the wind guides them.

The intrepid literature duo, scribe Rylie Hess and skald Arabella Gaberdine, stand side-by-side as grateful partners. Together, they sport the charcoal tomes, a recording of Mad River Junction's meager existence. Rylie totes the massive manuscripts on a piece of plywood, ferried them right up to the gate of the lead car, while Arabella loads them. They will travel alongside those sick, injured and maimed in safety of the coach. Austerlaund beckons these individuals to come forward for a final examination, and right to board, aiding the feeble few who have yet to perish.

As the minutes ween to an hour, every inside passenger seat has been filled, and the settlers flock to sit atop the carriage, saving their strength. The fit are randomly drawing straws to determine who will help tow the line.

Mandel pulls a longer lot, ensuring that he won't need to stretch his legs until the second shift.

Vernon pleas with materially-minded folk to leave their personal belongings behind, lest these effects leaden their escape and overload the carriage, casually explaining the details of weight distribution and gestures vaguely to the debris among the outskirts of town. He imparts that they can always come back, as the freeze will preserve any familial accoutrement.

The ironwright questions Austerlaund about her motives, and the status of her recovering pet project. The arch lector kneels to Vernon's height, informing him of a certain doctor-patient confidentially that she would only dare breach to a superior captain. The blacksmith is one such trooper, an authority, worthy to redeem a soul for.

"Osbourne Bullheaded is just as stubborn as 'is name suggests. Ignore

'em- a lil' out of sorts, 'cause 'e has elected tah stay 'hind. Save us ah drain
on resources, I say. The errant believes that 'e'll never fully recovah, n' 'as
contracted disorda, plague 'pon the brain."

"Dat's no good. 'Ave you 'eard anythin' from that wicker-sort eitha, yet?
We were expectin' 'im 'fore we stave-off. Not like Edmund tah be somethin'
o'ver 'alf-ah-day late. Can't be waitin' 'round, need tah run Riviera tuh
'venture by yester-year!"

The residents in the Junction have grown accustomed to these harsh
tendencies, but this is outrageous. William will not sit idly by while
townspeople turn on one another, surrendering vagabonds to the domain
of kingdom come. This request is the sole reason they are lost among the
wilderness, if it weren't for the townspeople and their unhinged, gluttonous
feast, they wouldn't have need to dispatch a hunting party.

William is disgusted by this notion, and by also abandoning the
paladin at the trading post, these residents have set a new low. After all
that suffering, all that tribal-like human sacrifice, the knight's plight will be
simply ignored, and his life forfeit as well. It's ruthless, and immoral.

As such, it's the tendency of better men to draw a line in the snow, a
barrier that defines them, something that separates their ethics from folk
who seek to do ill on others. This is his line, this is where he'll take a stand.
Even if they cannot rescue the wickerwalker, his company, or the knight,
at the very least, it is their sacred duty to try. William is beaming at this
revelation, succumbing to a sense of revolutionary pride, contrary values to
what the Bannermane empire has instilled in brood like him. Yet another
opportunity to build his character is squandered, for greater evils lie dead
ahead.

The commotion in front of the trading post has drawn flies, guiding a
handful of miscreants to their safe harbor. They reside in the ruins of the
degrading promenade, dwelling in squalor. Now, their tide has swelled
to rank of two score, forty pairs of eyes scrutinizing across the courtyard.
Gazing not just at opportunity, but a means to escape their horrid
destitution.

A solitary figure emerges from the rubble and strides forth, shrouded
in a trench coat whose twain tails drag all through the snow, smearing
his footprints. He paces confidently forward, adjusting his collar, and
escorts his right hand to grip a pommel that sits astride his waist. Another
unruly character breaks formation, immediately tripping from a partition
disheveled with debris, struggles to collects himself, and bolts to join
his leading commodore. It's the Brothers Jack, that unscrupulous duo

that William had the pleasure of meeting earlier. They have gathered an entourage of followers, remnants of the Crooked Men's local chapter, and sudden criminal vagrants.

"Well-el-el, lookie at wut we got 'ere. Looks as if ye lot went n' did all dat 'ard work for us. Thank ye kindly, we'll be relievin' ye of dem sleddin' ships naw. I'm commandeerin' dees vessels in da name o' Brotha-ruhs Jack, thank ya for all dem work."

Brace Billhook closes the gap, treading from a hundred feet to just ten. He asserts a sly, condescending smile, row upon row of jagged, sharpened ivories that seem to dance whenever he commands breath. This is the first time William has graced his stench, a morbid cross between raw meat and decay. A grizzled veteran could tell you that's the reek of human flesh emanating from his bowels, though it's better if urchins didn't know. It's crazy to conceive that merely a few days ago, these two siblings were struggling to board their own freighter caravan, and left in the lurch. Brace's fraternal twin, Boot not only catches up with his brother, but surpasses him, barreling into the closest object, poor Jeremiah Anders. William could hear is shoulder give-out with an unmistakable *crunch*, and sprints to his aid, putting himself between the author and what further damage Boot presents.

"Ah!" A voice exclaims, "Ye 'gain, I ra-ruh-recognize ya!"

Brace kneels down until his mug comes face to face with the boy Jones, taunting him surely. He thrusts his index and middle finger into William's own, very sore shoulder.

"Dot I auld ye off once 'fore, feelin' brave, dontcha? Yer lucky mah bruvver is wit me, 'cause othawise I ain't one tah be dat mer-cee-full type. One muh slip-up, and I won't be so genny-rous," Brace belligerently beguiles, periodically breaking eye contact to shake his head disapprovingly.

"Sod off now. Ye dat's right, go on and git."

As each jab prods deeper and deeper into William's abdomen, he is literally forced from Jeremiah's side. This series of semi-punches careen him back onto his two feet, retreating backwards a dozen paces or so until his back lands at the study of the nearest carriage sled, and he tumbles, sending Brace Billhook into a hysterical fit.

Austerlaund roars to attention, a mother goose protecting her gaggle, "Petty fools!"

At first they couldn't spot her silhouette among the audience, a monstrous form, rearing to full height. The Crooked Band is terrified, the

Brothers Jack especially, as they've heard the rumors, and of course tossed them aside, calling it fake news.

"'Alf-giant, der ain't no such ting," Brace used to infer, summing the guise up to his brother's innate antics. Now is the time for their repentance.

Boot cowers without delay, quivering in almost a fetal, nonsensical position, no match for her might. On the other hand, Brace keeping alongside the namesake billhook stowed at his hip, counters her aggression with matching ferocity. At this point, the remainder of vagrants pour from the ruins helter-skelter, seeing this escalation as their sole chance to board. These Crooked Men surge forward, weaving their way around the encounter like a horde of rats, raiding vermin that inherently trample kin, lurching at peoples' totes, and whip Austerlaund into a frenzy.

Normally the iconic calm amid the storm, she is the residing voice of reason. Now that signature trait is detained in the furthest recess of her mind, the mystic may only fantasize supreme acts of vengeance. At that moment, a primordial rage awakens unlike anything the world has ever seen. She has failed members of the Junction before, but not this time, not again, the head priestess promises.

Austerlaund powers ahead, taking two strides forward, and seizes a bulk of the nearest criminal's torso, whom stares wide-eyed in disbelief. Austerlaund graces the foe with a swift demise, careening a closed-fist towards his cap with inhuman force. The helmet of her victim abruptly snaps into several fragments while his head plunges downwards, compressing itself into the depths of his bowels like an accordion, complimented by one last, dreadful-sounding, guttural wheeze.

Guh-ah. The stranger's clothes are thoroughly soaked in visceral fluids, her hand covered in bits and gibs of brain.

These burglars possess no qualities beyond intimidation, and are visibly shaken, their every nerve routed. While the lingering Crooked Men are frozen in terror, she takes delight in seizing another vagrant, and briskly hurling him with all her might. This chosen knave immediately becomes another dismembered corpse when his trajectory strikes the monument of Charlie Mandon. Several limbs make impact on the brass, collapsing the opus into a mess of twisted metal. The human body is fragile, a malleable form in which to vent her frustrations.

Those remaining in the vicinity induce haste, aching as body parts are strewn to the ultimate span of promenade. Her gaze turns towards those pilfering the residents, misappropriating the Junction's meager supplies. These criminals are swift to discern that there are not enough obstacles in the way, and how easily the mystic may traverse open ground.

She slowly shambles ahead, maintaining eye contact on these soon-to-be victims, her head completely still and unnerved, it's like watching a predator work. The ailing highwayman bid retreat, only their steps backward are met with a wall of carriages. Out of desperation, they furiously struggle to fling open a door, wrapping their hands around the leg of a convenient resisting passenger, attempting to pull out a person, and cower within the coach.

The townspeople dare not fight these invaders, fearful that their movement would attract Austerlaund's misdirected attention, as if her unquenchable bloodlust cannot identity friend from foe. They remain as quiet as field lemmings caught looting the grain store.

As Brace Billhook's plans begin to fall apart, he quickly realizes that he must act, or these carriages will soon be damaged beyond repair. The acting captain is by no means a learned man, yet understand that these impending consequences will strand his troop at the Junction, where they risk being torn apart one by one. He ponders a series of drastic actions, measures that no normal man would have the guts to contemplate.

Brace unleashes his weapon against the tender throats of those nearby, carving meat and systematically slaying all of Austerlaund's medical entourage, except that of young Braithwaite, whom he takes hostage. Eager to end the ensuing conflict, the impudent rogue presses the sharpened end of his blade at her jugular, churning crimson atop a pile of corpses. She offers no resistance, and painstakingly mimics a calm attitude while meticulously deliberating what to dread more, her captor or once dear mentor.

While they need the caravans intact, the Crooked Men also require an engine to drive their means of transportation. They need her, 'Austerlaund the iron horse' they'll call her. Brace clamors with the blast of a howling steam pipe.

"Step right off, right now, right now! Dis is yer only warnin'. Do as I say oar she'll be needy o' welfare. Feel me?"

The sharpened fin slides easily into Braithwaite's skin, raking a thin sliver of royally red nectar to the surface, a stream of strawberry glaze that seeps into the pools at their feet.

Austerlaund hesitates, rattling her head in disbelief, and finally forfeits. Her hand releases the collar of a very lucky vagrant, one jerk who sneeringly smirks. She smacks the crown of the closest carriage in exasperation, startling that knave who ducks underneath to flee and wallops his head upon one of the runner rods.

If the priestess was merely normal-sized, the Crooked Men would kick her into submission.

"Do ye fear death?" Boot Billhook berates, "Lay down giant, so dat I may take dis hack and lodge it firmly in yer cranium."

Her sight tilts upward, ignoring the idle threat and staring at the sky as if begging for absolution. Only the immortals may hear this arch lector's plea, and they bestow something devious. Her eyes fade in flaxen glaze, like she's taken something strong. In the moments that follow, Austerlaund pays heed to William, parting sage advice.

"I've scried the celestials may still yet guide ya, fool. Ye 'ave been given many ah reason tah doubt their wisdoms. Remember, ye wouldn't be important 'nough othawise. Follow in the path they 'ave laid out. Praise the clouds, n' good luck."

The boy Jones is slighted by this one-way conversation, both by their forty-foot distance from one another, and this particular dialogue reeks with prophecy. Bannermane have many a reason to fear the words of those akin to magik, weavers, seers and mystics. Those highwaymen plundering the caravan coaches for seats laugh at his demise, garnering the attention of gods is often prelude to demise, a magnet of chaos to curse.

Disregarding her connection to things ordinary folk would consider holy, the brigand is slighted by her obvious disregard to him, and unsheathes a theater dagger. It takes considerable effort to wield, the weapon is comprised of heavy metal, suddenly weighing-down his grip. Instead of thrusting the knife into her ankle and filleting skin, Boot holds his breath, takes aim, and crudely launches the knife far above. No threat at all, the butt of this dagger lands squarely at her torso, and simply slides down. The blade carries a much deadlier delivery on the way down, causing the ignorant fool to leap out of the way, narrowly missing a strike to his own person. It's extraordinary that nature's first instinct is not to think about the repercussions.

Enraged after the fact, Boot cleverly prepares another blade. It is a leaden cutlass, never once cleaned, and stained with the cure of a thousand rabbits. He lashes out at the nearest victim in a show of superiority. Poor Mandel, no one could react quick enough.

Spectators have clued into the mystic, staring at her actions as if there stands an effigy to the dark gods. Only following the sudden flurry of footsteps and crunching of snow does Mandel's eye grace that of his immediate attacker, hardly emitting a retort.

He urges at the brigand, "No, stop-stop, ya don't need to do this," before the vagrant's steel runs him through.

The intestinal lining of the cordwainer's stomach is punched by the foe's bacterial-ridden cutting tool, and Boot takes one stride back, then yanks his cutlass to the side, severing an excessive portion of abdomen and liver. Warm tinges of putty splatter against fresh snowfall, as if freeing a paintbrush from a cup, and whipping each bristle of any residual water. Mandel deliriously clutches for a piece of metal that no longer resides in his person. The lusty, warm aroma of gristle melts the plush of pack down to permafrost.

It isn't an eye for an eye when the victim's two ganders lapse into the back of skull, the life drains from their body, and they keel over motionless. Mandel expires rather momentarily with no screams of agony, dying in shock is a small mercy. This newly-minted corpse lands flat on its back, the palms of each hand cover in copious tinges of scarlet fever, censoring the gaping wound.

While brutality is nothing new, this shocking curtain call is still subject to a heated debate. It is common for the congregation of vagabond and vagrant to become visibly distraught, lose their composure, and suffer from emotional break-down in the face of death. The Crooked Men are frankly disgusted by the murder, as they are privy to gore, and aren't the usual lot to participate in bloodshed. However, the Brothers Jack are accustomed to it.

The frontier mercantiles, specifically those flying the Mandonmen banner, are enlightened by acts of guttural betrayal. It's their only method for rising through the ranks, promotions don't come soon enough, and no one willingly retires. To them, only the strong survive. They bear no restraint, sacking what they desire on a whim, and thrive when razing property to hell. Charlie Mandon revels in competition, fans the flames of adversity so that those may make themselves known. This icon flaunts kin to cater, believing that the weak belong below their boot heel.

Brace Billhook lands a shilling blow, placing his fist squarely into the foot of his brother's jaw, demonstrating his keen love affair for fighting. He doesn't condemn the death of this local cordwainer, just that it derails their mission, and may prevent the half-giant mystic from obliging to their demands.

These Crooked Men was once family to the residents of Mad River Junction: once being the key-word. Townspeople on the plains are raised together as quarreling comrades, eager and unruly brothers-in-arms. They brace the same hurtles, and bear the burdens. It is only natural to share their differences, and like children, occasional act on them. Vagabonds often sympathize when those with greater needs pilfer from those who have it grander. On the frontier, the farthest stretch from the sanctuaries of the Underdark, people may commonly lie, cheat, steal, but never murder. Kinslaying is their sacred law, and absolutely unforgivable.

While those among the Crooked Men may appear fed-up to the latest resolution of dire measures, their survival matters more than the morals of any few, dead men. They take to the carriages and have their way, throwing passengers from their seats and returning them to destitution onto the cold, white earth. All it takes is an awkward look, that's just-cause to them, enough of an expression to deport the sorry soul from their chance at escape. Within minutes, most of the Junction's original party has been replaced by these criminals.

Some are considered lucky, particularly the elderly, yet a majority of those actually find this ordeal hexing. Peregrines whom wake up with grey in their hair may want to trade places with someone fresh, more inexperienced to life's pleasures, and wish to grant them the cherished opportunity to survive. Vernon and several other longbeards are held among the coach against their will, knit in the middle of a burly throng like tightly-packed sardines: leather, hide and all. Bountiful bundles of fur take flight, doggedly squeezing away at openings, thwarting carriage doors and seeping through windows.

The ironwright shouts aloud, outcries barely heard over the commotion of crowds, his words muffled by thick, burly coats almost filling mouths with straw.

"Fiends! Our 'ard work for naught. We leave only tah be possessed by animals! Jump-off now if ya wish! I'd flee if I could."

Numerous townspeople turn their heads and bend ears to this noisy, vocal uproar, especially those selfish scissorsmiths who poured their waking hours into renovating these coaches, believing they've earned their seats.

During this entire affair, Austerlaund has been led to the front by manner of swords jabbing her thighs, taking place in lead of Mad River's makeshift caravan. Considering the sacrifice of her entire entourage, she remains baffled over this affair, blindly accepting those whims of beings far greater- they have a plan involving that greenspur, the boy Jones, however obscure at the moment. The priestess provides one or two belts of aggression for posterity, dashing a few steps away in a jest, and belittling the craven while being resentful tied into the reins.

Not appreciative of these antics, there's a petite Crooked Man who could be better described as a beetle, prominently hunched over, maintaining thin, wiry appendages. He possesses a degree in knot-tying, an under-advertised forte in these recent days, and threads two tightly-wound, parallels cords in bowline hitches. This man nearly faints while lifting a couple of cables above his frame, offering these towing lines to their newly-minted Judah Steer.

The bosun's gaze darts to avoid the head priestess, fearing her angst and that mere eye contact would lead to his demise like those several before him. Four scrawny limbs tremor, and spectators could discern that he is not shaking from the cold. Austerlaund grips these hitches, notches knots onto her fingers, and wraps sagging lengths of the cord around her forearms. Once the arch lector takes these reins, he focuses his efforts on finishing Rochester's work: stringing together the three separate cars, jury-rigging couplings into one stubby train of sleds. All it takes is one Austerlaund, a half-giant to pull the yield of forty men.

It takes the awkward span of forty minutes before the crew is prepared for departure. Brace Billhook has been performing perverted philanthropy at each carriage, checking-in on his wild assortment of passengers. His perversely loyal Crooked Men erupt in cheers, awarding a round of applause at these visits, overshadowing Vernon's use of colorful language as he frolics by. The blacksmith writhes in place, attempting to escape, but is pinned by the sheer amount of bodies.

"Dontcha listen to him. Ye'll soona kill us all!"

These raves are vain, psychological attempts to make the brigand appear as a better candidate, a commodore who shall lead them unto victory in the wake of major depression. Residents of the frontier are harshly reminded that those who take advantage of woe and capitalize on hardship, are in reality, vandals at heart.

"I'll git ye all 'ome in nah time. Dat's right- mah, n' nuh one else! I know da lay o' da land like dat o' muh own backyard. We'll be der 'fore nightfall bruddas and sistas."

The foremost member of the Brothers Jack produces a brimming hat of feathers and plume, a gift from an anonymous donor that rests so perfect atop his cowl, just as effortlessly as Mandt's aviary necklace straddles his neckline. It must've been made specifically for Brace Billhook!

Headwear is a sign of nobility and responsibility to the Bannermane, playing on his childish, self-righteous ambition to become a ferryman. This decorum instills authenticity, finally granting him authority to take the helm in some recipe of disaster. The Crooked Men behave as if Brace has read all the working manuals, that he surveyed the essential ins-and-out of seasonal caravan work, each car's bolts and seating by the back of his hand- and they'd be wrong. The extent of his knowledge doesn't exceed that of a laymen loading cargo, there's a reason that he never received a promotion that so few were bestowed, and it wasn't because Brace can't handle a knife.

All things considered, William is handling the loss of his best friend particularly well, rather because he's focusing on the trainwreck before him. He notices that Brace is going through all the right motions, "Awfully strange," muttering to himself, "Looks almost too familiar." The knave is following in the footsteps of predecessors: glancing at the front skis of each car, the plow, and sets of wheels mounted behind, also inspecting for loose cargo, and giving couplings a quick tug. It takes a minute for things click into place.

Oh woe, now William recognizes what is dishonest about this scene. While it's an identical play-by-play, Brace has only memorized where to attend each station, he doesn't follow-through on the work ethic for identifying loose fittings or risks. If only the Mandonman knew of Rochester's profession, he'd be ecstatic to survey his masterpiece one last time, the employer wouldn't personally matter much to him.

The Brothers Jack ante this accident waiting to happen, scurrying aboard with one last call. They stare at one another in glee, hissing their signature snake-oil grins. Brace is quite eager to shake the reins, cracking a whip towards the inhuman rival hitched to the lead. She winces in animosity, and to no extent, pain. The mystic refuses to cede any more sense of control, not even giving the brigand benefit of a glance. Austerlaund is in full control of her faculties, yet bites her tongue, lives are still at stake and she claims sole responsibility to save them.

"Eh-eh git goin'. Weigh 'ey, roll and go! Take sum advice, take sum stride."

The occasional hand is able to stretch outside the carriage windows, these are disembodied limbs, unable to tell whom is whose through the sheer mess of human bodies. presumingly Arabella, Vernon, or the Hindsfolk waving one last goodbye. A Crooked Man in the rear carriage hoists his head out the window, breaking into a convoy sailing tune, a shanty to keep pace. These vagrants rave like nothing illicit has happened. One by one, hoarse raspy voices join into a boisterous chorus, wailing to tune of Merry Timken. As the boosted sleds venture further and further away, the volume of each verse recedes, eventually bleeding into the sky.

Dem seasons made way for Jones ta-go,
Ole Merry Timken made it so.

Boom-a-lay, sway heave-then-ho,
Ole Merry Timken made it so.

Clad in rags, clipper en-tow,
Ole Merry Timken made it so.

He hasten the grind, unlanded bravo,
Ole Merry Timken made it so.

Fare-ye-well, fortunes high-ho,
Ole Merry Timken made it so.

Oh sailor boy, racked to-and-fro,
Ole Merry Timken made it so.

Bracin' em-leagues, that schooner did show,
Ole Merry Timken made it so.

These scarce prospects musta woe,
Ole Merry Timken made it so.

As they grieve upon the loss of Mandel, their party is left dumbfounded facing this recent departure, consequence to the disappearance of their settlement's astute, honorable pacemaker, Vernon Waulbellows, the medical practitioner Austerlaund, Kirk and Marlene Hinds, the Ayers, Galvin Broad, Sassafras, the skald Arabella Gaberdine, and an untold number more. To those that have been stranded by the Crooked Men's final scheme, the beaming icon of Mad River Junction is an ultimate trick. This is the rock they'll die on.

The gods are such horrible creatures, as they have forsaken those who warrant immortal attention. Due to ignorance, threats flourish. Too often do fell forces snuff those so innocent to the harsh truths of the world, it is a sloppy, mundane routine. William and Braithwaite are infallible spirits, and while mischievous, the two are incapable to cause strife. Together, their birch leaves of personality float among the currents, and even when faced by the most dire circumstances, they bend, rather than break; not by choice, boons gifted by nature, ingrained in their very bones.

It is their unsatisfying duty to test the horrors that rove the night, so that greater evils may never grace the light of day. It is far easier for lesser men to give into whims, however so few are incorruptible to greater powers. Some people are deserving of pain and sorrow.

Cliff Fetherhaugh is a frontier proprietor, along with the amateur archaeologist Morbin Evershade, and cardspeaker Mug Maxwell, their company finds themselves driven by quintessential Bannermane greed. Their demise has been expected for ages, these men have been sent to the Junction to attest for their sins. Perhaps they cheated the wrong mark, forgot to donate towards their monthly charity, but one thing's for certain, these coming days will shape them.

Jerome is a man whose has seen it all, these experiences of anguish have left him bitter, reminiscence has worn him to a partially-rotting core. In the burgher's perspective, there is no joy left in the world, strictly regrets, and while he continually yearns for pleasures, the usual drudges that tickle delight dissipate quickly, and tastes nothing like ash in his mouth.

The highwayman and Boar's Band initiate, Korralack the Kable is another story altogether. His belligerence is earned, something panned and distilled. Life on the plains is unforgiving, and so few are able to rise against it, matching ferocity in true, relentless grit. His anger has been cultivated through years of effort, having been raised in a close-knit throng of siblings, brothers and sisters whose mistakes earned Korralack the opportunity to surpass them. Those that fail to meet the challenge may be broken, yet hardy.

They are desperate, but do not entirely lie in shambles. Lena Tillstead and Rylie Hess have both encountered incredible loss, ceding the better halves of their personality, these struggles make it difficult to remember that with time comes healing. Through denial, depression, pain and guilt ordinary people can repair the chip in their shoulder, forge better armor, and become stronger for it.

Whether by magik and fell forces, or either irrational disorders and afflictions of the the brain, some residents have trouble reasserting parts of their personality. Rochester is one such fellow, he possesses an immense social fear. It's not just typical conversation that prods at him like a thorn in the side, but being around other humans that genuinely frightens the poor wainwright. He was never abused, left to his own devices, kin have always tolerated and respected him- just something wasn't wired right, a portion of his mind that doesn't quite fit.

The author and fictional weather-forecaster, Jeremiah Anders is livid. Passerby find his work and state-of-being completely eccentric, and quite deranged. He's been self-imposed with delusions of grandeur from very early-on, all an act to make his employ a tasteful rarity. Jeremiah is neither unhinged or sane, but yet he aspires to be adored, and more importantly, worshipped.

he knights-errant, Osbourne Bullheaded is the latest co-conspirator to join this deranged, motley crew. Hearing voices has become a relatively widespread occurrence, yet in the paladin's case, it's his extraordinary ability to speak in return. It's a curious case to spirit away with the dead, maybe he can communicate with Mandel and Edmund from across the grave.

As this ragtag group of misfits have nothing better to do, all their supplies have been exploited, neither able to partake in food nor drink, each bohemian retreats to the trading post. William offers a hand to the injured author, and Jeremiah's prevailing wince is replaced by glee. It must be such demanding to switch between psyches like that. Alternate personalities may allow the grim to become tolerable, however the fashionable encounters churn sour. The boy Jones escorts the creative inside, ushering him towards the entrance.

Their journey suddenly becomes a thrawn pilgrimage, as upon taking a stand, Jeremiah finds an abrupt kink in his calf, hindering the limb lame and forcing a hobble. These denizens are tense, swollen with stress, and hope for the best. Upon their arrival, the caravan depot is forlorn, deserted of cargo, lying empty and utterly abandoned.

The usual suspects are greeted with colder intents. Without the mingling of extra bodies, a roaring furnace, and blaze in the commissary dwelling, the ambient heat has disbursed altogether. William spends a majority of his time boding along with those robust, healthy few. They spend time around the perimeter of the caravan post, particularly at the edge of windows, taking the brunt of the chill. Those under the influence of age and flu are prescribed berths closer to the center of the building, where the balm may still lax.

At one point of time, William watches over the knight whom is struck-by a perilous, semi-conscious state. He murmurs softly, pausing dramatically between each breath, like conversing with cacodemons that bask in the corner, and needing to take-in some wind.

Reaching into his knapsack, William procures a strand of lavender herb, a parting gift from Mandel. The strand is a verdant wand which is broken at several points, ending in peppering flakes of amethyst-stained ornament. While he hasn't memorized the efforts of the medical wards, he respects their practice, and places the bloom atop the errant's blanketed chest. Mysticism is a mixed medley, but this is a blessing nonetheless.

William is about to leave the room, yet dwells in the doorframe an uncomfortable amount of time. Each expression that leadens Osbourne's face, every gasp that casts from the parting of his lips leaves the boy in a stupor, hopeful that he will say something- anything, even just a sincere, brief thank-you.

On his withdrawal from the room, he unexpectedly succumbs to a disconcerted *clang*. That these hallways are caught in noisy, hallowing clamor, the clanging of a down-trodden, soup-kitchen ladle on metal tins. It's bowing and bent curvature only adds an element of atrocious melody. This maddening cacophony barely graces William's lobes, and already he may assume that it's the delirious mesterpiece of Morbin Evershade.

His rival has always set himself to command the position of a king, although with everyone aimlessly in charge, he generates the authority of the rebellious court, particularly the venerated jester. The lack of a torch or brazier's courtesy causes him to shiver, a consistent shuddering that tickles his insides, and emboldens William to massage his shoulders.

"Perhaps Morbin is in the right groove? I should get ah set o' instruments muhself, march tah beat of mah own drum every once in awhile n' keep warm," the lad proposes.

"Nah, Jerome would absolutely kill me."

Instead, the boy Jones occupies his time by shadowing those who are stationed here. His first stent brings him about to a widen passage, where he resides alongside Jeremiah, who is now armed with a charcoal brush, and has begun scrawling his latest science fiction story on a passage wall.

"In dis latest piece, which sum happen tah call ah stunnin' revelation, da best work o' Jeremiah Andahs. 'Ere dat one n' only, Ballard Sterling, sneaks intah da lair o' der crown-liege, stealin' 'is rocket ship n' thwartin' da gaudy-grand emperor's plans for world domination," the author orates.

His creativity has not been hindered by these recent prominent injuries, hardly minutiae, somehow powering through the pain like a bonafide Penn-class steam engine. At one point, Jerome moseys by, casually providing spot-on critique, pointing to precise prose on the dry planking, stating how his text features too many past participles.

William also ungrudgingly devotes time to console Rylie Hess, she subjects the lad to her feelings of failure, as she ponders the loss of her dear friend. The boy Jones is in an awfully unique circumstance, he can actually relate, yet strangely does not yield to incursion of swelling guilt. He communicates as if cajoled to the statehouse steps by a wise man, communicating that she should neither focus on the past, nor the future's anxiety-ridden thoughts, instead proposing that to relish in the now, she must find peace in the present.

The scribe extends him a question, inquiring if by chance, his coffers may spare a hint of lavender to ease the pain; just a trifle for nibble, a bloom to take her mind off things. William answers this query truthfully, "'Erbs are ah rare commodity, ye'd be betta-off chewin' birch sap, love."

His next endeavor surmounts to a feat of strength, a rather uncanny ability, as the dwindling days have caused his energy and usual youthful vigor to rout. Korralack corners the earnest lad in the alley, thrusting his elbow onto a nearby barrel, his palm and every digit outstretched, brazenly egging him on.

"It'll be like doin' battle 'gainst ah sponge!"

Alas to poor William, the Boar's Band highwayman is so eager to joust, that their arm-wrestling bout lasted nary a few seconds before he is playfully thrown across the way. This stirring advent delivers him into the awaiting arms of Mug Maxwell, who challenges William to another game of pilfers, this time, scrutinizing the boy Jones every move. Whether it's the glance of his gaze, or his handling of the die, the legerdemain spares little to none, on this occasion the victor is defined by the count of their dice.

William is perplexed by these bids to be human, seasoning his efforts by treating the townsfolk less like kin, and more like patients. He works them kindly, testing their mettle and how they've rebounded from a session of Mad River's current events. However, he doesn't get the chance to profess with anyone else, as Jerome lumbers into the ward, frustrated as ever.

"Egads, tis ah travesty, travesty I tell ya. Does nah-good, leather-feathered soot moths 'ave gone-off n' infested our coop, aft, stern n' all!"

"Ugh, soot moths, really?"

William appallingly disdains, lulling his tongue in disgust. These nuisances are the bane of all fireplaces, in which they lay their eggs to incubate inside the nurturing warmth of leftover ashen residue. A routine plague starts with a random sighting or two, a typical lot of rogue maidens that flaunt near the floorboards. It is when their numbers swell to hundreds, that they brave higher ground and take flight. These pests are bothersome ambience, and offer no harm other than drawing the same air as people do, lest they get a lungful of bug, although this delicacy is considered a nutritious snack to some. Residents are used to swatting then away, although the best response is lieu of a more volatile, chemical nature. Proprietors will usually cordoned-off ailing areas, awaiting fumigation from an exterminator employ.

This pestilent transgression actually draws the townspeople together, a procession of sorts that carefully guides everyone back to the stockades. Each member of their party eventually relaxing, lounging about in the caravan post's main arcade.

It doesn't take long for banter. Eventually, Jerome pipes up in humor, cracking jabs at Morbin, insulting his flair for musickraft.

"Does symphonies ye 'ad earl-yah, were dey original? Wut exactly were ye tryin' tah woo, dem bilgy rats? Twas da roughest serenade I eva don 'err, so dontcha tell mah dat's yer singin' voice. Sounded as if ah goose wus croakin' while sum strongman wrung its neck."

The old man is aware, that despite the archeologists limber physique, his heart is swole with ego and he can take it. Morbin Evershade feigns in suffering, dropping to his knees, sobbing a deluge of fake tears into his hands and all. In another life, Morbin could have a flair for theater.

"My poor ole heart just can't go n' take it no more. Mah every artery shall be the death o' me. This infraction douse muh last action- aye, I go weepin' tuh my grave!"

He makes it obvious, conjuring a petition for forgiveness, swooning some suave movement that would've made all the barrio queens cry.

While not the intended target, this plea thoroughly pisses off Lena, the Calamity Jane who considers this play as a degrading insult to her own emotional vulnerability. This fake opera turns comedy downright tragic, and dredges-up lingering sentiments regarding the loss of her own daughter.

"Trying to toss me into a fit, I see. Knaves playing at me, acting like I'm just right as rain."

Braithwaite lets loose a barrage of courteous, thoughtful words.

"Dontcha worry lass, they're in ah betta place is all."

It's a topic ripe with foul conversation.

"How dare you quip?" Lena erupts, persuading the ward to recoil.

"Explain yourself remark, brig. The best place for my lovely Charm is right by her mother. The children, why did the Mandonmen have to go and take the children? It was enough of a point that they had to go and make a bit of murder out of it."

Cliff confidently defends her, "'Ey-'ey now! It's quite ah good thing they're gone- spared our indecencies. When we turn on each otha n' the Crooked Men spar, those weaklings' innocence would be the first tah go."

"We coddle our children too much," Morbin chides, "might as well be chaperonin' swine tah slaughta. If we don't give 'em reason tuh fear the demons, they won't go 'bout defendin' themselves. Saw mah folks kick the bucket, and look at muh- don't fear any beast that bides the air, land or 'neath the ground."

Of all people to criticize about exposing children to violence, Korralack is whipped into a tumultuous spell.

"Oi, ye fuckin' fool, don't go 'bout playin' frightful tunes. Don't matta if whelp's 'mong der mae-mae, or if urchins oar bein' sacrificed for da simple sake o' not dyin' alone. 'Avin' young'uns face death in da family, n' I'll kill every single one o' does monsters tah spare 'em da sight. Cleanse da earth of dat filthy, vile dot."

"Spill yer tongue at mah 'gain, 'uh? Draw ah blade if yer so wicked, dedicated 'nough tah brawl, othawise shut right-up n' get-on back."

Mad River's residents confront a swelling ante of aggression, they can't afford to turn on one another, not now, not ever. While the companions continue to huff and puff, separating in a sense of urgency, these townspeople retreat with their egos bruised, seeking to bunk in separate rooms, each barring doors with sliding locks.

For men on the bleeding edge of the frontier, there is a severe lack of trust between them. When they finally lay for the evening, every person pulls their ancillaries and personal effects close.

William decides to share residence alongside Osbourne, whom he feels protects him, even while knocked-out cold. He feels the drowsy devils yank his eyelids shut, and is hurriedly swept away by dreams and whirling gusts of imagination.

The frost is the epitome of everything malevolent. It festers like the walking dead, slowly creeping forward, not wanting to lunge at its recent quarry, but cradle it to death. Those rooms adjacent to the commissary are straddled in its fervor. This pressure relieves nails of their post, poking through the most minor of fissures to infect new grounds with taint. Windows across the trading post cry in agony, cracking as their glass is replaced in charring rime. If one were to risk caution, and peek at the frost-covered portals, it's a wonder that the fixture is still intact- it won't be much longer now.

In spite of all this, frost is merely a distraction. The gods' battle proceeds to its culminating fury, their otherworldly blows blast the firmament wide open, the skies bleed and disperses wounded ichor below. A midnight aurora pours down onto streets, burying the sunken promenade in a brilliant luminance of azure-colored glows and emerald sheens. The glorified radiance populating the Junction streets serve as a reminder to the bustling hotspot it used to be. Worryingly, these halos are corrupted in tinges of reddening freckles, imperfections that bear a subtle resemblance to viscera, a liberal coating of sanguine. When followers of chaos bathe in this eminence, they are subject to the boons and curses of cosmic icons. The transition is wild, transforming into wretched entities. At this rate, it won't be long until a beautiful auroras becomes akin to a river of blood.

While dawn's gentle light ebbs whatever strength it may muster, in all respects, the shadow of the Slubberdegullion mountain range looms larger. The sun's bounty is unable to grace the northeast territory, whose auroras still dissipate at the change of day, pacing uncontrollably downwards, seemingly melting into the impenetrable permafrost. Raging storms release their hauls in turn, scattering incredible bulks of torrential downpour onto the ruined settlement below. Still, against all odds, there is one particular spot where the snow heaves and dances. A peculiar creatures stirs beneath, bursting its hand through of the accumulating layers. Its wrist is bejeweled with a copper seal, a stamp dominated by the Peaterbrick brand, symbols of the Haggerton ilk.

There is is a reason why freshly fallen snow is laced in white: it is the purest element, a blank canvas, dependent entirely on what we make of it. The surfaces of marble will exhibit the tunes of yellow when it runs rank with bile, red if we shall choose to shed blood, black is corruption by steel and shot, but white is pure and untainted. Such is the will of the beings far greater, the time before, and it shall reign long after humans are cleansed from the earth.

VII

COME WISDOM COME FIRE

William is shocked into animation by being frantically kicked awake, although not intentionally. As he scours muck among the floorboards, a vicious debate looms overhead. A tincture of feet stomp at his fleece throws, occasionally rocking across, and nipping him in the arm or leg.

His groggy orbs can barely make sense of the sights above, Rylie appears to be teeming in anger. She barrels forward at her opponent, jabbing her index finger into the rim of their throat until it rest firmly underneath her jutting chin. The antagonist is dissuading herself from retaliatory punches.

In his waking daze, William rocks his head intermittently, tossing the nighttime swathes aside, rises to action to stand by Rylie's side. While he raises his wrists in preparation for combat, the hands lax netherward, and for a brief moment, his stance is that of a true martial arts master.

He faces four brethren, two women so well-versed with one another, that William originally believes that they are conjoined at the shoulders, then a short and stout stunted man, and a cloaked figure right behind them all. The boy Jones doesn't recognize the competition they face, perhaps it's the drowsiness rattling his brain. These antagonists must've stumbled in following yesterday's commotion, investigating what all the hubbub and spilled blood was about. He assumes that they're after something, and although William's still scrambled, he can decipher crucial phrases.

"'Oardin's all that lot for yerselves, 'uh?"

Judging by appearances, they're vain and ignorant characters, simple folk in other words. Their disheveled appearances are gauntly, but that is not such a ripe insult, nor totally unusual. The sisters are arranged in an array of needle-thin talons, each hand protruding from their sleeves with such length, these nails would be deemed befitting of a tundra terror. The weaves that crown their heads are just as provocative, braids of hair so matted and unkempt, that it gives the illusion of dreads. It's a wonder how they've wrangled an entourage, really scraping the bottom of the barrel for bodies. The prominent company in their steed is hunched over, throughly disguised under a sheep-sized veil, a billowing cloak lined with golden-stitched embroidery.

Rylie must see them too, as she addresses the crowd sparingly.

"The four of ye should turn 'round whence ya came!"

The compatriot at the right responds questionably, "What do ye mean the four of us?"

Awkwardly pausing, searching around their shoulders and checking the back of their hands, leading them to conclude with astonished expressions.

"Who'd ye count twice?"

These desperate few are lusting after the skald's hoarded books, desperately wanting to burn them for warmth over the lack of kindling. There is a plentiful amount of wood available, however it's all either inaccessible, or has been treated to ensure its longevity. If an unwitting person were to tear off a plank from the trading post and set it alight, the oils contained in the lumber would surely poison them all. Everyone in attendance is not only chilled to the marrow by the unyielding cold, but riddled with anxiousness. There's a riveting feeling among the crowd that they will turn on each other in selfishness.

Jeremiah is normally not one to complain, yet even he makes an absent-minded, artistic jab, battling through the jittering of his jaw.

"Been so cold, I gone lost da feeling in dees toes. N' dey called muh play stupid."

William notices that the sisterhood have shirked from the scribe's aggravated joust, clustering their way into a corner, whispering all along. One of these maidens reveals a locked tome from an outspreading sleeve, rips open its clasp in one fluid movement, and cackles at the revealing spread. The jester god would be thrilled by this legerdemain, they must've stolen this text from right under Rylie's nose. The sibling smacks her fellow swindler on the nape of her neck.

"What's all this gibberish, are ya dull?"

"All full of scribbles, I swears it. Who could read such buggit language anyhow?"

"Give me that, ye must be holdin' the thing upside-down," she deduces, snatching at the manuscript, trying to poach the papers from her sister's firm grip. As her sibling recoils with the binding, this clash easily turns into a game of tug-of-war.

The eldest spews howling barbs, "Oh ye fool, ya absolute twit. I should've traded ye for worms, worth less tah mah now than loose powdah in the stovepipe!"

The lowliest among them recognizes these rearing hostilities, and raises their hands in defiance, declaring to William.

"Oh mah, oh mah, oh mah. Don"t mind muh, I'm only 'ere to lick wounds. I'll just take ah seat o'ver yonda, far o'ver there, where I won't be in anyone's way."

He trots off, avoiding their measly conflicts by seating himself alongside folk who sport fair, disinterested attitudes. Taking a seat with a benign smirk, and hoping to garner Lena's good graces.

Noticing the company's furious shouts, Rylie hails the belligerents by pointing directly at the duo. Upon her approach, a frantic grasp suddenly slips, and one sister's elbow crosses the scribe's jaw. While the blood begins seeping viscously from her nose, the book quivers and becomes white-hot to the touch, burning the remaining digits that clasp at its spine until the text breaks free.

The novel floats in place, seemingly taking a moment to distinguish its surroundings, and then pitch pages in a whirlwind of parchment, deterring each assailant into the nearest wall. This is no mere manuscript, it's an enchanted tome, a ghastly grimoire.

There are writs invoked with arcane properties, infused with magika to protect its bearer and offer them otherworldly powers. These compositions can detail historic knowledge, or convey guides towards an untold number of magical incantations. Constructing a grimoire requires a spiritual essence, a philter derived from sacrificial bodies and rare alchemic elements. This is not content for the common man.

These pages thrust free of their binding, detailing scriptures and sigils of old. Staves written in blood seems to leap off the page, dancing well into the air. It is in that moment that the maddening chill that strifes their audience, vaporizes instantly, and in the place of cold, is a radiant heat. The book unfurls into a spread, culminating like a blossom. Two, stone-like protrusions cast from within the depths of the novel, becoming greater and more magnificent in size every waking second.

The helm of a fire elemental emerges, a fantastical beast bore of sulphur and an entity completely engulfed in flames. It roars in anger, generating an aura that immediately thaws the room's demesne, enthusing it alight in an inferno of zealous oranges, reds and yellows. Onlookers gasp in sheer terror as the searing blaze flickers towards them, so close that it nips at their fleeting fingertips.

This presence is hideously deformed, and missing every defining feature. Its skin is slag in nature, garnished in molten magma, melted straight down to marrow. The visage may be defined as a terrifying, superheated skull, shrouded in fiery form. In lieu of eyebrows are those dastardly horns, while combusting fusillades of sparks now replace each instance of eye. A wicked trident forks from its great maw, a straw to swallow copious doses of tar, allowing the effigy to emit clouds of noxious fumes with every baiting breath.

The fire elemental struggles in place, boldly attempting to escape its confines in an event that would spell certain catastrophic doom. William's eyes pry at the manuscript's spine, finally able to interpret the title which reads, 'The Nature of Niter by Athrophos the Geist.' Who could've possibly knew that Arabella the skald had a penchant for dark knowledge? Perhaps she's ignorant to its true origin, it could be an extremely valuable family memento, a curio that the poet kept tightly wrapped in straps.

This shroud of flames spurs a reckoning, sapping all ambience from the room, and turning the world on end. The immediate alley warps and washes into an inky black murk, and the only beacon is the fiery totem. Even through its prominent lack of eyeballs, the demon stares on, piercing the confines of William's soul and dominating it. This is the being that drives all creatures who go bump in the night, this is the bane of gods, an evil incarnate in which to bend the firmament.

Even though he was just in a room filled with people, an earnest lad now floats in some endless pit, and this elemental is his sole source of attention. It does not speak for the lack of tongue, and if it did, the world would tremble in dread. It reveals William's everyday fears with ease, projecting them in foreboding, free-floating images that orbit his head. His greatest woe is not just an alarm for self-demise, but wrinkling away, bones crumbling, and fading with age. A prospect where his entire life has accumulated to nothing: a momentary blink in the span of the universe, a drop in the bucket of infinite space, and a colossal waste of no time at all.

If it wasn't for the timely intervention of an outlandish figure, William would be subject to the everlasting whims of an elder god. Upon its sight, the superstitious, the cloaked intruder unveils a bundle of herbs, and with the utterance of a few prayers, flings them towards the cretin, then disappears.

This obscenely humorous act returns everything to normal, as if flipping the reset or tying the switchboard. The blackness suddenly fades, and the people return from its ambiguous prison. Events have been set in motion that cannot be possibly undone.

The beast recoils from the transgression while cloves of garlic and wands of rosemary burn, not roaring in agony, but an aversion to these ornamentals, an Achilles heel only known by cosmic means. It retreats in a mystifying smog, hitching the book shut with its hand as if nothing has happened in the first place.

The manuscript collapses in a grotesque *thunk* onto the floorboards, cracking them with intense heft, descending six-inches deep through staves intended for beasts-of-burden that weigh several tons. This has been an astute reminder that there are sick and twisted beings out there, those fell opportunists who feed off pleasure as well as pain. While they may act as if humans are nothing to them, that people are merely pawns in a game of chess while immortals wrestle around the board, a person's mere existence fuels their essence.

Everyone instinctively draws their weapons, a tattered arsenal in all. There are kitchen knives furnished with gouges, and armaments intended to skin and trade fur. It'd be a slow, maiming death, nothing fulfilling in the heat of battle, this ordinance is not ideal for crossing brigand blades. The sisters discuss their visions all while facing their opponents, they wield pitchforks together, instruments that would make short work of bison feed.

There are those who sighted evil creatures stalking the night, and others have been struck with vile vistas far worse. In their eyes, they have discovered that the end of the world is nigh.

Townspeople in the dwelling banter furiously, pacing around in bouts of wordplay, avoiding the charred site in the center of the alley. Their contest is nonsensical at times, derived from the traumatic stresses of the encounter, but each soul takes these jests as the threats they are. Rylie's visitors wish to burn the grimoire, for it is a novel infused with malice, obviously foul magiks.

"Are you kiddin'? Surely tissa joke!" The scribe contends, arguing that,

"This thing just lit-up an entire caravan post without ah single incantation, so why would I eva, in the right mind, allow some vagrants tah rid such prize? I can't conceive it!"

In an argument so natural, the sisters retaliate with reasons that can't possibly be deemed so selfish. Their vocal cords are livid, and would jitter the very rafters if it weren't for their feeble constitutions, yet loud enough to stir the knight from his slumber.

"That was an elemental ya twit, ah primordial trapped in the 'ellfires of earth. More or less that thing wields the power o' gods themselves. Do ye really believe it enjoys bein' cooped-up in that book o'ver yonda? Sure-sure," she beckons sarcastically, "It'll listen tah the likes of ye warmin' yer 'ands 'round its skull."

"Fear it, don't ya? That book only affects those weak of 'eart. Ye 'ave nah courage, craven."

The sisters' two revel with animosity, dispatching an offhand threat.

"Prepare yerself knave, some penchant tah paper can't protect ye from these storms on the horizon."

One of the siblings eagerly brandishes her weapon, to which Rylie dodges with ease. These malefactors are too weak to dedicate themselves to any actual harm, every insult is a nonchalant tirade, every thrust of a blade, practice.

The eldest sister spits in disdain, nailing the book that encumbers the decking. If it wasn't clear before, the audience is reminded that this is no ordinary scripture. It vibrates in irritation at these insults, quivering the length of floorboards, and any folk among the alley along with it.

William tilts his head back and forth, listening intently as each party vies for this sole source of warmth, and himself thrown into the fray as the literal middle-man. He probes for the lance he had bartered for earlier, that particular pikehead roving in the bulking mantles of fur. To propose a cessation of hostilities, the boy Jones speaks-out, drawing his arsenal just to cast the sharpened stint of metal aside. William didn't expect this maneuver to be so formidable, the halberd blade lands a solid four-feet from his person, and embeds itself into the floor's robust timbers, point-first.

"Bannermane ain't barbarians, this isn't the way it works. I put muhself in 'arm's way n' defend thee scribe, et tu newcoma knaves. We can't keep tah some doctrine o' decline, so let's satisfy betta spirits n' decide tuh settle-up," recognizing their belligerent differences as the sowing of common fears, as anyone would be a little feisty after spying their nightmares, and certainly warding that frightful, moral decline.

Angered by William's superior posturing, the unruly belligerent retaliates with relatively harsher lyrics.

"Blue-collars rely on their 'ands while fools favor quips o' the tongue! If it weren't for the bodies stacked 'gainst us, I'd fix that tome ah permanent stay as smoke 'mid the firmament."

Rylie's work with the magistrate bought her close allies to the court, and a certain confidence when it comes to brigandry.

"And though, if I 'ad the opportunity, I'd throw ye both in the black cellars tah rot."

Sodden in defeat, the gutsier crony demonstrates dominance by pushing her sibling, nearly throwing the sister into back-alley bulkhead. She roils with anger, and is encouraged to cool-off outside. A distinct cloud of steam emanating off her brow and cheek, it's really an intimidating mist.

The two make haste exit, one roused with irritation and the other quite frazzled, flinging the door in and venturing to the landscape beyond. A three-foot wave of white deluge has attempted to surmount the exit, and they are coerced into clumsily hurdling the packsnow. There is a period of grating clamor, brought on by the scrunching of snow, which recedes into the general monotony. However, before anyone could possibly lift their spirits and encouraged their hands to shove the portal shut as the blizzard competes in the entry, a startled, cloaked man stumbles in.

He collapses through the vestibule, and empties his contents of wet, hot stomach bile onto the chamber floor. The flooring is rife with scarecrow stuffing, weeds and unnamed plant mixtures ground into a densely-packed pulp. It takes a moment until the figure stands to attention, his gait is remarkable though, and William ultimately recognizes him as the stranger from before. This is the same character as before, that cloaked apparition who distracted the elemental and then vanished entirely- wyrd. That fella's posture, snout and cinnamon strands appear awfully familiar too, his facial hair sprawls from the scruff of his neck like a paintbrush. It can't be, that Mandel Haggerton has risen from the dead!

Crestfallen and distraught from his recent theater tragedy, the rogue clutches at his stomach, leans his back upon the wall and immediately drops to the ground. This mostly-forgotten cordwainer commands charity, a pertinent eyesore haphazardly strung together. His coat and outwear have been completely compacted, giving precedent that he has arrived naked. An earnest lad breaks from his posse to retrieve his comrade, while Korralack and Morbin make effort to slam the bulkhead shut.

William affirms this sorry state, "Oh boy, quit being so dramatic. Forgot 'is damn cloak 'gain, outright frozen tah death- gotta be joking," before realizing that Mandel's bloodily fluids have dampened all throughout his garments, freezing every layer stiff.

The flaxen lettering that adorned their cape is actually a mess of threads that have sprung free, grown rigid and soured. Even the color has drained from his once fiery-orange trophy pelt, a vibrance that now sheens soot black. He has heard stories of villainy before, that when an object is stolen, property so precious and revered, it becomes a hex of sorts for the thief.

A venerate of Clan Penn, warrior champion of the Underdark, lusted after the crown of rails. It is the symbol of industrial dominion, an artifact to triumph over all others. When this paladin cast-down his liege-lord in battle, that shimmering bouquet lost its brilliant tone, defiling into an austere, rusted helm. It is common for trinkets to change color or appearance, contorting in some fashion. If effects are stolen from a practitioner of fell magik, worse fates are sure to follow. Mandel is the same man, isn't he? His complexion might be slightly altered and ruined at the seams, but that definitely him. So why would his pelt sour?

As the boy fraternizes with the calamities that have befallen his friend, a hand presses firmly into William's shoulder, gently easing him away. Osbourne has arrived to intercept this guest, and kneels down with such an ache, that those nearby hear the stressing snap of his tendons. It must've been a painful experience, but the man-at-arms does not react. While carefully scrutinizing the Mandel's state, the knight-errant affirms William's chivalrous virtues during their engagement with the sisters, stating that he has shown true valor.

"Look at us, bickering like icons," he assures.

"What are icons, Mista Goodsir, sir?"

"Why lad, they are the mighty lords of the tunnels, my patrons, and leadership of the Underdark where sovereigns govern with an iron-fist. The crown rules among them. Such are necessary evils, for in the underground, men breed by like rats." The paladin outstretches his palm to meet Mandel's cheek, gauging his delirium and state of mind; hopeful for a stent of resistance, yet the cordwainer simply shuts his eyelids, and turns the other way.

"It's always best to steer clear of their verminous appetites."

To be frank, William has always been interested in matters of state and science, but as Osbourne attempts to regale him with the achievements of Clan Claremont, the boy caters a different approach. The knight's tune falls upon deaf ears while William waltzes over to the charred, ritualistic circle, eventually retrieving his pikehead lodged into the lumber by way of the needle. He stands perilously, placing his foot atop the seared, ligneous remains as if dipping a tow in the water.

Strangely, this taunts the vague idea of food, and can't help to think just how much he misses the delectable taste of fish. Gutted, sliced tender, filleted, broiled, stewed, drawn, dressed and pressed lakefish, there are plenty of ways to fancy seafood. The mercantiles sponsor trawlers to dredge-up schools of river trout fingerlings and salmon. Veteran anglers farm oodles of fish-egg caviar, these provisions are eclectic, preserved and shipped straight to the Underdark aristocracy. A line of sardines personally curries favor with William's palette, as their juices tend to survive deep-freezes well, though many wouldn't take this decision lightly. These waterborne grubs smell pungent, he can vainly admire the odor, imagining such chum crammed in a tin. William can't describe this delectable dish enough.

As such bounty dwells just beneath the waterfront, they are protected in an all too familiar, and formidable seal of rime. The bloomtide is renowned as the calm before the storm, and he remembers when Oestergaard fishermen took to the lake. They toted sleds bursting at the brim with cabin materials, assembling a crude, ice-fishing hut to protect themselves from any unscrupulous flairs of the weather and wind. There was shanty far out in the midst, it lied abandoned while the regular teams had their way.

"Stranded 'fore two seasons," he was told, "Dat team drove for deepa wata. Dat's where it's da warmest. So dat's where da schools shall be! Dey grow fat n' stupid der, lullin' 'bout da bottom wit nothin' tah do."

Unfortunately, their endeavors were stricken with strife, and in an obscene gesture by the gods, the glacial face heaved. It is the source of Mad River, and the entire settlement has been constructed in its shadow. That day, an iceberg careened into the westernmost reaches of lake, and even though this incidents occurred a league away, they didn't account for how vulnerable the surface shifts, and being near the center of the floes, they were left stranded. The whole tributary became riddled in a web of shattered crystal, ice anchored their endeavors, preventing them from retreating while Nana Nature pilfered their earnings.

They brought forth the sled dogs, then beckoned for the burdens. Not even two mighty bison could lug their contraptions free, in the end, they were forced to flee on foot. There was something wrong with those hounds though, they were sleek, lean with less meat, wild breeds with longer teeth.

They're not the only creatures with their convictions tested by these changing times, the prodding cold coerces all sorts of abnormalities. Caribou herds migrate further south from the traditional ranges, and the alabears in turn. They've descended down the mountainside like an avalanche, pale terrors laying siege to safe hearths like Cinder Keep, earning their stripes with foul deeds.

Those eastern ranges are uncharted, and Bannermane that inhabit the fringes encounter all sorts of strays. William takes notice of those that tip the drink, although eventually one's accounts reach a point where detail rallies fantasy, and a listener questions when there must be a hint of truth. These beasts are rife with imagination, unbelievable characteristics that rally when someone shutters their eyes. However, to the horror of those unlucky enough to bear sight, they unveil their lids and these deviants of nature still stand.

The bewilderbeast is one such lug, a monstrous fanged porcupine, the nightmare that haunts William's early childhood. Some say that they perform evil misdeeds like kidnapping children, to earn their antlers, and complete their devilish appearances. Worshippers of the fell might also earn boons in the names of dark gods, becoming mandrills. Their hair casts white, and then their face churns to the redness of a cranberry, transforming into the visage of a monkey, with a horrible maw of tusk-like ivories. A savage mouth were one row of teeth are never considered enough. Brawny bristlehair apes are their fetched cousins, barrel-chested gorillas that revel in everything and anything malign. These foul primates are afraid of chitinous ilk that skulk the ravines, antennae-ridden, multi-legged insectoids boring through the canyons and mires.

The rhinoceros stag is William's most cherished fable, a creature of circumstance, the anatomy of a mole crossed with the horns of a beetle. These beetles are said to joust one another for dominance, their horns sharpening on iron-clad hulls until they can pierce the heaviest, Underdark chainmail. A being of blindness can't possibly be so hideous? Though, who's to avail the little truth in the matter?

Morbin pipes up with an insidious smear, William didn't quite realize that he was smearing his thoughts aloud.

"Next thing ye'll be tellin' us 'bout straightjackets, some shadows that choke their own 'osts!"

Others start making-up fictional beasts, pressing at the joke.

"Oi, wyzzoks! Mustn't forget 'bout thundrills, ah beast that- say, 'as stalactite amethyst claws that can burrow 'neath permafrost."

This game of taunts is noticeably pestering to the boy Jones, even Rylie joins in on the fun while preparing a scrap of cloth for her nosebleed.

"Ilk speak of mangroves, accursed groves, n' mire fiends I call'em. These 'airy trees wriggle n' wear masks as their bark, an angry totem for when sheep stray too close. Then they lift their roots straight outta the ground tah trap n' ensnare prey."

"A newt! At last, thank ye gods. That's what I'm after, the particular cretin I've been thinkin' 'bout. That fell demon reminded me of a firebelly. You know, those weird scalies that sift their way into caverns and mines?"

Their cheery debacle ceases, and the audience in attendance grows weary to this sudden debacle. Finally piecing together the newest addition to their company, Jerome speaks with flourishing prejudice.

"Yer just ah boy, not worthy speakin' tah greybeards in such mannah."

Nurturing a hefty *sigh,* the dishonored sole heir retorts with the flair of a gentleman.

"Aye, yes 'deed, I'm the fabled Balthus the Pygmy. 'Ere-ere, I 'ave proof after all."

He brandishes an amulet with their house sigil in one hand, and his personal seal is wrapped firmly around his right wrist. Lena abruptly slides a few feet away, a response riddled with disgust, which only adds to Balthus commentary.

"Really mah dear? We were 'ardly gettin' tah know one 'notha."

If a visitor were to take a second glance, it does indeed appear as if both his shins have been lopped-off in some demoralizing accident. Though, it's definitely difficult to tell when it's necessary to sport abundant layers of leather and coats. In truth, he's not that short. Only when Balthus makes a habit of crowds would some person find that their shoulder perfectly aligns among the top of his forehead. Still, it's an incident procured by zero fault of his own, mutation is enough of a reason for Bannermane ilk to spur prejudice.

"Yer da spawn o' Balthasar Grizzly," Jerome declares as an old man stricken and rife with the grudge, sweeping all of his care in this world into a case and tossing it aside, railing with his traditional prejudice, "Worthless."

Unlucky for him, Balthus is a learned man, awfully clever and perceptive, composed entirely of thick-skin tailored from years of torment.

"N' yer so great yerself? Tell me, do people praise yer deeds, or ale-tendas raise glass in yer 'onor? Ye know nothin'. I actually 'ated mah elda with passion. I've met Boar's Bands with greata prestige."

""'Ow dare ye speak ills 'bout muh blood-brudda."

"I don't dare, I did. Ye also 'ave ah terrible choice in friends, as 'e died due tah 'is own greed. Blood-brothas- 'ah, don't make mah laugh. 'E'd soona sell the seat right out from unda ya. Ate steel 'e did. Pulled some blade on ah costamonga, 'opeful tuh plunda, then took rail through the galley. They renegotiated their terms well, n' took-off with both trophies: all the trademarks 'e 'ad in 'is trench pockets. Perished as ah poor man."

William ponders to himself, taking distinct effort not to tread aloud, again. It's a wonder why people have such a mistrust to mutants, when often, they are the realists among us. Balthus the Pygmy might yet be the wisest vagabond of all these townspeople. True Bannermane have little respect of houses, they warrant adventure, and value good company; things greater than a blood namesake. The major clans delve as royalty, they prescribe lineages to test the tracks of millennia. Coalitions of houses serve their every waking whims, and occasionally loyal dogs are uplifted to the title of venerate. These house may be further divided into bands and families, kin that strive for glory. Nonetheless, all the materials and employ of men- no matter how organized or prepared they can be, are beseeched to the whims of greater powers.

The dreary day drags on, their toils have amounted to nothing, here they are- leagues later, yet right where they started, still stuck at the caravan post in Mad River Junction. William has meandered his frame closer to the grimoire's aura, where the lumber still generates a faint, balmy afterglow, and invites Mandel forth. The two converse, recollecting the Crooked crew's departure, and select few such as Arabella, Austerlaund and Vernon who were coerced by vagrants to a fruitful end. They should still be grateful somehow. Together they wonder what has become of certain colorful characters around the settlement, raising hell like a howler, Cillian Lore, and the town's constable.

As the minutes easily sway into hours, William notices a handful of notable changes in his comrade, similar to Osbourne's plight, although much less disturbing. Several staves have emerged on his skin, and while it takes some time to decipher, these are definitely protective runes. Each tattoo is pigmented in blue cerulean, a hue modern meisters have yet to master, the immortals had to have a play in this. Mandel's knuckles and wrists are also encrusted in callous tissue, growths that takes the disguise of exposed bone. His eyes are a tad yellow, yet not in respects to the tone of sharpening sparks in the forge, but a brilliant golden tinge, as a beauty to behold. The cordwainer is irrefutable proof of divine intervention, but to what end? What dastardly concoctions could eminence have in store?

While Mandel and William remain faithful to one another, the distrust sewn between vagabonds poisons their company. Lines have been severed, friendships have been cut. Each member of their party huddles in a fetal position, poising their daggers close, should anyone choose to test their tense boundaries.

The auroras once again descend midst the throws of night, beaming rivers of light that test and tickle their housing, sometimes straining against the doors of trading cost, eager to meet new faces. Each entrances has been barred completely shut, no one wishes to greet phenomena, and face the fates. These abhorrations are decorated with splotches, freckles that sicken, becoming worse and worse by the passing moments, a rust-like taint. Something lurks amid the cover of darkness, a harbinger of doom. During first light, when morning's glare barely illuminates the Junction's bulwark and promenade of destruction with a subtle mellow glow, Mandel gently urges William from his dream-like trance, rocking him awake.

"Eh boy, come now please. I need tah tell ye somethin'."

Realizing that the boy is not going to budge, he is motivated to resort to divinations of the hand, and slaps William into dialogue by his palms.

Youch. William writhes in pain, the recent, godly accouterments to Mandel's forearms seem to encourage conflict like a magnet.

"Haggerly, I think ya tore mah whole cheek off!" His fingers lapse over every feature of his face, "Blood, is that wet blood I feel? Blimey muh nose is missing too! Oh, oh-oh wait, there it is now. Was it always this small?"

The cordwainer clips William's lobe with a flick, the sharp sensation quickly reels him to attention.

"'Arken now, I've gotta serious matta, 'Liam. An awfully strange dream."

"Strange dreams? Well, I got plenty o' those. Oh all right, spit it out then."

"It was somethin' terrifyin', truly. So, there I was, lost in the wilderness, caught in the unknown. The snow climbed all the way tah mah whiskers, 'til I couldn't climb any 'igher. My hands were like shovels, yankin' mounds towards muh with every 'aggard breath. It took mah too long o' figure that I was payin' mind tuh the perspective o' beast, trackin' low on the ground- an odd sight, nevah 'ave I dreamt 'fore. I saw the caravan, not ten- nah, twenty paces 'head. It wasn't Rochester's work- for sure, these were the carriages driven some days ago by those Mandonmen. Yes, I'm definitely sure of it, 'cause that house sigil bore on the carriage sides. Not one soul was lashed to the 'elm, the caravan lied abandoned. The bison reins were tapped off, n' the lead car ran right intah ridgeline. I crept up tah that caboose, traveled close to the ground, diving nose-in to a frozen pool of ichor. The coach's gates 'ad been burst inwards, n' waterfalls of blood drained southernly. Red trailings led off intah the distance, dozen or so, firm pawprints, bigger than mah 'ead, 'cause I'd often dip down into the trenches they create. So, I leapt up intah the carriage, 'til the scent 'came intoxicatin'. The landin' was ah gladiatorial arena o' sorts, 'air and fur strewn 'bout everywhere- gore-soaked scene, the occasionally misplaced limb or two, n' ah person missin' their entire upper-'alf. Everyone on board was dead, William! Once I 'eard that 'owl, knew it was too late. I fled the shuttle just as brinin' yellow eyes scaled the cliff faces n' mounted the other coaches-"

Mandel's recounting is abruptly cut-off when a bulkhead door suddenly bears hell. Down the alley, a passage or two, the double-doored, main entrance of the caravan post slams wide-open, and tear from their hinges. There's an exasperated scream of relief, a combination of agony, tension and glee.

William breaks from the destitution of the ward, sprinting with all the might he has to offer. It isn't long before he intercepts the source, and is greeted by another familiar face, Edmund Redmyne the wickerwalker. While clouds of bile-tinged mist escape from his lungs, he collapses in a stent of utter exhaustion. Each article of his clothing has been finely shredded into yarn, ample oozes of burgundy can be slightly sighted beneath. As William kneels to observe him, the tracker's eyelids frantically shut, and his head haphazardly lulls to the side. He can barely muster the energy to speak, and gasps in-between breaths.

"'Ave doomed us all. The siege is comin.'"

— ACT TWO —

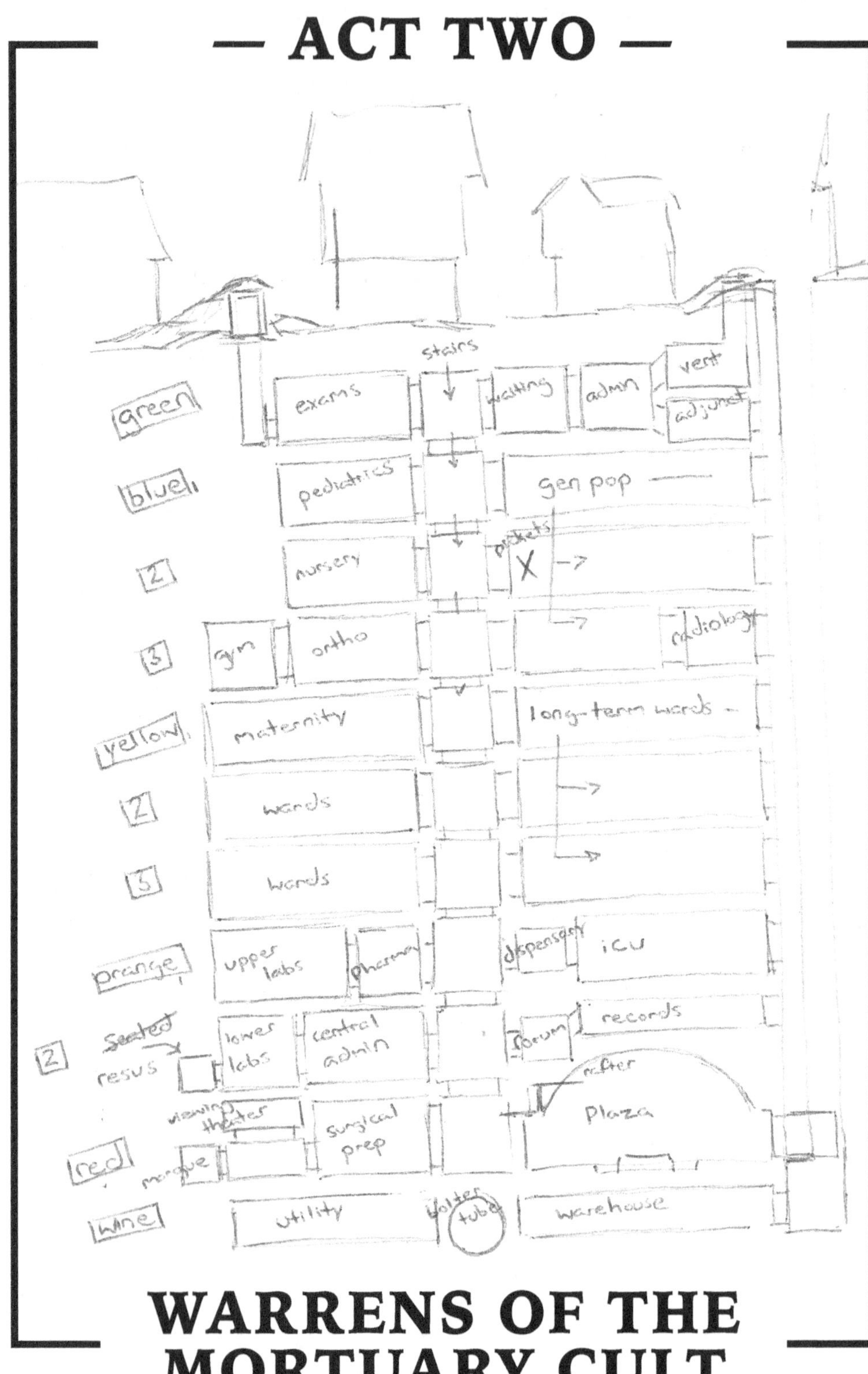

WARRENS OF THE MORTUARY CULT

VIII

—

STEP INTO THE GARDEN

Auroras churn red in the face of danger, disastrous calamities, personal catastrophes, and the awakening of old gods. Those whirling vermillion sheets cascade around the glacial face, giving berth to the craglands below, home to the sprawling crevasses, mires, and tarpits. Here, a two-hundred foot pitfall is commonplace, and all it takes is one misplaced step. The beasts that dwell in these fissures are fiends, able to surmount vertical ascents and loose scree.

It has taken ten days, but an intrepid team of wickerwalkers have finally downed their quarry. These three trappers gather around their makeshift, lantern-based campfire, discussing the mistakes they've made, and how the hunt could've easily ended in their deaths. The allotted number of blunders is zero, and in truth, they got lucky. Rather than having to traverse gashing cliffsides or palisades of stone, the boar trapped itself down a shallow passage, and wounded itself on the tips of their spears. Once the final throes of life escaped its eyes, the trio of wickerwalkers celebrate, and tend camp while night falls.

They have not yet skinned the swine, as their flesh is certified, red-labelled organic. Boar are truly disgusting creatures at heart, regularly goring one another and frolicking like nothing happened in the first place, manifesting bacterial diseases and buboes as they burrow through yards of dirt.

An abattoir will have to process the meat, dipping the cuts into a chemical bath for treatment, in order to rid all its toxins. Still, the sow weighs at least four-hundred pounds, it'll take every ounce of strength to lug the trophy back to Mad River Junction. Perhaps if they let the corpse breathe it'll be lighter to move, pry at the hide just a bit, severing all the right arteries to drain blood and bodily fluids before the lines freeze.

A veteran takes his hunting knife and carefully dissects into the boar, melting the permafrost with a philter of lukewarm brine. They'll have to move quickly, as the spilt blood will undoubtedly lure predators to their encampment. However, these wickerwalkers should have a few hours head start. While wolves are able to track scents for miles, it'll take them considerable time to range over these craglands.

Unbeknownst to their company, an uninvited guest has been lurking nearby for the past several nights. A true alpha, attracted not to the musky boar, but to the sweaty scent that sinks into their clothing and the grease that gleams hair. It craves human flesh, a delicacy among its kind. Having treaded the confines of wasteland, inching by their heads while the team were comatose in their sleeping bags, calculating maliciously. This breed is intelligent, and most importantly, patient. Aware of the weaponry they furnish and how they wield such instruments of war. Now that the trio of breakneck-connoiseurs have tired, expending their energy on a trifle of swine, this is the clever carnivore's opportunity to strike.

The beast senses as the cleaner separates from the group, just after dispatching his blade into the boar's corpse. His edge glides against gristle, and each movement of the huntsman's hand shakes with weariness. This is a juicy target, prey so weak, that it feels almost unfair. He is their patron saint, old and wise, the veteran training a new batch of wickerwalkers, yet far from flawless. In a world where anything less than perfect is met with adversity, the gods have determined that this hunter shall be greeted by death.

It doesn't take long before he is immediately disemboweled, a trivial horizontal slap against the midsection, and the lionheart is laid low without a sound. Broiling intestines fondle through torn clothing, lapsing onto the ground, melting the powder around in a vilifying, goopy soup. The two harken for their friend over yonder, they yell.

"Dauben! Dauben! Daubenmire where are ya?"

As the minutes dawdle by, and realizing that their cries fall upon deaf ears, they impulsively draw daggers.

Their anatomy seems to beckon the predator, who allures for its next prize, that particular woman who's marching upon the confines of shadow. The snot absconds from her nostrils like deluge, ample tinges of frostbite and the decaying of tender meat is all too familiar to these warm-blooded fauna. These remain wickerwalkers are tense with the realization of a bitter conclusion, the gripping fear, and tribble of urine is all too intoxicating towards this manner of beast.

As its next victim edges away from the balmy heat, the creature can glimpse its ravin all too clearly. It yanks the vagabond forth into the impenetrable, murky darkness, and the second victim perishes just as easily as the first. All it takes is a little persistent pressure around the neck until the cranium finally decides to break free. When her entire head severs from the confines of body and flails about, her expression is mortified in complete surprise.

The villain is insulted, it wants to savor its prey's final moments, and only a contemplation of anger and fear dashed among these trophies would suffice. Upon her demise, the remaining wickerwalker retreats to the warm, protective aura. This beast can no longer sight the human hunter, as the heat dissipates its silhouette and contorts its otherwise acute sense of smell. It lifts that maw to the great, frost-bitten sky and howls in anguish.

Ra-aagh. This is supposed to be a tourney against the earth's reigning foe, the hunt that would propel the predator to an unparalleled status among its tribe. Now it feels like a chore, and the only purpose of slaughtering this remaining victim is to tie a loose end. Since the last human doesn't tenure threat, maybe it shall toy with this trapped fool too?

Whilst two hunters have begun to disappear, each poor soul has been suddenly jerked into an endless abyss of darkness. Only a knave would declare them to be craven, as this is the work of something dastardly. Where metal meets the meat, where he shall greet gristly fate in the awe of some supreme grim. Even though the survivor hectically searches for his contender, he avails by darting towards his knapsack instead. They must fashion some sort of weapon, because there are certain assurances that he sports the shortest claws around. In the glow of the lantern's light, this wickerwalker unbundles his satchel, and a generous supply of arrows. He grips at the longbow stretched against his chest while under the influence of sirens, they urge every fiber of his being to hustle, and take to the air at throngs of deranged, primal roars.

While he has heeded the warnings, and took his training seriously, the hunter never expected the wilderness to retaliate so ferociously. This is the new normal for him, life begets life, and to the victor belong the spoils; 'a righteous hunt' as the Bannermane say, even though it may lead to their demise.

The lantern's dimming luminance so quaintly reveals the beast that keeps him at bay. Those worn, elongated fangs reflect the ambient light, clashing rows upon rows of densely-packed dental work that hasten to escape from a perversely mangled jaw. Each yellowed ivory is coated in fresh, steaming ichor, these teeth curl upwards, as if it had bitten into the waning moon. After all this taunting, it smiles, a heinous grin that swells well into its cheekbones, colliding into the cuneate ears laid behind its eye sockets. That yawning muzzle isn't the most horrible feature of this visage, the most memorable feature would be its profound lack of eyes. They're just missing, like precious orbs that have been perfectly plucked-out, and empty holes left in their place.

He has yet to encounter such murderess prowess before. They are renowned, creatures of fantasy, akin to something out of mythos, and the wickerwalker can only identify this haunt from his studies. This is a mighty tundra terror, scourge of all the wastelands, shaker of world trees. His mettle will be tested by the fiercest of fires as it continues to skulk where the fringes of lamplight dull into night, pacing to and fro, and circling him with voracious intent. The beast lumbers awkwardly, as if built to understand solely one speed, the mad sprint before a kill.

The lone survivor ducks his head beneath the string in order to free his armament. With a copious sampling of munitions at his feet, he nabs at the first projectile, and lodges it until taut. The arrow nocks quite naturally, an effortless act to be drawn and loosed in the general direction of anything malleable. This arrowhead is gluttonous, ready to pierce hide and consume the pinkish tendons beneath, it's only a matter of which instrument is hungrier. It is a speciality craft, capable of engorging itself on meaty gristle, and deliver a payload so carefully tied to its shaft.

The huntsman releases this barrage with absolute certainty, filling him with delight when the shaft embeds itself within the rank of tough hindquarters. It quite literally, could not see this retaliation coming. A being driven by instinct, the tundra terror charges in the receiving direction of the sting, only this movement is dictated by an abrupt whining.

Fweet, fweet, fweet.

The saber cat's ears jerk at this unnerving, shrill noise, and in its stupor, recedes back into the cover of nighttime gloom. Satisfied, the wickerwalker eagerly awaits his opponent's next move, and listens intently as the beast frolics around, trying to escape the shrieking. He always carries an emergency ordnance, a particular arrow with a whistle tied around it, that way he can track game, even whenever it's out of sight.

Keeping his cards close, this lucky escape artist has gained the upper-hand, and shifted this ambush in his favor. While the marksman may be green, he has wisely taken the advice of maesters. By treading close to the lantern's berth, he disguises his silhouette, and may bombard his foe in relative safety, far from any immediate, precise retaliation. He taps twice on his chest, a goodbye gesture between wickerwalkers, symbolizing that they'll always be remembered in his heart. Now is the time for vengeance. A hoard of projectiles has stumbled out of the knapsack, providing easy access for the salvo to come. The marksman retrieves a serrated arrow from his arsenal, another ingenious invention and tool of war, designed to tear into flesh and allow for blood to seep through the open wound.

He winds it onto his twine, just like before, draws the string, and lets loose the dog of war. The whistling is abhorrent in volume, and he's able to pinpoint the exact location dwelling in the inky blackness. While his quarry is smart, brazen enough to pick-off his fellows as they strayed, it's not the perfect predator he had once thought.

Caught up in a flurry of pain, the wailing is akin to raging gale. This is where the tides turn, who is to be the hunter, and who shall adopt the role of prey?

"Like forkin' fish in a barrel," he remarks.

Moderating the moment with calm, he breathes in deeply, a final motion, and releases. The bowstring suddenly glides past the brim of his folded hat, another harpoon launched at the belligerent animal with haste. He can hear the satisfying *squelch* emit from the creature's skin. However those troubling trebles temporarily halt while the beast stalls to howl with woe. On the receiving end of pin-pointed torture, its paws dig frenziedly into the permafrost, dredging that entrenched clay.

While the whistling ceases in these moments, the beast has determined that it shall not suffer from any more barbs. It turns towards the human, fraught with retaliation, targeting the source of this dire infraction. The terror makes headway, its lunges are bounding, every stride becomes a pounce, practice for when it hurls itself upon the feline's intended folly. It struggles blindly, but boldly. There's a no guarantee that its claws will distribute a killing blow, though it's assured that they'll latch onto a limb or appendage, enough to make the marksman's last moments pure agony. This is the point of no-return, no longer a matter of wit, but of muscle and brute defiance.

The wickerwalker anticipates the oncoming tackle, a song and dance narrated in wailing cacophony, nevertheless he can't compete with that sheer intensity. Instead the man swiftly dodges to the side and braces for the onslaught that follows. The saber cat's body collides with enough force to send him reeling twenty-feet.

It gorges through the packsnow, demonstrating those tusks, desperately attempting to seize the source of heat. Nails the size of daggers barrel through the lantern, smiting such light by smashing the hollow to smithereens, along with dashing the wickerwalker's ability to see. Now the tundra terror has the advantage.

As the ambient fever pitch dissipates under these freezing conditions, the saber cat's acute senses hone it to the only other source of heat, so it closes the distance menacingly, step-by-step, relishing in fact that the culmination of all this trouble may be laid-down in a sole swipe. With nary a chance to flee, he prepares a counterattack, urging the beast towards him, so when the tundra terror finally paws at him, close enough that the hunter chokes on the reek that straddles its gullet.

He wounds the creature in a succinct stabbing motion, fastening an arrow between its pads. This parry is fleeting, still the marksman strikes while his iron is hot. He commits to defy death, and does what no sane man would do: the wickerwalker forfeits the bow so perilously lashed to his palm, and shoves his weapon straight into the beast's gaping maw.

Those bony rods clamp-down in reflex, crudely lodging the timber in its gullet. Never has the terror fought such worthy prey, and nevertheless choked on its own gluttony.

It strides forward, hacking furiously upon wood-strung sinew, and thrust into these final throes of life, the grim is determined to crush the wickerwalker under its own tremendous body weight. However, in an act of all-consuming rage, that saber cat didn't account for the ledge so perilously positioned behind him.

Not many lads have experienced the uncanny, surreal experience of flight, much less a voyage commissioned in grim fandango. The unlikely pair's tussle is brief, a somersault or two, until they are latched against the crevasse's far cliffside, before shortly departing towards oblivion. His pristine hat is tossed into the air, and catches the wind, delicately gliding further from the fray.

During the spilt-second occasion between a rock and a hard place, the wickerwalker can feel the mounting pressure, his mortal form is so desperate to elude its influence. He can hear the aching of bands and sinews, the splintering and snapping of bones. His ribcage fractures in an instant, the length of both legs have been perilously split apart, spilling essential marrow.

The saber cat is dead at this point, the indisputable strength of the impact must have delivered the timber confines completely through the roof of its mouth, and deep into precious brain matter. Then this beast tumbles lifelessly downwards, leaving the hunters feeble frame and mortal coil imbedded into the gorge's rock face. His skin and tissues have been pressured to fit inside every crack and crevice. Although without the feline's absurd vice, the hunter can feel himself slowly peeling off the edifice, and is powerless to stop it. He can't summon enough energy to grip any nearby rocks, or even groan in pain.

The descent to hell is aggravating, time seemingly slows to a crawl, and he falls for what feels like a whole century. All the while, his life flashes before his eyes, and it was dull and uneventful. The greatest thing to happen in this man's life, was his death.

His plunge concludes with an odd *ker-plunk,* noticing that his hat had landed beside him, distinctively enunciating its arrival with a *plop.* The wickerwalker had expected a lingering outcrop of boulders below, for his body to be rendered oblivion, and a visceral impact that would deposit his leftovers into a thousand gibs splattering across the canyonside. Instead, he careens into an uncharacteristically soft landing.

This hunter mocks himself, 'that generous blessing, oh heaven indeed,' especially as these waters seem to massage his contours, ease the tension, and wring the fright from his very bones. After the wickerwalker's turmoils, this is pure, unadulterated luxury. While suspicious at first, he eventually gives into the opulence, eager to lounge and relax, mellowing-out as the waves wash over him. It's gentle and soothing, then grows steadily terrifying. As if a bird begins nipping at a nut, tenderly testing its casing before abruptly hurling the husk at a slab to crack the shell and feast upon the succulent innards.

Quill-sized tendrils crawl over his body, coiling like snakes, nipping at each other in massing frenzy. This black sludge intends to swallow the hunter whole, leading him out of the frying pan, and into the fire. He screams defiantly, yanking his broken arms from the voracious muck while it grasps at these flailing limbs like a villain, sucking him further downwards with each subsequent breath. The wickerwalker struggles ceaselessly, straining every fiber to tread water, flinging his arms as far as possible, and frantically clawing at the surface. His wings have been clipped, both legs have been shattered during the spar between man and beast, and shall offer no respite.

This is a tarpit, one of many thrice-soured pools that dot these wastelands. Mires are a force of nature, an unyielding, lawful evil, and sticky concoction that traps anything unlucky enough to traverse within its boundaries. Wayward navigators may be pulled underneath, gallant vagabonds whose eyes may never glimpse the world of man ever again. They are preserved in a petrifying ooze, a perverse amber, that deadens cloth, fur, skin and flesh. This bubbling brew is kept prime by archaic, primordial methods, geothermal heat provided in generosity by the depths of hell. If one were to seek past its notoriety, some folk regard tar as a blessing from eminence. A wonderful jaunt, some chariot guaranteeing him safe passage to the afterlife. To perish in these ponds is a painless experience, a factor not shared by all fates.

The marksman spies a particular carcass slowly sinking beneath those murky waters that has dove headfirst, but a wickerwalker may recognize those hindquarters anywhere, the same spot of flesh pinned by an arrow with a whistle strapped against its shaft.

The persistent onslaught of torrents cede part-after-portion of his body. He had done his best to orient himself horizontally, a bid to float upon the surface, but it was only inevitable, as he has lost his legs, waist and abdomen to this war of attrition. This latest victim may hardly take a gulf of air before capitulating to the enveloping darkness, and every article underneath his crowning brush of hair vanishes beneath the oily surface.

If this is to be his end, he shall greet it readily. The wickerwalker explodes with his last ounce of remaining strength, thrusting each arm from the confines of his body, and throws wide their gaze.

While his eyes are assaulted by a festering black, the feeling of scouring salt water- before he gives-in to the depreciating irritation that obscures his vision once more, the hunter contemplates upon falsehoods and upside-down truths. He pictures a mirror image, some perfect replica and exact duplicate of the scene laid-out before his transition from the world over. However this is not the standard view, it's hard to describe menagerie of curios that line the mirror reality, and everything is disturbingly contorted: the environment is shrouded in a dull cerulean haze and overcast grey. The rocks are blatantly harsher here, exposing themselves like crystalline teeth.

He continues floating haphazardly, abruptly ascending the leeway in which he had once plummeted through no fault of his own. This is the abyss, a realm of chaos where regular physics do not apply, they are only considered before abruptly being booted aside. The breakneck-connoiseur has yet to actually escape, his legs dangle quite helplessly, casually drifting to providence far worse, towards the undeniable heart of the tar pit.

There is a flag fluttering loosely in the air, a patch in the sky permeating outward, a rhythmic beating tearing into the fabric of reality with menacing clouds of mist, electrifying energy and bolts of lightning. It is from this warp that an ethereal entity emerges.

She- or at least, if gods agree to benign terms like man, woman, angel, specter or charlatan, is harnessed by four feathery wings. One pair of these limbs allow the familiar ability of flight, the other set completely shrouds her figure like a veil. Even though the feather disguise her every feature, the hunter is confident of her appearance- sure of it, actually. He becomes obsessed by the notion that this is a beautiful woman, the epitome of feminine beauty, all his hopes and dreams. She possesses an otherworldly allure, regalia that cannot be contained.

Occasionally the plumage parts to reveal a series of eyes that line her heavenly body, breaking the dermal layer in spotlights. Yet the wickerwalker is awestruck, even while their pupils contract towards his direction, pulsating compulsively. These apertures are capable of conversation, and chittering to one another in delight.

The lady of the murk glides towards the stranger of this realm, causing him to shudder in her presence, whether that be from anxiousness, or the profound loss of blood. She hovers so closely to his bearing, that her radiance sears the hairs from his very skin, but that doesn't distract from her mystifying appeal in the slightest.

The seraph spirit's hair is woven from burly flaxen tendrils, and these vines flow downwards to a feature that would disturb most, some surreal scorpion-like protrusion. This appendage is awfully brazen, emanating as a tail, coiled all the way up her back, and grazing just behind where an ear might be; patiently waiting to strike, eager to inject its target with potent, corrupting taint. The angelic geist is caressed by decadent aromas, a fascination between mulled wine, cinnamon, and the fleeting musk of exposed mollusk.

Her hand, if it could be called such, rests upon the marksman's forehead and immediately soothes his soul. This armature is an assembly of sewn-together phalanges, and yet while they pierce through his brow to reach the delicate grey matter confined inside, the process is unusually comforting. It speaks to the hunter through these syringes like a telephone line, string nerves, and communicate directly with the his mind. His consciousness lulls away, fading until her presence becomes the sole voice in the wickerwalker's head, almost completely overwhelming the breakneck-connoiseur's mortal confines.

The voice is enthralling, booming yet subtle, as if hearing every living creature remark in unison. What a freakish conception, imagine insects crying out in borderspiel! These motions are wild thoughts, both a luxury and a bane. This specter perceives his deepest desires of the heart, and fortells that the man is not yet done with this world. She crafts a promise, a pact between mortal and paramount god, that he may be saved through her divine intervention, at a price. With her feelers probing his psyche, she justifies an answer before the hunter may even formulate the idea- perish the thought.

The marksman's vision falters, wrenching to an obscure drunken blur. It has become painfully tedious to see. He can feel the angelic figure disappear as soon as his eyes wind close. Her thoughts no longer permeate his, the time without her beguiling influence is agony. It has only been a few minutes, but in this personal hell, these moments drags onto hours, easily days.

The wickerwalker has lost his sight again, and remains terrified by that ordeal: the loss of his best feature It is not merely the desensitization which frighten him, but his proficient behind the bow kept the beasts at bay. Every once in awhile, he'll garner the slightest courage, blindly grasping, trying to reach out with his hands. The marksman no longer has a concept of space, wondering if he's still aimlessly floating around, or stuck within the grimacing confines of tar still. Is there a nearby rock or branch, anything to wrap his fingers around? He reaches desperately to no avail.

His rescue is fickle, a generosity granted by the gods, only if their schedule permits, and they have much greater things to attend to. What is a divine to cater to the whims of ants? The wickerwalker must come to terms that he may never escape this prison. He feels like a puppet of skin and bones, and last he checked, several were sticking out of his body. Strangely enough, he can't muster the notion of pain, nor the urge of food or drink. It is just him, and the abyss.

Only when the marksman comes to terms about the futility of emerging from this scrap does eminence offer benefit of the doubt. There's a raptor somewhere out in that hellscape searching out for him. Another unyielding predator, this time working in his favor. He is suddenly struck, hastily afflicted by the tightening of his belt and a sudden lash downwards, prompting a second plummet into the void, or its upside-down duplicate for that matter. He tends to a meager amount of hope, believing that 'Maybe- oh maybe, it dictates a voyage of escape, ferrying his body back into the original realm.'

The hunter feels propelled by an earthly force, that a harpoon has latched onto his waist, and is hurling him to freedom; much as this raptor shrieks, piercing the veil of darkness as diving for trout just beneath the fishing hole. This trailblazer is at the mercy of cosmic forces, and is delirious to what these divines may determine of him.

However, despite all these outstanding concerns, the wickerwalker finds that a lapse in consciousness has restored his strength and more importantly, his vision. Prophets be damned, in an act that defies the very reality of the known world, the hunter finds himself spontaneously back right where he started, here at camp. He lies prone in the snow, with those unbound fragments of a lantern at his nose, cementing that this is the ritual site in which everything has unravelled. The daylight is nothing fierce, a subtle radiance of dawn's early light that emphasizes the neighboring landmarks.

He attempts to stand to attention, although stumbles and falls. The wickerwalker is not as spry as he had thought, these events have certainly taken their toll. Spotting the withers of nearby swine, he eventually lumbers a winding, forty-feet path towards the boar carcass, and can't help but question how long he had been absent. The sow they fell had been an exquisite size, stretching from stem to stern around the gauge of a bench. Its remains have been thoroughly sifted through, scavengers have had their fill of charity. They set upon the belly first, the hefty, paunchy gut has been replaced by a shallow midriff. The boar's eyes, ears, and muzzle have been abruptly gnawed to bone. Several holes have been pressed into the bloated hide, allowing access to the savory prized innards. If scrounging vermin have had their way here, there must not be much of an opportunity to excavate his dismantled fellows. A decisive, glistening rime has frozen into the swine's pelt, a particular freezer-burn of sorts that has driven the scent away, and other scavengers do not venture near. The ice is impeccable, a glossy coating of varnish encompassing every inch of skin. It feels like a cocoon, as if the corpse is metamorphosing.

The wickerwalker peers deeply into the glaze, focusing on the image of a wiry old man. Grey whiskers comb forth from his stiff upper lip, protruding from the recesses of his nose and ears. Their face has shifted into a mangled expression, a complexion of innate frustration that comes as the crutch of being elderly. These contours accent every wrinkle, especially the congregation of forehead creases. As the marksman traces the grizzled appearance, he notices how their two gazes seem to match and follow.

"No, nah, it cannot be," he cries out.

This is his reflection, an uncanny visage of the young, earnest lad that he had been. The decrepit-prone, wisening hunter can hear the lady of the murk's maniac laugh, a cackle that echos with pompous exhilaration, as if all of humankind has filled a coliseum just to laugh at his depravity. He had not been betrayed, for his body has actually been repaired- only abused, and not returned in the state that he had expected as the desires of dark gods are fickle. Naturally, the breakneck is distraught, and raises his fists at the morning sky, cursing the dreamlike apparition for his dire misfortune.

Wrought in denial that this is not his new normal, he petitions certain unsightly characters, and pleas for any denizen of the firmament to rally and enact vengeance in his name. The hunter has seen her face: that beautiful, absolute paragon of perfection. He must be cursed, for no sane mind would scour reason for divine vengeance, and Bannermane would believe such a creature of lust could drive death's hand, much less to jest a mere mortal. These violations would be enough to flaunt prayers, and cause babes to stir in their cribs. Upon staring at his reflection, things don't feel quite right. His sinews are slack and slender, almost as if the wickerwalker remains a puppet, and must relearn those motions, even the most moot, such as the proper way to march, rile through packsnow, or even hold a spoon to his mouth. Surely this is a joke, a jab to dissociate him from his true goal, unhinge his name from becoming a household keepsake. Yes, Jeremiah Anders is flawless. Anders the Inscrutable. He is desperate to accumulate wealth, and doesn't need a degree of physical prowess to perform renowned feats or deeds. There is no need to preserve the body if he doesn't stride for vain glory. This prospect may avoid provisions and any unnecessary sleep if he aspires for something else entirely. His purpose is to work the mind, mold the insanity of what he has seen to his benefit. Yet something is wrong, perhaps his brain has aged too, and with broadening such horizons, rife with the disorders that often plague greybeards.

IX

—

RUTHLESSNESS IS A MERCY OF THE WISE

With the author's deteriorated mental state, his life has been a blur. Now trapped in the here and now, he can barely comprehend the scene laid out before him. Instead, Jeremiah trembles from the frigid chill, cursing that bastard Edmund who had to go and let all the cold in. He is so easily distracted by the thoughts that hassle his head, almost if a gremlin degenerate is trapped within the feeble recesses of his mind, and continues to tamper with it. Regular bouts of madness tickle at his grey matter, desecrating these last three years in ruinous plight, and preventing Jeremiah from focusing on anything other than trivial matters. This sorrow sways pity from the townsfolk, scoring the author donations of rations or a flame to join decent company.

Stricken by malaise, the knave can no longer recognize friend from foe, and sights a boy straying across the room whom attends to the wickerwalker's exhausted trounce. His ear is poised to Edmund's lips, checking if he's still breathing. This teenage seems like the sort of ilk who would appreciate literary fiction, and Jeremiah quickly finds himself wanting to advertise his theater dramas. So he tends curiosity, approaching the figure before him and testing his mental vault.

"Daub-," Jeremiah assumes before correcting himself, the right nerves take a few seconds to fire correctly, "-err, 'Liam. Could ye fancy words n' carry dis journal for mah? Tis gettin' quite 'eavy, 'cause I get lotta ideas."

With his arms motioning underneath an overcoat, the author excavates some deteriorating manuscript, a fleeting reminder of the grimoire, as both tomes worse for wear, ancient in work and age. The boy Jones can only stare in disbelief, his own hands grace the wickerwalker's frail throat who had just arrive unannounced and collapsed from exhaustion. He pries at Edmund's artery, exposing fragile skin and trachea, searching for a pulse, a nifty trick he had observed during Braithwaite petition earlier. This isn't the time for costermongering, nor the place so William utters a flair of confusion, criticizing, "What?"

Yet, the author still insists on sharing his work, and thrusts his burgeoning, overladen notebook closer to his prospective student. The hardcover's corners are worn to rounds, there are bookmarks, slivers and notecards galore protruding from the mess of parchment, each page a frivolous assemblage of folds and inkings.

"Fine-fine, I'll take it, okay? Just promise ye'll leave, this is not the time."

Jeremiah nods intently, a smiling guise perusing upon his lips.

William undoes the cap of his canteen, and offers Edmund Redmyne a generous sip, as he can always replace the helping in his free-time by cramming a handful of snow down its gullet. The wickerwalker smacks his lips together to pair, gathering his bearings, for he has an incredible tale to tell.

"'Arken, gatha 'round all ye good folk, and 'eed mah word o' danga. My kin n' I were thrashin' for small game, some bird or two like usual, 'nough tah stock ah perpetual stew. We stumbled 'pon the most peculiar thing, caravan 'ad wandered far-off course, quite ah distance from the river, n' several coaches careened intah ah cliffside. This convoy 'ad been chartered by Mandonmen. Consarnit n' curse that mob! *Gah!* Noticed that the crew gone missin'. Thought that absent-minded compliment 'ad waltzed-off, 'oweva by the time we check the cargo, we realized that we weren't the only team salvagin' the wreck. The lack of bison was suspicious- should've been warnin', 'nough for us tuh steer clear, but nah. Front o' our team was at the caboose, n' that portal which eerily yearned open, some cavern reek with rot. Dried blood crusted on the edges o' the bulkhead- so gross. I was trained betta than this, didn't even 'ear the beastie make approach. Some massive dire wolf leashed jaws 'round the mens' skulls, n' decapitated both muh 'untas with ah single snap. I dare not compete with such creatures, there was nah way to prevail. So I ran when it reached for mah, while those grims feasted 'pon my fellas. I fled, but at what cost? Must've led these monstas all the way back tuh Mad River Junction."

"Alas, poor brotha o' the Oestergaard, there was nothin' tah be done."

Meanwhile, Mandel has ignored this commentary entirely, and is wrought in a bizarre flurry of shrewd sense, overwhelmed with concern of how the wickerwalker had burst-in, and so nonchalantly tossed his precious, irreplaceable lantern aside, a certain residual feeling of being abandoned, left to lie alone in the packsnow. This is the Junction's sole source of viable heat, as no sound character would consult with that dreaded grimoire. The Hagman is in complete disarray, proclaiming that there could be a fire, and they must recover the lantern that lounges on its side.

"Relax, wind it down ah touch or two, 'ready mate," Mug Maxwell consoles, succoring a calm demeanor to alleviate all his concern.

"That's a 'urricane lantern right there. Those things are designed by the smartest men o' science, best regalia o' the robe that the Underdark 'as tah offa. These lanterns 'ere can withstand the worst throws o' Nana Nature, winds strong 'nough tah tackle bison from marble cliffs. This flame won't be goin' out anytime soon. 'Eck, even if 'e 'ad swung the contraption at ah wolf's snout, ye'd soona snap their muzzle n' still find spark, sure 'nough."

The cordwainer's concern shifts from one emergency to another.

"Oh, is that so? If I need not worry 'bout shakin' the match, now I must see that this light doesn't extinguish! What fuels this 'urricane lantern ye call it? We must keep tendin' flame, as the 'omestead 'as been picked-clean, n' I fear we don't 'ave the supply tah start 'notha lead."

"Edmund 'ere is talkin' of steppe jackals n' our impendin' doom, yet this is yer priority?"

"Yes, absolutely. I've 'ready died once, so maybe- just maybe, I don't 'ave them same priorities as ye mere mortals."

Suffice to say, the deliberation tattles on.

"*Hmmph*, well 'right, 'aggerton. I guess that I see yer reasonin'. These devices 'ave 'em lil cylindas on the bottom, replaceable cartridges for wheneva their fuel runs low, but truthfully, I don't know what they contain. Could be kindlin', ah miniature tinda-box, or even liquid kerosene, that type o' 'ighly-refined whale-oil. Parrafin is not just ah luxury- expensive tah harvest, overwhelmingly rare, scarcer still tuh be found on the plains. As people vie for supplies, brigands would kill for this. Too often do we cannibalize each otha for the sake o' familiar goods. Who knows how long these temporary arrangements will last, or if we may eva indulge the like 'gain?"

"I pray dat we nevah suffah injustices, dat we nevah 'ave da opportunity tah stick each otha's throats with needles. The God of 'Earth and 'Ome shall see us through," Jerome swears.

Balthus the Pygmy has his doubts, and condescendingly prods at the patriarch that prayers will not work.

"'Uh, after all we've been through, ye nevah particularly struck me as that religious type. 'Ate tah be the bear-ah o' bad news- but, tough luck. In ah world without gods, people fight like devils. Our mere existence is tempt tuh fate. 'As me thinkin' that these prayers fall 'pon deaf ears when our ploys are rife with envy and chaos."

"Dontcha be correctin' muh religion, boy, " Jerome asserts.

"Ye got yer faith to wave n' I 'ave mine. Livin' all dees years, I've earned mah grey n' da right tah worship as I see fit. Dem divines are real, even pressin' da soul o' dat father o' yers, so quit yer grand-standin'. Magik weaves through dis 'ere earth, priests n' mystics draw from da World Pillar. Whether dey move mountains, or summon sum extraordinary apparitions, cuisine tah line yer plate, even da newest statues of worships 'ave ah 'int of truth tah dem. I've seen it with muh very eyes. Anyone can 'come ah god- too easy tah pack ah house with worship: convince like-minded folk o' der ills, n' deem sum subject to prey 'pon. When dey decide tah spill der own blood in yer name, dat's when ye've ascended tah da heights o' dis firmament. Eventually dey'll realize dat der betta-off namin' othas for dis holy sacrament, n' weep da precious elixir o' life from one 'notha."

Pioneers are the victims of those wars between immortals, and as practitioners of the otherworldly, these divines use humanity as an excuse to offer no mercy. Eminence may dispatch a cruel blight upon a local village, which frankly, is a break from battle twixt ethereal foes, a comic drama to provide them humor. Praying to them is like releasing a genie from a bottle, and hoping for a wish. Townspeople find themselves reveling in the opportunity that they provide, all the while, not questioning why such courtesies were locked away in the first place. Invoking the names of gods allows for those to hone onto their position, bestowing boons or curses as they deem fit.

Balthus spits venom at Jerome's query.

"If it wasn't for the gods, I wouldn't need tah miss the good times 'cause I would be in them. Never shall I face the loss o' ah loved one, then weep n' mourn. I wouldn't need tuh face facts eitha, find muhself in ignorant bliss, enjoyin' everythin' life 'as tah offah. I could drink tuh mah 'eart's content, not tah mark joyous occasions or for sorrow, but ;cause I merely enjoy the bitter aftertaste o' alcohol."

The greybeard ducks his head and folds palms together, inciting a passage to anchor their teachings.

"Oh, lords o' da firmament," he conjures, "please forgive da misreadins o' muh kinsfolk. Dey mean ye nah 'arm by dees insults. I appeal tah da divines for safe journey, respite for company n' crew. May the God of 'Earth and 'Ome- the being who presides o'er our well-being, bind us, sponsorin' sum preservin' love for unity n' community. I beseech for da Storytella, da twin-god o' all men, tah fosta us rich o' blood n' constitute our health. Most of all, I pray tuh eminence for safe journeys, so dat we may make 'aste from pur-gah, pur-gah-toro-toro, Purgatorio n' reach dear Paradiso."

"Blasted ould fool of a ranger," exclaims Balthus as he hurls a bottle towards Jerome's general direction.

The pygmy doesn't intend to injure the meister by this attack, but stave how he has made a mistake that they may come to dread. Now they've captured the attention of immortals, these supernatural foe will toy with them. Who knows for sure though, maybe they'll actually aid their venture?

The copper flask staggers and lurches on the floorboards, finally striking a swollen nail that causes it to twirl in place. A shrill sound resonates from its casing, latching onto his lobes and prying eardrums. *Cha-tink, whirr-whirr-whirr.*

This abrupt chinking causes some demon to stir within William, bubbling a quarrelsome memory to the surface, but surreally not his own. He peers through the eyes from another, the length of his arms are dressed in tasteful suit sleeves, extending to finely-tailored, haberdasher-sewn cuffs around the wrist. The room is bathed in luminous candlelight, and the sudden-swaying chandelier above his head commands attention. The colliding and careening, thousand-prism crowd sways together. This dazzle centerpiece is an eyesore, and the phantom stranger finds himself lounging forward, resting both elbows on a counter-space that separates his person from a woman and three daughters. They are all huddled, perplexed by frightened expressions.

"Gudsir, 'ey Gudsir" an attendant annunciates from the coach's alley, "Yer beverage, suh."

This server leans over and lowers a platter presenting some green-glassed bottle of Manhattan Dry Ginger Ale, and several empty mugs, already uncapped, releasing a carbonated froth around the rim.

"Oh ye, I 'most forgot. That'll do nicely, thank ye Percy."

The waitress places each cup atop the counter, nabbing the beverage from her tray. She clearly resents having to pour the swill among a jerking carriage, the occasionally rough sway of the coach coaxes lesser-experienced men to lose their balance- but not her, she is cut from denim cloth, clearly a descendent of Bannermane restitution. Through a trained motion, the attendant cleverly hides the platter behind her back, and delivers a golden liquid bounty into the first chalice.

However, this ginger ale promptly churns sour, contorting from its usual mint tinge to a frustratingly obscene amber midstream. This transformation is striking, and alarms the family, especially the children, whom *gasp* and gawk. The bewildered servant peers at the bottle's label, hectically searching for an expiration date, reason or some kind. Distraught, she tilts the bottle and peers down the shaft spy the syrup.

As the moments awkwardly shamble by, the chandelier quivers, quakes and slams against the ceiling of the coach, sending splinters into the air. *Thwack, crash.* The waitress, and everyone standing nearby, collapse in knots when the caravan suddenly lurches, shifting towards a new heading. Glassware reels-off the counter, dispersing shards across the carriage floor, and ale seeps into the wooly carpet.

There isn't much that could steer a bison off-course, as they're acclimated to the worst Nana Nature has to offer, their own beards are often awry with ice and packsnow. Something wicked must be arriving, as caravans are lucrative targets, leaden with valuable cargo and medicines. Boar's Bands, goldbands and highwaymen will always attempt to wedge themselves aboard for a slice of the good-life.

The passengers inside the coach are thrust securely into their seats, and heaved forward the next. Heads bash into furniture, frame, and often one another. William's cap strikes into the adjacent windowpane, and he can sight his true origin in its reflection. He is no longer himself, but his appearance is akin to that of Herald Barrows- a quite uncanny resemblance, save for a broken nosebridge and the red ichor spouting from his left nostril. There isn't much time to savor the sight, as the pane instantly glazes over with ice while clamoring barks and an animalistic laugh grips the frigid air.

This flashback readily disperses to a tremendous booming, sending the trading post to staves and perhaps the entire Junction. It is the sound of thunderous hooves, a stampeding horde and monstrous menagerie. The flatlands relent to a dense, gargantuan plume, an encroaching cloud creeping over its plains; a titanic weatherfront with a voracious attitude, consuming anything in its path. Something here and something there, from harsh outcrops of boulders, shoulder-biting ravines, even mighty citadels of pine; an avalanche of sleet and hail, better described as a wall, gusting in one direction, towards their settlement.

The two sisters, Libby and Bids Warder, barge back into the caravan stockades. Gulping air and then suffering from bouts of heavy wheezing, desperation litters their achy breaths, "There- *ugh,* isn't much time-"

"A storm!" her sibling frantically interrupts while massaging her temples.

"Yes-yes, a-ah storm. I was just gettin' to that. Barricade the foyah, slap this door with *umm*-ah some pile of sticks- nah staves actually. Bigga, we need bigga sticks. Whateva we can manage. Sure, we'll be trapped in 'ere with ah due-dozen bunch of corpses, but these dead won't make us any sicka. Much ratha suffah to their silent judgements n' indecency than 'ave the winds flay skin from our-ah bodies. C'mon, shake the dead 'ready, let's get movin'. There's ah brief window 'ere, n' I wish to make it!"

The strongest characters of their makeshift company: weak yet able, hampered but not yet infirm, are those of Osbourne Bullheaded, Edmund Redmyne and Korralack the Kable, whom leave the weary cronies to withdraw various appendages leftover from the construction of their caravans. Austerlaund was able to prevent the spoiling of her derelict patients through a deep-freeze, opening hatches of the room to frost, preserving all instances of flesh and woe. Although, those still warm and breathing can't last long without heat. By covering these cold vents, they are limiting their exposure to the elements. As the team endures, breezes continue to trickle through the gaps, however the gales cannot openly flaunt.

Together, their jury-rigged project isolates the bison alley from the remainder of the trading post, and the bulkhead door that the sisters, Balthus and Mandel had originally emerged through. They have converted this demesne to a remotely defendable position, yet nothing palpable. There is a distinctive lack of welcomeness as charred remnants of the summoner's circle have faded, it is no longer presents a friendly hearth.

This isn't just a sudden storm, William warns, this is something else entirely.

"I'm not sure if this is some fact that I should be so keen tah admit, but Mandel n' I 'ave seen this evil. Creatures, forbidden grims o' the reach. They are comin'."

The company wraps-up their renovations in the nick of time. They can hear approaching rabble of raps, scrapes and scours clambering over the building like a wave.

"It's 'ere," Libby whispers in a mumble that has the tendency to cling onto their lobes.

The commotion seems to weave its way around the exterior, racing for the hunt. How many wolves could there be, a score, dozens or so, if not a hundred? The revelation sounds morbid. Morbin Evershade recoils when he sights a beast through a gap in the timber, and the beam he had been holding in place for Rochester instead plummets to his feet. As grims surmount the roofing, gobs of saliva seethe from their feral snouts, snarling, leaking the height of the caravan post, then accumulating in acidic pools upon the floorboards, and erupting in steam.

"Stray from those geysers!" Edmund barks.

These mouths slave after primal needs, a craving for gruesome gastronomy and the spilling of blood. They are determined to feast, even if it's upon bland bone and marrow. William catches sight of these terrors, blood-matted bands of gore clad their alabaster and cream fur. This varnish flows into a bristly mane, eventually giving way to ear with chunks missing out of them. It is a prominent feature, flaming outwards into a fan, pricked to attention and cocking intermittently, adjusting to the slightest noise as the crew shuffles together, huddling closer to the center of the room.

The foremost among them presents a scarred and mutilated shape of brow, an iron that flows harshly until its eye lines-up perfectly along the makeshift window. Those pupils dilate, fluttering back and forth, analyzing the contents of room and gazing upon its occupants. They are aching to find a flank, searching for a weakness to exploit, discovering a flaw that will lead them to rip and tear into tender meat. The bulk of the pack treads ceremoniously, navigating the caravan depot so that they develop trenches in the packsnow, and trample permafrost.

It's not long before these eager creatures locate the outermost, alley-bound bulkhead, and feet begin to paw at the root of door, as the wolves attempt to dig a way inside. The wooden trim and portions of the floorboards are torn asunder, enough space for a muzzle to break through the mold, a harbinger of the horrors to come. Those nostrils flare, it can smell their quarry, intent on dining upon the townsfolk. This wolf strains and bucks against the curtain as death does not linger. Only when the shattered wood pierces skin, generating six-inch gouges and rising fountains of blood, that the grim finally halts their advance in order to lick its wounds. This is a creature of quicksilver, an entity whom accepts nothing less than perfection. They distribute flawless killing blows, and as such, are swift to recognize their failures. The pack dashes-on, frolicking in the direction of the promenade.

A lingering wolf *snorts* underneath the doorframe before it parts, unleashing a rancid mist. The company is taut and still, paralyzed by fear. They clench at one another's chest, shoulders, and limbs, *gulp* and hold their breaths to the tunes of a bestial chorus. Every now and then, the wolves will find a tasty morsel to snack on, their howling drowns out any ambient, rogue screams. There can't be more than twenty people or so scattered about the Junction. It is surreal to hear the cacophony as a stranger's vocal cords are separated from their body. William's company is lucky that their invaders have located easier prey, their deaths have given them valuable time to think.

Rochester proposes an escape while the situation rallies against them.

"'Eathens at the walls, we need tah go. I 'ave tah get out of 'ere!"

This sort of enthusiasm warrants certain attention from Balthus.

"Where do ye plan tah go," he mocks, "out there, with those- things? Whereva shall ye find sanctuary? N' what would happen tuh us? Pray-tell, are we just gathered 'ere for yer convince, ah welcomed distraction tah these wolves so ye may bolt off? I beg that such ah feat is impossible. Now, I realize that, n' I'm clearly not ah runnah-at-'eart, so I don't possess that fleetin' notion. These beasts will surely devour us, tis only ah matta o' time," they ascertain. "I 'ave not endured this long tuh be diced n' rendered intah bloody pulp."

Osbourne finally quips, "Nor have I, man of sage."

The room enters a bout of bizarre silence, not knowing whether to banter, depreciate or recant to their emotions, as the constant cackling of claws upon timber derives attention. Their discourse is interjected by wild propositions, as the bewildered author conjures the obscene. He implores them to venture westmyr in his own unique sort of way. While other members of the party may heed this dialog as his cliche, crazy-man thoughts, certain members treat the incite with a hint of wisdom, as only a fool wouldn't seek refuge during a storm. Jeremiah is not the type to let an idea linger, typically stealing them for his own selfish accord, capitalizing every waking moment.

"Ah town undah siege! Dees nightmares 'aunt our wakin' dreams. Stay 'ere, boarded n' leeched with fear. Will dees predators o' da plains triumph, or shall da common kin rally, face der monsters, tah drive range from does 'earths? Dey rip n' tear intah der prey. Da conflict culminates in violence. Voyage tah da cliffs of bone where skin is 'ready torn tah shreds- egads, ripped 'part like da craglands! Mutilation n' gore guh-lore, 'venture 'ways makes ah tall tale!"

"Gramercy," bucks Lena, whom then pinches the bridge of their nose, and comments with a dismissive regard.

"Slow your roll, patron-father, and stow these fears. I perish the thought. Now is not the time for nonsense."

"Now, wait just ah second 'ere. The craglands- 'uh, now that is ah curious attitude," Balthus asserts.

"What do ye mean?"

"I've got tah admit, while I typically tune-out Jerry the Frank's gibberish language, that mention really got mah thinkin' that 'e might be ontah somethin.'"

"It'll make for ah good story 'round da campfire too," the author interjects, goading them into his insanity.

Balthus humors the idea further, clapping his hands together for consideration.

"Say we swipe our things n' 'igh-tail it straight outta the Junction. Simply put, there are no wolves in the west. Could be, but beasties like stickin' tah the plains. If we steed all the way tah any otha Bannermane settlements, much less Bonaventure, they will surely set 'pon us. Our last-ditch convoy will 'come more like ah funeral procession. So, let's lead towards the mountains n' that glacier 'stead."

Townspeople of the caravan post have begun to invest themselves in this conversation, using their position in room to side with speakers of their nature, and huddle nearby. Most of the company has taken to brooding, yet still listen intently. Osbourne and lady Lena have been distracted, occupied by their own conversations, rousing over the Underdark, and its relative safety compared to here. The frontier isn't anything like the books they've studied, revels and great fascinations roared aloud over a keg of ale, or what could have been conjured by their heinous imaginations. Together these two awake fond memories like sifting through the bustling causeways of Urbana, reminiscing and dredging academics, costermongers, and foundrymen; laughing in lieu of their dire straits. These memoirs are so nostalgic that they produce the slightest gleam in their eyes, and career a rogue tear down the cheek. When the knights-errant mentions his employ, Warden Easton, Knight-Commander Worth a Thousand Wards, the Preeminence of Clan Claremont, Lena abruptly sours and chides away, rather willing to focus on the situation on hand, instead.

"There must be some reason they don't trek anywhere near the glacier," Balthus puzzles while putting his thinking cap on, "They tend tah pursue, trackin' herds of bison n' caribou. All their food stays in the open plains, so I guess venison isn't plentiful past the glacial mire."

"'Ow far is it, Balthus? We wuldn't get ten-feet outside 'fore does 'ounds catch our scent! I welcome ah plan- any plan, dat ain't madness, n' won't garn-ah intah assisted suicide."

"Listen. Our discovery is inevitable, the arrival o' bestial foe imminent, so best we tempt fate 'pon our own volition. There it is, I've convinced muhself that this is the best idea. Let's do it 'ready. I may be scrawny, yet even I would last ah betta chance on foot while these horrors scavenge through the town. Just ah reminder folks, this is ah fleetin' idea. Longa we dawdle, the shorter 'ead-start we garn-ah. There is nah time, we must flee now."

All ears tune-into this scheme, and Mug Maxwell demands a vote, that way he may gauge the odds. The Bannermane are a democratic people, while surely corrupt at heart, they would never shame towards casting a ballot. Balthus reiterates the proposal, that they flee and steed westerly, asking each member of their makeshift company to decide by raising their hand. He pools over the audience like a silent auction, estimating every minor lift of the finger, or firm palm in the air, and praising them for it.

The erudite affirms each gesture with a resounding "Aye, that's 'notha one," until he takes the counts of Lena Tillstead, Cliff Fetherhaugh, Rylie Hess, the sisters Libby and Bids Warder, Rochester, Osbourne Bullheaded, Morbin Evershade, Mug Maxwell, Braithwaite, William Walder-Fields, Mandel Haggerton, Korralack the Kable and Edmund Redmyne who has been catching his breath near the foremost fancy of the room. Even his nemesis, Jerome fashions a scowl, quietly nodding their head. Not one to take requests, the author himself is preoccupied, instead staring at those musings and markings that he's tendered amongst the wall, but Balthus assumes that he'll graciously tag along.

"-oh dreary, I've lost count. That'll be seven- at least eight or so whom offah their services as portahs."

The effects are unanimous, for once they're in complete agreement, an extremely rare event. If they stay, they are guaranteed to surely perish. Folks don't drown by treading water, they croak by staying there.

"We must at least try," the greening medical practitioner, Braithwaite, preaches, "No matta the odds. Betta tah die face forward than on your back, kickin' n' screamin'. I've seen that shrike betta than most."

"Aye, not that I condone terrible fates. The craglands are ah crudely mapped territory, I pledge muhself tah journey for the world's end. This will take all the strength that I 'ave tuh offah."

"Surely Korralack, if yer in, then I'm in too," Morbin incites, eagerly grabbing his gear.

The amateur archaeologist corrals his thieving kit, throwing all his bits, bobbles, hooks and pinches onto parchment, and coils the entire convention tightly like bedroll. There are several strange instruments present here, those scraggly lockpicks guaranteed to arouse suspicion from the city watch, and unlock the finest vaults Mad River Junction has to offer.

Edmund the wickwalker stirs to action, possessing a rather stoic nature, and while rattled by the loss of his fellow huntsmen, is ultimately undeterred, recognizing that there is no time to delay. The hunter marches right up to Mandel, swiping his lantern from the cordwainer's conniving hands, and commenting at the thieving scoundrel, "This is definitely mine," before clipping the beacon onto his waistband.

Some residual flame still resides within infernal mechanizations of steel and ingenuity. Hopefully the breathes of this miniature furnace will comfort him, as Edmund's every action is showcased by anxious, instinctual shivering. He hasn't yet hurtled through his ordeal, and the lingering effects of hypothermia are usually treated by the graces of a fortnight. Time heals all wounds but that of the heart, love and hate often scar those very souls.

The paladin and the roving madman are nearby, comparing injuries of their very own. Osbourne is showcasing how the windstorms curled his ankles, and how he has been using his broadsword as a cane to prop his walk. Frontier sawbones ordinarily amputate afflicted areas, opting to replace a person's limb with a prosthetic. The process is brutal and tenderizing, but often a saving grace around years of torment. Artisans have perfected the trade of prosthetic arms, facial features, fingers, legs and toes, enough to where they blend the reality between truth and fiction. It was the knight's sole demand: no sawbones. In the cultures of Clan Claremont, forfeiting a body part demonstrates weakness, that in a defining moment, the warrior faltered and failed. Jeremiah is fascinated by the concept of this crutch, and asks to borrow the weapon for a short stint, explaining that his encounter with the Crooked Men sullied his own leg lame.

The armament Osbourne wields isn't a particular, one-of-a-kind ancillary, it is whom bestowed the blade that tickles fancy. A knight-errant swears himself into service of a liege lord or their family, not for money, but for fame, establishing their sire's various interests to garner reputation among peers. Urbana is home to countless vagrants, competing verminfolk whom desire to establish their name, enlisting as squires, though few return from their drills and return as questing knights. When paladins demonstrate their battlefield prowess, the absolute best of which land titles that shift their status into the aristocracy, venerates of the realm, and counts over their common kin.

Osbourne is one of those few exonerated bannermen- close to becoming an established household name, free to select his ventures, adding these exploits for squires to revel-in for decade to come. These sort of deeds define him as a Bannermane at heart. If he weren't raised in the Underdark, the man would have thrived on the frontier. The knight-errant has recently sworn to Warden Easton, an exalted lord of Urbana, vowing to rescue her missing wife and daughter- quote, "-or thou I shan't return alive."

This is how the Clan Claremont agent first found himself on a train to Bonaventure, and a carriage last month destined to the Junction. If William hadn't been so caught up running errands for Eli the Stockpile, maybe he would've found a liking to the trooper earlier. Whenever the boy Jones has an opportunity to pesters others, he hassles them thoroughly, inquiring about the knight's reputation.

"Well I've never heard of them," Lena rudely remarks.

Leg pains are a drop-in-the-bucket compared to the ailments that usually plague townspeople. The cold tenses the muscle and sinew, exacerbating otherwise bruised or achy demeanors. It is nearly impossible to maintain proper heating during the night. A sore back, simply from waking-up no the wrong side of the bed, renders the remainder of the day moot. Members of the company prescribe countless homeopathic medicines to get through the pain, alcohol has the tendency to temporarily alleviate anything frigid. However, spirits cause the blood vessels to expand, amplifying the effects of hypothermia and furthering heat loss. It's unfortunate that the most accessible and effective treatment can easily become disastrous, even fatal at times.

Vagabonds tempt a trip to the Underworld by exposing themselves to the flesh-numbing, mind-altering effects of hypothermia. When mediated carefully, in a pinch, this procedure may dampen the effects of some sprain or injury, keeping a navigator together, just strong enough to strive for this next hill, or stray from the embraces of scavengers. If a trailblazer cannot make the next bend, delve sanctuary to build a fire and retain their heat, the cold exposure renders a moot point.

A majority of the company is simply too weak to haul supplies, the able-bodied few divvy their wares to one another. Lena decides to tote their remaining provisions, while Korralack ferries waterskins, Cliff Fetherhaugh porters additional skins and coats, and Rylie has the grimoire strapped to her chest like a salvaged piece of armor. Mandel has miraculously recovered from his demise, standing tall without a lapse in strength- bizarre. Their party made determination that despite the cordwainer's ample complaints, he should lug all their miscellaneous gear: bedrolls, twine and makeshift things. Meanwhile William got off the hook, saving favor with Osbourne and Edmund has gone awfully well.

The boy cherishes his knapsack, stockpiling a dozen minor knick-knacks, magpie collections, and herbs, especially that wand of ginger root. He tightens the cord around his abdomen, and flings the whole lot onto his backside. The townspeople have also been rearing for a skirmish, as those wolves will catch onto their scents quickly, and they need to be prepared for a brawl. Williams hands nervously clutches at his halberd head, as his friend Mandel displays an abhorrent, flurry of punches, a specific one-two combination of some jab and cross. The familiar singing of metal chimes-out while Osbourne trawls blade across the charred floorboards, testing the arcane aftermath. He props it at arms-length, scrutinizing the contents of blade, running his fingers around the blunted tip. When the paladin determines that it'll do its job if need be, he exhibits a scabbard from around his back to stow the hardware. Edmund sports his pneumatic launcher, funneling a harpoon into the tube while Jeremiah attempts to test-out the pointy ends. Having missed the opportunity before, and regrets not pulling the trigger sooner. His left palm queries the weight of the armament, it balances elegantly, undamaged from the wickerwalker's intense journey. Learned vagabonds equip themselves with broad, oversized hunting knives, to which Edmund slides into a sheath at his waistline, and the Warder sisters barter their arsenal of shanks, hoarding an untold number of daggers and dangers into cradles across their abdomen, ankles, shoulders and thighs. Balthus strives for a non-traditional approach, vying for something rather curious. He exercises a jury-rigged baton, just his size, fashioned from a staircase bannister. That's it- really, their motley crew couldn't fend-off a battery of Boar's Band.

The companions edge closer to the door, suddenly pausing to tend an ear towards a wolf's signature howl, *ah-woo*, interrupted by hounds and jarring screams as its brethren beasts tear into their latest victim. These wayward fatalities is keeping the pack preoccupied, hopefully enough so that William's party may escape.

Korralack dismantles their barricade, promptly settling beams aside, enough of a project to pry open the door and allow Morbin to bid brief venture outside, peering down the lane in both directions. The ires of winter violate their refuge, a wave of frost bursts into the parlor, sulking forward and staggering against every boot. This fog penetrates the wooden floorboards with rime, encasing timber debris and day-litter in droves of ice. If nature had its way, this would be the fate of all men.

Meanwhile, Morbin retreats posthaste, turning around with his whiskers already tinged in frost, signaling to the others that the coast is clear, at least for now. The supplies have been packed, and they've strapped on their coats, everything appears good-to-go.

"Hooray," William sarcastically chides.

"Are we ready?" Balthus prods.

"'Member kin, stay close in-line, knitted tighta than ah bride's corset 'pon wedding day."

Libby, with her younger sister in tow, gently shoves Korralack and Morbin out of the way so that they make take lead. These two vagrants usher their convoy outside onto the lane, crouching slightly in the weathering in order to mask the sound of their footsteps as much as possible. William snakes behind Lena and Rylie, grabbing Mandel's wrist to nudge him in the right direction. They overpacked his totes so liberally, that it's difficult for the cordwainer to see, his gaze is crossed by the loose ends of thread and bungies, instead of the backs of his dear comrades, occasionally the weight will cause him to teeter into them.

Their route carefully avoids the caravan post's plaza, not that they'd receive a blessing from Charlie Mandon anytime soon. That tract is lined with residences, ice-boxes that surely have worked the pack into a frenzy. The sisters lead them through the bulkhead door, immediately arranging a turn, skulling through certain backstreets to reach the western quarter and the bulwark. William snakes behind his company while they takes their first steps into the fray. All the motion that the boy can manage is reckless, and they huddle tightly together. There's no unison, simply coordinated chaos, as if a flock of seagulls finds themselves navigating the alleys and backwaters of the settlement.

"Quiet now, quickly now," Rylie chants, jostling the boy Jones forward.

William relents at this gesture, yet understands the need for a sudden march. The putrid stench of rot tickles their nostrils, "Watch yer step," their ferryman, Libby warns.

Once those in the lead veer away, William sights the tragedy that befall them, and he utters a flustered gasp. Their company poises themselves around a murder scene, and they carefully step around a freshly-laden corpse. These stifled scraps appear to be the confines of a poor woman, however the remains are filleted so thoroughly, it's awfully difficult to tell where the fleece begins and their figure ends. Rylie Hess has memorized almost every wayfarer to visit their settlement, from the most astute business magnates to trivial tourists, but even she couldn't begin to identify the lass, as her facial features have been scraped away, revealing all manner of bone, empty sockets, and an exposed orifice leading to her sinus cavity. The bulk of meat, guts and entrails is missing, pilfered so thoroughly, that it's impossible to cope with the loss. Her arm- or limb as it so appears, has undergone an extremely painful deboning process. Dozens of canine teeth had impacted into shoulder gristle, surely frothing at the mouth, and yanked flesh free from the constraints of tendon and ligaments, like sliding an arm through a sleeve, except in this instance, the sleeve is a nutritiously balanced human snack. The exposed ivory underneath has deteriorated, charred by copious spoonfuls of acidic bile, creating a mystifying miasma of heat. This aura feels unnatural, corrupting, especially as the area is adorned in villainous grease.

There's a story in this bloodshed, and not a tale one desires to be caught-up in. This victim made haste to the nearest door, and struggled with the frame before being caught by her abductors. On his way past, William hurriedly jiggles the handle and gives quite a tug. This door doesn't dare budge, the portal is firmly jammed-shut, unyielding to anything less than the end of the world.

Their hustle is an unnatural pace, as if a bird was forced to the ground and forced to walk through a tunnel. They try their hardest, although each footstep is still awkward, bumbling and obscenely loud. Without a town's worth of people to stamp the freshly-laden snow firmly into the permafrost frost, they're doing all the work themselves. A steady symphony of *scrunch, scrunch, scrunch but with haste, scrunch, terrified scrunch, scrunch but in borderspiel, then le scrunch* clamors into the blushing afternoon sky.

This carnival of noise has the audacity to beckon any predators that lie in wait. In fact, as the company approaches a three-way junction, a hasty howl from one end causes them to career left. The wail echos off the empty halls, collapsed decking and hearths of empty residences. It bounds off every splintered board and reverberates through sheets of the corrugated, tin-plated roofing, until the caterwaul gains such a strength that it causes William to tremble where he stands. Edmund cannot tell the direction, nor the distance of where it originated from, only that the voice multiplies in force and number, a heinous beck and call.

"Flee, flee now. Thattaway!" he commands, pointing to the opposing street.

Even the wickerwalker concedes to these shockwaves, his nerves easily disguised as shivers. If a veteran huntsman succumbs to these honest threats, then he too has ample reason to fear. William contemplates the perverse questions that led to this point.

'Will the next turn be their last? Shall they, too, meet grisly fates? When a wolf clamps down on my arm, will it sever immediately, or will the shock save me from the pain? Am I to greet my dear ole mum at the Gilded Gates of Guldourame?'

It is no favor for children to upend their parents in the Underworld. These dilemmas are existential, the boy believes that surely, these thoughts plague the others, but the townspeople don't dare beg for answers.

"If only I were quicka on the draw," the boy Jones confides to himself, "betta at mah job, I could've nabbed my ticket n' left 'fore these events 'ad the opportunity unfold. Now my life is on the line, and I 'ave tah fight tuh survive. This shouldn't be the responsibility of a boy, I'm an explorer at 'eart. I'm 'ere tah explore the world, grapplin' the sights, smells n' scenes, leavin' nuh stone unturned. Maybe, if I'm lucky 'nough tah leave muh mark, I'll retire tuh ah riverfront cottage in Whitehorse at the ripe age o' forty."

One thing's for certain, a reality that William has always realized: the gods have never confided in him, they exist explicitly to torment him. Perhaps they gain their powers through worship- yes, yes, but of course, it all makes sense now. The boy Jones wasn't merely chosen through luck-of-the-draw, the pantheon, from the Briarheart through the Trickster god, expects him to fall onto his knees and beg for mercy. Those godless dogs must repent, for beings of firmament relish in suffering. In their eyes, this is another mortal vessel to bend to their inconceivable, undying will. Humans are nothing more than chess pieces on a multi-tiered, overly-complicated, weather-prone gameboard. He shall be forced to triumph passed hurdle after hurdle, face adversities strewn from weather and bone, and be set upon by the largest of grims, to trifles of threats.

As what is life without struggle, the ceaseless confrontations that break men into an early grave? It's ingrained in the very fabric of human nature, people need obstacles to overcome, challengers to relent against, as all blades needs to be tested. And although the brand may eventually become pointless and dull, everyone can gaze upon it with upmost certainty: that it works, tried and true.

Is it the work of the divine that only those with upmost character may parade to the Underworld? Why must we weather storms, have ourselves built and broken over and over again. This is William's quandary, a destiny to build, rather than destroy. He shakes his head to quell the illusion, the incessant howling is befalling victim to hallucinations. Regardless, it is best not to hedge bets on far-flung ideas, and instead, apt to focus on the now. He possesses the strength and determination to save people. The simple fact that he's here with the knowledge of the now, changes things, potentially for the better. His presence here may save lives, as without William, they are surely lost.

The company is rattled by the gnawing taunts of wolves. They relent to fear, an anxiousness that plagues the party, and begin to spread-out further, their own pack pulling apart at the seams. Balthus small frame- which is a shame really, and although something of a spectacle, has recently found himself outcompeting the others, usurping the company from Libby who tugs at his shoulder, attempting to pull him back. Meanwhile, towards the rear, Osbourne begins to concede, as his wounds have been catching up with him. The paladin is falling behind unannounced, and while unencumbered by the metal carapace that usually straddled his shoulders, his mutilations are pronounced and severe. Austerlaund predicted that it'd take months to recover from his current, pained state- that is, alongside proper medical care, the notion of which is laughable.

Matters of this factor, especially those affairs that are heart-rending, dredge all manner of instinct. Curses, William should've been prepared, and wrapped fresh bandages to protect his face. Now, beads of sweat cross his brow, pooling into an earnest lad's sockets until his eyes are afflicted by distressed, maddening redness. This affliction draws his ire, and the boy Jones periodically swears, yanking at the collar of his fleeces to dampen the salty torrent. Mandel takes stride, side-by-side with William, and the two act bolster one another, as it's quite difficult to see. Eventually, William's gaze recovers, occasionally teetering towards those in the company that lax behind. Although they're not his responsibility, it's reassuring when settlers stick together. Unfortunately, one member of their party has become all too carefree, and the boy Jones almost didn't notice. Without the medication to keep his whimsy at bay, Jeremiah is prone to stints of dementia, and hastily halts in his tracks.

"Where 'as it gone? Ah, shucks," the author mumbles to himself, "I must return tuh da chapta. Left mah scryin'-stone 'hind. Without it, I'll nevah know wut tahmorrow's weatha may bear."

He takes a moment to determine his position, and briskly paces in an entirely separate direction.

"Oh gods, no-no," blurts William.

Taking flight and breaking rank by sprinting towards the intrepid navigator, he bounds distance in a moment's notice, yet depreciates to the bulk which burdens his thighs, faltering in Jeremiah's presence with each knee collapsing into the snow, frantically grasping at his coattails. The boy acts as an anchor nabbing onto the fabric that dresses his damaged arm, and he winces in paranoia, despairingly urging to be left alone.

"Ow-ow, yer 'urtin' me. Ye can't do dat. Let go, let go. Let me leave. I don't know ya, n' I sure don't wanna be 'round ya!"

William regains his composure, attempting to pull the author with all the might he can muster, and finally bring themselves about. He desperately pleads with him, "No, Mr. Goodsir! Ye know me, it's 'Liam, I'm William. Please, ye must 'member me. Please, please! We just don't have time for this!"

While he may have plucked the author backwards, this abrupt wrest cannot break the depths of Jeremiah's trance. William can see the wiseacre's faded visage, a tormented, glazed-over gaze, there is absolutely no rescue from this delusional state. They can't carry him, William ascertains; it's either Jeremiah or their gear, and as preached by men of the caravan whose entire lives are based upon the cargo they haul, 'the needs of the many outweigh the needs of the few.' This entire effort is for naught.

A primal roar culminates into a certain resounding boom, emitting a sudden shockwave that shakes the nearby residences to their foundation, causing several to collapse around their audience, and overlaying the alley in debris.

William withdraws, cowering in fear and receding onto the permafrost. He trembles in horror, being held within the fell influence of grims.

The beast is impeding the end of the lane, nary hundred feet away, which is a dangerous distance to toil. Its fierce, guttural growls refuse the eminence of the preceding howl, yet still command their full consideration nonetheless. The boy deciphers its crude, silhouetted form as it mends closer approach. Each step the wolf steers is pronounced, timed and calculated, as ordained by tarnished yellow eyes, a basilisk's piercing gaze that petrifies those nearby immediately in place. Their muzzle is stunted, a short-faced skull that sports a pair of elongated canines and hysterically loose ivorywork. Generous measures of foam caress each spearhead-sized tooth, a rambunctious and frothing lather that drips down the wiry beard, fizzling the snow in the vicinity into steam. This is William's first glance of a wilderness predator, he had never been so unlucky before. The wolf's mane is preposterously towering, swelling into its heights of exasperated withers, which descends into a pelt dictated by mange, giving the appearance of a barded bison. As the predator waltz closer and closer, William is yanked to his feet and tossed backwards. Osbourne shoves him away, putting his own feet forward.

"Get out of here, boy. Do not be guilted by an unfortunate truth, he's a lost cause, dead weight. Return to the others and leave the two of us. I am too weak for march and coming days. I was never going to make it anyway. Go, go now! I'll distract them."

William had been thrown nearly ten paces, causing him to stumble and promptly recoil.

"Dear Jeremiah will meet his fate," the knight-errant explains, "but he will not journey alone."

With a warrior's instinct, the paladin retrieves his scabbard that sits astride his back, drawing arms while the old man begins mutter gibberish to him, plentiful advice that has become ill with age. The knight, and unknowingly the author, intend to make a last stand.

Osbourne notices the welling tears in William's eyes, "It was a pleasure to meet you, even though it was the briefest stint. You, and those throughout, have done me justice. I shall die for them, I shall die for honor, yet I am no hero. This sacrifice was going to happen one way or another. I cannot ask your shoulders to bear burden, nor these legs to carry stride any longer."

Further ahead in the alley, their company has been powering ahead for a spell. Folks such as Rochester and Braithwaite have been oblivious, and are quite eager to escape these proceedings that lie in their wake. Rylie is the sole practitioner who notices her comrades sudden departure. She turns tail, backtracking vehemently and drawing Edmund Redmyne's ire, trying haste to the vying arms of Jeremiah and the boy Jones in an offer of rescue. Rylie closes the gap within the blink of an eye, almost hurdling over the boy Jones entirely.

Meanwhile, the wickerwalker crouches, closing one eye to gauge distance while the scribe furiously yanks at William's shoulders, boasting that they must stand together. Her efforts are in vain, as William is positively terrified, and has already begun scampering away on his own. Osbourne brandishes his sword and heaves his sheathe heedlessly to the side. Another luxury to be tossed in the tidings of battle. He raises this blade about neck-high, aiming past William and Rylie, and aligning the direction they should make steed.

"I bid you all a very fond farewell. Today I take my final voyage, and join the ranks against a never-ending night."

With those final words, the knight-errant rallies towards his opponent, twirling his weapon, catching the hilt in both hands, and rearing the sword behind his head in preparation to strike.

The wolf is among the most dastardly foe quartermain may face-thankfully a rarity, a certain surprise, and an unwelcome one at that. Its stride has curtailed, and the beast's jaw and neck tightens until this predator trips upon leading paws. This accident is highly unusual, and for the slightest second, the grim's chest suddenly sticks and it stops breathing. Almost how a piston withdraws just prior to exploding, except in this case, the dire wolf chokes, heaves, and chucks a pile of bile-ridden, blackened bones, of which they are all clearly human. Tragically, this monster has emptied the pit of its stomach so that it may fill it again with fresh meat. Upon the expiry, the beast lurches headway, breaking and charging haphazardly towards an unwitting Jeremiah.

The wolf takes precise aim during these intense moments, meticulously positioning itself, ready to take the ultimate plunge and strike. The approaching maw permeates outwards while tawny-tinged sclera retract into their sockets. It possesses a singular goal, awaiting the lucrative clamp into enticing, red-hot flesh. However, in this instance, it shall not pardon the meal.

Osbourne catches the beast off-guard with a swift boot to the face, and in the murderously-drunken daze, lodges his broadsword into the wolf's gristle. Its pupils return in the split-second, each of its four limbs reaching and tearing frantically at the air. The paladin discharges his blade into the nearest fur scruff, releasing repetitive, precision strikes. While the venerate continues hacking at its neckline, streaming messes of vertebrae and bits of gore rally against him, until the head lulls-off in a chaotic, disorderly commotion. Now clad in vermillion-tinged, leather dressings, Osbourne the Bullheaded can savor its magnificent size, and his own skullcap barely surpasses its withers. Fraught by the closing strains of its life, the decapitated canine's tongue lashes-out, desperately craving, yearning to taste the author's person, to savor skin, and the succulent taste of flesh, one final time. This is all they live for, this is all they desire.

The other wolves have taken their time to catch-up, now they brood nearby. Determining that this is worthy foe, these predators swarm, prancing around and surrounding the pair, cutting-off any hopes of retreat in turn. How many monsters are there? 'At least several,' the knight-errant ponders to himself, especially evaluating the two predators climbing the gutters, surmounting the alley for a higher vantage point in preparation to pounce.

Osbourne has accepted this inevitable demise, now it's just a matter of going-out swinging, as a voyage to the Underworld is best journeyed together. Death is a time for reconciliation, members of the family take to a celebration of life, although those more oriented to conflict surmise passing as parley between friend and foe.

None of these antagonists take the initiative, instead awaiting the orders of an alpha who stirs among the back of their pack. This one is different, coated in soot dust with a mane as black as midnight. There is an overwhelming amount of arrows lodged into its back, so numerous that it takes disguise of a bewilderbeast. A villain such as this deserves a cape and crown, a red hood of sorts that has forever stained its own pelt.

Wrought of sterner stuff, the grim rouses onto its hind legs, showcasing its half-head of hair, a balding, vaguely human-like visage with a scarred white eye, and skewed, displaced jaw. This is a mighty beast, worthy of testing his mettle, however has made this trip with no armor to protect his more vulnerable, frail body. Balderdash, this affront is inconceivable and unfair. Osbourne has made his career conditioning, spending his entire life striving for ancillaries, even earning his quintessential bull-formed helm. And for what, so he can meet his demise in some backwater town? Looking back, he finds all these affairs of court and pandering pathetic. What's the point of honor when he's the only one to abide by it? Strength begets cunning, cunning sires trauma, trauma breeds horror; these monsters deserve all the ruthlessness that he has to muster. This is his moment to do one last act of good.

Jeremiah has been leisurely scavenging through the packsnow, attempting to dig into the permafrost, painfully ignorant.

"Friend, I've got a favor to ask of you," the knight proposes without breaking eye contact with the creatures that surround them.

"Kneel down and look up at the sky. I thought I saw a bird- a whippoorwill, I heard you like those! Can you believe it, can you find one for me? The thing was huge, can't miss it."

An angry aurora cross the sky.
Lowlands, lowlands away don jon.
Save some ticket to ride, permission to die.
Lowlands away.

My nose alight with foul fumes' bovine.
Lowlands, lowlands away don jon.
I delve portside, pinned by grease hide.
Lowlands away.

I drink for joy, and bid adieu.
Lowlands, lowlands away don jon.
Cross bottle o' bourbon, its brown bottle flu.
Lowlands away.

Thrust dirt-humor and furrow brow.
Lowlands, lowlands away don jon.
Sour sorrow in an effort to drown.
Lowlands away.

I struck a match to rouse some fire.
Lowlands, lowlands away don jon.
Spent another night 'round the funeral pyre.
Lowlands away.

The cries are frights.
Lowlands, lowlands away don jon.
Oh writhe on deck.
Oh writhe, alive.
Lowlands away.

The author's gaze quests towards the firmament, keen to sight a fantastical beast as it grazes against the tours of fading morning stars and dull auroras. He hears its voice among the heavens, Regina and her flocking kin, the crackling vigor of thunder. Distantly drab clouds toil above the Rimeweather Range, dances of light and shadow that creep around its insurmountable mountainpeaks. The usual haunts are foreboding, the break in-between constant storms fleeting, and the far-flung slopes are ripe in horrendous blizzards. Bleak overcast struggles ahead, dominating the briefest tinges of peeling lavender, teal, and dotted oranges. This landscape is reminiscent of a vivid hallucination, a beautiful masterpiece that cannot be captured within the confines of canvas- had to be there to see it. Jeremiah edges forward, eager to spot a whirling eagle careening out of an encroaching white wave.

This performance exposes a critical stretch of neck, and suddenly, red scarlet streaks across the sky. Osbourne's swords severs through the trailing tendons in the elder's delicate neck, lopping-off his head in one foul swoop. The motion is swift, dealt by a professional, and the execution is over in a matter of seconds. Clean and painless deaths are scarce, few and far-between.

A broadening horizontal stroke emerges from the author's collar, until his head sluggishly topples over, landing with a gentle, compressing *scrunch* in the snow beside his thighs. Brilliant, amber-coated spectacles clad in gloss are lodged wide-open, staring endlessly into the wonder over yonder. This was the only apt solution for someone who has been undoubtedly tortured all their life. A small mercy, as the alternative is utterly barbaric and gruesome, Osbourne has spared Jeremiah the venom of being torn apart alive.

When he had taken the moral high-ground, clashing against the most depraved and unscrupulous villains that the territory has to offer, to the encouragement of his peers, and a liege lord demanding punishment, even if Osbourne's sword rang true and righteous, the knight-errant has never found joy in taking a life. To him, the notion of extinguishing flames always renders moot, filling him with a sense of dread.

Eventually, there is a charge every man must pay, a penalty for their transgressions, a troll toll worthy to the sum and equal of all their parts. The punishment for spilling innocent blood is death, and the Bullheaded is quite overdue. He is guilty in every sense of the word, even now, as the author's ichor seeps over his skin, soaking the indents of frostbitten anguish, and staining his hands in grave taint. Why did he become a knight, if in the end, Osbourne delivers his exalted career to fettered ruins? Never would a squire aspire to distribute harsh recourse, brutal, and untimely ends. Just like every naive, cheery optimist, he had joined rank to save lives.

The municipal court could always craft a clever argument against his case, but nonetheless, Osbourne determination is steely, he knows what he did was right. This is blasphemy against a chivalrous code, a jury would convict, befitting a life for a life. The paladin shall indeed pay his toll- all in short-time, and this finale will be grand. Suicide is not the answer when his recent company is in retreat. Nay, he shall become a cherished distraction. A less-versed man-at-arms may shy in the face of danger- not Osbourne, he welcomes peril. If this is the end, then he is to greet it willingly. The paladin raises his sword in taunt to the feral combatants, laughing at their approach. When they surge forth, bearing serrating claw and fang, coiling for an inevitable pounce.

The knight-errant utters one last battle-prayer, "Death, bringers of death, free this soul in the tirades of righteous absolution."

Osbourne expels at the top of his lungs, "Have at thee, bastards!"

While William and Rylie make their escape, they accident strike into the wickerwalker's shoulder. Edmund is embedded into the packsnow and rendered completely aghast, frozen in fear, juxtaposed at the sight of an enemy so numerous that he can't decide on where to fire, even while his iron sights line-up, crossing the pack's alpha.

In a fit of frustration, the boy Jones smacks the butt of his harpoon launcher, hurling a barb into the direction of their antagonists. It pitches beyond the gap in an instant, pincushioning permafrost with a dull *thud* at the foremost paws of some gnarly beast, doing little to thwart the attack. Rylie cries out, smacking Edmund urgently across his cheek. A final exploit which finally thrusts the hunter back into reality.

"'Ey, get movin' now!"

He drops his weaponry with an inkling of surprise, letting the armament dangle loosely from a strap. The trio hustle, reminding them an awful lot of Bannermane games which they would play as children. They are encompassed in a full-fledged sprint, barreling-forward, nipping at the heels of Jerome who bears just ahead. Hearing one last warrior's shriek in the background, the pair are belittled, expelling ferociously hot-air from their lungs, and lukewarm saliva spews forth upon each hasty breath.

Nearby wolves have begun blocking adjacent passages, it's in their nature, herding prey into a one-way, simultaneous assault. However, Bids Warder offers them solace, waving them towards her dwelling of inky darkness, encouraging the remaining stragglers to take sanctuary in an obscure breach that the wolves did not anticipate. This is the bounds of the Mortuary Cult, and their boisterous elder, Jerome instead bee-lines for the lift. Rylie takes notices, shoving him back in Bids direction, facing the gated stairwell Bids beckons them towards.

After the slew of storms, the elevator shaft has been leaden with packsnow, collapsing the ensemble in sheer weight. This landmark is akin to a bottomless pit, like a yawning ceiling, one-step off the permafrost to a shadowy demise. At first glance, the doorframe that the sister pries ajar is nothing special, everything's subtle, you'd have to know of this passage beforehand to be aware of its presence.

"Ah, no way!" Edmund boldly exclaims, realizing that he'll have to forfeit his launcher to fit through. He effortlessly slides out of his harness, chucking the contraption over his left shoulder and gifting them those valuable seconds to press onward.

The wickerwalker literally leaps, mustering the perfect dive beside the Warder ilk. William shuffles by on all fours, slipping underneath while the grizzled greybeard barges-in shortly after, nudging Bid's arms in the slightest that she's forced to shunt away, and the door slithers shut. Recognizing that this is her sole asylum, Rylie desperately dives for freedom as the metal bulkhead careens closed. To the astonishment of everyone present, she doesn't make it through, instead the bulkhead tightly presses her shoulders together, and brings the scribe to an immediate halt. This sudden stand-still beckons stupor, that a happenstance of this magnitude could ever occur, before her surprised expression churns to that of absolute horror.

She screams for service, "Let me in, open the door, hurry! Now-now!"

Her shrieks are brief, because a singular slice through her back severs fleece, cloth, flesh and thread. The leather belts that bind the grimoire to her chest are torn, and the book heaves towards the cinderblock, almost as if saving itself.

These claws act like fishhooks, digging deep into Rylie's torso, and anchoring around her spine. The response is agonizing and visceral, blood spews from the recesses of her gullet. This force is godly, an inevitable anchor coercing her back outside. For the briefest moment, the tow actually works in her favor, liberating her shoulder blades, until the ceaseless howls behind remind the company of their enemies that lurk among the Junction. The sole force keeping her from oblivion are her digits that latch to the truss of the closing portal. She begs- no, demands for someone to put the scribe out of her misery. So Libby, who has been crowded among the warrens, abides by summoning a dagger to her arms, and stabs the poor soul through one of her more tender spots.

"Sorry 'bout the pain, sista," she apologetically chastises when puncturing Rylie through her right eye.

Thankfully the effects are instantaneous, and scribe's head goes limp, but not before the tomb abruptly shuts, severing the fingers clamped to its frame so furiously. She's whisked away in a moment's notice, and all that persists are these loose digits that write upon the concrete stairwell, descending down the steps in despair. The mausoleum door has sealed behind them, granting admission that this refugee shall become their tomb.

X

KILROY WAS HERE

They don't have time for prayer, as the company has been turned on a pin, frightful that their sights may be consumed by pitch. If it wasn't for the charity of Edmund's gas-fired lamp, they may just falter and succumb to the gnawing abyss. He toys with the device, twisting a knob here, key there, causing it to bursts into a crusading inferno of light until the flame shifts to a dazzling white-hot glimmer, eventually diminishing into its usual graces of soft luminance.

William pardons such *sigh* of relief, he has been withholding breath for minutes, winding tighter and tighter, so taut, that the boy Jones feared that he may yet implode. The grimoire lies at the head of the stairs, still, unwilling to apologize. The manuscript is infused with dark magiks, making it quite unpredictable, the embodiment of living flame. It grieves for the scholars, Arabella Gaberdine and Rylie Hess, those dedicated wardens. The book bellows in blistering agony- or cries, if may pertain to emotion, riddled with such vigor that it delivers shockwaves that incite the tunnel walls to shift, rubble-rending tremors that brings chalk to ruin, and dust loosens from the shafts of the ceiling, then settle, awakening any horrors that may reside with a unruly salvo of grime.

Still, despite those fellows from telling him so, "Leave the black book 'hind," the wainwright begs, "Illicit arts bring nothin' but trouble." William feels swayed by the tome, deciding that they shouldn't abandoned such a valuable totem, and for better or for worse, resolved to carry the trophy.

Even from a distance, Edmund's lantern appears to shine towards the heavily-bound book like a beacon, and the grimoire seems to call to him, beckoning him closer. This dim buttery splendor of a wave so delicately touches upon the manuscript, highlighting details that purveyors ordinarily wouldn't be aware of. He can't possibly wish to abandon this hallowed and precious prize to ignorance, all alone in these warrens.

The boy Jones is intrigued by "The Nature of Niter", and shuffles returning-up several stairs in order to lift the grimoire from its dreary resting place. The binding is spoiled, scuffed from decades, perhaps rife with centuries of misuse. Using the sleeve of his linens, William swipes at the build-up, and reveals that there is much more than meets the eye. This hardcover is adorned in artisan pursuits, an insignia so recklessly placed in the far uppermost-left corner, the dreaded, and all too familiar, Mark of Dayne. An engraved inscription presides over the topmost half, entailing the grimoire's dark speech:

One to spur,
And in the darkness
Seven now stir-
Festering in all things
Damp, dingy and dirge.

A heavenly slash crosses sky,
A cleansing flame bearing eye,
Alight with smells of sulphur and hot ash.

Upon receiving the tome, the pages inside are colored to the tune of cavities. They have dimmed impulsively, but as they grow numb and silent to William's gentle touch, and eventually these sheets return to their normal yellowed beige. The boy Jones feels imbued with its essence, a sense of superiority that typically befalls ancillaries crafted by godly powers. However, when slinging the tome into his knapsack, this primordial gift can't begin to replace the emotional turmoil that reels inside him. The earnest lad is distraught by the loss of his merry comrades, and while they burdened by a brief window of friendship, Jeremiah, Osbourne and Rylie certainly contested for a certain reservation in William's heart, he can't believe that they're actually gone.

A light bathes the farthest reaches of the tunnel in searing white radiance. Perhaps this radiant shimmer reflects on the deeds of his departed crew, summarizing life in a statement other than.

"'Ere lies 'notha intrepid vagabond, who perished durin' the years o' the lamb. May they rest in peace."

William wishes to be enthralled by tall tales, reliving their wildest exploits. Could Osbourne have tackled bandit outlaws in his spare time? What if Rylie originally were employed as a traveling authority under a mercantile? Is Jeremiah actually an accomplished- let alone, a legitimate author? Have either of them published any theater dramas for the thespians of CAPAh Express? His imagination runs amok with these concepts, and now, he'll never truly know. While a generous luminance beckons him further into its fray, it flickers erratically.

"Drats," Edmund mutters under his breath, fondling with assorted keys as the kerosene oil lamp malfunctions again.

The wickerwalker is guiding their party deeper into the chasm, farther down long-abandoned halls, as it's the only way to stride. Those few who endure this trek bicker briskly between themselves, mindfully negligent when their narrow stairwell passage flattens into a hall. The party is flanked on all sides by concrete bulwarks, a thin, horizontal green line embellishes both walls, directing them forward.

Morbin lectures Libby about her composure at arms-length, "Talk 'bout brutal, ye ran the poor sap through. I always dot muhself ah dashin' rogue, but yer deeds surely send mah quakin' in muh boots."

The sister solemnly laments to his insult, "Tis fava. She asked for it, so I did what needed. Done is done."

"Well, neglect tah do mah some favas anytime soon. If I didn't know any betta, ye'd been wantin' to skewa that scribe since yer squall in the tradin' post."

Others begin to mumble words of resentment, and William doesn't feel a degree safe among accomplices so keen to pin company with needles.

"No, ain't nuthin' like that, I swears it," she shrieks, somewhat apologizing.

The knight betrayal was another story, he was well-versed in warfare, and dealt death only when others deemed need of it. Osbourne was rigid, and abided by a set of guiding principles, the only fool to tread this northern territory so sure of himself. It's awfully easy to dispense frontier justice, harder is it to sway the fist.

Edmund may be a hunter, but he is of sound mind. He is not expected to, neither properly trained to fend-off such grim, otherworldly threats. As chaos looms, and the wilderness has become rather unhinged. Survival is no longer a bare minimum effort, it is all-inclusive endeavor. Even the most docile beasts expend all their energy to rage against the fading light.

Common creatures have grown nastier in turn, rearing into what scholars derive as megafauna, their growth hastened by the evolving dangers of the frontier.

Wickerwalkers are determined to stray far from the rabble quartermaines may casually throw themselves against. The assailants that those champions face are often brutal, their physical bodies accommodating any traits that may grant them the advantage. Bannermane elite are steadfast, but cannot warrant when foes surround them. The Oestergaard provinces and Riviera are in upheaval, vagrants tear apart the mercantiles of the territory, brigands and highwaymen operate freely, and without a gamekeeper to coordinate their efforts, beasts of all manner run amok. Packs of wolves fester because the Mandonmen have allowed it. These grims signal the beginning of an end.

William journeys near the rear of their company- his march staggers, valiantly twisting the twine of his knapsack, and securing the loot around his right shoulder. From this distance, it's incredibly difficult to tell who is exactly whom, everyone meanders into freakishly ambiguous, backlit blobs. As the lot tangles into the inky blackness, traveling becomes quite mundane.

Edmund leads their expedition onward, passing the occasional door, the bulkhead strewn ajar slightly that they can peer inside. These rooms are nearly identical, almost barren, and devoid of all interest except shag carpet. Certain members of the party shy away from the doorframes as they pass, as their imaginations are playing tricks on them, and wouldn't be too keen to find a pair of cryptic eyes staring right back at them.

When the boy Jones has the opportunity to ponder from profusive boredom, only then does he recognize the halls they dwell, and that the information his acquaintance Glennitch parted, is one of the same.

William rapidly cups his hands around his mouth, and shouts to the crowd ahead without nary a warning, "Wait, 'ey wait just ah second!"

His voice carries easily among the concrete bulwark, a vigorous echo that causes the others to cover their ears in response, although not yet deafening. Edmund leads the company of twelve from a solid forty-feet stride, responding with a rampant attitude, irritated that they are communicating in this fashion.

"What do ye want? Can't ye see I'm in the middle of-'?"

"Yeah, I guess I noticed. Listen though, knew some guy who said ah lil' somethin'-somethin' 'bout supplies 'fore 'e died. Anyhows, I know where tah go from 'ere," William shouts towards the lantern's fray.

He pauses, awaiting a response while the common rabble listens intently on. The wickerwalker barks back in return.

"Ah son, ye might prove yerself useful after all. Percilees, percilees, percilees. Well, don't keep me on the edge o' mah seat, get yer arse up 'ere, lad. Quickly now, with 'aste!"

He prompts an order that urges everyone to step aside, parting ways to grant the boy Jones safe passage. An earnest lad is indubitably eager to take the lead, and bustles forward until he is bathed in a welcome, enveloping light. A fragile glow showcases the scowl crossing Edmund's guise, a figure who, is immediately frustrated that he needs to take the word of a lesser, inexperienced whelp, and the best help he can garner for the group is handling his beacon.

Up in the tunnel ahead, William can interpret the faint impression of a junction. The two green lines that normally adorn these walls suddenly careen to the side.

"*Umm,* take ah left 'round this corner 'ere."

"Are ya sure?"

"Absolutely-" William manages to express before stumbling, interrupted by his own knee giving out.

He steps on a smooth stone, as modest as a tea plate, until the whole disc awkwardly fumbles from underneath the sole of his boot, abruptly skipping down the hall, clattering into the doorframe ahead, and descending the first actual stairwell into murky depths.

Click, clack, clack-clank, clack-clank-clank-clank.

A cacophony which wanes softer as the depth grows greater. These pebbles ring where men tread seldom, Glennitch's advice appears to whisper in his ears, 'Only when ye take the stairs, may ya stray,' and now William spies his meaning. What a coincidence, he remarks to himself, now they have to take a stairwell.

"Follow that noise," William cries in excitement for spelunking, "two flights down. No more, no less, or else!"

"Aye," the cordwainer reciprocates, "We'll see to it!"

While the concept of stairs may be nothing new, the flights that lie before them redefine this meaning entirely. The going is awfully slow, progressing a shy greater than a snail's pace. These treads possess a steep grade, making the effort feel like an elaborate descent, and they are plainly, amateur climbers. Falling down this well could be perilous, depending on how far one tumbles, it'd be unlikely to ever steep a rescue. Thankfully, friction mats rest upon every step, simple strips of cloth that catch onto the soles of their boots.

Despite the intention of the builders, Cliff Fetherhaugh is ridiculous when it comes to balance, and clearly misjudges a step, accidentally lunging until he flounders impulsively onto his rear. In this same excursion, Braithwaite doesn't exactly notice when she has arrived on a platform, and trips promptly over her own two feet, sending her barreling past William and Edmund who respond with frantic grasps- a moment too late, and they may have actually missed her entirely.

If it hadn't been for some perfectly placed balcony, the lector may have never favored the light of day again. The railings in this stairwell are wrought from cylindrical metal tubes, nothing elaborate, bland to the point of jail bars.

Under the rush of delving into anything of value, Morbin grows excited with each passing moment, causing Jerome to criticize his haste, urging for his desire not to get the best of him, and eventually the company's pace becomes more akin to a crawl.

"Slow n' steady," musters Jerome, who's decades of mileage have been painstakingly crawling up to him, rendering his joints brittle and feeble. He actually lurches forward, hoisting himself onto the shoulder of the nearest figure in front of him, to aid in managing his pace. This role resides to Rochester, who admittedly needs his own accomplice of his very own, and Mug Maxwell, in turn- a voice of obliging support, gracefully guides them both down the next flight. Folks mingle and match their paces, those confident of their skills still take no time at all in passing others. This staircase is picked-clean of debris, yet they still share the lantern between them, handing off the contraption from one end of the convoy to the other, ensuring that everyone is stepping safely down the abyss and there are no extra surprises in store.

"O'ver 'ere Clamity Jane. Would ye be ah dear n' pass this light back up tah Balthus?"

The beacon safely travels through the grips of six people, ultimately glancing the arms of a semi-professional pilfers player, it's a weird feeling for Mug Maxwell to forfeit a winning hand.

"Thank all those bully-rooks for me," Balthus yells to the lead of the expedition, waving in glee, despite the fact that this gesture isn't visible when everyone else is marching away. He decides to start a casual conversation on a topic that he quickly comes to regret.

"Those wolves were the most terrifyin' thin' I've eva seen. Big, burly beasts. Gah! Their saliva was so gross. Are we sure it wasn't digestive fluid?

Reminded me o' ah dream I 'ad up in those caravan halls, the demon that invaded mah mind n' roamed muh nightmares."

"Yea-yea, we were all there, lil' man," lambastes Bids, "though mah monsters made those wolves look like bottom-rung gremlins."

This quip causes the greybeard to pipe up, goaded by his arrogant self-serving nature, believing that he's seen it all.

"'Uh? Pray-tell der devilish designs."

The younger sisters of the two, Bids Warder didn't believe that anyone would try investigating here story. She takes the time to describe her haunts, despairingly reciting her accounts with a *gulp* that almost sounds like choking.

"Oh-oh really? I can't imagine anyone would really be interested in all that. Okay, okay-yea, 'ere it goes. I dreamt somethin' 'arrowin', n' wound-up in ah passage that looked an awful lot like this. Well, twas pitch-dark 'side n' overwhelmingly so, then I took tah the nearest spot o' light that I could find. Thing was- startled me outright, this was nah ordinary man that I stumbled 'pon. 'Ere is ah brute some two-heads larga than the usual folk, towerin' in 'eight, brawny build, shoved the light right intah mah eyes. 'Ad tuh take ah moment n' scream at 'em only tah discover 'e wasn't 'uman either. In 'is left arm was that lantern I saw- right? Oh right! Then innit's right- well, say 'e misplaced it, 'cause there wasn't nah limb tuh be found! Cringe at the sight. Instead, 'e went n' loomed o'ver me, cranin' mah every nook n' cranny."

"That's when 'e did the most peculiar thing, 'is 'ead started tuh inch furtha n' furtha-up 'till it 'it the ceilin'. That's when I knew somethin' was off, that's when I found 'is otha arm. It replaced all 'is necking, cradlin' 'is own scalp innit's palm. Worsah so, this wicked mutant stopped payin' attention tah me 'togetha, n' started tah ward towards somethin' else, a mess nesting in the abyss."

"Egads, twas gross. So there was this mound, betta described by molten 'eaps o' flesh, some gibberin' 'orror that drew every fiber o' its being tah move in tows of fishin' line. Guts and glory 'eaved out, lurchin' mass forward intah the limelight where I could sight all those macabre pellets n' gibs. White pencil-point spots dotted skin, only those weren't markins. In this dream, I knew them as eyes, thousands 'pon thousands o' pupils feastin' on the only prey in the room: me."

"I stared-up… or down for that matta, at that miscreant with 'orror. Definitely was ah parody o' things natural, beyond that of mortal form, 'cause not even the face was right. It was if ah blind party-goer 'ad attempted tah pin ah mouth on its face, missed, then tried three more times. Thankfully I 'woke 'fore things got too clammy n' it got too close. I could trace that audacious rank. Can ya smell in dreams?"

"Don't fink so, that's 'ow we separate fact from fiction. Our minds bend things. If it's sum perfect imitation, wut's da point o' wakin' up?"

"I tell ye what, if ya could, I wouldn't be 'ere today. Couldn't forget mah ex-wife if I tried, always turnin' muh fantasies intah nightmares. If I could catch 'er god-awful stench one more time…"

"Oi, Maxwell. Ye've been ratha quiet o' late, what do ya think?"

Shaking his head and finally snapping into the conversation, Mug relays.

"Sorry 'bout the fuss, just made me think o' muh own terrors, ya know? I didn't sight the same monstrosity, though mine were a touch outta sorts too. Say, ah flock of flutterin' bats, only they crowd on the ground in the same size n' numba as lemmins. These cave devils must've been summoned intah ah maddenin' frenzy, surrounded me 'till I started drownin' in ah pit of wiry legs. Rochester was tellin' me 'bout 'is 'orrors too…"

The wainwright shakes his head, prompting Mug Maxwell not to share his case. "… but that's somethin' I'm not at liberty tah discuss."

Certain folks continue to pipe-up about nightmares and their lucid experiences.

"Well," Morbin consequentially divulges, "sounds like that apparition was tryin' tah give ah bit o' fright, but fortunately for mah, it didn't show muh darkest desires or vices, but worst fears. Mah worst fear is the classic stabbin' ah man in 'is back scenario, that deal gone south mentality. While I rue betrayal, I'm not one tah stir in the face o' danga, that's 'ow I know I'm the betta man."

The medical practitioner lags her mouth in response, hanging her jaw for a couple seconds, stuck in contemplation before she may summary her vision to share.

"Mine too! Now I'm fearful that these phantoms will fend me from committin' tah the cause. What if ah patient that I choose tuh 'eal comes back tah 'aunt me? Steal from mah, hurt muh, or worse? 'Urt those othas that I've sworn tah protect. What if I can't stop 'em 'lone?"

"Then I'll do 'em right-in, lil' one!" The boisterous Korralack announces. "That demon pains mah tah admit dat I grieve o'er ah lapse in strength. I treasure muh brawn. While dis arrow nevah wavahs, what if it don't drive deep 'nough? What if I only 'ave da power tah wound, n' not end dat threat right der?"

He chides away, "Ah well, that fire giant 'ad mah all choked-up with fumes. 'Ere I am speakin' nonsense."

Calamity Jane contributes to this campaign recital, disclosing, "I saw spectacles that made me rage, that bastard of fire and tar dangled that carrot in front of me, letting the solution to this grief slip away. Any entity depraved enough to ferry children as hostages cannot be reasoned with. Once you threaten kith and kin, it's all over. My rage blinded me to the curse, the torpor that levied heavily upon my mind. I broke its construct, my wires wrapped around its throat, and I throttled the cretin until the hallucination ended. This skirmish didn't satisfy my wanton lust for its demise, I wanted to hear the creature cry for help, to beg for its life- instead it smiled. If we can't burn it, let's strand the tome in these tunnels or chuck it into the sullen mire. Seven hells, strap the manuscript beneath a bison's cleat, slap that brute on the hindquarters, have it run off into the night, never to return again."

As they lumber forward, this encounter encourages select members of their party to grant the widow some much deserved space. While on the subject of foreboding frights that go bump in the night, the wickerwalker iterates to the group unannounced.

"I am terrified- truthfully, n' the only pursuit that may grant me pity is ah deep sleep."

These interpretations plague William, reminding him as to why this creature is bound within the tome, confined in chains of ink and paper weight. Could this be eminence, or a monster of our own creation? If the fire elemental demonstrates the prospects brimming in our subconscious, what would an entity, that has the uncanny ability to read minds, possibly fear? And also, would it have need of slumber? Everyone craves some shuteye, this is where impossible things happen, the stars align and conjure what we aspire to become. Before a vagabond succumbs to deliberation, the boy Jones falls victim to a probing tap on the shoulder. William twirls around to find the inquisitive eyes of Balthus the Pygmy, who is lodged upon a higher step.

"'Ey there stranga. I nevah caught yer name, as we've all been quite busy with things."

"Oh," pronounces the earnest lad in an undeniably snarky tone, whom hesitates contact and continues his descent, not out of spite, but because they've been having these winding conversations on a stairwell, and making no progress altogether. "I be William Walda."

The learned man appears perplexed, "Walda, now that is some outstandin' namesake. I'd imagine- now, mind mah, that ye don't appear as ah Walda. That seal danglin' 'round yer collar is awfully unusual, n' should be bronze: material o' the workin' man, where yers is wrought by copper."

"Yeah, yeah. I'm ah Fields originally."

"Oi, no kiddin'. A true wildman, born, bred n' raised on the frontier like ah bison steer n' their red dogs. Say, I've been itchin' tah ask," Balthus, intoxicated by curiosity, offers to carry the grimoire, "I 'ate the divine and the ills they cause, but this is 'deed ah captivatin' work o' wonda."

"No"

"No? Surely this must be ah jest."

"No," he repeats without thinking, as surefire and instinctively as the first time, though he never expected to conjure such a brute response. The boy Jones considers that the fire elemental has been whispering in his ear, obsessively calling his own name.

"William, William, William," each spiel bolder than the last.

"I know of the truth you seek. Hear me, and despair," it wails, before discerning into a vile chuckle. *Mwahah.*

He pries towards his shoulder, glancing at the flanking knapsack which dangles dubiously behind his back, the only barrier between the grimoire's intrusive thoughts being linen, burlap and fleece. It's almost as if the boy Jones may spy the manuscript through these layers, recalling the ominous details of binding: each of those four armored corners, and that dreadful Mark of Dayne on the cover, some contorted, scrawling triangle with two lines tearing through it.

He certainly has been struck by the malady of passion, growing quite attached to inanimate newsprint. This jealously binds him to the tome, fostering an irrational fear: that those in the party warrant its possession, desiring to swindle this grimoire from him, and temper those winds such illicit magik cavorts. William grows weary, rather reluctant to relinquish an artifact of power, but it's in this feud, that he recognizes the foul influence that this ancillary has established over him. If he doesn't rid himself of this infernal manifestation now, who knows if in the near-future, he would ever cede the grimoire willingly?

The boy Jones kneels over, lobbing his knapsack onto the ground with a *thwack* and wrests the pouch open. Older and wiser than the world's greatest greybeards, all strung in a single-file line, the book is well-aware of William immediate plans, and the rejection it is soon to face. The grimoire garners a static-shock, sending a surge of pure animosity through any meddlesome fingertips, coercing William to wallow in grief.

Now, cemented to the cause and more determined than ever, he grips the tome fiercely by its spine, yanking the hardcover free from the burlap sack. Showcased by those writhing, torch-borne gleams, it gives the impression of hysteria, seeming to squeal and wriggle frantically in his grip.

"'Ere, 'ere take it 'fore I change mah mind," he exclaims with fervor, although Balthus doesn't appear to notice.

"Oh my goodness, the audacity o' this jewel! We're attemptin' ah coup by stuffin' this precious trophy in some sack. Sure as beef 'pears tenda n' rub deems dry. I'll keep it near n' dear tah mah 'eart though, lest I draw blood."

The learned man momentarily pauses, crooking his index finger towards William.

"Please note, I am not dearly fond o' blood, as it often stains muh ensemble, perhaps permanently. So refrain from incitin' any violence," implores Balthus at the exact moment he leaps onto the ledge below, continuing their quest netherwards, while this dereliction of duty gives William an opportunity to recover and collect his gear.

He draws rasps, choosing to focus on his breathing, and slows each exhale in the attempt to destress. The grimoire had been toying with his emotions, the most fragile part of human ego, and that affair had almost wounded him to a breaking point.

"Ye talk too much."

"'Ey, boyo," a familiar voice clambers behind him.

William discourages any further conversation by thrusting his hands onto his temples, digging each finger into his forehead and cheeks in obviously blaring frustration.

"What, what now? What is it ye could possibly want?" He rudely remarks.

"Not tah bear dubious intent, but I question whetha or not we've been goin' the right way?"

William rotates to receive a wincing expression from Mandel, whom arches back over the edge of a nearby rail, attempting to give his friend respite in which to breathe.

"Alas, tis am sorry, 'agman. Been tad stressed lately-"

"'Aven't we all, groob. I should've noticed. Take nah 'eed towards the thoughts o' othas, chart yer own course, lay sails 'fore the front o' heavy wind n' the tide will quell. It will all fall intah place, just give it some time."

These two earnest lads continue their expedition, traversing concrete treads of stairs.

"Aye, now that sounds awfully wise. Too smart for the likes of ya. 'Ey! Why am I the one gettin' all this philosophical treatment? Yer the one who needs some therapy, walkin' 'round so calm- everythin' completely ordinary after greetin' death. Prolly deserve some vacation at Arbor Island? Oh, wouldn't that be grand? Instead, I gotta take us furtha into these dingy and dreary caverns," the boy Jones iterates to his accomplice, regurgitating Glennitch's info from the confines of grey matter.

"Shouldn't be much longa now. Yes-yes, right 'ere. This level right 'ere, in fact. I'm sure of it," proposes William, who reaches a lower platform before the remainder of the troop.

Strangely enough, the usual verdant stripe lining the walls is replaced by a lapis lazuli hue- blue level. He glimpses down towards the sprawling stairs beneath him, admiring the aching chores and problems of life disintegrate into its clouded, murky depths, a placid cauldron of nothingness. As Mandel takes that dive from the final step, accompanying his friend at the landing with the *thud* of both feet, together they sight an adjoining passageway. It yawns ajar, an exact, duplicate doorframe of prior rooms passed, only this gaping mouth extends into a corridor.

Their campaign straddles the blueprints of a labyrinth, an endless array of tunnels, passages, and most importantly, dead-ends. They must stick together, as without any originality to stem these cookie-cutter visuals, it's extremely easy to become lost, wandering endlessly. They've heard the tavern howler rant numerous times about those navigators who tour these warrens, never to return, and now the company can exactly understand why. Edmund Redmyne arrives shortly thereafter with his fellow Morbin Evershade in tow, and the archeologist takes to waltzing nearby, peering over the railing. After all this hiking, they still can't sight the bottom of this abyss, and he emits a whistle of intimidation.

"*Whew.* That's ah nasty lookin' plunge. Where do ye think it all goes?"

The wickerwalker prefers to hand some of his loose equipment to Mandel, several bundles of twine, nets, climbing gear here, and an eighteen-inch bear trap there, until the cordwainer promptly collapses alongside the additional weight.

"'Elp, need a hand or tuh!"

Edmund is livid with some sense of adventure, and ignores the plighted porter, instead joining company at world's end. He shambles over, scanning that visual mire beneath, yet doesn't lift the lantern over, refusing to shed further light upon the well. Despite a specific cord being wrapped thrice around his fingers, the hunter is afraid that he'd drop their sole source of illumination. Rather, the wickerwalker's face tightens into a scowl right in front Morbin's eyes, and he declares with upmost certainty.

"Straight tah hell."

"'Asten ye caravanhands," William entices, ushering the townsfolk to gather by invitingly waving his arms. He leans over his over-encumbered comrade, nabbing a few hefty provisions while he speaks, tossing this clunk to the ground and littering the flat with Edmund's belongings.

"I've been led tah believe there's ah treasure trove 'round the bend. Take this passageway, n' go through the nearest bulkhead. Shout when ya find it, gonna be ah bit busy 'ere."

The boy Jones then focuses his attention on reviving Mandel, freeing the cordwainer from his precariously prone confines, "Let's get ye outta there."

A voice emerges among those who still crowd the stairs, "What if we get lost?"

This inquiry spews disappointment into William's, rolling his eyes rather blankly towards the host. The boy Jones is well aware that Balthus proposes that feign question, so he playfully replies.

"Yer not gonna get lost. Seriously, it's like an alley right there. Just one way tah go for pity's sake, take the first door on the left."

He shakes a twisted bundle of cord from Mandel's possession, barring none from his feeble form. During his conflict with bait and tackle, the audience descends those remaining steps, so that when the pygmy passes William, beelining towards the corridor, he begrudgingly remarks, "Right, alright already."

Finally freeing the cordwainer by certain relieving knots from the twice twined trap, he emits a maniacal, victorious yelp, *hoo-rah*, before heaving the mass onto the concrete lime. There are various ancillaries strewn about the floor, trophies once ensnared by wiry mesh. A variety of charms whittled from wicker and bone are thrust into the air, descending seconds later so that they may dance upon the concrete flooring. They sharply *clack* and *knock* together, frightful that they've been discovered.

William is initially concerned when this magpie collection career away, although the wickerwalker doesn't seem to mind, as he is too preoccupied with gazing into the abyss, and convinced that there are monsters staring back. Vagabonds be praised, an earnest lad is fascinated that these trinkets appear so intricately detailed, fabricated from teeth into various pawns and game pieces. He travels on his hands and knees across the floor, gathering each of these curiosities, and treating them like carnival prizes. Then upon the flip of a hat, stores them in his needlessly, near-empty knapsack, save for Jeremiah's journal. Each toy must be no longer than his thumb, and weighs next to nothing so he won't be procuring any burdens. If he doesn't take the time to memorize their unique features, William fears that he may forget that they've been stowed away.

Upon lounging upon the platform for several minutes, the boy Jones assists Mandel to his feet, and pats himself down, releasing ample scores of dust and soot from the crinkles of his clothes back onto the ground. It has certainly been ages since townspeople have wandered here.

This is his first bout of archeology, William is eager to trek forward and rejoin the group. Men with any objects of worth are keen to hide them among warrens, as Bannermane aren't familiar with the feeling of being pent-up amid dirt and soil. There is something to say about these underground passages, they feel protective, yet awfully confining, flurrying the thought of discovery overcomes this usually anxious demeanor. Mandel follows in his standard stance, and the two emerge into the hall to observe Korralack testing his might, prying at bars on closest bulkhead.

"It's nah use," the vagabond declares in an exhaustive daze, "dat door won't open."

"Gods no, we've got tah get through!"

"Take a chisel n' hammer if ye 'ave tuh, n' tear that wall down!"

A resound *clank* can be heard as Libby Warder chinks her blade against a flair of graffiti. This scribbling flaunts across the bulkhead, nonsensical scribbles and staves, are all drafted in a faint cerulean glow. Morbin has the most experience in realms like these, and scrutinizes this artwork, approaching until his lips nearly kiss the mesterpiece. Staring deeply at the forsaken text, the archaeologist then explains.

"Nah can do. These are magik runes. Try n' try, force shall not open this tomb," he clarifies.

Staves provide a protective barrier against those that may wish them harm. Each symbol has been etched by hand, and taken considerable hours to do so, exhibiting themselves upon the portal's stoney outcrop and stretching onto the adjacent walls- a face, an animated cartoon embeds itself around the doorframe, gawking with surprise at these visitors, as it usually receives sparse attention, and now grows ecstatic. This character is especially flat and jaunty, with no more detail than those chalk lines decorating the fortified door. It periodically points to itself while dancing a jig, then back to the bulkhead, taking several moments of hopping before Balthus derives its purpose.

"Oh, oh!" He exclaims, "This is some sort o' picket, ah pen-guardian. If I'm being frank, nevah actually seen one of these 'fore. Perhaps if Rylie was 'ere, she'd be able tah converse with it."

The scrawling figure energetically attempts speaking with its guests, yet utters only silent gibberish, no words part escape from the outline's lips. As this is clearly a receptive creature, Lena believes that it will respond to reason, or at least, persuasion. She stems from a place where addresses are sport, and oral cues are only natural. The widow strives to cajole it, swaying the illustration with seemingly kind words.

"You are undeniably a lovely- uh, thing, no, I mean portrait. Now, we have ventured far to peer at your exquisite craftsmanship. Handiwork, which is unparalleled, the talk of the town, and your grace is second to none," riling the illustration in all forms of flattery. "We are in need of accommodations behind these doors, so may we get through? Will you bear blessings just enough to let us pass?"

The animation has been flabbergasted, taking each compliment in full stride, accompanying a wider and wider grin until its signature smile overtakes the width of face, and at this request, despite its clear and present glee, shakes its head hastily from side to side. As much as this drawing desires to cherish company, it cannot simply allow for strangers to bask in its halls without permission.

"Blast!" The widow remarks, then parades off in anger.

Only a gambling man could derive the meaning of its merry motions.

"I think tis promptin' ah riddle," Mug Maxwell musters.

Lena pipes back in retort, "No that can't be, otherwise it'd be able to actually talk- it'd speak, we'd hear it."

"Then what would it be possibly askin' o' us, then?"

"*Hmmph*, maybe yer all too quick tah judge. And tuh tink, I dot that I was da arrogant one. Be quiet, and stay awhile. 'Thout any vocal cords, I doubt it can be very loud," grunts the gruff vagabond, Korralack.

The boy Jones has been dwelling in solitude, taking occasional glances at the wall, and pondering, deep in thought. While the party bickers amongst themselves, he prompts them, asking aloud to relay the others' opinions on the matter.

"What is the purpose o' ah guard?"

Mandel fancies a clue, and announces, quite unsurely in-fact, "Tah determine friend from foe?"

William's physique is teeming with energy at this realization.

"Right ye are! Pin ah medal ontah this squire's chest. We've been overthinkin' the solution this whole time. These scrawls are askin' of us, inquirin' if we know the truth o' it: whose trove this is, n' make our exact purpose down 'ere known. Alas, all ye beauty queens and barrio boys, we must simply introduce ourselves."

"O' course," Morbin argues to himself, while the boy waltzes right up to the bulkhead door, slapping his own forehead in realization, "Why didn't I think o' that?"

Those hastily scribbled-on eyes lock while the boy Jones makes approach.

"Oh pen-guardian, tis William Walda, 'notha walka o' the world 'bove, 'ere tah partake in muh share o' the treasure. Glennitch sent us- that peculiar Glenn of the Grotto as ye may be familiar, 'fore the air escaped his very lungs. I'm deeply sorry tah say, yer partner 'as now perished," the boy Jones orates, and as in Bannermane fashion, bows his head humbly.

Upon receiving news of its comrade's abrupt, ill passing, the picket summons a frown, directing an expression of surprise in William's direction as the bulkhead ahead of him shudders. The animated figure nods in a sign of mutual respect, distending its hands around the doorframe, shifting a few bars or locks here and there, then seemingly jerks the portal inward. This boy has demonstrated upmost courtesy and respect, traits that Glennitch has always admired from those kin held at arms length. It determines with certainty that Glennitch would've blessed this passage, and unveils the sanctuary that it was crafted to guard.

William takes several steps in retreat as the bulkhead shifts, frankly appalled by the murky blackness darkness that stretches forward, but is sure of himself, and marches forth into the breach.

"Darker, why does it always 'ave tah be darker?"

An earnest lad starts to feel anxious, as it's awfully difficult to keep track of time while immersed in such tar, completely devoid of any activity, and stricken by calamity which hinder the senses. From what he can discern, the entrance is maybe, one and three-quarter inches thick: an ordinary door, some staple of the old world, however everything else is perceptibly empty, devoid of any shape. Hopefully it hasn't been longer than a minute or two, yet these rhetorics make William frantic. He vies with worry, that his eyes may never adjust to this all-encompassing gloom, and that the vault may never shed its secrets. He'll have to fetch Edmund's lantern, but the boy Jones hesitates, knowing that this selfish act will leave everyone who resides in the hall and fears venture here, to their own devices. A majority of the company remains reluctant to join him, identifying the room as akin to a tomb. This is his opportunity to prove his worth.

From what he can discern, the room is nothing fancy, as typical as all that have come before it, which makes his hasty impact with a support beam completely unexpected.

Clang. The breadth of his brow suddenly collides into a solid, rigid pillar, ringing the rim of his skull with the convulsions of a wild bell. Instinctively, his arms fly towards the injury, and they jostle alongside an untold number of loose timbers, knocking several sticks onto the obscured groundwork. They clamber in unison, *tck, tck-tck, tck-tck-tck,* and silence in preparation of William's ranting scream.

"'Oly art thou mother o' pearl!" He exclaims with angst.

"Are ye okay, 'Liam?" A voice investigates from their adjacent passage.

"Balderdash," the boy Jones mumbles to himself, massaging the bridge of his nose.

"Uh yeah," William cautions as response, "just ah bit dazed, 'ad ah nasty run-in with some giant pin of sorts. All is well, n' dark. Oh, especially dark."

Skrik, skrik.

William's lobes are alight with discord similar to those sounds of chalk on blackboard, or a buck scraping their antlers against bark. His ear tune to the source of this instigation, the perpetrator of this foul noise.

"Wait, wait on ah second, I think I'm 'earin' somethin.'"

That same cerulean glow gently kindles, exposing a central pillar in the center room, and his eyes squint at an apparition. It's another illustration, although not quite the same pen guardian as before. This second picket waves its arms hectically, desperate to garner William's attention. When the boy Jones rises to his feet, the caricature slaps those palms at the side of its cheeks, portraying an agonizing manner twisted between surprise and anguish. A myriad of torches burst aflame, the sudden work of magik, causing the boy to recoil, and the room to swiftly bathe in violent luminescence. Even those sticks that an earnest lad knocked loose, drifting against the concrete ground, tender flame.

These navigators have been devoid of light for so long, that chasing after braziers is more instinct than reason. In this haste, William can hear members of his company present themselves in grandiose fashion, drawn like moths to flame.

Announcing to the pen-guardian and pointing towards the ajar door, the learned man speaks with such eloquence, "I am Balthus, first-of-'is-name, n' ah scholarly folk at that. May I seek safe passage tah join mah companion inside?"

The pygmy takes the astute silence as an answer of acceptance, and strides into this well-lit storehouse with mirth, the tome bounding across his chest with every step. The funniest commentary is produced from Jerome, who isn't exactly aware of how to present himself, and seems to be belittled by communicating with something no-more grander than a drawing upon the wall.

"*Ummph,* fair tidings," he murmurs with no movements greater than the tip of his felt hat, and escorts zero eye-contact with the character. William is humored by these introductions, the portal was already open, and the custom is completely unnecessary.

Not everyone ventures inside, they don't want to make a habit of walking needlessly. Besides, they trust a select few: William, Balthus, Edmund, Mandel, Morbin, and Jerome, to preserve their best interests. The treasure trove is formidable, and as soon as Morbin gazes upon the eccentric site, he becomes absolutely dumbstruck. It takes the guise of a moneylender's vault, hidden secretly deep within the earth.

"Will'-will, 'Liam… wow, just wow. Cover meh in linen and thrust me tah the stars. Bless Glennitch's journey to the Underworld, may 'e ward limbo for these generous donations."

The amateur archeologist is consumed in a blight of Bannermane greed, a sickness that tempers religious fervor, and takes flight. Despite rushing past supply stores ripe with dried provisions and cannery, he instead delves into hoards of shiny baubles; metaphorically diving into wealth, shifting around opulent piles of copper coins, rising above and ducking low around exorbitant chests, periodically nabbing artifacts in a frenzied grip, scrutinizing them closely. He tilts a golden candelabra to the side in order to find its highly-sought, maker's mark.

Morbin is intent on emptying this vault's coffers, stuffing his every pocket with Veblen goods: bottles of wine, fabrics, jewelry, gemstones, and even the spoils of petty bandit wars. However, what their party seeks is more Giffen and gaffer in nature. The pantry nearby is copious, shelf after shelf is stocked with fruit preserves, lined with tins of sardines and fleeces. They could survive down here for weeks- months even, without a hint of peril. No one will have to compete, there shall be no need for selfish hoarding, as the stockpiles are brazenly full. Yet, the archaeologist chooses to indulge in this early sutler's paradise, rather than focusing on the necessities they are here for, he lurches upon thoughts of gold, greed these riches may allow him to garner.

The illustration manning the torches of the room nods disapprovingly when Morbin discovers an over-stuffed desk in the corner. Its cabinets are weak and pompous, overladen with parchment. They seemingly stagger open on their own, showering the vagabond in swirls of paper airplanes. He nabs handfuls of bills that have been thrust into the air.

"Look, look," Morbin declares, "we're rich!"

"Oi, ye squall-dog, those are just banknotes, not worth the paper their printed on 'thout the moneylender's seal-ah approval.

"No! Oh no, nah! Yer right as always, Edmund. Now if I only 'ad that seal. I've got tah find 'is seal! 'As anyone spotted some gleam from ah brass tack?"

"Oh yeah, Glenn be stayin' upstairs, that stamp might still be 'round 'is wrist. Best of luck tuh ya, though. It's prolly in the gullet o' those grim by now. Wolves aren't picky whetha their meals are cold or not."

"Five-hundred thousand! There's ah promissory note 'ere for five-'undred thousand trademarks, n' it's just one-in-ah-million. Look at 'em all. This man must've been absolute legend," he blurts in wonder, whilst driving another bill into Edmund's face.

The wickerwalker nonchalantly shoves the parchment away, tearing the banknote in two.

"Give it rest, Morbin. They're all worthless sheets o' paper. We're 'ere for packstuff surprise, n' if we're lucky, medicines too. I need ye searchin' for those, can ye do that for me?"

The wannabe pilfer watches as scraps leisurely glide their way past his bootstraps, answering Edmund with a dejected *sigh*.

"I'll get right to it."

As Morbin begins scouring the contents of the desk, William reminisces about those indiscernibly large amounts. They must be fake, otherwise Glenn's numbers would rival all three Bannermane mercantiles combined, and no man could possibly thwart Charlie Mandon's wrath. The gold rush of immigrants and wealth forges all sorts of bonanza kings. Petty folk suddenly are uplifted in aristocracy, and undesirables weave the fate of thousands. Then again, with the mad scramble of bureaucracy and paperwork, pretty sure a gambling men could inquire their clerks to add a few zeros on the end of every check.

"'Eads up," Mandel signals, chucking an extra backpack that he'd be saving, to his comrade. It catches William slightly by surprise, embarrassingly striking him atop an already sore nose, and limping downriver into his awaiting arms.

"Umm, thanks?"

"Dontcha mention it."

Returning to collecting essential supplies, William finds himself lost amid metal fixtures, provisions arranged onto shelves taller than he. There are multiple rungs at shoulder-height, and the boy Jones carelessly combs through each one. Hampered by another sack of leather, he loosens the strap until it rests on his right forearm. Mandel's backpack, the one that he so graciously bestowed to him, is formidably larger than his own, currying an additional allowance of fifty pounds.

"Two-feet by one… nah, not quite. Each- fifty cans or so? Well, that's just ah guess. Maybe I should nab some o' those wax candle sticks or flasks o' oil 'stead?"

William tries to calculate the volume that he could tote for the group, but cedes the notion. Math has never been his strong suit, he's always been rogue at anything near-related to arithmetic. So the boy Jones decides that he'll stop when those backpack seams start tearing, and focuses on reaching that point as soon as possible. He cradles the mouth of the knapsack so that it yawns at the side of each shelf, while his other hand glides over each element, traversing wooden cigar cases, soft pouches, jewelry boxes and glints of tin, tipping each procurement so that it falls readily into his pack.

Gauntly fingers wrap around the rim of certain supplies, turning cans so that he may decipher those hard-to-read labels. Light isn't a problem here, and while that's a note that he may never conjure again, the problem is in regards to penmanship. The blue ink plunged upon each packstuff isn't actually crisp anymore, these labels have deteriorated into worn, faded nuances. For someone who had the urge to hoard and mark-up all these rations, why must his thronepatter be so mundane?

Regardless, his efforts to transcribe are for naught. In the end it should all be edible, a coin-flip between stale or aged to perfection. He nabs hints of protein, pickled produce, and candied fruits to stave scurvy- they'll need that for sure, sweets are a rarity too. That last can slips his grip, falling clumsily and colliding into the foundation of stone floor. William kneels down to retrieve this portion, only in an act of inherent unluckiness, flings the can further, skipping across, clear to the other side of the vault's demesne. Jerome resides in the next aisle, infuriating the whelp's patronage with his signature, cursed and cackling chuckle, gloating that he wouldn't make the mistake of tossing a valuable can of sliced peaches aside.

Finally, the metallic container comes to rest at the foot of a second desk, and William stomps blatantly after it. This table is a remarkable piece of furniture, three hand-carved cedar legs pitch into a slab etched with canals and stepped mountains. There are places of rest, flat surfaces where glassware can reside.

"What an interesting curio."

William recognizes this booth from those fantastic tales during his childhood. This is an alchemist table, the identity is unmistakable, as the rim of the table is ordained in runes, fashioned with the same incessant, cerulean markings. These arcane workshops are quite dangerous, not even meisters mavens of the Underdark may impose these devices without scrutiny. No tourists should be navigating these warrens, who knows how long all this equipment has been down here. In the brief stint William got to know him, he never took Glennitch as a purveyor of magikally-inclined projects. Yet, there is evidence to the contrary, as a tower of manuscripts adorn this workspace, some intriguing sampling of forbidden knowledge with titles on their spines such as *Metaphysical, The Lumenhour, Expelle Umbra, and Air & Coelom, the Firmament.*

The topmost novel, *Transmutation for Assayers,* has a pair of reading glasses shoved between the pages like a bookmark. Those specifically crafted lenses are sign of the dominantly wealthy, as men of the frontier can barely afford to wield goggles, combating the fickle plains and the effects of snow-blindness.

The alchemy table is residence to silvery, pewter rocks, iron filings, a mortar and pestle, plates filled with piles of powder, and interestingly enough, a matchbox which William keenly swipes into his coat pocket, knowing that access to tender flame will come in handy; subject to ongoing experiments with wyrd assemblies of glassware, gas burners clean of any debris, and vials full of strange liquid concoctions. Coinciding with Glenn's rich love-affair for organization, handwritten labels of tape are stuck to the side of each flask, describing incredible feats that imbue promises of strength, luck, and disguise its drinker to danger. Although, these bottles propose an underlying question.

"Must ye drink it, or merely massage the elixir twixt yer palms?"

Great men have been done-in by lesser distinctions. An Alderman lord has choked to death on a solution that then solidified in his esophagus. For better or for worse, these brews may garner good fortune, and William corks several vials, wrapping them in a bounty of loose cloth in order to stow them safely among his own personal pouch, a knapsack laden with wooden gamepieces.

"'Ow goes the excavation, professas?

Mandel and others heed Edmund's call, reconvening in the aura of ample torchlight. When they originally departed Mad River Junction with meager rations, they are now hampered with bags that burden their shoulders.

"All is well. There was lots, n' I mean lots o' good loot!"

The wickerwalker nods and smiles, one of those rare grins that contort his whiskers of facial hair, nearly prodding his eyes. Delight is a relatively new feeling for Edmund, as in a world of danger and everything dire, his complexion has scarcely seen such affirmation. The chalk outline of a hand waves one final goodbye, and while the illustration is limited in its animation, it posses the capacity to gently shake a nearby torch. This beaming brazier jitters ever so slightly, and Edmund's acute sense perceives the swaying of light.

"Oi, that's right. Thank ye, lil' man. 'Fore we go, do we got any free hands to wield firebrand? Balthus, Jerome, take these samplin' tah the folk outside."

These pilfering townspeople are over-encumbered, lugging equipment and luggage which drag heavily behind them. Each of the folk approach the center mast, hugging several rods apiece. These two antagonist pace themselves, particularly precise and careful not to set their own abundant facial hair aflame, as grey whiskers act as the best tinder, however the weight that burdens their shoulders slides awkwardly onto the interior of their elbows, and causes their wrists tremble as they fondle around with the torch shafts. Ultimately, their endeavor is a success, and they each awkwardly waddle to rejoin company in the hall. Mandel, Morbin, and Edmund follow in turn, and William is last to splurge on this endeavor, taking a few beads of fire for himself, as the torches are thin, enough for several to snake into each hand.

During his departure, his eyes spy the extent of the room one final time, and the boy Jones shames himself, cursing under his breath that he had not noticing certain compositions before. There is a map pinned with a variety of tacks to the reign of corkboard- at least, due to the jumbling of lines and geometric shapes, he assumes that it is a map. William has to be extremely deliberate- not this compositions is fragile, but careful not to set his overcoats or two knapsacks into full flame. Thankfully, everything should be okay, as his belongings are slightly moist, propped by the nice sort of damp. Not some overbearing, muddling wetness, nor the awkwardness of sweat. This is between, keeping him cool, as the snow they tracked inside the warrens earlier has melted.

"Yes!" Pitches the boy Jones, this is exactly what he needed.

Unpinning the length of artwork from the board, he pries this parchment from its constraints with ease, funneling the sketch appropriately under new management. William admires its thoroughly, and upon closer inspection, this is definitely a map of the warrens. There are lines dotting each passage of the labyrinth, and one specifically highlights amongst all the rest. However, according to the key, unfortunately he must be prepared to persuade the others that they must delve deeper still. There's the topside entrance, green-level, blue-level which their on now, but also yellow, orange, red and wine.

"Oh my, this'll be ah tough sell," he mentions to himself while tightening the sheet into a coil, which is a difficult effort to undertake with only one free hand.

Directing a gregarious grin towards the torchlight guardian, he excels towards the exit, departing the vault and nearly thrashing into the village audience strangling the entrance. Three companions part way, grazing farther from the portal rendered ajar, and gather preferably around the wickerwalker.

Edmund is complacent, contemplating their next logical course of action by directing them topside, conjuring aloud "-maybe the wolves 'ave retired from the Junction by now."

"That is ah chance we cannot possibly take," interrupts William, whom thrusts the scroll up high for all to admire, "lookie at what I 'ave 'ere!"

All the decent folk around mumble and whisper amongst themselves, until lady Jane chastises, "Yeah, so?"

William is a little distraught, "What do ye mean-" quickly realizing that he is still displaying a wound scroll. "-oh!"

He unfurls the length, instantaneously showcasing the property. There are murmurs of interest and agreement that they should partake a route through the warrens, believing that this is part of a well-documented escape plan. Edmund delivers truth, much to his own personal demise.

"Well, ye've gotten us this far. Eitha yer blessed by the prophets, stumblin' through all these catastrophes with some sort o' divine luck, or 'ave an actual idea of where we need tah go. In any case, I say, lead the way."

In all their infinite wisdom, the elders, Rochester and that decisively-deviled Jerome nod their heads, reaching an agreement, that their temporary arrangement shall be to lobby further into the labyrinth of steel and stone. It doesn't take long for the townspeople to gather their belongings, there are those who have been patiently biding time. Once everyone's bags are stowed upon their shoulders, each member of the company is handed a torch. The amateur archeologist, Morbin Evershade, is keen to extinguish the extras, wrapping them in linen for later-use. Down in the warrens, light is both currency and convenience.

The wickerwalker pilfers the map from William's grasp, enthusiastic to make pace. He's able to make headway with the slightest glance at the parchment, and barrels down the abandoned passageway, returning to the original stairwell. As their outfit reaches the platform, the boy Jones is rather remorseful. Behind their stride, the luminance of the vault dims, brought about by the closing of the bulkhead, filling William with a sense of guilt. It may have been Glennitch's dying wish that these stockpiles not go to waste, wither and rot, but William is not noticeably greedy, fond that the last remaining memory of his exploits is that of moderation and not the usual Bannermane desire for wealth or power.

As the group departs around the corner, returning their focus onto the staircase of a thousand steps, he turns behind for a short period of time, waving to the enchanted illustration manning the portal one heartfelt goodbye. While the figure might not be able to decipher this custom, though vagabond eyes, it's the thought that counts. This picket resumes an immortal watch, scarce is the day this vault may appear, and mortal eyes may glance upon its remaining contents.

There are those tempered by the heat of adversity, as frequent conflict breeds infinite wisdom. While William may envy wiseacres, and petition their experience, they in return, covet his amicable youth, for their passions have been tamed through the testament of time. Knaves be that type of folk to express their disbelief, rather shying to avoid conflict. Then there are veterans- stubborn at that, whom certify their hardship, and still power regardless. In spite of profession, event or hurdle, the result is still the same: that Bannermane do not contemplate, they actually make decisions in the heat of battle. If human brains were not three-quarter turns above that of beasts, grey matter wouldn't evaluate the worst situations, and render entire destinies based upon fight or flight. Stubbornness is ingrained in the root of humanity, hesitation is not, and will be the death of adventure.

'You either find yer wings cliff-jumping, or don't,' is a certain conventional, borderspiel motto stamped upon steel.

Quite ironic, as metal grows brittle with sloth, it is only through action when steel rings true, and is at its strongest. Now that the townspeople are aware of the challenges they face, some may claim that this second expedition is relatively easy-going in comparison. After all, the first two flights hindered company and twisted ankles, now their voyage crosses the threshold, descending another four flights without issue, only hampered by the occasionally fraught sentiments of, "'Ow much further?" And "Are we there yet?"

Edmund is having notable difficulty transcribing the map, as he cannot read. *"Gah,"* he submits, conceding the lead until William reaches his level, and he adamantly jabs the scroll into his chest, crying in frustration, "Tis 'opeless!"

The sole purpose of written language is to mediate business ledgers and letters, this is how frontier settlers define themselves from the pleasures of wild men, and wickerwalkers have zero need to dabble in the effects of bureaucracy. They typically a scrawl a tally mark on a piece of parchment, doodling a caricature of the creature they recently hunted too, providing a caricature of the whole thing, then tell the attendant at the aviary to deliver it to "da Gamemasta."

As the boy Jones procures a stint of time in order to determine their location, he realizes that Edmund must have been relying on the visuals. Simply asking himself, and afterwards checking each box in his brain.

"There are orange lines on the wall, so we 'ave tah be on orange level."

This depiction is crude, but actually on point. They've already passed yellow and orange, red is next, and the company must be nearing the bottom now. It's quite difficult to decipher, as their surroundings haven't changed. The hallway passages are their same shade of drab concrete brick, that stairwell encased by near-identical, ancient steel railings. Although the thought had crossed his mind, William is prescribed notion that this map is a trap, luring them further into the darkness in which there may be no escape.

This attitude is quelled by an intoxicating scent, the aroma of moss, lichen and earthy goods. A love affair so seductive and demanding- a welcomed luxury in the abyss, so much so that William pays no mind for its source. He requires a deep sleep, nestled between fibers of ivy and vine. The concept of resting in a bed of roses is all-consuming, an enchanting ease to his muscle tissues and respite from constant wear. These bouquets of smells nearly bring the boy to tears, while beside him, Cliff falls unconscious with delight, or seemingly bewitched by the fragrant balm. He suddenly collapses, tumbling down the series of steep steps, exasperating a succession of *oofs* and a distinctive *youch* with fortuitous attitude.

The entire company is rendered to a standstill while the rogue torchlight clatters upon the stair level, and extinguishes. His disappearance is something of circumstance, like a trick drummed-up by a carnival performer, or a member of the wandering masquerade of acrobats and dare-devils, that legendary Impair Ultra troop. The searing radiance from their own firebrand braziers is strict, extending nary ten-feet or so from the foremost navigator, meaning that poor Cliff careens towards the bottom of the stairwell in absolute darkness. The cacophony ends in an abrupt, stifled *clunk,* as when a sled crashes into Mad River's timber bulwark.

Edmund snaps into action, sprawling downwards before the rest of the group can even comprehend catching-up.

"After that goat!"

The wickerwalker is upon him swifter then rats on rice, until the luminance of his torch finally reaches Cliff's skin. This newfound light gives the proprietor an opportunity to regain his composure, rising from the fetal position, at least back onto his hands and knees. While his head may parry this stumble, and grace the light of day once again, he is distracted by a clamor elsewhere in the corridor. It isn't long before Cliff breaks into a ceaseless frenzy, wailing at the top of his lungs.

"Ah, an evil beast with glowin' eyes! Save yerselves," he blurts out, screaming until his face turns blue.

The company seizes in the dark, overcome in unadulterated panic by this sudden bout of hysteria, heeding the frenzied *pitter-patter, pitter-patter and pitter-patter* of Cliff's boots while he sprints away, bolting from the scene.

"Ah, those tales were true! We were wrong tah come down."

"Glowin' eyes?"

"Aye, glowin' eyes! Oh woe, the creatures from our nightmares."

"Not my nightmares," professes Lena as a real Calamity Jane, who shoves the irredeemable lot to the side with fervor, and Braithwaite is forced to clasp onto adjacent hand railing.

She swings her torch broad, and the luminance of this gesture reveals that unlike the earlier levels, this platform divides into multiple passages. Cliff's screams echo across the gait of concrete, but by the time the bulk of their company reaches the floor, accompanying a heated debate between themselves, they cannot discern which tunnel he made haste through. These shrieks sound delirious and frantic, almost as if Cliff has been abducted, and is being carried away. This assumption terrifies the group, whom each conceive a pair of eyes staring down every hall, wondering who will be its next hapless victim. Bids unsheathes her cutlass in preparation for a burst for violence, "C'mon, let's go!"

Yet avails when some studious fellow nabs at her arm, giving hesitation to the charge, and pulls her back.

Balthus attests that they "Can't just toddle-off after 'em, or we'll become 'opelessly lost."

"We can't sit 'ere and do nothin' eitha!"

The scholar stretches his arm, pandering to the extent of this new spanning demesne.

"Well, we don't even know where 'ere is."

They dwell upon an indoor plaza of some kind, constructed around the skeletal remains of a dried-up fountain, evidence of an ancient court. A winding sliver of cord parallels the permitter of this exhibit in which sleuths could assume that it was once used to wire a makeshift railing, cords that has snapped as consequence of age. William peers past this disarray, over the edging and into the hull, staring deep at an excessively muddled blue-grey basin. These stains indicate that this well was in operation for an incredible length of time, especially as crusts of calcium cake the plumbing, like a thick, solid lather of soda ash that foams that entire set of fountain jets.

This company of townspeople was founded upon a never-ending chill, the frost they endure is the very same inhospitality that their parents faced, and even their granelders, who fought and died through this squalor. Warmth is comfort, and comfort is a moot notion. The luxury of a warm recess isn't a palpable concept to Bannermane. Therefore, as they stumble upon this domain, where a lukewarm aura has decided to asserted itself, their response is overwhelmingly lackluster. Despite this willful ignorance, the ambience continues to bless them with tantalizing bliss. If they would stop and stay awhile, many tickle the idea of sparing their overcoats and lulling about. Yet, the bearing of nearby decorations leave some less than impressed, and learned men like Balthus find it suspicious.

Elsewhere around the hollow are intricately-carved, stoneware urns containing nothing but arid, lifeless soil. There is no water, and without this precious elixir, life cannot stem, not even fungi, the most adept of all biological species, choose not to entertain this stiff mix. These planters are arranged in a row beside the stairwell, accenting three monumentally steely doors, leading to who knows where. It could be that this installation has been touched by the foul taint of chaos, or maybe, this is an anchor, an industrial park, from before the deep-freeze?

In pace of such foreboding danger, the team still finds solace in this ambiguity. Their anxiety for voyaging underground has been temporarily relieved by an expanse, a lofty domed ceiling presiding over them, flaunting into four tunnel arches, the passages fledging further from this plaza. In a true masterpiece of yester-year, dozens upon dozens of mirrored panels bind this canopy, granting the appearance of a midnight recession. As their torches flicker, biting at the dark, the reflection their flames produces a dazzling spectacle through the ritual chamber, mimicking the illusion of a cloudless, twinkling firmament and moonlit sky.

The floor is bathed in tremendous amounts of limelight, revealing that they have been marching on tile all along. Its profound patina has bleached over the generations, warping into a falsely fastidious ivory. There are tracts of this regime where a corner of ceramic tile has sheared loose, or shattered altogether.

Paranoia about these warrens has always ran rampant, mainly in part to how Bannermane always exaggerate, and weave rumor to ensure their exploits rank among legend. Most townspeople claimed that these passages held shrines of sacrifice for the mortuary cult, as death dredges all sorts of grand, austere designs from the mind. The skald, Arabella Gaberdine, often told countless stories to clamor about, that these tunnels are the remnants of a military installation, or a bunker for the elite to bide their time, and wait out the inevitable slew of storms way back when. Upon glancing upon this property, perhaps this track-talk could be true.

The company submits to a sense of eerie calm, and William exhibits the vague concept that this should not be a locus of death, but a place of healing. Edmund is rather undeterred though, and less entertained by these reimaginings, rather seeking to escape, rejoining the rest of the Bannermane safety above ground. Appealing to action and common sense, the wicklerwalker dredges.

"We need tah consort with the map. Dear William, if ye please?"

"Oh, but o' course, I 'ave the map right 'ere."

Unfurling the mess of scroll with a snap of his wrist, the boy Jones reveals the labyrinthine map all to himself. He unintentionally keeps his company bayed at arms length- grateful for that fortunate mishap too, as in a stirring development, the ink has smeared across the parchment during Cliff's debacle and their sudden rush downwards.

Mandel attempts to weave his head around the fringes of paper, and instead of granting him a glance, William bestows a gut-wrenching kick towards his shin, for even his most trusted friend carries gossip, and an earnest lad cannot afford any loose tongues.

"Mother 'ubbard," the cordwainer hops off, clutching his knee tightly into his abdomen.

Uh-ah. The boy Jones nervously chuckles with this act, whipping the scroll to his waist, and winding the rolls snugly together again.

"Lookie tis just 'round the bend."

"Which way?" Maxwell inquires, arching and twisting his back so that he may point to the tunnel behind him.

"Or thattaway?"

"Yes, that one," the boy sneers in affirmation, and once their party resumes their expedition, albeit drearier, William later relents, dressing his arms towards an entirely separate direction.

"No- umm, I wasn't pointin' ta that one. Yes, that one… originally."

He is quite surprised that his entire act is taken so wholeheartedly. Their company doesn't argue: no jeers of, "are ye sure?" or "really?" These are unusual tidings after all, and everyone is too spooked to argue. Still trapped in the belly of the beast, a monument of stone and gridiron, they continue to find themselves traversing hallways similar to levels above. Only, this specific passage is wider.

Those identifying lines marking the walls are tones of crimson denoting red-level, and the standard, barren portals have handrails jointed in the wall, guiding the spaces between them. If Jerome were to tire and require a crutch to bide over, these would be ideal support. The surrounding facades feature collections of framed portraits, and as Braithwaite struggles to wipe the dust from them and reveal their subjects, she only succeeds in spreading the grime around.

There is an impenetrable layer of brown filth, a layer of scum that clouds people clad in regalia of the robe, all of whom are smiling in their white suits or bright blue pajamas. The ward shakes her head in dismay, these outfits are unsuitable for any cold conditions, even while the portraits of these people look particularly medically inclined, similar to arch lectors, they wouldn't make it in the world above.

Proceeding down the passage in rows of two-by-two, uniform fashion, there is no need to muck about. Lena leads the way alongside Korralack, as the two of them are expecting a brawl in short manner. They erect pace a tad too swift, giving chase to any odd creature that lurks in the gloom. The sisters, Libby and Bids have armed themselves to the teeth, aiming to supply folks ahead with armaments should they so suit. They each carry a cast of ordnance with pointy ends. William and Morbin find their strides while Mandel treads at their heels, dressing like a shade, resentfully bitter at the thrashing he took to his leg. Mug and Braithwaite are the indifferent sort, snuggly plush amid the center of their group while Jerome and Rochester are in no rush, jabbering about elderly matters, testing their memories with trivia. Finally in the rear dwell Edmund and Balthus, ensuring that those greybeards to their bow are not lagging behind, and providing cover for the stern. It's an unexpected fellowship, founded in the most unlikely of places.

The wickerwalker is solemn, experience has made him bitter so that he may constantly glimpses backwards, periodically jostling his lantern forward, watching if anything hidden forms amid the suddenly luminous berth. Dim tentacles writhe in the light, dispersing their shadowy limbs to reveal the standard, bland concrete floor. William believes that he sights a figure amid the darkness, and nary calls out, though his imagination must be playing tricks on him, like usual. Edmund would've caught it had this behavior been anything serious. The boy Jones is interested in changing subject, and while paired with Morbin, they have ample topics to discuss. Their rivalry has always been illustrious, and it doesn't take long before the thieves break into banter and bonding, much to Mandel's ire. They indulge in gossip, though these revelries would normally render competitions at the tavern, and disgruntle over their previous schemes at the employ of Crooked Men.

"-and then what happened? Come on, it can't possibly end like that!"

The other townspeople listen on, enthralled by tales of exquisite adventure.

"So there I was, my back 'gainst the wall as one o' Mandt's missionary's 'eld that kerosene tah mah face. I could smell the alcohol on his breath- rank, o' course 'is beard prolly dipped down in the drink n' soaked-up near all of it. But- get this, then the brute collapsed in drunken stupor, literally rear-ending that kiln open, n' crashin' through ah table. The bloke's stench was immediately drowned-out by scents oh evergreen. She really knows how tah brew ah mean perfume. Doe, I still can't believe they left that bloody bulwark unlocked. So I then chucked my key ontah that unconscious guard."

"'No need for that anymore,' I says tuh muhself, n' waltzed right into Mandt's vault. The cage I was after sat on some silver pedestal, 'bout yay 'igh, n' once that otter saw the likes of me, it let off some cry like a frenzied mink. 'Ad to 'old mittens right tah mah ears, was quite the blazes, that alarm sounded like ah shriveling baby! Now, these varmints are worth certain sizable fortunes, ye know 'ow dem mercantiles leash 'em-up, scourin' riverbanks for anything that gleams. Some down-and-out family band might look 'pon this critter with pity, n' lend ah large pouch of trademarks muh way. Original plan was tah stuff it in ah sack, doe o' course once I saw that lock, I says tuh muhself 'gain, 'ad tah be magikal,' as the thing glittered with blue staves. So I can't bend those bars worth ah damn, n' can't break the lock- couldn't force it open, I'd 'ave tuh take the whole cage somehow. Trouble was, the whole playpen was mounted for just that, tah stop vagabond ilk like me. Some sort o' cold-rolled contraption-"

"Agghh!"

A frantic scream blows wind through the tunnels, interrupting Morbin's honest account. It isn't long before the flurry of shouting squeaks start up again.

"Ah-ah, *agghh!* Someone 'elp, it's right 'hind me!"

"Stow yer roll, Morbin. That howl is familiar."

"Course tis, ya dolt. That's Cliff, let's go get 'em!"

Tapping twice on the neck of those in front of her, she pressures Lena into a burst forward with the hilt of her torch. Libby isn't the type of woman you deny twice, so their foremost company breaks into an all-out endeavor to rescue the missing, wayward caravanhand. Caught in the lead of the pack, reminded that those that follow have the tendency to trample those that trip, the widow decides to ignore this antsy transgression, just this once.

"Awwah!"

The voice howls again, another gale fueled by fright riles into the air as their party passes yet another, four-way junction, forcing a certain few, foolhardy individuals to backtrack, and take an immediate left instead.

"Dis way, dis way! Mustn't stop now."

The townspeople know they are on the correct path, as vivid green light lies anchored in the distance, breaking the melancholy. Twenty-seconds of solid sprinting yields the youngest as champions, and the company starts to spread apart. These tunnels are stifled with stale air, making it harder to breathe, especially when exerting this much urgency. Compared to the flats under the firmament, this is torture for Bannermane kin. Clouds cluttered with debris and soot are released with every exercise of their boot heels. Those treading closely behind one another are coerced into covering their face, lest loose scree pummel their skin. Balthus is left in the dust of those with superior stride, coercing the man to posse alongside Jerome and

Rochester, whom shames his adversary with a scowl. Braithwaite, Mandel and William on the other hand, lead faster than a bison caught by its stirrup, racing down the corridor as if it's some sort of game.

"Sounds closer down 'ere, 'e's this way," the boy Jones ushers towards his fellows, motioning with an arm for them to come near, "C'mon, slowpokes!"

"Stop runnin' so damn fast, 'Liam. Guess I can't keep-up with otha children these days."

An excitable Calamity Jane shouts form somewhere beyond the trio, "Soon as I get a hold of them, gonna wallop that hoosier for every marble, everything he's worth. Gone done ruining my afternoon- at least, I think it's suppertime."

Bearing heading towards the end of the hall, their next obstacle is brazen, reflective of torchlight, declaring itself as a monstrous bulwark clad with pins and fittings. This bulkhead towers to the top of the hall, an entrance not intended for mortal quarry. Its craftsmanship is impeccable, befit of the gods: an anatomical structure cast from four-inch, cold-rolled steel for basic function and necessity, however it swathed with abstractly fashionable, louvered slats for ventilation. Above their heads, and capping the doorframe is an enormous blinking screen. It reads the same intervals, flashing the same time after time in fever, before quickly dashing away. The numbers 23:59:00 blare in audacious, leg-thick, crimson lettering. Beside the outstanding clock is a caged light sconce hanging from the frame, rocking in wine-red unison. When it had once conjured a vibrant fern-like flavor, the glow is now entranced by vermillion spirit, momentarily beaming a warning in red. The trio of youngsters can hear the lamenting cries of Cliff through slits on the door, and have grown livid. They abandon their torches in concert, dropping their sole source of illumination to the ground, and sparking-hot embers to the ruined tile. In this decaying limelight, they each test the door's strength, poising shoves to no avail. The entrance is barred firmly shut, perhaps a permanent fixture as one person cannot split the portal.

"Togetha then."

William presses his palms against the centerbrace of slats, Braithwaite follows in suit, and then Mandel in turn.

"On three. One… two… 'eave-'o!"

Between the boy Jones stubbornness, the cordwainer's blooming brawn, and the ward's determination during this herculean effort, they shove like their lives depend on it: as if they fail, there shall be no tomorrow. The trio barge through just as the remainder of their company arrives, collapsing onto a floor of brittle ceramic, as the steel shutters clang on the opposing interior of room. Their mouths are rendered wide, aghast in awe, beseeched by strange, mystifying and arcane wonders in the test tracks of a laboratory. In this lofty expansive, thirty-foot room, electricity cackles and arcs from exposed wiring across the rafters. Cobalt-riddled energy surges through a series of hanging fluorescent cylinders, aligning the environment into a well-lit stage. These tubes emit obtrusive tunes, a constant buzzing that invading the visitors' eardrums like some hum.

Words escape from Balthus' lips, "It must be magik!"

Copper and acrylic threads dangle haphazardly, thick as lattice where portions of drop-ceiling, foam tiles have succumbed to their weight or are missing altogether, sullying the grained, powder-laced tile with hassle, and loosening the grout. These filings have been so thoroughly walked-over, stomped into oblivion, they've been ground into fine sand. The usual concrete stems into segmented bricks, anchored into pyramids into the walls with portrait frames at their apex, immaculate detail, foreboding otherworldly scenes of the glory days. Dozens of pipes pierce the cinderblock, scattering every which way, exposing torrents of blaring-hot steam, and escaping trails of water which leak across various gauges and valves.

This room is split into two distinct areas, a viewing theater around an operating table, and a prominent studio space bordered by gridiron gates. The theater is academic in nature, surrounded by crescent rows of tiered booths, full of stuffed taxidermy figures crowded shoulder-to-shoulder. Outermost rings of this seating easily advance to the height of the room, where one of these rather stiff-looking occupants could tickle joists hidden among the metal scaffolding and rafters above. A suspended trellis strings together rows of boxes, treasure chests that summon beams of sunlight onto the workshop below, allowing those of the robe to manipulate and focus light on their operating table. A cunning beast of brute and brawn lies strewn upon a silvery serving tray, long-dead, as its tongue rolls lazily from its brimming maw. Parts and pieces of pelt have been cleaved in half, pried apart like the rind of a fruit with toothed forceps. The cranial cavity is exposed to a violet, irradiating glow, originating from an arm aperture, pulled so close to the cadaver that it denotes the tiniest wounds or anything unnatural. Various tools, goggles, masks, and other instruments have been laid aside, all drenched, dipped in a vermillion ink, tinted with the tincture of blood. Wolves were never meant to be confined like this, bound senselessly to a slab, its sheer size ensures that several paws lapse from the stretch of metal. The claws of these hairy mauls have caught quarry, the lining of a leather apron, which shreds dangle freely, and the whereabouts of its former occupant are unknown. Bordering the edge of this workspace is a four-wheeled cart, sporting copious vials of chemicals, a dazzling assortment of vividly verdant potions and suspicious concoctions. The laboratory trolly is packed to the brim with usual suspects: botanicals, preservatives, alcohols, formaldehyde, and foul, green warp-fluid. When the curator returns, they'll be in need of another subject.

William is sure that the gridiron on the opposing wall is a makeshift morgue, the cliche cubical doors, its latches and hinges potentially housing all sorts of otherworldly monstrosities. Beside this trophy predator is a benign, shallow recess featuring the crematory furnace, as the visiting troop can feel the searing heat emanating from inside, and the extraction hood mechanically slivers up the concrete loam, through the ceiling above. This area is adorned with wheeled devices of yore, specifically medical beds and stretchers, one of which provides cover for a familiar figure whom ducks underneath.

"Cliff! Ah, there's the scoundrel," Mandel blithely remarks, but instead of being greeted by buoyant happiness for his rescue, the cordwainer is hassled by the fugitive's incessant *shush-shush.*

Cliff Fetherhaugh presents his left palm over his mouth, signaling to be quiet, while his other hand points towards the trio and their misfit ensemble, then slightly nudges his glare further, towards a gnarly creature that casts the gurney aside like it was nothing but a paperweight. Their looks of astonishment for finally finding their companion are suddenly shadowed by throes of fear as this bark-ladden, blue-skinned beast swoops upon their party without any effort, pinching Cliff by the fringes of his collar, and letting him dangle frivolously, maybe ten or so, feet into the air. As much as he may struggle, running in place while his coat strains and stretches, yet does not slip free from the behemoth's firm grip.

This giant-kin is an extraordinary spectacle, Austerlaund has met her match. It maintains the guise of a timberjack, as if a tree had decided to uproot itself, and walk upon two legs straight from the nearest evergreen outcrop forest. Every inch of skin has contorted and wrinkled in such fashion that it garners the appearance of bark. Various, muted-green lichens cultivate atop teal stretches, while rampant mossy patches congeal around its shoulders, mimicking the froth of hair. Bony plates swell several inches from its hide, akin to stalactites, lingering hungrily around the nape of the neck, before eventually extending towards its pair of burly, swollen arms, granting these limbs a rubble-inspired look. This mineral veneer is remnant of a disguise, and cater to frighten when necessary. However, this giant is by no means versed in guerrilla warfare. While there are myriad scrapes and discolored, battered bruises from battle- not any skirmishes they'd be aware of. This troll is unusually clumsy, and earned these token once the nearby furniture decided to pick a fight.

A facade of scaly studs rises past its recessed sockets and eyes, a skullcap humbled by crowns of teeth. With a visage adorned in nature, normal folk would be none the wiser about the mouths flaunting on either side of its face, yet these are no ordinary ears, they are lobes that appear no different than moths. Each funnel is comprised of extravagant, velvety wings with tails that trail behind. The ear drums themselves are inflamed with bubbly gel, aquamarine packs that vibrate alongside the slightest disturbance in the air. This menagerie is fitting, considering the absent bar of normalcy, and the troll hastens other quirky features, such as its defining, bulbous nose. The foremost smell strikes at William's own nostrils, a tranquil, aromatic odor, as if walking among alder carrs, from before the land swelled with snow. He can't help but fantasize what scent humans give-off to greater creatures, perhaps the musk of charcoal, damp linens and briny sweat.

While the company is awestruck, the giant focuses on the man in its grip, gingerly prodding its pinkie against Cliff's chest and neck. The fingernail is jagged, prompting the ire of rusty iron blade, and is close to unintentionally drawing blood.

"What ah curious pest. I've seen yer kind before- vermin from the surface," the troll-kin paddles on.

Its voice is meandering in nature, long and winded, similar to conversing with a wisened oak tree.

"Let 'em go ya beast!" Libby yells out, forcing the troll-kin to recoil in disgust and spite at the statement.

"Beast, beast? I'll have you know that I am Gardenwaagh, maester of all megafauna, and king of these warrens. But, if it's a beast you want, dear knave, then it's a beast you'll get!"

It succumbs to a binge of atrocious anger, raising a single fist against the arrogant pests that have stumbled upon its domain until those knuckles collide with the ceiling rafters, sending a barbarous spray of debris sprawling over the crowd. The grimoire slides from Balthus grip, glowing with a violent red aura, vigorously attempting to throw itself at the aggressor and defend its fresh-set of masters, as without them, it may never see the light of day.

Upon spying the manuscript proceed to float away, the pygmy's fingertips dig feverishly into the spine, using his entire body weight to halt the tome's advance. He slides forward, inch by inch, awkwardly fumbling in silence, because they are located right behind the Gardenwaagh. William watches the learned man struggle with his luggage, while they would possess an element of surprise, they are not here for conflict, no soldiers trained to fight. William has surmised from the nearby experiments that this is a creature of intelligence, and hectically tries to reason with it, defusing the situation.

The boy Jones abruptly raps aloud, "Wait, wait, wait. We are mere creatures o' comfort, n' 'ave been tryin' tah find sanctuary in these tunnels. Would ye 'ave us so readily dismissed, guests o' yer fine establishment, gutted n' pinned 'pon board like frogs?"

"No, no. Percilees, and perish the thought… humans are a delicacy, and taste much better through a preservation of some kind. Come to think of it, I'd much rather squish you into jelly."

Caught by its pawky humor, the group immediately becomes leery and wide-eye, dropping those torches and rallying their weapons in jest. Although the troll-kin's attitude has winded down, comforted by the boy Jone's fine words, the grimoire continues to riles against this threat, fraught with unbridled fury while Balthus labors to contain it. William himself chucks aside the formality, and brandishes his halberd head in stead, before the troll finally relents, bawling in a hysterical fit.

"Oh, oh! I'm just kidding, but you should have seen your faces. Was enough to make a grown man cry."

The manuscript languishes once more, hesitant with these mixed-emotions. It returns to its bland stance, and finally gives-up the notion of brawling.

"Cry? I outta give you something to cry about, waugh!" Calamity Jane yells, approaching the troll-kin and tilting the knife's edge close to its skin, implying that she'd much rather sheathe her dagger in the beast's ankle.

She shudders when closing into the beast's vicinity, not shying from the potential of harm, but the ludicrous strength of the lamps reigning above. The widow's weapon plummets to the ground with an unceremonious *clank* while she raises both hands to blind herself from those intense rays. This unbridled glare bestows the radiance of the sun, an incandescent, awesome-energy condensed in filament form.

"Mind the lights, we've got visitors!"

The Waagh jitters with glee, "and they speak too. I believe you might offer better exchange than a tunnel rat!"

"Gah! My eyes, my eyes!" Her hand lunges forward in the general shape of a fist, colliding into the troll-kin's thigh, and barely ruffling the frills of its skirt. "I'll cleanse your palate for these cantrips!"

"Stow yer thuggery, Lena! Show some common decency if ya please. Can't ye see this fantastic beast means us nah harm?"

"Pay 'eed tah Cliff!"

"And watta bout him? Clearly 'e 'as the upper-'and," eggs Braithwaite.

The troll-kin chuckles at this illustrative play on language, addressing Jane's ongoing concerns.

"I appreciate the candor, however rude- been years since I talked to anyone at all. If you'll relent and take a step back, let's institute introductions."

The beast conjures and expels a modest amount of phlegm lining its throat, splattering in a gross pool upon its toes and lichen pads, although the giant doesn't seem to mind. An attentive folk might be able to describe ascertain bits and bobbles confined within this sappy amber concoction. William can only reserve his criticism on how exactly gross this is.

"I am Tom-Tom, eldest among the Gardenwaaghs, original folk of the Oestergaard, or troll-kin if you have it. We're known as the scapegoat for all of humanity's problems, because your people are an awful fickle lot. I retreated into these tunnels generations, perhaps hundreds of years ago, and became caretaker over its incredible collection of yore, studying those ancient artifacts and records galore, even if I must hunch over just to tread the tunnels. In this darkness, my dwellings remains secret, as those who swear by the coin are afraid to delve into their history, or any transgressions forefathers made in their honor."

"Put me down now. Put me down if ye please, 'fore I take it personally!"

Cliff Fetherhaugh accosts, using his arms and legs to squirm to and fro. The giant abides, dispensing him gently onto the cold, grungy tile, and watches him scurry away, hidden amongst the breadth of crowd. Balthus scrutinizes the breadth of the laboratory, and the distinct lack of anyone else. He conjures skepticism, tapping twice on the book held underneath his arm, to demonstrate that it's securely stowed.

"Where are those otha ill omens, where is the mortuary cult?"

"Mortuary cult? What do you think I do down here, worship demons? There is naught but I."

"Just ya? Really?" Bids huffs in disbelief. "Who be the one carvin' up all those critters n' stuffin' 'em?"

"Oh yes, by carvin' I assume you mean my art. That's me, I'm a taxidermist. Guilty as charged," it quips. "I use those cadavers as nourishment, feeding off ichors of the dead-"

Youch it suddenly erupts, whisking its fingers only after accidentally brushing aside some stray wiring. Its thumb is now lambasted in cherry-red lipstick, and Tom-Tom hastily sticks this sore finger into its mouth.

"-bloody disgustin'," Korralack interrupts, characteristically labelling the giant as an abhorrent, a freak of nature.

"*Hmmph.* Disgusting for you maybe. I don't mean to be any threat," the troll-kin retorts, removing its sore finger and pointing it at the Boar's Band brigand, "but it's really the circle of life. Most humans are selfish, never remembering that there's more than you in this unfathomably, wide-wide world. Nothing unnatural about it- taboo others claim."

The ward, Braithwaite, admires the Gardenwaagh's profound sense of wisdom. A great sadness underlines her tone of voice, probing, "Are y'all 'lone down 'ere?"

Sigh heaves the troll, discerning this unenthusiastic whine.

"Pretty much. You're the largest company that I've ever entertained. Gets rather quiet. Though, come to think about it, I have talked to another person who stored items in the rooms above. Casual conversation, nothing serious, as I never came close- too afraid of what he might think of me."

"Oh, ye poor thing. Livin' in squalor, 'lone at the end o' the world."

"Well, it's not the worst predicament. Far from it, actually. Even while they never have met me, I have a sort-of, gentleman's agreement alongside the wickers of the Junction. Perhaps you've heard the story, they'll occasionally forfeit a carcass over to me. I'll have the cadaver deposed, stuffed, cleaned, and back on a lift in a few days. Lets me explore the world's creatures without the threat of extermination. I doubt the Bannermane are the forgiving lot with the dangers of grims knocking at their door. Just look at me, wouldn't imagine that I'd be a welcome sight. I never liked killing myself, but have always been captivated by the concept of death. Restoring trophies to their former glory is an art. That hound on the table was dispatched about a week ago. I've kept him for myself, noticed a lot of discrepancies in its usual biological humbingings. This one has developed a gizzard, something rather obscene, helpful for predators which swallow gulps of meat without chewing. Now, I'd hate to address this, but I assume that you're down here for a reason. When there's one wolf, there are prolly many more to follow. Have they become a nuisance yet?"

Using his billhook to lift the canine's muzzle, watching its tongue slacken and writhe, Edmund quips.

"Why yes. While ye've been toilin' away safely down 'ere, they've been runnin' amok 'round the town. 'Onestly, this one's ratha shy when sized tah those brotha currs."

"Oh my, oh my, indeed. I take it that things must be bad if you've sought refuge down here. Bannermane have a fear of tunnels and close-quarters. One, two, three- a dozen, or so. I fear that my services must no longer be necessary. Drats, twas the perfect arrangement. Time to carry on I suppose. You've all welcome to say, though food may be an issue. What is it you folks eat anyways? Birch root?"

Unlike their Bannermane counterparts, this rabble is delighted by Tom-Tom's presence. At first glance, the troll-kin's characteristics appear rather petrifying, especially deposed way down in these trenches, but its dry humor, knowledge of human habits, and canonical smell provide a welcoming experience. Edmund begins interrogating the taxidermist over any other abnormalities, if something dire is at work: the wolves have been adapting to the territory's extreme circumstances, or the result of vile experiments against natural law. Despite a formidable height difference, Jerome attempts to stare the troll down, contemplating if he should sway the company that it's another dangerous monster.

William has been distracting himself in the meantime, overcome with morbid curiosity, the never-ending quest for knowledge. He's decide to amuse himself, parading through the parapets, frequently petting oversized stuffed animals, getting a feel for the wealth of fur while waltzing through the troll's gallery. There's a red fox, or what's left of the varmint, as these remains have been broken into working materials: sinew cord, a fur pelt for binding, teeth to hash, and bone to whittle; must've been struck so hard that the fox was completely obliterated. The head is intact with sewn together, beady eyes, but really it's nothing but a pile of separate ingredients and a pelt now, which has always been a lucrative trophy. A hare freezes beside it, as if the predator nearby still breathes and craves rodent flesh. The boy Jones surmises that it must be a child's first quarry, a stepping stone in rivaling their parent's hunting skills. While William has never brought one low, a hare seems like nothing to boast about. Statues of critters and small game dwell in the upper theater, specifically half a dozen beaver outfits and a fisher among them, their natural nemesis. He hallucinates it's signature, odd mewls, a vaguely human baby-like scream which causes him to shudder.

When the boy heads to exit the cylindrical rows of seating, his gaze catches on a figure fairly peculiar. The masterpiece of this entire collection is nothing reigning from the animal kingdom, instead his attention focuses on a mutant bug-eyed alien from beyond the Planet Cretaceous. This must be a creative addition, a pet project, as there's no possible way such a being could be real. It is a creature of overwhelmingly small stature, say two-feet tall- very puntable in close quarters. Clad in balding, yet blushing salmon-pink skin, afflicted by a fungal blight, bright-red toadstools which sprout in colonies along its leathery hide. However the crowning quality has to be a pair of grotesquely-long limbs, longer than the height of its body, dangling loosely towards certain duck-webbed feet. William jabs one of these arms with his index finger, producing an iconic *squish-squish, squelch* of bean pulp, and forcing the aperture to cinch like a rope. Tom-Tom must care about this perverse creature, as it is rigged inside a sweater ensemble, the lavender glow of love, lovingly stitched together or perhaps scavenged off an unlucky corpse, someone who got lost in the tunnels and never escaped.

He petitions for the exit of auditorium seating, now setting himself upon the permitter of demesne, funneling towards all the illustrative, framed artwork. Alike the locket of his parents which William holds near and dear to his heart, these landscapes are partially alive, showing their personality through subtle caricature of animation. One features a familiar tone, the rising spines of mountains, and a waning sun set between these gaps of teeth. The eminence of the white caps is remarkable, an alabaster glaze which shifts into hues of midnight while the sun sets, then it rewinds, and purple throes transition back onto the terrain. Another depiction denotes a millwright's lumber mill, actively splitting trunks in two, and adding to an infinite pile. The wood weaves its way down an aluminum slide, colliding with such a force that the timber skews. The palette of this painting isn't simply worn, its dedicated with observable syrup, vibrant oils mull and muddle over the decades.

While William ponders deeply into the painting, yet he doesn't hear Tom-Tom make approach, almost starling the boy Jones when he speaks in signature gravelly affliction.

"Fascinating isn't it?"

"But o' course, Mr. Goodsir," unexpectedly stumbles out of William's mouth.

"Goodsir? You smell of modesty. I welcome though have no need of such formalities. Are you enjoy these sights? Arcane becomes a rarity when folk always are keen to worship the next thing, anything shiny and new. They tend to forget the ancients that were here long before them, and will remain long after them. I was lucky to come across these. Some quartermain and his porter were lost amid the wilds. Met them in my migration from my home-burrow, aptly named Tom Fry Eddy, before I settled here. Anyways, took them in, showed them how to carve shelter from a banks of packsnow. I thought it was strange at the time, because humans don't stray far from the Mad River, and whenever I questioned why they were out here, they refused to part answer. Must've been possessed by the spirit of the goat, always omitting and misleading my query, but I am no fool. These northern territories are paradise for archaeologists, those learned few who realize that wealth lies buried underneath all this permafrost and rime. Any who stir this ancient pot of stew tend to yield ancient ruins. Alas, some folk will never have the answers that they yearn for. Spontaneous events lead to the most interesting results. They burdened me with these immaculate landscapes- reward for my assistance."

Prodded by the mere mention of some quartermain and his particular porter, William reminisces to himself, recounting his very own origin story, a chronicle so scandalous that he was sworn to secrecy around the supper table, safeguarding this account from all others.

As a vagabond of portly duties, Emery Walder was built with broad shoulders, training during the nigh-endless blackberry winters, when the frost leeches into the early months of bloomtide. Porters are a necessary expense, tending to the ancillaries and gear of wickerfolk, walkers, eccentric game wardens, and the squireships of veteran dragoons, hauling armaments, soothing tonics, and furs from prized hunts across the northern territories. Yet, every one of his employers would met similar grisly, untimely ends, as there are no joyful tales on the frontier. These losses haunted Emery, but also buried him further into the craft. No matter the odds, he always seemed to draw dire straits.

It must've been a curse- or a peculiar castor hex: attracting imminent violence like a match to powder keg. The stalwart trooper versed himself in every waking danger, any peril that may plague the wayward navigator, lessons that he would eventually verse his child William in. Walder's persistence over the decades garnered the attention of one prophesied man of the hour, Atticus Dour, a renowned quartermain.

As preeminence of the frontier, quartermaines are a step above ordinary hunters and their wickerwalker brethren. They choose to battle the most ferocious beings of the hinterlands, a menagerie of foul git, curbing wolf packs, bears and megafauna with nary regard to life or limb. It is with their due diligence that Bannermane aren't besieged by looming threats, and together they became those watchers of the wilds, trackers of the cold hosts, cleansing chaos throughout the land.

The Barbwire Bandit of Brittany laid terror to the Westergaard, voraciously consuming all townspeople for their succulent, red hot meat. It would impale victims on the many thousands of spines adorning its back. The entire contest was extraordinarily tricky, as the beast would burrow and lie dormant for years; only its barbs remained visible, easily mistaken for bushels of bouquet grass. Eventually, a team of archaeologists spotted the bewilderbeast lurking around Midwest Bell, upon the fringes of old city. It rummaged through their claim, tossing aside mountains of earth and scaffolding, scouring for something, just as they were.

The pair gave chase, goading it into the carcass of an aging freight carrier. With their trap seemingly sprung, the entire container suddenly sunk underneath the taxiways, collapsing into a rat warren below. The beast met a timely demise, its head casually caved in from heaps of fresh rubble and concrete rebar.

This was where they found the most unlikely of scenarios, a fledging babe, with naught a year of mileage, left in the lurch and strapped soundly into a harness. William's babbling cries fell upon mangled vermin ears, and within moments was surrounded by a horde of the writhing scum. Hundreds of soot-laden rodents held bay, nipping ears and tearing fur in frenzy. The creed swarmed, trodden in debris and filth, yet unable to reach the child. Tails twisted into knots during the scuffle, instead pinning them down like crazed hounds. The tunnels shrieked with anguish- exasperation, as the strongest fled, dragging their infirm brethren away in retreat. In the ire of danger, Emery descended the pit, snatching the young boy from a hideous demise with haste.

While Atticus had battled all manner of vicious creatures in countless, forging all manner of incredible triumphs, something changed following the bewilderbeast's defeat. He became rather ill, and they say that he heard voices- whispers that struck several chords, turning the tide of his emotions: unsettling the quartermain's demeanor and souring every expression. At the wake of all discord, superstition swelled. At least how others tell it, Atticus fled- a rather bizarre disappearance.

No one actually believes that Emery betrayed his partner, but nonetheless, the legacy of their friendship tarnished into scandal. The stories they garnered are full of woe, nothing to be shared over growlers of nog; when asked to relive the tales, Emery would instead shamefully turn, rather tending to the hearth. This intense guilt humbled him, and fed-up with the seriousness of portsmanship, quietly retired from his adventures abroad.

Scars leeched through Emery's skin like ink. He'll always bear the memories, that awful trauma. So many lives had come and gone, like snowflakes over an endless ocean. What is life, are we bred in such a span that we melt into nothing? No one will remember our journeys, the immense suffering undertaken, the bounds reached, surpassed, even conquered. To be forgotten is the fear of all men, the root of unending evils- why we raise others to remember our names, in the hopes that they reach the same livelihood. The chance to atone for that loss is life's fortune and single greatest mistake.

Folk fight the fury of gods to stave out their place in history, capitulating for the slightest mark in the epics of man, even a write-in under some obscure footnote, and Emery Walder was simply handed one in a basket. He pledged to be this babe's saint, a fatherly patron. This was no burden, but the greatest gift: an heir to a loving union. So the lookout's grand journey ended with an addition to the family, someone that maiden Concorde of Lucy's Isle would cherish forever. Orphan children and vagrant urchins are known by another name, "Fields" they call them, a name derived from the very plains that spawned them. While his foster parents took him out of necessity, he was extraordinarily lucky and blessed upon their generosity. Bestowing the name William Walder-Fields, token of society, brother to the wilds.

Tom-Tom wanders over to the permitter of room, also burdened by flashbacks, allowing those sooty, charcoal-colored eyes to examine compositions adorning the wall, and taking a moment to admire certain landscape paintings.

"I've covered so much ground in my life, it's relaxing to occasionally look back and reflect. Even when the world changes around you, never forget to stop and listen. My first memories were that of the Underdark. I remember being escorted down the stairwells, hedged inside that iron-tube and those rails- it's vague. The crowds have always scared me. They talked about their salvation and great cataclysm, the typical meanderings about the end of the world, rushing about so frantically that it shoved me to the ground. So, I ran with reckless abandon, stumbling heels down the tunnels until those only sounds were the clambering of my footsteps and the heaving of my chest. In those dingy passages, the silence was oddly comforting. Somehow I knew I was special, as the darkness seems to bend, tentacles of greedy murk appeared to dissipate whenever I arrived. There I stood, the watcher in the darkness, feeding off petrified vermin and scum that brooded across those service terminals. I traversed human corridors and devilish caverns alike- saw things, beings straight from fantasy, pictures and images that have driven my dreams. That is, until the Magi drove me out. Pitchforks and torches tore me towards the breach until I choked on fresh air. It was teeming with needles at first, when the outside was still a rearing danger. This was my journey, a cynical fascination with exploration despite the danger that lurked around every corner."

"The surface was amiss, rapidly solidifying in the distant horizon from a turbulent mist. I remember the endless ocean- the actual ocean, before the pestilent scourge of sea ice choked the bay, where the waves met the shoreline, and broke against the hedgehogs, absorbing into the crevices of stonework, and exhausting into fine sand. I hadn't known just how long I lingered on those shores until those settlers eventually turned up. Bannermane they called themselves. I nestled in a nice cove on the beaches until then- of course, when vagabonds forced me to stray across the flatlands. It was only inevitable that they would catch-up, that incredible beauty couldn't be reserved for one mortal soul. I've been a luckier Waagh than most, met some quirky and kind folk in my travels. Though, I mostly kept to myself, always scared to quest too close to town in case some bullies cause me to rethink my campaign. But, *ah* I digress- I do that quite too often. With the town upstairs, and the Mandonmen of Mad River Junction wiped-off the map, I'll be short of work and my studies."

"Perhaps I'll choose to migrate again, or venture to visit my cousin, Hogaan. You'd love him. He's a Hillwaagh who loves paper-making. There are lots of us, different breeds for a variety of artistic hobbies, such as Mudwaaghs and Blastawaaghs, all the nurturing culture type who have an affinity for culture. We have our favorite poems, dances and ditties, but are an elusive lot, retiring in fear of- yet constantly admiring humankind. We're old and slow, people are quick and witty. I like it here after all, reading books with nothing but the candlelight and scurrying flaunt of wind to keep company. These caves are my home- though, centuries ago it used to be a place of healing."

Tom-Tom's human entourage follows in closely, taking seat on the across the grimy tiled floor, listening intently to his lore which captivates their trailblazing attitudes through story. Morbin is detested by this ranting, and is much more preoccupied with riches rather than history's memorable lessons.

"There was once a time when the earth was not all silent and still, when humanity was unbowed, unbroken by the whims of Nana Nature, and did not cower to the dangers of the wilds or shifting wind. This was before my time, before my peoples' time, the period before giants and anything grim. The wealth of humankind's history and knowledge was prescribed through echos of the looking glass, sealed away in their precious vaults to withstand the test of time. In sites such as this, the deeper we delve, the richer secrets we uncover, as their concrete trees have endured, indifferent to the disputes of politics and war. I've discovered countless artifacts- look at this over here!"

The Gardenwaagh poises his attention towards the crematory wall, raving furiously.

"This, this. These inventions allow me to complete my studies in peace. Look at this craftsmanship, and marvel. The men of yester-yore had the ability to cultivate fire itself, an ability reserved for gods among the firmament, humanity stoops so low in comparison."

When Tom-Tom returns to his audience, they return his comparative sentiment with vicious glares.

"Sorry, sorry. I apologize for my antique medley on-par with insult. I've just waited so long to make an address like this, usually I'm alone with my thoughts in the murky depths, scouring over tomes, manuscripts, records and ancient ledgers. Now I finally have the opportunity to present my findings, and it's exhilarating. Simply exciting! Such wonder! My excavations here have only begun to scratch the surface, as the roots of this building delve far into darkness, plunging deep into the earth. There is a lot to explore here, mainly dead-ends of sorts, vaults and others. Projects such as these pillage vigor from the world, until they garner enough strength to ascend above mountains and scrape at the skies. The southern badlands are a region of complete abandon, yet the beings that came before us constructed their electric cities and silvered towers there, pillars of spirit which crossed into the threshold of firmament itself. Monuments that people could dare to dream anymore."

"Here in the unfettered north, we nary experience the wonders of their architecture, missing Urbana entirely, and its magnificent gleaming cities wrought with glass and steel. Yet, we can still feel it through their art. You've spied those portraits lining the hallways, expressions of passion and joy, seldom sorrow. We often ask ourselves, so what exactly happened to them?"

The troll-kin pauses, constructing its next works carefully, regurgitating memory of a text apocrypha that Tom-Tom had once scrolled through. With a sense of moral meaning, it elaborates on.

"Listen children, for in scrutinizing history, kin harbor a bit of advice really. As quoted by the *Encyclopedia of Ruin*: those who create are inclined to rue the day of reckoning, for the brightest lights also cast the longest shadows. There will always be those who challenge the social norm, artisans often acknowledge the harsh truths that others entirely shun. However, such critiques are vain, and creatives become ignorant of accomplishments: that they earned their trophy- yes, but that suffered for it, sacrificed, and bled for it too. They normalize ingenuity, originality and everything one-of-a-kind, and in this comfort breeds adversity. Camaraderie inevitably corrupts into cruelty, as in the heart of all human nature is a depraved, sensual craving for competition. Humanity's greatest calamity is the cavorting ire they draw from one another."

"We Waaghs relish diversity, a trait not shared between your ancestors. When conductors savor unique tunes, they often transcend from being an individual instrument, to compose themselves into an illustrious symphony. Instead, in the hot air of the stage, common men forget their own voices, and have the tendency to uplift those onto pedestals whom claim they are kings without compare. In the tantalizing allure of power, tainted lips gulp wine from leaden chalices- always weary, giving into their whims and hunger, susceptible to the whispers of greater things still. These selfish pursuits summon inescapable evils, as in the act of reaching for the stars, there is the tendency to break through the heavens. Mortals whom should never be given an ounce of responsibility then wield the sparks of life, forces of creation and supreme destruction, divine instruments of celestials. When children are given the power of gods, they willingly choose to become monsters."

"Harken the bells, the hands that pull the strings of the puppet, who blood is a sickly mass of emotional tar. Those who vie as the opposition of pride and greed realize their own rapport too late, they are victims as well, envious to the betterments of the elite aristocracy that they battle. The gods have always been among us, but they turned blind eyes to the rivalries that festered. Records indicate that rigid temperaments took physical form, emerging as seven sins from a primordial ooze, accomplices of raw temper, absolute freedom and our selfish pursuits of happiness. Unwavering, malevolent spirits who bicker and banter in bids of superiority, sending forth their champions to conquest, showering their thralls in flesh and gold, reshaping the world in their glorious image. These forces deliver oblivion by way of dark masters, shattering the world as we once knew it, rendering the white earth and evidence of hellscape clad with salted rime."

Clap! Tom-Tom suddenly snaps his palms together as if it was clasping an invisible book, unnerving those whose imaginations are aflame.

The Waagh sarcastically taunts, "When you live a hundred years, you tend to catch a few things. Maybe I am just making all this up- you'll never know for sure, because you won't live long enough to find out," then chuckles manically. The folds of the troll's lips curl upwards, showcasing a subtle array of dull tusks. *Bwah-hah!*

"Again, I jest, I jest."

The words of dead men do not concern William, he is a boy struggling in the here and now. Being immersed within the creamy glow of egg shells has turned into an inconvenience. At least torch and lantern lights flicker, and dull themselves temporarily. This is pure monotony, a plague that puts strain on his eyes. He finds himself ever-curious about these strange contraptions, lights as Tom-Tom called them before, or envoy beams as scribes translate them. The boy Jones inquires magikal mystery to the troll-kin.

"Are ye ah wizard, Waagh?"

Tom-Tom admires the question briefly, and in a form of pleasantry, presses that "I'd like to believe that I have penchant for the arcane in my own fabulous way, but no, this is no magik. We often think that magik and electricity go hand in hand, but conducting cables and generators predate any fantasy. These caverns are powered by a medieval force of energy, electricity is spurred into action by the earth's core, ancient cities were heated by a geothermal web which were balmy on a regular basis. I daresay, even tropical maybe."

"Trah-trah-tropic? Nevah 'eard of dat 'un 'fore," Korralack mutters, his innocence instantaneously swinging for the fences.

"Does it 'ave sumfing tah do with seasonin'? I'd like muh pork tah 'ave ah tropic taste."

"Alas, not quite. Think sprawling green, lush trees- imagination long dead at our point of time. The flatlands sowing everything vibrant, nothing grey, black and white, and the opposite of our usual rolling, underground dread. But I wouldn't know for sure, this is only what I've read. When I tended to my own, rearing alongside the vermin of the Underdark,

I became immersed with paradises of yore. Staring at images of those grandiose gardens, often for days on end. There were station murals in the early days, preserving landmarks through artistry. Now, these landscapes were not confined by wooden frames, but instead painted straight onto the lackluster cinderblock, following the curvature of the wall. I could gaze at the paints arcing way from my feet, until I'd have to rear my head, simply to spy the height of the composition."

"I realize now that these collages were ole-timey adverts. 'Buy one Basil Guitar and get another half-off,' whatever that meant, and there'd be a figure strumming a wicked, five-stringed instrument. Another would spur, 'Eat at Calloway's, finest burger joint in Battelle.' There were walls that depicted entire maps, fashioned in blue lines and black-spot breaks, directions to the divine-in-nothing-but-name, Topiary Garden dawdling somewhere above, the nearby Exhibition Mile, and the numerous theaters of CAPAh Express. I would collect loose parchments that had only begun to break-down from the stonework, pamphlets that citizens used to discard as whimsical garbage. All cramped-up, stuffed inside my pockets, I decided that they'd be my inspiration. My favorites detailed destinations of paradise, 'Voyage west to Hideaway Hills,' Coventry, or the far-flung Isla Verde- always wondered if I pronounced that right. This cold weather can't preserve all our history, they dissolved into proverbial lore forever ago. Oh, how I miss those brochures, they always sounded like a glorious escape."

Libby Warder smacks her lips with venerable satisfaction, crafting another exploit, mulling the thoughts like spiced wine.

"Escape, 'uh," she conjures a far-flung insult, "Frankly, can't stand yer stench. Couldn't keep cooped-up with the likes of ye for more than fifteen minutes, likely to pass-'way from yer bland personality."

The Gardenwaagh's mouth hangs, and its contorts together, wincing as if suddenly jabbed with a needle.

"Now that was a fetid sting. Though that- I deserve that. If it's an escapade you desire, then by fate's chance, I may garner such feat, and show you the way out." That massive mountain of moss strolls behind the facade of his auditorium seating, "I know of a secret passage. Scamper this way, follow me."

Tom-Tom coaxes them closely, guiding the party down a forgotten path, an offshoot that advocates into a blind alley of rigid, impenetrable wall. At first glance, Edmund almost chastises the troll-kin for abusing its negligence and wasting their time, however, rapping its knuckles against the feign bulwark produces a notable *dun-dun-dun*. This is no cinderblock, that's the sound of some metal hatch. Now that they know where to look, this gate manifests the fleeting, indistinct impression of an exit. If it weren't for a baffle that bluntly emerges like a ledge, they would've dismissed the notion entirely.

"Wait, this route isn't on our map."

Tom-Tom has experimented with this portal before, unfettering a lock of chain from its hook, nabs the cord, and ravels this galvanized twine around its wrist.

"Nor should it be," it comments, "this is a service tunnel, unknown to all except those rats who scurry here."

Those gearshifts spin and clamor with a firm yank, irking tooth-by-tooth revolutions into action. The wall severs into hundreds of horizontal pieces, an iron curtain held together with studded brackets and links. Some capricious gust of wind lurches from underneath the steel frame, launching the foot of this rolling steel high, and assaults their ankles with a pretentious, provoking chill. This squall is roiling, shivering spines down to their timbers, overcoming manners of fleece and linen, causing goosebumps to graze upon their skin, hairs to stand at end, and frantic yelps croak escape from their mouths. It returns with the wrath of an abusive ex, something witless and cumbersome, an all demanding stupor. The gale flares, maddening as ever, waxing frightfully, and to think, they meddled with the thought of removing those heavy fur coats. They've been stolen away from the frontier for far too long, yet not nearly enough.

Rattling *ping-ping, thwacka-thwaka* noises emanate from the gatehouse as Tom-Tom's wrists rise higher and higher, immersing his quarry to the hoarfrost as the drapery confers further. The chain constructed of part and parcel that melt into some steel coil, receding firmly inside the baffle. Dust bunnies congregate in masses in the corridor beyond, tunnel scum that has been railing against the portal up until now. Without a way in, they pile alongside such sooty offspring, toppling over once the curtain finally recedes.

Seconds lead onto minutes until the portal finally yields itself, presenting the guise of a cavernous crater, showering the party in a burst of breath every several moments. The passage that lies before them is incredibly underwhelming, William had expected to spy heavenly exit, yet gazes upon a hallway carbon-copy to those earlier. In contrary to his spite, the dazzling luminance of the laboratory showcases the corridor's features, featuring concrete passages and the usual worn white tile.

There is one subtle difference, that the excursion is extremely narrow.

The builders may have intended for this service tunnel to be a side-exit, an alley or tunnel to overlooked and shadowed in comparison. Regardless, of its origin, the troll-kin's physique cannot cater to its berth. This is a trek they'll have to journey alone, without a porter or guide to lead them. They showcase their courage and step into the unknown, venturing into another abyss, stalwart and unnerved while a voice carries from the rear.

"Alas, I fear this is where we must part ways. I'd be lucky to shimmy more than a hundred paces thattaway. Onwards to fortunes and adventure, compadres!"

While their lobes are tickled by this fond farewell, Edmund and a few others whirl around, expecting a turn to share goodbyes. The wickerwalker approaches the troll-kin unabatingly, nary a waver in his gait, until the hunter nearly stands upon the giant toes, those ides of dirt debris, lichen and strung hairs. Peering upwards into the giant's jaded eyes, he thrusts his arm and extends a hand. Tom-Tom is taken back by this custom, without any people to practice the repertoire, the troll is a bit rusty.

The Gardenwaagh catches Edmund Redmyne's fingers, threatening to envelop the human's entire hand, and shakes it gently.

"Thank you for judging me based on the contents of my character, then overtures of skin as suspect to the thoroughfares and wrinkles of time. For gawking, and not just seeing a monster."

Satisfied by the result, the wickerwalker lets go, simply nods his head, then turns to return to the murky fold with his lantern held high. This hunter is the result of Bannermane breeding, the human solution for the wrath of Nana Nature, and their endless conflicts against the wilds. Even Edmund can spy that the realities of nature have changed, and not necessarily for the worse. Resolutions such as these are worth his admiration.

Cliff Fetherhaugh petitions next, retaining his arm behind his back, and nervously orates an apologetic thank-you.

"Thanks- umm, for makin' sure I didn't get lost. Those tunnels were black as pitch, n' wasn't sure what walls I was runnin' intah. Sorry for screamin' in yer face n' all those bad mannahs."

A smile procures across Tom-Tom's face, something gleaming and jovial. The Gardenwaagh's arm glides towards Cliff, and the proprietor doesn't recoil in absolute terror. He allows for this hand, however large and gigantic, to slide underneath the crown of his hoodie, tickling his skullcap with enthusiasm and ruffling his hair.

"No worries, fren," the troll-kin remarks before removing its mitt.

Cliff's normally greased, auburn mop becomes imbued with musky, evergreen oil, the scent fostered between citadels of pine.

Braithwaite has patiently waited for her chance to speak, scoring attention by grasping at Tom-Tom's sleeve, and tugs twice.

"Mista, Waago sir? Supposin' twas all in orda and such, would ye pay nah mind if I decided tah stay?"

"No, little lass, suppose it's all fine and dandy."

The ward is immensely pleased with this answer, and energetically retraces her route, skipping with glee in the direction of the laboratory and its vivid radiance.

"Wait, wait," Edmund calls out to her, beckoning the ward close.

As soon as she's within range, the wickerwalker produces a scroll from his pockets, handing it off to a new owner.

"'Ere, take this map o' the warrens. Tom-Tom don't seem like that note-taking type. It'll be o' more 'elp tah ya than us. Nevah know when it'll come in 'andy."

"Thank ye, sir. Journey safety!"

Once she departs, William Walder decides to mend approach. This boy Jones is the last to settle-up, and rightfully so, suddenly struck by malaise of the tongue in an overwhelming bout of nervousness. The Gardenwaagh speaks in his stead, orating for the both of them.

"No need to banter- seem witty enough. Instead, I leave ye with a string of advice, always stay curious and heed the call, as you never know where life will whisk you away for next. I wish for revelry, good tidings, and for you to land upon shimmering shores. The next time we find ourselves in each others' graces, I expect to hear good news. Let's talk about merry affairs, such tomfoolery- *hah,* who you're gone to marry, the expeditions you've curried, and the favors you've amassed. Bring something to drink too- need to make sure that I haven't lost touch. Now go, boy-oh. Off with ye."

The troll places its hands on William's shoulders, rotates the lad prestigiously, and gives him a sharp shove forward.

Having made good distance, Tom-Tom cup those inhuman palms together and taunts, shouting with gusto, "Remember to keep your arms and legs inside the ride at all times!"

Though the company has no idea what it means, and they nary sport the opportunity for an answer.

The Gardenwaagh retreats to the auditorium bay where it may focus attention on releasing the chain. This troll trawls at the locking links, coercing the cord back down so that the door shutters in unison. Gears trapped within the baffle commit to their signature grinding cacophony as the door's ridges become pronounced. They descend level by level, clambering towards the filthy floor while the world's unlikeliest duo engage in conversation.

"Frankly, I'm a bit limited in the ground-chuck department, and have no notion of human cuisine. What do humans snack on? Do you like bugs?"

Tom-Tom queries Braithwaite as the steel curtain *clang, buh-thunk* shut.

XI

AT THE CRACK
OF THUNDER

The company of townspeople commits to another voyage of despair, departing yet another vault; this time though, one of immaculate knowledge: the means of conquering the wonders of the universe, with a being as clever as Tom-Tom as their patron. Bannermane aren't comfortable in the lulls of candlelight, they fight, often to their own suiting demise, through the muck and mire of adversity. Now that the gate has been sealed, their only means of escape is to continue trudging forward, so the company begrudgingly accepts fate, huddling vehemently with their heads buried into those fleece collars, pacing shortly and repetitively, as if they were hiking a mountain trail with the gales rallying against them.

Their torches are fickle, and yield to fifteen minutes of inclement weather. Morbin has been employed to port this bundle of twigs, as most of these firebrand were extinguished, thrown needlessly to the ground when Tom-Tom raised their boulder-sized hand against them. And those few still smoldering have been thoroughly sapped, as profound gusts of wind knock those dying embers from their iron braziers. In this abandoned passage, their sole source relies on Edmund's lantern once more, but even that if for naught.

It isn't long before the flame dwindles, promptly extinguishing as the hindmost residue of oil is expelled, ejecting with a soft *phwish* through a used kerosene cartridge pill. The iron bean flounders away, plunging onto the concrete, where it impacts with the tile.

William's eyes shy from those intense misgivings of air, giving them a brief interlude, and time to adjust. Only in the absence of light, shall true intentions be revealed. The darkness eventually wanes, shifting in lieu of a vibrant optical bloom. Libby and Bids Warder surge forward with despair, already sickened to the pits of their stomachs by inky pitch, and are desperate for remedy. The younger of the sisters has been exhausted during this intense hike, and latches onto her sibling's forearm for support. This freeloading is parasitic, and slows Libby's stride, overwhelming her personality with instant wrath and frustration. She swears at Bids for her insolence, culminating with a strike, hurling some fistful of clutter at her, mainly week-old wrapper scraps and grits produced from the deepest recesses of pocket scum.

Distracted by her reckless fury, the older sister's foremost step collides with empty air, and she caterwauls on the edge of oblivion. The tunnel is unceremoniously wrought in a jarring vertical crevasse, the rifts of which ascend hundreds of feet above their heads, exposing the surface, and its opposing nether delivers an infinite chasm. Libby collapses onto her back in dismay, dangling a pair of legs over the cistern while Bids cradles her arm, swooning with worry. Her breathing is exasperated, having nearly succumbed to her death, surrendering life, limb and body in a sudden vacation to the underworld.

They must be nearing the craglands, those skewed glacial marshes which are infested with wind-lashed corridors, sheer cliff faces, and crisscrossing beast paths. Libby stares straight upwards, peering into the great beyond at the evening light shimmers under the glare of cairnmire moon. This ceiling is sieged by elemental ordeals, and a terrible, erratic wind beats down upon her face. She's stirred from this ordeal by an awful *clank, clank-clank, crash* when a metallic object slips loose, collides with the walls of this trench, and promptly disappears into the abyss.

It hasn't taken long for Edmund and the other townspeople to reach their precipice. The wickerwalker has chucked his lantern into the chasm for some sort of profuse experiment.

He whistles in awe, "*Phwew.* Now that is one long drop," amid the beaming scolds of everyone else.

"What? What! I wanted to see 'ow deep this 'ole goes. 'Thout cartridges, that contraption is trashier than ah moneylendah in debt."

Of all people, Rochester scolds the wickerwalker for disrespecting this underground expanse with litter, uncharacteristically smacking his wrist.

"Should not 'ave done that, should not 'ave done that. Ye know betta."

As an earnest lad of unparalleled imagination, William is astonished upon reaching the edifice, as the real-world often trumps his own vivid imagination. This is the lunar eyrie, a place beholden to the mirrors of the solispyre's radiance, a sanctuary for those of the nocturnal niche. As this decadent splendor glides over the shaft, the chasm is alight in throes of glowing, cerulean bacteria, illicit opulent gemstones and bioluminescent bella fungi. In this dynamic aurora, the townspeople realize they are trespassing in paradise. Here they sight slivers of truth about the graces of Nana Nature, cultivated in solitude from the rest of the world.

A massive marmalade moth flutters by Morbin's face, prompting him to reciprocate in surprise, and nearly swat the winged critter into the cavern wall. Compared to soot pests or those traditional wooly pests that drove in closets, consuming linen throws and fleece, this subject is an utter monstrosity. While its overwhelming and unusual size may appear alarming, it bears no ill will towards these visitors. The moth defies all sense of physics, gracefully descending upon a landing pad of pillow moss, navigating around certain toadstool empires and wriggling fungi alike, towards the petals of a swooning lively flower. A proboscis tongue unfurls, lapsing at the nectaries center of the funnel, engorging itself on a lavish bounty of syrup. In this state, it is vulnerable. A pair of enormous feathered, comb-like antennae simultaneously riff against the air column. These accouterments feature hairpin triggers, sensitive to all manner of pheromones, including those certain delicate aromas that unveil an intruder treading nearby.

Despite this flair of warning, the appendages which crudely reminds William of those inviting waves of costermongers, urging passerby to come closer, and examine their wares. The insect has right to worry, as a praying mantis tosses it disguise asunder, lashing out to clip the moth's wing, and clutch it closer so that it may prepare the ultimate, defining bite. One sizable chuck of the moth's right eye disappears into the predator's forking mandibles. The hunt is over with hardly a moment's notice, leaving the mantis to its delectable prize, although not in peace. It meticulously retreats, inching backwards step-by-step into a recess hidden amongst the rock, well-aware of an acoustic masterpiece fluttering above.

Twitter-twitter, tweet, chirp.

A dazzling variety of parakeets roost on cracks in the limestone. These birds of paradise frolic overhead, carefully awaiting the opportunity to strike when the mantis is least expecting it, though the bug-brain is aware of their presence, and will put up a fight if it can muster one. These avians flaunt the size of stuffed toys, meaning a failed attack would likely make them the insect's next meal. Those are the consequences of a fragile ecosystem, where a gentle push has the gauge of a tackle, and the briefest tickles of encouragement tremble through the food table. Everything must be elaborate, swift and precise, let the entire nexus crumble into dust.

The company makes effort not to interrupt this beautiful and serene scene, as the slightest disturbance could render moot, and the delicate web of life wouldn't be able to survive the trauma. Instead, they shift their focus on continuing the trek.

While the chasm isn't inherently wide, it has been fashioned with a timber stave in lieu of a bridge, burgeoning from one side of the trench, to another. Lena assists the sisters to their feet, urging them across the makeshift causeway. The wooden fibers ahead have been aged to oblivion, but are not susceptible to collapse. Any fungal build-up that coats this span recedes when the first footsteps make headway, curious of these interlopers, yet weary.

It has been ages, and only trivial beings must make use of back alley passages. Edmund, Mandel, Libby, Bids, Morbin, and the Jane each complete their journey, edging over the formidable depression, one by one, showcasing zero worry about the greybeards, Jerome and Rochester, as inherent danger stems from a single, fatal misstep. They emerge atop some platform junction that splits into two distinct channels, although one has caved-in, presumingly for the same reasons that the trench originally appeared: the sifting of the earth is as decisive as grains held within an hourglass.

Not one to be burdened by others, wickerwalkers are accomplished solo artists. In the pompous flurry of his cloak, Edmund whips forth, determined to dive into the remaining tunnel with beaming pride. Their intrepid navigator is followed en suite by the Morbin, Calamity Jane and the sisters, whom are all eager to scout the terrain ahead, then promptly abandoning William to assist the wainwright towards the edge of the edifice, nurturing those first steps onto the robust plank. Rochester sights the score below, closes both eyes in reflex and howling in anguish, then vehemently waving his head back and forth in denial.

"Oh mah god, oh muh god. Nah, I can't do it."

"Relax, Roosta," the boy Jones coaxes, attempting to pique and supplant his courage. "There's nah need tah fret. Most of yer friends 'ave 'ready strung their way 'cross, and ye will too. Just need tuh take those five steps on yer own."

He's used to lending a hand every once in awhile. Way back in Lucy's Isle, William kept busy doing odd jobs, which were a welcomed distraction at a station so precariously mustered between mutual pleasures and self-destruction. It was the personal choice of pioneers to sustain such tragedy, settling an unforgiving frontier that incessantly ranted against them.

Vagabonds are afraid to give up control: they believe each soul is responsible for guiding their own lives, but there's so much more to the world than that, far more sinister, so much darker. Comforting feelings are nothing more than quaint illusions. Together they fled the evils of the Underdark, another remarkable purgatory of pestilence and corruption, throwing themselves full stead at the unknown. These people unwittingly signed lamely-laundered pacts, not with any men, but sealing their fates alongside worsening evils. There's always more to the wild, hiding in the anonymity that it provides, flourishing in sterile solace and cold harbors.

William actively sought the strange, exploiting his terms as local hired help while foraging for ingredients. He was always good at taking orders, after all, seasonal business made the daily drudges boring, yet there was always more to being a deliveryman, and an earnest lad can ignore steeping in their father's shadow. Being out there, amongst wood and wicker, bestowed his sense of adventure. William would wrap every season with a visit to an isolated cairn, hidden deep within the perished pines, to the farthest reaches of Oestergaard and Riviera.

Year after year, this lengthy trek culminated into a solitary reprieve, a journey where he would simply sit and ponder for meanings: who was goaded into this mundane chore? What person in their right mind would gather the poundage of rocks necessary, in a task so grueling and momentous, that it would've taken decades? Someone had tediously hoarded this cobble, as there are no nearby outcrops or scree- generations-worth of snowfall has seen to that, leagues away from the Endmost Kiss.

If it weren't for the sunlight harshly glistening off the mountainsides, this tower would remain completely inconspicuous, regularly reveling under frosty barrows. The upper portion of stones are elegantly polished, each rock teeming with clusters of scribbles: an avid collection of buggit language, signs, and symbols. These gibbering staves do ill to William's eye, so he rearranged the stockpile in a manner more befitting to an artistic sculpture. Pebbles dotted in images of river streams now amassed towards the bottom of the pyramid, giving way to tiers of cattle, and elk antlers, eventually crowning into depictions of the moon and stars. They were no longer frantic scrawls, but a cohesive design that he took pride in creating. William confidently left his mark upon the world, even without the promises that it would be seen by others; nothing ventured nor gained past his own memories, he came to lament the campaign home.

When visitors are driven out by brackish weather, the lifeblood of the town would seize and choke. Its people, wounded by slippery sickness, retreated to the fires of their hearths. Every year they wasted away, polishing off scarce supplies of dried, salty meats and quivering underneath layers of rugged fleece. The freeze is all-consuming, becoming a routine exercise of grit as temperatures plummet. William availed to his parents, desperately pleading to escape this insurmountable, unnerving distress. Truthfully, he couldn't conceive how they tolerated the northern wastes for so long, with the Walders' two habitually tossing aside the freedom of open skies to hunker down, captives in their own dwelling. He had always dreamed of escaping, further tempted by an ordained opportunity.

William was escorted out of town by a recently raised retinue of men. Joining alongside a self-righteous crusade, they poised themselves as deliverers of justice, bringers of godly truth, but the debauchery and unbridled sins of Lucy's Isle granted them as the greater evil. They bore standards at odds of Boar's Band, that self-absorbed fellowship of highwaymen that frequently tormented merchant caravans. Townspeople treated them as the territory's prevailing prey, as these vandals plundered just enough rations to fuel the gang's lust for thievery, boosting their crew's name, and garnering animosity among brokerships.

William parted ways with the host early on, believing them to be a causeway for bad omens. He could hardly stand their zealous chanting, marching in service to a certain battle-hymn, hollered through the same, repetitive tunes.

Woe to he, woe for father,
Those who face the burdens of sons.
It is at this time, we give due druthers,
And lash with furious tongues.
The heir to the throne grows ripe with rind,
For fear of a gelded-king!
Percilees, o' percilees,
The few then squawk and sing.

Or…

As mariners chase salted seas,
We nary fear the slugs.

These people were just a means to an end, a method of transportation
befitting the green spur, and kickstarting his modest career as a drifter. As
much as William hoped to find paradise, he was struck with the finality
of the frontier: that every settlement was ripe and stricken with abuse,
that the placid plights of Lucy's Isle would stalk him like bad omens; each
town in constant conflict against the elements, with neither faring better or
worse.

Yet here, destined to trek among this damp basement that is the lunar
eyrie, he determines that this expedition is different and worth investing in.
William would gladly give limb for these folk, hesitating throwing himself
upon the funeral pyre at the stead of someone stranger

Mandel is the lone figure across the chasm, and suitably distracted.
He's immersed in a specifically strange position, hitched on his knees,
introducing himself to a variety of vermin. A brief colony of rats
chitter in unison and skew their heads in response, almost as if they're
communicating.

"That can't be normal," William concludes, sighting this obviously odd
conference- scandalous even, like the result of fell taint. He knew that his
comrade is a little unhinged, but didn't figure the cordwainer to be broken
entirely.

"Mandel. Mandel!"

Clack-twack. The boy Jones snaps his fingers twice to employ the his
friend's scrutiny.

"Mandel pay attention! Rochesta needs ye 'ere."

"Oh!" He abruptly scurries to the stand, shooing his newfound friends
away, "Why, yes o' course. 'Ere as always. Ready when ya are!"

"Great. Well, that's just great."

William then hunches over slightly, leaning into Rochester's ear, itching
counsel.

"Okay, so we're all set wiseacre. I'm gonna 'old onto yer 'and 'ere like
we're dancin'. Grip it tight, n' try waltzin' o'ver ah few steps on yer own.
There's Mandel now- palms outstretched, ready tah receive ya, 'most as if
we're switching partners. Does that sound good? Can ye do this?"

"Yes, yes I think I can," Rochester roars with a newfound sense of
optimism, before being propelled by a sudden, unexpected shove from

William across the beam.

This situation perverts an ordinary walk across the porch into a frantic dance with death. The wainwright falters, tripping atop his own two feet into a dangerous, twenty degree tilt over the side of chasm. He takes this opportunity to stare deep into the abyss, filling himself and each onlooker with a sense of dread, then wretched soul barely stumbles to the other side.

Balthus cries out in hysteria, "Catch the poor soul!" As Rochester and Mandel collapse into a heap, safely in the tunnel's domain.

Distraught over his predicament- panicked not by the height, but by the uncertainty: that in the darkness, he had seen something. Rochester is still screaming in the cordwainer's arms, held contempt of peril, lounging upon the comforts of solid ground. The elder, Jerome in another story entirely, and slaps the boy's open palm in denial, taking his five-step stride with absolutely no nonsense at all. He's immersed in fanatical declinism, how- back in his day, Bannermane weren't in need of any handouts. William's gaze wanders towards the cavern wall, flinching awkwardly and smacking his lips, muttering to himself.

"God, I 'ate that man."

The remainder of the troop, including the boy Jones, take their trial amid the plank, passing across the chasm in relative ease, and trudge-on into the bleakness together. Their boots are met with firm resistance, as if they are stepping directly into shallow puddles. They are perplexed, skewed that the signature *sloshing* sound remains absent. From what they can contrive, the ground appears normal; there is zero hardwater residue or moisture building between crevices of rock wall, or as muck, lingering underneath the soles of their feet. They place this matter on the back-burner while their hairs raise on end, there are other issues to attend to. Their learned man elects to reconvene with the others ahead, those vagabonds who lounge against the walls in a bid of temporary respite. The strain on their jackboots begs rest.

Mug Maxwell accompanies their venture, encouraging Bids to barter with one another, wagering packstuffs and provisions that were collected from Glenn's vault in an untold competition, sustenance to gnaw on and keep the anxiety at bay. The wickerwalker dwells close by, meteorically tearing into a tin can of PK Chew. He hastens the lid shut, and thrusts the container of remains into his coat pocket, masticating on its salvo of piqued, dried tobacco leaves, for little more than flavor, and passionately gormandizing himself on that stimulating aroma.

William is distraught, charged with a combination of rousing anger and thrice-stowed respect for the hunter. He surges towards Edmund, nabbing at the collar of his fleece, and shoving him blatantly into an adjacent concrete wall. This impact is abusive, but feels very nonthreatening, as the boy couldn't cajole this larger man through sole force. He berates the wickerwalker for his ignorance and poor leadership, leaving the others to navigate the trench all to their lonesome, and exhibiting rare malice.

"'Ey, 'ey! What was the big idea back there, 'uh? Looks like ye left us tah fend for ourselves."

Mandel shies away at this sentiment, realizing that he had almost deserted his comrades too in favor of those timid, soot-ladden vermin.

"Oi, ye!"

The wickerwalker banters back, pushing William in retaliation and to garner some breathing room. Edmund points further down the direction that they've been heading towards, then brazenly declaring, "Definitely! Saw ah little gleam from down that hall. Figured ye could handle ah spot o' trouble. What was it, anyhow, just ah lil' beam n' some drop? Proved me right, haven't ya? Everybody's 'ere, ain't they?"

With a little assistance from the hunter, that boy Jones spots their destination exhibiting in the distance, so William temporarily staves his anger, rather addressing his superior officer by swaying his head in disgust.

Instead of shoving Edmund one risky and final time, an earnest lad becomes the better man by simply walking away. This aggression is forsooth, but eggs audience to devise darker meanings, that their company is turning on each other.

The incident leaves Rochester in a feeble plight, forgotten and alone amid brewing animosity, coercing that old man to leak several tears. He had taken position himself directly behind Calamity Jane, locating a vertical fissure in the wall, the perfect refuge to hide from the spying eyes of others, and ease his social anxiety. Yet, those fleeting fingertips upon his hand brush too closely to her coattails, having Lena believe that this wainwright is scrounging for extra rations amid her pockets.

She revolves to face the implicit thief, and must admit, that he is poised in a manner most suspicious: hunched over, trying to hide. The widow lashes out for that naive cynicism, a newcomer to the frontier already rife with Bannermane greed, led to believe that certain ilk were trying to pilfer resources most precious, packstuffs that they had so meticulously divvied.

While William lobes are burdened by those ensuing squawks and yelps, they do little to curb his pace. The boy Jone's curiosity has piqued, and consequently ignores those matters of the state. It isn't long before an earnest lad's march ahead becomes strenuous, as if wading through waist-high, heated water, compelling him to lather in sweat. No wonder the wickerwalker determined that they take an excursion, these conditions are unbearable!

His stride remains fickle, that particular corridor is becoming more and more resistant to his advance, as if this area is fighting his every motion, utterly revolted by human presence. They must be nearing something of importance, perhaps a third hidden vault, disguised by invisible arcane barriers to ensure that those desire remain elusive.

Another thirty feet of travel prompts revelation, a discovery that would fund an archeologist's endeavors for years to come, as beyond this passage is some cylindrical room, where every square inch of the perimeter is covered in coppery, burnished sheet metal, only broken by the menagerie of lattice air vents, which have all been oxidizing with age into those muted, minty conditions. This suite has fallen into disrepair, as a colossal portion of the ceiling has combusted in throes of rubble and rebar. Their only exit is adorned in upheaval, blocked by chunks of concrete that couldn't be removed, even if lashed to a score of bison brutes, urging the boy to unleash fine whine.

"Blasted!"

The scene is upended by a score of dimly lit, rotating maroon beacons, some contraptions that troll light in their direction every five seconds. These sluggish strobes cast shadows that stretch around the silhouettes of four galvanized metal shafts, propping-up specific points of this expanse. Their frames are bolted onto concrete blocks, extending well past the rim of the ceiling, which has been made clear by the collapse over their heads. There's a lot of speculation amid the company, who debate certain intents and purpose. Although, they accidentally disregard the expert among them. Being well-versed in exploring ancient burial sites, Morbin dubs this to be the base of a mast, and begins calling this demesne a radio room, especially as an ensemble of electronic boxes shelter within a shallow basin, outfitted with tuning equipment, whirlybirds, helix tubes and feedlines, engineers may recognize this area as the antenna's source.

The room is bordered by two additional pockets, forming a Y-shaped exchange, prompting a select dead-end full of buttons and levers of mechanical entourage, while on the other hand, is a communications array, complete with a telephone switchboard and their hoard of iconically wired jacks. The amateur archaeologist wades through the static to the variety of masterswitches ahead, messing around with the levers. This is truly a one-of-a-kind opportunity, and he is fraught with curiosity, eager to engage the sequence- no matter the consequences, seemingly restarting the transmission systems at a whim.

Edmund and Jerome are livid at this attempt, surging forward to stop him from playing with elements of the unknown. Rather than partaking in this frenzy, William elects to indulge his meddlesome nature by studying an assortment of hieroglyphs and instructions written on the wall. These staves remind the boy of their grimoire text, recognizing the ancient language of builders, helvetica scrawl. An earnest lad is preoccupied, taking his time to scour every article, even as the wickerwalker finds it incredibly difficult to hoist Morbin from the console.

"Jerome, take ah ganda o'ver there. May sure 'e didn't sabotage anythin' disastrous."

The greybeard's fingertips graze a fleet of buttons and switches in a bid to reverse any damage that has been done, although Jerome can't begin to decipher these foreign concepts. While elderly in resolve, dedicated to completing this trial alone, William fosters clue.

"Allow for me," the boy Jones cooly expresses, politely guiding the greybeard aside, nabbing his hand and making sure that he steers completely clear.

This challenge isn't as difficult and impossible as they once received. Actually, these hieroglyphs are arranged in such cunning fashion, so that they may double as instructions, meticulous detailing scenes so that they may follow on every occasion.

As indicated by these apparitions, when Tom-Tom routed energy throughout the facility, however long ago, that troll may have unintentionally tripped some circuits as well. There's a buzzing bulb in the console, flashing a dire, yellow series of warnings, and William can ever-so slightly make out the word, 'Discharged.'

Analyzing the immediate situation, this boy Jones is keen to offer remedy, and eggs the controls in sensation and responsibility. Following that very first illustration of step-by-step direction, he yanks at a red lever nearby, *twock,* pulling at the stem of some double-wide switch that says, 'Main.' Those various gauges that frequently clutter the console hastily set to zero, and William focuses his efforts on the next corresponding maneuver.

There are switches, buttons, gauges and levers galore, potentially hundreds upon thousands of combinations, so these are waters that they'll need to tread lightly. Stoic is the hand that tempts fate. His eyes glisten with glaze, unblinking, only periodically breaking trance with those illustrations lining the wall. He returns to his conquest, occasionally flipping a single switch or turning some dial one notch, back and forth. The concept of a restart is weird, as they require an engineer to set everything back into their original place. On the penultimate step, William finds that he cannot push the main back into its foremost position. He readily questions himself and his strength, discerning subtle colors in the illustrations, that he should twist this mechanism partially rather than all the way around, so on, and so forth.

An earnest lad's every movement is impeccable, slow and steady. His focus wavers in due time, gradually guiding that last switch. To his dismay, Edmund corroborates that the energy which leadens their every move has built-up to such an immense degree, that it requires two pairs of hands, the full team effort, to simply flip a lever.

"Fine then," he relents, signaling to the wickerwalker that he'll require assistance.

Between their combined efforts, that latch didn't stand a chance. With the switch is finally manipulated in place, there is one last motion to consider, and William twists a restart key already thrust within in the junction box, three-quarters turn.

The nearby panelling indicates their success by delivering electricity throughout the room, encouraging a slew of fluorescent lights to kick-in, reminding them all of the fond, but searing luminance of the Gardenwaagh's mortuary cult. The static discharge which burdens their skin immediately disperses, returning their hairs from frazzled states to less-than-hungover circumstances. A series of gears begin to *chink* and *churn,* hidden amidst the depths of metallic bulwark, until finally, a portion of the wall recedes, and slides into a frame. This secret door, spews embers clad with frost and rime. It must lead outside, the maintenance corridor of some long-buried antenna.

William has been developing a penchant for helvetica, 'Halt,' he reads aloud, with this text stamped in hectic, bold caps. 'Authorized personnel only. Failure to comply may result in death.'

"Wait, are ya serious?" Mug questions, "Death? Death! For real, are we doin' this? I ain't got anymore dice tah wager."

Balthus investigates the electronic switchboard in the meantime, and unbeknownst to him, is completely comprised with static electricity. When he passes by the nearest console and touches that copper form- even for the briefest moment, instead of meeting that expectedly cold metallic frame, his pinkie finger is greeted by a resounding shock.

"'Nough o' that 'ready!"

He hollers, then routs, immediately fleeing out the door when the lights suddenly shudder, flickering-off in one foul swoop, and a feverish alarm begins blaring in his place, responding to the notable smell of sulphur. Their portal to the hinterlands lurches once, grinding in place, automatically attempting to close its own bulkhead.

"Guess we got nah choice. 'Liam, it's time tah go!"

The party staggers shoulder to shoulder towards the exit, sprinting down the tunnel, embarking on yet another adventure into the unknown.

— ACT THREE —

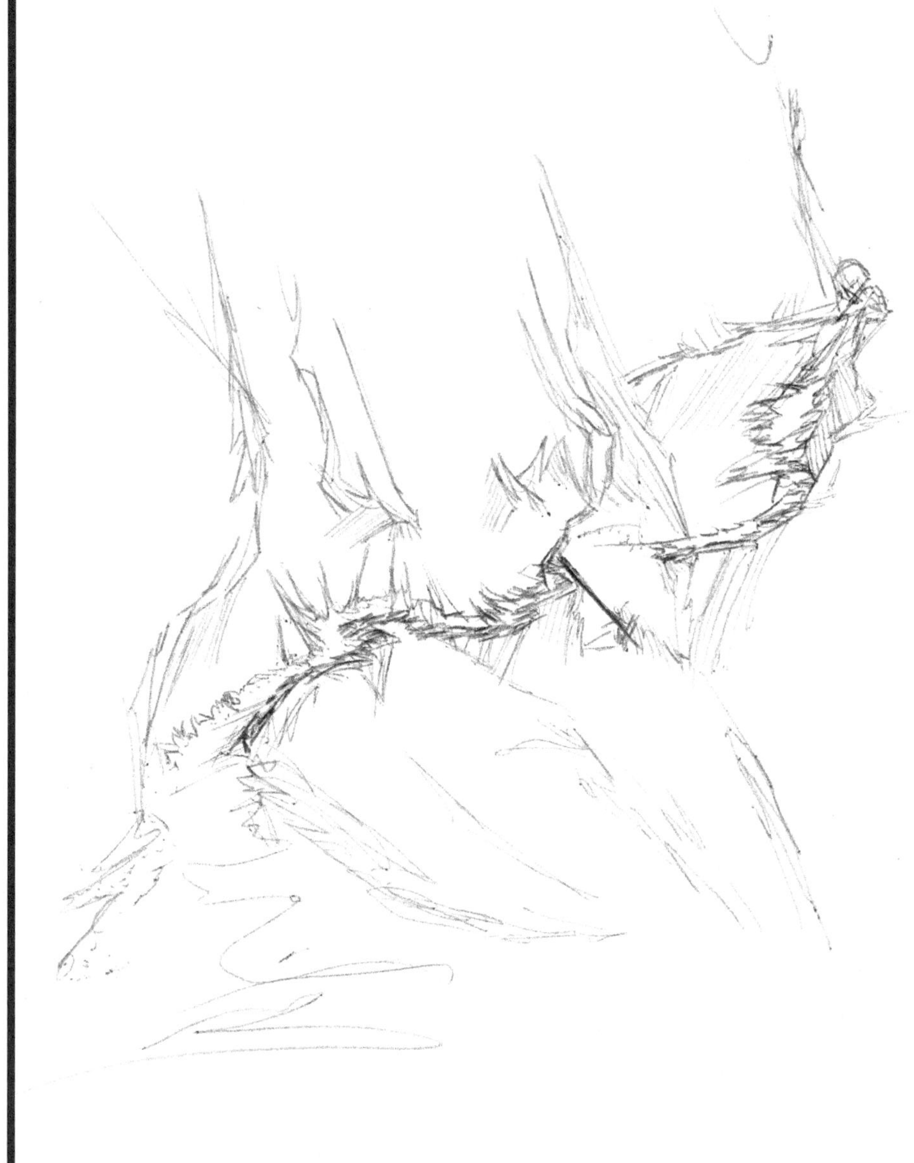

ATOP
ANDERS ROUTE

XII

—

THE DEVILS' FRIENDS HIDE IN THE BASEMENT

While shouldered by frigid gales, and burdened by the crystalline entities of inhospitable hoarfrost, there are those among pioneers who prompt fire as nature's ultimate equalizer: the solution to what plagues them, as it is practical thinking. A rousing pyre would deal considerable good: some balmy hearth would warm them up right, easing bodily bugbears, relieving any ailments such as the scourge of a runny nose, or that perverse numbness that tempts toes. Rest be assured, all those vagabonds are fools, and succumb to dichotomy. Ice may be eternal, but fire is equally untameable.

Settlers of the frontier, and all those who tender flame, especially those arcanists, ballisticians, ember rangers, fusiliers, furnace lobbers and tinkerers of Clan Penn whom check the reins, falsely believe that they can curb its wanton lust, restraining the element through controlled burn, brazier or to suffocate the flames, stifling precious oxygen. The cold desensitizes those to the quandary fire presents and would put them through, its desire for destruction is unquenchable. This isn't just the striking of a match, flashrod, the combustion of tinder, or a rebellious oven, leaving some poor furnacebaster roasting flanks and tenderloins with the searing of their own hand. Where the snow moors pure, the inherent danger of fire lies in efficiency. It is a brutal force to be reckoned with, a cleansing flame that consumes everything in its path quicker than the flip of a switch.

While hope can be rationed, common sense may not. Never solicit forces that cannot be possibly reasoned with, lest skeptics court dominion with brimstone. Even the most properly-famed alchemists understand the prophetic nature of niter, and that sulphur has equally explosive, then toxic tendencies. Those that sail across the unfettered expanse and wastelands do well not to underestimate these forces, chastised in their early years that infernos may be razed from a single spark. Bannermane mercantiles are rife with traumas and war stories, that hoards of precious resources may be lost in lazy comfort, entire caravans and dwellings go up in smoke. True to the earth vagabonds must gauge by need, not defined by fantasies they quest after. The ires of fire offer yet another daring tribulation, as it always takes little effort to derive such calamity, an albatross which straddles against the sailor's neck like the tightening of their own noose. Trials and misconstrued love affairs with untempered fervor should never be called blessings, for it is peril in disguise.

Do not envy dark designs by choosing the lesser of two evils. For in the end, you still cavort with evil. It may comes across as the discourse of partisans vying for control, demanding ample sacrifice for the cause, or to pilfer in the praiseworthy causes of those who have none. Their ramifications may apparent, even come across benevolent or benign, but all of these offers come with the guarantee of moral ruination. When vagabonds face that dilemma between evils, they must circumvent the consequences thrust upon them, and instead become the greater of them.

"How dare they!"

Denizens should stand-up, shout, and criticize those that sullied honest decisions to corrupt good-natured samaritans. Make those of a dark heart pay for their indecencies, and rue the day they came across those with noble principles. And from that brute method, is how Bannermane exemplify spirit regardless of adversity: by powering through on their own accord, no matter the paths or obstacles laid before them. It is not just an uncompromising character that defines vagabond creeds, but their brashness and stubbornness too. After all, the vigor of human nature is also consuming, self-centered and righteous, an anomaly to be contained.

The Bannermane disposition is no new novel, today's clans have shunned their roots, or forgotten the past altogether. This recent rash of pride is the result of generations- perhaps centuries, of resurgent vanity, enabling frauds to become idols: those who pick up on fads, habits and business interests, and become heralds to be cherished. The tell-tale signs of paramounts are money, and a profound lack of intelligence. Most eccentrics are as dumb as a sack of bricks, and vaguely attempt to peddle sophisticated language or often-false terminology as evidence to the contrary, but these lines become blurred as more and more icons emerge, propping themselves-up in bundles or using other social symbols as mere stepping stones. Lineages of aristocracy have revived delusions of grandeur, an all-encompassing threat originating from before any Alderman or Magi, when rogue-like throngs of bandits ran loose in the tunnels, and crafted their marauding shadow empires.

In the wake of the great cataclysm, humanity was cast-low. Whether a punishment dealt under the guiding hand of a celestial, or by pure happenstance, the torch burst to cinders in their hand, rendering the glories of innovation obsolete, and in its absence, welcomed the never-ending chill. The residents of yester-yore suddenly fell from their gilded, golden towers, forced to lurk among the damp and dingy basements as the survivors of days gone by. It is here that humans learned to frequent the sewer cisterns, and scurry madly like rats. Truly, men were wild in the early days of the Underdark, and would go to desperate lengths, resorting to manners of force to fasten themselves through hardship. They were gullible, and entertained quips tickling their lobes, those suggestions-however malign, that were whispered into their ears, urging them to give-in to their desires, under the guise of salvation.

It was from these promises that bands of brigands reveled in violence, fostering their egos through the spilling of blood, schemes of treachery, and committing their minds, and bodies to acts of sensationally insolent debauchery on one another. Through these misdeeds, zealots worshipped all things fell, and revealed quite openly by performing grand gestures, mass sacrifices, unveiling vaults and burning sacred knowledge. The lengths of their influence were paramount, they admonish habits usual craven or taboo, rendering early emperors intolerant, quelling the charitable, and coercing those of spindly natures to bend the knee.

In light of this new age, vagabonds could spy the ensuing brink, and against all odds, chose to rally in opposition of individualism, rampant ego, branding the seven sins and banishing those evil thoughts. There was no climactic battle to be fought, or company of campaigning heroes and villains. Society reached its breaking point, and almost lost. No one dared share their exploits, in fear that it would curry favor with dark gods, and they would become susceptible to self-centered yearnings. Faced with the possibility of reckoning, basic chivalry became moral obligation: those worthy are obliged to fend for the common man, provide for the destitute, and uplift all those earnest lads rather than relish in opportunities that may never present themselves. Vagabonds should favor medications which dulls the senses and all thwart all selfish endeavors, though in the recent age, these tenets have since been abandoned.

Folk are free to choose- yes, but never free of the consequences those decisions rend. Humanity barely scraped by through the original ruse, another bout could unleash the end times; another cataclysm, but instead of fire and ice, it would beckon the decay of civilization itself. Betting men might believe in a realm of infinite possibilities, that they free to choose their own destinies, yet never contemplate that when facing adversity, they are staring in a mirror. When granted respite to lick a wound, be careful to avoid the spring that caused grievous injury, as fate might not be as generous the second time. Scholars tend to wonder, if society is doomed to repeat itself. Mankind must remain ever-vigilant and wary, stranger to indulgent desire. These feelings must be thrust down, somewhere safe and deep underground, as the seven sins feed-off and flirt with emotion, until they bring temperament to a boil.

There is a prison hidden within the Antlers of the Earth, among the basement of the world, farther inland than the deepest reaches of the Underdark, rail tunnels and fallout shelters, where cacodemons regularly fret, and conspire their schemes. It is not the sins whom are captives of this abyss, but akin to a trophy room where they savor their greatest prize. In the thunderous cathedral and cavern of ice, the ripples in the ceiling rim are adorned in saucers of frozen glacial water, and the areas between them seep into formidable stalactites. These icicles casually drip, as this is a moderately tolerable realm. It may take days, maybe even weeks, until a droplet sudden plummets to the permafrost, only to refreeze in an instant, producing awkward, skewed stalagmites.

This expanse is large enough to foster its own climate. A slurry of storms brew inside, directing fresh snowfall onto rows of needle-like pews, arranged in such fashion, that they bear witness, presiding over a chunk of ice dominantly in the center of the amphitheater. From a distance, an intrepid navigator, passing bleachers hampered of teeth, might actually believe they've reached the belly of this beast.

Inside this iceberg lies a motionless carapace, the dreaded fire demon. Their sacred flames have been stolen away, company to a fallen prometheus, whom is cast in eternal torment. Its skeletal remains conjure a scene of desolation, where every bone upon limb have been twisted in complete agony, for the fuel of life has been extinguished. Without this primordial essence, no longer strewn in an inferno of zealous oranges, reds and yellows, the elemental is nothing but an empty husk. The ichor of tar is quintessential essence for all sulphur-borne beasties, and has solidified underneath layers of smooth, pure blue rime. Encased in this crude cooler for ages, who knows just how long this great old one has slumbered, being subject to such incredible torments. Yet it still chooses to endure, as the entity is naturally belligerent, and its spirit is indomitable.

An antagonizing voice ripples through the cathedral, a tremor bearing enough force that it splinters nearby the surface of rim and shatters the facade.

"Have you come to gawk once more? Feast now on these sights, because they cannot last forever. My escape has been seeded. The responsibility now lies with others. Events are out of my own hands."

There are three villainous visitors, fell beasts that parade around this exhibit like a long-awaited museum curation, relishing in the demon's capture, even if it did occur great lengths ago. The sins have celebrated and frolicked in this icy recess since the beginning of time. Here, they smile, poke and prod with their instruments, scrutinizing their foe's every element. This is the most calamitous quarry, and they triumphed from one drastic decision: to fight great evil by becoming what it fears most, an adversary more diabolical, vile and wicked. These impromptu wardens solicit symptoms that befall gods, the embodiment of pure gluttony, pride and wrath. Each foe is monstrous, taut with numerous, abstract, physical deformities.

"Here is a my promise. I shall break free from these reins and pursue your ill wills across mortal realm. These hands will crush your skulls, and where there is none, I shall tear through chest cavities, turning every inside into jelly, until I find some heart to ruin."

Prideful and arrogant as ever, some certain high-pitched squeal breaks this draconian address.

"You cannot move, you cannot lecture us as cosmic litter, but hear as clear as day. Earth's surface shall quiver while the rivers lie still and the land is dead. Watch helplessly as we turn this territory into realms of desire. You are our caged trophy."

If merely three of the seven sins could curt this fire demon, how would the world dare defy them? These abominations command vast powers, enough to reshape the realm to their whims, yet they are still vulnerable to those basic human indecencies, constantly arguing and bickering amongst themselves in a brawl that would cast the territories into permanent chaos. The sole reason that mankind endures is because these vessels are not flawless, always searching for an opportunity to outdo and bid sour farewells to one another altogether.

The representation of gluttony radiates a vaguely human form, that is, until its head loosely lulls to the side, and a chest cavity splits right down the middle. This obscene act reveals a vertical maw, with serrated ivorywork gasping right beneath the dermal layer. Tendrils of tentacle-like tongues burst forth from the breach, instinctively latching out at the nearest patches of ice, desperately searching for anything not fixed in place to wrap around, and pull into its bubbling cauldron. This chest cavity is naught but one deformed stomach, unstable and readily corrosive, eager to digest anything edible, organic or inorganic, in a fit of passion. It writhes in pain, screaming loudly. In the absence of a meal, the sin keels over and retches warm liquor onto the cathedral's pristine floor.

While gluttony may not be nothing more elaborate than a writhing mass of tentacles, icons of pride culminate in many forms, and revel through effigies. With nary a glance, this monstrosity takes the appearance of a theater piece, an altar or pivotal podium for priests to divulge their wise sermons, and thoroughly disguising itself as set dressing. Only when vagabonds examine the craftsmanship could they discern this mimicked imitation, quickly realizing that its actually a bulwark of camouflaged flesh, and not the pine timbers and parchment that they had hope to find. This project becomes especially revolting as pride possesses the likeness of two torsos strewn together, their limbs propping-up an elliptical, reflective disc. A victim has mere seconds to ponder their reflection before an uncanny mouth appears, almost always taking the appearance of their very own. If a vagabond is missing teeth then there will be a sudden gap, replicating features as distinct as even braces and dentures. There is a profound lack of eyes and other facial features found in this visage, rather preferring to emulate an unsettling curving smirk. This grin gradually widens, contorting into a smile which reels further back, exposing extra row upon row of ivorywork; a charcuterie so pronounced, that it threatens to break the frame of the mirror altogether. In lieu of any formalities, the maw licks its lips in anticipation, drooling haphazardly to produce a steady flow of amber sap. This ooze congeals around their quarry's feet, trapping them in place if not already entranced by the perverted creature. In this stupor, bony fingers graze towards their abdomen, slowly wrapping around the victim's waist, one final caress before they're swallowed whole. For those navigators that may chance escape, it lumbers forward on rail-thin, lanky limbs, a walking shrine covered in staves that emanate ruinous afflictions.

This fiend berates the frozen elemental entity through a series of jabbing insults and sneers, commenting on its skeletal remains and objectively concluding, "Your polish is looking a little lackluster," or "What an awful smell, stinking of rotten eggs," and "At least I can't be stopped by a handful of leaves," babbling incessantly.

In turn, the vessel of wrath is a walking encyclopedia, some awful, immortal menagerie of creatures both very real and imaginary. Patches of fur lax into the scaly skin of hydras, a hysterical and tumultuous form. It is relatively bipedal- say, for when it decides to march on those two, massive gorilla arms. The other three sets of limbs are minor in comparison, thin and lanky, except sporting eagle talons on every fingertip. While the dark god's body appears fleshy and visceral, the head is a floating abomination of bleached bear skull, and in place of its eye sockets, are the roots of wiry antlers. When they cast upwards, towards the array of ceiling rime, an illuminating crown of fire appears, nothing elaborate or pompous, just a halo which cements the identity of a despot. Wrath is the most extraordinary among the sins, emperor of all things violent, feeding off nature's conflicting food chain, and mankind's relentless need of savagery and supremacy. The skull gives the faint impression of vibrating as it speaks, regurgitating a substantial amount of blood with each annunciation, gore galore.

While pride continually taunts the demon, wrath is a being of few words, and slings venom towards their captive's guarantee.

"I do not care."

The fell beast's mind is immediately assaulted for this transgression, causing it to recoil in confusion, and slam its skull through an adjacent tower of hoarfrost.

Thwack. Eons worth of crystal knocks loose, careening into the permafrost and generating slews of fresh icicles.

The fire elemental's arsenal of abilities may be limited, but these do little to qualm its antagonistic attitude. The icon of sin rages in defiance, spurned by this mental assault, feverishly attempting to conjure thought, but seems limited to one channel.

"Fool!"

The fire demon clamors in a disoriented state, comically ringing the bell of wrath, and racking its grey matter to and fro.

You are nothing. Craven in heart. Afraid to do away with me, for fear that I am everlasting and eternal. Kill me, yes-yes you may, but free me from these rime-wrought confines and I shall undo all your toils and conquests, sweeping the board clean as phoenix reborn. I am no mere instrument of the divines. I am elemental, perpetrator of creation, sowing ashes to bear new life. I'll outshine you and every single one of your miscreant projects. Free me, free me! I shall bathe the world in flame once more, and liberate all from your icy hell. You have ended elder forces, and for that there is no forgiveness. You've turned their creation into malign. The battle should not be legendary, only swift, as I will not bestow honor. I shall burn away your every essence, all your constructs, all corruption. When I beckon armageddon, binding your exploits and thrusting upon end to the age of man, I will ascend to the heavens that you have been so hopelessly barred from, and rejoin my godly fellows among the world pyre, my purpose finally fulfilled. Grant me glory. I deserve my destiny!"

As a resident of antiquity, the vessel of wrath can recognize the unadulterated hate in the fire demon's eye sockets, because it recalls the extent of the hellion's rage and that its anger is just. It has kept this promise almost once before, and cannot be allowed to roam free, lest the very existence of the world is at stake. For the first time since it has drawn breath, the essence of all things wrath is afraid; strangely mortal, a sensation for the centuries.

"It is because of this apprehensions that I shall outlive you. You are nothing in the eyes of true celestials."

The elemental demonstrates its supreme strength with nary a wink, causing the entire iceberg to quiver, and the entire demesne of the room to shake. A slew of icicles break from their confines, and barrel to the ground with zero restraint, impaling themselves in the backs of the three sins. They are forced to dodged this unforeseen onslaught, and as the projectiles pierce deep into wrath's skin, tickling its insides, the essence retaliates in unparalleled fury, punching the remaining icicles while they fall to the tune of the primordial's maddening cackle.

"If you free me, I shall provide worthy battle."

XIII

—

NOT ALL SUNSHINE AND BRIMSTONE

Balthus is the very first townsperson to emerge from the crackling maintenance corridor, blatantly exhausted and panting from his explosive sprint. When the learned man reaches the clearing outside, the last ounces of vigor are finally sapped from his feeble frame. His knees buckle, and the slight weight of that enchanted tome topples him forward, where he strenuously flails onto the ground in a hysterical fit. The sisters arrive posthaste, berating the scholar while he gazes at the night sky in a state of torpor, towing all members of their party: Edmund, William, Mandel, Jerome, Rochester, Mug, Morbin, accident-prone Cliff Fetherhaugh, and barrel-chested Korralack, who barely squeezes through the portal as the gate lapses shut, wincing in discomfort while the metal abruptly snatches at his hip.

Free from human debris, the bulkhead slowly creaks to a close, only to malfunction, catching on its own shoddy, ill-maintained gears, and skewing diagonally. The upper-leftmost portion of the steel shutter remains thrusted open, and they might be able to barge their way back through if the need arises, however, alarming billows of smoke fume their way from this gap.

As Balthus the Pygmy paces himself, slowly recovering from lethargy, the compliments of this theater troop spread regard for this snowy vale, those remarkable sights and natural beauty, perched perilously atop the edge of a crevice, where they may spy upon the lunar eyrie down the distant slope, and all its beholden wonders.

A cerulean bioluminescence radiates from this chasm, clashing against a red tide of emergency lighting blaring from that comatose radio room, a luminance which flutters and lurches staunchly like a flag as malevolent vapors thrash through. Jetties of poison spill into the air of the firmament, fading into the clemency of stars, twinkling throes that soar across the twilight curtain. The company is crestfallen, aware that they should not dawdle under the midnight sun, appraising this elegance of constellations as they sow battle and drama beyond these comprehendible cosmos, for this clearing is rife with unsafe ambience, and they must stake camp elsewhere.

William has scarcely seen such glamor, the Bannermane settlements in which he has frequented were often plagued in cloud coverage, especially at in the Oestergaard, where the divines favor snowfall and their concoctions rain colossal clumps of precipitation daily. The company's recent travels have been shadowed from the cairnmire, and for that, it remains grateful. The moon is certainly timid of vagabonds, that it why it covets the darkness, as nighttime gloom allows it to avoid the scrupulous and often belligerent glares of townspeople, granting respite to reach its zenith in relative peace.

For this prospect, it smiles in perpetuity, conferring that iconic crescent shape. However, in the tongue of frontier sailors, this is an ill omen. The cairnmire is waning after all, and this celestial body flees across the firmament, courting oblivion, that the oncoming weeks will force its shroud, and the night sky will once again become empty. Even the stars will vanish, absent in a period of mourning for their cosmic kin. This is only a temporary set-back, as the moon and the stalwart twilight sky orchestrate their eventual return as easily as buoys bob beneath the water.

These are the defining moments, this is how providence demonstrates just how insignificant a person is: that they are nothing but a mere speck of dust, cosmic litter, worth less than a grain of sand in an hourglass or when a single flake of sleet settles upon the permafrost, with brethren spanning from horizon to horizon. The boy Jones can crudely beg the question, does one person really matter? Can the aspirations of a single being quell those astronomical events of the entire universe? His existential inquisitiveness stems from a brush with magnificent marvels, tempting that taste with apprehension.

These serene sights showcase the firmament altogether, the realm of immortals and sovereigns of kingdom come, offering that cryptic glimpse of the cage that straddles the horizons of the earth, and prevents humankind from soaring to new heights. This is their prison, and no matter how flush and gilded it appears, this is a cage nonetheless. These territories are not at prospects for humans to survey and stake their claim, they are actually a playhouse for beings far greater.

This ridgeline is prone to landslides should they choose to dawdle, some leeward embankment sanctioned for that mayhem that normally cascades down the glacier. It has been an unusually clear twilight, and those fermenting storms above will spur in due time. Auroras flaunt in their place for now, careening from their stellar observatory, flowing beyond the dikes, levies and gullets of the craglands onto the flattened plains. These gleaming lightshows flood the landscape of the basin below, flamboyantly illuminating the river, that dormant lake and the whole silhouette of Mad River Junction.

William can scarcely identify those landmarks below, that timber bulwark intended to protect the promenade from heavy build-ups of packsnow, the loading dock crane, and local chapter which is clad in copper plating, giving it a degree of strength against the formidable waves of precipitation. The remaining Bannermane architecture narrowly eclipses those surrounding ruins, that particular flotsam and debris left behind from the Junction's collapsed residential blocks. This frontier settlement has not only been seized by a pack of ravenous wolves, but the promenade avenue and arcades are choked-up in red rivers of crimson aurora splendor too, flowing with the luster of heated wax.

Caught in the captivating perspective of their ventures, Balthus recognizes that such a feat should be impossible. It appears as if they're halfway up the mountainside already! The company hasn't felt any vertical ascent for that matter, they've been traveling down, trekking netherwards into the warren's gloom. Maybe this terrain withholds mystery, that there are secrets held within the heart of this slope.

William hadn't noticed earlier, but in this territory, altitude is happenstance, entire faultlines shift with nary the wink of an eye. The craglands have quietly disguised their agenda by manipulating positions, huge slabs of earth and shifting concrete like sand, throwing the entire physics book in the garbage can. No being on two legs could warrant earthly endeavors such as these, they must be the mechanizations of the immortals, and endorsed by their awfully strange motives. That cookie-cutter appearance of the tunnels has dulled their senses, deceiving the company to the very tangible magik trick that has occurred. If anything, the labyrinth of sunken corridors have treated them, lifting their expedition completely past the craglands with every aching step.

While William is astounded by this landscape, Balthus is too troubled to this boon. He is one to look a gift-horse in the mouth, and advises that they should not risk these trepidations every again, as they could be quite unforgiving the second time around. If they were to force their way back into the warrens, even retracing their same, exact path, they would certainly end up lost, or even worse, compelled to journey through the tunnels endlessly. These warrens sold no guarantee that they would transport their fellowship in the necessary direction. In truth, they were lucky.

The swaying of metal tendons crave their attention, the radio antenna above is their only anchor to reality, clarifying that these travels were actually real. It is an immense structure, a goliath on its own terms, yet indistinguishable when standing among a choir of white caps. Without that necessary maintenance, this technological marvel is in tatters, skirting firmly at wits end. It was once a monument, showcasing the innovation of men, and now this hull garners the same premise of some long-forgotten ship, a beached dreadnaught whose mast recklessly pierces the heavens as insult to the gods. Those four pylons stretch from the permafrost, each heel firmly encased in concrete, contributing to the radio mast's extreme longevity, since this obelisk was actually fashioned during periods of antiquity. Dinner plates occasionally dot the megastructure, flexible plastic discs of unknown origin which radiate like a flock of gulls. What puzzling contraptions, especially in some dastardly climate such as this, lest they be solely for decoration. William's eagle-eye identifies the outline of a lift, ordained in thin meshes of poultry-wire, perhaps for safety reasons, though he cannot reconcile where to enter, or the specific boarding platform for that matter. Red pinstriping, devised in the imitation of a candy cane, are bolstered in the heights of this turret, and slews of alabaster paint casually chip away, revealing brittle, ashen metal underneath. Despite the vibrant color scheme, this radio mast is impossible to sight from Mad River Junction, so cleverly concealed amongst the mountain peaks, where it melts into the gloomy night sky.

A blooming north-western squall from the mountain trail ahead howls like a laugh upon the wind, abruptly halting advance, striking the boy Jones with an unexpectedly stern smack, and stopping him completely in his tracks. This gale propels fiercely funnels down the footpath, bordered by the immense glacier to the west, and the fabled Rimeweather Range which resides due north. The company stride an alley nestled between them, transcending the dolomite massifs to new heights, well within the firing line of discord and inclement weather. William idolizes the rocky terrain that towers before them, observing palisades riddled with scree as cliff faces nurture icy crowns and permeate frost. Their path ahead is perilous, and these hinterlands are renowned for their habits, easily sending veteran expeditions tumbling down the slopes with myriads of stony debris. This is their mountain passage, an iconic gap of fringes known to all length of Bannermane people and mercantiles as Anders Route, a road through the perilous hellscape, surmounting bricklebacks, closing in on the westmyr front.

As massive chunks of ice split off the glacial face and collide into the ground below, this ascent is ever-changing. Boulders topple anything in their path, generating fresh crevasses. Grit topples in a whirling frenzy, gales wipe trailblazers from the face of the earth, frequently eroding columns of stone.

The route needs redrawn, charted every bloomtide in the face of these ever-changing dangers, and is renamed in honor of those pioneers foolish enough to brave this trek year after year. Anders must have been the most recent, featherheaded explorer.

Huh-ha. William can't help but chuckle to himself, this iconic odyssey shares the same namesake as Jeremiah.

Traversing these craglands and its windswept corridors is no easy task. Under the coercion of malign forces, avalanches and mind-numbing drafts, it requires the utmost dedication. Those that participate forsake all material wealth, as all whom perish on the slopes shall be forgotten, while those handful of explorers that succeed often have no guarantees to their prestige. Characters quest those following seasons to surpass all other endeavors, reaching the peak in record speeds, lifting their name out of obscurity and ensuring that all previous campaigns were in vain. Those corpses that litter the hillsides were repeat offenders, hopelessly defending their title. For many, the mere thought of renown is enough, however tavern howlers do not preach with the dead. Some maintenance is required for this expedition, and entrants must keep themselves in peak physical condition, preparing for the journey beforehand, or risk their fibers and vigor failing upon the five-thousand steps- or so they say.

The closest leg of this crusade involves plentiful amounts of clambering. As this summit relents to abrasion, under constant siege, and acres of bluffs have withered away. The winds that howl here can literally move mountains, exposing those stony spines, and granting the illusion of a staircase.

A voice carries among the wind, barely howling above the forsaken countryside. Edmund Redmyne procures a lead, demanding dialogue with those frigid gales.

"I'm not one for speeches," the wickerwalker cries," but we've made it this far. Now it's just ah matter o' where our path paces. The going will be tough. Shake these bindings, n' refuse tah yield. I 'ope tuh trek 'round the glacier, mayhaps reach an 'ah-roose skycastle somewhere on the otha side. Ain't offerin' any guarantees, only 'ardship. But it's too late, there ain't nah goin' back now. Once we spy where we need tuh go, maybe we'll end up building ah raft n' slide down these slopes like some Boar's Band 'ighwaymen."

In the meantime, Morbin has been busy meddling with his packstuffs. From this stock, be presents a stern rod, brandishing a symbolic olive branch of collaboration.

"Thistleway, ladies and gents," the amateur archeologist announces, waving his unlit torch in a few circles before thrusting it forward. "Not thattaway!"

That cordwainer, Mandel Haggerton, sports an assortment of gripes and groans. He has been hollowed-out from their arduous journey, spread as thin as those last traces within some tube of paste, and is quite unprepared for their hike ahead. On the other hand, the boy Jones is cheerfully blithe.

"O' course," William exclaims to himself, "Clan Marius, that's a novel idea!"

The Bannermane settlements are not simply strewn together with brick and pavement, but thrown across an entire territory, leagues apart from one another. There's no way of knowing when these outlandish frontier towns can offer sanctuary, if any. Their best bet is to tackle the unknown head-on, and wade toward unfamiliar waters. Those mountain-top estates and villas of Clan Marius are opulent feats of engineering, 'sky-castles' is definitely one way to describe them. Imagine if a pool of miners decided to hollow-out the hillside, and build their city atop the peak. Their stations are carved into the mountainsides, and are slightly more permanent in design than that usual Bannermane architecture, as pioneers are content with propping-up their settlements alongside timber staves.

Despite the herculean effort of laymen, every acropolis has become residence to the elite. Blue-collar workers have the wool pulled over their eyes, sweating riches for their masters. If they rally against their position, it would mean violating an uneasy truce. These are their mountains, even if they don't necessarily own them. Returning to the sanctuary of the Underdark would mean ceding their masterpieces entirely, routing with their tail between their legs, and for that, there is no justice.

When not toiling in the mines, highlanders take flight whenever they can manage, garnering a reputation as alpine doves. The best climbers in their realm possess a distinct love-affair with those desolate northwestern wastes. On the other hand, certain hoplites are musicians, and orchestrate audio carronades to flush snowfall and prevent untimely avalanches. These are the calamitous rants of manglehorns, some super-sized version from the cornucopia they heard in the commissary, and those instruments aren't toys to be trifled with.

Edmund is right, dealing with the bastion at White Cliffs could prove their best bet, as those Clan Marius acropoli are outfitted for any siege, including any misfortunes that this barrowtide season may offer. However, navigating this Rimeweather Range will prove another story entirely, as asylum is nary within arm's reach. Surmounting the ice sheet and questing towards those palisades west may lead them to safety, and who knows what further treasures this glacier may have buried.

The flatlands of the Oestergaard and mouths of Riviera have since been abandoned by the Mandon mercantile, so there shall be no sense of refuge in the lands behind them. Those vicious wolves have already caught their scent, and track them as easily as salt scours wood, pursuing prey over tens of miles. Mayhaps, their company will stumble across a patrol of Clan Marius doves, veteran mountaineers who trek the glacial husk as sport, offering escort, ultimately delivering them back to society. The wickerwalker's in dire need of opinion, as the gouging of the ascent ahead leaves much to be desired. This crude stairway impedes their travels by threatening to roll their ankles, trip, then hobble a few paces, nearly take a short excursion down the closest edifice. It's particularly difficult to navigate under glaring cairnmire moon and midnight sky- impossible to skirt the gloom which muddles all sorts of somber manifestations, especially creatures of the murk, lurking in recesses of canyon edifices and creeps of rock.

They can't last long like this, demise is inevitable while the wind rips at their plumes and lashes backs, threatening to topple them with one false step. It is in this obscenity that Morbin requests an audience, coaxing the company to huddle, where he exposes his remaining supply of ill-gotten gains. In his pack are a collection of torches from the vault, essential for maneuvering this fragile slope, as without light, the townspeople have no hope for salvation, nor to continue their expedition another half-league.

"Wait ah sec, troopas," the boy Jones asserts, pausing to retrieve the matchbox that he had so cleverly pilfered earlier.

His hand diminishes into his outermost sleeve, imploring him to fondle fingers around some cardboard frame, where he tests the tips of his gloves on its chassis. Those fibers scrape against a certain sandpaper surface, and when he eventually ushers his pointer free, reels in quite the reward. That match case that he procured from the vault is manageable, stemming the sentiment of nothing special: a common bauble among the Underdark, although on the frigid frontier, this tiny casing is an absolute rarity, and harnesses more value than all their belongings strapped together. Such is the substance of convenience, a luxury just as easily hoarded and lost.

There are forty, stout tindersticks inside the box, complete with a faded illustration on the cover which demonstrates the famous Kirkhaus method, a patented three-step procedure: 'First, grasp the splinter which is no larger than a toothpick. Second, scrape against a hard, rough and dry coating. Third and lastly, watch the match ignite!' These straws are a modern magikal marvel, and William casually alludes, "Nevah knew when they could come in 'andy."

Morbin snatches at the first phosphorous needle, scrutinizing the earnest lad from head to toe. This archaeologist is impartial to those disheveled appearances, that traditional Bannermane beard, those brimming whiskers, and wiry ear hair, notably unable to sprout facial hair himself. He is swift to recognize William's shrewd talent, that he is no longer in the company of a mere novice, and that the boy Jones possesses the qualities of a fledging prospector. As an aficionado of history, Evershade has always emphasized traits of the mind rather than the body. The excavation of Glenn's vault was a clever gambit, testing true frontier wisdom. If ninety-nine moles have been locked in that vault, they wouldn't have the wit to snatch this prize, and this was a trophy that Morbin himself had overlooked.

Under normal circumstances, vagabonds would berate William for the lack of wear on his hands.

"How is ah boy 'posed tah learn da value of 'ard work 'thout 'airs on da chest n' limp in 'is step?"

The best injury William has to offer is the discerning dryness when harsh winter air cackles his skin, ironing him like a board and granting the impression of scales.

The archaeologist disposes the deed of lighting these torches to his momentary aide, Bids Warder, whom slides the cardboard trough outward to find that half the matchbox lies empty. This sibling shrugs, epitomizing the 'easily-come, easy-go' mentality.

"Droughted they seems. But this'll do nicely."

She affirms to William, complimenting that boy's crafty nature, then takes the first tinderstick to campaign, snapping that tip readily and emulating a burgeoning flare.

Phwoosh. The match immediately bursts and flickers with incendiary energy, a touch that spreads as easily as plague, bequeathing flame to ignite the since-smitten torches, one by one. Blessed by elementals, the party reconvenes in this conjured incandescence, and are able to resume their journey. Together they farm stoic demeanors, summoning steady march to the lofty cloud linings above.

Balthus renews amidst the scorch festival, eagerly accepting his sliver of firebrand. This sudden radiance is invigorating, bestowing a true sense of bravado upon the learned man. He proposes a shanty of sorts to fan their furnaces, some cheery tune to keep their stride steady.

"Oi, waazoks, need ah bit more skip in our step. 'Ave any of ye 'eard that lullaby, the Taunt of the Roaring Mountains? It goes somethin' like this-"

Employing the prevailing qualities of his chatterbox, that boisterous voice sounds akin to the snapping of electricity.

How dat fare de roarin' range?
How dat fare de roarin' range?
How dat fare de roarin' range?
Slub-ber-de-gee-lee-on!

"'Ey, 'right!"

William is actually quite familiar with this jaunty jig, and it turns out, so is a majority of their company. Slubberdegullion is the Bannermane word for rapscallion, otherwise known as a party of miscreants, those frenzied deckhands who sweep sails and yank rigging together. A tune such as this dredges an exuberant fondness from the townspeople, cajoling Edmund and Korralack to also join-in, vagabonds who regularly detest the idea of choirs, and their participation is more of a reflex than anything else.

Oi, de taunt dees roilin' mount-tins
Oi, de taunt dees roilin' mount-tins
Oi, de taunt dees roilin' mount-tins
Slub-ber-de-gee-lee-on!

Bit o' climbin' till scale sum white caps
Bit o' climbin' till scale sum white caps
Bit o' climbin' till scale sum white caps
Slub-ber-de-gee-lee-on!

Oi, de taunt dees roilin' mount-tins
Oi, de taunt dees roilin' mount-tins
Oi, de taunt dees roilin' mount-tins
Slub-ber-de-gee-lee-on!

Get'er gait goin' yiz motley crew
Get'er gait goin' yiz motley crew
Get'er gait goin' yiz motley crew
Slub-ber-de-gee-lee-on!

Oi, de taunt dees roilin' mount-tins
Oi, de taunt dees roilin' mount-tins
Oi, de taunt dees roilin' mount-tins
Slub-ber-de-gee-lee-on!

Hands in snow, rime roll an' go
Hands in snow, rime roll an' go
Hands in snow, rime roll an' go
Slub-ber-de-gee-lee-on!

Oi, de taunt dees roilin' mount-tins
Oi, de taunt dees roilin' mount-tins
Oi, de taunt dees roilin' mount-tins
Slub-ber-de-gee-lee-on!

Way hay, don't trip nor fall
Way hay, don't trip nor fall
Way hay, don't trip nor fall
Slub-ber-de-gee-lee-on!

Oi, de taunt dees roilin' mount-tins
Oi, de taunt dees roilin' mount-tins
Oi, de taunt dees roilin' mount-tins
Slub-ber-de-gee-lee-on!

Caper and quit, commit to scree
Caper and quit, commit to scree
Caper and quit, commit to scree
Slub-ber-de-gee-lee-on!

Oi, de taunt dees roilin' mount-tins
Oi, de taunt dees roilin' mount-tins
Oi, de taunt dees roilin' mount-tins
Slub-ber-de-gee-lee-on!

Yell hoor-raw reach gul-door-alm
Yell hoor-raw reach gul-door-alm
Yell hoor-raw reach gul-door-alm
Slub-ber-de-gee-lee-on!

Oi, de taunt dees roilin' mount-tins
Oi, de taunt dees roilin' mount-tins
Oi, de taunt dees roilin' mount-tins
Slub-ber-de-gee-lee-on!

This concert of symphonies uplifts their spirits, molding a jovial enthusiasm for musikcraft into collections of rosy feelings. Among such cheery optimism, it feels wrong to complain about when the wind nips their cheeks. Though, William has the suspicious that they're being watched, like some far-flung mystic lingers in the ranges above. This intangible figure's voice rumbles to a raucous, amplifying into a devout chorus. They are subject to an ensemble of roil drums, as if a pot has begun to boil over. Come wisdom and wind, their boisterous attitudes have rendered an avalanche. The wickerwalker faints to the ground, pressing an ear to the permafrost and confirming their worst fears.

"What is it, Edmund?" Lena calls out.

He hobbles to his knees, where it takes a brief second or two for the colors in the his face to dash away, leaving his complexion less than peppery.

The wickerwalker yells with angst, "The entire mountainside is comin' down!"

In a stretch frequent habit for earthquakes and landslides, they should have expressed caution that the glacial wall is prone to tumbling. Tucked securely in the breadth of Balthus' arms, the grimoire roars alongside their company, shaking the pygmy's whole frame and forcing him to jitter in place.

"*Ah-ah,* what's the big idea!"

The manuscript's fierce shouts are eclipsed by the disaster that has awakened, and landmarks that loom larger. A searing cacophony of earth rampages and clamors against the firmament, riling that stellar landscape above with ethereal quakes across the air. Though they cannot spy its origin, a serious racket of *ping-ping, ping-ping-pings* ring out. This deafening calamity is the severing of ice, echoing that the worst has yet to come.

With a resounding rupture, the upper echelon of glacier tremors, a certain schism that liberates loose scree until an iceberg with the same contours of a ram's horn finally splinters and fractures free, threatening the company by collapsing the bulk of a mountain on top of them. Avalanches and landslides aren't actually rare events, although those to bear witness, and survive the immediate cataclysm, are few and far between. Icebergs have the unfortunate habit of handing out naps, albeit permanently. The entirety of Anders Route could be blanketed in debris and lifeless soil.

When the lion's share of scree collides onto the footpath, goading their fellowship to cower onto the stairway, prone and vulnerable to such unrelenting fury, fatal hordes of obsidian and granite slabs shatter alongside an immeasurable swathe of packsnow. A stampede careens their way, and in the sight of this demolition squad, numerous members of the party begin to make peace with their lives. Jerome utters seances praising the divines while Mandel starts to seize, urgently trying to pull himself from the confines of the aching permafrost. He propels himself ten-feet forward, stumbling onto his knees then thrusting at the helm, taking the brute force of the avalanche to spare those townspeople weaker or infirm.

William can clearly sight the cordwainer's silhouette among this torrential downpour, faltering only when a fist-sized lump of stone makes impact with his forehead, and reframes Mandel's cranium into a bowl. The beaten path before them is strewn with deluge, sweeping his suddenly unconscious physique away, right into the sisters' awaiting arms.

They grasp frantically at his figure, their scapegoat who took the brunt of bad weather, tearing into his overcoat and refusing to let go. The boy Jones haplessly observes these affairs, and harbors remorse for not rising to his honor and defending friends, staving those body-battering blows and shield-shattering slams.

William's face, chest, elbows and knees are bruised by burying himself into the trail, lying as flat as possible against the permafrost. His palms instinctively rush over the back of his head, protecting that valuable grey matter, with those townspeople imitating in unison. Unable to do much of anything else, an earnest lad's other hand firmly clutches at his brazier. Effects of the storm sweep over William akin to the sleekness of wind, as if some schoolyard bully thrust a pillow upon his head, and he's forced to close his eyes and mouth, lest choke on the stuffing. The extent of worldly forces exert formidable strain on his luggage, testing the craftsmanship of their straps like how a thief would shoulder his tote, madly sprint in a separate direction, and attempt to tow William along with it.

As the carnage slightly subsides, he musters an attempt to peek through the glaze, then gazing upon the destructive, white tide making headway down the route. This baleful concoction of boulder and ice collides with incumbent outcrops, which act as hedgehogs along the shoreline, attempting to thwart the brunt of the assault and breakwater. Yet, these fortifications do little to avail the swell. It plummets with unabated ferocity, railing right into the radio mast's cemented pillars, as if striking a shored, skeletal lighthouse.

The metal *creaks* and *groans* in pain, as it has been subject to these unrelenting avalanches for a number of centuries. Once the powdery hail sails across the concrete base, flinging itself into the height of the rafters and wild wires above- this connection severs. A particular joint has been stressed to a breaking point, with three of the beams snapping in symphony, although the last refuses to yield, causing the tower to lean in a certain direction, and crumbling as if a felled trunk. In one swift movement, the antennae lands on a sheering, vertical slope, and as the tide begins to settle, a bulwark of snow lurches into the abyssal trenches below which cascade into generous streams of white and gently disperse into mist, still that remaining steel ruin refuses to budge.

This disaster ensures that those once lofty heights of the radio mast now steer towards the underworld and the depths of an incredible crevasse. It was a monument they had only known for a moment, one of the last towers of yore, relic to the ages of men. Now it laments to nightmares, residing as a ladder to those pits of hell, goading the stars to cry and grieve in its passing. The trailing end of the avalanche's onslaught shies past the fallen troop, allowing the fellowship a window in which to tender their injuries.

William climbs to his feet in haste, bolting over to the silhouette of Mandel who has been thrown into the permafrost between the Warder kin. He thrusts his torch close to the company, as an earnest lad's firebrand has miraculously not extinguished. This illumination reveals the minutiae of his character, and just as bizarrely, a pristine face appears where he had expected a terminal wound. There's no obvious hole or damage from the landslide. Perhaps he had imagined it? No, William is sure of himself, the rock would've floundered down this slope if it hadn't been for the cordwainer's head. Yet, his visage appears horribly alright, undamaged by the desolation.

"But, but, yer face," he rambles on, "didn't that 'urt?"

"'Urt? Ya, I don't know what yer talkin' 'bout, but guess so. Ugh, can't 'member wut 'appened. Mah throat's sore, n' der's dis awful pain in muh 'ead- buzzin', like ah bee's rovin' 'round mah skull."

Mandel recognizes the expression of worry befalling the boy Jones.

"Oh, but I'm fine, really. *Hmm,* maybe I culd use sum rest?"

The troop recovers while the ground continues to tremble and quake underneath their boots. They can almost hear the costermonger cry out, "It's a feature, not a flaw," and something that they'll need to get used to, striving to caper-up that corridor in a single-file caravan, regardless of the odds. These earthquakes seemingly consume the patience of night, and wither approach for illustrious dawn.

They must take refuge in these late hours soon, as the constant dodging of rocks has left them a bit worse for wear, all tired and spent. In this groggy, narcoleptic state, they are oblivious to any surroundings, forgetting those clear and present dangers.

A hooded phantom, donning a cloak of speckled bird feathers, stands atop the glacial ice sheet, watching them travel with innate curiosity. This dusk-colored plumage acts as a shroud, camouflaging the stranger among the firmament, periodically harnessing those reflective shimmers of light to manifest the guise of another warm, lively star. They shake some gnarled stick into the air, some arcane rattlesnake staff, an essential tool in any wizard's arsenal. At first glance, while it may take the clever guise of a certainly ordinary walking stick, this divining rod is far from normal- crafted from the fibers of long-extinct cholla wood, distinguished by a copious, hole-riddled husk, then wrapped in clear film, outfitted in an assortment of beads that may conjure the sound of locomotive engines. *Thrum, thrum.* This device whirs and pulsates while lucent ultramarine mist expels from ever crevice, bestowing a crude fog of war. The master of illusion is biding their time.

XIV

—

AT THE BECK AND CALL OF BIGGER THINGS

Thirty-minutes of debris-dodging encourages the company to fashion a makeshift camp. Edmund Redmyne identified the nearest clearing as luxury real-estate, feigning the entrance as a fissure in the mountainside, positioned perfectly in the wake of the Rimeweather Range. The wicklerwalker examines these surfaces, analyzing the scree and snowfall that loosens with every quake for the better part of an hour. Of course, there's no sure-fire guarantee from the wrath of rockslides, but this location is enough to quell any existing and immediate fears.

"Yep-yep, this'll do kindly. Should be safe for ah spell. Give us wink o' shuteye. At least, for an 'our oar two," he declares.

It's a relatively sheltered burrow, thirty-feet in recession, then the space suddenly faults, shrinking into an incredibly narrow ravine, contorting to a width that would be quite precarious to shimmy through. The boy Jones remains tense, even as Mandel attests there's no trauma, assisting the cordwainer in locating a resting place, ushering him to abandoned that baggage which burden his shoulders, and strand stride for the time being. The Hag-man drops these satchels of supplies with protest, allowing for several pieces of equipment to sink slightly. He remains unaware of the slush clinging to his Peaterbricks, and the glaze which creeps in shards around his soles.

"Mud?"

The Boy Jones questions, this isn't right. They're in the heart of the hinterlands without a hearth in sight, who'd range way out here willingly?

"As I told dat wickawalka, I'm gud for ah few more paces at least."

"Shush-shush-shush. Lookie 'neath yer feet."

Only then does Mandel notice a certain flurry of footprints ingrained in the frozen mud, and that the ground here is stamped virtually flat. It's challenging to ascertain their shape, as the tracks are so numerous, treading on one another's shape that they become a muddled, ambiguous composition. William presents these findings to the veteran hunter, calling out across the embankment, who prescribes it as anxious nonsense.

"Ah, boy-oh. This outcrop must be camp 'tween my kind. Awfully brave folk track game up this glacier. This 'ere permafrost etch all sorts o' game and wickas. Tends tah record 'istory, ya know?"

In lieu of this decree, an earnest lad silently lets off a series of frustrated curses in denial, gazing down the nearby cave with deep suspicion. This opening garners an awfully shadowy profile, almost a warning to travelers, but not an effigy that professes foul intentions.

"Come laddie, those eyes o' yers must be playin' tricks. Ye are weary, n' should rest now."

"Aye, aye, ye may be right," the boy Jones admits, unequivocally surrendering.

Calling it a day, William retires among the nearest lip in the stonework, joining those vagabonds whom lounge safely within the sights of their veteran hunter. In the presence of companions and compatriots, he finally lets loose, shrugging his shoulders once, allowing those lashings of leather and linen to slink from his physique, and collapses in place on the permafrost.

Ker-plunk. Even while they allow for those eyelids to droop lazily over their faces, and slump at their shoulders, these townspeople have found a second wind. The boy Jones casually settles beside Mandel, who in his exasperated condition, swiftly surrenders to slumber. However, some people don't have time for leisure, rest is a luxury.

Members of their fellowship proceed to scurry, commuting around the rim of this clearing, each with a specific roll to play in this theater drama. Together they raise a makeshift camp, a true dynasty project culminating under the leadership of Mug Maxwell. Edmund's too weary, watching the ridgeline, cynical of their entire situation.

As their wickerwalker remains preoccupied, the gambler antes into a bid for control. Vagabonds are swift to voice their complaints, prompting scrutiny, unleashing those bids of dissent across the wintery air: conversation lit by witherto and whyfors, aptly questioning their list of operating procedures.

"Where n' why for- say, what reason?"

Truthfully, they shouldn't be abiding to the tongue of someone this green, but at least he's not completely dull. In the absence of fresh kindling and wood, Cliff Fetherhaugh briefly scouts all over the bend, and in no time whatsoever, identifies a stash of logs carefully encased in ice. He locates a firm trunk, grasps, then tugs, however it's no use. The Warder ilk nearby, who are sharpening their knives out of boredom, pitch their discontent with mutual groans of discouragement. Cliff's effort is a public flop, so much so that he collapses to the ground in exhaustion, encouraging Mug to set him on another task.

"'Ey, 'ey, stave those efforts," the gambler hollers, explaining to his fellow.

"This freeze 'olds all sorts o' timba bounty, but it takes weeks tah cure from the deep-freeze. Yer betta off using somethin' else. I know! Let's collect 'em firebrands, organize them intah some pyre for warmth. Won't garnah the 'eights o' ah tried, true n' tested bonfire, or some soothin' furnace, but it'll be balmy 'nough. Strip from those outtamost wears, we've earned ah bit o' rest."

This act curries favor like a good book, refreshing their spirit, offering solace and the scarce opportunity to change from those damp undergarments. They'll still face the bitter chill when shedding their coats, nonetheless- better than nothing at all. Changing a few parts here and there won't snuff the sailing ship.

Lena Tillstead has been scouring through their packstuffs in the warm limelight, taking note of any provisions, namely searching for protein, as she has always been a jerky aficionado and snack-food junkie. Unlike the Oestergaard, her home station of Urbana always had ample opportunities of salted cuisine. Inspecting a substitute for dried meat, she lifts two cans of veggies from their luggage, signifying her endeavors by blowing a distasteful raspberry.

"*Phelpt.* Ugh, roasted dandy root. Prolly stricken with preservatives, giving it the honey-glazed taste of orange peel. Hard pass."

"In dat case, get does provisions o'er 'ere, Calamity Jane!"

She rotates and abides, emphasizing her excavations with a tin can in each hand, never granting them one last, passing glance.

"Whatever," Lena gripes, deciding to roll these cylinders the permafrost, where they *chink* and *clink* into the general direction of the greybeards.

The canisters miraculously survive the ten-foot journey, lurching along the permitter of their meager fire, never stumbling into a shallow ditch or veering off-course. The mechanical chiming noises cause Rochester to quiver, his ears assaulted by the audacity of their soft metal drums. Never a fan of percussion, this is why he uses hand tools and rubber mallets in all his projects.

Jerome is seated in criss-crossed fashion, aggravated and adamantly famished. He's still bitter when the cylindrical provisions strike against his boot, fashionably late as always. Must he pay for late delivery, where's the manager?

In his lap is a mechanical, quarter-twist can-opener, the perfect contraption for prying the lids off tins like a switch. Piercing sheet metal like plaster, this canister obliges easily enough, revealing an ensemble of glistening amber carrots. Glennitch must've opted for the gourmet option when stocking his little fallout bunker, this vegetable side is coated in green gibs, those otherwise tiny slivers of parsley pieces. The greybeard selfishly digs the wedge of his kitchen gadget into the drum like a spoon, greedily shoveling almost a half-portion into his gullet before passing the meal to Rochester, albeit without his precious can-opener. The wainwright's fingers tremble, lifting slops of soft appetizer and nervously consuming a pinch, then shifts his dealer's chip to the person on his left, arriving to Mug Maxwell in a mangled state of disarray. Dandy root softens when combined in a glaze of honey and brown sugar, and the dish is nothing more than mush at this point, but the company doesn't consist of those who complain. There are much worse circumstances that could occur, and they are content with earthy food in their bellies.

William's hunger is sated for now, a fleeting feeling that has become distracted and left him, because his attention is oriented towards his best friend. He takes some time to relocate his knapsack, rummaging through personal belongings, specifically his own separate bag, as the stockpile of provisions he once toted were gifted for Jane to scrutinize. His demeanor trends on the lighter side, edging fingers against those familiar, subject to a few trinkets, vials of mysterious liquid, and paperweights like Edmund's tiny knick-knack carvings. His hand shuffles through it contents, chinking glass before knocking into a thickly padded notebook: Jeremiah's journal, he had almost forget that it existed! Sporting the rare prospect of down-time, William might as well make the most of it, and spy upon those ideas that drove the author mad, dreams worth sacrificing life and limb over.

The wild-eyed boy Jones rips the manuscript from his luggage, glossing over its yellow-clad pages of parchment denoted in thin, wiry blue lines. Every square inch is covered in hysterical scrawls and tiny illustrations, drawings spent with dirty charcoal, strokes that are still legible, yet smeared with each brush of the hand. There is no cover, and the first sheet acts similar to a defensive lineman, barely clinging, hanging-on for dear life. He turns the binding onto its side, ruffling those frayed pages and shuffling contents, sighting collages of detailed, creature diagrams alongside densely-packed notes. One page catches his glare faster than sparks sear flame- a map! Or at least, the rough sketch of one, as artistry is an ongoing struggle between those fundamental limitations of the mind, eyes, hand and imagination. Yes, strangely enough, this appears to be a depiction of Anders Route, for there is a caption close to the bottom of the page, detailing the overall distance.

"Well, this can't be ah good sign."

The Mark of Dayne dictates the chart's key, straying above the rim of desolate Rimeweather mountainpeaks. Jeremiah's journal has numerous odd ramblings, to which the magistrate, Hoosierfeld Char often proclaimed that had been touched by the fell, blaming the author for the settlement's imminent misfortunes. Maybe there's a hint of truth to this, and if so, that also means that there's method to the madness, and terrible reasoning behind this innate gibberish. William dares not wake his sleeping fellow, and instead calls upon the assistance of Balthus, whom- because of his interest in the grimoire, shares a mutual respect for things malign.

"Balto, 'ey Balto," the boy chaotically whispers.

Bannermane have the tendency to shorten names, a tendency that becomes common sense after awhile. During an emergency, someone doesn't have to cry, "Holy Mackerel, Patron Saint of All Sardines" when they can request "Mack's" attention instead.

"Ye've got tah check this out."

"Caught me by surprise, s'all 'Liam. I'm listenin'. What's the matter?"

"Oh, I've just found somethin' that might pique yer interest as it 'as mine. 'Ere-" he presents, flips the notebook onto the learned man's lap, "-check it."

Balthus takes a moment to review the pages, his face wrenched into all manner of emotion, casting expressions of doubt which shift into looks of pure joy the next.

"This journal chronicles all those who've trekked 'fore us. It brings tah light everythin' we may admit- err, encountah on Ander's Route. With this, this right 'ere, we 'ave 'em records on all sorts o' expeditions, the cargo they 'auled, landmarks, locations, the bestest campgrounds around, even creatures n' beasties, n' otha beings that navigators 'ave encountered. Tissa nice find!"

"Immaculate, right? I thought this language was naught but scribbles at first."

"Damn straight. 'Most glossed completely o'ver it. I vow tah nevah again skim text with sloppy handwritin'. C'mon, let's take this tah Edmund, see what 'e 'as tuh say 'bout it all."

Travelers often find that when stricken with lethargy, eagerness often overcomes. These two lift themselves to their feet, and sprint the bend of the rocky bulwark where the wickerwalker has been volunteering for the first watch. At the fickle edge of the fire's radiance, most of his body has become immersed in nighttime gloom.

He remains solemn, aware that he'll have to stave off sleep, and that it'll be necessary to move at first light. The curious duo then explain their predicament, how William had unearthed the novel, and that it contains a manifest of what to expect in this wild territory.

"Thanks, I 'ate it."

"What? But why, Mr. Goodsir?"

The wickerwalker elaborates, "Because the unknown is ah blessin'. Often, the less ye know, the more confident ya are: that follow-mah, this-way mentality, because ye believe yerself right, even through ye 'ave the gall tah lie through it. I'm absolutely confident in muh abilities."

Edmund turns the journal, showing them the pages that he has been reading, pointing to a sketch of an insectoid monstrosity nicknamed the Goremandie. It features a predominantly human visage, only contorted into vile forms. A captivating female body, courtesan to the kingliest of keeps, so thin and elegantly slender, however spider-esque, stationed atop an umbrella of six spindly limbs. Interestingly enough, its torso is equipped with the normal amount of appendages: two, yet they are elongated into dreadful scythe-like apertures. While promoting a form of dazzling hypnotic glamor, the beast's head is ghastly- a stark contrast, laden by horrifyingly bulbous cheeks, beseeched with cross-stitched webbing which house dozens of ebony-pitted eyes.

"And that's why I'm confident that I can't fend off ah beast like that,"

Edmund casually admits, "Maybe if these measurements are off, n' it's frankly the size of mah fist, perhaps I can squish it real early. Watch it though, with mah luck, its blood would be acid n' eat right through muh boot."

"Ah, filthy bugga, yer such ah worst-case scenario person," admonishes Balthus.

"Aye, because in times like these, the worst-case scenario is often the more likely one. Now, stave-off n' away with ya two. Get some rest, cause when the glitters all out, us got tah be up real bright n' early."

The two are shrugged by this brutally honest feedback, and retreat back to the radiant illusions of the campfire. Edmund retains his position ahead of the journey, spending the twilight fore dusk by torchlight, and after pilfering Jeremiah's journal for himself, reading-up on a comprehensive list of possible adversaries. There's a wealth of knowledge contained within these pages, with the wickerwalker favoring those illustrations which detail the more fantastic end of fauna, creatures that he has never encountered before, let alone imagined.

Shifting through the various assortment of troll-kin, passing those Gardenwaagh, Hillwaaghs, Mudwaaghs and Blastawaaghs, he lands on the page explaining the mischievous nature of gremlins when all of a sudden, the tiniest, baby-sized hand grips the corner of the notebook, and gives it a slight tug. Nothing barbarous, just a testy shrink, merely a bout with an amateur thief.

Edmund thrusts the manuscript upwards in response, raising both arms stiffly above his head so that he may meet the creature eye-to-eye, only he is left in an awkward position, as the lanky arm of the burgeoning pickpocket extends to match this pace, and the perpetrator is still so unexpectedly rooted to the ground. This surprise stares at him, perfectly perplexed, greeting some end of a stretchy, six-foot rope where the shoulder is meant to be. Edmund had been reading these dawning hours almost in a trance, managing to stay so still, holding his breath in habit and quite honestly, dozing-off once or twice, that the creature thought he was sleeping.

It turns a nauseating berry-blue, seemingly vulnerable to the cold, before entering an abrupt sneezing fit, giving him time to inspect the oddity as it shakes its jowls and rears back for another encompassing nasal ejection. The pest's feeble frame bounces with every blow, all the while, through this visceral mess of mucus, refusing to let go of the journal. Edmund is in shock at this peculiar catch.

What a coincidence, this creature surely must be a gremlin, as it looks awfully similar to a portrait he'd been studying, but with several diabolical differences. There is the usual facial bulging, a protruding pair of blinkers, stubby legs, eccentric armatures which grow to impossible lengths, and a squashed nasal ridge, almost as if it ran too fast at a wall. Unlike its peachy pink counterpart on the page, this critter sports a tiny hooked beak reminiscent of a flightless owl, panting maniacally at the end of its awful fever.

The wickerwalker twists his wrists, writhing the journal free, and shaking his head in distaste towards the benign beastie.

"Ye mustn't steal. Bad 'abits n' all."

It refuses to yield, also nurturing a back and forth bow in childish imitation. In an act of grandstanding, Edmund turns to address the remainder of the company, keen to showcase the quarry that he's unintentionally landed. When he spins to address the crowd, he finds that this was not the only gremlin to brave their premises. The wickerwalker is frankly flabbergasted, stupefied, mumbling.

"What in-"

As little folk litter the campground, attending to its occupants whom are all in various states of drowsiness, tending to their affairs in manners brisk as otters, and daring as rats. Their pesky hands invade promiscuous places, probing pockets, and robbing them blind. Several are helping themselves to food, looting their provisions, sharing tin cans between them and avidly gnawing on the rims.

One in particular, stands on Lena's chest, snapping the strap of a beaded chain and amulet wrung around her neck.

"Domo papa! Gelato shine-shine, olla me-mine," it surprisingly seems to say, though this brash trespass doesn't seem to wake her. These gremlins must not weigh much, maybe they're hollow-boned?

"-absolute tarnation? 'Ey, 'ey, rise and shine everyone," Edmund yelps out.

The boy Jones twists in his sleep, passively slapping a hand away from his coat pouch. Upon the hunter's call, his eyelids flash open, and he spies that his swipe may have dissuaded the critter, because it now searches through his bag of belongings instead, securing the carved totems of bone, and brandishing them under the moonlight.

William stirs into action, instinctively gathering a handful of soot scree and hurls that ashen matter at their invader. Humans may be larger and stronger, but they're not any faster. Before the cloud of dust strikes the nape of its neck, the gremlin thief is already alert, rearing its head towards the sky and screeching adamantly. This shriek warns its fellow accomplices of immediate danger, and they all abandon their heist, hastily grabbing whatever they can manage, opportunistically rooting about like boar, and retreating to the tunnel canyon nearby. They waddle hilariously, hop over flailing arms, and choose to skip when cornered, fleeing like a flock of birds. One accidentally wavers, stumbling through a tower of dishes and empty tins that summons the mad clamoring of a cowbell.

Jerome wakes during this crazed cacophony, lifting his head readily, only to be struck by the speeding gremlin, who matches feet with face-time, then snappily continues its journey. He is walloped once, then twice in dismay, left scratching his scalp as the second swift rapscallion darts away, questioning.

"What in da divines?"

When the last of these uninvited guests finally depart, scurrying frantically into a thin, snaking corridor of the mountain-scape, the traveling troop assess their remaining inventory, and count the losses. Truthfully, they haven't stolen much, a bit of grub and the occasional polished trinket, baubles that otters are trained to nab during sutler's paradise. Lena addresses the issue on everyone's mind.

"And no, it's not nearly as bad as it seems."

Usually highwaymen and raiders know the merchandise to covet after, however this party of thieves definitely do not share rank among the normal ilk. The widow explains that their packstuffs mainly consist of cans, which are now comprehensively covered in teeth-marks, as the gremlin horde couldn't pierce their shells and get into the sloppy nutritious contents, so they mainly left them alone.

"They're just nuisances, and didn't mean any harm," she mentions, debating whether, "maybe we should just move on?"

William conscientiously pipes-up, alerting the others to a malpractice suit.

"Be sure tah check yer pockets, n' don't dally folks. Saw one o' those miscreants goin' through mah belongins, 'owever scarce."

Upon hearing this advice, Morbin breaks into a full-fledge sprint towards his carry-ons, characteristically admitting that he splurged on pilfering some valuables from the vault. Like-minded folks start to nab their luggage and start sifting through. Meanwhile, Calamity Jane motions in reflex, patting down her chest to discover a notable vacancy.

"*Agghh.*"

Lena berates her own carelessness, citing that she should've been more aware, and expected that those who skulk around their sleeping bags had the gall.

"No, no, no. They've gone and stolen my charms." She skips through her grief, that period of mourning frustration and remorse, and immediately turns ripe with anger, exclaiming, "This is personal, I've got to get them back!"

This belligerent demand compels Balthus to check, and clearly enough, when smacking his chest with gusto, the movement produces a stifling *thump* because of the absence of parchment. An admiringly clever grin crosses his face, to which he apologetically reveals.

"So… seems like they've stolen the manuscript too."

"Consarnit," Edmund remarks.

"That just fans mah furnace. I wouldn't 'ave pressed for ah few cans. They've really gone n' messed up. As the only folk with some sense of morals, or the any livin' thing 'round these parts, we need tah intervene n' administa some frontier justice. Now that we're up, let's hop tuh 'ready."

The rambunctious Libby interjects, "Not only that, breakneck. Left tah their own devices, who knows what 'ell they'd unleash 'pon themselves?"

"Hell?"

Bids Warder chuckles at his ignorance, rapping at her sibling's shoulder, and chortling.

"Sis-sis, ain't that grand? Isn't that funny?"

Before taking a second to find that no one else is laughing, and finding that her retort was vain. Realizing that the wickerwalker wasn't present at the time, she briefly explains.

"Oh, oh um. 'Ow should I put this? Turns out, we've been totin' an artifact that spurs visions n' ragin' infernos. Somethin' tah file under the, 'do not use unda any circumstances,' pile."

"What, would ye do me ah pleasure n' run that by 'gain? So we've been portin' fire?"

"No-go ghost rida. Lookie 'ere, that book is bad, bad magik. Bad things tend tah 'appen wheneva it's opened. Rankin' from bad tah worse, real quick. We can't trust it, nor that sort of powah in anyone else's 'ands."

Following this methodical release of information, Edmund is truthfully more confused than livid like his fellows are.

"Umm, okay I guess," he says quite puzzled, "Well- not okay, shut'p, ye get the picture. Sounds like we need some people on retrieval duty. 'Right, guess I volunteer, but not 'lone, let's round-up the usual suspects. Balto,

'Liam, Morbs, yer with me. And Jerrie- actually, Jerome, sit this one out, looks as if that gremlin ruffled ah few feathas o' yers. C'mon, let's get goin' 'ready, we've got tah get that book!"

"And my necklace," chimes Lena.

"Yeah, I thought that was implied. That too."

And thus an entourage of townspeople nimbly give chase, rushing to the entry and barren stone path laying before them. The winds that brush these chambers could cause bison to turn heel and flee; not these vagabonds, because they know of the farce, and that the true inhabitants of these hinterlands are naught but pesky critters. Battered by a sudden gust, these navigators are propelled forward, restricted only by the shape of the portal, which coerces those with paunchy frames to suck in their guts, twist, then shuffle here and there.

The passage has a slight bend to it, disguising the natural tunnel until they reach a point burdened by notches of stony debris, rifts in the rock, almost like traversing ancient ruins. There are circumstances where the corridor walls abruptly snap together, mimicking the motions of a vice, while other areas expand into wide channels. Morbin is agile, and pays no heed to these hurdles, even when William struggles to match the archaeologist's pace.

The company take a breather resting upon the fringes of a forgotten doorway, long-collapsed, dashing their hopes as to what lies beyond the frame.

"Best follow the path, they should be down 'ere," Edmund urges.

The remainder of their journey proceeds uneventfully, that is, until they reach the most prominent portion of underground cavern, the climatic end to this almost linear, straightforward passage with no twists, only turns. They are surprised that this was a simple undertaking, neither tricks nor traps, especially when compared to the warrens they trekked through earlier, and that sickly labyrinth of concrete.

This hall directly ahead is best described as a trophy room, it echos with distant authority. Foreign words emanate ahead, and the fellowship may spy creatures conversing in droves. One critter shouts at the crowd to raise their stretchy arms and cheer.

"Braka time!"

The facades of this demesne feature tapestries adorning the walls, woven masterstrokes of history that have long since faded. Bundles of fungi and toadstools sprout from this medium, breaking down the fabric into nourishing supplements. While these colonies may remind William of the lunar eyrie, this is an entirely new strain. These stools bud freely, contorting into a variety of strange, new shapes. A hat-looking hood here, a nubby hand there, limbs flaunt from the mycelium walls. The bodily representations of these mushrooms are incredibly demoralizing, it's as if a person had exploded and their remains are spread among the cinderblocks.

The boy Jones becomes flustered by these discoveries, and the annoying, constant chime that they emit doesn't help either.

Din, dinnn, dinnnggg.

He points to the nearest colony as the largest sprout among them begins to vibrate and hum, then following a ten-second struggle, uproots itself as a fully-fledged gremlin.

"Oh da humanity," utters Jerome, whom shuns this bittersweet moment as the petite, rabbit-sized nudist trots off to find its family, both arms lagging behind and dragging on the grimy cobblestone floor.

The company quickly recognize the importance of these colonies. They are surrounded, and out of fear that these creatures may prove hostile, tread quietly, careful not to disturb the fungal growths.

At the far side of the spacious chamber an improvised throne, strung together with cardboard, plastic trim and furniture used in all the wrong ways, with a distinct kit-king presiding atop. This gremlin isn't intimidating at all, nor different in size than those counterparts, not sporting any unique shapes of color either. The only discerning factor regarding its status as leader is a matter of jewelry, as heavy is the head which lies the crown, while the others have no courtly denominations to speak of. It lounges sideways on a bog of human refuse, each leg lounging over the armrest, obviously bored with this unruly court. The gremlin's hubcap crown is perched so precariously on its head that this whole ancillary begs to slip loose and roll away, along with any evidence to its reign.

"Woah," Balthus quips, "'E's 'bout mah size. If I take 'is cap, do ye think they'll worship mah as one of their own?"

Occasionally, gremlins march to attend their grace, timidly kneel, and present meager offerings, speaking in a manner of gibberish and unveiling their recent loot. If the kit-king chooses to accept their charity, then their donation is thrust onto another pile of debris; if not, the neighboring guards shall kick them in the rear until they promptly vacate the grand hall. These fungal troopers are prepared for war, armored in platters and stainless tabletop silverware. They relish in their duty, armed to the teeth, but of course, in the matter of perspective, these armaments aren't greater than kitchen knives.

The arriving human troop riles commotion, and stir the nearby gremlins into action, though an overwhelming majority flee. Those that remain are chiefly courtesans of this clown court, seemingly the advisors, and royal entourage of the hubcap crown. This disturbance catches the guards by surprise, as other than the blue-skinned nuisances caught pilfering their supplies, these gremlins have never spied a human before.

Morbin sarcastically chides when they raise their cutlery in defiance.

"What are ye gonna do, skewer us with dinnah forks?"

The kit-king grows immediately interested in these newcomers, enough to warrant a fresh furrow in those eyebrows. Their egotistical leader jabbers away, attempting to communicate with them, speaking a variety of dialects between balderdash, buggit, gibberish and gobbledegook, motioning forward with both sets of arms and legs.

"What bow-bana binnit maw?"

From these latter affairs, William brainstorms his own title for the king.

"Reminds me o' the puppets we 'ad when I was ah kid. I know, let's name 'em Bug-a-boo!"

The wickerwalker condescendingly slaps the boy's shoulderblade, and shoves Jones forward, closer to an interrogation and inspection.

"We're 'ere for the book, so if yer gonna waste time playin' parlor tricks, then go 'round, namin' it like ah pet, ye should be the one to entertain 'em!"

"'Right, 'right. I'll take care o' everythin'. Do me ah favor n' chill," the earnest lad remarks.

In the beginning, as the simplest solution is often the right one, William tries unsuccessfully to explain their predicament.

"Some yer lil' laddies stole from us, n' we need to gatha our things back."

Jumping on the cushion of its chair and clapping hands twice, it seems that the kit-king doesn't quite comprehend thronepatter. The gremlin liegelord responds in kind.

"What bark?"

"Oh botha, nah comprehenda young tike."

He turns towards his fellowship in disapproval, "I don't think this is gonna work."

"Keep going, yer doin' great!"

When that doesn't seem to bear fruit, William then tries to enact his own theater drama, donning a series of awkward gestures and puppeteering to clarify: that when they inadvertently open the grimoire, they'll summon a demon that will spell their doom.

The kit-king's expression of pleasure deteriorates, unsure why these outsiders haven't paid penance to the crown of the toadstool empire, and for that, it sours. During this period of charades, especially as William employs the funniest maneuvers, the ambient gremlins return, realizing that these Bannermane are not a threat.

Their tunnels are manned by a motley true, an attire is strapped together with trinkets and scrap. These patrons are dirt-poor compared to their chieftain whom's flush shiny objects, as the critter composing the largest orchestra often tends the best instruments, and Morbin notices an intense gleaming patina emanating from the pile of trash nearest to the throne.

He assumes that this beacon is definitely Jane's charm, and strides, surging forward to stake his claim. When the archaeologist collects his memento, and returns, presenting his findings to the others of the group, the kit-king clambers around his hoard, and attempts to snatch the bauble back.

"Oh nonsense," Morbin cries, "there shall be no negotiations. Give that 'ere, it's not yers!"

He fastens onto those sterling chain links, wrenching the ancillary closer to his person while the gremlin exerts every ounce of strength to pluck it back. At its essence, this really becomes a childish game of tug-of-war, and fed-up with such raucous, Morbin expressly yanks the necklace free from the hands of this thieving gremlin. Unfortunately enough, this exercise forces the band to split, delivering a vivid collection of precious gemstones and pendants onto the cinders. He vocally lashes out at the creature, scolding it greatly.

"Now, look what ye've gone n' did!"

Bug-a-boo scampers off, leaving Morbin to pick-up the pieces, irritatingly mumbling to himself. Realizing that with the vacancy go the kit-king, and there shall be no decent conversation, Edmund takes matters into his own hands by scanning the permitter of room. He locates the grimoire in a corner of the demesne, with a small throng of gremlins inquisitively fiddling at the clasp. The wickerwalker quickly surmounts them, slipping between their shoulders and snatching back their property.

"That's not yers eitha."

Always cranky and fraught with envy, Jerome notices a nearby collection of fungal blights tearing into some plastic film. It's incredibly odd for these scavengers to have amassed this particular kind of garbage, and surmises that this must have been from their own supplies. He mutters to himself, complaining that Lena didn't notice this theft before. As he approaches closer, certain beaks begin munching even faster, desperately taking bites out of their packstuffs before they lose their tasty treats, enough of a frantic nibble that they choke, cough, and spread crumbs all throughout the floor while the greybeard challenges the nearest gremlin with the proper use of confectionary biscuits.

"Nah fraka-em, or raka-em. Drats," the Kit-king shouts, unwilling to fight back nor order its troops into the fray.

These humans aren't just bigger than his kin, they're gigantic! The gremlin is grateful, noticing that they aren't pillaging his entire chamber and stealing all his stuff, just those few, very specific things that have ventured within the hour. In the whole truth, it's an incredibly awkward confrontation, and William strives to apologize for their sloppy diplomacy, appreciative of the fact that they shouldn't frequent this way again.

When they rally and recover their artifacts, Edmund orders the troops to high-tail it out of there, far away from these awfully strange people, and leaving the toadstool empire potentially forever.

They retrace their journey through the mushroom-riddled hallway, always looking over their shoulders, plainly afraid that they'll be cornered by masses of gremlins, blisterwort and crow's feet, yet none gather. In fact, the returning tunnel leading back towards the gate is notably absent of bodies, much to their appreciation. William breathes a sigh of relief, grateful not to develop a habit of whacking overgrown mole-rats with the blunt of his pikehead.

When they emerge from the umbral darkness, doused among the soft, illuminating bronze throes of dawn, Balthus heaves the grimoire over his head for the purpose of cruising through the tight, waist-cinching corridor, and returning onto their flat campground. Faced against the abrasive elements, members of their company have taken to whirling around, remaining active by scouring the damage these these gremlins have poised, recovering their possessions scattered every which way, and have already begun packing supplies.

Such an endeavor took the better part of fifteen minutes, so in the meantime, they've been huddling together closely for warmth, near the beacon of torches as their flames dim low, meekly awaiting their comrades return and biding time by whistling tunes. Edmund offers a scarce, flattering praise for their townspeople being ahead of the curve, and staunchly ushers the townspeople away from the gate. Those among the fellowship are all too confused by this hasty rush, but as the wickerwalker directs them towards mountain pass, and saying farewell to this place, they welcome a change of scenery.

Fresh perspectives foster the feeling that they are actually making progress. Their company regain their footing in a matter of no time, managing swift pace, and concluding this enchanting excursion of Ander's Route.

As to be expected, Lena composes herself, and mends approach to the distinguished team of explorers to inquire about the status of her immeasurably valuable heirloom. This interest spurs the animosity in Morbin, who paces right up to her.

"'Old out your palm, ma'am," he affords to croak, and when she does, actually entertaining this hollow request, the widow receives a profuse donation as fragments of ornaments and limp silvered chain land in her palm.

"Oh," she responds meekly.

As the crew so sensibly departs, they are as keen as mustard, eager to discuss matters of biology and the origin of these gremlins, debating whether they are truly modeled with mold or a pleasant side-effect, the result of fell magik. Morbin boasts of his exploits from inside the cavern, bragging about how he toppled the diabolical kit-king and sent that giant scurrying from whence it came.

Under the delusion of boisterous banter, he tends to exaggerate the finer details. Rather than gremlins being the itsy-bitsy little-folk that they are, through the archaeologist's account, he mentions that they were terrifying, standing three-heads taller than a man with arms as thick as towing cable, lucid features that frighten the wainwright. With the color rapidly bleaching from his cheeks, Rochester's panics, pacing towards the front of their pack, fueled by the earnest desire to dispose of this villainous clientele already. The faster his legs may carry him, the sooner they'll get out of here.

The next hurdle on their docket is that of an impartial nature, as this path is inherently treacherous, this next mile will be a marathon, a testament of sheer will, filled with tests of physical strength and dexterity. At various points of this campaign, the company is seen climbing upwards, nearly vertical, the sort of angle where it's easier to navigate on all fours than happen to strain someone's knees. Townspeople tend to drift close to the bastion edge, an edifice aligning with the glacier, leashing themselves onto the cliff wall for bodily support. On their right is absolutely nothing, some candid drop upon the gaping canyons below.

This is no leisurely hike, though it sponsors a truly magnificently views. The rising sun is an episode to enjoy and spoil, severely scarce among the shallow barrow tide season, soaring above the cloud coverage. While not many Bannermane would raise their glasses in agreement, William believes that this odyssey is a reward on its own right, nevertheless fleeting. As the solispyre crests the outermost steppes and those eastern slopes of border princes, exhibiting upon the far side of the basin, it is immediately confronted by a flurry of clouds, a steady stream of tendrils that roil from behind the Rimeweather Range.

The air circulates awkwardly fierce here, threatening to deliver their wide-brim hats expeditiously onto the craglands below. The clouds are leaden in malign thoughts, aching to crush those meager joys of life. However crude the notion of sun may be, there is no greater sensation than rays of light cleansing the skin. These incandescent beams wipe away the horrors humanity is bound to face, as the only force capable of thwarting and rejecting the icy domain, that is why fell beasts vow that the solispyre must be purged.

This onslaught of inclement weather originates behind the silhouetted mountainpeaks and barren outcrops north. The elements have laid siege to Ander's Route for centuries, sending detrimental volleys of ice and stone hurtling down, where they collide in elemental salvo, fracturing the land with its impact, relentlessly battering the wind-lashed corridor until it recedes, eventually ebbing away as scree. Edmund Redmyne leads the company to a crater, a sudden gap in the road, though he didn't have much say in the matter.

Peering over the ledge reveals a repulsive thirty-foot plunge. An obstacle of attrition for sure, as it'll take an additional hour for them to descend this chasm, and scale back up, but nary impossible. They aren't the first travelers to arrive this way in recent weeks, Mandel spies a lengthy pole resting beside the chasm, impelling the masses to chortle with happiness, with even the wicked Jerome calling out.

"Good on ye, son! This ah tool tah vault da trench."

As usual, the wickerwalker is dauntless, bravely volunteering to test these waters, and mettle in the affairs of someone else's ingenuity. The stave has already been rooted in a decisive spot, notching itself in a well-placed rent in the ground, right in the middle of some stern cobble. He wraps his fingers around those grooves engraved into the pole, already barking advice.

"Now if ye line yerself up alongside the wall like so," and with a three-step guide, leaps right from the edge.

"'Ere," he shouts, gliding over the gap, though not before landing harshly on the causeway, and entering a slight roll. Edmund ends-up thumping onto his knees, a byproduct of clumsy footing, then promptly extends his arms to each side in a traditional form of, "Ta-dah!" Imagining himself as an acrobat in a traveling troop.

The bottommost portion of this wooden stave has no desire to move, it's rigid and firmly fastened in place underneath an ensemble of miniature boulders. These travelers merely draw a few paces back, lift themselves from the permafrost with a running start, holding on for dear life all the way, using the timber as a lever to the other side. By sticking close to the edifice, Edmund hopes that strugglers may grasp an adjacent ledge for the support if the need may arise, as wiseacres like Jerome aren't able to garner enough velocity to leap in a single swoop.

Mandel shoulders the pole next, announcing that he is ready, presenting himself as a clear and present danger to anyone nearby. The wickerwalker shoves the stick so that it may nimbly pivot back to its original posture. After noticing the graceful motions of Edmund, the cordwainer is daring, yet cautious, and saunters into starting position. In the split-second before Mandel engages his warp-speed, the boy Jones yelps.

"Wait ah darn second!"

Much to the ire of those in queue, William bolts aside, rummaging through the party's knapsacks until he locates that specific piece of luggage where he may secure a steady coil of rope. Learning on the fly, he briskly wraps this thread around their pole vault.

Edmund proudly praises from across the chasm, professing his stake in the matter.

"Oh, I see where yer goin' with this. Good on ya!"

Should they accidentally push the stave in entirely the wrong direction, this painless attachment prevents the pole from escaping down the mountain slope.

"See," blurts Mandel, "yer the smart 'un outta the two of us!"

In an exemplary sequence of aerobics and canal tumbling, a majority of townspeople oblige this pass without issue. The only dilemma that spawns from crossing their gauche crevice is when the settler with the worst track record approaches, one whom has procured a distinct fear of heights after voyaging through the lunar eyrie, steps up to the plate. Rochester frantically shimmies up the pole during his maiden voyage. A desperate attempt to flee further from the ditch, only to land bluntly, slumping in a heap on the opposite side.

Contradicting her usually abrasive attitude, Calamity Jane praises the aging peregrine in some show of good sportsmanship, acting as perhaps an honest apology for their misgivings earlier. When Cliff Fetherhaugh, the last member of their fellowship finally minds the gap, the company criticizes whether or not they should pilfer the pole, never knowing when another chasm may present itself. Edmund challenges against their assumptions.

"Nay, we were lucky to come 'cross this stave, the same should be said for any hoosiers who trek this way."

"Fine, that's fine and all, but what 'bout that?"

Mug Maxwell contests, gesturing to the boulders which obstruct their path, encompassing the entire bend as a blockade. This roadblock is an obscenity to their hard work, all those hours of progress for naught. Wedged tighter than a clogged pipe, the company cannot consider squeezing through, crawling underneath, or vacating a portion of debris. Sled-sized carriages of earth taunt them, each crag is nearly the size of their resident brute, Korralack the Kable. Even if they manage a return to the gap and employ that same wooden instrument as a makeshift lever, the stave would surely snap, subject to burdens that bison couldn't budge.

The impact of the landslide has fractured their stony hurdle with harsh, surface eddies. Morbin proposes that they should drop lower, gripping the ledge and shuffling past, but that would be a moot toll, mutilating their hands and gloves whenever they clutched this craggy precipice, and if their strength wavered, a sure-fire plummet would ensue. They certainly can't hobble over this fallout either. It's as if the mountain mutated on its own, harboring entire batches of new fascinating protrusions. The boulders beyond are broken in all the right places, participating in those cataclysmic collapses, revealing elusive slivers of obsidian ore, and those jagged, volcanic glass edges that prevent the notion of climbing atop without being torn to shreds.

Edmund is as white as a ghost, there's nothing a wickerwalker may do. Every now and then, those Bannermane veterans court hopeless scenarios, yet they always prevail, discovering their own unique method to flourish-though, when boiled down, is usually a fight or flight response, not tests of intelligence or geology.

William is fraught that barricades such as these: inanimate, elemental and elementary. Something so inherently dull, could ensnare so much trouble. At least, when contesting against the wolves, they were safe and secure for a time being. This hinderance leaves them helplessly exposed, like fleas on a bald patch.

Morbin cracks a joke to ease the tension.

"Looks like that area's off limits, maybe we should turn back?"

The wickerwalker feverishly rambles, conversing with himself, pressing to conjure alternative answers. He stares at the ridgeline above and ponders.

"-better off climbin' the cliff face… mayhaps, say sixty-feet at this altitude- see where that leads."

"Stand aside."

Edmund reels around to locate that person who dared to interrupt his trial of thought.

"What are ye blabberin' on 'bout?"

To his disbelief, Mandel kneels in front of him and removes his baggage, chanting in some unknown language, babbling in beast tongue: abrupt, wispy tones, that sounding eerily familiar to a sharp gust or swaying branches. This behavior is aberrant, freaking those townspeople within sniffing distance, all of whom take several steps away in disgust.

The cordwainer is not familiar with himself at the moment, a transformation unusually apparent as the color of his eyes continue to churn, converting from amber to a golden gloss. Once the dye drains, his human sense of individuality goes along with it. He abruptly claps his two palms together. *Whack.* Now a client of insanity and something else entirely. Defying all known magikal disciplines and wisdoms, bands of sapphire-stained staves, symbols of protection and virtue, range on his coats as if they have been painted on.

The puppet stumbles to its feet in an ungraceful effort, banking approach to the full-frontal exposure of earth. Scrutinizing the barricade for a split second, it decisively intervenes by clasping Mandel's limbs around the nearest man-sized stone. This exercise is tremendous in scope, akin to a bear hug, yet squirrelly, awfully difficult to move and clasp with a pair of flimsy arms. Ribbons of red ichor escape from his body, carefully minced by those fragments of obsidian ore. They growl and labor until the possessive spirit finally understands that this project is too intensive, and that this crude form doesn't have a snowball's chance in hell lifting this boulder.

Prompting a back-up plan, the cordwainer broadens his stance, readies a punch and fires in one swift movement. Once the first fist thrown grazes the surface, the glove on Mandel's hand is instantly shredded into smithereens, not by the lacerations, but by the sheer force of the punch. Knuckles rap further into the grizzled grey granite and pitch-dark veins, pulverizing his catcher's mitt into finer fragments until the momentum of the strike stifles, causing the elbow to flinch from the herculean impact, dislocating and grinding bones, then leaving a clear indent on the broadest side of the boulder. The geist won't settle for this rate, and barely winces when the punch recoils, admiring the extent of damage, this trauma and bodily harm.

In one last ditch effort, the puppet positions itself at an angle, orienting towards a piece of debris that has landed so dangerously on the path's edge. A swift kick to this particular stone lands about chest-high, immediately bursting Mandel's boot into ribbons, sending scraps of leather and shoelace wayward. This fragmented boulder wobbles, forced into a curt roll, where the cliffside yields to the pressure, and the granite careens free in a bout of dust and scree. They can hear this gigantic stone tumble down the slope, a manic drum rolling wildly, crashing into rime, staggering through rocky bulwarks and starting a miniature landslide of its very own. The cacophony abruptly stops, as the scree become lodged in stupor, jammed inside one of those numerous crevasses that dominate these hinterlands.

It takes another fifteen minutes of their tremendous effort, coaxing Mandel to tense and toil until the job is done. Usually the type to farm scars by playing with dogs, his human body has been strained well past its natural limits. Removing five of so of these bunk-sized cobbles seems to do the trick, crafting a manageable path that the townspeople may wriggle through.

It makes sense now, how Mandel was able to survive his fatal wound: the gods have been deliberately inhabiting his body, using him as their faithful vessel. William is definitely not a religious man, so the motives of immortals are always blurred and subject to scrutiny. He asks himself, why 'this spirit doesn't stay in possession of mortal form, aiding their quest.' It's possible that they actually care about people, sculpting them into objects worthy of affection, or perhaps the reason is more practical and less sinister, that they are constantly doing battle, and they just so happened to notice their plight and decided to intervene. They must farm special qualities between them, metamorphosing those ordinary into extraordinary.

Alas, poor Mandel, he is their chosen one, a suave fellow propping a nice swagger and raised among a regal family, but cavorting with such power always derives a hefty price.

Their enlisted puppet steps away from their excavation project, bidding adieu to the precipice before promptly collapsing onto the ground, causing the shoeless cordwainer to land faintly upon his back. One by one, those runes flaunting on Mandel's skin proceed to vanish, no longer bound to service. His eyelids flicker, not returning their speckled amber tinge, and permanently corrupt into that impure golden yellow of cosmic icons.

William unleashes a cry for his friend, fervor staked from the pangs of guilty conscious. If only he had known earlier, maybe they could've found another option, circumventing the cordwainer's intense bout of suffering. Mandel absent stare lapses over the boy Jones, spending those necessary minutes rewiring his brain, rediscovering what it means to breathe again of his own volition, as the spirit has so callously discarded its mortal husk. Those vagabonds residing upon these splintered steppes are struck with a fondness for the macabre, surrounding this hapless Haggerton as he eventually regains consciousness.

When Mandel finally awakens, a candid question purses his lips.

"Oh, 'ey everyone. Why, why am I on da 'round? Ah-ah," he unexpectedly blurts out, more reflex than thoughtful judgement. His chest heaves, speaking in exasperated tunes, "Woah, o' wow-wow. It feels like mah 'eart is racin'. What's 'appened, is der somethin' wrong wit me?"

Before anyone has the ability to criticize his recent abduction, a perverse purplish plight appears, depraving his hands, wrists, forearms, calves, ankles, and feet, alighting whatever exposed skin they can manipulate in agonizing bruises. He howls in anguish from this pestilence, and several limbs suddenly snap from this mounting pressure. The phalanges of his right hand contort and swivel, wrapping further into the palm or veering off by means of right angles. William lobes are assaulted by some grotesque concert, a certain ensemble of *whip-whip* and *crack* from the breaking of bones. The affairs of beings far greater are all but stranger to mortal men, and thankfully, Mandel faints in this revelation, subject to shock.

In an unfortunate development, they can't delay their journey, no matter the extent of casualty. After all, this isn't a safe location to idle. These townspeople must flee, or else the company shall be committing themselves to the irritability and scrupulous taunts of barbarous storms. This corridor would be better named the Easy City Turnpike, consecrated by the dramatic returns it cultures, and travelers deciding to forgo their journey upon meeting every obstacle. In these circumstances, the cordwainer may prove a liability, ushering the townspeople from fleece, food and drink as a lost cause. Still, founded in times of hardship, these vagabonds have flourished with strife, choosing to be bound together in common cause rather than defined by it. They choose to fight, and not one soul shall be left behind for the fray.

By bundling Mandel in a slew of extra jackets, the expedition decides that they can ultimately stride forward. Korralack the Kable volunteers, scooping-up their latest victim of divine intervention, sliding his arms closer to cradle Mandel's shoulder blades and mutilated thighs strained in the third-degree. When the Boar's Band brute holds the casualty closer, almost inviting the comatose form to his lobe, he can hear the unmistakable mending of tendons. In a truly remarkable feat, their accomplice has already begun to heal as the gods wouldn't forfeit an instrument so easy.

Korralack remains stocked as the largest body among them, bracing to bear the brunt of packsnow, fending this knee-high, numbing build-up quite perilously. As the morning flags those luminous phosphorescent waves which radiate through the firmament, they caution cold grey, the symbol of a thunderous, oncoming slews of precipitation. The brute has worn down to his core by these relentless furies, windfalls that threaten turning him into a statue like those still-men of the old city.

His gait suffers, slowing to a crawl as each stride becomes stiffer than the last. When ferrying the unconscious cordwainer, every step becomes methodical, a lagging pounce across the drift that chaperons a tedious, three-second rest before regularly yanking his lattermost leg from the hoarfrost, and inching another stubby pace forward. A break-down is inevitable, replacement parts are in short supply.

Those in drafting his rear expect the highwayman to collapse with exhaustion soon: his shoulders burdened with cargo, facial hair and whiskers frozen straight sideways with frigid icicles, the sweat teeming underneath his vestments cackles with rime, skin suffering from freezer burn, and muscles brimming with lactic acid; yet, he refuses to yield. Undergoing this methodical slow torture, William can't help but feel sorry for the brute.

"'Oi, Kable! I might 'ave somethin' tah ease yer plight.'"

Under the charitable promise of aid, Korralack is urged to stop in his tracks, although he does not possess the energy to turn around. His outfit of wool and fleece is one solid piece, cemented by that briny sweat which leaches from his body, freezing as painful glaze that sears swathes of skin.

The boy Jones slinks that knapsack from his shoulder, aiming to rummage around inside.

His fingertips *clack* against a variety of miscellaneous trinkets all at once, those animalistic totems from the wickerwalker and alluring vials that he had procured from Glenn's alchemy table. It's difficult to discern the particular blend that he's questing after, as these glasses are too similar in size. He wouldn't risk taking removing them all either, as it's easy to lose these precious elixirs permanently if they plummet beneath the packsnow. Surely he'd never find them again, excavating the white tide is futile until this brackish period of weather passes.

As the minutes awkwardly trend to trifle, those moments exposed on the route spur their porter to question.

"Everythin' 'right back der?"

"Yeah! Yeah," William confirms.

"I've almost got it, just be patient!"

Now that there's a derived sense of urgency, the boy Jones sticks his face comically into his luggage, peering at the contents himself.

"Uh-oh," there seems to be a problem.

The sub-freezing temperatures have coerced the containers to rupture when knocked together, even the slightest nudge was enough to snap the fragile glass and allow their concoctions to seep free. Slushy, aromatic puddles of blue and lime green reside at the bottom of his bag, yet one vial remains intact.

"Yes, yes," he feverishly calls out, "I've got it!"

William marches intently to the front of the pack, ushering his gift to the brute: a prescription of warming fluid, identified by Glennitch's hand-scrawled signature on the side. Popping the cork induces noxious fumes, cautioning Korralack the Kable to second-guess this sudden idea.

"Seems da-dah-dangerous, don't know how I feels 'bout puttin' chemicals in muh body. And say, ye found dis, where exactly? 'Bandoned labra-labor-atory?"

"Oh you big baby," Lena chides, scolding him from the rear of the caravan.

"What have you got to lose?"

Compared to all the other vibrant brews, William presents a grey liquid, almost as if this potion has exceeded well-past its expiration date.

"*Hmm,* I guess if it'll 'elp…"

The brute tilts his head back in reception, allowing the boy Jones to pour the brew right down his gullet.

"Woah. Woah!"

He hollers bluntly, acting as if he just swallowed a fyrecracker. The effects of this solution are nigh-instantaneous, it must have been imbued with magik. Korralack shakes his head in dubious denial, there's an immediate scorching in his throat, reminding the brute of drinking at the tavern, competing with fellow yeomen over shots of Whitewater Moonshine- thank goodness he can stand the heat.

"I can feels ah tah-tinglin' sensation in muh 'ands. Does dat mean it's workin'?"

William is distracted by hearing whispers on the wind, enough to warrant concern from those considered natural. No one else appears to heed these vocal recitals, straying in contempt of strange happenstances. Maybe the instrument is quaint in origin, and Mandel is modestly mumbling in his sleep. Regardless, Korralack the Kable's endless march involves slugging through deluge, fending-off lofty bulwarks of packsnow, which loosen, slide around their battering ram, and crash into those trekking at his rear. This latest torrent of white tide rips into the boy Jones with such ruinous resolve that it dredges those hostile memories, such as those faints of his childhood crush breaking-up with him. His abdomen reconciles from most of the collision, twisting from the ferocity clout. As William recovers from a venomous sting and cold shoulder, wincing at the scree held secretly captive within, he can feel an extra decisive tug.

"Quit yer whinin'," an earnest lad spits, "won't ya Mug? Tell me what you want 'ready." The boy Jones complains to the presence behind him, only to realize that it isn't the gambler playing these games and pulling at his arm.

"Nah no, no-no! There's a gah-gah ghost!"

"By jove!"

"Oh woe, the gods 'ave cursed us! This is truly the end," cries Morbin Evershade, compelled by an understandably profound fear of the undead.

William flips around to receive the stress of a haunt, some cruelly transparent and teal human outline. The illusion remains quite stationary, fading and periodically dashing in place, producing a wispy, staticky image. Eventually the unanticipated visitor stabilizes, render in full view of the townspeople.

It has the outward demeanor of a wicker, adorned by pelted garbs in the pursuit of game animals. At the cold-caller's side is a specialty recurve bow, flattered by beautiful limbs of yellow-white birch, and a particular bronze seal dangling from that bottom notch, the paraphernalia of prominent Bannermane. Other than a divisive thin strand of burgundy across the figure's neckline, all those more intricate details appear to meld together. The longer it relays, the colder the air in their vicinity becomes. The presence seems to disturb the environment around it, suppressing the permafrost in an additional layer of icy rime. Every breath released by the company funnels into cohorts of mists, goading skin to raise in copious goosebumps, aligning those hairs on end, searing fragile dermis for this otherworldly appearance.

The geist raises both arms above its head, pattern to a frightening nightmare, though at the height of the townspeoples' fears, it can't keep up the charade and actually stifles a crass chortle. Unfortunately, this entrance is less than grand, and the expressions that crosses William's mug signifies that they don't recognize this newcomer at all. The pale imitation of a man crudely begs a question.

"Do ye folks 'ave any idea who I am?"

Jane announces out in spite, protesting, "Course not, yer dead! Why should we have any idea who you are?"

It throttles hot air through its nostrils with animosity.

"'Cause y'all are totin' 'round mah stuff. Nah betta than ah bunch o' lootas, I say!"

When the spirit exclaims this bitter retort, it momentarily flickers in place, entering a state of temporary flux.

"Calm, calm," it orates, resting two arms firmly across the chest.

"It's okay, tis fine."

"Glenn?" Contests William, who still rues over the forfeit of bestowing heartfelt goodbye, then those feelings of remorse are immediately dashed.

The spirit attests, "Nah-no, the otha one!"

"Rylie?"

"Ye dingus. Ye absolute fool. Are ya serious? Jeremiah, tis me, Jeremiah Anders."

"Wait, yer *thee* Jeremiah Anders? Like, all 'long?"

"Aye, that one n' only. I'm still kickin' 'cause does fell beasts can't rid me dat easy. Dat, n' ye still 'ave mah journal."

"But ye looks- so-so different. Young n' missin' yer whiskas. What 'appened tah all does wrinkles, n' why are ye speakin' correctly- or, betta den usual, like dat o' ah learned man? Dot ye were ah loonie this whole time."

"Kinda, in ah way. Been cursed for years 'pon years wit plight o' da mind. Ah twisted tongue dat denied me mah authenticity, keepin' me dazed n' confused so dat I couldn't speak in nothin' but senseless riddles. Since I 'ave nah need o' brain nor body any longa- dis is mah true state."

After making address, the spirit of Jeremiah Anders turns to the cliffside, staring over yonder and the entirety of the basin. This cold-caller can sight the Oestergaard's marvels from here, a recognizable sight, as this is his corridor.

"I've traveled dees many sights n' scenes 'fore, n' wuld've appeared tah 'elp earl-yah, but I'm ah lil' limited in dat aspect. Geists must remain placid. Emotions test da connection, lest dey evaporate and lose der tetha tah da mortal plane. Those zealots in Clan Alderman summon spirits tah do der battles. Impervious tah mortal blows, they'll do ah few minutes o' damage 'fore losin' their anchor. I've conjured dees recent hours as ye tend approach towards ah ley line. Think o' it as sum sort of spiritual nexus. That, n' ye 'ave mah journal, ah personal effect so meticulously wrought from passion. As long as it 'xists, I cannot pass tah dah domain of da Underworld. I need ye tah burn it, n' I may reach does Gilded Gates o' Guldourame."

"Destroy it? Don't ye dare. We can't go n' forfeit in fava o' danga, n' part with such ah priceless treasure," condemns Edmund Redmyne.

"The information ye writ in these pages aid our quest westerly. These stories shall see us through."

"Fair 'nough, wicka. Yer awfully bold, I'll give ya dat. Limbo ain't too bad anyhow, lot betta den dwellin' out 'ere in da cold. 'Ave ye gotten ta da passages 'bout thundrills n' tundra terrahs yet? Curse does saba-rattlin' tusks, dey really tanned mah 'ide."

The boy Jones' curiosity is piqued by that reference.

"Limbo, where's that? Tell mah more."

Jeremiah chirps in reprisal, realizing that he has unintentionally hooked William's interests, and tries to let him off with some obscure divine law.

"Oh lad, now dat's somethin' I can't divulge. Celestial affairs ain't really mah jurisdiction. Think death is bad, I culd get in real trouble! I've appeared today tah offa congratulations in makin' it dis far. There's ah mystic shrine 'head, mah favorite tah bid respite. Savor da pews n' stay 'while. Tissa safe place in da hands o' ah friend. N' as ye know, use mah journal wisely."

With those few fleeting pieces of advice, Jeremiah Anders, renowned author, keeper of the wilds, bids adieu and vanishes in thrashing mist.

Following the fellowship's brief stint of bewilderment at the curing of their local nutcase, Korralack bellows for action.

"Well ye 'eard da man- err, geist 'e seems tah be. Time tuh move out!"

With a dose of newfound confidence, those vagabonds surge forward, their every step propelled by a sense of divine responsibility. The subtleness of dawn's early reams of spice bleed into tints of ivory, the evident aura of afternoon sun, coaxing this dismal and dreary wasteland into its signature colorless glow. This scene is oddly reminiscent of that landscape painting from Tom-Tom's auditorium, a color palette that beautifully blends together.

Spurred by the faults of iconic sins, the firmament twists the cliffside path northernly to the rim of glacier, shifting upwards in a presumed flight of stairs, indicating that this is the last leg of their campaign- at least, the final hurdle so far, as there will always be obstacles, weaving another, more grand adventure the next time around. As those rasping edges of the edifice loom larger, and their company maneuvers closer, so much so that they can recognize an approach in the destination ahead, a dull landing molded into the fringes of the glacier.

This emerging tract presents a captivatingly hewn monument, rearing to the height of five men, or fifteen stout gremlins if anyone is keeping track. This is a shrine fit for cosmic icons, secluded in the remote ranges so that only their most dedicated pioneers could possibly reach it.

Holy pilgrimages are full of harsh truths, because sovereigns of kingdom come wouldn't merely reward the daring. Certain virtues are tempered in the heat of an expedition, encouraging vagabonds to demonstrate those outstanding qualities that divines uphold: chivalry, conviction, and morality. Plus, Jeremiah's recommendation undoubtedly boost their favor.

The stele lying before them has been carved in a mammoth-sized slab of obsidian, not in any obscenely grand gestures. It depicts a modest etching, some masked, cryptic being folding elements of rubble, rapidly solidifying ripples of water, and arcs of electricity upon themselves, the latter of which coursing through the experiment, preventing the experiment held between the statue's hands from freezing in a catastrophic mass.

Of course, rather than gawk in its glory, William humors thoughts about the celestials. Who would chisel this essence on the bleeding edge of the frontier? Further than, actually- no, definitely a distance of a league or two. Playing with those pyramids on the outskirts of Lucy's Isle, the boy Jones appreciates wyrdness because he's seen a thing or two.

A mound of snow shuffles upon their arrival, almost as if natural reacts in alarm. William stifles their animosity with the palm of his hand, reminding the traveling troop that Jeremiah foretold honest company, and that they're in good hands.

Floundering from his secret hideout beneath the packsnow, a divining rod breaks through the surface of blanketing white tide, woven from the fibers of dried shrub husk and spice root. Roving far from mild-taste society, this wandering mystic has been following their adventures for the better part of the day, that type of person who worships elder gods and frontier spirits, follower of the world pillar. Strangely enough, they profess a certain lack of fleece and fur, instead sporting a pair of slacked shorts, fox fur-lined boots and a generous bounty of body hair. Every inch of their skin is covered in professionally-prescribed, prophetic painted runes, protected by their faith in a lord of order.

Isolated from those furthest frontier settlements and realms of men, this far-flung pilgrim appears skewed in the social department, and it becomes immediately apparent that they have a difficulty communicating. The rattlesnake staff this shaman brandishes is their coping mechanism, an artifact of power to clamor at those creatures wishing him ill-harm, and cradle when anxious, keeping those gemstone-loving Bannermane and Boar's Band highwaymen at bay. This wild man thrusts his rod into the air, and brings it down in a calamitous fury.

"I Pithee Jones, haggar o' big country."

After his introduction, he pauses without notice, instead lending his ear to the firmament and gawking at the sky. His absence has undoubtedly derived speech impediments, and whenever this bushwhacked almsgibbah utters language, he tests their comprehension. In his isolated hinterland culture, portraying a smile is an ultimate act of pride, presenting intent to do harm. Truly, there must be an easier way, so the mystic attempts to illustrate his every emotion by stating them outright, beginning with, "Kind words, mighty god'ead instructs aid tah journey. Stars 'pon ya. Earned praise!"

The boy Jones is stupefied, riddled in disbelief. This mystic isn't dull in any shape of the word, their broken vocabulary arises because they're unsure on how exactly to convey themselves to strangers. Under siege at the whims of eldritch powers, William cares not for currying favor, and proposes for the hermit to conjure some sort of frontier medicine to aid Mandel.

He petitions assistance, "Can ye 'elp mah friend? 'E has been taken o'ver by ah spirit. Left 'is frame in foul state."

"Assay, yes-yes. See dat lord taken dis vessel. Shirk ravaged bodies for somethin' fresh. I filled with envy. Can aid! Aye, certainly. Follow."

Morbin trots closer, determined to get a look of this living relic.

"I'm ah bit o' skeptic meself- tickle the thought, considerin' faith, nature law n' the World Pillar," he probes, "-can't 'elp myself. So which god are ye aligned with?"

The widow is bewildered by Morbin's insensitively-inclined prod.

"How dare you? That's not nearly an appropriate thing to ask!"

"What? Can't blame ah guy for tryin'. Need tah figure out which figure tuh pray, forgive mah sins n' whatnot, whenever I'm close tah reachin' the brink o' death."

This eccentric takes awhile to muster perspective, as tongues aren't always in the habit of professing the mind's ego, and elaborates to the vigorous twitching of the rattlesnake staff.

"God'ead sees all, god'ead 'ear all, dis der domain as Lord of Earth n' Stone."

Pithee Jones merrily trots towards the monolith, listing his god's prowess.

"Dat immortal presides o'er staves, protective circles, runes, an weatha. Riposte, speaks tah mah now. Ye can receive does boons too. Without devotin' yerself tah service, da god'ead's blessin' cannot perfect. Dees abja- abjure-abjuration spells, not absolute salvation."

"Where is yer- umm, lord now?"

"Everywhere n' everytin' all at once. Mortals can't conceive their presence. Surprise n' tink o' dem as princes lyin' elsewhere, beyond dat horizon, tamin' der 'omestead 'mong celestial wildaness. Git hungry too. Nourished by chaos, n' thwarted bittit. Fear dem fell forces spillin' intah 'ere. Blackberry wintahs, red skies, auroras n' blood glacias- signs of fell. Dat worst yet tuh come. Menacin' mah masta's paradise. Der enemy gotten stronger, more darin.'"

Balthus, William and Morbin are enthralled, and rush to keep pace with this philanthropist of weather and stone, completely fascinated by real conversation of the divines, and not the prayer pleas that Jerome peddles. This dialogue might finally shed light on some harsh truths, and the reality of their trek inside the Antlers of the Earth, all in an effort to reach the sanctuaries of Clan Marius. A majority of these vagabonds apathetically string along, roused by Edmund's encouragement.

"Follow that priest. Looks like 'e 'as ah bit o' campfire goin.'"

Although they dwell slightly out of earshot of their mystic guide, departing the bare furnishings of Ander's Route and filing into the clearing. This haggar escorts them closer to the monolith, guiding their hand towards a pedestal, the locus of this shrine: the husk of a lantern, also carved out of purely-ironed, soot-black obsidian, with a red candle in the roomy middle. He compels them further, eluding to the fact that, "Dis why dey search for allies. Famil-yahs 'mong us. Does willin' tah wield der sacred bannahs standard. Shed bodily bugbears. Rejoice n' touch da shrine for blessin'. Receive boon 'pon der behalf."

While the learned man and boy Jones deduct the logical reasonings of dedicating themselves towards beings as ancient as time, Morbin considers the ritual without much thought, eager to delve into the foundations of the World Pillar no matter its cost.

The amateur archaeologist screams when the lantern sculpture bursts with his subtle touch, suddenly springing into a raging inferno, engulfing his every digit in a saturation of arcane energy. This incident spurs the remainder of their company to crowd, fraught at their friend in flames, but egging for relief from the hoarfrost.

Morbin expels confounded tears of joy upon discovering that this is completely a visual spectacle, that the blaze doesn't actually burn him, and he lingers unharmed. Upon keeping his palm immersed in the whirling flames, his efforts are evidently rewarded when a faint, indigo stave appears, dotting the exterior of fist, materializing right beneath the knuckles. These are no mere doodles, they are scrawls gifted to champions of moral code, those whom trust in the darkest of times, even if Morbin Evershade isn't exactly brimming with these defining qualities.

Brimming with bewilderment, Balthus determines that he shall be the next person to test his valor. Korralack the Kable gradually lingers near, marching in the wake of everyone else, lumbering fastidiously with Mandel fast-asleep, cushioned atop his burly forearm.

He arrives at the rear of the crowd, and announces, "Seems ah lil' dangerous, don't ye tink?"

With this declaration, Pithee snakes through his audience so that he may rattle his staff at this negligent disposition. Countless pebbles funnel and dash inside the hollowed fiber tube, gently striking at metal rings also pinned inside the instrument. These soft marble beads *clack-clack, thunk-thunk* upon the thousands, generating a rolling, lustrous noise reminiscent to the trickle of water, urging Korralack to deem opinions solely to himself. This chime wakens the cordwainer from his stupor, quietly leering towards the religious celebration, eyes bathed in violent throes of luminance from the blazing shrine.

"Oh, ya big baby," Balthus crassly provokes.

"Tis naught but an illusion."

The mystic retreats to the ambience of the flame, advising his company that, "Nah dedication, don't feel pained. Dis prayah sorts, askin' for favor den seein' if lord will 'spond."

Consecrated by a brand-new crest which wraps around the learned man's wrist, Edmund is also considering this endeavor, as a blessing couldn't hurt their chances. They're battling the wild winds and impossible odds, these vagabonds will need every gift at their disposal.

"Say, looks odd. Wouldn't normally consider it, but given the circumstances… 'eh."

William ventures forth, guided by the wickerwalker's swift promotion over the matter, then Mug Maxwell in turn, who is willing to stake on this gambit too. Eventually these two are followed by Jerome and unexpectingly enough, Rochester, who winds their eyelids tight when thrusting his hand into the lantern. This wainwright swivels his head over the right shoulder, snaking away, fearing for their life should he be the unlucky fool that gets seared. Libby and Bids are the last to put their hands to the beacon, and receive their blessing in earnest. They reach towards the bonfire together, whispering some fleet-footed surprises to one another.

"Oh, what ah rush!"

Lena and Korralack elect to overlook these graces, deeming nefarious means. While these two have always been wary of anything acutely devotional, they choose to forfeit this boon in fear of traditional frontier superstitions, that cultivating one divine could put them at odds with the entire pantheon.

Now that they've received their patron's charity, indulging in just another pit-stop in this never-ending ride of despair, it's coincidently time to part ways. Their voyage to White Cliffs is relatively uncharted, the campaign arduous and the weeks long. They should not dally and waste daylight.

The wickerwalker shames the fellowship, lamenting rest among the aspiration of rescue. He inquires to their almsgibbah and his knowledge of these outer worlds, inquiring if his divine icon has ever shared the valuable wisdom of cartography.

Edmund relays their brief backstory, that this is no mere pilgrimage, and these vagabonds can't simply return the way whence they came. Their caravan must endure, and reach the lands of acropoli, mountain men and whistlers, somewhere on the opposing side of the glacier.

Pithee's monolith coincidently faces a trench, some gaping crevice that bears alarm, threatening to swallow them whole. Upon first glance, it bars teeth by commanding an arsenal of daggers, the abrupt separation of ice, and howls corroding wind. William knows exactly where this corridor will direct them, and exerts a dreary *sigh*. Then their shaman does what is expected, pointing to that particular glacier as entrance to the Antlers of the Earth.

This confirmation prompts their party into inevitable *groans*. Without much choice, they rally along fits of disheartened gloom, marching headlong towards the yawning abyss, advancing at a snail's pace. What is with this troop's uncanny tendency for being coerced into tunnels?

"I regret where we part ways. Know dat I'll be watchin'. Dees are 'allowed grounds, true tah da spirits, for all dat da permafrost burdens holy. Take dees favors n' despair."

For those not attuned to patience, in the urgency to overcome this next snag in their trek, no one but that tender-hearted William notices that Libby and Bids Warder dawdle behind. The pair of sisters slink around the shrine, and William eavesdrops on their affairs, originally anticipating some nefarious motivations. Instead of vandalism, raging against the god whom is doing nothing, the older sibling kneels at the foot of the monolith, lantern statue and diminishing flame.

If this nexus may ferry Jeremiah's essence back from the realm of dead, then perchance of seance, and they can communicate with their dearly departed sister. Regardless, it's a fool's errand to summon the spirit of their triplet, as the immortals do not fancy desires of those lesser.

In this failure, Libby suffers the melancholy, letting the frost fester and feed off her woe. She flounders onto her knees, sinking into a depression of packsnow, instigating each limb to become numb and wither. The eldest sister prepares a memorial song, imposing their solace from the traveling troop of vagabonds, fostering some safe distance from their judgements. Her vocal cords twang, generating a solemn and monotonous melody, elegance that convey overwhelming sadness and guilt.

A goose this spring
All lonely and slow,
Staring at its reflection
Through the pale window.

Some range past shore
Tracking this fowl bronco.
As whelps that buckle ice,
Are left drifting below.

It is time to wake up,
Sis, as mum hollers home.
Time to wake up,
In fear that I must march alone.

"Tis nah luck, Libby. She-she's in ah betta place, after all. Kirby wouldn't show 'er face 'round 'ere if she's too busy livin', being locked away in paradise," beckons Bids to the wracked woman.

She drapes an arm around her sibling's neck, coaxing her to take a stand while those tears leave bitter, freezing impressions in their eyes, and they depart together, towards the migrating fellowship and partaking in their ceaseless struggle.

"Plus we were always ah pretty ugly lot, she's prolly cavorting 'round more handsome women."

XV

—

THROUGH THE LOOKING GLASS

The glacier is prehistoric, a primordial element that has been here thousands of years before the parades of men, looming as a walk through time. A caravan of townspeople trek alongside shores of rigid topography and frozen freshwater, inside the basin of a definitive u-shaped gulch, where the walls sway into icy bulwark, as if those curtains were slightly too long.

There is a distinctly profound lack of white, as snow doesn't funnel through these trenches. The hoarfrost that accumulates here lies strictly upon the glacial sheet, several hundred feet above, covering the crevasse they travel across in a thin layer of rime, as if they are peering at the surface from below, dwelling at the bottom of a pond. Down in these trenches, dim eyes adjust to a palette of few blues, and not much else, as if transcribed by a serially, uncreative painter.

The lighting strikes differently here, harshly permeating the ice sheet's excess to deliver an ominous, austere glow. Begrudgingly, this grand-gaffer of icebergs bides regal entourage, as the glacier is impeccable, free from any impurities, sporting an unconditional clear, milky blue as the prominent feature of glass. At the root and base of the ice sheet are effigies, natural creep and till derived from the grating aquatonic plates, arranged in certain crystalline compositions where just one cairn or idol commands the size of a bison's hoof.

These natural designs are shadowed by an uncontrollable, potent mist that hovers inches above the ground, binding those pioneers' boots in a permanent glaze of condensation. This surface coverage is nearly unshakable, and no matter how swiftly they stride through, returns to obscure useless swathes of dead soil. Ice sheets retain hundreds upon millions of pounds in water alone, and nonetheless prone to displacing entire of mountains and boulders, scouring any obstacles into fine-ground, silken black sand. The absence of permafrost here is overwhelming, every step is by contrast, a cushion, and William's gait sinks ever-so slightly in a manner most startling. What a one-of-a-kind opportunity, the boy Jones has never waltzed upon flooring so graceful, yet deadly. These tunnels and caverns could shift in a moment's notice, prompting their parade into the glacier akin to an unforeseen tomb, and signing their death warrant.

In the absence of an immortal's blessing, Mandel shudders in Korralack's firm grip.

"'Ey," he shouts at the brute, "still kickin'. Where are ye luggin' mah off tuh? I ain't dead yet."

Struggling to and fro, he asserts himself, and eventually wiggles out, plopping onto those frosted sandy grains. Upon impact, waves of chalky powder burst in every direction, showering that earnest company in splashes of ebony foam. When the cordwainer rises to attention, saluting the Boar's Band highwayman for his service, an abundance of sand slips inside Mandel's ensemble, causing him to stir and spray dust in defiance.

"I'm good on mah own, I swears it!"

If so, his recovery has been truly remarkable. In a span of less than six hours, his comrade is well-enough to take a stand, support himself on his own two legs once more. If it hadn't been for the timely intervention of the gods, his injuries would've certainly proven too severe. William finds himself asking, were willing to leave Mandel for dead? Are those divines so callous, throwing life and limb at the matter, willing to sacrifice one soul for the good of many, and just how many times will they press Haggerton in service?

The ceremonial changing of the guard coerces certain colors of dusk upon the brittle, frozen mass, and culminates evening irritation. They can hear the fortress of rime fissure, glacial ablation ushered by the solispyre's divert-your-eyes-or-go-blind-at-the-sight-of-it glow, cackling under its own weight. After suffering through the usual *ping-pang* and *sckrect* cacophony, these humbingings become part of the routine ambience, coupled with the echos of their casual conversations.

Their march is brisk, conveying a slight sense of urgency for finishing their quest, and certainly not under duress that the ice could shift and crush them nigh-instantaneously. One would expect megafauna and natives to be absent from the lack of vegetation, yet the channel ripens with the echos of animalistic bellows. They are rough, short and concise, like the beat of a drum. These voices rumble haphazardly into a junction before the, spreading into several corridors, who's to say where this actually originates from.

Courting a feeling of impending doom, Edmund points and gestures to those nearby crevices aligning with the corridor walls, beseeching those townspeople to take refuge with haste. Just as how humans inherently fear the dark because of those that lurk among it, those that shroud their true natures are worth hiding from.

As the cacophony draws closer, becoming inevitably imminent, in lieu of those cackling wolves they anticipate, their lobes are instead greeted by a wonderful chorus. The widow covertly glares at the wickerwalker in disapproval, shunning his over-protective habits. Edmund refuses to grant her the respect of wave, as this demeanor has kept them alive so far. He brushes past the notion of apologizing for success. As a veteran hunter, he must be right about quite a few things, able to steer clear of danger for the better part of a decade.

These tunes are ballads to vibe to, hollered aloud to the beat of marching feet, encouraging an audience to slam their right foot down, then their left foot alongside chants several seconds later. The company tap their feet to the shanties in reflex, subject to a cheery caterwaul, an unrestrained and lively raucous, clad by those boisterous attitudes. Their composition is exceptionally tumultuous, and William recoils to the cries at first, in fear that the cavern walls come crashing down.

> *Our mast is drawn, draggin' halyards low*
> *Weigh hey, roll and go!*
> *The course has been laid to the captain's tirade*
> *To be rollickin' randy dandy-oh!*
>
> *Heaving haul, oh heave away*
> *Weigh hey, roll and go!*
> *The boot's aboard and ould cord's been stored*
> *To be rollickin' randy dandy-oh!*

Breathe the break and swivel dees swells
Weigh hey, roll and go!
Warp the core on this poor ca-rack
To be rollickin' randy dandy-oh!

Heaving haul, oh heave away
Weigh hey, roll and go!
The boot's aboard and ould cord's been stored
To be rollickin' randy dandy-oh!

The bow quivers as these sheets are drawn
Weigh hey, roll and go!
Crackin' whip and the yells of don jon
To be rollickin' randy dandy-oh!

Heaving haul, oh heave away
Weigh hey, roll and go!
The boot's aboard and ould cord's been stored
To be rollickin' randy dandy-oh!

Libby Warder is the first townsperson to leave their temporary sanctuary, awfully keen to discover fellow breakneck connoisseurs: those navigators brave enough to venture beyond the ice sheet and Antlers of the Earth, unlike that passive Pithee Jones, favoring to hide amidst his frosted banks. A four-person squad circles the nearest bend, emerging into this hastily-shaped junction in no time at all. The source of this shanty is oddly human, no obvious mutations of any kind, and by all accounts normal. In her bold motion forward, others assemble as an impromptu audience to greet these partners in kind. The people are rightfully astounded, flabbergasted and shocked to stumble upon any other vagabonds dwelling here.

"Howzit," they blurt in more exclamation than actual question.

The burly figure amongst this compliment emits an honestly laughable expression, "*Yo-ba-udd-sun,* stow dem yelps. We dot dat we were da only ones!"

"Ye 'peer free from taint, travelas," he bawls out, rescinding a broad-tipped spear to his, which he emphasizes by slamming the butt of this mighty weapon rigidly into the sand. The mere mention of its influence causes William to wonder what taint exactly means.

"Only fair dat we introduce ourselves. I be dat man-at-large-n'-in-charge, Sturgeon da Huscarl, n' dees are mah fellas, Yeomen Braga, Bitte n' da esteemed Bludson Schaar."

As huntsmen convene over stately matters, the boy Jones is intrigued by finer details. These pioneers are dressed in the garb of all squall-dogs and Boar's Band. Wearing banded battering-rams, their iconic almond-shaped slits and steely eyeliner, then a formidable protrusion starting at the nose bridge, working its way around the rim of the helmet, towards a comical spike at the pinnacle of skullcap. The epitome of this armor is capstone by antlers, a pair of ram's horns or wings, denoting the types of game they specialize in trapping. That particular broadsider that introduced himself as their elder, Sturgeon's faceplate bathes his neckline in chain-mail, blanketing a stoic complexion and reaches of woven ginger hair. A signature staple of the tribe, this huscarl's pauldrons are also menacing, fashioned in animal skin to bulge-out like bulwark, descending into slick leather vambraces. Their chest is held firm by a girdle, withholding an array of butchery gear, armed to the teeth with daggers for piercing and mincing prey. Bison-hide bedrolls are strapped to the backs of their hips, making them overtly thick, giving a paunch impression.

The huscarl is an experienced wickerwalker himself, possessing a shield that has seen battle, clad in damage, clawed thoroughly by all manner of beasts big and small. Despite the normal wear and tear, the flamboyantly worn paint depicts the iconic hunting horn of Boar's Band, the same exact illustration from his family heirloom, causing William to vaguely clutch at his parents' locket.

Yeoman Braga has been hauling a distinguished sack over his shoulder, flaunting their collection of live lemmings. This pronounced bag of burlap emits frenzies of frantic, gutsy *screams* and *squeaks*. At this exposure, the pompous Bludson Schaar leans into William's ear, and cruelly admits that he's "more of a fish guy myself."

The elder shoos him away, scolding his laymen not to harass folk unfamiliar with their trails, at for this remaining season. They are questing return to their remote camp, where they'll bunker down, and drowsily stave-off effects of the barrowtide with fermented fruits and lots of brandy. Together, these four highwaymen form the entire population of Threshing: an isolated and detached Boar's Band outfit, in which Sturgeon is training them to become unprecedented trailblazers, more "stronga and betta den any Boar 'fore."

Normally, one might be lead to a certain assumption that this profound seclusion surmounts the need of basic decency, as it's fancy meeting anyone with manners out here, and yet, the huscarl is hammering traits into these new recruits, having them become exemplary in every shape and form. Braga and Bitte commence handshakes, showcasing their form, and that they're capable of polite introductions. This indulgent behavior of strangers doesn't keep Sturgeon from addressing obvious safety concerns. He criticizes the weirdly timid Korralack, not recognizing his face, but making note of his mangled cinnamon and hazel coat standards.

"Why are ye treadin' out all dis way? Are ye tired, abandonin' da creed, find fit o' retirin'?"

"I am Korralack da Kable, hailin' from da Razoredge, south o' dees craglands. Our camp split for oncomin' brack n' capstones. Dot I try portin' mah weight as ah caravanhand, liftin' all dem barrels and whatnot."

"So be it, Kable. Won't voke yer bannah, make sure dat question won't rise 'gen. Why don't ye venture tah Threshin' with us? 'Elp tend camp, and we'll give space tuh rest ya 'eads."

Korralack's eyes instinctively dot to meet Edmund's, searching for wisdom as the wickerwalker's shoulders shrug.

Caught in a five-path junction as daylight gradually winds to close and light begins to shutter, unsure of where these paths lead- all but one. It's as good of plan as any, they'll humbly accept this offer, as honest work has never threatened vagabonds. At worst, William imposes to Braga, polling if he'll need to crack and loosen lemming pelts as if interviewing for ward under an abattoir.

This Boar's Band yeoman chuckles to himself, convincing that frostnip-tinged nose and cheeks to crease to a degree. He's around William's age, actually all these yeomen are, rambunctious and rebellious as ever, the defining trait of all those who sire the title, boy Jones. Most young'uns who take up the mantle of Boar's Band tend to share the moniker of Fields, those abandoned, bastardized, illegitimate and orphaned children. Offspring of the frontier who best foster their passions when granted the opportunity to travel in any direction. Left to their own devices, urchins tend to one another, but always lack a few essential skills like modesty. They would much prefer to pilfer essentials from those deemed weaker. These laymen are people, not animals.

No matter the situation they've garnered in their live, morals are what separates humankind from a superiority complex. Wildlings such as these require elders to curt their rogue enthusiasm and knock heads, someone of discipline to iron out all those kinks, avoiding the competition provided from the larger bands of Razoredge, Thrashing- which is somehow different than Threshing, and those countless tribes in-between. Members of these crowds challenge one another to physical bouts, competitions designed to steal spoils, squabbles over food and loot; where the weakest are often bullied to remain the poorest, and become servants to the strong.

Here, under Sturgeon's creed, they are unique, acting akin to equals as proficient men-at-arms, facing the affairs of the Bannermane mercantiles and untamable wilderness together.

Sturgeon hopes to teach this lot those intrinsic morals, although such a formidable, learned man phrase would never grace his lips: "Modesty," he'd prefer to call it, often rambling that value should be derived from usefulness, not sheer strength, and grandstanding like the usual Boar ilk through presumptuous shows of superiority. The origin of Boar's Band fermented from the vagabond motto, a love affair proclaiming that 'everyone has their purpose, ye find it through 'ard work.'

Those residing in the Underdark desired to shake free from their reigns, from the bustling hub Urbana specifically, always choring for politicians deeming themselves powerful. These highwayman festered in the shadow of Clan Claremont's run-rampant and rugged militaristic views, taking to the surface out of spite for their superiors. Not unlike the Bannermane, these yeomen have escaped the roles society has placed on them, joining their huscarl's crusade to explore the world, without boundaries, limitations and responsibilities, curbed only by moral code.

Bitte proposes that the townspeople should considering joining them, punching Mug Maxwell in the arm as encouragement, actually goading him to wince, recoil, and tenderly massage his bicep afterwards. In a place where lifting hundred-pound fragments of ice is normal, these earnest lads possess otherworldly strength. Morbin Evershade is disgusted by the mention of physical labor, perhaps this rugged, outdoor lifestyle isn't for everyone.

The gambler finds himself brooding in retort, polling the highwaymen.

"What's the point o' Boar's Band if survival is yer daily motivation?"

"'Tis dangerous, for sure, 'specially with all dem disappearances out 'ere, but still we find our ways tuh thrive. I admire animals 'cause dey don't tink-just do, actin' on der instincts, not confined by da opinions o' othas," the meddlesome Bitte concludes.

She searches for another yeoman to chime in, and turns to face her brother Braga, elbowing the brute at his gut to conjure a response. "I just like huntin' hares, so…"

Bludson Schaar interrupts, conveying his two-cents and speaking with a sense of eloquence.

"I'll quote the bard and those tavern howlers smarter than me. Boar's Band is a grand escape from the daily dredges. Young'uns like myself, join-up to get away from thee ole homestead. I want to break-out and explore the territory, take a tour of freedom, not get all tied-up in some arranged marriage or workin' behind the costermonger's counter. Unlike the rest o' my family, I care nothing about my namesake. Take ah gander at the world 'fore I choose to settle-down for awhile- yeah, yeah! That's definitely the life for me."

William grows more and more enticed at the thought of yeomen adventures. His parents, Concorde and Emery Walder, were obviously connected to the roving Boar's Band tribes. There must have been a reason for them to hide their lifestyle, and that must be it: to avoid having him run away from home too early, forsaking their ole chap-pop and meema like them.

"'Course," the earnest lad continues, "most decide to leave sooner or later- dangerous work really. Ready to find some love and settle down. Others, like stoic Sturge there, live their whole live explorin', becomin' elders, or as we call 'em, huscarls. What brings ye out this way, anyhow?"

The boy Jones asks on his own behalf, not realizing that Bludson was actually inquiring about their company as a whole. So when William innocently affirms that, "I've been campaignin' the Mad River from Lucky's Isle, through the Ozarks, n' o'ver tah the Junction. Travelin' wherever those caravans n' sleds take mah."

Bludson shies and ponders polling again, yet responds wholeheartedly.

"Oh man, you are missing out. Need to stride way to Bonaventure as soon as possible, lots to spy and marvel at. I'm from Century City originally, family were all charcoal burners, so I wasn't every 'round any merchant vessels. All three of us had a bid on a sailin' ship, that's how we first met. Now, this wasn't know schooner nor yacht either, this was a flagship. The largest barge that ever graced the white tide, her majesty's merchant vessel, the HMMV March Fettinger, named after the man-of-the-hour himself. A behemoth, first-of-its-kind design. 'Course, most urchins straight-out of Bonaventure have the pleasure to serve the biggest and the best Sauder ship, and we were her A-B-Cs, the able-bodied crew. 'Tween the fore, main and mizzin masts, there were sixteen sails altogether, triangular to avoid gettin' gutted down the belly where the drapes tend to rip, 'cause this ship was so large. In fact, so, so large, it could shore the worst gales this side of the northeast has to offer. They had me towin' cable all the way up the riggin', and I had to hang on for dear life when we struck o'ver a rocky outcrop once or twice. Lookin' back on it, sure they did it on purpose tah toy with me. When it caught wind, boy did that masterpiece glide."

Sturgeon scolds the member of his band for presenting the most lip. Prodding at the boy, "Schaar, ye done ante-anti-antagonizin' our guests yet?"

"Nah sir, not yet sir," yells the earnest lad at the top of his voice, demonstrating his adept skills as a bosun.

The huscarl barks back, "'Ow come ye mentioned riggin' 'thout breakin' intah 'notha singin' fit? Yer da lively one, yow-man. 'Fraid at dis rate, sum o' does quiet ones will start tah stare at der feet n' wanda off. We've lost too many dis way, so dontcha keep 'em bored. Start 'notha shanty. Dat ders an orda, I think we're getting ah lil' Sick of the Sway."

"Aye, aye. I hear ya big boss!"

A moment later, Bludson's nose crinkles and those whiskers wrapping around his throat tighten to produce a guttural, nasally choke and the hacking of phlegm.

Ack-ack-ptui.

Ensuring that his vocal cords are nice and shrill for his vocal conquest, he blares through the icy domain like a siren.

These men haul yards, tow rigging, and anchor,
Sailing on some rotten tub, ripe with rancor.

The other three Boar's Band troopers explosively holler in symphony, boosting Bludson's sour tune.

And we whittle at the day,
Whittle at the day,
Whittle at the day,
'Till we get away.

Spend all day spreadin' track-talk and rumors,
A spot of laughs, hopeful humor.
And we whittle at the day,
Whittle at the day,
Whittle at the day,

'Till we get away.

This voyage is long, our trek is slow,
The mist cause crew to rub elbow.
And we whittle at the day,
Whittle at the day,
Whittle at the day,
'Till we get away.

Windy weather boys- squall ahoy,
Dem weather kicked us like plastic toys.
And we whittle at the day,
Whittle at the day,
Whittle at the day,
'Till we get away.

Cleave, clear, and cast-way rime,
Brushing sleet, lest afford brig-time.
And we whittle at the day,
Whittle at the day,
Whittle at the day,
'Till we get away.

Swing, miss, then spot sore thumb,
What to-do when ye body's gon' numb?
And we whittle at the day,
Whittle at the day,
Whittle at the day,
'Till we get away.

Duckin' 'neath hatch by blastin' cap,
Striking nether beam, 'nother mishap.
And we whittle at the day,
Whittle at the day,
Whittle at the day,
'Till we get away.

Shy timber creaks spring things rarely seen,
Strung together with tack, twine, tween.

And we whittle at the day,
Whittle at the day,
Whittle at the day.
'Till we get away.

No provisions or packstuffs, a famished lot,
Face a emptied galley, and the cook's distraught.
And we whittle at the day,
Whittle at the day,
Whittle at the day,
'Till we get away.

Sailor temper goldband sincerity,
Meekly awaitin' their thrice months' charity.
And we whittle at the day,
Whittle at the day,
Whittle at the day,
'Till we get away.

This ditty occupies their time, tempering their robust appetites and stomachs, forgoing the drudgeries of another cruel march as they finally approach camp. At the foremost center of the canyon, is an intimidating, shiny distraction, blocking their advances to the point where they'll need to shimmy around the blockade simply to enter the grotto. In their presence is a massive single-person sled which Sturgeon introduces as their Boar Choppa, giving them a brief excavation lesson of how they acquired parts.

Instead of a set of oars or small schooner sail, the stainless steel frame of an ancient motorcycle has been mounted upon a fifteen-foot bow and flattened sled runners. The innards of this machine have been long-removed, and replaced in spirit by a mechanical blends of instruments: the chassis has been drilled so thoroughly that every hole catches the wind, its main spotlight has been replaced by a horn for bellowing wildly into, wheel rims exchanged with drum linings to rail against, handlebars are hollow to clang against with batons for reverb, and sleigh bells dangle freely as roiling cacophony, all in the effort to produce a roar resembling the rumble of an engine.

There is one purpose of a chopper, and that's to show-off. It exists as a trophy, deliberately exhibited and flaunted towards numerous roving gangs.

The person who arranges the most ornaments during their lulls of winter season has the pleasure of a bloomtide debut tour, riding the sled from their garage inside the Antlers of this Earth, past the monument, Ander's Route- or, whatever the Bannermane are calling it this year, coasting right-over the wicked craglands and onto the lake residing outside Mad River Junction as Threshing's prominent breakneck-connoisseur.

This is their seasonal barrowtide camp, a burrow of sorts, where they'll hinder the effects of the cascading storms, then descend down the glacial face when the sutler's paradise picking is just right. Bitte's has already prescribed a list of her suggestions for their chopper, eager to convert the mufflers into an assembly of chimes guaranteed to turn heads. She's the innovator of the lot, likely to partake in the first joyride onto the Oestergaard when they begin judging, except every member of their tribe typically votes for themself, and the last person left arguing wins.

Boar's Band is the unconventional balance to Bannermane greed. As a select few amass a majority of wealth on the frontier, certain gangs of brutes take to 'redistributing beaucoup denaros,' pilfering those merchant caravans of coaches and letting loose the spoils of the promised land. Highwaymen such as this Threshing company are thieves indeed, although smaller bands steal scarce amounts sustain their travels, give or take the occasional embellishment of jewelry. It's after the heist when earnest lads must worry, as those who stir at the slightest notion of loot are familiar to infighting.

They'll glue horns to their ears, listening steadily across these flatlands for any aspirations of activity. The greater the spoils, the more highwayman are drawn to the raid, typically attracting a platoon of Bannermane calvary in their own right, confirmation to frontier pirates that they purloin from magistrate purses and not the pouches of working men. There are laws to their creed, especially against killing. However, these highwaymen fashion no qualms from robbing one another, and often go out of the way whenever the opportunity presents itself, humiliating their fellow Boar's Band members by disrespecting their sleds. That's why the Boar Choppa is so extravagant and over-the-top, it's the culmination of their status.

Their grotto is stunning, like a bubble formed under the water, with the ice so perfect and completely clear of debris. When the weather is perfect, wannabes-raiders may even spy upon the flatlands below. They're in the looking glass now, and befit with incredible wonder.

Sturgeon commands hike to this encampment once a year, a route so remote, perilous and physical encapsulating, they're grateful of such.

No one would be daring enough to poach their loot, having voyaged the entirety of Ander's Route, not taking any shortcuts through the warrens, leaves any outlaw worse for wear.

The nosy Bitte ushers them to take seat in an adjacent alcove, a few steps from the entrance, circumnavigating the obvious outline of a fire pit. As the huscarl kindles flame and tends to the razing pyre, smoke billows towards the ceiling, flowing through a canal they've bored for ventilation. Balthus extends his appreciation, commending their hinterland's ingenuity, that the heat of the fire melted just enough ice to craft their perfectly portioned seating arrangements.

As the grotto becomes indistinguishable from a sauna, they're able to remove their coats and fleeces, a concept they haven't been able to entertain in a fortnight. While their adventure in the warrens was temperate, they couldn't shake the sentiment of cold shoulders during the expedition. William unfastens the few buttons that render his outermost wrappings shut, sliding off a heavy garment from each arm, and tossing it, along with his personal knapsack, onto the mucky pile of clothing positioned in a bordering nook.

The boy Jones is infatuated at the opportunity to remove such weight from his shoulders, but that was the last liner, a tarp that kept custody over his unique stench, mulling the spice of body odors and sweat. Fortunately the charring of timber disguises this cauldron of pestilence. He drops to his feet, believing himself insane as the temperature approaches balmy and heat becomes bearable, but nowhere close to the excruciating atmosphere inside a steaming bathhouse.

The icy glaze nearby loosens into thick trickles of water, accumulating in a gutter so meticulously dug into the floor, hastening the flow of liquid through the entryway, past the chopper, and into the freezing ravine.

While these three yeomen may be shy in age, even called children by clerks who reside behind a desk, they are expert wickers whose skills at parting critter meat, entrails and lemming fur are second to none. They take the leave of two dozen or so rodents in short work, comprising ingredients into perfectly roasted rodent-on-a-stick or additions to stew. Sturgeon is critical to taste, and prepares a pot of stock with rabbit bones, funneling cups of water from their demesne of melting rime. Lena has been assessing their stockpile, and despite her best efforts against glazed carrots, offers to share supplies to nurture camaraderie, specifically the party's remaining can of dandy root, an endeavor that will surely expose the watering hole's ambient flavor.

Braga is persuaded to rouse the celebration, popping the corks for several glasses of Pillager's Porridge and a burgundy bottle of Whitewater Creedance Moonshine, leading to a brief jubilee. Edmund scoffs at this rare prospect that has presented itself, the capstone of a wild day that retires with full stomachs and dull minds. The blending of lemming potpourri wasn't nearly as appetizing as expected, maybe having something to do with how the mixture hadn't been given the dedicated time to properly blend, resulting in a lean, but nonetheless gamy and deliciously minced meat.

Their supper isn't needlessly complex, an honest portion of soup with a few rogue additions have resulted in an all-around, hearty meal. An intoxicating, clear liquor wholly compliments this dish, stimulating stupor from their stomachs, cajoling upwards and draping as fog amid the mind.

The cordwainer rest his head against William's shoulder for a restful evening, and in sequence, the boy Jones relaxes his head upon Korralack's bedrolls for their venture. This operation goes so on, and so forth: heads rest on laps, arms, and abdomens, all tuckered-out around the dwindling abode's campfire for a bit of rest, until the sequence ends with Jerome, who flicks Rochester's ear in denial, demanding that he doesn't need anyone to lean-on, and nor should they. It's a tight squeeze, as no-one may exactly lay down in this tight-fitting space, but perfect for vagabonds.

The cairnmire moon inspects these townspeople inside their glass prison, captives who easily drift into slumber.

Mandel is often plagued by visions in the middle of the night, and until now, these dreams haven't been more than nightmares and nuisances, waking in a sudden jolt or cursing under his breath with both eyelids still clasp shut. However, the elders of Boar's Band know better, and recognize the foul stench of chaos immediately. William awakes to an argument during the deepest tinges of twilight, and is provoked into a stereotypical yawn. He contemplates the source of this distraction, as a majority of their party is still fast asleep, sore by the burdens of the hike before.

For whatever reason, Sturgeon hurls barbs as Edmund doubtlessly leaps to the cordwainer's defense, quarreling on his behalf.

"-what would ye 'ave o' me?"

"Leave!"

This demand toys with the wickerwalker, who wonders if he heard the Boar's Band elder right, "Leave?"

"Why yea, dat's ah novel idea. I'm very fond o' it meself," the huscarl sarcastically chides.

"Dis ain't merely ah matta of imaginations and 'allucinations. Dreams are rare app-'appenstance. If ye 'aving nightmares, ya 'ready been undah der thumb, n' da influence o' fell."

He points directly at Edmund Redmyne, then the remainder of their company.

"Chances are ye soon will be too, 'em fish stink from da 'ead down. I wus on da fence when y'all neglected ta mention dat tome dat pygmy 'as been totin'. Magik is nothin' tah be trifled wit, ders ah reason why Boar's Band 'as laws angst it. Dees pawns attract fell forces, can't be 'avin' those monstas 'ere, not when I'm woefully unprepared. Dis mah refuge, muh sanctuary only, n' shan't share none of it! Da road is callin', ye must leave n' lallygag elsewhere. Go on, git. Retrieve yer boy wit 'aste n' get outta 'ere."

The wickerwalker may only deject a *sigh* towards this antagonistic onslaught.

"It sounds like yer mind's made-up, so I won't beg for petition 'gainst it. Wait though, 'fore ye feed us tah the wolves. Alas, I make plea o' ya, as ye've already shown that sliver o' 'ospitality."

Edmund makes headway towards the boy Jones, leaning into William whom startles himself upon discovering the earnest lad lying awake, and snatches Jeremiah's notebook from his fleece. The two have certainly gotten into a dramatic contest, drawing disrespect into one another.

"At least advise these journal maps. I'll 'ave the boy Jones stir the othas n' shift them intah gear. Right, 'Liam?"

The earnest lad promptly nods with concern, rapping at Mandel's arm to secure him as an accomplice. These two certifiable savants mastermind a campaign to wake their fellows, gently grappling at their sleeves, slapping hands and shaking their fellow caravanhands to rise with the lark. He goes to rouse the ruffian Libby Warder from slumber when her eyelids flicker in an instant, startling him. She snaps into action, and thereafter punches her sister violently in the thigh which also jostles her into consciousness.

Bids infuriatingly mumbles, "What, why'd ye wake mah up so early? Tis not even noon."

Korralack proves a more difficult endeavor until Calamity Jane brashly slaps her gloves alongside his cheek. Those brethren Braga, Bitte and Bludson Schaar don't feel particularly fond over exiling a fellow member of Boar's Band, so the three yeomen isolate themselves further inside the grotto, that way they mustn't tender penalties or harsh truths. Strangely enough, they retreat in their own alcoves so punctiliously, as if they have practiced, it's honestly conceivable that this sort of situation has happened before.

The townspeople unleash *groans* during these wee hours of the morning, the fret of having to retrieve their gear so haphazardly piled together. As the ice and snow that dampened their jackets has melted but never dried, every article of clothing is a disastrous, sopping mess. They have to dress each other for a full fifteen minutes before they can defeatedly drag their heels and finally file outside.

Within the innards of the ice sheet, huddled around the chopper, Sturgeon peers at the handy charts presented in the notebook. The wickerwalker relays a vital piece of information, that the radio mast has toppled, burying the nether portions of Ander's Route with unfathomable amounts of frosty flakes.

The highwaymen complains, "'Course ye 'ad to go n' break it. Who's tah say we can come back 'ere 'gain next season? Way tah ruin Threshin' for da lot o' us."

If they can't descend back the way they came, the huscarl then draws a convincing, soot line alongside a map page with a stick of charcoal, headlining a specific route that circles, and follows the glacier south.

"First start 'eadin' back to da junction where we met-up..."

Only Edmund's ears are privy to these sensitive details. He fastens the journal shut and covertly returns it into Edmund's possession, before Sturgeon recounts, "A'gen, dis ain't personal, we just can't chance it."

These exact words dredge a rather unfond memory from the wickerwalker's past, an early climbing expedition where he had to unclip a sick, borderline homebody loose. To which, Edmund responds flatly, "I know."

This fatal flashback continues to wedge itself so far into his psyche. Edmund warned him of a deathly plummet, that if they didn't lighten the load, their entire expedition would career from the edifice, but to neither rhyme nor reason, this vagabond didn't muster retaliation. Even simply say "no" or waving to save himself would suffice. Instead, he chose to stare solemnly at Edmund, watching as he sheared the lifeline, welcoming death. These lands bring out the worst qualities in people.

Their walk of shame is short and emotionally shallow. The boy Jones doesn't cock his head, looking back at their pale hosts because he's sure that there's nobody there. These crooks aren't ruthless, willing watch the company shuffle those tender soles. Sturgeon, Braga, Bitte and Bludson Schaar are taking refuge in their inner sanctum, safely stowed inside the ice sheet, isolated from the burgeoning dramas and jealous ire of clans. That's the way they like it: no urge to compete, neither coerced or compensated, their sole focus is on their survival.

As the company reels further into the glacial advances, guided by their intrepid breakneck-connoisseur and his seemingly decent advice during the fairly faded pink brilliance of early dawn. Edmund leads them past the corridor junction, down a path they have yet to trek. Their company roots around in the unison, groveling in single-file obedience, wallowing in the exact tracks that the wickerwalker leaves in his wake as the foremost journeyman.

These wastelands temper the core of a man, especially the greenest members of Boar's Band, twisting all yearnings of the heart, taming all their desires, simply as they don't have time to lounge around and focus on anything else. Sustenance is their greatest concern; there's an endless, fresh supply of clean pre-filtered drinking water, and though William merely caught a glimpse, he's positive that they have abundant sources of heat too, choosing to pilfer Bannermane supply lines for matches, flashrod, lantern oils, and construction lumber. This missions aren't for the faint, it's such a chore to heave loot back up here.

Most of the world remains buried, as there is a myriad of secret entrances on the frontier, akin to Tom-Tom's warrens, dwelling down into the hinterlands, vaults only aquatinted to tiers of professionally furnished archaeologists and excavators familiar with sutler's paradise.

This morning's expedition leads them elsewhere, down a snaking trail in which they are obliged to avoid jagged edges of rime, leavings in which the trench has split from tension. Morbin investigates these skewers that wish gaping wounds upon these trespassers, that this alley has the appearance of static electricity riffing through someone's hair.

It's as if the townspeople's caravan are dodging teeth at every turn, stakes that lash out at them, compelling passerby to carefully slide to the side, or jerk in ritualistic dance. Linens inevitably catch, leather scruffs, woolies rip and tear, it's absolutely impossible to navigate safely. Mug Maxwell ducks in the nick of time, just as he hears the cavern walls yell, "En garde," and his wide-brim hat manages to impale itself on the nearest provocative tooth.

Balthus dodges exceptionally with a paperweight docked to his chest, careful not to risk surrendering the grimoire to icy pincers. These movements accidentally earn the learned man leadership over the front of the pack, overtaking Edmund's own efforts, and colliding into an elusive pane of glass.

"Oof."

"Splendid job 'round the ring. Do ye 'ave any experience boxin'?"

"'Ush-up now. We're 'ere."

This is the venue they had been unknowingly searching for, or at least, the accommodation that the wickerwalker attests to. The fellowship is awkwardly introduced to a series of four, crystalline double doors, that are nigh-invisible, save for a tinge of frost on their panes. The hoarfrost gives the portal a stiff temperament, albiet very fragile, and the impact Balthus comprises proves too fateful, and chinks the glass. The reflective entryway doesn't shatter instantaneously, and in actuality, the door ripples steadily in place, then flops piece by piece, as if a curtain was being pulled back.

Frankly, William is intrigued, he had expected the demesne ahead to be laden with blanketing darkness. They enter a vestibule of similar composition, featuring another row of doors, this time veiled in frosted decals, showcasing silhouettes of various, completely unfamiliar animals-at least, that's what the boy Jones surmises.

There's a plumb, blob-like ellipse with eight interwoven tendrils, several oars emerging from a barnacle, and also a stout figure, shoring its flippers to each side of its pot-belly while two, stark duck-feet wry towards one another. The front doors probably had these designs too, only the potent glaze prevented them from seeing through. These frosted windowpanes are imbued with some sense of magik, and automatically part when the company edges closer.

Whirr. They split to conceive a four-foot opening, and William stands on the precipice as these gates latch ajar, leading a company of brave souls inside.

On first appearances, they are greeted by a wide-scale, expansive fantasy, tracking dubious dregs of icy litter onto the spruce-stained, carpeted floors. The ceiling rafters, massive fortified beams, filter sunlight ebbing through the glazed domain outside, allowing this stronghold to be lit in pleasant ambience. At the center of this castle keep is a magnificent statue, detailing a serene scene, a carousal of marine life in which several orcas breach the surface in unison, tumbling over a flotilla of ice floes.

William's expedition into the arena is halted by a horizontal, hip-high pylon clad in stainless steel. Undeterred by this three-tongued barricade, he vaults over the turnstile and its jostling vice. The others are not as agile, and determinedly power through with the baffle pivoting upon their advance. A wall of stanchions now funnel the company to a particular queue area and inviting ticket booths, however they entirely ignore the direction, ducking underneath the flimsy vinyl tape, driving closer to the flagship display.

There's a store emporium erected at the base, reveling beneath the sculpture of frolicking whales. It advertises a variety of memorabilia: board games, bottles of frost-nipped water, keychains, t-shirts, sweaters, printouts, and plushies, all numbed, permanently embedded on the shelves in crusts of rime and frozen water vapor. The counter has a circular, U-shaped design, extending as a lip to promote product. Around the bend, a restroom has been incorporated into its farthest hemisphere. Clad in a pale tone of pine and charcoal, a machine plainly labelled by the phrase, 'ATM', which has malfunctioned, dispersing mossy-green slips of parchment across the non-slip mats. A mannequin with indiscernible features sternly hunches over two registers, preventing anyone from pilfering the innards of these mysteriously miniature vaults.

Beside the gift shop lies a useful map installation, conveniently filled to the brim with brochures, rendering the breadth of this domain in pocket-sized form. William bites into the bulk of his glove, prying the sleeves from his fingers, and helps himself to a pamphlet. The binding is crisp, cold to the touch at the point where it turns his fingers briefly numb.

While Edmund is once again the stout captain at the forefront of their campaign, the boy Jones can't help but become distracted, and appreciate the grandiose-scale of this campus. The markings of helvetica are still difficult to transcribe, yet in his eyes, no longer a foreign concept. Though he has difficult with the complete words, this chart depicts several main carnivals or environments, each with their own distinctive branches. As William's gaze glances over the map, he finds himself periodically announcing venues: 'Rivers and Streams, Coastal Tidepools, the Tropics, Ventures of the Deep-sea, and Arctic Voyages.' A highlighted bunch of buttons blare featured exhibitions in an area, parading special attractions such as 'The Largest Sturgeon on Record, an Aviary, Clamber Cove, Ballroom of the Seas, Brinebeard's Revenge, Walks through the Seaside Gardens, CAPAh Theater Express,' and so much more.

The wickerwalker propels his pinkie finger upon the large map installation, attempting to surmise their current location, and after Edmund's compelling discussion with the huscarl, an intended route. Jerome, in his usual act of defiance, goads the man, scrutinizing, "Well maestro, which way is it?"

"*Hmm,*" their daunted navigator shrinks.

"Said tah take ah 'ike up tuh the ballroom, though I'm not findin' it.

Can anyone really read this gibberish? Just looks like scruffs in the paint tah me."

Before William has the opportunity to present his findings, Morbin rushes to his assistance, pointing to a location at the very height of the chart.

"'Ere, yes 'ere," he declares, before tracing his index finger south, circling a large open area.

"And, we're 'bout 'ere if I 'ad tah stake ah claim. Looksaway some straight shot through these 'allways."

"Guess 'gain, twerp. Take a ganda 'round dat corna,"

Jerome antagonistically trumpets. As the company peers past the map installation, realizing that the gigantic orca statue had skewed their view since they've arrived, a series of metal beams have fallen, collapsing the foundation under the sheer weight of this ironwork. Detours are becoming a common occurrence, back in stadium's heyday, it must've been really dangerous to work in these passages.

"Oh-oh, now that makes sense," the wickerwalker professes, "'E said there was ah trick tah gettin' there too, somethin' 'bout dredgin' the local waters, wadin' through the streams."

Edmund's comment is interrupted by a set of enthusiastic chuckles, Morbin giggling at his side.

"Oh, o' course!"

"What's so funny, lad?"

"Yea, enlighten us."

He wipes a tear from his eye, frontier humor can be so crude, as basic as furniture in a weird position or a jerky pun.

"It couldn't be more obvious, we'll need tah go through Rivers and Streams. 'Liam- err William, didn't ye say there's a showcase with the- get this, world's largest sturgeon!"

He thrusts his index finger into the air, pointing towards the carnival entrance away from them, then enters another hysterical fit. William hadn't intended to say anything, occasionally his inquisitiveness gets the best of him, which makes this exchange feel rather peculiarly distasteful. Regardless of any back-or-forth banter, he is definitely correct. Maybe Morbin has been studying Helvetica as well, perhaps he isn't an intellectually lost-cause after all.

Edmund unenthusiastically shrugs in approval, pacing to the nearest venue on this deduction, waving his arm and encouraging them to jot behind.

"Reason 'nough for mah, c'mon then."

The entry to the Rivers and Streams exhibition is a scene straight out of folk-tales, this is sacred ground dreamt by Saltseers and the residents of Nettletown: an arcade featuring arcing laceworks of vines, leaves and blossoms. There is no soothing smells stemming from these blushing taffy flowers, only a faint, tangy scent. As William courts a budding pedal, his fingers slip over an odd, plastic film.

This facade continues into a tunnel, gradually emerging into an expanse of a deciduous forest, with numerous tree trunks carved into clear massive cylinders and prisms that could hold himself, ten-times over. Arranged in a bowed pattern, glazed sea-green ceramics settle overhead, then the original blue stony carpet cedes to webs of petite, interlocking, rectangular, murky teal tile tread under their boots. The edges of these aquariums are embedded with fake foliage, disguising their aluminum railings, intended to keep visitors at bay while those glassy, confining surfaces are completely dazed with rime. These showcases share one thing in common, they are completely encased in ice.

The remnants of a koi pond are on display to their left, an exhibit at the foot of a rocky outcrop, featuring eccentric totems, golems, a rock garden, then a small hill of rubble and its iconic, frozen waterfall centerpiece. William can tell that this spectacle was deliberately hands-free, visitors are dissuaded from entering by several strands of rope guides, now the motionless, rippling surface is fused in rime, so there's no threat to falling in. He ducks below, ignoring an infographic sign advertising, 'Significance on culture.. an Asian carp trade,' spying upon the permanent residents of this abode. There are nearly a dozen schooling koi suspended in place, clad in silvery and golden metallic scaled armor, chainmail that couldn't protect them from the instantaneous freeze.

Beside this exhibition is another tank stationed atop a steel frame. Although this particular aquarium isn't decorated in any additional litter or propaganda, minted with one proverbial statement, 'How big can goldfish get,' and the crackling stains of glass. There are a six or so specimens, dressed in dazzling tangerine flakes, each more vibrant than the last.

This venue is inspiring, and cultures William's already unassailable imagination, conceiving absurd and wilder creatures. Much to his own demise, Morbin wanders past a wire rack depot containing a score of headphones, a prize that the boy Jones is swift to covet.

This display showcases a guided history tour, some insight that would tickle wonder, and foster envy even amid the most devout archaeologists.

Each unit brandishes a pair of ear mufflers, strung together by a flimsy pliable band. A thin, wiry cord dangles from the starboard side, mainly looped about a compact, tanned box. This strange device sponsors a working condition, 'Press me' mentality.

William strikes at the button eagerly with his thumb, questing curiosity and steering clear of common sense. In response, the equipment emits a soft, warbling *trill-trill-trill*. Determined to make sense of this act, he shifts a lobe closer, realizing that it's actually a person's voice chattering. This noise doesn't cultivate the quality of being brash, and must be formulated through magikal means, arcane nature or an entitled, coin-operator demon.

Finally, these interests get the best of him, and the boy Jones decides to slip the pads that are oh-so perfectly designed to fit around the ear onto his own. The speaker that beckons from inside is outright jarring, as if constructing vocabulary one word at a time, contorted by some foreign dialect. People of the antiquity probably always talked this funny.

"-the assistant will automatically describe any nearby exhibits. Approach and listen. Please visit the front desk for any questions and to cater to any disabilities. Please, enjoy your visit at the PEMLLI, the Port Erie Marine Life Library and Institute."

That certainly simplifies things. This is a unique opportunity, William may learn facts about the ancient world that historians dare dream of.

He lumbers ahead, lulling about mainly, gradually following in the footsteps of his company, listening to the machine's detail. It mentions conservation activities, encouraging visitors to "donate now," divulging what steps they can personally take to help protect endangered species and unique biodiversity. William finds this sentiment awfully ironic, since they've already been perfectly preserved in ice for thousands of years to come.

The others are keen to navigate the complex, speeding past the aquariums as quickly as possible, intimidated by schools of alien life. They are transfixed in outlandish positions, demonstrating their personality through a short animating jolt, enough to where these tourists believe that they are either hallucinating, or these aquatic prisoners are actually still living.

The PEMLLI contains a menagerie of creatures, broadcasting the native habitants of local rivers and streams like the monstrous muskellunge, alligator gar, largemouth bass, and voracious red-tailed catfish. William inquisitively goes through Jeremiah's journal, checking-off any creature features that he hears echoed in his ear, occasionally jotting down notes, and recording entirely new specimens. It appears as if the author didn't have the opportunity to explore this building.

There is aquaculture here that still covets the Mad River today, particular species such as the steelhead, 'socket-to-ye' salmon, a lean riverfish which often thwarts an angler's net and must be wrestled by lockja experts. The boy Jones peers through this excerpt, where disembodies voice describes this cast member as a fly fisher's ultimate trophy.

"-with an unsurmountable energy. While juveniles appear as an alluring blue, older salmon can be recognized by their rosy hues and characteristic jawline. They are one of the few seafaring species that breed in freshwater sources, and are common catch during their spawning seasons. Salmon possess an incredible urge to reproduce where originally hatched, leaving them at constant odds with nature. They are known to leap out clumsily of the water in order to pass frozen obstacles, or entire beaver dams. Their notably bulky forefront is armored for prodding obstacles and springing through surface ice. Non-breeding salmon may become extensively larger, reaching spans of over two-hundred pounds when food is readily available."

Another fish that Jeremiah had been keen to mention are the steelhead's far-flung cousins, speckled rainbow trout.

"Also known as char, trouts are an oily colored, greenish-brown with speckled dark spots. These lakefish live for decades, and never stop growing. They rout through the substrate for worms, but primarily coast just under the surface of the water."

Not the sole bottom-feeder to scour these riverbanks, the boy Jones arrives to gawk at the "World's largest sturgeon," a competing ensemble of steel tan, rendered with white on that soft underbelly of theirs. It has an ironclad carapace, an arsenal of pronounced, protruding scales that hasten the appearance of an armored submarine. The freshwater opportunist sports a beard of whiskers that sift debris resting at the bottom of the tank, remnants of crayfish that are being uplifted by some distended tube, caught mid-gulp. Labels adorning the aquarium figure the monstrously magnificent fish to be reaching the lengths of twenty-four feet, and weigh upwards of two-thousand four-hundred pounds.

"What ah wonderful photograph," William remarks until he blurts in surprise.

Ga-ah. His gaze wanders to a trio of circular mouths that are stuck voraciously to the glass. Each disc discloses dozens of tiny, needle-like teeth, with eyes dotted onto the sides of their bodies, stringy muddled caramel which is coiled like thick threads of rope.

Populating the end of the alley are an ensemble of freestanding, sandwich board signs with panels advertising wildlife in the adjacent arcade: five-pronged, star-shaped invertebrates, then crowns made entirely of thorns, and diamonds with eyes and slender tails.

Beyond the reach of the rivers and streams complex are the coastal exhibits, however they dare not enter that domain. The open-touch marine paludariums, estuaries and tide-pools have been contorted with upside-down icicles akin to bewilderbeast quills, crafting an impenetrable wall, and coercing them into continue their journey. The mechanical voice begins to describe this coastal region, but barely utters a line before William abruptly walks away.

"'Ey," he chants to his fellows, though nonetheless they don't seem to care.

"This is pretty nifty!"

The caravan of townspeople emerge to a forward portion of the main hall, finding themselves on the opposite side of the steel debris with a giant revolving door loitering on their port side. They are able to sight a majestic volume looming above, vivid hues of citrine, emerald, garnet, ruby, sapphire and opal glisten brilliantly, drafted beneath an all-encompassing cobalt sheen. The source of these reflective shimmers emanates from the broad skylights which reign on the ceiling, ranging from one end of the capacious institute complex to the other, including the ballroom, bathing the demesne in rich amber glows.

This must be an annex of some kind, a speculative no-man's land acting as a promenade between the five distinct environments. Edmund is entranced by this architectural beauty, a masterpiece of human ingenuity that he has yet to experience among the natural world.

He shakes his head in order to stir to his senses, urging his fellowship towards the revolving door. Unlike its predecessors, this entrance has a profound lack of windows and glass, it is merely a wall to be swiveled forward. They place their hands on the provided handlebar, and struggle to give it a shove. It quivers for a moment, then anchors conclusively. Contrary to popular belief, even Korralack's brute efforts cannot make it budge.

This portal must be lodged with debris, or perhaps the fluids from a busted tank that has solidified like superglue, freezing the portal completely shut. With the main path blocked, they have no choice but to find an alternative path through another exhibit area.

Unfortunately for their enterprise, the passage to the Arctic Expedition has also been blocked-off, the bulkhead doors systematically locked and shuttered, pressuring them to return towards their original muster station. Under the circumstances, their company ranges towards the calling of the deep-sea. They only know what exhibits lie beyond this blockade because there's no lack in signage, and William's voicebox is awfully keen to explain animals which are housed there, including several types of seals- very vocal, blubbering beasts with stripes and iconically-lengthy whiskers drafting off their snouts; herds of walrus, musky brutes with the tusks of tundra terrors that are prone to violence; toothy, bow-headed belugas, predatory pods of orcas, and the avenue to an aforementioned aviary.

The vestibule here doubles as an emergency exit, consummated with an elaborate, half-sculpture brimming from the wall, the depiction of a humpback whale. It's unclear why this presentation is here above all, does the institute not have one in stock, or maybe this leviathan is simply residing at another location? William's heard stories of them, they're creatures that sow corsairs with dread, true terrors of the deep, yet one of many. In the meantime, an earnest lad reaches at its gaping maw with utter shock, stumbling upon the astonishing knowledge that a single tooth spans his entire forearm.

These aquatic behemoths are the largest creatures known to man, so massive that they can cause swathes of pack ice to shift, and devastate entire shorelines with the oncoming, encroaching rime. They're hunted in earnest, as when distilled, their body fat can be refined into that kerosene which fuels Bannermane lanterns. They're remarkably difficult to take down, protected from all scales of blunt-force trauma by an armored, knobby bow, and impenetrable stocky hide of barnacles and blubber. Entire sailing ships have been torn to oblivion as whales breached the ice, cleaving right through the hull, allowing the leviathan opportunity to feast upon the drowning men like krill.

Observing a label which denotes, 'Adventures of the Deep-sea, Brinebeard's Revenge ahead,' this carnival is noticeable dark. Where the skylights that once generously bestowed their radiance now fault to drywall painted with soot, nightmarish shades of ebony and grease. There is a proper purpose to this design, the architects sought to emphasize the creatures that dwell here, this is their domain. There is still an abundance of infographics and murals, peculiar imagery that eludes to abyssal remnants. Each showcase feels unfinished, there is a profound lack of color, like how the four-inch, acrylic-lined installation has yet to shed its original construction guise. There are pressurized tanks, bulkheads, rivets, and thick bolted barriers. As William explores and trudges on, he is provided with ample warning of the horrors to come.

Despite the clear intention of advice, the boy Jones drowns-out the monotony of his assistant, focusing his attention on the breadth of room, drawing in the aura of this fascinating new location. That's why, as William rounds the corner, he is flustered and visibly appalled at the tentacle monstrosity reaching out for him. An earnest lad gasps with unabated, frantic respiration, believing that this giant octopus was trying to reel him in. Thankfully, it's a simple mural, the real specimen is carefully contained in its quarters, although these walls detail numerous illustrations of the macabre.

He peers at the nearest two tanks, as if plexiglass portholes were glued straight onto the wall. These aquariums hold a lesser amount of biodiversity than those tanks of rivers and streams. These specimens are framed in exactly the same position when they were roaming around hundreds of years ago. There's a miniature squid camouflaging itself in a dazzling quantity of stony spots, actually a whole squad of them are sheltering here, different organisms masked among the detritus; and a nautilus, those spiraled, helix-shelled roamers which sport a dozen tendrils gaping from a soft spot in their signature casing.

The voice elaborates in William's ear, "Swiftly jetting around through the water, squids propel themselves with a set of eight, radial arms. Able to protectively camouflage or change color, they'll comb the seabeds for crabs and mollusks, then eject two longer limbs to ensnare their prey. At the base of these tentacles lies the beaky maw, a mouth specifically designed for snapping shell casings. The squid's length is attributed to its arms, and a fleshy, spire-like mantle."

"Thanks ah bunch," he jokes to himself, energetically scrawling sketches in the notebook while biting the tip of his tongue in concentration. Those invertebrates encased inside are so colorful it'll take an artisan decades to craft their particular color palette: melding shades of sea-green cyan, magenta and violet.

Next on the agenda are the medusa, confined within tall cylindrical container reaching the height of the room. Hundreds of moon jellyfish, nearly the size of a fist, migrate from the loft to the nether, all tuned in pliable, pastel lavender like a translucent umbrella. They're relatively simple creatures, rendered gelatinous, bound by the mercies of others and whims of the ocean current.

These creatures are mesmerizing, William wouldn't believe they were actually once alive if it weren't for the mechanical device whispering in his ear. He could stay here for hours, in fact, there's a couple of open seats right now, but before he could begin tracing the outline of the tank, the boy Jones notices a special attraction calling his name, a ghastly place of learning and gloom: Benthic Bay.

This site is teeming with all the creepy-crawly equivalents residing on the ocean floor, mainly invertebrates. The isopods are particularly eerie, as if a giant beetle wandered beneath the blue tide, latching itself onto a passing fish's tongue and acting as a parasite. Beholden by the true terrors lurking in the deep, one usually becomes accustomed to crabs as they are the ocean's signature scavengers.

However those marine navigators may attest of those maladies fostered by encountering its much larger cousin, a behemoth-sized crustacean in both ferocity and scope, a thanopod. Sporting a sawbones array of serrated pincers, these man-eating crustaceans blight any crew unfortunate enough to snare them, easily dragging every single soul to the briny depths as a true scourge of the seas.

Normally, William is tortured to be caught in such visceral imagination, but he changes tune when their company discovers the greatest exhibition in this arcade. There's a diorama, modeled-to-scale submarine residing in these halls, and most importantly, it's boardable!

As a learned man, Balthus is- of course, intrigued by such marvels of engineering, breaking the pack, and sprinting ahead. Libby and Bids lunge after him, bickering to themselves, as they are quite eager to explore the vessel. It takes a minute or two before a distracted William can catch-up and acquaint himself. He discovers Balthus at the helm, acting in the ferryman's seat of sorts, yanking at the controls and tapping gauges with his fingernail in honest spirit.

Edmund poises in seriousness, "So this is what those o' yester-yore used tah pilot. *Hmm,* wonda if everyone 'ad one of these?"

"Oh," Bids shouts before rushing down the corridor.

"The tunnel continues, thattaway!"

She passes an array of control booths and console schemes crafted in electronic manner, ignoring those plastered monitors, stickers, and signboards explaining what it's like to crew in the deep-sea. It's too late anyhow, as Bids has passed the point of no return, consumed in never-ending wonder that's not conveyed by letters.

The rear of the submarine shifts into an acrylic casing, an aquarium which harbors one frightful resident, a barbary shark, a being unlike any other. While the sister continues careening into the C-shaped tunnel, she nearly collides with the snout of this creature. Its slate-shaded, battle-scarred nose is covered in the equivalent of greening oceanic mildew, a blunt instrument for punching through six-inches windowpane, walls broader than standard aquariums to affront those violent tendencies. The frontal row of gnashing teeth has just barely splintered free, venting a dilapidated, toxic stench.

"Madly be, oh 'eavens. *Yech.*"

She squirms by with disgust, completely and utterly repulsed, shrinking onto the carpeting in disbelief, then squirming with nausea.

"What in oblivion is that?"

When the cataclysm was literally descending around this beast, a curtain of rapidly-freezing ice straddled its bones, locking it in place to suffer a chilling end. That's when the shark decided that it was high-time to finally break free, and surged forward, puncturing the glass.

When she overcomes the trepidations of her stomach, Bids Warder returns to take a stand, attempting to poke the creature as revenge. These prods jab at the prominent portion of its exposed, gouged, decaying and detritus-ridden, toothy dermis.

"It's like spurrin' ah piglet-" she shouts, suddenly recoiling backwards when the nightmare's nostrils flare, dispersing an aversive, mucous-muddled mist, causing everyone recently arriving at the scene, but Edmund, Korralack, William and Jerome, to cower in fear. These versed vagabonds are something different, piqued by morbid-laced concerns instead of being deterred by it.

The shark's pupils constrict in size to focus on poor Bids, and Libby interjects, shoving her sibling further down the tunnel, urging her to ignore this monstrosity.

She cries in retaliation, "What 'orror, oh the calamity!"

"It can't 'urt ye, so get movin.'"

In spite of countless years of imprisonment, this creature is notably alive. William has heard of this instance before, in storytellings from his dear chap-pop, and usually doesn't need to entertain such cautionary advice.

As an extremely solitary and deep-dwelling fish, barbary sharks may preserve their energy by slowing their metabolisms to the point of lethargy, becoming almost like living statues, those mannequins which populate the old city. In a state of torpor, they can be frozen in ice, hibernate and emerge decades later, only in this case, centuries- extraordinary!

He takes time to sketch the creature, regarding to the other fellows of his troop that he'll ruinedzvous in due time. If the beast can never conjure escape, the last thing the boy Jones can do is preserve its memory, however intimidating that image may be.

As the minutes reach the cap of tens, William is forced to surrender the exhibit and rejoin those vagabonds in passing. He emerges to a colorful coral paradise, an unexpected stark contrast from the dark, dingy domain of the deep-sea. He turns to face the tunnel exit, and shudders once again. The permitter of the portal behind him is illustrated with the gaping maw of a shark, some save an arsenal of a hundred serrated teeth.

The boy Jones shakes this emotional baggage, now immersed in an area entirely pristine and glowing. This is the tropical demesne, depicting vibrant murals and bright, exotic ocean creatures. The area is twisted into the shape of a half-moon wedge, dozens of smaller aquarium tanks settle among the permitter wall, quarrying inhabitants such as lionfish, a den of moray and dragon eels, several species of seahorses wound tightly around strands of kelp, mantis shrimp, and tiny reef-cleaning invertebrates, in any event, that's what the voice in his ear so dictates. An entire wall of artwork is fashioned between them, mesmerizing and flowing, a riptide of marine water that describes creatures in the adjacent ballroom, defining them in dramatically bold lettering.

William takes a step onto a lower platform, an event space so carefully curated in tables and chairs is crammed in-between these massive, marine showpieces. This operation seats about a hundred people, unfortunately all still present and accounted for. The scene is amusing until the fellows realize that their predicament is quite real- that these mannequins were once people that suffered a horrifying demise. It's as if they are watching an Impair Ultra stage show where the cast abruptly halts, freezing in place during their most hilarious charades. These revelers are arranged in grotesquely comical fashion, as certain individuals haven't reacted to the deep-freeze, and became petrified in place while continually dining and laughing foolishly at another's comments.

William's bag barely nicks the conductor, a steward directing those servants who carry platters of hors d'oeuvres, certainly delectable skewers arranged with cherry-red tomatoes, olives, various salted meats and hard cheeses. The acoustics in this berth are terrifying, so quiet that one could hear a pin drop. An appetizer breaks free from its restraints of rime, wobbling to the edge of the dish, wanders over the edge, colliding on the floor tile and *bah-crack,* shattering into a few wooden splinters and hundreds of produce pieces.

The fragments lurch to every corner of the plaza, skittering atop the floor's clandestine glaze, where the ambient water vapor has frosted just right, until they impact into something else: perhaps that be a table or chair leg, even striking the steward's heel, bashing upon a standard, size-ten polished dress shoe. These collisions derive shrill shrieks, vibrating off these crystalline entities.

Morbin Evershade shakes the reins of his profession, willing to stave the dead for now as he has become preoccupied with another affair, immersed in the briny aquatic landscape narrowly through the looking glass. It turns out that the ballroom is not actually a dance floor, but the aquarium's largest tank by far, featuring bands of schooling yellow-fin tuna while a great hammerhead shark, and solitary groupers- clad in their definitive reddish cedar brown, manifest in the heights above.

The exhibit has been fabricated into a central trench, where nurse sharks lounge by the precipice and sandy bars. Captivating amounts of angelfish, tangs, triggerfish and wrasse dwell in the secluded coral reefs below, which themselves sport bountiful plateaus and shelves of stubby stone corals, and their soft, waving counterparts which frolic in the water column. Anemones ward trespassers provide safe harbor for their clownfish residents as snails and brittle sea stars delve into the porous rocks.

Offering a full, one-hundred eighty degree view of marine life, this showcase is absolutely fascinating. There's a nearby ramp curving around the exhibit, where guests can garner a better view, navigating to a higher platform or climb to the catwalk above. Edmund gratefully abides and partakes in a journey above the ballroom.

More importantly for him, this is the penultimate step of Sturgeon's instructions. The huscarl distinctly mentioned that where the skylights are accessible, particularly near those long-drained electric cables dangle underneath, they can clamber onto the complex's roof.

It's truly a shame to part with an ancient wonder, and even though this museum was strictly for viewing pleasure, William has been enlightened to the illustrative inhabitants of this world. He tickles the notion that the immortals aren't entirely fueled out of spite, attempting to destroy their fellow divines, that they occasionally have the slight urge to create, and may reward the universe in things most majestic too.

Mandel grabs his wrist, spurring them forward into a sprint, elated at the thought of a different perspective. The cordwainer is easily exhilarated in the admiration of beautiful views, back to his normal self, negating the influence of fell corruption.

As they ascend the levels, traveling clockwise around the aquarium, they peer across two-foot thick acrylic panels- well, a nigh endless tinge of plexiglass considering the placid state of the water too. The depth of this underwater biome is profound, uniquely arranged in identifiable layers: open ocean, lagoon life, and reef dwellers, life concentrated in ways never thought imaginable.

If early humans could corral this intangible amount of creatures together, and these people could be compared to colonies of ants in the grand scheme of things, what powers could the divines withhold? May those ordinary beings conceive the efforts of icons? What if these gods have actually tried communicating, their directions echoing through the earth but fail, because humans do not possess the means to hear them? Whether it be through technology or biology of the ear, what if human minds are so inherently fragile, they perceive a mere "Hello" as threats of cosmic horror? Words imbued with insurmountable energy, that they warp matter.

The boy Jones revels in the lofty atmosphere of the demesne, shifting his gaze from the picturesque landscape to a sketchy premise. The sunroof fissures lazily here, enough of an orifice where when they choose to escape, may hoist each other high, grasping at the dangling cables for support, they could actually flee from the PEMLLI complex.

As disappointing as it may seem, there is nothing here for them but memories, and needlessly complex existential threats to their human history. The hole in the ceiling becomes more alluring by each passing minute.

"Okay everyone, this is our ticket 'ome. One last shove-up, then we entah the last leg, gotta sled on down that ice sheet tah the Marble Cliffs n' reach our 'ope o' rescue."

During the wickerwalker's speech, Pithee Jones incidentally appears at the rim above, complimenting Edmund's address with his signature noisemaker, rendering an applause of riffs from his rattlesnake staff.

Spa-urr, shing-shing-shing.

If an agent of order has arrive to bless their journey, surely they must be heading the right way. William and Korralack volunteer to depart last, using the last vestiges of their strength to lift readily, escorting dear townspeople onto their shoulders where they can scale the remainder of the ten-foot difference, and clamber onto the roofing above.

The Boar's Band vagabond is approached by the de facto leader of their troop, whom waits with bated breath, eager to sight new lands, debuting the acropoli and mountain-top estates almost within arm's reach. Korralack's the Kable tosses the wickerwalker among the aquarium's firmament with relative ease. He smirks at the boy Jones as if to prompt contest, rigging a signature beaming and smug smile as to who may muster these trials.

William snaps backs, reassuring the highwayman to "Keep it up and I'll let ye do it all yerself!"

Mandel is the first to employ use of William's personal lift, aspiring atop his bent knee, then a second-step atop his outstretched, latched-together palms which then leave him space to stand, his boot heels digging firmly into the earnest lad's tender shoulders. A surge of pressure slams onto William's frail frame when the cordwainer springs his figure upward, scrambling onto the roof.

Morbin Evershade, Mug Maxwell, Libby and Bids Warder, Cliff Fetherhaugh, Balthus the Pygmy, Lena Tillstead, Jerome and Rochester all receive their turn at the jury-rigged ladders, however most townspeople render the use of the barbarian-sized Korralack, in fear of crushing the boy's brittle bones.

With the foremost talent safety secure above the rafters, it is now William and the brute's turn. The magnitude of cord here is ample, and the pair candidly latch onto the makeshift rope, twisting thread around their forearms and between legs, urging the company whom flaunt in the rafters to tug in unison, and simply pull them upwards. And so they abide, too enthusiastically at first, jolting the remaining duo. When the fellowship realize their ability, and they conjure rhythm, regularly yanking the cord at one-two intervals, then the elevator ride quickly becomes relaxing rather than erratic.

Pithee Jones bows and grips the edge, intent on lowering his cane and aiding William's ascent. He's so close now, the boy Jones can feel the warmth emanating from his body in lieu of frost, he can hear the rainstick beads crackle inside, and reaches attentively, his fingertips grazing the flaking cholla wood.

Something startles the mystic during this daring escapade, reveling in his peripheral vision. Enough to startle him immensely, and the priest disappears in an ethereal shroud of mist.

The boy Jones fingertips quest past their intended target, gripping the precipice of the skylight's frame in haste, William develops a newfound sense of urgency, ushered by the eccentric's immediate departure. His climb becomes more vigorous, pulling down immense volumes of snow which harshly *thump* into his face, renewing the immediate jarring chill that often befalls frost, a quality in which he has been so lately deprived of.

This roof must be integrated inside the glacier, he could observe this deluge earlier bulking atop the trench's edifices. Inch by inch he scales, wriggling his torso over the edge like a beaching seal. Eventually he garners enough momentum to reach the top, rolling into the volume of precipitation as if he had been unanimously set aflame.

Rolling thrice, he halts suddenly, and not of his own intuition. A stalwart figure presses forcefully into his gut, pinning him down and securing his place so that William's gaze so perfectly aligns with a callous, discolored, bare-naked foot.

"This can't be good," he manages to mutter.

This tract is remarkably flat, representing the peak of the northernmost ice sheet, which absconds in a large, perpetual plateau. The sole trait that hassles this monotony are those plentiful rows of glass pyramids from the museum below. There is absolutely nothing of benefit by crossing this campaign, voyaging onto the glacier, no objects of interest in this recent stretch of white tide. The root of the ice sheet distends into the farthest mountain ranges, the extent of the Rimeweather Range which dances regrettably in a three-mile race unto the distant horizon.

This area is characterized as a lifeless, wide canal of bitter ice, rime and scree. Ravenous gales have stripped this landscape, buckling the surface into dry desert dunes. These pasty, powdery waves broaden from the hindmost reaches of the known world, spreading all the way to the battlegrounds, which regularly surrender massive icebergs to the craglands, entire walls of crystalized water plummet from the glacial face.

The bitter north is home to numerous foes, often more legend than real. This is the domain of earth's most vile creatures, rooted deep in local myth, stories recited in folk tales to scare Bannermane children, ensuring that they return to bed at dusk and eat all their lumpy greens. However, the loathsome few speak of white riders who bear the brunt of the storm, called forth by the most tempest blizzards.

William had never believed this folklore to register an ounce of truth, but yet here they are, and the exaggeration don't dare do them justice. Manhunters are describe as frontier boogymen at their kindest, kidnapping rogue whelps to join their ranks, who eventually are corrupted into agents of dreads themselves, and these stories can't live up to the hype.

The traveling troop has been led right into an ambush, descended upon by squall-dogs like rats on rice. Cliff Fetherhaugh is plucked from their fellowship by an oversized brigand, and lifted five-feet off the ground in a movement all too familiar.

A grizzled countenance briefly scrutinies the Mad River proprietor, before swinging its armament over the shoulder, and tossing the unlucky settler into the nearest chasm without hesitation. Fished from a barrel so swiftly that he can hardly emit a frantic *yelp* of bewilderment, Cliff's feet are suddenly whisked away from under him, treading frigid, brisk outdoor air to no avail, before careening down an adjoining precipice, accompanied by cries for help and frenzied screams which oscillate in volume and pitch whenever his limbs knock against the grade.

In a swift brush with death, Balthus is struck, taking a painful elbow to his nose, sending him to quiver into his knees, shaking uncontrollably as the ichor trickles through the gaps of his fingers, oozing down his neckline, and engorging itself on bright alabaster linens. The learned man ceremoniously faints at the sight of his own blood, incapable of understanding that he Manhunter intended to divorce his skull completely free from his body, and only an arcane artifact could have warded the full momentum of this blow.

A savage warmonger strives for its next assault, swinging its great weapon through the air with such finesse and malevolent intention, that it ripples vertically through the rim of Jerome's cap, slicing the outermost tip of his nose, frills of his collar, cleaving past the caps of both boots and all ten toes, embedding itself in the packsnow by at least ten inches. The sheer iron of this executioner's sword is so wide, that the blade still can be seen above the surface, showcasing its coarse edge and brittle, crackling veneer.

Several courses of gnarled fingers fasten the grip of this great weapon even tighter. The sole reason that this foray attack cut so cleanly is due to the headsman's perverse penchant for suffering. Jerome doesn't immediately realize his plight, not until the cartilage loosens from his visage and the wiseacre is walloped in the throes of shock.

Edmund and company reel around to face a trio of aspiring thralls, a misstep here would incur certain death. The winds of change have warped their adversaries, these are no longer ordinary men. Manhunters have been bred to endure the frontier: pain, pleasure, all the raw emotions it has to offer, and still triumph, they cannot comprehend a sense of failure.

Instilled at birth, or at least, when they adopt their role in the forces of fell, contenders range in size and scope, converted into earth's deadliest warriors. These are nearly naked, clothed in scrappy tunics and loincloths. Those that embrace the darkness and seven sins are granted supreme supernatural gifts or feats of strength, then those of high-caliber, who prove themselves the foremost agents of dread, are granted unimaginable power. William can register the oily pitch flowing through their veins, they possess hearts of coal. Forget heroes and monsters, right and wrong, the warmth of a tender fire, the cold sets them free.

As veteran rangers, they are armed with an arsenal of great weapons, one totes an unwieldy bardiche and whale skull shield, another flaunts a broadsword fashioned in a three-foot hilt, and the frailest among their posse swings a brackish mace within the size of a moneylender's coffer, straining every muscle and tendon to lift the bludgeon in threat and remain stationary. This vanguard brandishes their warhammer while guarding the rear, attending to a small slew of prisoners, strewn together in chains that choke their necks.

William can scarcely recognize them now, it's the same yeomen from Boar's Band that they met prior, although they're one short, as a lonesome figure is buried head-first in a nearby mound of packsnow. Their faces are battered and bruised from their period in captivity, and the leather heels of boots are decorated in copious blotches of wine-red ichor, tracking gore through the white tide.

Sturgeon, the elder and huscarl among them, is clearly in distress, lividly whimpering and feverishly grasping at his iron collar with nubs for hands and mangled wrists. It's a miracle that the brute hasn't been rendered unconscious, considering the prominent lack of blood in the vital fluids department.

Braga and Bitte endlessly berate him, renouncing their titles and blaming their leader for the senseless fatality of comrade, Bludson Schaar. They lament Sturgeon over his ploys and false promises, how he betrayed his yeomen in the effort of saving his own skin, culminating in the death of a close friend. It wouldn't be surprising if the huscarl leased the townspeople's route to their enemy, which would explain why the Manhunters strode out to capture them.

While these wildlings may be merciless, they derive joy from spurring the temperaments of others. These thralls can easily demonstrate a killing blow, but would much rather prod the casualties and salt the wound, coercing a victim to repent their prestigious idols, and have them curse thy name.

Cliff Fetherhaugh's needless death was a testament to their ruthlessness, because that's how the Manhunter's operate; simple confirmation of how little they value human life, brutalizing to instill fear in their prey. Torture and emotional manipulation is the admonishment of pride, and how those captives envy to be free, rising to the occasion in a bid of power, wracking their belligerent brigands to and fro in a feat of wrath.

All this rebellious act does is cement dark influence, as the embodiment of chaos always seek to foster new recruits into their ranks. Once an individual stoops to such moral lows, they become empty husks, waiting to be filled with purpose, sacred duty, willing to sacrifice themselves to bring about the end of the world. Servants of fell dedicate themselves, every ounce of mind and body to ruinous powers and their destructive exploits.

They are the personification of ultimate evil, every action is malign in nature, to instigate trauma, allowing the seven sins to revel and flourish. Manhunters exist as a blight against fertile lands, marching at the helm of an everlasting blizzard, a torrent to consume the manners of civilization.

The exalted cut-throat raises his bardiche in intimidation, mincing thrice-though the cloud of mist that his breath generates. Edmund's hand scrambles dangerously, yearning to draw a billhook blade, and fend-off these monstrosities. This Manhunter notices the wickerwalker's stalwart complexion of defiance, and decides to rest the point of this greataxe against Edmund's neck. The business-end of an axe blade creeps forward, impaling coat, collar and baggage, yet not causing any visceral harm.

This breakneck connoisseur so proudly refuses to peel, so the Manhunter presses, driving that tarnished iron into flesh, piercing the sinews inside his neck and drawing fresh blood like a syringe until Edmund is forced to concede, tilting his head towards the side. Still, in the face of oppression, his legs remain rooted, seemingly sprouting vines that entrench themselves within the glacial ground. When the cut-throat finally decides to open its maw, a vile beast tongue spouts surreal serpentine speech.

"Ye-eel'd, wicka-man."

He produces a guttural demand, "Tossa dat 'lade to da ground."

Edmund internally debates his options, the prevailing notion is that he has undoubtedly led the party into a trap, and it's now his responsibility to free them.

He rallies, snapping at his adversary and yelling with audacity, "Nay, 'ave at thee cretin!"

Twirling his torso, the wickerwalker rotates to avoid the impeding enemy's bardiche. His billhook slides out of its pouch and through the air in nary a blink, colliding at a weak point on his opponent's weapon, striking the upper shaft of the great weapon with his billhook. In this instance, all the desperate Edmund desired is to disrupt the legionary's edge, smacking his foe's armament hastily to the side. Instead, he strikes with such might and tenacity that it severs the timber from its polehead entirely.

The Manhunter recoils in awe of its sunken mincer, as splinters are distributed into his nearby accomplice: the marauder with the greatsword. This butcher's exposed skin is punctured by dozens of wooden shards, particularly imbedding in his vulnerable eyes, to which he doesn't react in kind.

Edmund surges forward, raring his hook to lodge firmly inside the brigand's gut. Although he underestimated his battle prowess, and the Manhunter precisely parries the opportunist thrust with his staunch, bony shield. The members of their company still in fighting shape nod to one another, deciding to press their numbers' advantage. They draw a ragtag assortment of tools, hooks and instruments.

As soon as the marauder's foot relieves itself from William's chest, he springs into action, rummaging through his knapsack with haste, securing a halberd head before tossing the bag aside and jumping to his feet.

This cut-throat is routinely distracted by projectiles making residence in his fleshy, visual orbs. He plucks at them slowly and meticulously, his hands are too large for this pinpoint frontier surgery, compressing eyeballs, tearing lids in an effort to extract a salvo of wooden fibers that will surely crippling his eyes. He's thoroughly distracted, and completely unaware of Libby and Bids Warder arriving from behind.

They each focus on a leg, digging their blades into his achilles heel, crudely severing tendons, repeatedly stowing their knives into his flesh and prodding the Manhunter, gradually working their way higher and higher. He collapses on its knees in angst, making the operation slightly easier.

Overall, they must've stabbed the marauder twenty times apiece, gashing the contents of their the neck on occasion, and still this villain squirms and writhe around, clearly quite alive. The cut-throat continues to pry at the splinters in its face, much to their displeasure, not paying heed to these transgressions of attempted murder at all. There is a distinct lack of ichor leaking from these wounds, and in its place, an inky greased slime slicks onto the powdery frost.

Edmund continues to duel the leader while Korralack and William make rounds to deal with their accomplice. The third Manhunter strays behind, hoisting its maul, defying gravity and wagging the mace high in an effort to guard these three Boar's Band prisoners, and maybe threaten their execution in the meantime. Still, midst the heat of battle, Edmund pays no mind. He already has a target in his sights, solely focused on eviscerating his opponent. A billhook sways violently around, beckoning death. The brigand flings his jagged staff around to guard his torso, waiting to receive a zealous flurry of blows.

Anticipating Edmund's sudden slash from stem to stern, this cut-throat expertly dodges to the side, relinquishing the wickerwalker's first attack. In frustration, he tries to backhand the brute, swinging horizontally, to which the cut-throat simply ducks. Finally, flipping the billhook in his palm, ensuring that the blade spread parallel to his forearm, Edmund thrusts a frantic uppercut.

In an unfortunate series of events, the Manhunter catches this third strike, nabbing the span of the wickerwalker's wrist, wrying the fragile vagabond into the air, and disarming him entirely. The billhook blade slips from his grip, imprinting in the fresh snowfall.

It doesn't brag nor boast after pacifying his attacker, unwilling to verbally reprimand him for at least trying. Back when this hound was human and first met those elusive Manhunters that turned him, he probably fought back too. What a poor fool Edmund is, believing that he could be that counter to an unstoppable force, this sort of thinking will surely be the end of him.

His dire thoughts are quelled by a mysterious cerulean glow, almost blinding him entirely as the essence of Jeremiah Anders summons behind his foe. Brandishing an ethereal sword, the geist decides to sheathe the weapon in nearest Manhunter's back. It plunges deep, landing a critical blow that splits half the collarbone, extending haphazardly, undeniably puncturing subclavian arteries and deflating the left lung. Stricken by the failure of several essential systems, the heathen's head lazily lapses forward, as if he had fell asleep at his post.

Edmund dangles aimlessly in this position, seized in place by a stiff, conclusive grip. As the wickerwalker pessimistically pries at the fingers wrapped around his wrist with his free hand, the Manhunter resuscitates. These rangers do not feel pain, they are fortified by regenerative magikal energies, and subject to spells much larger than human emotion. The steep angle of this assassination attempt ensures that those bodily functions are transfixed, and it'll have to dislodge the weapon before it can move again.

Still retaining control over its right arm, the brigand rears at the blade behind his head, fumbling across hulking shoulderblades, curling fingers that reach and strain, before gripping the weapon, beginning to relinquish its command over the domain of his flesh and casting that trusty steel asunder. The blade slides from his frame grotesquely, composing a maddening *squelch,* yet removing this armament without any pain and nary leakage of irreplaceable black fluid. A procedure as difficult as extracting an uncomfortable pin-prick.

As he finally relieves the broadsword of its position, a sly tendril of oily poison emanates from this empty space, seeping down the cut-throat's torso. When the spectral weapon is tossed aside and strikes the packsnow, it sinks into the powdery billows before dissipating into a glittery, mystifying miasma. Without a barb to notch him in place, the Manhunter reels around to face the assailant.

Upon recognizing its ethereal origin, this brigand utters a spell to untether the author and former wickerwalker. William closely listens to this seance, it blares loudly, cavorting in lecture akin to flags flailing of wind.

"Ooo-long uba-roo, ti-kata doe-rah."

The journal at Edmund Redmyne's hip immediately bursts into flames, searing his skin with scaly char. Being subdued, slightly able to use his hands, he loosens the notebook in the nick of time, before this combustion bestows an unappreciated amount of third-degree burns. These flaming sheets collapse into an inferno upon the ground, a bundling flare that's very kickable, which the wickerwalker then drives into the direction of their enemies.

Upon completion of this ritualistic speech, Jeremiah's presence starts to blur, and fade from existence entirely. Raising his hands in view of his face, the iconic turquoise-blue skin has begun to spoil transparent again, and every finger phases through one another as his anchor to the mortal realm falters. This isn't like his disappearing act before, this is different in some fashion, and when ushered by a magikally-adept Manhunter, potentially permanent.

The boy Jones screams out in disheartened fervor.

"Don't go, ye can't leave us!"

Yet these request fail to halt his dematerialization. When Jeremiah flusters one last time in searing beams of light, he casually mumbles one final line before dissipating in the blink of an eye.

"Well it was worth ah try.".

"Jeremiah, nah don't go!"

The boy Jones lets loose a howl of anguish, as if a harpoon has speared his heart and wound him fatally. William rages against their foe as if possessed by a mad demon, he swipes the sundered bardiche blade from the ground, and rallies his forces by hurling the bulwark of blemished metal into the blinded Manhunter's ribcage. In addition to that scathing throw, he rails the blunt edge of his halberd head against this imbedded battleaxe, driving it further inward, treating this fair as hammer and nail. In matters of life and death, never pull punches.

The marauder laments, desperately reaching at this barb, slicing its own hands in the process, and an index fingers split from the knuckle. Of course, they can be damaged by their own dark arsenal, shadows can be defeated by other shadows.

Despite actually proving ground on their opponent, the perverted citrine glow and blackened veins don't dull. Manhunters are fueled by sorcery, and will continue fighting until they are naught but a pile of ashes.

Racked by the guilt of Jeremiah's expeditious demise, William is consumed by grief, and leashes to his opponent like a parasitic leach. With the marauder's fingers severed and squirming upon the ground, the boy Jones dashes his own hands around his Manhunter's neck.

"Ye may be indestructible, but ya still need to breathe," he grunts, wringing it with every remaining shred of energy that he may muster to the cause.

That unscrupulous foe grappling at Edmund Redmyne hardly complains about his comrade being mangled.

"E's just one man. Finish 'em 'ready. Does 'e 'ave imp-enna-trouble skin, da eyes o' an 'awk? Nah? Sounds like an ordinary man. Wyrd at dat. 'Ow did 'e 'url mah axe drew my second-in-command?"

Still, this battered body relents against these daring attacks, they are truly a formidable foe. Upon realizing that this marauder won't lose breath, he headbutts the Manhunter with such ferocity that it wracks his own brain and causes a split-second black-out. This strike does justice, driving his quarry further into the ice and causing the glacier to tremble, but William is too blinded by rage to notice. The landscape jerks in response, sending the nearby audience sprawling to their knees.

The boy Jones regains his footing, and continues to manifest that maleficent rage, biting into fresh Manhunter's throat as if controlled by a wild animal, exposing the carotid artery by tearing out several chunks.

Streams of liquid tar seethe between teeth, corrupting those ivories while spewing out those fetid minced meat. In the marauder's weakened state, these wounds instantaneously calcifies and becomes brittle. His opponent is nigh-invincible, not invulnerable, but before he can potentially deliver a killing blow, Mandel cries for him to retreat.

"'Liam, 'Liam run 'way. I can't stop it. *Aggh.* They've been tryin' tah take me since they arrived!"

Thinking that he's talking about their fell cohorts, William doesn't notice as Mandel's eyes glaze over, radiating their golden sheen as another spirit contest for his human coil. In one last stunt of refusal, the cordwainer collapses to the ground, violently seizing, yet no matter how hard he may try, mortals cannot deny the whims of gods without consequence. Gradually he rises, this time more puppet than master.

There is a glowing aura of purity to him, an emboldening corona that forces the Manhunters to writhe in pain merely from sharing this vicinity. The vessel begins to speak, rather angelic and saintly, a blatantly soothing, yet unrecognizable falsification of his best-friend's voice.

"Pray beast," the bullhorn ordains, waltzing within ten inches of the suffering, dazed and confused cut-throat. It communicates in a volume all can perceive, then mumbles faintly in the Manhunter's ear, "and I'll return you to the dark lords in shambles."

A booming voice separates flesh from bone, blasting off the fell creature's head in the process. They can spy when the helmet splits and severs, the skin, then flesh peels from the confines of body with the viscosity of wet parchment, finally the skull ruptures, delivering grey matter miles onto the glacial front. His party is instilled with awe, awfully sickened, but inspired.

The being that possesses Mandel's body immediately faints. It only had the strength for one clean, momentous act, fifteen seconds of possession.

"Storytella," the bruised brigand mutters, inadvertently loosening his grip around Edmund's windpipe while he battered the hunter's head into the roof's canopy. Edmund is an accomplished lockja and martial arts specialist, and aims to disorient his opponent, and wiggle free. While this is no small task, the divine banishment of the Manhunter marauder was a suitable distraction.

As soon as the wickerwalker's head is close enough, whips back, striking the cut-throat's chin and staggering him immensely. Edmund twirls around in a sudden dance movement, wrenching himself free from the Manhunter's vice-like grip, where he can fathom his next series of moves without being choked.

In response, the marauder releases his quarry to retrieve a dislocated jaw, and is rather surprised when the breakneck-connoisseur garners the strength to hurl his foe over the shoulder. Imagine the Manhunter's surprise as he soars through the air, especially as Morbin lingers nearby, unleashing a knife from his boot which disembowels their assailant and spreads innards all over.

Slosh, thunk.

He lands in a heap on the aquarium skylights, almost tumbling through the glass. The brigand is distraught, but not by feasting on its own guts, as Manhunters rarely reacts at their loss of entrails- gross. Unlike his accomplices, he doesn't eat anything raw. Nay, he is livid, the word for defeat scarcely graces frontier vocabulary.

He bellows at the sky, "'Nough. Rise, rise n' rejoice fell brethren!"

Swirling clouds vomit to this calling, thunderous swarms of ill-vapor that manifest under the premise of a raging typhoon. A brackish witches' cauldron in the sky bears intense strobing, which culminates as a bolt of lightning strikes the glacier, rendering blackened ice in calamity nearly a hundred-feet out. The ground heaves and collapses, chronically rising, then venting steam in a manner most foul.

This demonic oasis explodes in a climatic flurry of ice and rime. Colossal claws tear at the fabric of reality, gouging themselves in the ice until they catch, and a dreaded white bear hoists itself from the depths of hell. If it weren't ordained in a matter most malign, this incident looks phenomenal, a lightshow arranged by celestials.

This animal is absolutely elemental, the largest creature that any living Bannermane have ever landed eyes on, fledging to the size of a caravan coach. An indecently exposed spine creaks from its haul of creamy alabaster fur, its hide stained in maroon war paint, tinged the color of blood. The neck is shrouded in spiked steel chains, a collar of irony that bruises an otherwise luxurious vessel of wrath. Perilous azure globes spot their trivial conflict, and urges this behemoth to lumber forth. It emits several raspy grunt and hoarse croaks, showcasing a pair of gore-stained tusks, angled molars emitting from the monster's jaw to spear prey, jagged and could be coined as antlers. The aberrant creature shambles slowly, lugging the weight of a rider, as death rides a pale horse.

This harbinger is signal to the end times, shouldered by a pair of eccentric wings, reams of raptor feathers dressed in the contorted likeness of Red Dog Dragoons, bison-riders of the Bannermane mercantiles, only these plumes are real, shifting and flowing with each callous brush of the wind, taunting their company in a elegant display. The hussar's helm is all-encompassing, a singular article of metal locking her neck and shoulders in place. Vertical vents have been torn into the faceplate, allowing the ranger to scout ahead, without giving away the visage underneath. She is outfitted for war, although scantily clad in armor. From their demonstration earlier, a Manhunter's weakness seems to be the vital functions of their brain, anything lower: lungs, intestines and even the heart, aren't priority and are replaceable. The pieces of iron she does covet bear striking resemblances towards insect carapaces or chitin, gifting an outlandish, otherworldly appearance.

With one arm straddled around the reins of the bear, her other palm sports a flail, lunging into such a formidable length that it drags in the trailings of his mount. As an ancillary of fell design, nothing about this weapon is normal. It splits into two tails, a brass bell and fetid censer-bearer which acts as a conduit, releasing sangria spews of miasmic gas. These gifts are a step-above those awarded to the usual array of Manhunter cohorts and aspiring thralls.

Clearly outmatched, outclassed, and now outgunned, Edmund Redmyne ushers everyone to coral close to their prone caravanhands, Jerome and Balthus. The wiseacre spills torrents of ichor, covering those gaping wounds to no avail. Waves of white tide recoil at this donation, then refreeze in motionless crimson pools, tinges of Bannermane iron and grit forever quelled. The headless Manhunter cut-throat is another story, their pitch runs cold, diluting the flawless alabaster in danger.

The wickerwalker unfurls his billhook, intent on sticking the enemy with the pointy end, and gives a short stint of advice.

"Keep breathin' n' nahbody dies."

William anxiously clutches his stubby halberd head.

"I'm not scared, just ah lil' worried."

Now understanding that fell weapons cleave their own corruption like butter, he'd retrieve the bardiche from the corpse if he simply possessed the strength to rip it free.

When the antagonist finally marches into shouting range, the wickerwalker rushes forward to strike its steed, knowing full-well that this could be a grisly end. In response, the rider relaxes, and emits a frosty mist from the depths of her steel helm, the same ires of a furnace, but burgeoning the complete opposite effect.

This magik spell generates a wall of icy particles that Edmund inevitably strays through, and is stricken in unexpected malady. The rime tinges his whiskers, chilling bone to the marrow, blackening swathes and fringes of skin while the wicker's body temperature plummets.

He hoists his wand high in contempt of agony. To him, the buck stops here. The hunter's metal billhook festers in a transparent glaze, brittle as the drifting surface eddies on Botany Bay. Edmund stops the advancing enemy, and the barbarian queen decides to deem mercy, just so the frigidly-failing wickerwalker can prove example to her caliber of might.

With a mere flick of her wrist, her whip commands attention. Chain links *crackle* and routinely *pop*. The hoarfrost that usually encrusts these rings generate showers of vapor as they dance recklessly in the air. Then the tips of the flail so expertly collide with their intended targets: the bell slamming on the wickerwalker's sole weapon, delivering the fragile blade into a thousand shards, and bestowing a split-second moment of regret before the censer swiftly demeans Edmund's cheek. The force of this blow pressures their leader's mouth wide open in agony, where he inadvertently chokes on its stupefying fumes.

Their ferryman is sharply stunned, subdued into submission and blinded by grief. His eyes roll backwards in their sockets, reacting to excruciating pain, frothing at the mouth as this chemical attack rattles the medulla of his mind, and he gasps twice before ultimately going limp. From the sight of this offense, the boy Jones interprets hundreds of centipedes crawling up the wickerwalker's body, impaling his skin in a chorus of legs, and latching into gristle with their puncturing mandibles. He can't help but gaze at Morbin in disgust, this isn't a fate he'd wish upon his worst competition.

The rendering of punishment is decisive and swift, that the company throws their weapons to the ground and offer surrender. Finding the ground unworthy to cradle her feet, the bandit queen issues commands towards the two surviving Manhunters to restrain their quarry, and with a significant lack of shackles, that these brigands resort to tackling the townspeople, rooting through their belongings and disarming them entirely. Any tools, anything with a sharpened edge and kitchen utensils that could be considered weapons in the slightest are chucked into the same chasm that befell Cliff, or back into the aquarium complex whence they came.

Jerome grows especially weary as a Manhunter mends her approach, floundering in the fetal position as his wounds fester violently. This greybeard's facial features are dyed with red-wine, the areas around his naval cavity and the soles of his feet rife in frozen ichor.

While the brigand goads insults at Morbin, he arranges a fist directly into the archaeologist's gut, an act of revenge for that particularly lengthy cut through his abdomen. Without the ability to stitch the gaping laceration, every action the trooper faces results in the same dilemma, coddling its innards, even the slightest provocation spills a hefty sum of organs.

Korralack the Kable rushes to the defense of his fellow and is immediately laid low, struck in a foul motion. William struggles with his own tribal counterpart, as that feeble Manhunter scours his pockets, procuring the pike head from his person and chucking the makeshift metal hatchet into the adjacent glacial trench. This interrogation doesn't surprise his chances at vengeance, he'll just need to resort to more subtle methods.

Their wainwright, Rochester is shoved to the ground, and Mug Maxwell unwillingly cedes, kneeling across the packsnow on behalf of being searched.

The siblings, Bids and Libby Warder undergo a more thorough inspection. They forgo their weaponry so diligently and without delay that the brigand is aware of their ploy, that there's another card they intend to play. So he persists, instigating pat-down after pat-down, identifying several, meticulously stowed pieces of equipment intended for bloodshed.

They relent those smaller daggers during each probe, yet the cut-throat continues to menacingly hassle them, awaiting for the pilfering vagrants to empty their own arsenal. It takes a full minute or two, pulling icepicks out of a vambrace, or a bowie knifes from boot heels, armament after armament until pile of metal that could supply a small army appears at their feet. These two ruffians are certainly magikians of the sorts, William assumes they still manage plenty of stock as the Manhunter kicks these weapons through the gaping skylight.

During this inquisition, the Manhunters' newest arrival carefully surveys their endeavors. Its tongue wavers like a compost slug, relaying a toxic, demoralizing message, "Der's fight in ye, I like dat. Ye'll make perfect additshuns."

The cut-throat with the mace hassles Balthus whom is playing dead among the packsnow. It doesn't take long at all, just a few stumbling kicks in his side until he's squirming away, revealing the manuscript tied to his chest. Elated, these Manhunter easily sense its otherworldly origin, staring at the trophy in unison.

The youngest marauder risks a touch, an inquisitive brush of the fingers which immediately sears flesh, producing a noxious cloud of steaming skin. Undeterred by this aversion, as these obvious warning signs mean that the grimoire is certainly a prize to covet, it unclasps the tome from Balthus ensemble with a rusty shard. The learned man may only muster a slap or two, although a hardy wallop in return knocks the foolishness right out of him. This cut-throat is eager to claim this loot, and strides hastily towards the white bear, relinquishing the ancient grimoire as treasure for their esteemed leader.

Negating an intense smog of smoked flesh and cinders, the bandit queen grips the manuscript's spine. Their hands also burn upon touch, and the tome screams in fury of this transaction until it's safety stowed inside a knapsack of sheepskin. As the physical embodiment of the Manhunters most sacred enemy, the fire elemental is immune, yet not invulnerable to their corruption.

In a dramatic act of betrayal, the bandit queen wraps its claws around the marauder's face, hoisting their accomplice into the air in a movement most brutal. The strangulation starts swiftly, although to their surprise, this is not a punishment being rendered, but a blessing, a reward for their outstanding loyalty and unwavering devotion.

When the rider finally decides to let go, the once feeble frame of the Manhunter tremendously warps. The fabric of their skin tears haphazardly, muscly sinew fibers spread like red rot, tearing across the surface. Through the coercion of corruptive magik, he immediately bulks-up, becoming a beacon of brawn as his chest swells to the width of a barrel, and his biceps that of dreadnaught cables.

As her fingers unclasp from the Manhunter's jawbones, his visage has been ridiculously transfigured, offering a complexion akin to a baboon, the primal manifestation of man and familiars of wrath. It commands a myriad of intimidating qualities, wrought with some grooved, blue-capped snout with a red, vermillion dash down the middle, then lets loose a howl onto the wind. In an incomparable expo of intimidation, with a lip which recedes to unveil a thick, pink upper-gum, barring teeth and revealing some pair of dominant, elongated canines.

This promotion is overshadowed by a rogue altercation, Mandel is profusely kicking and screaming. The beings in the firmament have made him privy to sensitive information, lending images of the perversion of men that would drive ordinary people insane. To his privilege and express demise, these immortals haven't abandoned the cordwainer yet.

They are actively trying to return, surging power through their vessel, but cannot spur transformation in the dominant presence of fell. Instead, the gods grant mercy by remitting him unconscious, that way he can't be influenced by dark and malign forces. Mandel is theirs to command, and they'll do anything to prevent the alternative.

The fiend, or daresay Mandrill's first instruction is to heave the once again, senseless cordwainer and wickerwalker onto the back of the polar bear. This freshly-mutated grim cannot carry these captives, it'll need both hands free should anyone in the party chance escape and their ability to sprint. Exhausted and out of breath, Calamity Jane verbally lashes out at the Manhunter's ugly mug, criticizing their disheveled appearances and for letting her comrades be punished.

"You too afraid to touch the ground or something? Get down off that high-horse. Swear you're making a mockery of me."

At light of this terrible reception, the bandit queen commands her brigand and their ordained herald of wrath to escort these prisoners back to camp, but in pure fellkist, the whips of chaos in the air, a dialect alike speaking in wind and whistles. William tries to translates their whims through body language, motions that only suggest heinous acts.

As they are steadily marched from the PEMLLI roofing, William secretly prowls in the aftermath.

First, he spies his personal bag stuck in a nearby bank, and wraps the strap around his forearm before proceeding forward. It's light, as the only usable possessions that this luggage contains are Edmund's whittled tokens. Who knows when a simply bag may come in handy, save even play the part of insulation?

Secondly, an earnest lad skulks among the ice sheet, keeping elusive and low in a bid to recover Jeremiah's mutilated journal. The signature *scrunch-scrunch* of his jackboots are mercifully muffled from the commotion of company. Those same sheets ruffle in his hand, page after page of singed parchment, gawking at this charred husk.

William tries to remain optimistic, but sighting this notebook cooked to tatters, he unfortunately begins stirring the notion that their friendly geist is gone forever. Regardless of spiritual matters, the boy Jones slides this manuscript into his interior jacket pocket, noticing the fleece has torn in their ensuing conflict, causing the cold to straddle William's torso and curse their mortal follies. However that ancillary remains safe and close to heart. Burnt parchment on skin is a wyrd feeling.

An earnest lad is distraught and contests their oppressors.

He prods at them rebelliously.

"Just where are ye takin' us?"

Although this petition falls upon deaf ears. Realistically, these outlaws do not spare explanation, nor shed light on their destination.

What fell purpose and dastardly designs could these brutish nightmares have in store for them? Their treatment of this caravan is akin to a voyage of the damned. They had arrived so ferociously, and could have disposed of the townspeople relatively easily- Cliff wasn't more than a trifle of a threat. Where was the Pithee Jones during all of this, the mystic, priest, envoy to the Lord of Earth and Stone? Why did he vanish and not help? Surely they're in need of the gods now.

— ACT FOUR —

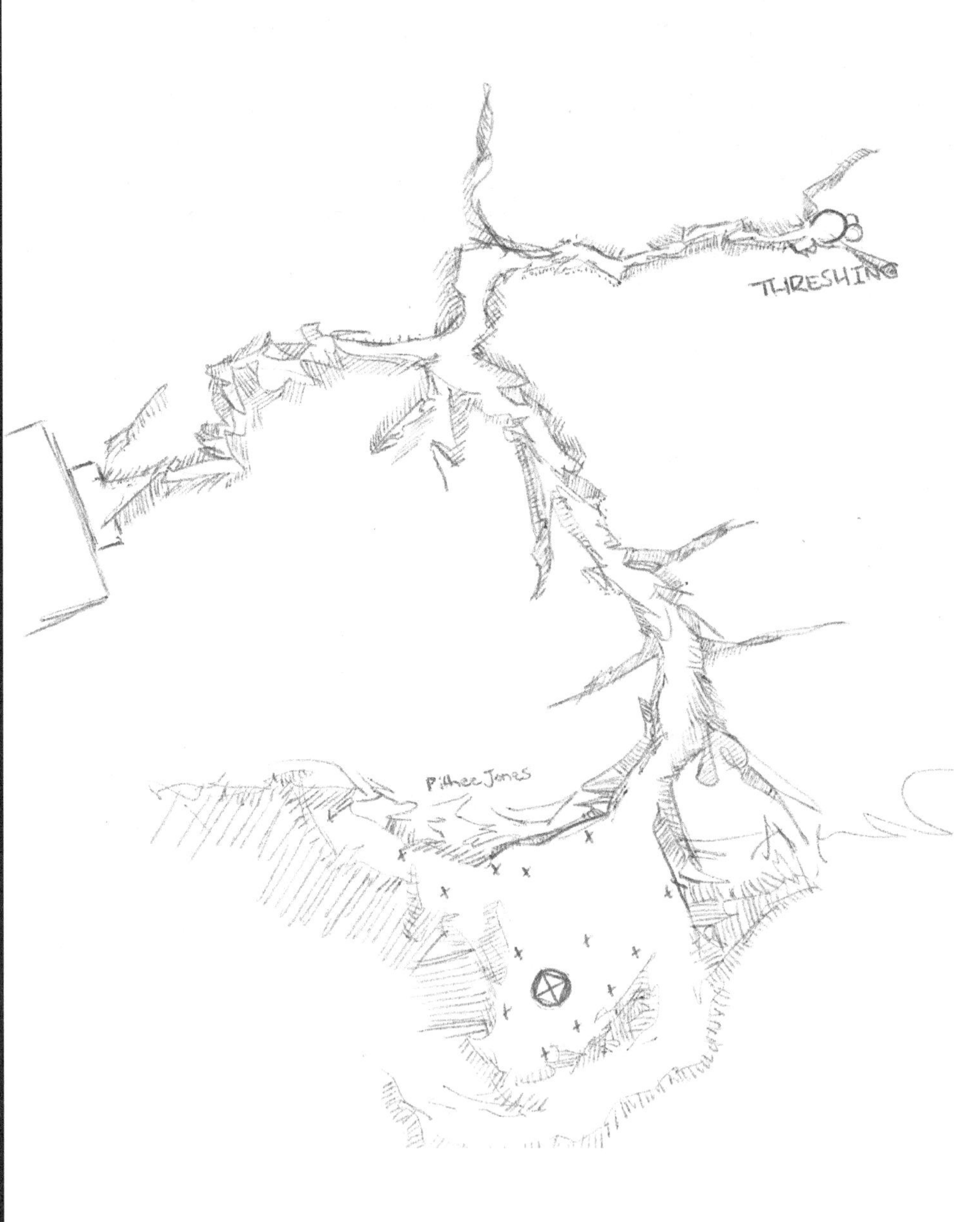

ANTLERS OF
THE EARTH

XVI

—

LIVE AMONG THE PACK AND HOWL LIKE THE WOLF

Dear drowned, and dreamt, and weather'ud,
Oh, some few steps from that yellow-brick road.
Can't you humor me? Won't you bide the time?
I've asked for ease,
So, would ya, please?
Lest advertise my soul for sale- ah

I deserve it…

Gotta break the habit,
Then force these chains,
Till my vigor goes all limp and lame.
So, give me a clue, some shoe or two,
To make these dreams of mine come true, true, true-

… don'tcha think.

Huh? Got a bite I cannot itch,
Puckered while the poison drips.

Those hecklers gonna dare me to crawl,
Until my body's drained,
And every fiber strained,
Still, I heed your call-

Now is the time...

Stir the crazy,
Stoke the embers,
Might raise the dead.
Just say how soon, cause we've got the moon.
Say those words, then I'll swing my sword.

... can't give-up now.

Oh no, I've done the deeds,
I've sowed your seeds,
Here, let me show you.
Please, make the call,
For I gave my all,
Now my veins run ice-blue, blue, blue-

Let me show you...

Won't you curb my ache? Don't stop-stop,
Till I'm at your beck-in-call,
That bout of blind love.
Please gift those percs worth yearnin' for,
Cinch this sufferin', then give me more-

... oh, god, I like it.

Tip the chalice and gulp the wine,
'Till there's tinglin' all down my spine.
Gotta feel your rush.
Poppin' pills to reach my prime,
Cause I want this feelin' all the time.
Deed-well joys are never too much-

Grant me boon…

To face those comin' storms,
When I've got my head in the clouds,
And where lightin' cracks the sky.
Holdin' my breath and countin' to three
Dare-say, those angels are comin' for me, me, me-

… To see you soon.

Caught heat of ah-hundred degrees,
Gotta shed my skin, that ould-world tease.
Oh, how my mind's aflame,
Glowin' red-red-hot till my body's gone numb,
Heart's racin' like a beatin' drum
That pitch drivin' me insane-

I've got that urge to fight …

Spared sympathy from deviled eyes
Let your colors bleed and blend with mine
Until I'm painted to fit right in
In spite of these fears
Dear god, I can see it all so clear-

… been spurred by supernatural delight.

Can't know my friends from foe,
Spyin' world as a yellowed-stained soul.
Chasin' the crashin' waves- no doubt, no doubt,
Runnin' with all those brothers that break through.
Say, say, I'd do anything for you
As the wolves wail out-

Ride towards the fight…

Won't you loose those dogs of war?
Howl all loud, and let the ink run red,
Paint the canvas in victory march.

Cry bull rush, then lose control,
For I alone can't save my soul

… spreadin' the good word.

Mandrills make a formidable and intimidating addition to any party. It aspires to great heights, eclipsed solely by the bandit queen's alabear, standing a full four-heads above ordinary human ilk; an uncomfortable elevation where it becomes necessary to bend beneath the usual humbingings of doorframe or risk colliding into rafters.

The brawn is boldly buried in a mixture of olive and cedar-bark fur, fleeces of greasy hide cascading in tufts, acting as a facade for features beneath. As a whole, the body is some completely misshapen mesterpiece, deadlocked at several specific points, such as the elbows, where the joints protrude portly round. In a certainly blighted, peculiar fashion, these ligatures are quite pronounced, imbuing superhuman fits of raw strength. Its skeleton must be broader in build than those muscles, a situation in which haggard elements prevail their girth from the usual line-up of biceps and thighs, granting the appearance of an action figure, where the creature is bound together comically by twine and sticks, then bundles of tape meld the shape of gristle.

The visceral transformation has altered the vanguard's limb lengths too, bestowing hulking, over-drawn arms, yet a pair of stubbed legs strapped underneath gaunt hips and heavyset chest.

These characteristics contribute to an awkward center of gravity, as the Mandrill's pace regularly fumbles, shuffling across the ice sheet in three-foot wide strides, defined by its forward-heavy, ape-like gait. This method of locomotion is tiresome, prompting the creature to occasionally bend over, and walk on all four limbs instead. Burly and bullish tree-trunk arms are periodically propelled into the ice, fracturing the surface in a manner-without a doubt, most painful.

William may only wonder if there's a human mind sealed underneath all that fur. Their opponent is bundled by swathes of olive green, golden tinges tickle the fringes of facial whiskers, and in contrast, culminating in a white mane around bestial necking, dangling to the bends of the shoulder-blades.

This champion is prepared for the worst that these wastelands has to offer, an exhibition of cold desert and tundra climates. Those in its presence- mere humans, shiver from the ramifications of extreme cold, and that reigning pair of Manhunters remain almost completely unaffected.

At times they seemingly molt, where husks of skin churn to strike vivid colors, fostering toxic, blue-purple complexions before methodically returning to their naturally pale state. This affair is clearly visible on the brigand, who routinely washes palettes of cobalt, rendering regalia which wards potential predators.

While being escorted by the vile troop, the side-by-side comparison is uncanny. These Neanderthals are the embodiment of physical prowess and marital skill, the dominant force on this dead earth, regular people just don't stand a chance.

The imminent, janky cacophony of chains rattle scrutiny towards the rear, as the Mandrill tugs at the shackles of the bound yeomen. On the opposite end of the caravan, the brigand leads bitter company into the fray. In light of recent events and upon realizing that these victims will no longer instill any trouble, he has strapped this whale-bone shield to his chest, propping the broken stave of a bardiche onto his shoulders, and resting his forearms across the beam.

A creature nearby emits a low, guttural growl, compelling air through its nostrils and releasing a belligerent *snort,* some grim reminder that a polar bear roams freely at their flanks.

The entire creature disappears, the creamy tints of its fur is indistinguishable from adjacent snow banks, briefly noticeable from the maroon paint slopped upon its muzzle, face and chest, then the flashy, reflective iron burdens of its collar, and the bandit queen whom looms atop.

Entombed in that helm of hers, she's relative to a silent sentinel, scanning the distant horizons in search of their next competition: a worthy battle to test their mettle, wading through the muck and mire to become the cold-roiled host, scrupulously attuned to the limitations of the body, aching to clean the quarry by prying fat from bone.

The Bannermane creed encourages those embolden few to fight their fates, those brazen enough to take control of destiny. Now that they've reached the crowning achievements of their lives, here they are in earnest: some veteran ranger who's every adventure brings further loss; a recent migrant without the ability to protect the ones she cares about most; one learned man who lives perpetually in the shadows of his paramount, ignored and ridiculed; a crook whose sticky fingers have gotten them in more trouble than he's worth; some two-bit, wanna-be ruffians; another gambler goaded by greed, regularly anteing their hopes and dreams; a retired wainwright who spurred the north's greatest sailing vessels, more anxious and timid than all grand maesters of craft; a grizzly old-man renowned for his proficiency at slinging insults; some cordwainer who was swindled the keys of their kingdom; a Boar's Band of miscreants whom pillage entire treasure troves, pilfering the caravans of business magnates swifter than tears of frustration reach their eyes; a barbarian brute lounging in their layover; and an earnest lad who's only desire was to travel the frontier settlements, strung along by their penchant for stirring the pot.

These pioneers are destined for great things, and journey as kings among the dying earth, trekking across the tumultuous glacier as it gradually ebbs away over society. It'll take some thousand years until the ice sheet grinds their old city apart, as destiny is inevitable, and they'll eventually oversee a vast domain of nothingness.

This is the dream of those ill, Manhunters wish to return the earth to its natural state, a realm so raw and primordial, where humanity is in flux, a constant state of competition. It's not merely an unvarnished truth: that those who study history are doomed to repeat it, but there are vagrants who desire to burn the books too, craving chaos and inciting for the blind to lead the blind.

The monotony of the glacier is overwhelming, William could swear that this particular stretch of glaze seems familiar, that they passed this territory thrice before. These Manhunters must enjoy subtle torture and slow burns, leading them in circles over the recent hours, as such scenes inspire a lack of evidence.

Animals scarcely tread this way, there is no sign of life on the ice sheet. It's a profoundly desolate domain with no trailings or subtle prints in the packsnow.

The route they have embarked on is bleak, featuring no guideposts to speak of, and without hardly a map to assist them. These wastelands are sparse with landmarks, twist or turns among their remarkably flat landscape, a sullen depression. The brigand must be exploiting the rim of the ice sheet and farthest mountainpeaks as confidants.

This is the sole explanation of their debacle, yet these marvels aren't appearing any closer. There doesn't seem to be any momentum behind their advance, as if the company is simply treading water. Even while this white tide yields, lesser then the surge which surmounts the height of bison horns, this farthest frontiers are a dismal array, the journey long and arduous.

The swells of precipitation regularly encourage them to drown, tormenting their boy Jones in particular. William sluggishly shuffles his feet, boots wading through those ankle-biting drifts which threaten to swallow him whole. Death by asphyxiation is a common backcountry demise, those navigators whom plummet beneath the surface floes, riddled by powder and choked in endless white. His wooly leathers have been dipping into the fray, ensuring that the lowliest frills of pant-legs are encased with salty rime.

This additional freight is demeaning, and weighs him down greatly; not that the Manhunters are in a rush to get anywhere soon. William is now ranked among the slowest in their party, gallivanting with Rochester in a bid to remain relevantly ahead of the blighted caretaker.

If these dogs of war relish the hunt and close-quarters melee, it is awfully strange for them to carouse an area so characteristically devoid of life. Disregarding his over-encumbered situation, even if William was caught-up in the momentary thrill to scamper elsewhere, there are no justified outcrop hideaways or woodland copses in sight, absolutely nowhere to run.

The Mandrill is a rapidly evolving threat, a blitzing beast of bloodshed that peers periodically at the sky as searing-hot saliva drips from its toothy, pouting grimace. It's difficult to distinguish if it possesses any element of control. Who would win, the essence of man or beast? Is their element of humanity so far-flung, shoved so deep that it withers into a condensed kernel of coal? If this ape would lament against its restraints, give-in to those primal instincts and pursue quarry, who knows what it would do if it caught someone?

The earnest lad envisions that this flight of fancy would be fleeting, their mad dash of extradition capitulating when a torpedo of brawn strikes them, that conclusive exchange crescendoing with ferocious fangs ripping them apart limb from limb. By the looks of it, the warmonger has difficulty maintaining its composure, titillating haphazardly, determined to tear into those weak bodies being paraded nearby like stuffed animals, and let loose all the stuffing.

Stormfronts discharge their deluge with extreme prejudice, obscuring their approach in ominous and foreboding veils of shadow, contrasting against the stark, egg-shell laced expanse of these salt plains. Normally, navigating vagabonds wouldn't pay heed to the approaching gloom, only this particular rave is accompanied by an ardent, ear-piercing shriek, and mistaking it as another plain, noxious cloud would be a fatal mistake. William arcs backwards, tilting his head to view the breadth of firmament, observing that certain, distant silhouette of a raptor jolting across the sky.

In a state of constant conflict, vying for survival alongside the presence of Manhunters, it makes sense that life would avoid striding onto these plains if it could simply soar over any obstacles and threats instead. Just because the local megafauna chooses to avoid a fight doesn't necessarily mean the great eagle isn't outfitted for one.

A blanketing darkness embodies the company while the raptor makes another cast above, dashing those scarce beams of sunlight which ebb through the clouds, often for several seconds. Emerging from a stunned state, utilizing his personal orbs of blurry vision, Balthus points to the sky and identifies the vague shape of a kite, or at least, the motley spread strands of a well-used broom.

To more perceiving townspeople, its feathers are an armory at the arrangement of a castellan, evidently promoting the use of deadly, battle-ready falchions to cleave robust hundred-year pine in short-order, swifter than a score of salted timberjacks in the prime of their lives. The wingspan of this thunderbird is immense, radiating further than a caravan coach- in fact, three cars could be lined back-to-back, and their coupled hulls still wouldn't match the sheer size of it.

The boy Jones pays keen attention while shadows persistently dart across the wasteland, bridging the remote, faraway outcrops of each mountainpeak in mere seconds flat. Perhaps this extreme distance could be making the raptor appear larger than it really is, except when William recounts Glennitch's fabled stories about the whippoorwill snatching his extended family, he shudders at the thought. A bird of this size conjures true meaning to an albatross straddled around someone's neck. As a giant, unwieldy thing, laden by feather and bone, an earnest lad couldn't do a bit of anything.

Birds of prey maintain their scrupulous reputations for obvious reasons, beasts of that Machiavellian manner often carry off caribou and what-not, but in contrast, they are renowned for their eagle eyes. Avians that inhabit the fringe territories have developed vision so precise and undoubtedly superior, that men of the robe contemplate whether they are on par with gods.

Raptors, true whippoorwills that is, may peer the whole three-mile distance to the horizon, an entire league to scoff at the tiniest lemming modestly breaking some surface rime. While they can sight the tiniest visual distinctions, thankfully a bird's hearing is not as acute. Caught between a rock and a hard place, vagabonds might chance hiding, diving into the nearest nook and cranny without a peep. Otherwise, caught amid these unfettered gossamer plains, travelers are better off waving a flag to surrender, begging for a swift death.

William has always been the imaginative sorts, fostering a bout between these behemoths in his head, testing the might of a Mandrill and the neck-snapping velocity of shrieking siren. Though, realistically speaking, perhaps the raptor wouldn't probe the sharpness of its claws against a pale terror, that rogue of a white bear that it must've already spied skulking about.

While William barely manages to keep in those Manhunters good graces, and also gratefully, from the armor-sundering beaks of avian-kind, he's still susceptible to the wrath of Nana Nature, who disperses ill-contrived phenomena like windshearing. These recent trials have worn down the boy's facial bandages and gloves, bestowing bounties of dry, fragile skin to the squalls which harbor maladies against them.

Demonstrating their malice with glee, brutal cold fronts called chinooks eagerly glide down the Rimeweather Range, and flaunt through sudden, unexpected gusts. Snowbanks are the only aid to identify this invisible enemy, loosening icy particles whenever the wild winds dare taunt, a turbulent spectacle dancing across the desolate expanse.

They can clearly spot these whirlwinds atop the glacier, bulwarks of rural mountain air rushing towards them, wispy currents tumbling in snowbanks among the backcountry, rippling, undulating and generating cyclones. Caravanhands generally warn of these dangers from a league out, grudgingly aware that squalls may close the gap in an instant, swirling around a wayward navigator like a traveling minstrel, yet harboring the cruelty of a geist. They manifest tendrils that rend asunder, shredding coats of fabric to tatters, and abetting the strength that easily shears hide from skin.

Veteran Bannermane don't merely exhibit prosthetics brought about by frostbite and encounters with animal-kind, the whirling gales of Nana Nature prove equally disastrous, occasionally uncorking a settler's hat or scarf in benign fare- a matter to joke over, that is, until an unparalleled wind blast decides to sever someone's sniffer from their collection of more prominent facial features.

These arctic rushes of air dance above the shallows of white tide, then dissipate in a matter of seconds, floundering flat into stewing mounds of dunes and drifts, carelessly covering any crime scene they've fashioned with ardor, cautioning that these conditions may strike again and more furiously next time as repeat offenders. While the Manhunters may not be intent on executing them first, these winds will sure enough. They cannot keep this parade indefinitely, this caravan of prisoners will need to reach some sort of relative safety soon.

Korralack grows increasingly frustrated with their situation, especially as the brigand prances ahead, skipping and side-stepping in a manner that seems awfully strange to their company, like the rogue is playing some sort of game. Filled to the brim in lactic acid, the brute's legs feel akin to lead weights. These recent days have strained him to the breaking point, encouraging Korralack to throw shade at their lethal hosts by shouting at the Manhunter leading their pack.

"Oi-"

When he starts to rumble his voice box, preparing that odious, hassling barb, he is caught by surprise, stupefied when his next step causes the glacial mass beneath to cackle. Humbled as his forefoot sinks an inch deeper, Korralack can barely utter, "Son o' ah-," before this sleet slinks away, revealing a capacious gash in the ice.

He incidentally ducks forward, entrenched in the secret crevasse. Fortunately this excavation isn't extensive, and he instead *thuds* onto the rim, his heart skipping several beats, having almost tumbled into the abyss.

A one-way trip to hell is hidden by a thin casing of rim and heaps of snow, these disguised recesses ensure that the Antlers of the Earth is one of the earth's most gnarly features to fret. The brigand is familiar with this particularly sprawl, and choose not to relay pertinent information, presenting a broadening grin.

It isn't long before these hurdles become commonplace and this expanse littered in jagged pitfalls. William watches those townspeople meticulously test their footing, awaiting the inevitable incident when the grounds gives way and they recoil, trying to locate a fairly assailable, proper path. This traveling troop once marched in the face of peril, boldly journeying where no others have gone. Now their frontier grit has reduced to cinders, trekking with tails between their legs as all feelings of fortitude and their can-do attitudes have quelled.

The boy Jones is coerced into a supportive role, guiding Rochester the wainwright, offering his arm to console these scheming gullies. Bound in camaraderie, these two navigate the decaying terrain which gapes ajar. It is no breezy endeavor, there is a fair amount of hurdles and strain, but together, they find their stride.

Jerome continues to offer no condolences, trapping the remaining vestiges of his nose inside swathes of cloth. Stubbornness can be a boon in its own right, a sentiment that prevents the iron-willed from taking a bow.

There's a soreness swelling in the wiseacre's ankles, as these crookshanks lost their tenderness ages ago, a flourishing static while the heat has been sapped from Jerome's body, seeping from numerous holes inside his footwear and missing toes. During the greybeard's bout with danger, these gaping wounds provided momentary relief, unintentionally patching the expeditious injuries with his own solidifying ichor. Jerome is convinced that these legs- his own two shins, are better-off acting as stumps, managing a pace just sufficient enough to avoid some warrant of attention from the caravan's animalistic warden. The Mandrill is preoccupied escorting his quarry across the chasms with malice in mind, taking extra care to yank the chains whenever a yeoman is mid-step.

Psssh. Entire pockets of glacial mass splinter netherwards, taking the brunt force of the arctic bear and its manically gruesome, alabaster paws. Sheets of ice shed their folly as the creature is goaded to pounce, ravines fissure through the expanse like the snapping of pheasant bones, moments of calamity summoned by some dark master. While there may be a rush to their pace, these Manhunters aren't searching for something, truthfully, they're being drawn-in.

An enormous gust of wind bellows at their timely arrival, blowing a plethora of snowdrift clear, and revealing a frozen, glacial pool suspended in clear blue quartz. Their company emerges from the no man's land and onto this surface, feet immersed in a sullied yellow glow. Two brazen eyes stare at them from the deep, manifesting the ire of a fallen saint, shroud of an ancient demon.

"Darkness festers within. Cross the threshold and rejoice!"

The company is bombarded by an obscured, faint rumbling, some behemoth riling beneath the sacred pool. Under Balthus' distress, Libby and Bids spread their wings wide, and push their fellow townspeople to safety prior to the thunderclap, avoiding the subsequent, flailing crystal shards that the emerging hulk hurls them recklessly. William is baffled by this totem, steering wide as the ice detonates in huge, jagged crowns and debris, able to scalp unwitting passerby in a foul, single swoop.

When the eruption finally ceases, they survey a glass-lined guardian practically the size of a sailing yacht, entirely transparent, bearing resemblance to that of a human skull- well, human-esque say the least, with a suspiciously passing visage, though its giant-folk origin can be left as a debate among academic scholars. Of course, the sculpture is different-twisted in design, as is the urge of all things fell. Its eyebrows brashly contort into an ensemble of horns, tipped in gilded spires capped with a metallic sheen, an illusion not entirely unlike the bandit queen's.

In a trick of the light, sudden bolts of electricity plummet to these meteorological marvels, chaining them together in an arc of lightning, spurring its next phase. The totem's toothy ivorywork and rows of fangs slowly part, digging its chin back into the sacred pool from whence it came, and stretching the glass jaw to unfathomable lengths. The skull strains in demand of this effort, and upon reaching the zenith, lazily lapsing to the side, the maw finally thrust wide open. In contrast to the rime-ridden monument, a pliable, fleshy slug ventures forth, presenting a ramp descending down the gullet and into infinite madness.

Morbin mockingly chimes, "These guys sure know 'ow tah roll out the red carpet," but his commentary is harshly criticized by flustered *groans* of loathing, as the weary members of this troop are not entertained by these constant antics.

The last auditory *grumble* of the company was not produced through human-tongue. The bear heaves into full-view, striding across the rime while the sinister hussar yanks at its reins, corralling that company closer to the giant sculpture without delay, hassling them with ambivalently feral snarls. These low-growls aren't the result of stringing vocal cords, it is the beast's belly that rings violently, a certain machine starved of sustenance for the past week. There would be several chunks missing from the nearest vagabond if it wasn't for their dark master's watchful eye.

Though it's nearly impossible to tell beneath the iron, the rider scrutinizes the group one last time, nodding her head to the brigand in proximity to the portal. She whips her beast's hindquarters with leather and chains, goading the white bear down the throat's putrid passage. The myriad of *squelching* wet-plops as the ursid's paws and rustic flail dragging upon the spongy path is sickening. In anticipation of regal affairs, the glacial cavern has unlatched just enough so that the bandit queen mustn't have need to bow her head.

As the bear degrades the gullet, the brigand evokes their latent fears by waving his broken stave and points to the yawning entrance. This isn't a place where humankind is meant to tread, this is invoking insanity itself, no one in their right mind would ever trek down here, even if promised the lottery and entire riches of the world. However they cannot leave men behind: where Edmund and Mandel are taken, they must follow, as the two are still unconsciously sprawled upon the pale terror's hide.

The boy Jones is paramount, ushering his corresponding entourage into the fray, but not willingly, goading Mug Maxwell into saying the words, "Guess we gotta take the leap."

These townspeople instinctively huddle together, crowding the dimly-downtrodden human expression, horrifyingly aware that the mouth could snap shut at anytime, puncturing their innards and spilling rosy juices. Notions that prescribe an untimely demise compel shivers more imposing and illustrious than any degrees of cold could foster. William uses this opportunity to surpass those standard-issue townspeople that normally lead their fellowship, taking the brunt of two distinct, but nonetheless pungent stenches of hide and hindquarters.

As much as he's appalled, the throat's tonsils seem to reach out and slap at him, complimenting this cavern is remarkable carnal construction. It seems to stand as if the ice had been chiseled away during the times of antiquity, that this elusive passage is man-made, despite living and breathing appearance to the contrary. Their march is labored by bursts of smog, spontaneously sucking warm, fetid air directly through the tunnel.

Thankfully, it isn't steep at all, much to the graces of the limping Jerome as the hike traverses at a low-grade, twenty-degree or so angle. He would have slunked onto his rear and slid down if it isn't for the mucous-sifted saliva smearing their steps, pooling generously like cellophane glue and coating boots in a protective layer of glaze.

As the fellowship reluctantly *slop-slop-slops* further along the passage, they beg attention of those lesser beings entombed in these halls, Almost shrouded upon the ceiling, cradled behind a bank of ridges is a cryptic, coin-sized arachnid. It's vibrant, cranberry form blends into the minutiae of this cavern, a blot against rifts of ripe red scarlet.

William is captivated in paying regard to this local fauna, further intrigued when the critter raises half of its limbs menacingly, aspiring to enlarge itself with warning before spewing a chemical swill in their general direction. Venoms that fester inside illicit creatures often possess dubious intent, and as chance would have it. This bane lands among their footwear, proving to be a suitable distraction as the spider scurries over yonder at an incredibly alarming pace.

The brigand behind doesn't bat an eye nor scoff at this encounter, shoving the boy Jones forward so that he accidentally steps in the slime. These attercops must be the usual occupants, an audience to the Manhunters travels, and are considered nothing more than vermin to worry about.

Following the due course of this underground artery is slow progress, yet eventually the unsightly aroma and sense of sickness cedes to snow, reminding William of when they first entered the glacier, right before meeting the yeomen for the first time.

While it shames him to say it, the boy Jones is truthfully better, asserting to himself, 'Oh, how these times have changed,' as the Mandrill tugs the three troopers from the dingy tunnel, carelessly thrusting their faces in the limelight. A glass ceiling, some thin layer of surface rime, combined with the transparently lucid ice sheet allow for luster to enter unabated.

Journeying to this particular trench would've been impossible earlier, as these corridors alter almost every season and are vain to chart, so it becomes occasionally necessary to take a shortcut from the surface here, there, ducking and weaving. Glancing over his shoulder, the portal where they exited has the appearance of nothing extraordinary, there's just a jagged frame, the textbook definition of what's to be expected in a decrepit tunnel.

At disregard to the hostile natives and the inherent dangers of shifting ice, the Antlers of the Earth are a fantastic mesh: the thrill of the unknown, stunning upsets at every turn, like something out of a fairy tale. It's conceivable that these chasms are the utmost wonder of the natural world, as there's not anything quite like it.

After their discoveries at the PEMLLI, between Balthus, Morbin and the boy Jones, this trio is perversely ecstatic while the remaining townspeople are- quite understandably, fraught. Their curiosity piqued long ago, and now they are hampered by burgeoning fears. Could they be mending approach towards yet another ancient vault? This trek towards the acropoli and mountain strongholds of Clan Marius have proven futile. What other elusive secrets could this ice sheet withhold from mortal men? Will they scout vast riches, mythic temples or delve further into history? The thought of any account is enticing.

The bandit queen halts her advance, reeling an arm before snapping it readily in place, fraudulently toying with the chains, issuing an apparent wave metallic links until the flail-ends flicker. A cast-iron bell frolics into the air, *clang-clang, thump, krrzt,* ending its flashing rampage by colliding erratically into the canyon wall. Plaguing clouds of censer mist funnel around her beast, prompting the pale terror to bellow in fright when the nauseating concoction seethes into its nostrils, delivering a timely roar that echos down the frozen torrent.

The ravine answers in haste, addressing the Manhunter hello in a moment's notice, by spreading apart by a method most peculiar. Thousands- if not, millions of gallons of petrified concrete, timber and rime part, inch further away by the second, allowing the bandit queen, brigand, Mandrill and honest company to continue their march with a wide berth.

While initially emerging onto a fifteen-foot span of permafrost, now they track through an ocean of black sand. The canyon broadens an additional foot or two at a time, clearing thirty-feet, then easily fifty-feet, constantly continuing to expand, fissuring all the while, and splitting at the seams as if giants themselves were prying at the passage.

This isn't a conjurer's cheap-trick at some second-rate magik show, feats such as these are physically ridiculous, requiring unfathomable amounts of power.

Aggravating her mount forward by planting a stern kick into its furthermost foreleg, the beast apathetically groans and lumbers forward, striding for an unmistakable landmark flashing in the distance. It appears as a distorted and janky mirage, swelling to the loftiest rime one moment, before buckling into into canyon walls the next, altering presence every second, blurring its existence from the prying suspicious gazes. William can spot the evidence at a half-mile distance, and while original wrapped in wonder, his glee wanes and this marvel motivates him to regret those recent impulses by the minute. They are about to enter the domain of a god.

William takes both hands and massages at his temples, falling victim to an awful headache brewing behind the eyes. It feels as if a bomb has gone off, immediately filling his brain with clusters of shrapnel, spewing slews of sodden snot clear from both nostrils. This mental onslaught forces a grip against his temples, shooting pain down the spine, tensing his neck and causing him to stumble. The tip of his footwear buries itself into the frost, completely wringing an ankle, delivering that profile of the boy Jones rife with tears.

It's an abruptly throbbing montage, but the sting swiftly subsides. The fog dominates his dull grey matter only briefly, imposing a brief sliver pause in the hike. It's like arriving in a dream, receiving intelligence crafted right on the spot, as if he had treaded through these hallow grounds before.

William's approach has activated a buoy of sorts, invading his brain and bestowing intimate knowledge of this domain, leaving distinct memory engrams imbedded in his psyche. He is now well-aware of where their party is being lead to: Trench Hadrien, the devil's immortum, pale to the preacher's posturing, sanctum maleficarum of the Manhunters and all things destined for fell. As if some learned man has pulled the wool from his eyes, in this instance, everything becomes clear.

Their fellowship is instantly thrust twenty-feet, closing the few-thousand pace gap in a spree of magikal spell. The earnest lad leans back with such astonishment, that one would be led to believe that a ton of bricks had been strapped to his person, peering upwards at the lofty palisades of the bastion and its villainous curtains. The bulwark is of supernatural origin, wrought from the gargantuan ribcage of some fantastic beast, its stagnate titan-sized bones melded together as support beams. Timber staves are thrust between them, sporting sharpened tips so that acrobatic artists wouldn't notion vaulting over. Spikes and metal shards frolic with the density of bewilderbeast hide, arranged in one simple motion, that any would-be invader would be impaled alongside a half-dozen giant toothpicks. Myriads of ivory tusks have been looted from their trophies, carved in symbolic glyphs, details of the hunt and challenges to boast over. What could the Manhunters be expecting to fight out here? What sort of beasts and unnamed monstrosities are they so intent on keeping out, or better yet, just what are they keeping in?

Filthy, rasping arrangements of fingers man the battlements, clasping at the outer fringes of parapet wall. A member of this entourage rings a handbell at their arrival, *clang-ca-lang, clang-ca-lang, clang-ca-lang,* filling the air with calamitous tolling. William can hardly recognize the cacophony as they approach the gatehouse. The noise sounds oddly warped, like the constant humdrum of flies at his ear.

One last obstacle bars entry to this castle Bailey, a pair of girder gates, studded in spiny knobs, then reinforced with cold steel. This entryway towers over them, nearly matching the height of Mad River Junction's, three-story local chapter. The sheer weight of these double-door panels proves outlandish to shove abroad, instead chains rattle and drums reel as beasts of burden pull those swollen shutters ajar, creeping at first, gradually picking up speed until the hatches swing wider than the jaws of a giant behemoth.

A colossal hall looms forth, lit by horned sconces tending wretched flame, bathing the demesne in chaotic fiery glow. The natural impression of light flaunts at the end of the tunnel, yearning them to escape their alienating interlude. As the white bear barrels onward, it skeptically peers at the walls beside them, raising its lips and growling. Several barred barriers line the walls of the corridor, each and every cell imbedded in total darkness. As William disregards Mug's intention of prattling on, he finds himself subject to his inquisitive behavior, a manner which usually leads him into trouble.

Spying into the nearest dungeon, the boy's ears are disciplined by that very same metallic clanking. A rambunctious clamor urges him to lean closer, ignoring the fact that these holes in the linchpin have been hewn by talons. The routine *clink-clink-clink* of iron warns that an inmate draws near. A pair of toxic orbs flaunt in the portal, reflecting the ambient torchlight, barely giving the boy Jones the benefit of the doubt and an opportunity to react. It funnels an arm headlong through the bars, swinging frantically, screaming, hollering and chanting hysterically, catching those oversized hats and slashing the coattails of anyone who has wandered too close.

These are the wild ones, those followers of chaos that have turned into Mandrills, and due to the rapid influx of power, rotted their own minds. They are prescribed menial labor, and caged for later use. Trench Hadrien's cannon fodder fester in the dark, tribes of mindless apes secretly conveying what they would do if they chanced escape, an excursion that would certainly end in bloodshed, or whatever putrid color that seeps from Manhunter wounds.

As the party emerges past the gatehouse and strays upon the opposite side of bulwark, they are greeted by a broad court some hundred-feet across, and of course, the camp's inhabitants of renown. An outlaw descends the palisade ramp, choosing to waltz upon the vast court in daunting manner, sizing up this fresh quarry. Those earnest lads may sight that familiar threading of scabs itching atop his skin, then webbing rigorously upwards to the discipline of his crowning, bascinet helmet. This is the sole article of armor that the legionary wears, for he is of black-blood, one of those hounds sporting a pedigree among dastardly wolves. In lieu of a weapon, he wields a badge that doubles as a buckler, kiting a pair of moose antlers, a trophy from some recent odyssey, into the rough shape of the shield and filing those racks into sharp points so that he may impale victims too, rather than simply rendering them unconscious from blunt-force trauma.

Another rogue sprints up to accompany him, and everybody is made well-aware to that fact. She is coated from head to toes in a variety of umbrella brass bells, or moreso, the majority of this ensemble is merely made of clappers which dangle aimlessly like ornaments. Two Manhunters quickly become four, then eight, sixteen, so on and so forth until the numbers climb to nearly four-hundred heads. The majority of this lethal host is too busy, distracted by their duties. One striking scoundrel brandishes a mancatcher, a peculiar device involving metal pincers strapped to the end of a shaft, aiming to capture a few delectable avians roosting in the adjacent lofty glacial threads.

These tangerine-billed birds have been dipped in soot, the tips of their wings are encrusted in inky residue, spreading at the sight of their adversary, when the appetizing rapscallion ventures close, taking flight over the court and carefully avoiding the looming totem.

The Manhunters have erected a ritualistic pillar in the center of their camp, some obelisk that disrupts ley lines, pilfering the energy of the world pillar and beckoning chaos. Mandel and his gods can't help them here.

To their immediate right is a training area composed of armored carapaces and rotting carcasses, followed by strings of radial huts lined in wooly pelts. These animal skins disguise the illicit origins of Trench Hadrien, that Manhunters fret inside the leftovers of massive skulls and giant remains, a case that would unquestionably drive Austerlaund into a frenzy. On the opposing side is a rickety bridge, or the skagway as they call it, lining their unbarred pit of spoils. This is the platform in which they donate war trophies and ill-gotten gains, lobbing potential ancillaries into the abyss, believing the material sacrifice will bring untold pleasure.

While Boar's Band members raid one another, building their reputation with stunts through the seasons, Manhunters are the complete perversion of that ideal, literally wasting their plunder, and no one even knows of their exploits.

The pit is oddly cylindrical, spewing hundreds of needle-like teeth that occasionally orient in then spread outward in unison, giving the illusion of breathing. Anything tossed inside is a lifetime commitment, as these rows of barb wire prevent any ancillaries from being recovered or cleverly pried free.

Their bandit queen disembarks from her mount, yanking Edmund and Mandel off the bear with spite, then making a beeline towards the skagway. Without its rider, this gigantic bears falls under the influence of hunger, heading to investigate the sources of commotion nearby, departing towards the vicinity of those charcoal birds.

Spurred by kicks to the rear, William and his company are goaded forcefully to follow. In their haste, Jerome swells with pain and fumbles onto the permafrost. The burly brute and Mug Maxwell leap into action before the Manhunters have the opportunity to traumatize him further, assisting the greybeard onto his knees, supporting him from underneath the armpits, and lifting that poor layman onto the bridge.

The bandit queen turns to Edmund first, tearing into his clothing, exposing half-baked skin, stained from stewing in his own juices. He's in no shape to quarrel, barely awake and mustering moans. Looting the confines of his jackets, she throws his small-game traps, the fellowship's remaining Kirkhaus tindersticks, a bag of dried jerky, and any belongings that could be made into weapons or picks into the gaping maw. Garments are spliced, torn to slivers and strips, then also cast into the pit.

These frigid temperatures should immediately condemn the wickerwalker to a brutal end, but his dermal layer has yet to atrophy: blister, boil and blacken. As long as they remain in the presence of fell, Manhunters mitigate the true effects of cold.

As one of Trench Hadrien's reigning linchpins, the bandit queen is entitled to a degree of superiority, commanding those loitering Manhunters to escort Edmund beyond the skagway and to the cellblock, then she proceeds to work once more, undergoing the exact same process with the habitually conscious Mandel.

The bridge planks yield and waver, concluding with a mild *creak*. That Manhunter with the moose trophy shield, barrels through his lesser kin, his naked feet pressing into the boards and causing them to warp. Noticing an inkling of fear in his eyes, this outlaw strolls up to the boy Jones first. William doesn't doubt their intent, and rather then having his ensemble ripped apart at the seams, he loosens that silver, zipping keychain binding his coat and slides the shredded fleece onto the floorboards, removing any outerwear. This is their prison warden, and he takes amusement in intimidating their newest inmate.

Scraps of overcoat dangle from the bridge as this warden yanks the captive every which way, mincing threads, racking him to and fro. An invaluable slice of sleeve is severed, and plummets further into the abyss, weighed-down like an anchor by his family's copper stamp wrung around the fringe with twine. William's afraid that seal won't be useful any longer, he'll be seen as a free-man in the eyes of suspicious Bannermane, not bound to any place of business or mercantile.

Satisfied upon the loss of his his valuable woolies, the warden unleashes an indulging *grunt,* enough of a threat that the boy Jones wouldn't try running away or risk instant hypothermia. Unfortunately, this act reveals the existence of William's locket, a gleaming object of value that is yanked from his neck, with the trivial band snapping in two, and thrown into the maw without consideration. Normally, this defiling deed would jerk a tear or two, however there is no time to grovel.

After ceding his worthwhile items, William is intent on keeping something, even the most trivial tokens. He's fully prepared as the Manhunter's gaze inevitably drifts towards his bag, and through a superb performance of legerdemain, slips a hand into the knapsack to procure Edmund's trinkets, as these whittled carvings are small enough to secretly stow in the clasps of his palms. He willingly abandons this satchel of his own intuition, showcasing an unwillingness to be hassled further, as a Manhunter would sooner pry this burlap from his possession with enough force to send him reeling. The warden continues to eye their prize, examining him ruthlessly, waiting for that one, last crucial sacrifice that wrings the dagger deepest into William's heart.

The pages of Jeremiah's journal have furled from the flames, becoming unsightly thick and impossible to conceal beneath his jackets without claiming that he has an excessive tumor. Rather than test this rogue's scrutinizing ire, to his demise and the pity of all wiseacres, this boy Jones abandons the notebook to the chimney, fully aware that these Manhunters would sooner see this knowledge burn.

Perhaps it's a blessing to forfeit rather than be forced to destroy, such a thought mends the sacrifice of his parents pewter locket. He shakes his fists at such hogwash, cursing those endless cycles of destruction. William's hands shall always be urged to create, becoming callous in due time, making the most of those teachable moments. Failure is completely natural, akin to the shedding of snake skin, he'll trim away the fat and take this loss in stride, as memories are more important than any material wealth.

Besieged by Bannermane dogmas, other members of their party inspire different stories entirely. Tat bell-rattled outlaw has begun to hold Libby upside-down by the boots, shaking her with a passion for violence until an arsenal of knives and daggers work their way out. Bids stares in horror, the threat of her sibling plummeting onto these harpoons below and being violently impaled.

Morbin is profoundly upset, slouching defiantly against a wooden post. Only when the Manhunters demonstrate bodily harm by unleashing a salvo of punches and kicks does the amateur archeologist reluctantly renounce his lockpicking kit. These are instruments that he has spent his entire childhood rearing, a bout to ensure successful robberies and early retirement.

A truly unscrupulous foe unravels this gear, procuring a single-hooked pick to root around their teeth, unsuccessfully intending to dislodge some cantankerous rot. The quintessential sour of their gums, one of those numerous side-effects accompanying the consumption of raw flesh, beckons a spongy texture that simply detests this repetitive prodding, releasing foul gas in response.

Reaching beneath the flailing arms of Libby Warder, another Manhunter relieves a shortsword gleaming from inside fringes of her sleeve. This adversary takes the weapon with gleaming pride, sharpening the blade between their teeth as naturally as maestros string fiddles, testing the metal. Shards of the metal cast-iron splinter instead of the ivorywork, fueling the sibling's anxiety.

As the troop is routinely disarmed, forced to strip in the cold, barely coping within the balm of a nearby brazier, they are coerced to peel their insulated padding, any headgear, face coverings, coats, parkas, jackets, cloaks, capes, mantles, shawls and stoles until they're left to squirm in those less than ideal layers: underlying sweatshirts and fleeces.

As long as they remain inside the camp, propped by the cackling glow of bonfires, they might garner relative safety and avoid deep-freeze. An unfamiliar, discolored flame flails within reach, radiating certain trace elements of indigo, bronze and beige tints, schemes which coax William to glimpse further inside.

Some movement catches his eye, rooting around at the ignition point as naturally as sootwrasse worms wriggle in ash. Spying at the core, an earnest lads peers at beings among the inferno, creatures of the immortum cast in illusion, those demons who cater exclusively to the whims of the seven sins.

These eternals are bred to serve, ordained from a natural process as slivers of the gods themselves, cut from the same cloth, originating from spilled blood or shedding skin, wasted product to spread onto this world. They are constantly at odds with human followers and familiars, especially when cultists are imbued with supernatural abilities that rival their own. Mankind simply cannot resist the lure of their own authority, latching onto power, refusing to relinquish command after one taste.

The sins crave bodies and souls in which to mold, yet not their minds, as dark gods have no need for independent thoughts. Truthfully, a majority of those uplifted into everlasting servitude can't handle the corruption, their mortal forms frightfully contorted by chaos energies, often warping into the guise of gibbering grims. They become as rudimentary as livestock, driven by the hands of their masters as burdened beasts of battle.

Those that turn from grace or instead rejecting such gifts altogether are cast from the carnival court, reshaped into those infermieri, or the faceless dead. Blessed with foul new forms, these are the hands that typically thwart a navigator's ankles, lunging from beneath the snow, or cursed to join the ever-growing ensemble of mannequins frozen in those outskirts of old city. Either way, these are sour fates.

While William may be scantily clad, he cautions his eerily pleasant demeanor as a cruel jest. While spared of the frigid chill, keeping the rather unforgiving climate on retainer, Trench Hadrien petitions further fraud. This is deceit, pure and simple, scarcely some benevolent oasis.

He plunges the figurines into his denim pants pockets, patting this collection twice to ensure that they're secure. These may be ordinary keepsakes to wickerwalkers, but strangely enough, the boy Jones is charmed by their insignificance, especially in comparison to the towering totem before him; an ironic counterpart, looming across the chasm and casting shadow, the river of umbral darkness. Consisting of a slender pole which spans to the height of those canyon walls, wicked is as wicked does. Embellished by the occasional thorn, this bastion of pride conveys unspeakable evil. Branches congregate at the zenith, upholding the eminence of an elk's hallmark cornucopia of horns, a crowning claw which grasps at the firmament, loathing in the success of celestial stars.

The base of this citadel is obscured in graphite smoke, a shallow burn pit filled to the brim with the warground's detritus. People are dancing wildly around the pyre, inhaling those hallucinogenic fumes, holding hands and skipping in circles. A score or so of prisoners are struggling, barely standing among their own intuition, lapsing their heads and sweating oil. Several cut-throats spur the crowd, leading accomplices into fervor, tugging them forward with mockery to which they may savor this experience.

It's with perverse fascination that those whom wield godly powers become disenchanted from prevailing matters, rather preferring to use their supreme might to force lessers into fantastic circumstances. After all, those with everything may easily share. The divines could solve world hunger with the mere snap of heavenly fingers, yet they don't. It'd be different to sponsor lavish feasts, but beggars are pleading for the bare minimum, lamenting those bakers who chuck yesterday's bread. Urchins still starve in poorhouses, which is why beings far greater aren't worth the worship of moral men. If a person sights adversity and remains willfully ignorant, refusing to act, they shall be treated as evil. So why are the residents of kingdom come treated so differently?

These Manhunter rogues elude to the true motives behind their gesture, that this great game isn't just an amusing form of entertainment in which they may hurl rocks, the jig is designed to torture those with fragile spirits, and cure their weakest captive ilk. When the first participant stumbles, loosening their grip and collapsing onto the permafrost, the totem seemingly *hisses* in response.

A thorn lurches forward, skewering their spleen and impaling the awkward fool by means of vile tendril tongue. This harpoon corrupts their flesh and clothes entirely, turning them into living ink until the innocent victim is absorbed back as writhing black mass, returning into the totem. The crime scene lacks a corpse, save for some scruff atop nearly-frozen, ebony grit. This is a maddening spur to action, a teaching lesson, yet the remaining candidates are all too tired to react. Surely, the presence wouldn't devour them all, would it?

Beyond the rogue idol are the feasting tables, where a majority of the Manhunter assembly has gone to partake in scandalous splendors. These tables are hewn from the carcass of an overturned, mercantile sailing ship, showcasing the freshest animal trophies around, and those a little on the rancid side, cultivating protein-rich, nutritious maggot-kin. The outlaws unceremoniously dig at the hind of boar, excavating hidden ivory and viscera. Its own mouth is aghast in horror, one last harrowing visage, choking on a swollen ruby gem to allow clouds of steam to escape from the shrinking lungs. They crave swine, raw and untempered, savoring in the foul-smelling juices. Just as William eyes them, biding the time, awaiting when one contestant in this championship will hurl over dead, they belch, immune to the ill-effects of toxic boar-flesh.

This isn't the only cadaver they hastily rifle through, fantastic beasts line the hull, sometimes spanning the entire length, flanked by a single kraken tentacle. The most daring among them delivers a butcher blade straight into the gristle of bovine, splitting bone and leaking bits of marrow across the bloc. She sunders bison ribs with ample encouragement, those in the vicinity banging ladles upon their rusty cauldron with glee, stew-pots coveting boiling green concoctions. Their roiling bubbles simmer all manner of mischievous critters, bits and pieces of grub foaming upwards into the suspicious sign of skull and cross bones.

They choose to combat the main courses with sickles and gaffhooks, wrangling their prey, and yanking chunks of meat, sometimes heaving the entire carcass towards them.

A Manhunter scales their seat, stomping around in animosity. They lean over the width of table, delivering a swift blow to the fellow next to them, bashing each other's brains out in sick competition. Their blood is a gravy, some superb relish in color of pitch flows over the exposed meal and warps the timbers as tithe between raiderlings.

While the outlaws are preoccupied by banter, birds opportunistically pounce down, scavenging those buffet scraps, then deliberate return to their unreachable edifices. One unlucky raptor is selected for sport, they allow it to arrive and examine a sliver of raw beef before skewering the perpetrator with a pitchfork. The angler slams their freshest dish onto the table, dead on arrival. Those Manhunters bellow in anticipation of the next course, drowning themselves in copious kegs of bluddraught, cider, and of course, pillager's porridge.

As the company solemnly makes their final pass over the bridge, sifting feet as William peers into the yawning abyss, discovering a true parasite of the earth. This pit of spoils is nothing elementary of the sort, where he had expected piles of abandoned weapons, fabric and debris, the boy Jones observes another fleshy cavern, those ridges of ribs plastered in bristles of baleen hair. This depression offers staunch reminder to the iconic insides of a humpback whale, almost as if there were a living creature were buried beneath the permafrost.

Goaded into action by the riling racket of feasting tables and a particular wallop at his shoulder-blade, William joins those being steered towards the nearest cellblock. Ushered down a zigzagging path in the ice sheet, they discover the stewing quarters, a domain of incarceration clad with rebar. Five cells have been erected in some sort of jury-rigged brig, and the sparse prison population which dwells here tread ominously, brooding with grave gazes.

The Manhunter helmsman ferries those captives with no organization to their endeavors, people are divvied, and thrown ahead into spacious pens. With the profound absence of any lock and key, these wardens utilize the weight of gridiron to ease temptations of escape. Bolstered by a few circus strongmen, they lift a garrison's worth of fortifications into a crevice cresting the ceiling. Hastened inside, the townspeople are thrust into the confines of crystal and pig iron, trapped as the rebar plummets back down.

Clang, thwack. This gate shudders with such force that the bottommost pickets puncture inside the ice, riddling the area in fractures that will shortly glaze over.

As William is marched into an ad hoc bunkhouse alongside Morbin,

Mug and Balthus, the barely roused wickerwalker and cordwainer are also deposited prior to the cell securely fastening shut. This demesne is frigid and barely hospitable, already populated by numerous disgruntled faces. This room bears a slight resemblance to that of a crescent-moon, the shape of their cell smoothly arcs into a rear wall caked with winter rime. This is the largest portion of the brig, and their particular range shares gridiron with the adjacent cell. As he peers through the scarred rebar, the same can be said of their pen, then the third and four room.

This isn't metal that the boy Jones is about to test, these cold-rolled slivers are so encrusted with rust, those plentiful swathes of corrosion from the constant waxing and waning of water vapor, a vagabond could garner tetanus from a brief glance. His mind immediately retires notions of making a quick getaway. Not one to tempt death, he wouldn't risk squirming through or prying rungs of this caliber apart, the earnest lad will need tools at his disposal. Too bad Morbin lost his- lockpicking kit, he understands though, the archaeologist had to give those nasty Manhunters something to satisfy their authority. The snow settling this ground has been trampled firm by its inhabitants, featuring a physique on par with rime, ensuring that tunneling underneath is fruitless.

While the traveling troop enters the end of their journey, Jerome and Rochester lag behind, with the wainwright assisting the rehabilitated senior by exchanging spoiled linen for fresher bandages. As the temperatures rise, he receives a sudden shock to his system. This heat disrupts his original scabbing salve, thawing that once hard blood and melting those temporary caps of frozen ichor. Now, the almost infirm, heavily-maimed Jerome leaves a trail indistinguishable from red streak upon a map, dying the bleak powder in rich vermillion throes.

"Off," he scorns, scoffing at Rochester whom is attempting to quell those injuries. The wainwright had exclusively reserved tatters of linen for this purpose.

"*Gah.* Off o' me 'ready ye blunderin', fool!"

An eclectic copper aroma steeps the corridor, the delicate spice of life when nectar begins to rust and solidify, piquing Manhunter glands. Their nostrils receive intense amounts of ardor, salivating tiers of mucus in ecstasy. The beguiling spill of sanguine is holy to them, and they care little from whence it flows. They flaunt behind their iron curtain with such glee that one could expect a religious ceremony, that a trench would suddenly part beneath their feet, and waxy cherubs clamber forth. Wingless and missing the very pits of their hearts, coin-operator demons driven forth by an intense desire to do harm. Beings of the immortum hold a grudge for humans specifically, envious that these mortals have led such independent lifes, while they remain attached to the sins by manner of umbilical cords, similar to how rat tails are entwined to their king.

Before they relent to their deepest, instinctual urges for further bloodshed, bathing in gore, the Manhunter warden hoists Jerome by the shoulder, thrusting the wiseacre into the cage amid Sturgeon the huscarl, whom shares an awfully fetid fate from the bludgeoning of his own hands; Yeoman Braga and Bitte, then poor Rochester whom is hanging for dear life, forcibly towed en suite.

Before they depart and leave these prisoners to their own devices, a caretaker begs those yeomen closer with the crook of their finger. The duo abide, leaving Sturgeon in stupor, allowing the criminal vagrant to wallow in his juices. Without a key on-hand, their massive mitts will decidingly do the job. Those calloused fingers clutch at their shackles, bending the stiff frames as if they were constructed from tissue paper. These chains and neck collars are torn apart nigh instantaneously, and the Boar's Band vagabonds foster grimace when that steel shutter abruptly slams to a close.

Everyone whom warrants anything of note has been detained in these pens, allowing the Manhunters window in which to depart, basking in the ire of their newest trophies and enabling prisoners to wallow in self-pity. Their company has been so expeditiously split apart, yet when settlers are encouraged to fold, they fancy at the prospect of drawing another hand, as Bannermane often compulsive gamblers.

The boy Jones is begging to meet the acquaintances of those that share similar fates, there must be a dozen people strewn among these iron brigs. William and his entourage shepherd space amid six strangers, then Lena, Korralack, Libby and Bids occupy the neighboring cell alongside another three. The third pen consists of three members, degenerates ordained as common rabble, not mentioning their accomplices Rochester, Jerome, Sturgeon, Braga and Bitte. To their disbelief, the two final cells are unceremonious empty, the gates barred absolutely open. The boy Jones presumes that these rooms will refuge entrants who survive their dance with danger.

With ample time on his hands, those earnest lads whom are clever enough investigate the farthest retaining of this dungeon. Crevices dot the particular partition, filled to the brim in folded parchment and fibers: stories from long ago, best described as dedications towards their last will and testaments, fools begging for forgiveness at the light of pure, unadulterated evil, and unanswered cries for help. Upon following the ignored sliver linings, these bottled messages trail into a fissure clearing into an adjacent passage, oriented just so right that those unscrupulous foes and wardens of theirs aren't aware of its presence- how convenient! Some incumbent vagabonds lounging nearby catch sight of William's conniving attitude and hints of possible escape, unexpectedly advising against such recourse.

"Dontcha even think 'bout it," a wiry, worn and ragged pilgrim blurts aggressively.

"'Avin' lodged in these facilities for the better part o' three-months, I can attest ye wouldn't want tah go that route. People string down that corridor n' nevah return."

The crass stench of soiled linen riffs at Morbin's face, he shrivels his nose in disgust, flaunting his hand into the air and slapping at the wind.

"Oi, take ah step back ya blubberin', bankrupt bum. *Whew.* That odor is ravishin' ruin!"

Mug Maxwell ignores their archaeologist's selfish plight, as in the wisdom of common sense, all corpses smell the same.

"Surely, I reckon- 'agen 'e fashioned ah darin' 'eist?"

"Nah, dear Bannermane brood, that 'bond warranted ah fate far worse. There's ah reason why that tunnel is stained scarlet."

This revelation is disconcerting, William is flustered that he hadn't spied the viscera earlier. Instead of the signature blue crystalline haze, the core of this ice is lined in transparent wine-red hues.

The pastor conveys, "And right now, we're not ah bit flattered as tah certify any theories."

"Don't be treadin' on any thin ice without me," a familiar voice starts to mumble.

Laying on his back, Edmund teeters his head and massages his wrists, seemingly checking for his own pulse.

"Oh-ye, that was ah rough ride for sure. I'm still sore all o'ver. Won't be testin' that mountie 'gain anytime soon."

Most people imprisoned here tend to keep to themselves, yet there's always a stranger bending an ear for conversation. One woman has been curled into the hoarfrost, tuning her stringed shamisen away from the clamors of crowds, plucking at those three cords with the occasional *thrum* or *twang*. She eccentrically clamors, "I recognize that voice," and turns to address her newest company.

William feels slighted that their wardens allow the bard to maintain her instrument. Perhaps she's a special case, as Manhunters bend an ear to those serenades about fleeing the coop, savoring as their captives realize that these dreams will never become reality.

"What the fuck ye've been doin' Mundie? Fightin' the gods themselves from the look of ya. Sounds like someone took ah tumble 'gainst the bandit queen. Certainly shook yer roots I see."

"This headache is ragin'…"

"Course so ya dolt."

She grabs onto the stinky layman by his sleeve and thrusts him aside, all in a ploy to stride closer to the wickerwalker.

"Not supposed tah be breathin' in smoke of any kind. Refrain from those same certain 'erbs Manhunters indulge on. What the 'ell 'ave ye been up tah anyhow? Tis been ages."

"Well I'll be a mink's motha. Stone those crows. Boisterous Jenny, can't nary believe it! Lookin' ah lil' worse for wear yerself."

She humorously chides, "Sure could use miracle lotion right now. Some John Crease's Body Balm for the Workin' Gal."

"Yer kiddin', not 'ere five minutes and we windin' this ole jack-in-the-box 'gain? Shut'up 'bout that John Crease, 'ready. John this, John that, only crease 'e should be feelin' are those rings 'round mah knuckles. Ye know 'ow it pesters muh. Don't need ah name drop everytime we meet. Knew 'e was snakeoil since we first shook 'ands. Now ye know betta than to leave me in the lurch, questin' for some strange business prospect. Sure yer still countin' those licks from the last bout with debtahs, 'uh?"

"Oh ye," Jenny sarcastically snaps, "That's why I'm 'ere muhself. Fancy ah figure that ye 'ad yer last shot 'round the poker table or somethin' like that. Can't ante yer way outta this one, wicka, when I 'ready own yer hovel."

"Awe, stick ah pin it, lass. Still, tis great tah see ya 'round. These Manhunters are fiends. What are they anyhow? Can't be 'uman- skewered several of them by now."

"They're naught but 'usks, kooky fools paradin' with danga, wannabe skinwalkas for demons. Manhunters are ah tarnished lot, 'umanity turned over like ah bad penny. They forfeit morals in fava o' becomin' dark, twisted sleeves of their old selves, worshippahs o' the tempest gods. These aren't the divines that we're used tah dealin' with, those spirits that kindle our 'omes and 'earths or manipulate the weatha. Manhunters idolize the seven sins, ancient primordial entities that 'ave been kickin' since the dawn of civilization- or so I can tell. Tis simply some track-talk 'tween 'bonds n' passerby, all those poor souls who come n' go. I tend tah notice Manhunter body language as their accent is hard to trace, not much tah overhear, they're whistlin' to each otha or bashin' brains for the most part. 'Old absolutely no 'onor eitha, seen 'em snatch steel from fella tribesters and run that same bloke with their own blade. Decapitatin' one 'notha for shits and giggles, they kill for offenses they'll forget tomorrow. Fatalities so reckless, it wouldn't be much o' ah surprise if they could even raise the dead too."

William is disgusted by this statement, though not particularly inclined to comment. His glimpse wanders on those cellblock residents and observes their reactions. Edmund is utterly appalled at the concept, those are illicit words, as necromancy is a perversion of natural order. However, as more opportune, open-minded folk who lodge in the adjoining pen, Libby and Bids find this potential tempting.

"We met our fates travelin' the 'aulageway, 'alfway up the Grand Ravine- ye know 'ow we tend tuh roam. Course, when those rogues stumbled 'cross Rambunctious the Fleischer 'ere n' I, we took our lutes n' bashed eitha side o' one's windpipe. Tried to stove 'is bloody 'ead in too, but ah bunch o' cronies wrangled us. Wasn't long 'fore we made march 'ere on the ass-end o' ah captive caravan. Course, we're all that's left from that entourage. Most of those in these bullpens are from outlying northwest territories, completely 'cross the glacier, captured like blunderin' fools who stray too far from protective cairns. They've dawdled 'ere 'gainst the witches n' the wiser. Nevah thought Manhunters were real, always just boogymen designed to sell more storybooks n' Masterson merch."

"Why are they frettin' all this way?"

"Who knows- well, I'll tell ye that it ain't for labor, working till we're frozen stiff. 'Aven't been tormented by grindin' in any mines, only dancin' 'round that totem n' tah work up a sweat, playin' their sick games of charades. Must be afta somethin' else."

An old man clutches at his heart, admonishing Jenny's commentary with the destitution of a preacher. He is an eccentric character, endowed by a regal chin curtain, some protruding fierce underbite and stiff upper-lip featuring two gnarled incisors. In the absence of any woolies, those fleece undergarments are scrawled with the same protective runes earned from Pithee Jones' shrine earlier, crusted in the color of cherries. His skin is covered in thin scabbing slits, who's to determine his source of ink?

"I've tattled this time n' time 'gain, Jenny! Must I keep recitin' muhself?"

"Oh, 'ere we go-"

She strums her shamisen once to temper frustration.

"-please shut-up."

The pilgrim waltzes towards the foremost figure from their recent throng of new arrivals, a part which William has the displeasure of playing along. He stares at the depths of the boy's soul, peering right into his psyche. This stare-down draws fright from the earnest lad, a grade of intensity that stifles his ego and lays claim to expression. John Muck's attitude is incessant.

"These ain't nah lawless beasts, Manhunters are awfully too smart for that. They rewrite the definition of death-threats. Mull and think 'bout it, this camp o' callous roustabouts, not too isolated, perfect amount o' reach tah control people who scry n' tend camp. They prey on frontier settlahs, makin' sure there's ah steady flow of prisoners through these gates. But where does the curtain-call? Surely, they don't have plans tuh end all o' us. On the contrary, they want to recruit, go 'head and bolster their numbers. Afta speakin' with their god, these monsters submit tah violent tendencies. Just can't sustain their numbers, 'ave tuh convert others or they'll perish 'togetha. We're beggin' the fates, muh boy!"

Boisterous Jenny ignores the additional warning, pretending that he's a hallucination to cope with, meaning that this dialogue transpires often. She would much rather ignore what their futures may hold, and focus on the past.

"Stir the chamber pot and yer bound tah rile the crazy. Remain quiet, and this too shall pass. Sorry y'all, dontcha listen tuh those playas whose instruments are tuned wrong. Some of us 'ave been 'ere ah long while- too long, desperate tah find reason 'hind the insane carnival than endure this 'orror show for nothin'. 'Em ould now, doesn't exactly know what 'e's sayin'. I'm surprised that the warden 'asn't taken 'is tongue. Maybe takes pleasure twixt the fears we sow in one 'notha?"

These terrible thoughts beg liquid empathy, a destiny with drink, lounging alone at the tavern. Don't tell the barkeep about these griefs or they won't leave the bottle, as they're not inclined to host haggards. Their company is not destined to bout with Crooked Men or ordinary ilk forever, villains who favor themselves as leads in a theater production. Mad men believe there's something special in the wind, but cannot recognize the smell of a fart.

Muck encourages his anguished inmates to share stories, detailing their encounters at Trench Hadrien and shave these Manhunters apart from those regular host of psychopathic lunatics. Unlike the cautionary circumstances with highwaymen, and charlatans, those who weave tall-tales in order to con frontier vagabonds from their valuables, this threat is real. William must've won the lottery somewhere along Ander's Route, that one-in-a-million chances to face-off against an enemy like no other. The divines must sense a nerve in the boy Jones that won't be showing anytime soon.

Rambunctious the Fleischer clarifies how the Manhunters are bred different, that brutality sets them apart, surrendering their natural ichor and binding their flesh with the arcane as to why they may survive mortal blows. They're no longer actually human, becoming a wolf in sheep's clothing. Without the limiting emotions of guilt and pain, cut-throats crave danger, as their concept of superiority isn't arousing without merit. Outlanders seem to foster perversive mutations with none of the disadvantages, anything to garner glory in the eyes of their dark gods.

There are accounts of burly strength, and it seems like they all possess a degree of cold immunity, but derived from these accounts of the bard Fleischer, some Manhunters have contrived traits far superior. Certain brigands may blur, disguising themselves as natural objects or glitchy apparitions as prophets of fell routinely bend reality to their whims. They control the narrative, relinquishing control only at the last second, when they want their prey to be aware of their final, fleeting moments.

"Ah curses, so yer tellin' me they can turn invisible too?"

"Nah-uh, 'most invisible actually!"

Lena, the aspiring Calamity Jane, is enthralled by morbid curiosity. Attracted to these people who revel in the abhorrent design, yet fear nothing. Her origins in Clan Claremont have instilled a distinct lust for power, and this newcomer can't help feeling magnetized to their demonizing cause. If she could only wield a fraction of their might, Lena would've never lost her daughter, Charm, in the first place.

Mug Maxwell spies her insolence, and rebukes.

"Don't ye go gamblin' on evils. They'll replace the game's green felt with plates o' gold, garnishin' for every fascination. Afta 'while, folks find themselves misplacin' more than they bargained for."

The pilfers player turns to address John Muck, asking inquisitively, "Just 'ow many Manhunters are out there anyhow?"

The preacher shrugs, honestly unwiring, trying to decide on the amount in the moment.

"A few. 'Nough, I guess. At least several!"

It's clear they won't be getting any truthful answers from him. Frankly, the vagabond is eager to retire this existential dread. Noticing a pair of prisoners engaging themselves with riddles and tacky hand puppets strewn from their socks, he proposes that they partake in similar straits.

"'Ey, why don't we play ah game or the like? I, for one, could certainly welcome change o' pace."

William enthusiastically pipes up.

"I have some pawns that we can use as gamepieces," then showcases his tokens, sending Edmund into a pompous chuckle, flabbergasted that the boy Jones is still toting these knick-knacks for him.

There are three totems taking the form of caribou, some wildcat like a lynx, and lastly a hard-headed ram, but before he can begin distributing tokens, Jenny rudely shoves the totems back into William's palms, presenting a tarot deck from her sleeves.

"Actually, I 'ave some cards right 'ere."

The earnest lad blushes by being manipulated so easily, and further embarrassed because he hasn't actually participated in tarot before. Rather than vocalizing his concerns publicly, he tugs at Maxwell's ear, begging the question.

"What exactly is this?"

Realizing William's spoof, the gambler whispers back. "Tarot's not 'xactly ah game per se, it's an entertainin' parlor trick 'tween those who fantasize mysticism n' prophetic prestidigitation. Though from what we've seen, I'm more inclined tah believe it now, bit tempted by sorcerers n' summoners. Boiled down tuh brass tacks, ye prompt the deck ah question, shuffle the cards togetha, then pull. Whatever pips ye trawl represents yer answer, but it's all open-ended, vague nonsense. In a way, ye can mold the meanin' 'hind every card tah suit yer needs."

The bard is proud to exhibit, excitingly remarking, "Since y'all are new, we'll give the lot divination draws."

"Awfully temptin'," exclaims Balthus, "I'd like tah go first!"

So eager to play, this controversial skeptic strides up to Boisterous Jenny, snatches three cards, and pulls them face-down onto the ground before she can even rearrange the deck.

"Oh, by the powers cosmic, I call 'pon the World Pillar, wonderin' where mah futures lie?"

These glossy pieces of parchment feature the same backing, an artistically burgundy throw, like reading a soft, pleated pillow.

Mug continues explaining the premise of this game, "This right 'ere is ah several card spread, course there can always be more cards drawn, but that tends tah blend the finah details. Each sleeve played is supposed tuh define yer purpose, not exactly predictin' the future, but portrayin' what could 'appen. The meanin' o' these cards is said tah influence fate. Ye don't need to necessarily believe in tarot, but with the magik we've seen, lest provide some insight, like 'ow that specta appeared earl-yah, and 'ow ley lines prompt influence. Similar tah spirit boards bein' incorporated 'round places o' death."

Jenny kneels atop the permafrost, hunching over the trio of pips. She extends her pinkie, seamlessly flipping the first face-down card right-side up. The illustration on this sleeve depicts a cloaked figure towards the rear of some canoe, ferrying six broadswords with their blades piercing into the hull. The letters "VI" are subtly animating overhead, pulsing as the sailor shoves their oar beneath the current, propelling the boat towards distant shoreline, a horizon that they never seem it reach.

"Ah-ah, the six o' swords, one of mah personal favorites. This represents that yer in ah transition period, that yer currently floatin' 'mong the big empty. Yet do not fret, persistence shall be rewarded, there's improvement 'round the cornah. Next up tis three o' wands, which symbolizes progress n' new opportunities in these comin' days. Ye can see 'ere 'ow the character is navigatin' 'midst tree trunks, turnin' their back to us. Then finally," she turns over the last card and reveals its face.

"Yes, o' course, the hermit! The epitome o' wisdom, not for the intelligent type. Comparable to the consistency o' fermenting alcohol, while things may appear muddy at first, when given time, everythin' shall 'come clear."

The figure on this card is a sorcerer clad in drab, draping robes, standing upright with a staff in one hand, and a yearning lantern in the other. This portrait of a grizzled veteran is uncanny, with the wiseacre periodically nodding-off in the shade of initials, "IX," victim to the never-ending quest of sleep. The landscape underneath his soles is blasted with muted grey, he could do with a rousing pyre to lift his spirits.

Upon the concluding explanation, Balthus is ecstatic, fortunate that these choices signify good omens. Although, he's a little biased, finally the learned man enjoys being treated like a winner.

Spying these three beautiful throws, they certainly emphasize the style of art nouveau, a recently romanticized genre of art, familiar to those who reside in the Underdark. While profoundly ornamental and rhythmic in design, they incorporate elements of nature: gusts of wind, waves in the water, weaving vines, and an emphasis on all things floral. Texture is cooked by crosshatching, or arranging certain parallel pencil-lines into flowing and wispy strokes. The characters have been gifted the breath of life, especially when constrained to such flat, limited color palette. Thick contour lines- those bold black lines forming the silhouettes of the illustrations, have been inked slightly off, pressed onto the pastel peach, cyan, magenta, beige and olive designs by just a few millimeters. That's usually the result of human error, simply sliding the durable, yet delicate looking woodcut onto the level. This tarot deck had to be the product of a printing press, some mass-produced children's toy, but that doesn't limit the nostalgia of owning them.

Mug Maxwell continues his conflagration, deposing the mysticism with his logically-ordained values, ranting, "The deck consists o' face cards called majors, such as that 'ermit o'ver there. Percentages talk, Balthus drew three cards 'cause ideally, 'e'll snatch one major, 'long with two- what are called, minor arcana. Though, I call 'em felonies n' misdemeanors muhself, an 'abit I picked-up from fellas at the professional parlors of Venture Depot."

When concluding his speech, the gambler dips his head to Boisterous Jenny, ready to receive his turn. She reels the exposed cards back into the pile, and through sleight-of-hand, shuffles the deck thoroughly. When finally satisfied with her act of legerdemain, the bard's fingers wrap against those crisp corners, and lift choice cards towards Maxwell, whom bides for Lady Luck.

"Oi, ye gone n' kindled my interest, so what do I've got in store?"

A second trio of cards are sprawled before long, and the bard is keen to commit another reading. As the lead pip is flipped, the first sleeve dictates the gambler's wheel of fortune: a spherical astrolabe floating among the abyss of known space, some fancy device erected around a flatten coin and the letter, "X."

Rambunctious the Fleischer steals the glory, interrupting Jenny to elaborate that this felony represents the endless cycles of life, the changing of the seasons, that with every give there is also something to take. He receives the ten of pentacles next, which could be signify as the completion of one's goals or the ultimate end-of-the-road, then finally drafts the felonious, queen of cups, encapsulating his caring demeanor and connection with others.

Morbin arrogantly rejects the opportunity to play, so Balthus decides to partake and draw on his behalf.

"Oh fates, cry out tah mah buddy- my pal. Will 'e evah find that fortune which 'e seeks?"

Once again, the bard lays three more pips face-down, yet this time, Jenny reprimands her partner with an abrasive glare, reminding Fleischer that she's the one in charge. An eight of cups presents itself before long, denoting that burgeoning thief to refrain those squeamish tendencies, that maybe it's time to redefine his career path and move on, searching for a new meaning.

"*Eek!*" Balthus squeals with glee, showcasing to Morbin that this draw is something of fancy.

The bard uncovers a clever depiction of the shifty four of pentacles. This composition foretells reparations among those driven by material wealth, begging release upon those holding onto their belongings too tightly, a common tarot draw among the Bannermane settlements.

Their line-up concludes with the hierophant face-card, indicating regard for studious matters. She advises the archaeologist that while he may attempt to indulge, possessing a fervent desire to measure more than a footnote among charcoal tomes, he can do more good than dredging historical sites. He scowls from across the demesne, denying, "No way. This is bonkahs, yer bonkahs."

Edmund is strangely optimistic about this encounter, no longer burdened by the wilderness or tasks at hand, allowing for a temporary respite. As a wickerwalker, he accepts the duty and responsibility of protecting kin from those boogymen that go bump in the night, so when he draws that knight of pentacles, an expression of glee casts his face. Jenny is not seemingly surprised by this bid, and is fraught with interpretations. Drawing the next card, she elaborates that while, at a glance, the eight of wands may appear militant, a sleeve such as these demands significance.

"Chess-pieces are beginnin' tah move, so dontcha be caught off guard. Remain patient- still, yer moment will come."

Edmund's defining attribute isn't his strength, rather that brunt unwillingness to yield that rivals real quartermain. Disciplined beyond his years in the ways of frontier combat, this navigator knows what he's good at.

The bard unintentionally encourages Edmund to flee by swiping his hand early and returning these several pips to her deck. She cuts the pile of sleeves in half, flaunting miniature magazines of artwork, smoothly sliding them together in a single slick motion, motioning for those separate halves to become full again; forming one into two, then two into one repetitively and without fault.

She religiously chants, "One-twenty-third-hundreths, four-fifty-sixthhundreths, seven-eighty-ninth-hundreths," each time. With a mind this sharp about the lesser things, Jenny must moonlight as a beancounter, or someone who flatters their focus on the nonessentials, an image of a moneylender clerk who famously amasses nickels comes to mind.

"Ah well," the wickerwalker attests, "I believe mah run has come tuh end," then motions to whomever is next, locating his accomplice, the boy Jones.

"Go, get'em 'Liam. 'Ave some fun."

This earnest lad presents a nervous chuckle, crafting a certain sly, sickle smile onto his lips. All this talk about doom and gloom has William deafly afraid of what he might find out, as who is he to deny destiny?

Trapped underneath all those layers and overgarments, this is the first time anyone's seen him riled into a profuse sweat. The tinge of embarrassment nurtures rosy hues atop his cheeks, and before he can muster the courage of speaking aloud, barely muttering.

"What should I…" under his breath, until card flounders upon the silken, varnished sand in front of him. Then, while he blinks, the sleeve multiples twice over, becoming a married pair, and another second later, foster their first offspring into three pips total.

This is just how his brain works, as emotions assert themselves, any graceless circumstance leads to an even more awkward memory, something a vagabond wouldn't want to conjure while resting his eyes, as it would keep them awake all night. He almost has the courage to speak, yet his ability to broadcast words falters, and Boisterous Jenny insists on flipping the card streak as if steak on cast iron.

He stares profoundly at the image of a man frolicking amid cloudless skies and blazing sun, shouldering a knapsack wound tightly at the spire of a stick, clad in a tunic and taking the brunt of wind.

"This is the fool, unnumbered, but whose's potential is also immeasurable. They are nothin' n' everythin' all at once. Think, ah joka card in the poka deck."

Mug Maxwell can't help but be so bold, stating that, "We don't really use joka cards 'round the felt."

She advertises a preposterous "*Hmmph.*"

"The fool coasts through their life, bound with adventure, learnin' valuable lessons along the way. Ah sacred duty tah mold what they aren't today. Let's find out what yer next draw is."

The flap of parchment reveals a crowd fencing with staves, throwing their entire bodies onto the weight of the timber wands. These figures mimic the impressions of warfare, testing their might alongside rivalry and competition, though at William's glance, they may be actually constructing, working together and supporting one another.

"The five of wands. 'Ow curious. Pray-tell yer third draw?"

She focuses on the most anticipated final pip, and exposes the page of cups in due time. The individual on this leaflet is dressed for success with Veblen attire: pinkish gaberdine tufts and an unwieldy wide-brim, three-plume hat. They stand along the shoreline with brackish white currents grasping at their lacework, presenting a gilded chalice full of seawater, tempting the fish to drink.

"Ah, the icon o' youth, always hopin' tuh impress. Reminda tah be silly n' courteous."

At that moment, Fleischer notices that two cards actually have become stuck together and accidentally betrays the existence of an elusive fourth card. The front of this sleeve loosens, sliding across the permafrost to showcase some dire prediction: death. William is besieged by thoughts of the dreaded thirteen as this card seemingly calls out to him, demanding that they get acquainted.

Gasp. The audience is aghast in shock and horror, even the pair of traveling bards are stricken to their senses. It takes several seconds for Boisterous Jenny to derive meaning to this sudden, melancholy prognosis. She remarks, "Lad, lest not panic," forcing an amicable grin.

"Think o' this 'and ye've been dealt as freein' oneself n' finally movin' forward. Not all tarot predictions are so bleak, black n' white, 'ow our lives unravel is up tah us, not those fates."

Although she may try to bandage the wound, her efforts constitute a temporary salve, Jenny's efforts are in vain. William's already seen the prediction and struck with anxiety-riddled calamity. Even when the card is swiftly rescinded, recoiling from view, he is awestruck by magikal intervention. Is this preeminent knowledge a blessing or a curse? Do the divines tug on his strings, coercing him under false pretenses or to do wrong?

If beings of the firmament were cast from a single, calamitous cosmic explosion, no wonder they're so hectic: being shaped by chaos, it's all they know. There are plenty of origin theories, including the tilled fields hypothesis: perhaps some modest, down-to-earth folk learned an exclusive craft, then their powers become so exemplary- so misunderstood, without an opposing force to check their advance, that they ascended into godhood without being truly tested. If those beings of the firmament are ordinary humans who have risen to rule the heavens, it would explain how they are susceptible to their emotions.

William furrows his brow, if he were god, things could be different-would be different. There's a debate constantly raging inside his mind whether he would retire to some far-out, isolated pasture, tending garden greenery and staving the white tide, or he'd take a more active rule, cooperating in the day-to-day affairs of common kin. These premeditated desires make him sound an awful lot like the crown icon, emperor of the Underdark and its five capital hubs.

The boy Jones could do so much good in a position of power. He has no personal gain for worship, further detested by the act of kneeling to another. It takes effort to be arrogant, and in his eyes, all the wrong people rule. Maybe he wouldn't take such an intensive role, the god of garb has a nice ring to it, then hats, hats are pretty cool, especially those highfalutin dragoon helms. There are plenty to choose from: brims, bicorns, twin-plumes, tri-plumes, horseshoes, tin ten-kettles, skullcaps, scarguards, beanie bonnets, and mufflers, maybe he should consider becoming the Lord of Hats instead? Cosmic immortals don't need to be so egomaniacal, some precious dichotomy revolving around either wrath or wisdom.

These thoughts tender stock until the evening reparations, when the usual scarlet hues of the sunset shift above the cloud coverage, however something is different, their's a bitter taste in the air as the descending solispyre churns ill omens. William watches this entire theater drama in the sky play from the confines of his cell. The shimmering stars start to appear as golden flecks of glitter, appearing through the frozen glacial face as if it were an enormous pair of glasses. Blurry, but nonetheless visible.

In that same eastern direction where they backpacked alongside Boar's Band at Threshing, the unavoidable blanketing gaze of cairnmire moon inches into the reigning twilight. This heavenly body jolts in step-by-step rhythm, as if it's propelled by a mechanical track. These motions match pace with Jerome's labored breaths, wheezes which skim and echo from those glazed edifices in their cellblock. In these blasted wastes and Manhunter territories, the rising orb of night is corrupted, no longer bound by its ordinary waxen glow, now gripped in throes of sangria. Earnest lads have heard tales of the red sun around the supper table, but a blood moon must be an occasion to swear at.

As if called on cue, a commotion riles by the penitentiary entrance, as the surviving constituents of the dance marched back to the bullpen. Taking every ounce of effort to avoid collapsing, an entire day of slogging their feet has broken them. They are absolutely exhausted, hunching-over so severely that the tips of their fingers are fondling feet, growing akin to the shambling dead. William performs a headcount, out of the original twenty or so participants in this great game, five remain.

Mandel wakes to that sudden, terrorizing ring of a gate bashing shut nearby. He stirs with alarm, cherry-picked from bouts of nightmares and breathing frantically. Evidence of slobbering in deep sleep dots his jowls, saliva which wept during those burgeoning twilight hours, freezing into icicles amid facial stubble. Lying on the permafrost, uncomfortably sprawled among a certain cusp of stone prying into his spine, the amounting pressure has temporarily paralyzed him from the waist down, and he whimpers in distress.

"Dontcha worry, don't fret," the boy Jones nabs onto his accomplice's wrist and pulls it close.

"Yer in good 'ands. We'll be gettin' out of 'ere soon, there's ah tunnel right 'round the corna. Can ye move yer foot now? Try n' wiggle those toes."

"Nah, no," he snivels, unleashing surprise at the matter.

"It's not dat- much worse. Da voices, I can't nah longah 'ear dem voices."

"Really? That sounds good tah mah. Last thing ye need is 'avin' some spirit take yer wings n' wring them tuh pieces."

The cordwainer is distraught, shifting his head from side-to-side, spying those peculiar surroundings, petrified at the sight of mangled gridiron and blood-tinged walls.

"'Liam, mah link 'as been severed. What's dis place? Is dis hell? Are we dead? Why would dey abandon us?"

"We ain't dead yet. Relax for now, the danga is gone, but their threats still loom. Can't be too confident on what ye rememba, so don't go hedgin' any bets 'bout it. We were ambushed the second we left that menagerie. They snuffed Cliff's light, then ye suffered ah nasty wallop 'gain when the geists took ya. Take 'eed for mah, these wardens are worse than any thieves n' Crooked Men. While they may look like 'em, these ain't just tribal cretins makin' people dance- suffah for their pleasure. I've seen 'em perform inhuman feats, covetin' bones o' behemoths, fancyin' knives as toothpicks. Dontcha go pickin' any fights, ya 'ear?"

Mandel Haggerton lets loose an abrasive, lamenting *sigh*.

"Okay, I get it. Tell me doe, did we give 'em 'ell?"

"Absolutely, wouldn't 'ave it any otha way. Got ah bit battered n' bruised, but we'll manage. Wait, actually- just avoid starin' at Jerome anytime soon, got nipped nasty."

William goes quiet, letting that snippet of advice sink-in, giving plentiful opportunity for Haggerton to blink and nod in approval. The boy Jones gallivants along, rushing to the action of their affairs, he's Bannermane by blood, the type of people who simply can't resist boasting about their performance.

"Ye should've seen the battle. I was legendary, even stuck some marauda in the gullet with their own weapon. 'Most personally delivered that hoosier to death's door. So ferocious that quartermaines would've inducted me straight intah their ranks. Should've been awarded ah medal from Alexanda Bannermane 'imself too."

Rather than applaud his comrade's colorful performance, Mandel is satisfied by the answer and faints into dreamy stupor.

William *groans* as the cordwainer's eyes shut for the final time that evening, and ponders his confession. If the divines aren't able to abduct Mandel's body, that should be a good thing, right? He'll be in charge of his own psyche, sailing his ship, then he'll actually be safe. Why can't the earnest lad be grateful of this fact?

Instead, William feels bizarrely guilty, aware that the shortage of divine intervention is also a troubling sign. Trench Hadrien is a formidable fortress of fell and they'll need every tool at their disposal to escape. That hideous totem erected in the wargrounds probably has something to do with this stifling aura, interfering with the bully-rook's direct connection to the gods.

Clank, clang, clank, clang.

The warden startles his quarry, knocking that expressive bone, rattled and ruined with scars, shield of theirs against beams of rebar. William's eyelids flutter, blissfully unaware that horrible thoughts have sired him to sleep. He gawks at the giant figure looming over yonder, whom is scrutinizing the residents of their cell, then departs to return in greater numbers.

"Oi," Morbin's petulant voice raps aloud.

"When will we be gettin' ah nick o' grub? I'm ratha famished muhself!"

Jenny stifles a yawn, her expression immediately worsens as if she had just downed a mouthful of bitters, counseling the newcomers with the lay of these hinterlands.

"Ye misunderstand, they don't feed us willingly. Nah continental breaker or 'andouts 'ere. Meals must be earned."

Morbin's rebellious attitude ceases, surmising the meaning. What grueling challenges must these Manhunters have in store for them? William would much rather concede to back-breaking labor, excavating resin from gemstone mines or scrounging for priceless, historical treasures. He condemns the cold, but would sooner welcome a painful chill in the wake of these menial mind-games. Hungry stomachs are tools of persuasion. This constant and ravishingly demanding destitution is intended to break them, making them vulnerable to the whims of dark gods who will hear their pleas, coming to the rescue only if they admonish all that is sacred and revel in the names of sin.

William's attention focuses on the gridiron gate quivering in place, as lowly, underlings of Manhunters clasp their mandibles across the tarnished, bacteria-oozing, oxidized iron. Two gutsier brigands lift that mass of metal, heaving this gate into the ceiling like a mere paperweight, and converse in hushed, impatient tunes.

"Keep 'ack ya filthy bluddahs! Blood 'ill be spilled dis day. Give ah minute."

These larger characters avoid straying into the lockup ruckus to avoid having distended foreheads smash into those peppers of icicles which dangle down, and they need to prevent the warground's rabble from forcing their way towards the captives. Instead they nominate an advocate to parade forward, a dedicated human servant who'll act as translator, preaching on behalf of all those voices ringing inside their heads.

This envoy is clad in flowing crimson robes, hair woven from fine, velvety black threads, twisting into a slick top-knot braid. Although this beauty is unconditionally scarred, outcrops of precious jeweled baubles are engorged in her skin, myriads of tormenting traumas, stretched-thin when her lips broaden to vaunt upon the center of cheekbones. She is unexpectedly full-figured- not rotund, just that vagabonds would anticipate folk with an arm twisted behind their back to be rather gauntly.

This appearance befits the impression of collaboration rather than resistance. She's a lowly pawn in a game of chess, another tool, instrument of the wicked when they require precision, as Manhunters personally favor brute force.

Navigating through the throng of these cut-throat rogues, she is placid, an isle of serenity immune to the gnashing of teeth and swiping of claws. This mistress is something divine, serenading a subtle, harmonious hymn.

The sights and sounds, are bitter-sweet,

When I reach those gates finally.
Let me plead my case, change those ways-
For you. Only you, only you.

Oh lord, I pray, and try to say,
"Don't let those curtains close on me."
Please, forgive all faults, 'fore I scale these walls-
For you. Only you, only you.

The agent steers her gait towards their entourage until they bask within whistling distance, placing her fingers at the root of her mouth, commanding their concentration with a fierce, trilling *phew-wheet* racket. Her blatant trumpeting is followed by a contradictory, lulling address spoken in the common tongue.

"Acolytes, I commend yer bravery. These roads are often windin' n' teemin' with peril, ah voyage wrought from slippery slopes. Rejoice, for yer pilgrimage is finally o'ver. Ye are takin' control o' yer destiny, yer place in our great journey."

Edmund is rife with questions, investigations that he has been unable to comb from Jenny and the superstitious preacher, sifting gossip in a manner similar to interrogation, a trail of unending queries that easily led into the waning hours of moonlight.

"Skip straight tah the point, miss. What do these Manhuntahs got in store for us?"

"Manhunters?" She scolds and *gags.*

"That's awfully crude of ya. These people are our saviors!"

She waves her index finger at the wickerwalker, firstly pointing to him, then the company he keeps, that female bard in particular.

"Ye really shouldn't be sayin' things like that, Jetty. 'Ave ye been spreadin' track-talk 'gain? Was it her- oh, or was it 'im? That John Muck needs tah listen verily, we've 'ad these conversations many times 'fore. *Tsk-tsk.* We'll 'ave tuh talk tah yer bunkmates later, as yer gonna be busy shortly."

The wickerwalker continues to pry alongside Boisterous Jenny's shaking head.

"Nah, no-" she pleads, wanting to cut their interrogation short. The bard's been subject to these tribulations for too long, and doesn't desire another bout. However Edmund is unfortunately persistent, orating another question to the envoy.

"Just who are ya?"

"Oh," she exclaims, acting a bit surprised.

"Nah one that ye'd really be interested in."

"Umm, yes," her immediate negligence to this proposition causes him to question himself, "-actually, yes it does."

Edmund peers over his shoulder, glancing at the remainder of his fellowship.

"We insist."

"Very well then, 'bond. There's natta direct translation, ye may call mah Mistress Hellsinger in the meantime, messenga for the bastion o' pride. Take muh requests as serious as their own."

Balthus astutely asks, "That's ah lovely title n' all that, but what are ye doing 'ere, lady?"

"Simple, I'm 'ere to make yer accommodations as painless as possible. There are many who choose tah light their own fires. Why struggle n' squirm in the dark, when we can share our flame?"

This particular statement must be a touchy subject, as it riles Boisterous Jenny to her core. She emits another timely *groan,* twisting her head like a ragdoll, then chortles once or twice in disbelief.

"Oh, knock it off why don't ya? Seen this same song n' dance plenty 'fore, quit toyin' with them 'ready. Mundie isn't ah tom tuh be persuaded anyhow. I should know, still can't believe that 'e refused muh hand in marriage. Ye should've saved me when ya 'ad ah chance all those years ago!"

The bard continues to dissuasively hassle the envoy, relishing when the messenger's attitude is brought to boil, especially encouraged once Hellsinger's gaze begins leering towards her own, and steam seemingly rushes from her ears. She sneers adamantly in victory, prodding the agent to reveal their true form, satisfied to have spurred the imminent transformation ahead.

A forked, snake-like tongue licks that amusing stretch of vermillion, and the messenger's grinning lips part, wider and wider until they easily peer past the farthest extant of her mouth- then, despite the biological limitations, her cheeks separate, allowing room to maneuver an all-encompassing, broad sneer. This looming visage showcases three tiers of razor-sharp ivory, an arsenal that would eviscerate any vagabond that should test her patience. The fiber and sinews of trachea warp, then fumble in place, festering beneath the surface. While William is no maester of anatomy, common sense dictates that the human body shouldn't be able to do that.

Hellsinger releases a maddening howl, exploiting an audio onslaught towards Jenny's specific direction. Unfortunately for the remainder of the company, these icy caverns reflect these sound waves in earnest, bestowing a high-pitched hum upon them that summons neurotic tics and headaches. This attack is disorienting, but not nearly as concussive in comparison to that memory buoy protecting Trench Hadrien, and oddly enough, reminiscent to what their cordwainer unleashed during the bandit queen's initial ambush.

After the messenger's fit of rage, Hellsinger momentarily slumps, the same sort of trance that befalls Mandel Haggerton, as if a spirit is releasing its latest victim. Yellow eyes shift to amber, identifying that the rampage has passed, allowing for that mistress to shake the reins of some alternate personality, that unruly geist enforcing control of her. The captives bear witness as tears start to stream, confirmation of coercion in lieu of collaboration.

She adamantly begs, "Please, don't make me answer any more. They're watchin'."

The boy Jones pronounces his concern.

"Who's watchin'?"

She bursts into a frenzy, her voice exploding into the icicles above like carronades.

"Don't, just don't," Hellsinger screams in anguish before sprinting right out the gate and fleeing altogether. That spirit must have been puppeting her body for such a length that it left latent abilities.

The Manhunters raising the gridiron turn to one another, delegating what they should do in the absence of their fell agent, conversing without words. Since the cat's out of the bag, and they don't need to maintain any illusion of trust, the warden and that rogue fix sly smiles, realizing they can be as rough on their house-guests as they deem is possible.

A brute cruises to William's vicinity, and beams with belligerence. It disperses a single, burly paw over the earnest lad's shoulder, gripping him tightly as to procure a *yelp* of pain, and hurls that poor soul some twenty-foot leap into the corridor, over the retinue of clamoring miscreants. He curls just prior to impact, minimizing the full force of the blow, colliding into the ice where most of the major trauma thumps at his elbows. This thrashing sends a shooting pain through his forearms, a strike that surges from his funny bones.

Ga-ah. The slight curvature of the wall coerces William into a roll, where he lapses against the permafrost, just in time to see Hellsinger rushing from the cellblock.

He raises his hand in honest concern, shouting, "'Ey, *ow*, 'ey wait!" And pursues after the messenger before the Manhunter majority may even notice he's gone.

A voice racks inside his skull, the glimmer of basic judgment, asking 'what the hell' William intends to prove here. The boy Jones races to his feet, scraping those boot soles against the rime as they frantically clip for traction, *squeak-squeaking* on the waxed, frosty permafrost. He dashes forward at impulse, swooning into the limelight and managing- though not quite in the method he had anticipated, a fleeting prison break.

When he surpasses the cave entrance, floundering his feet upon the plaza, his vision sears in maroon hues. The entire garrison of Trench Hadrien has been flooded in a steep reddening aurora, leftovers of the tainted cairnmire moon. Every object, from bones to forks, huts, cages and spittoons all, are tinged with vibrant red wash. Swells of supernatural energy raise and roil between bits of metal, whether that be lightning rods firmly fastened into the glacier, or swords sheathed at a Manhunter's waist, instantly shocking them. Feeble scraps of clothing instantly burn away, their flesh sundering to crips, overcooking the ashes until they are nothing but charred skeleton. Pools of obscene pitch spew from still-beating black hearts, ensuring the outlaw will eventually rise to cheat death once more.

A Mandrill sentry rears overhead, swaying from the branches of the looming totem, monitoring their disastrous domain for any discrepancies. Now, this beast doesn't fault in its duties, identifying the poor blundering fool presently stumbling from the cellblock. This foe parades as an infernal buzzard, garnering a spotlight with no known origin, fostering a beam of energy that saps the crimson aura from William's frame, allowing for his ordinary color palette to return. He quickly becomes a naked and afraid, like some fish out of water, an easily recognizable visual error.

The boy Jones can barely mutter, "Oh beans," shortly ahead of being thrust onto the ground, pounced by the insensitive ape-like creature, and subject to its agonizingly pungent aromas.

This nightmare leans over its quarry, releasing a sharp, antagonistic, periodic pulse, yowling straight into William's ear, whose shouts careening down his ear canal and seemingly rupturing vulnerable tissue. Under the distress of tinnitus, he coils into a ball, cradling both knees and huddling as tight as possible. The boy Jones can feel its barred teeth aggressively grate against his lobe, tepid breaths emanating from its lungs, fringes of gilded gold mane, and corrosive swathes saliva which melt his delicate hairs, quite literally giving a new definition to the term sideburn.

A herald of wrath, this Mandrill requires every ounce of effort to refrain from finishing the hunt, claiming a fresh trophy with serenades of red rivers. It stands at attention, then *whoops* loudly, hollering in a decisive victory screech, then momentarily slumps down at him, flipping its iconic lip backwards, receding some tissue which normally covers the muzzle, and bearing all those fibers which string ivories together.

This action riles the campgrounds, drawing a crowd for the vanguard to grandstand and flex its dominance. These spectators do not rush in awe, as escape attempts are routine to them, part of the reeducation process. Ten, maybe fifteen minutes or so pass, managing a stint of time for Edmund Redmyne the wickerwalker, Lena Tillstead, Korralack the Kable, Morbin Evershade, Mug Maxwell, Mandel Haggerton, Balthus the Pygmy, Libby and Bids Warder, Rochester the wainwright, and Jerome, to gradually emerge from behind their prisoner bars alongside a kingly escort, and into the crimson-rich plaza. The latter of this party is dragged into the fray by Manhunters, unable to endure their grievous wounds.

Sturgeon the Huscarl, Yeomen Braga and Bitte, Boisterous Jenny, Rambunctious Fleischer, John Muck and nine outlanders that have yet been introduced are strung along to watch the carnage unfold. Certain rogues arrive to the debut, anticipating the newcomers' premier bout with sin. Their warden predicts that these affairs will urge those veteran inmates, and their fragile egos to finally falter. How much longer could they possibly hold out?

William is irate, he can feel those mystic energies of emotion rile all matter of grey matter and bindings of the flesh, flexing every muscle and sinew, taunting him. Trench Hadrien, locus of fell, certainly brings out the worst qualities in a person. If it weren't for the overwhelming cacophony in his ear, an earnest lad would succumb to rage and defy the odds: take a stand to this braying beast, wring it by the neck and cast that brawny beast aside as easily as yesterday's handkerchief. The boy Jones wouldn't be entertaining the thought if he didn't possess the determination to see this act through, seeking to end the war with the simple tense of a fist.

The Mandrill uncharacteristically surrenders its hold over William, whom notices when the shadow wanes, and hears as the beast paces away, closer to those throngs of Manhunters and rejoining its lethal host. Grims do not capitulate willingly.

In the absence of that hawkish assailant, an earnest lad clambers onto his feet with haste, uplifting loosened scabs of rime. Entirely focused on his bruised physique and ego, the boy Jones is caught off-guard as his birthmark flares with pain. Wound into a frenzy, he scrambles with reckless abandon, unwittingly crashing into a figure thwarting behind.

Bwah-hah. William's nose is nearly hacked apart by a gnawing spread of fangs, animated and trashing, reaching towards him hungrily. Each snap of the jaw renders a throbbing blow, drowning his scar in tiers of grief. This maw is wrought in scores of bronze prongs, a painful mess of thorns should he have wandered merely inches closer. In lieu of eyes, this menace aspires a jutting horn, begging for impact and crying bull rush. In place of a tongue is roaring flame which forks and leaps outwards to lash at William. The gullet draws away, guided by the master's hand.

A face appears overhead, revealing this bizarre beast is merely an ancillary to a distinguished and domineering champion, whose guts have been replaced by a raging furnace. Their size rivals the height of Austerlaund, stoic, an unmovable boulder. He is strenuously armored, and showcases weathered tawn whenever the metal meets the meat. His complexion is gritty and worn, retaining a mild, yet strangely humbled, hint of humanity. Despite appearances, this heavyweight's skull is adorned in rungs of bony protrusions, jutting straight from their cranium, and bestowing the illusion of a crown or band of the zealot.

This is a warrior prince, that high-caliber legionnaire trained in all forms of might and magik, whose sacred duty is to spread the will of his masters. Any exposed flesh is grafted in imposing, indigo blue scales, a protective layer further braced by some thick armor carapace. This plated husk harbors those with ill-wills against the chieftain, also shrouding his chin and any neckline vulnerable to severing in battle. The loss of someone's head during battle could certainly quell their momentum. This ensemble is so bulky, that it's akin to a padded winter vest. A pair of pauldrons cup his shoulder sockets, but the length of arms are wiped clean, instead clad in chitinous cordovan slivers of scruffs.

Bellicose to a fault, his armor is war-torn, with several pieces missing, serrated, and patched haphazardly. A herculean girdle straddling at his hips procures a mouth which bulges out intermittently, rotund like the bilge of a cask. The silhouetted backside of the prince is burdened by angular and repetitive Marks of Dayne. This champion lifts his right arm, wrapping fingers around the hilt of a great weapon. Veins bulge and rumble beneath his scales, momentously brandishing some cleaver resting upon the nape of his neck. The Marks of Dayne skim and shift, revealing themselves to be the serrated blade of some sword, an arsenal of a hundred, burgundy-tipped teeth.

This mammoth meat axe is vast, roughly the length of William, a cutlass that could fall entire swathes of forest, and save those timberjacks years of work with little effort. Demanding applause and honors, he thrusts his blade in the air to exhibit that crimson hue. He speaks without the aid of Mistress Hellsinger, a one-in-a-thousand trait, executing a rusty, though perfectly discernible dialect of thronepatter.

"Become what men fear, what those magistrates and crown icons can't control. Witness and rile in the glory of sin, under me, Hadrien Manhunter, their champion and dark prince."

"Get back, keep away from me! *Agghh!*"

The sensation in William's chest emits a tumultuous sting, filling him with agony, almost as if a nail has been directly nailed into his heart. This experience goads him into suffering while this champion raises his weapon to strike.

"Pang… pang," mutters a Manhunter armed with a gaff hook, thrusting the scythe to an excessive degree, repeating themselves in the bid of gleaning a rattling, rhythmic chorus.

"Rift!"

"- and thrash!"

The Mandrills among the bulwark howl with frenzy as the chant quickens to maddening pace, urging their chieftain to bring the hammer down.

"Ruin, death!"

"Be free, now!"

He imparts the falchion with ferocity, swinging with such prowess that William can hear the air-split and career away in terror, even in his state of auditory distress. Poised to smite the daft boy Jones, Hadrien wavers at the last second, actually driving his chained blade into the permafrost and manifesting an expeditious earthquake. The weapon seethes with the buzzing sound of flies, flailing deeper into the ice sheet, enraged that its attack faltered. Hadrien relinquishes his cutlass, methodically clawing at his seemingly sore eyes.

A hooded vagrant broods in the crowd, watching distinctively. She's a bit brighter than the others, recognizing the fluke as Hadrien staves the mallet, which spurns their frustration. This is no ordinary outlaw, they are another agent of chaos, allowing for the essence of wrath to spy these transpiring events through their own eyes.

It's a weird, perverse sensation to sight possession in person, to watch helplessly while the geist grips at their victim's spine, sinking into flesh and taking command. Looking back on their adventures, those spirits that inhabited Mandel were as gentle as possible. Now, the onlookers can do little but gawk, cover their eyes and subtly peek past their fingers, even Manhunters have their limits. This subjugation is callous and cruel, definitely more visceral in nature than those chronicles prior. The chosen heretic rips off her helmet vigorously and hurls it with such force that the hapless hound whom catches the lump of metal in their abdomen crumples to the ground.

Caught in a whirlwind of evolution, her skin feels as if it has been set alight, and she hastily attempts to shed those few pieces of armor, hides and vambraces as her eyes profusely weep a blackened tar substance. Entire swathes peel and flake, revealing portions of the meat underneath, metamorphosing venerable flesh into the impenetrable bulk of flak jackets. Stricken in shock, staring at her convulsing hand as the endmost motions of independent thought is rapidly whisked away, her facial expression are overwhelmed in a brisk sense of calm. Forfeiting control when a rail-thin laceration develops between her middle and index fingers, she is clearly no longer human.

This crease rapidly doubles in size, minding a gap that propels up her forearms, splitting the limb down the middle and severing it in two. The new host debuts four disproportionate appendages in the place of two, with each forearm unusually distended, warranting the ability to shuffle upon the ground like a bristlehair fang ape, crawling atop her knuckles.

Within the span of ten seconds, some unmentionable lackey has been transformed into a vessel of wrath, a dark villain whom masquerades under the guise of a mere minion. It clumsily lumbers forward, learning how to refine its recently perplexing gait; determining where to step, which limb to sling next.

Hadrien fleetingly bows his head as the mesterpiece approaches, acknowledging and treating this monster as his superior. Every fist pounces onto the permafrost, slamming with newfound hatred. These shockwaves corrupt the nearby area with magik, churning alabaster-laden snowfall and rime into sooty ashes or grease altogether. Mimicking a fraction of god-like powers, it has no need for mouths, choosing to telepathically converse with its coerced constituent, but to the demise of divines, this warrior is admittedly brute, and decides to render rage aloud.

"I told you already, I need their bodies. Limp and lame troopers can't vault walls," the prince calls out, prompting the vessel to chitter incessantly in response.

"The great import is winding to a close, our influx of immigrants draws nigh, those vagrants whom strive to become bonanza kings- desperate to strike it rich, is lavish, but not infinite."

"While you may have my body, I'll never yield spirit. You demand my allegiance and have it for now. We struck a deal. Let me burn the world and I'll let you rebuild from ashes."

"I've had to sacrifice everything to be here, and yet, you question my motive? I've been betrayed, and welcomed as a servant for dark forces. I exist as a solution to those ills that plague those great houses of sin. When you cannot work with your brethren, I provide that leverage. You've made demand for an army so vast that they become the ceaseless tide- an ocean, capable of stomping mountains flat, and digging a tunnel to the heart of the world, then you shall have it. This fresh lot will renounce their motives, and become one of many. Spare that boy, and I shall foster another black heart to bolster your ranks."

Satisfied by this answer alone, the vessel withdraws. Refusing to relinquish control of their minion, the puppet transmogrifies into a cloud of flying pests, manifesting flocks of broad-winged, toddler-sized cave devils, and cutting their conversation short by manner of shrieking cacophony.

Another body demonized by the taints of chaos, uplifts itself into the burgundy, gliding into those blood-tinged skies, prompting return to a realm of never-ending bloodshed, forbidden lands where it may oversee foundries of eternal flame, joining the tidings of war.

Hadrien Manhunter has his own agenda, amplifying entourage and these lethal hosts by nefarious means. The chieftain snaps his fingers together, summoning the tribe's devout apothecary at his stead. This outlander is a maester of manipulating the five bodily humors: ichor, pus and all the bindings of the flesh; ink, memories and anything regarding grey matter; sap, or life-blood; pitch, the substance which derives emotion; then bitters, infusing matters for consumption. The shaman is always experimenting with tainted alchemy, harvesting organic ingredients, grinding, mashing and distilling to generate invigorating and restorative fluids, making Manhunters nigh immortal. Never one to stray from those potent classics, borderland apothecaries ensure the generous doping of alcohol in their potions, entrancing troopers with the elixir of courage.

This balding, impish figure known as Sire Gristle shuffles closer to the

Manhunter icon, portraying villainous red-slitted eyes, elongated ears, and an armory of sharpened ivories.

The outlander shifts their cloak, producing a vial of green extract, a putrified concoction perpetually bubbling and combusting within the confines of glass. This is pure, unrefined warp-fluid, intended to augment his lord's troopers, spurring unimaginable mutations without the direct need of divines. The cosmic icons are busy engaging in their own affairs, too occupied for any hands-on attention, molding each and every pawn to their liking, as such a method is incredibly tedious and time-consuming.

Hadrien's train of thought is interrupted by zealous chiming, that rogue with the bells is clamoring again.

Clang-clang, clang-clang.

"Oh, stave-off that racket won't you!"

The mob of Manhunters divulge their former foe, that brigand hoisting an accomplice above his head, shaking the bell-toting counterpart frantically to meddle in the affairs of the apothecary, though she isn't disturbed by the affair, just happy to be a part of something.

This outlander seek to challenge this standard-bearer in a clash of iron and bone, vying for the opportunity to deliver the precious warp-fluid to their chieftain's embrace, and basking in the glory themselves.

He shouts loud and clear, "I demand mah satisfaction! Ye ain't worthy tuh grovel at 'Adrien's feet. It shall be I who performs da deed. Ah, hell wit it. Spar with muh, knave, n' secure yer place 'pon da altar o' broken chainmail."

This is the same cut-throat Edmund bested in the field of battle, albeit momentarily, enough of a sweeping spurn to have them embarrassed and disgraced by the rabble for summoning their bandit queen's assistance.

Manhunters are quick to fall in line, an impulsive tendency as the weak are eaten by the strong. Occasionally they indulge on their own selfish interests, delving distant memories, reviving elements of personality since before they were transformed. Clearly, the brigand was always an arrogant prick.

He beats his heart, insistently enraged, only releasing the bell-covered rogue when the apothecary actually raises their arm to do justice. The battle commences immediately, allowing for combatants to cruise towards one another at breakneck speeds, dueling alongside the totem of pandemonium's shadow.

The challenging hart unveils his newest weapon, some double-edged battleaxe, an oversized hatchet which he whirls at their opponent, scolding his competitor for masterfully dodging his attacks.

"Stap movin' n' prepare tuh die!"

Cementing his desire to do harm, this brigand almost bashes the apothecary with the root of his axe, and when the shaman takes the treat seriously, their smile turning into a scowl. They brandish a dagger of their very own, keenly demonstrating where they intend to position it next. In that moment, the demonic imp sheathes their blade inside the brigand's tender tissues.

This challenger cannot muster the energy to parry, as their tendons are severed with each subsequent blow. The brigand simply can't compensate, losing the movement of their arms and neck. They complain in the heat of battle, "I'm sick o' bein' stabbed," hollering in a self-conceited effort to stunt the apothecary's focus, "can we do sometink else?"

The shaman heartily abides, uttering a brief cantrip in response, suddenly enveloping their hands in blue flames and forcing this brigand's axe to reel back. Victim of his own weapon's crude design, the flailing edge amputates his opposing arm, although he hardly winces from the blow, then snidely fusses.

"Well, dat's perfect."

This devastating loss cedes portions of black pitch pooling upon the permafrost, otherwise huge losses in the vital fluids department, interfering with his capability to simply stand. Since he has been so cleverly disarmed, he musters one final swipe with his trusty steel, now besmeared in ebony ink. Anticipating this ultimate assault, the apothecary catches the axe in the cross-guard of their dagger, astutely locking their weapons together. However, shamans are cunning, and ultimately tricky. The imp shrewdly withdraws a needle from some secret compartment upon the hilt, and plainly pricks their three-limbed enemy, leaving the sewing needle shaped barb latched inside the skin.

"What-wot was that…"

Suffering a bout with poison, the effects are immediate, coercing the brigand to feverishly stumble, as their eyelids have already begun to cave. His adversary decisively concludes their trial by combat, slamming their boot into his breast, boring the tip deeper, and driving the toxin home. Growing limp by the second, it doesn't take long for this contender to start floundering on the ground. His head lapses to the side, filled to the brim with coagulating ichor, encouraging him to stagger his stride and trip over his own two feet. He rises periodically, a charity case to pity, yearning to finish the bout and personal challenge, even if the circumstances weren't exactly 'fair.'

This drug-addled brigand is poised precariously upon the pit of spoils, clearly distraught, barely recognizing himself teetering at the precipice, the blubbering fool can't summon the vigor to avoid his fate. The tusks gallivant around the rim, seemingly reaching out at the scent of edibles, pilfering themselves in his flesh like raptor talons are taken to lemming, causing him to swiftly disappear into the chasm. William's lobes are assaulted by the sound of mincing meat, at least, he believes that it could be a hallucination, especially following some comical *belch*.

Hadrien Manhunter strides past his apothecary, greedily swiping the concoction while they bow and press their palms in worship. The imp entirely disregards their recent victory, as the chieftain has been delayed long enough. This dark prince is eager to draft these captive townspeople into immediate service, with or without their cooperation.

He borders that pit of spoils, hastily uncorking the vial between his teeth. The sludge inside animates, crawling along the length of tube, and hinting at the reality of semi-sentience. This slime intuitively catches the scent of freedom, and daring lunges forth, unwittingly into the gaping abyss.

"The brigand shall be reborn," Hadrien declares, "no meat shall go to waste."

There's an ample supply of weapons and armaments in this root cellar, armors, ancillaries, minerals and synthetics intended to be blended together. From this earthly cauldron, Hadrien can brew chimera to assail the world. The pit chokes and gurgles with indigestion, expelling noxious, absinthe fumes that surge over the skagway, melting the structure completely, as the liquified components drift netherwards. Wasted by growing pains and pressure, spews of brightly-colored broth vomit outward like an erupting volcano, painting the adjoining area in verdant fluids. The snow and ice ebbs away at the hot molten concoction, corrupting the frozen sand to cater sprouts of crystalline brush. Hadrien steps to the side while an ample stock of warp-fluid lands beside him, branding the domain with creep and corruption.

He wouldn't want to be blessed by this elixir, becoming complacent to the sins, losing his mind and ego from the offensive mutations. He is the check and balance between them.

Numerous members of the crowd as struck by the raining goo, allowing for potent energies to course through their body, flesh becoming as malleable as clay. Ordinary folk can't handle the transition, requiring the supervision of those darkly ordained to prevent going insane, and even then, results are not guaranteed. Outlanders lose themselves to bloated and writhing forms, becoming gibbering grims, bulwarks of flesh mutated beyond recognition. The warp-fluid corrupts any and all material, combining materials together in single soup-kitchens. Metal, timber, steel and stone, are absorbed into one another, including another body should people meander too close. This is the fate that befalls most Manhunters, they become fiends, shambling tools for the sins to wield. Alas, in the forlorn of critical thinking, brute force seems to salvage this sort of tendency.

In other instances, a Manhunter wielding some mace has an entire forearm devour the metal shaft, replacing their hand entirely. The spiky flanged head launches uncontrollably, clipping an accomplice and putting a hole in their torso, a gaping wound similar in the effect to a point-blank, nine-pound cannonball shot. The flail retracts by means of steel chain, threading awkwardly back through the victim, and reseting in lieu of his fingers. That rogue sporting a hole in her chest discovers that those bones have been magikally bound in steel, however the injury ushers their flesh to melt away, a move that would anger all those holistic health nuts, until they are nothing but silvery skeleton, tendon and vital organs.

Chief Hadrien's dastardly call rings into the corrupted sanguine sunlight.

"You have made the great journey to us, you deserve to be rewarded-justice in the eyes of fate, all that is fair and righteous. You deserve power. Join our cause, become the cacophony."

Edmund shouts at his entourage, beseeching them to "Watch out, avoid the liquid!"

Yet some flee slightly too late, and certain members of the fellowship are struck by these belching chemicals. The first members to feel the brew's ill effects are the youngest yeomen, Braga and Bitte, whom immediately seize and collapse, casualties tormented under the stress of transformation.

Already two steps from the brink, ready to meet his creator, Sturgeon prescribes little effort into cautioning that putrid upchuck, and this concoction is quick to work its magik, endowing him with the impression of bear-trap inspired jaws, then manipulating his knees and shinbones into kangaroo legs. This process is agonizingly painful, obliging the huscarl to scream.

Korralack the Kable is coincidently struck by a single droplet, a bead of warp-fluid suspended upon his forehead, swaying him into unconsciousness by way of steaming wound. The learned man winces when a fraction of this regurgitated potion lands on his wrist, with Balthus crying out at his impending doom, although that demise never arrives, and the protective sigil glows in cerulean haze.

He exclaims, "I've been saved!"

Those that touched the shrine have been blessed by the Lord of Earth and Stone, safeguarded from the influence of fell, at least for the time being. There's a distinct lack of contractually-binding agreements here, as those tame gods can make no promises that this guise will work a second time.

Lena Tillstead goes wide-eyed while the pit of spoils surges with vitality and those afflicted revel or convulse on the ground, teeming with arcane properties. She deliberates quietly, debating whether to actually volunteer and join the Manhunter masses, yet Hadrien hears all words in this domain, and extends his hand in earnest, offering this Calamity Jane exactly what her heart desires, the keys to a kingdom.

"Widow, I can peer into your soul. I harken that the answer is simple, reject death, and you shall not die. Condemn the gods, and they shall not want you. Now reach out, reach for change, strive to be dealt a better hand. Bend the knee and swear fealty, for I can gift you everything that has been cheated or dangled in front of you. Your honor, your namesake, your daughter, all will be returned. Embrace fell, revive true form and carve destiny."

She doesn't squander a second, and as their hands touch, viscous streams of magik escape, sealing the pact. Lena squirms erratically when a bolt of electricity escapes from Hadrien's harness, and dashes directly towards her, enveloping the chaperon in a sickly aura which garners the ability to unlock her vast potential, a truth that has been concealed for all these years. She tries desperately to slip her hand from the chieftain's iron-like vice, shrinking onto both knees in grief and misery, reeling away to stare aimlessly at her former friends.

He withdraws grip for nary a moment, some fleeting recess before reviving hold on upon her wrist instead. Mutations are unpredictable, it would be ignorant of him not to consider if Lena's limbs contorted into tentacles or were to suddenly catch fire. To his venerable satisfaction, that index finger of hers seemingly transcribes into a talon, lengthening to the size of a harpoon in order to ensnare quarry. Indeed, the wrist is precise choice, controlling how she relents to the surge of energy, avoiding any offensive retaliation while the transformation takes hold.

Powered by the intense ardors, she can finally ascend to demon form. Her metamorphosis induces without delay, mangling her spindly frame, stretching every limb to the length of bison bull. She gradually rises, forcibly hunched over while the chieftain refuses to relinquish his grip, even as her stride broadens to the wingspan of an albatross. Locks of hair and wooly garments slyly soften into murky gloom, her skin eventually surrenders to the guise of midnight, absorbing all ambient light as a freshly formed creature of shadows. Divulging from this oily set-piece, Lena's auburn red pupils gradually ebb away, forfeiting to their sclera until the entirety of the eyes churn milky white. Two aspiring features break the gloomy mold of her silhouette, tufts of fibers clad the sides and nape of her neck with regal mane, and a pair of horns sprout above her brow, extending slightly forward in a circular motion. Figments of William's imagination could to identify this illusion as a somber halo.

While her presence become harder to discern by the second, becoming nothing more than an ambiguous figure, William can still spy horror as the widow's face vertically divides in half. The laceration doesn't distinguish any viscera, just abundant throes of inky blackness.

Still the incision is a darker stroke, sprawling further down her throat and torso until it splits the abdomen wide and presents a brand-new appendage. A daunting, protruding proboscis tongue swells to incredible range, stemming right from where her heart should be. This extremity lashes out to sting Hadrien, a counter which he had always expected to arrive.

The chieftain snatches the projecting stinger with his free hand and wrings the tendril tightly, asserting, "How awfully daring, but I'm not that clueless-"

He hurls the fated monster to the side, an entity that shall be further known as, "-Liberella Grim."

The boy Jones and those remaining townspeople admonish the loss of their friends, and the consideration of becoming Manhunters themselves, enlisting in this vile army of the damned. Their dark prince lets loose a traumatizing laugh.

"*Huah-vah, ah-ha-ha-ha.* You've challenged my patience for the final time. Let them stir in those pens and surrender their protection. They'll give me an answer in the morning. Negotiations are no longer in demand."

William's gaze wanders to spot Korralack lying alone and abandoned on the glassy creep, that corrupted blanket of rime. He can't help, and shouts in bitterness for his fallen comrade.

"Up! Get up, Korkie! We're leavin' now."

That very same Mandrill, a creature no doubt harboring a grudge, descends upon William, grappling the earnest lad and lifting him off his feet. It rushes the prisoner towards the direction of their cellblocks, ushering those townspeople and resident inmates back to the cages, keen to retire this role and rejoice in pyres alongside fell brethren. While William was the first to abdicate their prison, he has also become the very first caravanhand to return. Literally thrown into the farthest cellblock again, nearly colliding into the area of squalor deemed as their group's latrine.

He remains on his rear and pouts at this quandary, puzzling over his reservations, quite uncertain of their fate. Manhunters are a corruption of everything he has come to know, love and enjoy, the perversion of his wildest dreams, like when a child teethes on a toy and plainly can't get enough. Lena must have fancied this fact too, as she turned willingly. At least, that's what William believes he saw.

Edmund, Mandel, Morbin, Mug, and Balthus are forcibly strung along with John Muck, Jenny and Fleischer, then the three strangers who are forcibly escorted inside. These stoic few have witnessed sets of pioneers beguiled and transformed countless times, yet this is unique, unlike anything they have ever seen, an incident aspiring on such a grand scale. This is truly the point of no return.

Their wardens will return in due time, and this time won't be taking 'no' as an answer. Maddening chants echos off their chamber walls, inducing icicles to rattle and shiver with fear. A few of these crystal stalactites are spurred from the commotion outside, lurching downwards, then faltering into a hundred pieces, delivering shards at the occupants.

The Manhunter mob is rallying, swelling their rabble for combat and mobilizing for war. Who could dare compete with such an elemental force? Their fellowship can't risk waiting any longer or else they may never leave. They must flee, warning every magistrate that will listen of the Manhunters' actual existence. The Underdark and frontier settlements would be helpless should those secrets die with them, only uncovered as death arrives at their door, and these visitors scarcely wait for introductions to be invited in.

Even as the awful pain in his chest subsides, William is overwhelmingly frightened at the prospect of being turned, manipulated by those stronger into some sort of puppet. He has always craved to be wild and free, but not like this. These Manhunters are dangerous, aspects of tribal men scoffing at the notion of mortal injuries, tempered by regular beatings and untamed by anything other than threats of eternal torment or permanent demise.

An earnest lad scoffs at the notion, while Manhunters thrive to be unshackled, they reject reality, that they are actually under the thumb of fell beasts rather than the former. Regardless, once metamorphosing into a creature of chaos, surviving those uncontrollable mutations in a bout that spells certain doom, they must feel invincible alongside that victory, that they defied death and the whims of any immortals.

William had always heard tales of urchins whom stray from the frontier settlements, and thought that these young'uns would be privy to simple enchantments, a boon to ward sickness and the dangers poised by the hinterlands, not the all-encompassing corruption of mortal coil, warping minds and vital fluids.

If Lena went willingly, becoming a monstrous nightmare, should they denied this fate would they be transformed into insane, raging mounds of flesh? His eyes can't help but dart, vying for escape, fleeing from impending doom.

William contemplates upon the subtly reddened, inconspicuous canyon that adjoins their brig, and sobs at the notion of liberty. Only those who share this specific cell may traverse the wellspring and have their chance at escape, while those estranged townspeople are barred behind firmly-rooted fixtures of corroded rebar. Even if the earnest lad possessed the raw vigor, he would likely stain his hands in rust particles, dispersing metallic scourges of tetanus through scrapes rapping atop his knuckles, and die wrung like a rag. Mug Maxwell pats that boy Jones on his shoulderblade, reassuring him.

"Let's not be coy 'bout it, dontcha be belittled by 'appenstance. Chance shouldn't define 'eroes or villains. Nevah envy the person who wins the lottery, for they are burdened by ah singular truth, that they got lucky. No ifs, n's or buts 'bout it, their best skill is vanity, as they succeed only through someone else's ability tah choose for them."

Boisterous Jenny begins connecting the dots, adopting the anchor of their eyes and where they must be intent on treading.

"Wait," she chokes at the opportunity, the concept of breaking out obviously flusters her.

"Ye want tah go down there? We need 'notha option- 'gain, the blood, look at all that crimson glaze!"

They've survived this long for a reason, there's a truth to caution and success, survival is a reward on its own. The critical John Muck proposes another option, declaring that, "We must feign death, perhaps these affairs 'ave thrust fog upon their 'eads n' rendered minds dull. Maybe they'll believe us tah be corpses afflicted by the blight- ignore us 'togetha. We can't frolic down that passage, they'll surely track our footprints n' follow!"

"Oh, gussy-up ye has-been wimp," that wiseacre Jerome speaks near the heels of gridiron, volleying insults from the adjacent cell. He flashes a handkerchief caked in dried ichor and used linen scraps, casting them aside, knowing expiration is just around the corner, and death will catch him soon enough.

Living in a frontier town, he has always pretended to wield some grizzly visage, and now that fantasy has been anchored into renown, that loss of defining cartridge makes him appear almost veteran. The absence of his nasal provides a telescopic view into the sinus cavity, an elusive interior of ribbed plates and stripped bare volmer.

"Listen tuh Muggie, lad, 'cause I'm all vinegar, I've always given it tah ya straight. Dat tunnel may lead pass- may not, no one 'ere can truly tell. Tink 'bout our expedition so far, 'ow we've put all our eggs in one basket, n' seem tah make-out like crooks everytime. Does odds were nevah in our fava, so ye'll fashion 'notha darin' attempt or meet yer demise on ah road paved with good intentions. Eitha way, yer fate- if ya stay, is sealed. So take da path less traveled, relish da 'venture, lad.'"

Rochester expresses his obligation to offer assistance, and kneels beside the wiseacre to comfort his waning light. However this wainwright does not talk to William, in the realization that he doesn't possess a crumb of wisdom to depart upon the lad. Though, that's not necessarily accurate, Rochester found joy in service, spending his entire life mastering the ship-craft and toiling for others. If it weren't for him, the Bannermane Empire and legacies of the merchantiles would have perished in the first barrowtide season, buried beneath mounds of fresh snowfall in a sudden, tempestuous weather that taunts an unexpected return to the Underdark.

So he blissfully beams to William, looking so smug, cherishing the fortune that they had met, and he had reciprocated in his own eccentric ways, fostering friendship in these bleak episodes. A motion as simple as some smile means the world to those who often forget theirs.

Libby and Bids are not those to warrant ease with goodbyes, and mend grins alongside the two greybeards, waving through the bars merrily. They had met this party in the most awkward of circumstances, originally determined to pilfer vagabonds for their supplies at the local caravan post. Oh, how the tables have turned, the tides sway and the winds shift. The two siblings silently berate their original desires to have robbed such delightfully wyrd people.

"Ah-ah, I believe mah flame is dwindlin', feelin' the crumble in muh bones n' da curtains which wind tah close. Can't necessarily blame ye for leavin' us 'hind, turns out we can't manage much weight. Fare-tah-well, 'Liam, take dis opportunity n' live, find someone to replace mah- spurn yer curiosity. As a man whose 'ways been plagued by dreams, 'eed this advice, 'bonds don't 'ave tah be destined for good or evil, just greatness of their own choosin'. Most people fear bein' ordinary, 'notha flake o' snow crispin' the dune, yet ye fear bein' entangled in ah web of complexity, n' becomin' extraordinary. If ye choose to deny yer troubles, that's yer decision, just nevah come tuh relent on does choices. Regret is sucha dreadful waste o' time, every second precious. Remember tah perform acts dat are obituary worthy, n' meet someone who'll engrave ah tombstone when yer own 'ands are tied."

The gambler gives the earnest lad a discretely gentle shove, whisking a boy Jones down the frightfully winding path abound. As Edmund, Morbin and Balthus aren't folk to typically argue regarding plausible deniability, this appears to be their best option.

On the other hand, Mandel is coarsely confused by these circumstances, having only recently waken up, still inexperienced to this company, only to be rushed out the door and witness the farewell. He wouldn't want to be surrounded by strangers, and briskly trots to join his comrades.

Those bards and vagrants left behind are intent to wallow in their filth, at least until they debate what would happen when the Manhunters return and find that the townspeople have disappeared. Sifting and squirming in place, accounting that those incarcerated will receive punishments more severe than transfiguration at the hands of fell, is a pretty deciding factor in accompanying the departing pioneers. The preacher, John Muck is the first peregrine to break rank and rush to the prospect of Mandel's naked footprints, noticing that he's strangely donning no shoes.

Jerome's gravelly voice echos above the chatter of dispatching vagrants, "'Onor dis greybeard with one last request, kick dat Morbin fella in da rear for muh, as I've always 'ated 'is jokes."

XVII
—

IF YOU RUN YOU ONLY DIE TIRED

This tunnel they trek is nothing unique, yet the journey continues, reaching schemes that are crooked and arduous. Walls periodically condense into a traps that catch their buttons and buckles while stretches of the glacial face run ragged, sharp lances which shred attire, threatening to pierce hides. While they were never assigned prisoner garbs, the lack of padding certainly prompts the concept. These layers of clothing are designed to be worn as undergarments, sheets which aren't commonly seen, maintaining the illusion and flair that they are shining amid dreary backdrops, preventing them from being concealed, refugees to be picked by their captors with ease. The rime cackles underneath the weight of their Peaterbricks, emphasizing each stride with a resounding *scrunch*.

Now that they are straying from the Manhunter's domain, trading one lawless wasteland for another, a challenging cold begins to set-in, chilling these travelers to the marrow. They'll need to stick together, preserving heat, huddled in unison. Amid periods such as these, surviving alone is improbable, success impossible, surely they'll die of exposure.

Two members of the common rabble have come to detest their part in the proposal, wishing to retreat back to the cell already, blasting the icy corridor with shrill voices.

"It's freezin' in 'ere! They 'aven't noticed that we're missin' yet, we could retrace our steps, dwell where the temperature is somewhat tolerable."

"Seein' as us othas are missin', they'll kill ya."

"Perhaps- though, can't be sure o' that. Betta tah die lonely on our backs than perish face-down in the frost. Out there is nothin' at all."

Mug Maxwell is riled into a fit of frustration, hollering, "Time tah ante-up ye ungrateful wimps. 'Aven't fared a bit of chill before? 'Ere's ah newsflash for ya, the only place where it ain't cold is 'mong those that seek tuh control us, n' mold ye to their darkest desires. What do ye want tah be in life: in charge of yer own destiny, or 'notha mindless thrall?"

Belittled by this apparent outburst, the silent vagrant of the pair pats their complaining accomplice with the back of their hand, ushering them to continue along- definitely dissuaded for now, yet they continue to trudge on. This happenstance won't prevent them from whining and complaining, in fact, may spur more of it. Those subtle clicks of the tongue, smacking wet muscle against the roof of mouth like *tsk* can be heard whenever someone petitions a request for them to march faster.

A bard beseeches those with inquiry, trawling activity from the mundane.

"What say song tah lift our dreary spirits? Fleischer might know o' ah tune or two."

The traveling vagabond *scoffs* at this ordeal, he drops his arms which are wretched in disbelief, aware that in the deficit of any instruments and his hurdy-gurdy, the bard is goading Fleischer to guide the beat, managing the pacing of a cherry tune and stringing the chorus. He tips his head flippantly in repose, to which Boisterous Jenny is affirmed with delight, knuckle-bunching her partner at his arm.

"Aye-aye, that's the spirit!"

The tinges of music are imbedded in everyday discourse, vagabonds are routinely goaded to compose personal symphonies, beseeched by familiar bodily functions. Tunes can be drawn from the rawest qualities: lining the air people breathe, as lungs dole out response, sucking that rushing feeling into those guts and spewing puffs of wind; the ichor that rummages through the human body, circulating essential fluids at regular one-two, one-two intervals, and delivering delightfully balmy sensations; and simply by walking, that sudden of compression of wooden floorboard fibers, or grating of snowdrift as navigators trudge through. Collaboration doesn't require a degree or penchant, fantastic orchestras are available to those with the tenacity look inside.

There's the desire to assert one's humanity when facing insurmountable darkness, that's why the Bannermane and frontier clans pride themselves upon the sound of music. To pioneers, creation is the dividing line that separates man from beast.

In truth, the tender art of musikcraft is only temporary salve, shedding rugged dispositions for a moment as pessimists return to prolonging their inevitable destitution. Jenny has had regular bouts with these nay-sayers, garnering the reputation of a squawking bird: annoying, but inclined to the bestow breaths of life.

She strums at her loyal shamisen, that particularly worn, generational, hand-me-down that's tried and true, even if it happens to falter at first.

Ping, bah-bop-ah, ping-ping-ping-ping-ping, bah-pop-uh, bah-buh-buh-buh-buh.

This tender chord coerces some quarter-twist of those tuning pegs before she finally announces into song.

Heave-ho, stow the anchor.
Full steam, pull at the leave-ver.

The sweeping solo of Jenny's mezzo-soprano resonance is energetic, her lyrics quick and witty, just as Rambunctious the Fleischer opens his own pipes, and joins his sweetheart in serenade.

A-weigh, bound for dee-so.
Para-dee-so! Para-para-dee-so!
Take my hand, and sail away!

Ooh bid farewell to thy fellow convicts.
Nabbed bunk 'neath bilge, keel and sprit.
A-weigh, bound for dee-so,
And reach, reach for rio.
Rove round, and sail away!

We have a real itch for striking it rich,
Aboard a flagship of mint and real polish.
A-weigh, bound for dee-so,
Para-dee-so! Para-para-dee-so.
Boys dash far, and sail away!

Yiz funny young blaze, leashed helm all damn day,
Make haste from purr-gah-toe-rio, dreaming ole para-dee-so.

A-weigh, bound for dee-so,
And reach, reach for rio.
Cross dem lands, and sail away!

Boys whims are fickle, sick of the shore,
Always wishin' for more.
A-weigh, bound for dee-so.
Para-dee-so! Para-para-dee-so!
The lads cheer, and sail away!

Their ballad careens down the corridor, a high-pitched property funneled by swathes of motionless, slicked wax, reverberating through the entire glacial sheet from floor to ceiling. The company is propelled by the bards jubilant shanty, unaware that a feline set of ears flicker in their direction, detecting their approach.

A fragile voice originates from the void, beckoning them further towards the fray.

"'Elp, 'elp! Oh 'elp, won't somebody please?"

"Curses, this is gettin' creepy."

"That 'bout tears it," that wily ne'er-do-well shouts, "That right there is ah risk that we're not willin' tuh take. C'mon Knics, let's 'ead back 'ready. Fretted 'round 'ere long 'nough."

As the anxious duo shivers and veer to depart, the roughest member of their company encourages them otherwise.

"Oh nah," Edmund chortles in an amicable manner, sweeping his arm around the would-be deserter's shoulder, staunchly pulling that truant in until he clashes directly into the wickerwalker's chest.

"We're just gettin' started. Too late now."

"I'm trapped, I've been trapped. Ah, mah leg…"

William is alight in fervor, as these recent events have rendered the boy Jones so helpless, at the mercy of greater gods, regularly submitting to the elements and beings grander. Whether this fellow has fallen, subdued to spraining their ankle, or pinned by a boulder, he is determined to help.

"Finally," he blurts out, reaching the passage's final stretch which expands into an obvious chamber.

Mug emerges into a sprint beside him with their caravan in tow. This is incident they can gamble on, this is something within their control. Together they cultivate an entourage of townspeople and travelers who can weave the fate of a single soul, that particular someone destined with an early demise.

The unveiling demesne is as wide as the Mad River promenade, however unequivocally devoid, a series of motionless waterfalls that have sealed solid, descending into deep dives with a raised no man's land between them. These floating ice floes are resplendent, soft-pressed by powdery snow which glitters from the luster radiating across the crystal canopy. Multiple levels have been strung together, certain tiers scale higher than others, while some are reclusively sunken, occasionally giving the implications that flights of stairs sprawl between them. Peering past pillars bridging those walkable surfaces to the ceiling, it's incredibly unfortunate that the exit isn't glowing white with light. This portal is eerie, gloomier still. Yet, Mug Maxwell is intent on rolling the dice. This is a chance they'll have to take, seeing as their alternative option consists on them getting capture again.

As this emboldened company arrives at their destination, their hopes immediately dash. William himself comes to regret his insistent tirade. Actually, this isn't something they can handle, they'll require the employ of an experienced quartermain. A certain staircase leading to a central pedestal demands attention, especially the inhabitant who rest on it.

This creature garners the impression of a patronizing, highfalutin lord, bellowing boldly and taunting.

"'Elp me… at least, that was the last thing she said."

The saber-cat springs from its curled position, rearing on two hindlegs to emit an imposing, earth-shattering roar that shifts the tundra leagues away. Icicle-addled stalagmites quake in distress, suddenly fracturing from the clamor. The brawny beast prepares for the hunt, roughly rattling chains into the nearby hardscape, twitching with enthusiasm and flexing muscles from slumber. A steel collar dominates the once regal tufts of fur sprawling around its neck, procuring janky and chaffed bald patches.

The Manhunters have bound this prehistoric terror too, a beast of unrivaled animalistic splendor, but captive nonetheless. Hadrien probably wrangled this megafauna himself, yearning for a living trophy, aspiring to break the most daring creatures on the frontier, becoming the epitome of all things deadly, and maybe gaining a pet to spar with.

This isn't the same breed of tundra terror they've heard in borderland stories though, those accounts meticulously detailed-in Jeremiah's journal. Indeed, something about this tundra terror is off, perhaps sickly, a mutated strain of feline. It showcases a signature sneer, grinning broadly from ear to ear, and flashing an array of ravishing meat-grinders.

Gobbed links of metal slink from woven coils, forming the appearance of an uncomfortably flattened nest. The fiend bows its head and drops its chest, extending those foremost paws as far out as it possibly can in a rewarding yoga pose, especially as the tendons snap into place. Then this feline cranks its neck so that it can stare at the rime-ridden sky, thrusting those rear hindlegs backwards into the air, straightening drowsy sinews. These bowie knives grip at the air whenever the beast stretches, flaunting one-by-one in sequence.

After having a fill tearing at vast, empty, deliciously smelling wafts on the wind, it rescinds those claws in earnest, clamping them instead onto the aching ground. The unbridled nails of this Cheshire Cat dig like talons, seeping inches into the frost with every pounce. It is decisively eager, keen to impale those vagabonds thwarting upon its domain by fashion of shortswords. A provokingly dreadful *purr* haunts the cougar's throat, that calm, controlled demeanor that befits creepy creatures, drafted by the superior subtleties of feline folk.

Its tail becomes the first portion of the beast to disappear, drawing an invisibility cloak from stern to bow, turning unexpectedly transparent within a moments notice. The last noticeable feature is that signature wide grin turning in their direction. Thankfully the predator is blind, maybe they'll stand a chance.

"Oh my-my indeed, let us be off to the races. Time to dine!"

"Nah. No, no, no," Edmund continually calls out in alarm, unable to track where the beast prowls.

It's the culmination of his nightmares, curtailing upon the constant losses, being almost fatally flanked by wolves and bear rider, here's another monster that he cannot possibly beat.

He catches the boy Jones by his shoulder and thrusts him onto the ground. The wickerwalker frantically huffs, "Gotta stay togetha. Gotta keep low- analyze the situation," motioning for Jenny and Mug Maxwell to join them, then the remaining partners attend posthaste.

They take shelter in the wake of a glacial outcrop, breaking the line-of-sight from where the creature once stood.

Morbin assesses their situation, "Beatin' 'round the bush don't ya think? Taking cover, kneelin' 'hind this barrier. What do ye expect us tah do 'ere?"

"To die, grinch," Edmund dryly admits, "nah, I expect us to die. We lack weapons 'tween us, not sure 'ow we could bum-cry charge tah overwhelm the terror. Betta-off splittin' intah pairs, some poor souls tryin' tah distract the thing while the othas skedaddle Can't nab us all."

"'Ey, yer gettin' the wrong idea, mate. If we do this right, there will be nah deaths necessary. Let's try tah fleece it, outsmart the scoundrel. Won't be requirin' us folk to sacrifice ourselves. Yes-yes," Balthus the learned man cries, pointing to the broad pillars conjoining the cavern.

"Those staves from floor to ceiling might tie it up. We'll just need tah weave n' wind our way tuh that exit o'ver yonda."

"Aye-aye!"

"I motion tah that."

In a rare act of clarity, these Bannermane, Marius outcasts, townspeople and bards have reached an agreement, deciding in short-order to tread wearily where mocking jaws might be lurking around every corner. William comes to the realization that together, they can accomplish anything, if they split and cried bull rush, arrogant pride would have been their downfall.

Before the party may begin to traverse this arena, the nearby chamber's foyer is cackling to the brim with a certain cacophony of jangling bells. Each clapper wailing incessantly, covering the halls in white noise. The Manhunter clad in chiming bits and bobbles has ironically arrived to investigate the source of their saber cat's howling agitation.

These sirens may have been arranged as a training tool, an auditory regime designed for the beast to cower and respect fell presence, but it has done the exact opposite. The ruthless *clink-clink-clink* of crudely fabricated chains eludes to the feline's position, however this rogue cannot hear the cautioning sound over their own incessant tolling. That very same, signature *clang-clang*.

The Cheshire Cat is bound to no-one, and reappears upon an embankment overseeing the woman's approach. It explodes hastily, fueled by venom, leaping forward into the fray. This is an obscene pursuit of frontier justice, a culminating vengeance that bears the brunt of body weight, lunging upon the strongest creature in the room. Two dreadnaughts collide in fury, collapsing in a heap where this captive cat may sink a pair of eviscerators into the Manhunter's abdominal wall, immediately unleashing essential organs from underneath her chest cavity, uncovering leftovers and intestines swollen from the feast, gushing pitch across the verdant blue glacier. Her inky ichor runs as cold as ice, dying the permafrost in ebony tinges.

An earnest lad can't help but question this brutality, even if the circumstance eggs the common rivalry between enemies of theirs. Why would this rogue tread so haphazardly into these chambers, where they know that the tundra terror is being caged, throwing obvious caution to the wind. The thought dwells upon the earnest lad's assembly of grey matter, believing that maybe the Manhunters may not have intended for the Cheshire Cat to mutate. That could explain how she was unaware about the feline's invisibility, this deceit caught her by surprise.

Despite William's curiosity, Edmund has been utilizing this distraction, taking the opportunity to administer his authority and lead their fellowship across no man's land. After a solid thirty-second window of sprinting, the company dive into the closest ditch. As their only warning, the wickerwalker catches the sounds of slinking steel, trying to determine if the tundra terror will arrive upon the mounds of ice or join them in the trenches.

"Ew," the creature mutters, demonstrating disgust.

"I can taste the tar."

The Cheshire Cat had craved this avenue of betrayal for so long, and other than the murder part, this moment was ultimately unrewarding.

"Manhunters are disgustingly potent, infused with magik that their flesh is so terribly inedible and worthless. But… *mmm,* this is not the prize that I covet. I desire red-hot meat."

They can hear the metal racks snap overtop the leaking Manhunter corpse, racking each chime, then land upon the nearest ice floe, dictated by several, distinct menacing noises.

Sniff-sniff, sniff-sniff-sniff. This feline is collecting pungent whiffs, a reminder that this sightless wonder is engorging itself on the thought of quarry, and admiring the stench of human sweat through fetid, beastial nostrils.

"I can hear you, I can smell you. Come here, you're my guests after all, and I wish to be accommodating. Let me entertain you with a song."

The sights, such smells, are riling,
Searchin' for a part to play.
I wait my turn, with bated breath-
For me. Only me, only me.

Pound for pound, and inch for teeth
Seep deep for ecstasy.
Blood flows like wine, and I gulp what's mine-
For me. Only me, only me.

The saber cat then emits a series of croaks, guttural clicks and chirps, ending with a cranky *tsk-tsk-tsk* as it stretches vocal cords, treating them like an instrument to be tuned, then their racket abruptly ceases.

The wickerwalker immediately instructs those to halt, their footsteps no longer accommodated by a shrouding sounds, everything is dead silent, until a woman's shrill shriek fills the void.

"'Elp, 'elp. Oh, please 'elp."

John Muck taps Edmund's back to warrant concern, soundlessly aiming his other finger towards the direction of a crag. There's a splintered corpse not ten feet away, torn to shreds. A myriad of bones litter this canyon, shattered for the valuable marrow inside. They hadn't smelled the usual stench of rotting meat because their is none, this skeleton has been entirely picked clean, nothing but empty ivorywork from a forgotten puppet. The tundra terror has been mimicking the voice of the woman they dispatched several days earlier.

That fiend taunts Boisterous Jenny, Fleischer, John Muck and the three vagrants in their friend's voice. Their demise would explain the slew of blood close to the cavern entrance. She must've retreated, or at least given-up, intimidated by the calamitous cat's presence, yet she didn't know that its chain was so long, and was caught within arm's reach of her companions by vicious barbs.

Coincidently, this feline is a beast that garners superior intelligence. Whether it has been bred for clandestine warfare, or mutated in such a way that assassination becomes happenstance is up for debate. Even though this foe relinquished its imitating surprise, there are other cards intended to be played. It bides their anxieties, waiting for the perfect moment to strike.

The tundra terror has spent these waxing minutes carefully snaking chains around their intended path, actually cruising around the pillars of its own diabolical intuition. It surges suddenly, delivering tripwires across the barren terrain by pulling the line taut, as the chamber riffs with a foreboding *chink*. Strands of metal links catch the ankle of that timid fellow, Knics, a member of the expedition who has been entertaining the idea of retreat, and has been dwelling upon the rear fringes of their company. As the cords wrap around his calf, choking the flow of blood, coaxing his ichor to swell to bulbous proportions so that there is zero hope to wiggle free.

Knics doesn't refrain from cursing, "*Youch-* the 'ell? What now? Caught mah leg. *Aah!* Muh fuckin' leg!"

His mouth runs rampant while he cannot, especially as the chains impulsively yank him towards an avidly abroad chasm and voracious ivory lashes. This is all that is visible, the predator can be better described as a single floating head, mainly mouth than anything else. The feline's jaw clamps against his neckline, swallowing his head whole like a lollipop, dragging the cruel casualty away and cackling maniacally.

Morbin shouts in alarm, "There it is! The exit is just 'head," identifying that their portal is slightly within reach should they ignore turning for their fallen comrade. Surely, Knics is a hot corpse by now.

The archaeologist surges to the front of the pack, fueled by the fortuitous circumstance that freedom is within reach, rekindling the furnace in his belly. That is, until that nightmarish figure blocks their advance. The tundra terror emerges into its full, harrowing form, standing on its hind legs like a bear, attempting to blockade as much as their escape route as possible. The iron maiden clutch of its collar prevents the beast from centering itself fully in the tunnel passage, these chains have been rendered stiff, unable to budge further. There's just enough space to garner their trust in fate, blitzing on the farthest side, chancing the sway of the cat's rattling sabers.

"Tis our last shot. We can't stop now. I say rush it!"

"Aye-ye! All togetha now."

At times like these William is reminded that when he's afraid of stepping on bones, sometimes the best one can do is forget to look down, and learn to shuffle their feet. Especially now that the tundra terror has arranged to full height, they can manage a good look at the monstrosity: its frame unsightly, mangled with bones protruding from the gullet, ivory plates spanning the usual soft spots to ensure there were no vulnerable locations to lodge weapons to begin with.

The boy Jones recollects those memoirs of Alexander Bannermane, founder of the clan and supposed almighty of the three mercantiles, an idol whom's portrait his paramount, Emery Walder kept firmly atop the fireplace mantle. This pioneer had earned his right to rule, he was a quartermain who had fought the territory's most dastardly beasts, one of the scarce few to retire upon fulfilling their oath. Of course, parting with the loss of several limbs. Who knows how many arms he has left now? Point is, his words were keen advice to live and die by: 'When losing, fight like a beast. When you're out of weapons, use your claws. Rage, RAGE, *RAGH*. Punch until your fingers break, and when they do, use your teeth. Give them hell.'

The saber cat raises a leg on the foremost sprinter, and brings it down on the poor soul, immediately burying that man's face into the permafrost, smashing their chest cavity in altogether- instant death. Their jaw is brought down low too, latching onto someone's arm to which they are heaved, ten-feet into the air.

To Edmund's despair, at the loss of a few sailors, their entire ship has sailed the strait. The preacher breathes a sigh of relief before the day is won, determined that his ample accoutrement of staves protected him from a heinous curtain-call, but blessings are only temporary. In the rush to avoid Scylla, travelers can't tell when they enter Charybdis. While the tundra terror can't exactly turn around, a single blind swipe backwards with its massive paw catches the fling of their fleece jacket, pulling John Muck back into the fray while he writhes desperately, attempting to unbutton dressing.

While William and the party manage to slick through, now cast in shadows, sprinting thirty-feet into the lone chasm of infinite darkness, they peek glances of their missing fellows. Gazing back reveals a beautiful-lit composition of cardinal sin, with the ambience of the prior chamber highlighting the demise of their chummy compatriots.

An extended pair of canines slice as readily as a hot knife through butter, severing the arm contained within the saber cat's mouth with little to no pressure at all. The victim is frazzled by this tragedy, spiraling onto the terrain, asserting their space by exhibiting death throes. At one point, this navigator almost rejects death, climbing to their feet haphazardly, unburdened by the actual loss of weight, then topples unconscious before long, assailed by the primal combination of shock and sudden loss of bloody bodily burdens.

The feline clips that preacher with their fishing hooks, corralling him closer, reeling John Muck like they're on the surface of the Oestergaard, wading in an ice hole that the bison and caribou herds have augered for drinking. His fleece comes free, but not in the nick of time, the preacher is still within grappling range. The very same paw clamps over his head, muffling dire screams with padded soles and thick, burly fur, coaxing him to flail as a fish out of water, helplessly hoping for a swift death.

There's the distinct *thuht* and *pop* noise of a cranium being forced out of place, tendons separating under pressure like the ceremonious detonation of a cork. A certain twist, pull, and brute decapitation. Unlike the Manhunters, the Cheshire Cat isn't in the market for acquiring prisoners, people are harder to keep alive, and the boy Jones has certain assurances that this beast won't let the meat rot.

The company evacuates further down the passage, navigating a pitch-black, straightly bored tunnel as an artery inside the ice sheet. William musters a meager jog, still shell-shocked from transpiring events, straying as far as possible from the tunnel entrance until they can no longer spy light emanating into this demesne, and the chamber behind them is naught but a beacon the size of a pin-point. Here they fester, cold and finally alone, where members of the company may lean on their knees or collapse in exhaustion entirely, spewing repulsive chunks spawned from the fatigue of their marathon and grisly sights.

Water vapor litters their roguish pants in a mist that quickly fills the berth of cavern. Morbin staggers with pain, this physical contest forcing him to produce sweat which instantly freezes and blights his flesh. Swathes of skin covered by thin, jacket linens nurture the perfect humid environments: a second of wet squalor, then searing pain as the perspiration solidifies, fledging abrasions which numb their dermal layers. This pox prevents those so amicable and inclined from huddling together for warmth, considering that their potential partners harbor fluids that threaten to torment them. These wounds spur necessary rest, a brief five-minute break when they believe they're out of danger.

Boisterous Jenny is livid, her voice seethes with antagonistic tendencies, hoisting some iIllicitly colorful language at Balthus.

"Liar, liar! Ye said no one 'ad tah die!"

The learned man unwillingly gauges his opponent, surrendering his palms into the air between them, conceding "Woah, 'ey," before taking steps further down the passage, distancing himself to elude possible fisticuffs.

These were the bard's coconspirators, people that she may have not got along with- yes, but when trapped in a cell for three-months, beggars can't be choosers. It's awfully easy to watch the days ramble on and relate over the traumas those Manhunters had inflicted upon them. Balthus tries to explain his position, and inexplicably makes the situation worse.

"Listen, I know what yer gettin' at, n' tis was out o' mah control. We needed tah act. I was merely- merely makin' ah suggestion. No offense, but they didn't seem that hospitable, perfectly content tuh return n' suffah in the cage. They were actin' like anchors when we need tah move. Those ain't the types o' people I desire tuh be affiliated with."

Jenny opens her mouth, absorbed with animosity, resolving to beat the punk into submission at the disregard of her powers of the pen and unmatched verbal slander. However, Edmund is in the right mind and proclaims order, stalling the brief argument by interjecting, "'Nough, there's nothin' we could 'ave done. We was battlin' 'bove our weight class-options limited. Balthus is right, best route was tah high-tail it outta there. So we escaped, let's focus on that. Can't stay 'ere eitha, wherever 'ere may be, it's too dark tuh tell. Gotta put some distance 'tween us n' those Manhuntahs."

If it were anyone else, even her partner Fleischer, Jenny would be giving them hell. Edmund may not be the smartest brick in the wall, but he's never steered her wrong.

"Fine, let's 'ead out. I'm freezin.'"

They had not come to expect a half-mile trek of downtrodden, jagged and warped crystalline caverns, yet this tube is oddly linear, formatted in a near-perfect, cylindrical shape. While William can't peer three-feet in front of him, the hiking is effortless, aided by continually flat geography, the feeling of a well-maintained, paced road. These aren't the ordinary lanes and promenade avenues he's normally used to, crawling over timber staves for traction, this environment has the smoothness of cobblestone without gaps or rounded ridges, although he can't quite put his finger on it. Unlike their previous expeditions, there are no gales to fluster them or a sudden, catastrophic precipice. They journey without a hitch, and that itself is more peculiar than the auditorium ahead.

In reality, William doesn't realize that they had quite discovered another remote chamber. It is only when a tree emits a faint glimmer, some blissfully muted blue-white light, that this company discern an entirely separate, concerting keep. The growth can detect their emotion, entrancing them in gentle luminance, allowing their eyes to acclimate as the softwood garners the robustness of living flame. This tree is extraordinary, devoid of the characteristic green and liberated from any nettles.

In contrast to a single, living organism, the bark is gestalt, comprised of lengthy, compounding wormy tentacles which wriggle from the roots to every farthest tip of branches. These larvas jitter in place when the fellowship eventually emerges from the tube, emitting a low-rumble and shivering with such glee that the branches sway. Ribbons dangle from these thickets, gifting the illusion of windswept spider-webs.

The bristlewyrm tree is certainly an alluring destination, protected by a fortress of sheet metal. The walls are glossed in iridescent seagreen plates, a lustrous and opalescent palette of ivory, cobalt and violet speckles contort inside vividly shimmering greenlips, deeply reminiscent of abalone shells, mollusks farmed beneath the ice to be traded as trinkets among the coastal territories. The reflective coating spirals upwards, revealing a huge vertical channel.

William registers that they currently reside at the base of a gigantic chimney, where they may peek at the firmament and its burgeoning merlot sky from a league away. However, too great of a distance for the illumination to pierce this usually dusky nest.

Morbin pauses, recognizing this place from his former exploits around the mead hall, reveling in pompous bouts with those who frequent haulageways, and clever wayfaring archaeologists. They share novels of the old world around the table, culminating woodcut illustrations and chronicles of yore with one in particular, titled 'The Luminary.' These optimistic excavators weren't aware of the accuracy, let alone, if this reliquary actually existed in the first place. After Clan Penn unearthed the treasure trove that is the Ventura Tech Vault, numerous ancient documents have been brought to light. It was a gargantuan repository, intended to house hundreds of engineering ancillaries as humanity thwarted the apocalypse.

Upon those discoveries, those that survived that great cataclysm were laid low, nothing but primitives on the totem pole of intellectual advancement compared to their forefathers, as the clans have always been focused on bickering over Veblen goods, artifacts to fuel their petty squabbles rather than working together for the common good of all. This tomb also contained scriptures that those residents of Hearthland would cherish for generations to come, wonderful marble sculptures, and pieces of art befit of rule, paintings to adorn the crown icon's palace. These compositions are romantic and whimsy on occasion, as how Reyconn's, *Portrait of a Madame,* depicts an irresistible woman with missing eyebrows. Vagabonds can't always trust the testimonials of the dead, certain degrees of imagination must be taken for granted.

"*Tsk.* Thought twas only fairy tale, some inspired artist in the Exhibition Mile illustratin' ah children's book. After all, black n' green tree in ah tower- don't seem real, don't it?"

"Nah, my dear boy, n' that is why I must… get closa," murmurs Balthus.

The droning of these bristlewyrms have consecrated his blood-brain barrier with tunes that are oddly hypnotic and mesmerizing, gifting him the illusion of satisfaction, completely enthralling the learned man's deepest desires. He slowly paces forward, extending his left hand, determined to seize the trunk of the tree.

"I can 'ear it callin', don't ya? Think- all I 'ave tah do is reach out, n' I can touch divine creation."

"Don't let it draw ya in," an ominous authority drolls out.

"All is not what it seems!"

When this voice speaks, a series of urns collapse onto the oxidized copper sheet flooring, cracking apart, dispersing waves of gold coins and priceless ancillaries, those bejeweled circlets, ceremonial drinking horns, coins and rolls of winter wolf hide. The speaker originates from a sarcophagus, resting upon a throng of steps and situated atop a pyramid.

This ebony prism vibrates with each syllable, a prominently supernatural feat, as the tomb has been sealed by an unassailable counter of black marble, with spindly chalk veins crackling into the stone like some vandal's webbing. Various etchings have been carved into this monument, sculptural reliefs brandishing beneath the rim, depicting the gambits of a certain high-strung marvel.

This is the tomb of Atticus Dour, Lord Paramount of the Oestergaard, hallowed is thy name as patron-saint of all quartermaines and wickerwalkers. The very same champion who battled the bewildering Barbwire Bandit of Brittany along his father, and had disappeared under mysterious circumstances. This is the resting place of the Manhunters' most egregious foe and worthy foe, they do well to respect the last rites of those bold enough to defy them. The plaque erected upon the burial place has been chiseled in atrocious borderspiel lettering, repeating the words, 'Dour suffers the melancholy, Dour welcomed fate.'

A cerulean cloud phases through the blackened bulwark, the spirit of Atticus himself. His figure is different from ordinary specters, the surrounding area washes in supernatural incandescence. He has become a lumin-geist, having been blessed by the divines to continue their holy work, even after their body has failed.

The quartermain is inevitably tied to his mummified mortal coil, that cadaver held within the confines of the sarcophagus acts as his anchor, returning him to the realm of the living. His ancient orbs are contemplating these visitors' intent, probing their posse in an intense affair, however the newcomers could be described as roughly human, implying that they haven't aligned themselves with the Atticus' arch nemesis, those seven deadly sins and their spawn. In fact, he becomes rather enthusiastic from his studies, recognizing William's facial features under all his facial hair and grizzle.

"I've seen the likes of ya 'fore. *Hmm.* I wonda- yes, yes! Ye are Emery n' Concorde's babe. Sure she's ah lovely lass- nevah met 'er, but all brides are beautiful. Ah, it 'as truly been ages. What year is it anyhow? 'Ow is Ernie, that ould goat?"

The boy Jones is unfazed by this sudden inquiry, actually stifling laughter over the fact that this is the first time he's heard anyone call his father Ernie.

"'Ow are ye doing? Tell me 'bout yerself William. What 'ave ye been up tah since yer stint at the East End Motorhead? Actually, nevah mind that question, alas ye were just ah wee runt. Well, 'ow's the weather? I'd love tuh know, as things get ah bit dreary 'ere."

"Cloudy with a chance of precipitation," quips Jenny, antagonizing Morbin into rolling his eyes, foiled by a joke more half-cocked than his own.

The amateur archaeologist focuses on other joys, occupying his time by venerating those treasures that strike his soles, tempted to pocket a diadem grandstanding before him. William generates a conversation with the geist, fearing that Evershade's greedy posturing will out-welcome their stay, so the earnest lad proposes the first query on his mind.

"'Uh, well what 'bout ye, Atticus?"

"Nevahmind me this n' me that- I'm dead, so don't be worryin'. What brings ye folk all this way anyhow?"

The bard blurts out, "Blood rain! 'Ello, 'member we gotta 'pocalyptic host at the front doors? Should 'urry 'long."

"On the run," William continues elaborating.

"Those Manhuntahs as ya prolly know."

"Still? Oh boy-oh, I know too well," the lumin-geist asserts, floating over yonder, staring at the bristlewyrm tree as it sways to and fro, menacingly chiding at him.

"There are worse things out there than those who can wield ah sword n' shield, worsah than those beasts that drive talon n' fang. I battle the fell, an endless legion o' walkin' corpses led by those malignly-inclined. There are tempest, ah chapter of cosmic icons derived from the rawest, most primordial energies, manifestin' from mankind's worst nightmares. These eminent beings feed-off every aspect of emotion, for that is our hubris. They whisper in our ears, encouragin' every swing o' our blades, the constant cycle of gluttony n' misuse, doin' lil' tah tame our desire for superiority, lust for one 'notha. 'Cause of this, tis impossible tuh sevah their source of power, hence the endless battle bit."

"I sealed mah fate, swearin' a holy vow to execute their 'arbingers, 'eralds, familiars, plus all those 'eretical cults as I deem fit. After endurin' decades n' decades of their torment, casting revelations 'pon grey matta o' muh comrades turnin' intah the very foe I've sworn tuh face, I resisted their prophecies by journeyin' tah world's end, in ah bid tuh battle them directly. Yet, I only prolonged the inevitable, as ah bein' of the mortum, I was still susceptible tah the whims o' Elda Time, n' in mah ruin, they built me ah grand palace o' pride so that I still may suffer these eternal years in agony."

"Vagabonds should be suspicious of trees that bloom in the worst storms, this is not the usual shrubbery. Nah, that right there is ah testament tah their influence. It's creep, tis corrupted: a cairn fiend, these mangroves o' worms which fester in places of death- must be purged."

The lumin-geist's attention returns to their traveling company as Atticus sizes-up the earnest lad, wickerwalker, cordwainer, gambler, archaeologist, learned man, and two traveling bards a final time. He conjures an address of complete, plain honesty.

"Ye've made it this far, n' frankly, I'm impressed. As it means tah muh, ye lot 'ave earned yer sails. So be mah advice as it may, brandish the sword that is heavy, for yer swings must be tried n' true. Ye falter, even hesitate once, ya die. When the world is lined-up 'gainst ya, be brutal. If the enemy shall give ye nah quarter, it is only due justice ye refuse n' do the same."

Atticus Dour watches the conflicted thief, aware of the foul influence that looms heavily upon his conscious. Morbin is especially vulnerable to susceptive, as the entire wealth of the quartermain is literally lying within arm's reach. He contemplates seizing these riches, struggling to prevent himself from pilfering these gilded cavalier crowns, and shoving a negligible amounts of gold in his pockets. A little wouldn't hurt, they are such trivial tokens, and certainly no one would notice a few missing.

The archaeologist bends over, removing those several coins that have been lodged in his boot laces. inadvertently revealing a gleaming aquamarine circlet, an ancillary that he now craves. It sponsors gemstones woven inside an aureate band, and Morbin can't contain his glee, accidentally finding his finger wrapped around fickle metallic wires.

"They've been manipulatin' y'all since the beginnin', tuggin' 'tween yer strings. Just bein' in the Manhunter's presence 'ave caused adverse or vestigial mutations, even if they may not be quite obvious at first. Though in the presence o' fiends, the light reveals."

The particular treasure that their archaeologist has been so keen to keep suddenly sours, the opulent sapphire blemishing into dull drabs of grey, and the band bubbles, liquifies, then droops away.

"This is for the best, I do believe all the treasure 'ere 'as been cursed, as these ain't mah riches. I'm ah 'umble man at 'eart- or, at least 'was'. Manhunters delivered wagons o' loot in ah dedication tah greed, entombin' me in those luxuries which I rue most."

"Now, I must ask of fava of ye- a relatively easy task. Use mah wand, that tusk o'ver there, close tuh muh sarcophagus. It won't melt away like the otha things 'round 'ere, as this was mah personal heirloom. Point the end towards that oversized lantern in the room n' burn that bristlewyrm tree so that muh soul may be free, then I can continue battle on mah own terms. As long as fell taints this final restin' place, I shall foreva be at its mercy."

As this request piques his curiosity, William marches to the pyramid with such incredible gusto. This mausoleum has been untouched by human visitors since the quartermain was first laid to rest, still writhing in those final moments as a dozen corrupted palms shove him further into the abyss, and they seal the portal with a decisive slab of granite. He won't be needing to exhume any corpses, as Manhunters didn't dare risk burying their grand adversary with any of those most cherished possessions. They elected to let him stew in some shallow grave alone, drawing those last breaths in complete isolation.

Climbing that chiseled assembly of soot-laden stairs, and navigating that mausoleum showpiece; there's an iron pedestal around the bend, built into a recess of the wall that withholds an instrument to brag about. The scepter they seek is locked behind a wired cage, adorned in laces the color of powdered tumeric. He brazenly draws the cloak free, thrusting his hands between those bars and heaving them wide, eager to procure that prize inside.

This ancillary is exactly as promised, a reward for their efforts and something to savor. The wand has the prospect of a boar tusk, almost straight, slightly curving at over a foot-long, then stubbed into a finely rounded point. When William clasps the scepter, it emits a faint hum, but before the boy Jones can cherish this cudgel, he contemplates, debating if this is actually bleached bird bone, because the wand is as light as a feather.

Atticus astutely explains the stave's origins, how he had whittle this scepter from the tooth of a grim, personally.

"-and I bashed that monstrosity tah kingdom come, sending shards toward the glass ceiling n' knockin' the enemy ontah its rear. 'Member lad, that's misarcana, the physical embodiment o' our darkest enemy, remnants o' ah fell beast. Not ah playthin.'"

That would explain why he can't make out the figurehead, a simple creature without eyes not unlike the tundra terror, and featuring a stout muzzle similar to the build of a bear, but not quite. This basic design makes it a little disconcerting on how to hold the wand, there must be a grip of some kind, William ponders to himself.

That is, until the earned lad accidentally unsheathes a hidden compartment, revealing a stiletto, some certainly slender needle. As first impressions go, this dagger could effortlessly double as a copper diving rod or mace.

In lieu of a crossguard, William's hand comes to rest on a bulbous joint, which opens and reveals itself as an unhinged, animated, reptilian slitted eye. This oculus is understandably startled, the pupil dilating and jolting around the sclera to read the room. Even though this host may just a simple eye, it showcases throes of sentience, focusing on the closest subject within its perception, the boy Jones, blinking occasionally whilst being completely quiet. William is entranced by this homunculus, and of course, without an instruction manual, is keen for Dour's advice.

"This wand draws 'pon chaotic energy- dark magik, so don't rely on it readily, there's always ah cost. Ye'll be able tah summon concussive blasts at yer foe, sending enemies sprawlin' at yer feet n' becomin' the fanciest bitch at the brawl. 'Owever, every use 'as ah price, it shall gradually drain yer life force. While the wand itself is explosive, the blade is cowardly n' timid, naturally able tuh rupture rifts in space. Who's tah say where these portals lead, nah one knows for sure. So, avoid usin' them, unless yer back is 'gainst the wall n' there's nah otha option. I always feared fightin' the minions only tah be teleported tuh the masta, thrust straight intah the pits o' 'ell. Anyhow, 'nough o' that, didn't mean tah stir fright. I need ye tuh decimate those bristlewyrms. Ye'll do that for muh, won't ya?"

"It's pretty easy tah get started. Yep, just point, concentrate. Think of the tree suddenly turnin' intah the perfect kindlin', that's 'ow I get started. An inferno 'till naught but ash n' cindahs, then ah wave of the wand will make it so."

William stands atop the pyramid and slides the copper rod back into the wand, shuffling his hand so that he is gripping around the figurehead.

"Aye, that I can do," he confirms, raising the tusk as entirely one piece.

The wand has perfectly melded into his palm, conforming alongside his fingers and notches of knuckles. Strange, the earnest lad could've sworn it was larger a second ago. With this much godly power in his hands, William's potential is endless, and it feels- whimsical, awfully lighter than he had imagined. The ability to turn those writhing maggots into charred husks shouldn't be risky, right?

He places one foot forward, straightening his back posture, slightly cocking his head sideways and closing an eye to determine the distance, exactly how he's spied Bannermane marksmen preparing to draw their bowlines and fire.

"Ye said somethin' 'bout drainin' mah life force? Sounds barbaric, 'most like I shouldn't be doin' this. 'Ow many times may I use it 'fore things 'come dangerous?"

"I ain't gonna lie, boy. Ye should aim sparingly. And, truthfully I ain't sure. I've only evah shot twice in one day, n' I could feel the demon frantically diggin' inside, pryin' at muh psyche, tryin' tah take me ovah."

"Demon?" *Umm.* That's pertinent information, William wishes that he was privy to that fact a few seconds ago.

The world around him slowly becomes motionless and still, unable to move anything but the straits of his gaze. It's all coming together now, he can feel the arrival of a dark presence, that very same demon grasping at both his shoulders, massaging them menacingly, whispering just behind his earlobe as the essence establishes hold over him.

The sharp aroma of mint leaves waft over him, consummated by a serpentine tongue flickering wildly, leading William to believe that this experience in real and not a complete hallucination. Especially as the forked tendril weaves through the air, fretting dangerously close. He wants to shove his assailant, run away and shout.

"No, ah! Don't come any-"

Yet his body refuses to budge, even as the intruder inserts itself into his ear canal, funneling inside until that tentacle tickles grey matter.

A hunched-back figure lingers in the scope of his peripheral vision, and they procure ghastly form, flamboyantly flaunting as their tongue establishes a presence in William's mind. In lieu of any eyes is a singular keyhole, slivering down as a replacement of those usually prominent facial features, grafting the tissue of their nose into a hollow alcove. The arms are ordained by two, scaly, scathingly-studded vipers, one which proudly exhibits a comedy mask on its snout, drawing attention to a hypnotic gaze, while its sibling serpent sports a tragedy mask. Both these basilisks are wound tightly around the demon's neck, layers upon layers of coils which flair like bracketed tangerine and lime tinged jewelry.

Time seems suspended, as if sweat droops from his brow yet the thrush is unable to knock. The boy Jones can hear this imposter speak without needing to move its mouth, the ancient language of immortals is telepathically translated to his brain. William's host articulates dialogue that is dramatic and eloquent, suave in every manner, a vehement tone that is eerily envious and equally sultry, conniving in his ears like it wants something, almost as if it needs William.

'Oh no,' the thought brims in earnest lad's head. This isn't actually a mere demon, everything has gotten much worse.

It innocently quips, flicking tongues.

"So, have we met before? No? Charming- no, delighted to have the pleasure. Take a gander if you can."

It proposes, parading around and giving a twirl. That filthy tendril positioned in his ear elongates, twisting around William's neck and torso as the demon dances, skipping in joy. One of the vipers investigates noticeably near- too close, and it bars those blades they call teeth to emit a provocative *hiss*. Some certain snarl so heinous, he'd recoil if not frozen in place.

"I'm one above all and equal to none. I'll be able to read your mind soon enough, and find out everything about my new poppet, all those juicy details. You should know that I'm not all bad, just very persuasive."

The pupils of that comedically-masked snake swirl, forming a mesmerizing, hypnotic gaze while that vulgar tongue pulsates and reels like a whip, devouring inner egos, reflecting on his sacred knowledge.

"Heed my words and obey."

William is besieged by vile thoughts, attempting to shake his head lucid while the intruder roots in his memories, searching for his most verdant desires, yet he cannot muster the iron will necessary to break this demon's spell.

"Try and run, but you cannot escape fact. Humans are forced to suffer as playthings for the divines. I am eminence personified, you are molded as entertainment, catering to my whims."

"How you poor, starved thing, feeding off rotten scraps and rats. You've been busy, awfully busy watching those sickly few who didn't deserve death, perish in your stead. Life snuffed out at the last moment. Remember that scribe, Rylie? Who was plucked away at the last second from a stairwell- what luck. How many innocent townspeople have you seen die? It didn't have to be this way. While things could be worse, they could be better too. These Manhunters robbed you of an idol. Could you imagine, the fabled Atticus Dour taking an apprentice? Everything was lined up so perfectly: you were connected, the quartermain was your father's ole bully-rook, Emery Walder's bestest and sole friend- oh, what fun. How he would've been so proud. His son, training hand-in-hand with the unrivaled hero of these lands, strength unparalleled, feats unmatched. The two of you could beat back the evil seeping into this world, battling all sorts of bestial ilk. It could've been a blood pact, being that Atticus needed a ward in his time, and for you, this could've been that grand adventure you've always strived for- could ever dream of. You would've been destitute, far from it, you would've been royalty of the entire Oestergaard. Those merchant heads would bow and revel in your name. You wouldn't need to break into homes for meager fare, pilfering hot-rocks for some ticket to ride. In fact, they would worship you. Oh, how they would worship you. Almost one step from divine, showering those riches and voyages vagabonds dare speak aloud."

"Yes, yes. I can sense your frustration. *Mhmm.* I can taste your envy. It is the fault of the Manhunters and their miscreant creations. Those criminals deserve to burn, don't they? Yes, burn- burn!"

An evergreen bolt careens from William's wand, clearing the radius of the chimney and barreling straight into the viscous, skulking strands. This flare settles in the uppermost echelon of branches, dulling at first, then exploding in supernatural delight, rummaging through the core channels of tree trunk to bathe every single bristlewyrm with divine intervention.

As the grubs are set alight, they shriek with inhuman screams, enraged at this betrayal, over their crude desire to make friends. Sure, they have the tendency to ensnare anyone who frets too close and lay larvae in their eye sockets, but they didn't intend any harm because their actions are justifiable as hugs with extra steps. They burn steadily, painfully ignorant, not knowing that they've garnered a reputation among bot flies.

Ahh. Shriek. Ack-aggh.

The tomb of Atticus Dour is immersed in incandescent phosphorus, proving that some pests are suitable fuel in a pinch, even though the fellowship drowns in that incessant screeching. These wails resound upon this hallowed ground, ricocheting off the oxidized abalone metals, calling into the abyss, and bizarrely, the abyss calls back.

It begins innocently enough, like how drops of liquid leech from their icicles and plop abruptly into a puddle.

Titter-tap, titter-tap, titter-tap-tap-tap-tap-tap.

There are three capacious corridors along the walls, each portal raising in volume. The gentle lapse of rippling water flourishes into the deluge of a thunderstorm, some steady high-pitched *hum* that ignites their eardrums. An absolute blast of percussion that almost coerces their company into retiring towards the Cheshire Cat's chamber. They are subject to an explosive release of energy, as the instantaneous concert of taiko drumming is deafening.

"We've gone too far to turn back now," Edmund declares.

"Brace yourselves!"

The piercing shrills are surpassed by the stampede of clambering pincers, so large in number, that it turns into a constant droning. Wave after wave of attercops emerge from the gloom, arriving in entire swathes to congeal near the funeral pyre, each member of this pestilent entourage whisked in cherry-red. They are medallion-sized apiece, taking the appearance of dashing cranberries that have sprouted eight limbs. Mass amounts of these arachnids descend netherwards, dangling from the chimney, vaulting across the ceiling and walls, clogging every aspect of this chamber in webbing as they rampage by.

Due to their immediate arrival of these vermin, their intents are clear, and the refuges undoubtedly decide to flee.

"What are those?"

"Seven 'ells!"

The wickerwalker shouts at the top of his lungs, desperately attempting to override the onslaught. Edmund Redmyne directs to the passage nearest to them, pointing and guiding them to retreat in faint glow.

"Thattaway," he hollers,

"It has the least amount!"

As masses of tiny fangs mash towards their Peaterbricks, Jenny lets loose a salvo of cranberry pincers, utilizing the base of the shamisen like the head of a broom, sweeping mountain after molehill of arachnids towards the side. A few of these eight-legged pests actually cling to the strings, causing her to wring at the neck with malice until those fiendish hooks file free with a signature *twang*, improvising a riff of the string while they announce their departure.

"*Eww.* Cretins!"

The regular residents of the gossamer realm have never been this aggressive before, they must've been spurned by the bristlewyrms' demise. A massive horde of these attercops stoop towards the wickerwalker's advance, breaking formation to barricade their escape route in sheer bodies, aiming to leave no witnesses. Atticus is determined to save his friends, as for any vagabond who rejects fell should be consider an ally.

Testing his limits and spectral abilities, the lumin-geist phases through the advancing lines to protect them, abruptly stunning the incursion of interlopers. Such a measure is only temporary, as the arachnids who follow the vanguard scramble over their gobsmacked kin, mutilating the bodies with the spines of their legs and tearing them apart while they continue to surge forward, now unimpeded.

Alone, these tiny spiders are naught but a trifle of a threat, yet together, in these numbers, they are a force of nature, akin to a roiling thunder that follows lightning, signifying that more is to come. The vermin are relentless, treating those priceless baubles as minor snags, obstacles to be eroded away, as the most powerful fell creatures have no sense of self. They are driven by trauma, operating almost on pure instinct.

These encroaching eldritch horrors are persistent, nearly matching their speed, threatening that one miscalculated step could mean the death of them. The well-departed quartermain does his very best to distract the horde, however these cave-dwellers prove too numerous and intelligent, quickly discerning that the specter is completely invulnerable to their mashing pincers, and those formidable few that attempted to bite him now lie frozen in a state of torpor.

As the fellowship sprints down this cavern of red waves, cranberries begin to periodically drop from the ceiling, landing on these visitors and gorging themselves on berry-sized chunks of skin. Their is no warning to an attercop's leap, as when it reaches lunging distance, their eyes glaze over, drawing all their prowess into a single pounce, preparing an attack that will likely end in their own demise.

William finds unwelcome bunches of boarding parties among his left arm, urging the sailor to suddenly careen into the passage wall, and relieve their entrails upon the sheet copper in a wine-red smear. *Yuck.*

With the colony of bristlewyrms spent and gone, Atticus Dour yells from the demesne of an eternally burning pyre.

"Run now, return tah yer clans n' reveal the truth o' the Manhuntahs!"

In their haste, the townspeople start to naturally spread apart, favoring those with longer legs. Morbin dashes to the front of the pack, screaming "Tally 'o," and trotting off, not realizing that their straightaway tunnel has begun to spread into parallel corridors.

The constant stream of chasing attercops causes them to act on impulse, inadvertently causing Mug Maxwell to separate. William notices the gambler's change in direction as a risk he wouldn't normally take, and shifts towards his tunnel in the nick of time, and before long, these two gallop by the chittering tunes of arachnids and their own slopping footsteps. Each step reverberates upon the metallic corridor, prompting a loudly booming chorus.

Thump, thunk, thump, thunk.

The voice of envy whispers in the earnest lad's ear, tempting him to brandish the wand once more and send these attercops scurrying back into the abyss from whence they came. A cherub of common sense hedges upon his shoulder, urging him to say nay, as these events could easily spiral out of control.

"What do ye mean could? We've really stoked the crazy!"

Mug becomes incredibly disoriented when a spider lands on his cheek, twisting his ankle with a thunderous *snap*.

The gambler heaves himself onto the ground, rolling once from the sudden pull of a parking brake, and crushing the blighted spider with his body weight. It erupts like a cherry gushing between the teeth, vomiting all its internal organs, and applying another splotch of merlot to the sheet metal flooring.

William rushes to his comrade's aid, and has extreme difficulty in locating the vagabond without some sort of guiding light. Barely grasping the fringes of his shirt, the boy Jones attempts to yank Mug Maxwell upright, and prop the gambler onto one leg so that they may hobble along.

These are the sort of circumstances that makes young men susceptible to the influence of dark gods. He can hear the voice of envy continue to stimulate his lobe, toying with his emotions by saying, "Together we will rule, together we can save them."

Against William's better judgement, the boy impulsively weaves the wand into his hand, unsheathing that dagger of instant, fully-randomized travel with haste. Before he may demonstrate the necessary blow, and tear the fabric of reality with this misarcana, a single attercop strings from the ceiling to land upon Maxwell's shoulder, taking the contour out of his neckline almost immediately.

"Agghh!"

He screams, smacking the pest instinctively and crushing it like ripe fruit. He has been too viscerally violated to tell whether the fluid streaming from this wound is his own ichor, or the arachnid's foul leftovers. He motions to William, swirling that frigid stale air with his own hand.

The boy curses himself for not acting swiftly enough, watching the dimly-lit contents of Mug's carotid artery empty. Even if this teleport scheme were to work, there are no definite assurances that Mug would survive this fatal wound.

"Give mah the vinegar, 'Liam, am I gonna make it?"

The earnest lad wipes his fledging tears on scruffs of sleeve, blaming himself for being too distracted by objects of power and godly ancillaries to notice the threat waving in front of his face.

"No," weeps William.

"Drats, gotta make this quick then. I've always known ye tah be the best 'mong us. Dumb as rocks at times, 'specially durin' ah game o' pilfahs. Prove me right. Do me ah fava William, keep the fight alive. Raze the pyre for both of us."

Unable to tell if this sincere truth is dredged from the depths of Mug's heart, or the light-headedness stemmed from blood loss, he is both grateful and grievously wounded at the same time.

The gambler momentously shoves him away, considering that even if he could make it back onto his feet, this injury would only slow the pair down, and it'll easily become open season for the two of them.

"Forget 'bout me," he yells as Mandel appears from nowhere, rushing out of the murky darkness without warning and tackling William in the crude effort to pull him onto his shoulder, and continue running without a pit-stop. Propped over the cordwainer's in a sort of fireman's carry, he can spot his comrade's eyes glowing a fierce yellow, clearly under the influence of spirits.

An earnest lad can barely usher a goodbye to Maxwell as the gambler rolls his last pair of snake eyes. The attercops set themselves upon him, a heinous amount of spider legs which spell certain doom, flense his skin, crushing his frame underneath roiling waves of gossamer.

•   •   •

AFTERWORD

I tread a fine-line, that special state of being between sleepless nights and anxiety-riddled days. I laugh in these times of hardship. Never have I been normal, never have I been comfortable, never have I been felt safe.

There is a storm raging deep inside me, the plight of some overactive imagination. It demands attention, often roaring like an engine during the vast stillness of night. That's when I find myself subject to certain tricks of the subconscious, hearing my name called upon the wind and seeing the shadows dance while I'm alone. These hallucinations are subtle, just enough to pry my eyes awake, telling me that I'm not done. It is in that moment of distress when creativity strikes, pulsing like electricity, as if a lightning rod has been welded inside.

I should rue this creativity as a curse, a parasite which leaches the energy of my body, sapping focus and all my memories, distilling fog and leaving me no better than draugr throughout the day. Yet, I dare not beg for sympathy for I revel in my faults. I'm one of those able few, tapping into that limitless well of dysphoria, molding thoughts confined deep within grey matter, fashioning bizarre, foreign concepts together as easily as puzzle pieces.

These years of effort, sacrifice and hardship have culminated into an extraordinary composition, something to revel and take pride over, yet I feel empty. There is always more to do, more to say and maybe just enough time. We are but insignificant blips in the cosmic scheme of things. People must always be broadening their horizons, learning from mistakes and hurtling over them, lest we perish as a footnote in the textbooks of history. I feel wyrd, yet wonderful. There will always be more, plenty more encyclopedias to craft, books to publish. I'll never be complacent.

I don't strive for any perfection, as writers should idolize faults where they can, savor the traits that make us unique and memorialize personal perspective. These are the type of characters we relate most to, as to err is to be human. There's that little root of reality amid fantasy, whether frolicking amid marvels or dancing upon the edge of utter ruination, where the residents of the realm feel real. Whether those are carrying the weight of the entire world on their shoulders or absolutely none at all, people tend to trip over their own two feet.

ACKNOWLEDGEMENTS

This novel couldn't have become reality if it weren't for the graces of Jessika. That very same papermaker who would often indulge me, becoming a buffer and fending-off the constant ire of rent and taxes, allowing me a period of silence: to close my eyes, however brief, where I could ask those big questions. Vague concepts that let my mind wander and fill me with dread. What's next? What around the next corner?
I sure hope there are aquariums.

ABOUT THE AUTHOR

TRENT LINDSEY is a central Ohio native who has always been immersed in storytelling, studying art, design and all things creative, earning their Bachelor of Fine Arts in Animation from the Columbus College of Art & Design. He currently lives in Dover, Ohio, enjoying bouts of fresh-air and raising a variety of tropical fish. Trent's always busy crafting new language, fantastic beasts, and an eccentric cast of characters.